The Courtship
of Nellie Fisher

By Beverly Lewis

HOME TO HICKORY HOLLOW
The Fiddler • *The Bridesmaid*

SEASONS OF GRACE
The Secret • *The Missing* • *The Telling*

THE ROSE TRILOGY
The Thorn • *The Judgment* • *The Mercy*

ABRAM'S DAUGHTERS
The Covenant • *The Betrayal* • *The Sacrifice*
The Prodigal • *The Revelation*

THE HERITAGE OF LANCASTER COUNTY
The Shunning • *The Confession* • *The Reckoning*

ANNIE'S PEOPLE
The Preacher's Daughter • *The Englisher* • *The Brethren*

THE COURTSHIP OF NELLIE FISHER
The Parting • *The Forbidden* • *The Longing*

The Postcard • *The Crossroad*

The Redemption of Sarah Cain
October Song • *Sanctuary** • *The Sunroom*

The Beverly Lewis Amish Heritage Cookbook

www.beverlylewis.com

*with David Lewis

BEVERLY LEWIS

The Courtship of Nellie Fisher

THREE NOVELS IN ONE VOLUME

The Parting, The Forbidden, & The Longing

BETHANYHOUSE
a division of Baker Publishing Group
Minneapolis, Minnesota

Published by Bethany House Publishers
11400 Hampshire Avenue South
Bloomington, Minnesota 55438
www.bethanyhouse.com

Bethany House Publishers is a division of
Baker Publishing Group, Grand Rapids, Michigan

Printed in the United States of America

Library of Congress Cataloging-in-Publication Data is available for this title.

This is a work of historical reconstruction; the appearances of certain historical figures are therefore inevitable. All other characters are products of the author's imagination, and any resemblance to actual persons, living or dead, is coincidental.

Scripture quotations are from the King James Version of the Bible.

Cover design by Koechel Peterson & Associates, Inc., Minneapolis, Minnesota

12 13 14 15 16 17 18   7 6 5 4 3 2 1

To my uncle and aunt

Amos and Anna Jane Buchwalter,

who gave us many happy memories

in their wonderful-big house

in Brownstown, Pennsylvania.

And

to our friends

John and Rachell Henderson,

who received the unexpected gift of a child.

The Parting

PROLOGUE

Autumn 1966

For as long as I can remember, I've eagerly awaited the harvest. Oh, the tantalizing scents wafting from *Mamma*'s kitchen, come autumn. But it's not my mother's baking as much as it is my own that fills the house with mouth-watering aromas. Each year I entertain myself, seeing how many ways I can use pumpkin in an array of baked goodies. Naturally there are pumpkin pies and pumpkin breads. But I also delight in making pumpkin cookies with walnut pieces and brown sugar sprinkled atop. And there is spicy pumpkin custard, too, and gooey pumpkin cinnamon rolls—sticky buns, of course—cinnamon pumpkin muffins, and the most popular item of all: pumpkin cheesecake.

As I wait for pies to bubble and cookies to turn golden brown in the old cast-iron oven in Mamma's kitchen, I thrill to the world beyond our tall windows, watching for the first hint of shimmering reds on the sugar maples along the west side of our lane. I catch sight, too, of the glistening stream as it runs under Beaver Dam Road and across our wide meadow. It's here, near Honey Brook, northeast of White Horse and smack-dab in the Garden Spot of the World, where I live with *Dat* and Mamma and my two older sisters, Rhoda and Nan.

But garden spot that this may be, this year I am not able to use our own pumpkins for baking, nor am I as aware of the usually melodious brook, or the growing excitement of the fun to come—youth frolics and hayrides. All the pairing up beneath the harvest moon.

Sadly our own harvest has already occurred—stunted stalks of sweet corn, acres and acres of it all around us, cut early. Dat said the fact it never got taller than knee-high was an omen of bad things to come. *"Time will tell, as in all things,"* he declared. And time did tell.

9

Accepting our loss, we salvaged what was left of the lifeless stalks, using them for fodder. Even so, some are still standing brown in the field. Rows of short scattered stumps, a cruel reminder of what might have been.

Though I'm only seventeen, I've already made some observations about the passing of years. Some are marked by loss more than others. As for this season, never before have we lost so many of the People to jumping the fence to greener pastures—our own cousin Jonathan and his family among them. But losing a crop, or some of our own to the world, pales in comparison to the greatest loss of all.

I still remember clearly that early June Saturday. The day had begun with anticipation, as all market days do. Grief was the furthest thing from my mind the morning Caleb Yoder smiled at me for the first time ever. I was minding my own business, selling my baked goods to eager customers, when I had a tingling awareness of someone nearby watching me. I looked up . . . and there he was. I felt a rush of energy, as if something inside me was saying: *Is he the one?*

Caleb's admiring gaze lingered after his handsome smile, and by afternoon, my next oldest sister, nineteen-year-old Nan, was telling me something Caleb's own sister Rebekah had whispered to her—that Rebekah wished Caleb might court me. Such a wonderful-good thing to hear!

Now, if I hadn't secretly liked him for several years, the smile and the whisper would have meant little and the day would have been like any other. Instead, it was the collision of the best and worst days of my life.

My sister Suzy died that evening. Younger than me by just eleven months, she drowned before she had a chance to be baptized and join church—a giant strike against our souls. Mamma and I were alone in the bakery shop when the policeman came with the wretched news, and I could not stop shaking long into the night.

Nearly a hundred days have come and gone, and at times it seems Suzy's untimely death has started a whole chain of unusual events. I'm aware of a hole in my middle, like someone reached in and pulled a big part of me out. This, mixed with a measure of anger. Surely the Lord God and heavenly Father could have done something to protect her, to keep her from dying. Yet I must learn to accept this terrible thing that has come across my path. It is our way. At all costs, we must trust in divine sovereignty, even when, secretly, doing so is just plain hard.

Am I alone in this?

My sister was daring, truth be told. Mamma sometimes said such characteristics in a pretty girl were a recipe for danger, and trouble certainly seemed to follow Suzy during her last months. Losing her was bad enough, but my own guilt tears me apart, too. I've heard tell of survivor's guilt—when you feel responsible because someone you loved has died, and you've survived. But that isn't my guilt. No, mine is ever so much worse.

Most times I'm able to push it deep down, where I can scarcely feel it, but every so often the blame rises unexpectedly. If not for me, Suzy would be alive. *Jah*, I know her death wasn't my fault, but if I'd stopped her from going with her friends that day—and I would've done so if I'd known she'd a mind to take dangerous risks—I could have saved her. I can only hope someday I'll be able to forget all of that. Forgetting Suzy will be impossible.

As for dear Mamma, it seems she can't think on much else. All of us miss Suzy's presence dreadfully—her constant whistling on washday, as well as her cheerful, even mischievous smile while weeding the vegetable garden. Like she knew something we didn't.

I daresay it is Rhoda and Nan . . . and myself—all of a sudden the youngest—who must help carry poor Mamma through this sorrowful time. Nearly all her energy still seems spent on Suzy. I see her pining in the set of her jaw, the way she shies away from social gatherings, longing for the comfort of silence . . . for her cherished aloneness. No doubt she yearns to talk to Suzy again, to cup her freckled face in both her hands and hold her near.

Sometimes I want to hug Mamma and whisper, "I'm so sorry. Please forgive me." But she wouldn't understand, and my words wouldn't change anything.

Truth is, Suzy's gone. The ground holds her body now. The ground holds her diary, as well. I broke my promise to burn it if anything ever happened to her, the kind of talk between sisters who never think they'll have to honor their frivolously spoken vow. Instead, I walked to the wooded area behind the paddock and buried it deep in the ground, as good as destroyed. Better that we remember the Suzy we all knew as sweet, innocent, laughing—the truest friend—and not who she became.

While Mamma grieves in her own way, Dat scarcely talks of Suzy. He acts almost as if nothing's changed, as if he isn't affected by her death. Yet I can't bring myself to believe he is cold toward the loss of his youngest daughter. Surely he is merely sad and simply unable to express his grief openly as his womenfolk do. I see flickers of pain and worry around his dark brown eyes. *Jah*, at the heart of him, he must suffer the searing, constant ache the rest of us feel when we whisper amongst ourselves of lovable Suzy and the mystery surrounding her life . . . and death. Daily, we struggle to face the future without her.

There's but a single bright spot on my horizon: Caleb Yoder. Now, I must admit to having spent time at Singings and youth frolics with plenty of fellas, but none who holds a candle to Caleb as I imagine him. Though the days continue to pass, I'm still holding out hope that he might yet invite me to go riding after a Sunday night Singing or other gathering. Such a fine driving horse he has, too. He might chuckle if he knew I thought such things!

I may be just fuzzy brained enough to think my affection for him is enough to keep me going when I feel this sad. Maybe Caleb has figured things out for himself about Suzy's final weeks and her death—who knows what he's heard, what with the rumor mill hard at work. Could be that's why he hasn't asked me to ride with him sooner, unless he is seeing someone else. If he is, I can hardly blame him.

Even so, I hold my breath, reminding myself that he might be honoring my time of grieving, a noble thing if true. Then again, maybe I'm mistaken that he ever noticed me at all, and I'm simply engaging in wishful thinking born of a wounded heart. Either way, I realize how important it is to yearn for the best, as Mamma used to say . . . before she lost her Suzy.

To my thinking, Caleb *is* the best. He is admirable and good from the inside out. I only hope he might choose to smile at me again, for hope is all I have.

CHAPTER 1

She sometimes wondered what her life might have been like had she been given only one first name. Instead, she had two—Nellie, after her great-grandmother on her father's side, and Mae, for Mamma's youngest sister.

Despite the near-fancy ring to them, Mamma had often said the names were a good fit, and what with the special attention Nellie Mae gave to creating her pies, cakes, and other pastries, she guessed her mother was right.

But I'm not fancy, not one bit! She hurried across the drive toward the bakery shop set back behind the house, where Dat had made an area for parking both automobiles and horses and buggies. Nellie Mae glanced at the hand-painted sign atop the bakery shop and smiled.

Nellie's Simple Sweets.

The cozy place was considered hers because of her near-constant baking as a girl. By the time she could roll out pie dough or see to it that a two-layer cake did not fall, she was baking more than her family could possibly consume. It was Dat who had suggested building a small shop right on the premises to offer Nellie's delectable treats to the rest of Honey Brook. Of course, it never hurt to bring in some extra cash, which the shop certainly did, thanks to word of mouth from Nellie's many satisfied customers.

This nippy September morning, Nellie Mae raised the green shades on each window and quickly turned the sign on the door to Open. In less than five minutes, the regulars started to arrive, all *Englischers*, two by car, and the other on foot. The brass bell on the door jingled merrily as they each entered, all smiles.

"*Willkumm*," Nellie greeted first Mrs. Hensley, a woman with a distinct southern accent; then Miss Bachman, who was known for her peanut butter cravings; and Rhoda's employer, Mrs. Kraybill, two of her children in tow.

Not wanting to appear overly eager, Nellie Mae stood primly behind the counter while the ladies perused the display case. Mrs. Hensley scrutinized the array of baked goods, a canary yellow dress resembling a sack beneath her sweater. Rhoda had spoken of such tent dresses, as they were called by the English, and Nellie was polite not to stare at what surely was the brightest dress she'd ever seen. With her swept-over bangs and pouffy hair, Mrs. Hensley couldn't have looked more like an Englischer.

Mrs. Kraybill blinked her pretty eyes over her rimless glasses and asked, "Would you mind if I purchased all four dozen of the pumpkin cookies?"

"Why no, not at all," Nellie was quick to say.

Mrs. Hensley pointed to the cinnamon-raisin cake front and center on the counter, tapping her manicured fingernails on the glass. It was nearly all Nellie could do to keep from leaning forward and telling her how wonderful-*gut* the cake tasted.

"How do you bake all this yourself?" Mrs. Hensley asked, her fingernails still resting on the glass. "It's perfectly lovely."

"Melts in your mouth, too," added Miss Bachman, eyeing the peanut butter fudge on the left. "How you manage to bake everything without so much as a recipe amazes me, Miss Nellie Mae. You're a walking cookbook!" Glancing at Mrs. Hensley, she smiled. "If you want the recipe, just ask. Nellie's as generous with her know-how as she is with the sugar on her cookies."

Nellie Mae blushed. She had always had a good memory. When it came to listing off ingredients and correct measurements, she could do so in her sleep.

Rooting in her purse, Mrs. Hensley pulled out her wallet and a small tablet. "Would you mind terribly, dear? I'd love to try my hand at that cake." Her eyes pleaded for the recipe.

Quickly Nellie rattled off the ingredients and the measurements, feeling somewhat self-conscious, even though she didn't mind one iota sharing such things with her regular customers.

If only Caleb Yoder would stop by sometime, she thought before catching herself. It was wrong to boast, and she would surely be doing so by showing off her baking ability for the sake of male admiration. Still, Nellie could hope.

She turned her attention to making correct change. When she'd finished with Mrs. Hensley's purchases, she assisted the other two women, who, much to Nellie Mae's delight, were now fussing over who would have the fudge.

———

Nellie Mae sat fidgeting in her elder brother Ephram's carriage early Thursday morning, thankful Mamma had sent Nan to oversee the bakery shop so she could make this visit. She adjusted her black outer bonnet while Ephram sat silently on the right-hand side of the carriage, his eyes focused on the road as they drove toward his house.

Snug under her heavy woolen lap robe, she tucked her hands into the gray muff and shivered, wishing it were summer again. She daydreamed of lying in a green meadow, the delicious scent of wildflowers perfuming the air.

Will Caleb ask me home from Singing by next summer, at least?

So much time had passed already. Regardless, she was tired of going with boys she didn't much care for, even though she had been guilty of stringing two young men along. While she'd enjoyed their company, most of the boys she'd gone with were ho-hum; none of them made her heart sing the way Caleb had the day he'd smiled at her. As with every boy around here, all had plans to farm. That was right fine with Nellie Mae. She wasn't hoping for someone who would do things differently. All she wanted was someone who had opinions of his own, and was not only appealing but who was smitten with her, as well.

Is that too much to ask?

Lots of girls married simply to get hitched, and she had no interest in that. She would not marry if it meant settling for someone to cook and clean for and having a whole string of babies. She wanted what Mamma had with Dat—a steady fire between them. Even after all these years, she could see it when her parents looked at each other from across a room.

Willing herself to relax, she sensed the buggy was warmer today than yesterday, when she'd gone with her mother to the general store in Honey Brook after closing her shop for the day. She always felt more secure when either her father or one of her five older brothers drove the team. Of course their driving was not nearly as much fun as the wild buggy driving the fellows she'd dated liked to do. No doubt such recklessness was partly to blame for several fatal accidents involving buggies and cars in recent years, not all on the more congested main roads. Surely it was good that today her elder brother—responsible husband and father of four, with another on the way—steadily held the reins, just as he did for his family.

Who will hold the reins of my life?

She shifted her feet, conscious of the tremor of the wheels on the road through the high-topped black shoes her mother had insisted she wear. *"Too late in the season for bare feet,"* Mamma had said before sending her off. *"Tell your sister-in-law hullo for me, won't ya?"*

Nellie sighed, watching the trees as the horse and buggy carried her along. She dreaded the coming winter with its lash of ice and wind. She wriggled her toes in the confining shoes, longing for the freedom of bare feet.

Farmers up and down the long road—Amish and English alike—were busy baling hay . . . what little there was, due to the regional drought. Farther up the road, the neighbors' apple orchard came into view. Immediately she wondered if the orchard had been affected, too. Would there be enough fruit for cider-making frolics and apple butter, come late fall? The apple harvest always meant a large gathering of young people—perhaps Caleb would be among them. A work frolic was one of the ways the young people mingled during the daytime, but it was under the covering of night that courting took place.

She tried to shut out the surroundings and let her mind wander, imagining what it would be like to encounter Caleb at such a lively get-together. She found herself lost in the reverie, wishing something might come of it. Hoping, too, he might not be as curious about Suzy's death as certain others seemed to be.

Her brother spoke just then, startling her. "You're awful quiet, Nellie Mae."

Ephram did not gawk at her the way he sometimes did when they traveled to and from his house. Though the visits were rather infrequent, he had been kind enough to offer to bring her back with him this morning, sparing her the two-mile walk to visit her sister-in-law Maryann. If time permitted, Nellie wanted to see her best friend, Rosanna King, too.

Her brother's blond hair stuck out beneath his black felt hat. The straw hats of summer had recently disappeared on the menfolk, something that nearly always caught Nellie Mae by surprise every autumn.

"You're brooding," he said.

"Maybe so." Absently she rubbed her forehead, wondering if her frowning into the morning light had given her away.

"Aw, Nellie, what's troubling you?"

But she couldn't say, though she hadn't been brooding; she was simply pondering things.

She glimpsed at him, averting her eyes before daring to ask, "Did ya hear anything 'bout that meeting Dat went to two weeks ago?"

Ephram turned right quick to look at her.

She smiled. "Seems you *did* hear, then."

His rounded jaw fell and he turned his attention back to the road. Even though she rarely interacted with him, Nellie could see right through this brother. His dairy cattle and growing family kept him plenty well occupied these days, but Ephram had always worn his feelings on his plump face. "What're you talkin' about?" he asked.

"I heard there was a gathering. All hushed up, too."

He shook his head. Whether it was in disgust or out of reserve, she didn't know. Fact was, she wanted to know, but she wouldn't press him further. Not fitting for a woman, Mamma would say—though Nellie didn't always embrace everything Mamma thought or suggested. Even so, today there was no sense dredging up the tittle-tattle she'd heard at the bakery shop about the menfolk and their secret meeting. Likely they'd meant it to remain just that.

Nellie wondered if this summer's stunted crops hadn't caused some of the recent turmoil. She'd heard there were some who were convinced the failed crops were a dreadful prophecy to the area of Honey Brook. Limited as the problem was to their area, it was as if God had issued them a warning.

She recalled the upheaval the phenomenon had caused. As farmers, their very livelihood depended upon the success of their crops. Feed for livestock and chickens had been trucked in. And the bakery shop felt the pinch, as well, from the need to purchase ingredients, tapping into the family's profits.

Shifting her weight a bit, she stared out the other window. The heavy dew looked much like frost, with the biting cold to go with it; the harsh air must have sneaked up on them and fallen into the hollow while they slept last night. Summer's end though it was, it felt like the middle of winter. And even though that meant ice and snow and wind and cold, Nellie Mae longed for this year to be over and a brand spanking new one to begin.

Looking at her brother now, she wished he would say what he surely knew about the meeting in the bishop's barn.

What's the big secret?

Ephram was turning in where the tree-lined lane led to his house. Right away Nellie spied Maryann standing in the door, clearly in the family way as she waved a hankie-welcome.

"Now, don't be fillin' *her* head with your s'posings and all," Ephram warned, stepping down to tie the horse to the hitching post.

Nellie wondered why he hardly ever referred to his wife by her name. So many of their men referred to their wives as "she" or "her," instead of by their lovely names.

I sure wouldn't want to marry a man like that.

Nellie Mae thought again of Caleb, wondering what he would say to all the gossip. Should he ever be available to talk to, would she dare ask? Or would he treat her the same distant way Ephram seemingly treated Maryann?

CHAPTER 2

———

"O h, Nellie Mae, ever so nice to see ya. Do come in." A glowing Maryann kissed her cheek as she came through the door.

Nellie gave her tall sister-in-law a quick hug. "Hullo, Maryann. Nice seein' you, too." She shed her shawl in the welcoming warmth of the house.

"You should come more often. Before you know it, we'll have another little one in our midst." Maryann's hand briefly went to her middle.

"Jah, and I'm looking forward to meeting him or her." Nellie sighed. "Ach, but it seems so hard to get away these days." With Mamma grieving hard and tongues still wagging about Suzy, Dat had made it clear to Nellie that she and she alone was in charge of handling the bakery's customers—at least for now.

"How is your dear mamma?"

"Well, she struggles." *We all do.*

Maryann reached for her hand, her hazel eyes serious. "'Tis not surprising. Tell her I asked 'bout her, will ya?"

Nellie nodded.

"It's good of you to visit." Maryann ushered her to the kitchen, where some sassafras tea was brewing and a plateful of warm oatmeal and raisin cookies graced the long table. "Care for a treat?"

Nellie sat down, glad to be inside after the chilly buggy ride. Maryann was known to bake new cookies well before the former batch was eaten. "Don't mind if I do." Nellie reached for two.

Maryann eyed her. "Oh, take more than that. You can stand a few more pounds, jah?"

Nellie was content with what she had, as well as the cup of tea sweetened with a few drops of honey. The pair talked of all the canning Maryann had already accomplished, and the recent sewing she was doing for the children, especially for the two older ones enjoying school this fall. As they sipped tea, Maryann periodically added more honey to hers, her fondness for sweets evidently heightened by her pregnancy.

Mindful of Ephram's earlier warning, Nellie shied away from discussing any hearsay. Even so, she was on pins and needles trying to comply with her older brother's wishes, all the while anxious to discover what Maryann might know.

The house seemed too quiet, although she was sure Ephram had camped out in the front room—doing what, she didn't know. Aside from that, the house was a large and comfortable place with a small *Dawdi Haus* built on one side for Maryann's grandparents, ready for whenever they might need to live closer.

Nellie made small talk. "Katie and Becky must be napping?"

"Jah, tired little girlies they are. Katie's tryin' to catch herself a cold, seems."

"Sure would like to see them before I leave."

"I wouldn't expect them to sleep too much longer," Maryann said with a smile. "By the way, your friend across the road would be happy for a visit, if you have the time," she added, as if she were aware of Nellie's intentions. "Rosanna said as much this morning . . . almost like she guessed you were comin'." Maryann chuckled. "The two of you have always known each other so well."

Nellie nodded at that. Though never as close to her as Suzy, Rosanna was as dear as a flesh-and-blood sister. The only girl in a family with a whole line of boys, Rosanna had frequently sought out Nellie's company over the years.

"Rosanna works hard makin' all those quilts," Maryann said.

"Jah, close to fifty a year."

Nellie had sometimes assisted Rosanna and two of her sisters-in-law to get a quilt in the frame and done up right quick for customers. But since Suzy's death, Nellie had been too busy with her own work to help out or visit. Now that she was here in Maryann's kitchen, she realized how much she'd missed both women, especially Rosanna.

Nellie finished drinking her tea silently as Maryann began talking of upcoming work frolics and the November wedding season, an obvious twinkle in her eye.

Of course, it was best for Nellie to follow tradition and keep her interest in Caleb to herself, especially with Iva Beiler and Susannah Lapp fondly glancing his way at the last few Sunday Singings. Caleb was mighty good-looking; no one would argue that. And while he wasn't one to flirt like some fellows, he certainly had an engaging way. No question that the deacon's pushy daughter was set on capturing his attentions. Nellie would never admit to disliking Susannah, but watching the way she batted her eyes at Caleb made Nellie's fingers tingle to wipe that syrupy smile from her pretty face.

For all Nellie knew, Susannah had already laid her trap and caught Caleb. Maybe that's why Nellie hadn't heard from him—he'd been stolen out from under her nose while she was mourning Suzy . . . before she'd even had a fair chance.

She accepted a second cup of tea and glanced out the window, captivated by the first hints of fall color. "Seems autumn has snuck up on us, ain't so?" Nellie said wistfully.

The splendor of the season seemed less important to Maryann. "Have you heard any of the latest church rumors?" she asked in a sudden whisper.

"Some."

"There's dissension." Maryann was solemn, leaning as close as her grow-ing stomach allowed. "Some of the brethren don't see eye to eye on the *Ordnung*."

Nellie moved nearer, pleased Maryann had offered this without any prompting.

"Trouble's brewing, Nellie Mae. For nearly a month now."

While Nellie was sure such trouble did not concern her and her family, she tensed up at this admission from Maryann. She chided herself. *'Tis a sin to worry.*

Afraid Ephram might overhear them, Nellie purposely stared down at the green-checked tablecloth. "Best not be sayin' more . . ."

Maryann slowly rose to pour more tea for herself. Then, sitting again, she glanced at Nellie and tilted her head nervously toward the doorway between the kitchen and the large front room. Likely Ephram was but a few yards away.

Nellie changed the subject. "When do ya think you'll be goin' to an-other quilting?" She hoped to finish their gossiping elsewhere, far from her brother's listening ears.

At that Maryann held her sides, seemingly bursting with repressed mirth. "Aren't you a good one, Nellie Mae."

Nellie smiled and gave an anxious little chuckle. She lifted her teacup to her lips, hoping her eyes might relay what was on her mind. There was precious little freedom to visit in *this* house.

For that reason, she could hardly wait to bid Maryann farewell. In a few minutes she would hurry across the road and look in on dear Rosanna, who would give most anything to be expecting her *first* baby, let alone the fifth, as was Maryann.

Reuben Fisher wouldn't have thought of telling a soul, but he found himself grinding his teeth whenever one of his daughters got to talking about missing Suzy. Heavyhearted as he felt, especially when Betsy wept in his arms for their youngest, he could not bring himself to speak of Suzy. Not to anyone.

He had heard the whisperings of the grapevine—Suzy had died because of her contrariness . . . her sightings with worldly boys, her growing secrets. It was becoming all too common for young people in *Rumschpringe*, the running-around years, to sow wild oats; their Suzy's mistake was dying in that carefree state. For that and for missing out on baptism into the church, she was damned for eternity.

He was a father in need of solace, with no one to turn to. No one who might offer understanding for the increasing fear that filled him. No one who might give him hope. No, all he was offered was the standard answer: "This is our belief . . . and 'tis the sovereign will of God."

Everything within Reuben cried out against the image of his youngest burning in fire and brimstone. She was young, for pity's sake—just sixteen . . . not quite ready for weighty matters such as joining church. Betwixt and between.

He considered his cousin Jonathan and what he might have to say on this matter. Recently Jonathan had embraced beliefs foreign to the church's guidelines for living—their Ordnung—and was therefore deemed dangerous. What a man chose to think about such things independent of the membership was not trustworthy at all.

Jonathan's wife and grown children had followed in his beliefs, standing with him in his choice of an "alien gospel," as the bishop had declared whatever nonsense Jonathan now embraced. In fact, Jonathan's offspring had so united with him, the People had voted to excommunicate the whole bunch.

At least his kin sympathize, thought Reuben sadly, wishing there was some way around the shunning practices that meant ostracizing long-standing church members, treating church brothers—in this case Reuben's own relatives—nearly as outcasts. The longer Jonathan refused to renounce his new belief and repent of it, the harder life would become. The purpose of the *Bann* was to bring wayward ones back to the church, where they were expected to obey the Ordnung, never to turn away again.

Yet as dire as Jonathan's present circumstances looked to be, Reuben could not ignore the fact his cousin fairly reeked with joy, even after suffering the shock of excommunication at the vote of the brethren and the membership. Reuben often wondered exactly what had gripped his cousin so thoroughly that he had found strength to walk away from all he knew and loved.

Could it help me cope with Suzy's death? His grief intertwined with an intense curiosity, driving him now to visit his errant cousin. Such fellowship was still allowed by the bishop, for the time being, provided there was no exchange of money or eating at the same table. Eventually, Jonathan would be cut off.

Jonathan and his wife, Linda, greeted Reuben warmly, and after making small talk about the weather and whatnot, Reuben had nearly forgotten the bishop's prohibition—that is, until Jonathan began reading Scripture.

Despite Reuben's protestations, Jonathan insisted on holding up the Bible and reading portions of it Reuben had never heard. As was their way, the ministerial brethren preached from the same biblical texts each time they gathered. Even Reuben's own father and grandfather had kept to those limited passages during nightly Scripture reading when Reuben was growing up. Only certain chapters were sanctioned by the bishop.

Jonathan continued to read from Galatians, chapter one. " '. . . the gospel which was preached of me is not after man. For I neither received it of man, neither was I taught it, but by the revelation of Jesus Christ.' " He raised his eyes toward Reuben. "See? It's right there." Jonathan sighed, tears welling up. "The Lord's in those words. He's revealing himself directly to us."

"You're sure it says that?" Reuben leaned over to have a look-see. He peered at verses eleven and twelve, muttering as he read them aloud. Jonathan was not pulling his leg about what the Scriptures said, but Reuben felt his mind resist. This was *not* the teaching imparted to him in his youth.

Jonathan gripped his arm. "You should look at the third chapter of John, too. It could be the difference 'tween—"

"What?" Reuben shot back, suddenly alarmed. He'd never before witnessed such intensity in his cousin's eyes.

Jonathan released his hold and ran his hand through his dark beard. "Just read it, cousin."

Reuben was torn. Here he was talking with a blemished man, one who was no doubt trying to recruit him to the wrong side of the fence. It was a line Reuben wasn't willing to cross.

"You goin' to please the Lord God or the brethren?" asked Jonathan.

"Ain't that simple."

"Well, 'tis so . . . the way I see it." Jonathan held his old Bible out to him. "Everything we need to know is here, Reuben—*all* we need for life and godliness. I beg of you, read it. For the sake of your children and grand-children. So they don't end up . . . like Suzy."

Reuben trembled. "What's that?"

"I'm sorry, cousin. I never should've—"

Reuben felt his ire surge within him. "Getting myself shunned won't bring my daughter back," he interrupted, putting on his hat. "Sorry to take up your time, Jonathan."

He bade his cousin a terse farewell, hurrying to the horse and buggy.

Out on the road, he seethed, needing the space of miles between Jona-than's house and Bishop Joseph's to quiet his thoughts. He'd brought along his eldest brother's shovel to return and was mighty glad he had. Time to put some distance between himself and his shunned cousin.

A group of steers were on the move near the side of the road to the south. He noticed several cattle bunched together, vying for clumps of green sage. The yearlings stayed close to their mothers, some of them bawling as they went.

It was hard to take his eyes off the cows and their calves. His sons raised large herds of cattle, though he had always preferred horses. He observed the cattle crossing the stream, as if following him, some eyeing his horse while others paid no mind.

At the next junction, Reuben spotted a row of bedraggled late roses, the last blossoms of summer hanging on. The bishop's place came into view, and he looked forward to exchanging a few kind words with his eldest brother before heading on home to Betsy and his work.

But as he tied up the horse and headed to the bishop's barn, he happened upon another spur-of-the-moment meeting—the second such debate over the Ordnung in two weeks.

Several men were talking about tractors, and others were raising their voices in favor of electricity and cars, too. "We don't just want 'em, we need 'em!" huffed one man.

Reuben's own first cousin, Preacher Manny—short for Emmanuel—shook his head in response. "We can't be unified for the upcoming communion if yous don't stop and listen to yourselves. It's impossible to make any headway with the order of things . . . not with such discord."

Ephram's neighbor, Abraham Zook, seemed bent on change, his eyes squeezing nearly shut as he spoke. "I call for an altering of the Ordnung come next month, before communion service and foot washin'."

The bishop next district over and his two preachers—all from Chester County—raised their voices in accord with Preacher Manny against what looked to be a growing faction of discontented farmers.

But Abraham ignored them. "It's high time we get some help. That freak summer drought nearly did some of us in."

"That's God's business," said Preacher Manny.

"Well, I say the Good Lord gave us brains and we oughta use 'em." Abraham turned toward his three sons, who muttered their agreement. One of them egged him on by cuffing him lightly on the back. "We could use the tractor power. Now more than ever."

When will it end? Reuben wondered, slowly stepping back to remove himself from the ruckus. Struggling from dawn till dusk was the expected way of the People—the way things had always been done.

Then Old Joe Glick and four of his brothers, along with a handful of their fired-up cousins, started defending the Ordnung. One of the younger men pointed his finger, and several more near Reuben mimicked the gesture, their eyes intent on Abraham and his sons. For sure and for certain, this meeting was even more heated than the last one, where many of these same men had gathered to voice frustration.

Placing his hat on his head, Reuben turned to go. But right then his brother spoke up from behind him. "'Tis time all of us head on home. We've got plenty-a work to be done, seems to me," the bishop said.

Abraham frowned. "Jah, we've plenty-a work, Bishop . . . and tractors would ease the burden. We're losin' ground in more ways than one."

"Such things are of the devil, the way I see it." The bishop caught Reuben's eye as he faced Abraham and the others. "'Tis best to do what you know you're s'posed to, following what we all know is right and good. And, Abe—and those of you of like mind—you best be watchin' your rebellious spirit."

Abraham looked down at the floor, working his foot on something Reuben couldn't see.

Their sixty-year-old bishop shook his head. "I must say, there's far more to this than meets the eye. And it can't be solved in these dog-and-cat fights."

Reuben was moved to speak at last. "Why not call the membership together? We'll put this thing to rest."

Both the bishop's and Preacher Manny's expression changed mighty fast. "Reuben, you have no idea what you're talking 'bout," said his brother.

The preachers from Chester County nodded, seemingly in agreement.

Then Bishop Joseph spoke again. "The die is cast . . . no turnin' back to voting and such. Here lately, if it's not one thing, it's another: men wanting tractors . . . others wanting to do away with shunning practices." He folded his arms over his stocky chest. "Seems we need more than just another gathering."

"Jah, but 'tis best to keep the women out of this for the time bein'," Preacher Manny said, eyeing Reuben.

"Well, our wives ain't deaf, nor are they dumb." Reuben stepped forward. "They surely know something's a-brewin'." He was tired of all this talking in circles; time to draw a line in the dirt. He was *for* the Ordnung as it stood, so why was Manny singling him out, anyway?

Manny's eyes shot daggers. "Best be keepin' your thoughts to yourself, cousin."

Ach, I'm with ya, Preacher, don't misunderstand, Reuben wanted to say.

Well, he was with Manny on *most* aspects of the Ordnung. He thought again of Suzy, departed before she could take the kneeling vow. It was impossible to erase from his mind the painful knowledge that baptism into the church was essential for any hope of heaven.

To think that some folk, in other churches, were allowed to say they belonged to the Lord—*saved,* as it were—and could rejoice in that assurance. His cousin Jonathan believed exactly that. Oh, to know where you were going when you died!

Poor, dear Suzy . . .

Reuben had a gnawing emptiness in his very soul, a festering grief he refused to express. Following the Old Ways had not fulfilled his spiritual longing, and his discussion this morning with Cousin Jonathan hadn't made things any better.

CHAPTER 3

B etsy Fisher, mother of nine, thought of herself as a perceptive soul, though she would never boast of it. Reuben had surprised her once by saying she had an uncanny way of deciphering the things folk said, could cut right through to the truth.

Fact was, she sometimes felt most everything right and good had ceased when her youngest daughter drowned. She assumed this was how other mothers felt when their children's lives were cut short . . . taken away too soon from those who loved them.

Sighing, Betsy gazed out the kitchen window at the clear sky, as blue as a piece of fine pottery she'd seen over at a shop north of Strasburg not so long ago. The color had stood out because it was so unlike the blue of the fabric sanctioned by the brethren. Not the royal blue of their cape dresses, but the soft yet distinct blue of a robin's egg.

She found herself glad for the lack of rain this day—the weather made traveling pleasant, and Ephram had already come to drop off some preserves from Maryann, offering to take Nellie Mae over to see her when he was headed home again. It was awful nice how that worked out, seeing as how Nellie scarcely got a chance to visit with Maryann.

Betsy realized anew that she disliked having Nellie Mae farther away than the bakery shop. Since Suzy's death, Nellie was the daughter who had watched over her most closely, as if more aware of the depth of her mother's loss. When Nellie left a room, she took something along with her. *Something I sorely need*, Betsy thought.

There had been times lately when she felt sure Nellie Mae was stronger than she herself, even as a grown woman. Betsy had known it in her bones from her daughter's earliest days just how confident Nellie was—at least since Nellie's first determined baby steps at only nine-and-a-half months. It was no surprise that such a determined child had grown into the kind of young woman capable of running a shop almost single-handedly. Few girls could handle such responsibility, let alone thrive under its weight.

Jah, Nellie's a strong one. Ever so steady on her feet . . . and otherwise, thought Betsy. *Till recently.*

She wiped her hands on her long black apron and hurried down the center hall of the farmhouse, heading for the back door. She had been awake since before sunup, glad for the few tender moments of Reuben's usual morning natter and nuzzling before he arose for a long day of work.

Sighing once more as she opened the door, Betsy breathed deeply of the crisp air. Just yesterday she'd noticed moths had clustered in the dark trees like tiny umbrellas, foretelling the cold snap. She looked out over their vast spread of land, a gem of a place nestled in a green hollow—"away from it all," as Reuben liked to say. His grandfather had bestowed this land upon them when they'd decided to up and marry nearly the second they'd started courting. Their youth had stunned the bishop, but he was happy enough when the babies started coming a full year later.

Betsy smiled. *Such a long time ago, but, oh, the good days of hard work and raising youngsters.* The familiar lump in her throat threatened to return, but she willed herself not to cry. *One step at a time,* someone had told her. You didn't get over the loss of a child in a mere three months. It could take years and even longer.

Whatever might come, Betsy must not let this crush her heart as she'd seen happen to others. Grief-ridden mothers, some who'd lost little ones at the hands of Englischers who drove recklessly around the buggies, speeding up on purpose, or so it seemed.

Does this pain the Lord God, too?

She was squinting hard, knowing she ought not to give place to anger. Even so-called accidents were the will of the Sovereign One, Jehovah God, whose ways were lofty—higher than her own. Trials made one stronger, didn't they?

The Good Book itself spoke of such profound sadness—weeping only lasting so long, then joy coming in the morning. Even for her, the time for the singing of the birds and spring would come eventually, if the Lord God saw fit to turn her sorrow into gladness. When dear Reuben read Scriptures like these, she often felt comforted, and she took refuge in the fact.

Betsy whispered to the air, "Are there others who fret like me?" She expected there were, even though they, too, had been taught to adhere to the Ordnung; many of its rules had been handed down for generations. They embraced whatever life brought, knowing that in God's providence, it was meant to be.

Forcing her mind on to the task now at hand, Betsy headed toward the chicken house. The old frame structure had recently been made sturdier by her husband's frugal ingenuity. She recalled her days as a young bride, gladdened by Reuben's natural skill in breeding and raising horses. He had gotten his start by purchasing half a dozen lame racing horses at local stock-yard auctions, mostly Morgan trotters, taking care to flawlessly mend their injuries. Over time those horses and their offspring became some of the best for harness use, thanks to Reuben's gentle, yet persistent nature and knack for training colts. His reputation was such now that Amish farmers from all around the area turned to him whenever they required a reliable horse. Truly, Betsy knew she'd married a good man; one with a good heart, too.

She caught herself in a rare smile and stopped to glance across the yard at the bakery shop, all freshly painted and done up. *Wonder how Nan's faring today.* Most days, she'd much rather help Nellie Mae's customers than tend to the chickens. Who wouldn't? Nice warm, cheery room. Friendly faces, pleasant chatter . . . a bit of gossip. She felt too alone here lately, but all of that was another thing yet. 'Twas Reuben's say-so where she spent her days for now.

She made her way across the yard, still wet in patches from the heavy dew. She remembered sitting there on the lawn with five-year-old Emma, her son James's daughter. How she'd enjoyed eating strawberries from Kauffman's Fruit Farm in the shade of their old maple.

Was it just this past June—before Suzy died?

A sudden longing sprang up for the youngster who looked ever so much like Suzy, but who possessed more sense of right and wrong, hopefully. She wished Emma would slow down some and not grow up so quicklike. The times she crawled onto her *Mammi's* lap were already becoming scarce. *Thinks she's too big for that now,* Betsy supposed.

What was it about summertime? Children and weeds.

Sighing loudly, she pushed open the door to the chicken house. The hens flapped and cackled greedily. "*Kumm* get it." She reached for the sack of feed, knowing right then why she cared not one bit for this job. She'd only begun doing Suzy's chore the day after she'd drowned, reluctant to let anyone else take it on.

Several times since, she'd considered stepping aside. "Think like Nellie Mae . . . be strong," Betsy urged herself. Still, it was all she could do to complete the chore and get herself back into the house to sit awhile. If only her now-youngest might somehow sense how much she was needed at home.

Rosanna King's blue eyes shone brightly with tears, and her blond hair was pulled back tightly in a large bun beneath her white head covering—her prayer *Kapp*. The expression on her face made it clear to Nellie her friend's tears were joyful ones. "Oh, Nellie Mae, you'll never guess what I have to tell ya. You just never will."

"Well, what on earth?"

"Nearly too good to be true, it is." Rosanna reached for Nellie's hand. "Ach . . . but my cousin Kate has offered Elias and me a most remarkable gift."

The first thing that came to mind was Kate Beiler's antique hope chest, which was a lovely sight to see. Handcrafted from the finest wood, it was perhaps the prettiest piece of furniture Nellie had ever seen. Was Kate going to part with it?

"Kate's in the family way—due near Christmas."

She's had many-a baby, thought Nellie, not quite sure what Rosanna meant to say.

"Kate wants to give the baby to *me* . . . to Elias and me."

Witnessing the joy-light in Rosanna's eyes, Nellie Mae's heart leaped. "What unbelievable news, Rosie!" She had heard of an Amish mother in another state offering to give an infant to relatives, but learning her barren friend was to receive such a gift was another thing altogether.

"Ain't it, though? And to think the Good Lord told my cousins to do this—well, put it in their hearts, I s'pose I should say."

"Jah, 'cause God scarcely ever talks to folk, ya know," Nellie said.

"Well, in this case . . . He surely must have."

"I'm ever so happy for you," Nellie said, smiling at this woman who was as dear to her as the day. Though Rosanna was but twenty-one, she knew too well the sorrow of losing her babies to miscarriage. This last time, the presiding doctor had declared she would probably never carry a baby to term. The shock of the news had been terrible for both Rosanna and her young husband, and Nellie wondered if Rosanna had confided the doctor's startling conclusion to Kate just as she had to Nellie.

Suddenly she felt nervous as worrisome thoughts flitted through her head. What if something happened and Kate couldn't . . . or didn't follow through with her offer? But Nellie held her peace, not wanting to bring a sad thought to her friend, who had yearned for a little one with no success.

"Please sit, Nellie Mae. Have some hot cocoa with me. Time to rejoice."

Rosanna didn't wait for her to agree. She scurried over to the stove and set a kettle on the fire. "'Tis such a gift, ain't? There's no other way to look at it."

"I should say so." Yet Nellie could not understand how Rosanna's cousin and her husband could give away their own precious baby—their flesh and blood. She'd seen the adorable wee ones Kate had birthed over the years, six youngsters in all.

How can Kate relinquish her baby? Won't she pine for this child all the days of her life?

Despite her questions, Nellie's spirits had risen at Rosanna's news. She couldn't help but think, and hope, that just maybe Kate's promise of a baby—a Christmas babe—might somehow dispel some of the ridiculous church tittle-tattle. *If a baby can do such a thing.*

CHAPTER 4

B etsy rolled out the dough for her chicken and dumplings dinner, glad Nellie Mae was back from her visit over at Ephram's. She had tried her best to chat with Nellie upon her return, but her daughter had seemed distracted. She wondered if Nellie Mae had taken the opportunity to open up to Maryann and share her secret. Close as she had been to Suzy, surely Nellie knew more about Suzy's death than she was telling.

Sighing, Betsy expertly shaped each dough ball, washing her hands at the sink when she was through. How convenient it was to no longer have to carry well water indoors from the pump.

Reuben's doing . . .

Thinking of her husband's insistence on bringing water into the house two months back, she hoped Reuben would not fall prey to the urging of his farmer friends and relatives' current progressive talk. Yet her husband had voiced nary an interest in modern farm equipment over the years, despite their living alongside English neighbors who owned such things. Of course, as a newly married couple, she and Reuben had sometimes talked privately of the hard reality of doing things the Old Way, which kept them working long hours, day in and day out. Truth was, Betsy did sometimes envy the Englischers, who could plow, plant, and cultivate their fields in record time.

With time left to rest of an evening . . .

Momentarily she wondered what that must be like, but immediately she rejected the thought, just as Reuben certainly would. It was not the path they had chosen.

She wrapped her arms around her middle, making her way across the backyard to the paved path that led from the dirt road in front of the house all the way back to Nellie's cozy and quaint bakery. The shop's sign perched above the solid structure, beckoning passersby to drop in. Like the rest of the building, it had been built by her husband and their eldest sons—twins Thomas and Jeremiah—both as strapping as they were dependable.

She smiled thinking of her double blessing, still recalling all the fun—and the seemingly endless work—she'd experienced as a new mother of only eighteen. How thankful she'd been even then for a husband who'd added to her joy with his thoughtful ways. Truly she had cared for handsome Reuben Fisher right from the start of their courting days.

Betsy suspected her daughter Nan was equally ripe for a similarly intense romance, although she had no indication from studying Nan's blue eyes, a striking contrast to her rich brunette hair. Nan was as guarded about whom she liked and disliked as any of Betsy's girls, just as a discreet Amish girl ought to be. No, this daughter was not about to give away any secrets with the stoic look on her face.

But now, there was definitely something going on with Nellie Mae. You couldn't miss the blush on her cheeks. She had always enjoyed playing baseball or volleyball with the boys in the church . . . even climbing trees at times, too, which had never set well with Reuben. He wanted his daughters to be young ladies—none of this tomboy business. God made boys to be tough and hardworking, and girls . . . well, they were supposed to be soft and sweet and mighty submissive.

Of course problems arose when there was a lip and an attitude, like Nellie Mae had at times, especially here lately. Thankfully it wasn't as obvious when Reuben was present. Betsy wished Nellie to be compliant and pleasant, but Suzy's death must have triggered something in her. Betsy had discovered the same angry struggle within herself. "Does the Lord God see the darkness within me?" she muttered, looking at the way the light from the sun cast parallel lines on the lawn.

Suddenly she noticed a black automobile with a white top slow down and stop in front of the house. A tall man got out and stood near the mailbox, as if checking for the address. He eyed the signpost poked deep into the ground—Nellie's Simple Sweets—the only advertising needed on the road, as word of mouth was the best source of customers.

Another Englischer, she thought, glad for the additional business. The Good Lord knew they needed to sell all their baked goods each and every day—this fall especially.

This worldly man did not look like one of Nellie's regulars, however. He had a purpose in his stride, and a stiff brown hat on his head. Even the long tan overcoat that looked like it had leaped off the pages of a Sears, Roebuck, and Co. catalogue spoke of business.

"Hello, there, ma'am." He stopped to tip his fine hat. "I'm looking for Reuben Fisher." His eyes were black coals in a too-pale face.

"Who do you say is lookin' for him?" she spouted before she could stop herself.

"Why, that would be me—Mr. Snavely, ma'am." He quickly extended his hand.

"My husband's runnin' errands, but he'll be back after a bit." She wanted in the worst way to ask what this fancy man wanted with Reuben, all dressed as he was in creased black trousers and a worldly sports jacket beneath his open top coat. Even his long plaid tie was looped just so.

"Would you mind giving this to him?" Mr. Snavely handed her a small white card with the silhouette of a small tractor up in the corner. "I've been in the neighborhood. This tells how to reach me."

She glanced at the telephone number, wishing to set him straight: They did not believe in using the devil's tools for either business or pleasure, no matter the convenience they provided. Besides, the bishop would put the nix on such goings-on in a big hurry.

He continued to stand there, looking her over curiously. Surely it was her Plain attire that he found interesting, being a modern fellow and all. Some Englischers weren't accustomed to the sight of Amish folk. "Thank you, uh, Mrs. Fisher?"

"Jah, that's right." She wasn't about to volunteer her first name, although she herself seldom went by her given name of Elizabeth. Better she encourage this unwanted visitor to be on his way.

When Nellie spotted the Englischer shortly after she'd returned home from Rosanna's, she ought not to have been surprised. After all, it wasn't the first time a stranger had rolled to a stop in front of their roadside sign. All the same, she did wonder why he remained out in the yard talking with Mamma, of all things.

"What the world?" Nellie went to the shop window, glad for the short lull, and watched the man lean forward while talking with her mother, apparently handing her something. Was he someone her father knew?

The moment the man hurried back to his shiny car and took off down the road, Nellie ran straight to the house.

Mamma was shaking her head, fanning her pink face with a hankie. "We've got ourselves a tractor salesman in the neighborhood."

"He wants us to buy *what*?" Nellie asked, shocked that an Englischer like that would feel comfortable going door to door.

Evidently the discord among them had already reached the ears of outsiders. Nellie should have seen this coming. Yet she dared not say she'd hinted at such things with Maryann over tea earlier.

Mamma rose. "Well, we Fishers will be havin' none of this nonsense." She opened the cupboard beneath the sink and dropped the business card into the rubbish. "You're not to breathe a word of this, ya hear? Not even to your Dat. No need for him to know a Mr. Snavely even exists."

Nellie Mae had never seen her mother's eyes so dark. The pupils were nearly black—odd, since Mamma's eyes were normally ever so blue. "Next thing People will be wantin' electric and cars and who knows what. It's the evil one at work among us, I say." She reached for the hem of her apron and began again to fan her face.

"Mamma, you're workin' yourself up." Nellie pulled out her father's chair at the head of the table, helping her into it. "Just sit now."

"You've got a mouth on ya, child."

Nellie Mae huffed. "Try and be still, that's all I'm askin'. You know Dat's not interested in such things."

Her mother kept fussing. "Promise you won't speak of this to anyone. We don't need any more worries."

"Oh, Mamma—"

"Right now, promise me!"

Nellie was silent. Then slowly, she shook her head.

Mamma glowered. "Nellie Mae?"

She gritted her teeth at her mother's resolve.

"Give me your word, daughter."

Nellie had stonewalled long enough. "There—you have it." Abruptly she hurried out the door.

Frustrated by her mother's seemingly irrational concern, she noticed a huge flock of red-winged blackbirds appearing out of the dense grass to the east of the house. Like a small black cloud at first, the flock took shape and flew low to the ground across the expanse of pastureland and meadow before flying up, up to the tallest tree. First one bird, then another plunged in and out of sight, settling into the branches of the mighty oak tree.

Suzy had always been so fond of birds, fascinated by their migration each year, their patterns of life.

If only she were still alive . . .

What would her sister have thought of the tractor talk between their mamma and Mr. Snavely? Life had become complicated indeed since Suzy's death.

Nellie cleared the table after supper, glad she'd taken time for a walk to calm herself down after her tiff with Mamma. Glad, too, she'd gone back inside after a while to apologize.

Presently Nan was busy heating some water while Rhoda began sweeping. As she carried dishes to the sink, Nellie observed the contrast in her sisters' hair color—Nan's such a rich brown and Rhoda's a buttery blond. Like Nellie, Nan could eat anything and remain as skinny as a stick, a trait the pleasingly plump Rhoda did not share. Yet despite their physical differences, her two older sisters could not have been closer.

The way Suzy and I used to be . . .

"Mamma's talkin' of having Emma come over for the whole day tomorrow," Nan said suddenly.

"I'm not surprised," said Rhoda, reaching under her Kapp to poke her chubby finger at her blond hair bun.

"Mamma can't seem to get enough of *that* one," Nellie Mae agreed.

"Well, one good look says why." Rhoda had a knowing smile. "She's a little Suzy."

"Just so you know, Emma will have to sleep with *you*, Nellie," Nan said, handing her a dish towel. "Will you dry tonight?"

"Why, sure." Nellie meant she'd dry the dishes, but she didn't mean the wiggle worm could share her bed. "Emma's all over the place when she sleeps."

"Well, why do ya think I suggested you?" To this Nan added a giggle.

"We could put her in James's old bedroom," suggested Rhoda, who stooped down to brush crumbs into the dustpan. "How's that?"

"If she doesn't mind sleepin' in a haunted room," Nan said over her slender shoulder.

"Ain't haunted," Rhoda insisted, pushing up her glasses and heading right to Nan at the sink. "Why do you make up such things?"

Nan grinned. "Ach, I say it is."

"Well, *why?*" Nellie asked, bewildered at the turn in their conversation. She'd never heard Nan talk so.

Nan looked at them both, eyes serious. "Guess you didn't know it, but Suzy went in there sometimes. Quite a lot, really."

"Whatever for?" asked Nellie Mae.

"Maybe to hide the . . . um, smell." Nan held up two fingers to her lips and took an imaginary puff.

Nellie felt her neck burn. "You don't know any such thing."

"Ach, are ya sure?" Rhoda piped up.

Nan shrugged. "I wouldn't be surprised."

Nellie was stunned. "I never saw Suzy smoke."

"Then why did she change clothes in there so often?" Nan smirked.

"You know this for certain?" Nellie asked.

"Jah, I saw her." Nan rolled her eyes, as if to say, *you think I'm fibbing.*

To Nellie the whole conversation seemed irreverent. They had no right to speak of their dead sister this way. Nellie wasn't surprised at Nan's seemingly jealous streak, though.

Nan had always been envious of Suzy's popularity, especially in school in years past. Not to mention the way Dat and Mamma had always held Suzy up as a standard of innocence, much to Nan's consternation—at least until Suzy's last half year.

Still, would she make this up about Suzy?

The teakettle began to shrill. Grimacing, Nan scurried to the stove and carried the kettle to the sink. She poured the boiling water into the cold and added the dish soap, swishing it around to make plenty of suds. As she did, Nan leaned over to whisper in Rhoda's ear, but not so softly that Nellie couldn't hear.

"I daresay Suzy was ready to jump straight to the world," she whispered, "just weeks before she drowned."

Rhoda's hand shot up and clapped over her mouth. "You don't mean it!"

Nan nodded, a glint of sadness in her eye. "Seems so."

Before Nellie could object to the foolish speculation and attempt to scold Nan for such disrespect, Mamma came into the kitchen, hushing them all up.

But for the rest of the evening and long into the night, Nellie thought of Nan's startling words. In some ways, she was glad Suzy's secrets were buried with her—whatever they might have been. She trembled a bit. No, she didn't really mean that. She would give most anything to have Suzy back, laughing and enjoying life, sharing her infectious joy. Nellie Mae would even put up with her apparent fondness for fancy English friends, if only Suzy were alive.

CHAPTER 5

The first thing Nellie Mae did Friday morning was bake more chocolate chip cookies than usual. Recently they were flying off the shelves, and she wondered why. Were fancy mothers too busy to bake once school started? *Seems they'd have more time, rather than less,* she thought.

Later in the bakery, she set about arranging the day's offerings and considered the number of pies and such she could make through the autumn months if she only had more pumpkins. Perhaps Dat or one of her brothers might pick up some more at market over the weekend.

Hearing footsteps, she looked up and saw a young man wearing a black work coat and black felt hat walking toward the bakery shop. He leaned into the breeze in such a way that she couldn't make out his face.

When he came in the door and raised his head, she was stunned to recognize Caleb Yoder, hazel eyes smiling.

What on earth? She thought her heart might stop beating.

"Hullo, Nellie Mae." He removed his hat.

"Hullo."

He fumbled for something in his pocket, and she assumed he was fishing for his wallet.

"I baked lots of cookies today," she said quickly, wondering what he might like.

He fixed his gaze on her. "Frankly, I'm not here for the goodies." Despite his words, he glanced longingly at the pies. "I stopped by on my way to do an errand for *Daed.*" He handed her a piece of paper folded several times. "I want to give this to you personally." His smile spread clear across his handsome face now.

"*Denki,*" she said. The note felt warm in her hand, and she wished he might stay.

But Caleb glanced nervously at the door. Was he worried he might encounter other customers?

"Well, I'd better be on my way." His eyes lingered on hers for a moment. "I'll be seein' ya, Nellie Mae." With that he left.

She moved immediately to the window and watched him fairly march all the way down the drive and out to the main road, where she assumed he'd left his horse and buggy.

Jittery with excitement, Nellie Mae returned to her post behind the counter, the folded paper with her name scrawled on the top still in hand.

I was absolutely right last June. He did smile at me!

Trembling, she opened the note and began to read.

Dear Nellie Mae,

Will you go riding with me after the next Singing? If so, please meet me alongside Cambridge Road afterward, about a mile southeast of the barn. There's a sheltered area among some trees and shrubs that will keep you out of the wind.

Sincerely,
Caleb Yoder

He was asking her in a note? This was rather unusual. Even so it was quite sweet, and Nellie felt ever so happy.

"Ach, this is unbelievable!"

She imagined how blushing pink her face must be, and just now there were customers coming up the drive, having missed Caleb by a mere minute.

She tucked the note into her pocket, her heart singing as she went about helping her customers that morning. *He does like me . . . he does!*

"A true miracle," she decided of the invitation. Up until now Caleb had kept his distance, attending the same Sunday Singings but always talking to others. She would have given up all hope if it hadn't been for that single June smile.

And now this note . . . after three months of waiting, it certainly seemed as if he'd finally decided to act. Yet could she allow herself to fully hope? Caleb had caught the eye of nearly every girl in the district, after all.

But I'm the one he asked!

To think he'd stopped by personally to invite her to ride with him after the next Saturday night Singing—one week from tomorrow!

When a break from customers presented itself, she wondered if she dared run to collect her writing paper from the house. But no, Nellie Mae didn't need to drop everything to give Caleb her reply. *He can wait for the Monday mail*, she decided.

After Mamma's noontime dinner of creamed dried beef and pan-fried potatoes, Nellie Mae was glad for some time to write her response to Caleb. Here, in the quiet bakery shop, it was private—although with its being the start of the weekend, there was no guarantee things would remain so.

She wrote the date on her lined stationery ever so neatly. How she wished for something prettier, but this paper would have to do. There was no extra money, hers or otherwise, for frivolous things like fine writing paper.

Not like Deacon Lapp's daughter surely has. Truth was, Susannah Lapp's father was earning himself a bank full of money raising tobacco, even in a dry year. Others in the community grew the crop, as well, including Caleb's father and all of her own married brothers. It was the cash crop of choice and had been around Lancaster County for longer than Sam Hippey's ring bologna.

Nellie Mae was glad her father had never grown the smelly crop, for she disliked the suffocating scent of tobacco hanging to dry in the shed. She would never understand why on earth her brother Ephram had decided to take up the pipe when their own father had shunned the habit.

Nan startled her but good, rushing in the shop door. "Do ya need any help?"

"All's quiet for now."

Nan's gaze fell to her paper and poised pen. "Takin' inventory?"

"Not today."

"Writing a circle letter, maybe?"

Nellie held her breath. Since Nan had been the one to bring in the mail today, she surely knew there hadn't been a single newsy letter from their cousins. Nan was pushing.

"What, then?" Nan asked, eyes probing.

"Just a little note is all."

Nan nodded. "Ach, if you'd rather be alone, just say so."

Nellie wondered if she'd seen Caleb come and go, but she wouldn't fret over that. Even if Nan had spotted him, she couldn't know his reason for stopping by. Still, she was relieved when her sister left nearly as quickly as she'd arrived. Only then did Nellie resume her writing.

Dear Caleb,

I would be happy to go riding with you next Saturday. I'll meet you where you said to after Singing and wait there in the thicket along the roadside.

Sincerely,
Nellie Mae Fisher

Perusing Caleb's note to her once more, she was thankful Nan hadn't returned, although she could always use help if business picked up. Typically it did this time of day as English folk stopped by on their way home from school or work.

She folded both notes and slipped them into her dress pocket. There would be plenty of time for addressing an envelope later in her solitary bedroom. She'd always thought Suzy's and her room was large enough for only one person, whereas Rhoda and Nan shared a bigger room. Sometimes she could hear them whispering and giggling into the night.

An uncontrollable shiver caught her off guard as reality sank in: Caleb had finally asked her out. Even as wonderful-good as that was, the feeling was tinged with the ever-present underlying sorrow; in happier days she might have shared her news with Suzy.

She missed sharing a room with her younger sister, something they'd done since their earliest days. The many nights they'd talked quietly late into the wee hours seemed precious to her now. At times she felt as if Suzy might simply come walking through the bedroom door. Today surely she would take one look at Nellie and say, "Ach, you look ever so cheerful—who's the lucky fella?"

Suzy had seemed quite eager to become a wife and a mother, to make a home for her family just as all Amishwomen did . . . just as Nellie herself would someday. Truth be told, until lately, Nellie had been rather contented living in her father's house. A comfortable family abode—large enough to bed down the whole family, including the married brothers and their wives and children. Now that there were only three young women left, the place seemed rather empty.

Sometimes while Nellie Mae baked in the early-morning hours, she considered the house and the comfort in its walls to be a safeguard of sorts. She had always loved their home. *A home with character,* Rosanna had said of it years before, after spending more than a week when her parents visited friends in Sugarcreek, Ohio. She and Rosanna had been exceptionally close even then, sharing not only a love of baking, but of quilting. Yet it was not merely the connection to domestic things that tied them together in close fellowship; they simply liked being together. With Suzy gone, Nellie longed for time with Rosanna all the more.

She rose and circled the display counter. Everything had changed, and nearly in the blink of an eye. Their loss of Suzy was enormous.

Perhaps it's missing her so that makes me less content, she thought, knowing she longed for more. But not for material goods. Rather, she yearned for things out of her grasp. Sometimes she went walking deep in the grazing grass or out on the narrow road, heading as far to the east as she could before coming to the busy intersection, then turning again toward home. At times she even caught herself muttering aloud, as if perhaps, in some peculiar way, she was expressing her thoughts to Jehovah God.

She did not quite know what to do about her ongoing yearnings. Often as a girl she had dreamed of the hereafter, wondering what it must be like in God's heaven . . . if the Lord God would see fit to say to her, "Well done, faithful servant," on the Judgment Day. To think Suzy must surely know the answers to these hardest questions of all.

———

With the shop closed for the day, Nellie made her way to her bedroom, aware of the coolness seeping in through the walls of Dat's big house. The second room down from her parents', hers was a cozy place with plenty of space for a loveseat in one corner, for whenever she might entertain a beau, as was their particular courting tradition, come engagement. Might Caleb ever be of a mind to visit her secretly? But she was getting way ahead of herself, she knew.

Already she was in over her head with hope. Who knew, once they spent time together, if she'd even like him? Or if he'd like her?

Standing now at the dresser she and Suzy had long shared, Nellie Mae put Caleb's and her notes safely inside. He had gone out of his way to hand her the invitation. *It could be the beginning of something special*, she thought. *Or will I be just another step in his path to finding a wife?*

She lifted the pretty blue plate that graced the dresser. Between the size of a saucer and a salad plate, it had been a gift from eight-year-old Suzy for Nellie's ninth birthday. Suzy had spotted the sweet little thing at an antique shop, and Mamma had purchased it. Over the years, Suzy had used it to leave notes for Nellie, and vice versa. Sometimes a joke or a funny saying . . . something for cheering up or saying merely "good-bye, till later." Even as a youngster, Suzy had always been thinking of ways to express her love for Nellie and others.

Nellie traced the plate's floral border before returning it to the dresser, wishing now she'd saved the last few notes Suzy had ever written.

Always wishing . . . wishing following the death of a beloved one, her good friend Rosanna said. Rosanna, too, had regrets, never having gotten over her own mother's tragic death so many years before . . . nor the deaths of her unborn babies.

Nellie picked up the hand mirror. Her eyes looked tired and her hair was a little *schtrubbich*, so she smoothed it some on either side of the middle part.

Her sadness often came in waves. Just when she thought she'd healed a bit, she would begin to miss Suzy all over again. Setting the mirror down, she opened the small boxlike compartment on the right side of the dresser. There she found the strings from one of Suzy's white Kapps . . . the last one she'd worn, on the day of her drowning.

Nellie trembled, knowing she had done a wrongful deed in snipping the ties from the sacred covering.

Mamma might not forgive me, she thought. *Yet my deed is nothing compared to the full truth of Suzy's final months, whatever that may be.*

Standing there, she recalled the night of Suzy's viewing here in the house. Mamma and Mamma's sisters had taken great care to bathe Suzy's body. They'd curtained the kitchen off, locked all the doors, and laid Suzy out in the pine box after lovingly clothing her in her best blue Sunday dress and long white apron. Poor Rhoda and Nan could hardly bear to be present and left together after a time to go upstairs. Nellie had suffered through it alone, scarcely knowing how to compose herself.

Not long after, a stream of visitors began coming and going, some staying longer than others. All through the evening this went on, some folk partaking of the great spread of food the women had brought in. Others took nothing more than black coffee before sitting by the open casket, heads bowed. A few of the younger relatives wept softly.

Nellie had kept to herself, wanting to be near her departed sister yet unable to grieve openly. The news of Suzy's death was still terribly fresh—a death she wholly believed might have been avoided.

Long after midnight, when she saw a momentary opportunity—the room's being suddenly empty of people after Mamma stepped away to the outhouse—Nellie crept to her sister's casket. Aware of her own breathing, she felt compelled to place her hand on Suzy's thin wrist, now so cold and lifeless.

Is it really her?

For a moment Nellie was frightened by the lack of vitality, recalling how she and Suzy had reached for each other's warm hands while sharing their bed upstairs. Nellie groaned, her deep sadness enfolding her as she stood, bowed and frozen, so terribly close to her dead sister.

The darling of the family . . .

Nellie refused to cry. She must hurry, for Mamma would not be gone much longer.

Swiftly she pulled the small half page out of her pocket. There was no need to reread the words she had penned earlier, words that had emblazoned themselves onto her heart.

Dear Suzy,

I wish I could've told you this while you were still alive. I'm sorry we argued the morning before you drowned. I was harsh with you, and I wish I could ask for your forgiveness. I miss you, dearest sister.

With all my love,
Nellie Mae

She shook, tears falling fast. Then, hesitating at first, she managed to reach under Suzy to raise her slightly, just enough to slide the folded note beneath her.

With a sorrowful sigh, Nellie stepped back. Suzy's body lay resting on the heartfelt apology, things she'd longed to say since hearing the devastating news. Little good they did her sister now, but perhaps almighty God would see the words she'd written and take them into account. No matter, Nellie had done what she'd set out to do, her heart and head all tangled up with grief and regret.

She moved nearer again, peering down at Suzy's face, so close. "Oh, Suzy . . . why'd you go with them? Why?"

Overwhelmed with both guilt and love, she leaned down and kissed Suzy's cheek. It felt as smooth and hard as the lovely painted faces of English dolls she'd seen and touched at Watt and Shand's department store in downtown Lancaster. She and Suzy had gone with some Mennonite neighbors, but only that once. Nellie remembered observing the many modern teenagers on the sidewalk—boys with hair cut nearly like her own brothers, and girls with free-flowing waist-length hair wearing long, gathered skirts—as though they were trying to be Plain somehow. She'd never told Mamma about their outing, not even to this day.

With a faltering breath, Nellie ceased her reverie and lifted the white ties of Suzy's head covering from the small wooden cubicle. She slipped them into her empty pocket—the same spot where she'd kept Caleb's wonderful note.

She sighed. *When, oh when, will my joy over Caleb overshadow my sadness for Suzy?*

CHAPTER 6

Talkative little Emma *did* come to visit that evening, just as Mamma had wished. As Nan had guessed, it was Nellie who was asked to keep the inquisitive child, and she bedded her niece down early in an attempt to get her settled in.

True to form, Emma had more questions than Nellie had answers. "Where's Aunt Suzy right now?" she asked, lying in bed on the side where Suzy had always slept. "When's she comin' back home?"

Nellie was shocked that her brother James and his wife, Martha, had not explained to their young daughter the finality of Suzy's passing. Or had Emma's young mind simply failed to understand?

Emma began to whimper. "Suzy didn't take her doll with her."

Nellie looked around the room, unsure what Emma could mean.

Still sniffling, Emma rubbed her eyes. "She left her little doll behind. She'll come back for it, jah?"

"Aw, dearie." Nellie leaned forward, kissing her niece's soft forehead.

"*Aendi* Suzy made it last summer . . . during Preachin' " came the explanation. "She made a dolly in a cradle with her white hankie."

Nellie lifted Emma into her arms. "Of course she did." Nellie knew exactly what Suzy had done to entertain Emma during the long, hot Sunday mornings. All the teenage girls and young mothers knew that useful trick.

"I kept the dolly in her cradle, Aunt Nellie Mae." Emma leaned back on the pillow.

"Did you bring it with you?"

Emma shook her head, her blue eyes blinking sleepily. "She's in my room at home. I'll show you next time you visit, all right?"

"Why, sure." She felt as tuckered out as Emma seemed, her energy for the day spent.

"I named her Elizabeth."

Nellie smiled. "Didja know that's Mammi Betsy's name, too?"

"Jah. Mamma told me." Emma closed her eyes. "It's a right perty one." She opened her eyes again. "But I still want Aunt Suzy to come home."

Nellie considered the rote prayers she recited in her mind each night while lying in bed—prayers she'd learned as a child younger even than Emma.

Now I lay me down to sleep . . .

She wondered if Emma was saying them now, too. Or had she succumbed too soon to sleep?

O Lord God and heavenly Father, is my little sister truly in heaven? Or that other place . . . ?

———————

Betsy was glad for the help she was getting with breakfast preparations this morning. Rhoda hummed softly, gingerly tapping the eggs on the frying pan to break them open while Nellie stirred the pancake batter as the griddle heated up. Betsy found it amusing and baffling that a girl who loved to bake sweets was so thin. She supposed it was because Nellie worked so awful hard.

Reuben liked his eggs fried over-easy, with plenty of pancakes on the side. So did Emma, a chip off the older block. She was balanced on her Dawdi's knee, her hands folded expectantly on the table. James was due to come for Emma sometime midmorning, and Betsy hated to think they must say good-bye very soon.

"How many pancakes can you eat?" Reuben asked Emma.

She spun around in his arms. "Ach, you know, Dawdi!" A chorus of giggles spilled out.

He played along, frowning a bit. "Well, now, let's see, was that six or seven?"

Emma grinned and jumped off his lap, going over to watch the pancakes rise on the big griddle, stepping back when Nellie cautioned her.

Betsy moved about the table, pouring freshly squeezed orange juice into each glass. Truly, she couldn't keep her eyes off James's next oldest, such a delight she was. Much blonder than even their Suzy, Emma had oodles of freckles, with one almost exactly where one of Suzy's had been—just left of the tip of her petite nose.

Emma came running. "I wanna wash the dishes, all right, Mammi?"

"You'll have to ask Aunt Rhoda and Auntie Nan. Aunt Nellie will be out at the shop."

As usual, Betsy had heard Nellie Mae rise in the wee hours before dawn, quietly pulling out the many pans in preparation for baking her cookies, pies, and other goodies. Every day she performed the same ritual, except for the Lord's Day. This day, Nellie had baked an abundance of bread, too. How she managed with only a minimum of help from her sisters was anyone's guess.

Rhoda had been employed for quite some time now by the Kraybills, their English neighbors down the road. Other young women in their church district had started doing much the same, with Bishop Joseph's grudging permission. Even Reuben had stated his opinion against Rhoda's arrange-ment, but by the time he'd known about it, Rhoda had already been working there for several weeks. Truth was, as an unbaptized young adult, Rhoda was to some extent at liberty to do as she pleased.

As for Nan, until recently she had helped Nellie fairly regularly at the bakery shop, although reluctantly. These days she more often cooked and cleaned alongside Betsy in the house, stepping with ease into Suzy's shoes.

"Can I help Aunt Nellie, then, after I wash the dishes?" Emma's question broke into Betsy's thoughts.

Reuben smiled broadly at the wee girl's persistence. "You're a busy bee today, ain't so?"

"Only today?" Nellie Mae commented from across the room. "You should try sleepin' with her." Suddenly she seemed sheepish, like she ought not to have hinted at her sleepless night with Emma within earshot. But the truth of the matter was Emma didn't seem to pay her any mind.

Emma leaped off Betsy's lap and headed over to Reuben again. *Such a busy girl is right*, thought Betsy, getting some paper napkins for Emma to put around the table. "Here, girlie . . . help your ol' Mammi out."

Emma stood and took the napkins, turning her face up to look right at her. "Aw, you ain't so old, Mammi. You're just awful sad."

The innocent words unlocked something inside, and lest she weep in front of them, Betsy inched toward the doorway and stepped into the sitting area. Behind her, she heard her husband call to Emma. Going to the window, she stood there almost out of habit, as she could scarcely see for the tears.

Rosanna set to work after the noon meal crocheting a baby blanket with pale yellows, greens, and blues. *Just right for either a boy or a girl*, she thought, although she hoped for a son for her husband, Elias. A firstborn ought to be a boy. Besides, if they were to have only one child, then a son would be ever so nice.

She pressed her hand to her heart. Ever since Cousin Kate's visit and the splendid news, Rosanna had been unable to sleep because of happiness. To think dear Kate would offer up her very own! And now beloved Nellie Mae knew the joyous news, as well.

'Tis God's doing, Kate had told her several times that day she'd come so unexpectedly, her face shining. The day had been one of surprises, to be sure, beginning with Elias's bringing in a whole bushel basket of oversized cucumbers and butternut squash. Rosanna had already set about to making pickles—both sweet and dill—when Cousin Kate had shown up, astonishing her with her words.

"I want to give you a baby, Rosanna," Kate had said. "Seein' you struggle so . . . losin' several wee ones to miscarriage, just nearly broke my heart." Kate had gone on to say she and John had talked it over. "Right away John was in agreement. Something that rarely ever happens, to be sure!"

Sighing now with all the love she already possessed for Kate's little one, Rosanna took pleasure in the feel of the yarn—the softest she could find at the yard goods store. The beauty of it, the way the pastel colors blended so prettily, made her hope this blanket might be as lovely as some she'd seen at Maryann's. Nellie's sister-in-law seemed to have a knack for making baby blankets.

Just as she seems to have wee ones nearly at will.

Rosanna brushed away the thought; she didn't see how she could be any happier if she were expecting her own child.

"Ach, if Nellie Mae wasn't awful surprised," she murmured as her crochet hook made the yarn loops. She let out a gleeful laugh as she recalled Nellie's brown eyes growing wide at the news. Nellie knew well of her pain . . . the heartache of waiting and hoping, month after endless month, for a babe that never lived to see his mother's face. Truly, Nellie was like a sister to her. She remembered the many long-ago times she'd stayed with Nellie and her family; and the same for her friend, spending time at Rosanna's father's house with Rosanna and her brothers. Though life was keeping them farther apart nowadays, their dear friendship had remained strong. For this reason, Rosanna had wanted Nellie to be the first after Elias to know.

As she began the next row on the baby blanket, Rosanna wondered how her friend was really faring here lately. She felt a tremor of sadness at the thought of her own losses, particularly her mother—much too young to die.

And Suzy Fisher dead now, too . . .

Nellie's sister's drowning still caused Rosanna distress from time to time, and she rose and walked into the kitchen. She set her crocheting down on the table and went to stir the beef stew simmering for dinner. How Suzy's death had come about was not at all clear to her. The Fisher family had said only that she had gone boating with some friends and an accident had occurred, although Nellie had shared a bit more privately with Rosanna. More than was necessary to be told around, she had added.

So an Englischer had been Suzy's downfall—her boyfriend, no less. Rosanna leaned over the pot of stew to taste it, adding more seasoning. What would possess a girl to go that route when there were so many nice Amish boys?

For certain, Nellie Mae knew more than she was saying, and it wasn't Rosanna's place to pry. To Nellie's credit, it took some amount of restraint to be tight-lipped—especially when Nellie had always said she felt "ever so comfortable" with Rosanna. From their first encounter as young girls till now, the two had shared openly.

Yet Rosanna had noticed that despite Nellie's sorrow, she looked almost radiant at times. Was Nellie sweet on someone? And if so, why hadn't she confided it as she always had before with every boy Nellie'd liked even a smidgen? There was an air of mystery around Nellie lately, which wasn't like her. If there was a young man, Nellie Mae had evidently decided to keep this one a secret.

Lovingly now, Rosanna touched the unfinished blanket that would warm her baby this winter. Unexpected tears sprang to her eyes. She thought of the last infant she'd seen, at Preaching service last week, and the way the baby had snuggled so blissfully in her mother's arms. She could only imagine what it might feel like to hold the wee one who was to be her own.

"Will it be a son for Elias? Or a daughter for me?" she said softly, bringing the beginnings of the crocheted blanket to her cheek and holding it there.

They'd all had their Saturday night baths, thanks to Dat, who'd built on a small washroom at the east side of the kitchen two months ago. Nellie was most grateful for a bathtub with running water where she could enjoy the privacy of bathing in a locked room. And she secretly liked having the medicine chest with its small mirror affixed to the wall. Having such luxuries certainly spoiled one.

Nellie and Mamma were sitting on Nellie's bed after Bible reading and silent prayers, their long hair still quite damp. "'Tis best not to yearn for what used to be," Mamma said. "Even though I'd like to turn back the clock somehow."

"I think we all would, ain't so?"

Mamma nodded sadly. "Every day." She paused and her face flushed as if she was eager to say something private.

"Aw, Mamma." Nellie touched her mother's hand.

Her mother sniffled. "I dream of Suzy so often."

Nellie rose and picked up her brush from the dresser, feeling a twinge of regret. *Why don't I dream of Suzy?*

Oh, how she'd longed to. The fact that she hadn't—or couldn't—troubled her greatly. Did this happen to others who grieved? Was it because she kept pushing the guilt away? Was she pushing away the memories, too?

Her mother reached for the brush. "Here . . . sit awhile. I'll help you get your tangles out." She stood and began to brush through Nellie's long hair.

Nellie sighed, enjoying Mamma's gentle brushing. She dared not tell a soul, but she had begun to forget what her sister looked like. Try as she might, Suzy's features were beginning to fade, and Nellie felt panicky at the thought. For the first time, she yearned for one of those fancy photographs. Yet even without it, how could she forget her own sister's face? So many things didn't make sense . . . starting with the stunted sweet corn . . . and now all the talk amongst the People.

Was this a sign of things to come?

CHAPTER 7

P reaching service seemed longer than usual. Nellie and her family were cooped up in the deacon's stuffy house, instead of gathering for the Sunday meeting in the barn, where the breezes could blow through the wide doors. The weather having begun to turn, it made better sense to meet inside today.

From where she sat, Nellie Mae could see the back of Caleb's head. Susannah Lapp and her mother and three younger sisters all sat primly in a row, off to one side. Normally Nellie wouldn't have paid any mind to the other young woman's whereabouts, but Susannah kept glancing at Caleb.

Wouldn't she be surprised that Caleb likes me? Nellie thought, feeling more smug than she probably ought to on the Lord's Day.

Forcing herself to listen carefully, she wished she could understand the Scripture reading. Both sermons, the shorter first one and the much longer second, were always given in High German, which only the older people like her Dawdi Fisher understood. Her father had also picked it up from hearing it again and again over the years. Nellie, though, would have much preferred Preaching to be in Pennsylvania Dutch, with occasional English mixed in, the way the People communicated at home and at work.

Because the sermons were not comprehensible, one of the only clues Nellie had as to the subject matter was the preacher's facial expression—at this minute Preacher Lapp, Susannah's uncle, wore a scowl. Susannah's family was certainly well represented among the church brethren, with both a preacher and a deacon in this generation. Of course, that had everything to do with the drawing of lots, the practice through which the Lord God divinely ordained their ministers.

What else will God choose? She hoped Caleb wasn't of the elect, at least not for Susannah's future husband. She wondered again why Caleb had written to her instead of Susannah. Every fellow surely knew Susannah was the prettiest girl in the district.

Nellie pushed the gnawing thoughts away. Slowly she began to relax, the monotone of the preacher's voice fading more and more, until . . .

Nellie's head bobbed, but a hard poke to her arm from Rhoda jolted her. Hoping not to draw attention to herself, she sat up straighter and inhaled deeply, then held her breath, doing what she could to try to stay awake from now till the end of the three-hour service. Why was it so hard?

On the other side of her, Nan seemed to be choking down a chuckle; either that or she was struggling not to cough. No, Nellie was pretty sure Nan had seen her doze off during the unending sermon—just like their mamma, who was nodding off herself. That at least made Nellie feel some better, though she was thankful to be well out of Caleb's view this Preaching service.

During cleanup following the common meal, when the women and some of the older teen girls were putting the kitchen back in order and the men were folding up the tables, Nellie came across two men talking heatedly on the back porch.

Not wanting to eavesdrop, she walked past them with the bag of rubbish she was carrying to the trash receptacle behind the barn, but the angry words followed her across the stillness of the barnyard. For the most part, the People were still gathered in the house.

"Listen here, I've got fifteen children, and four of my sons are out seein' English girls," one of the men said. "Can't get my boys much interested in farmin'—the minute they turn sixteen, seems they're out getting themselves an automobile . . . and, well, who wants to join church after that?"

"'Tis a bigger problem ev'ry year," said the other, an old-timer. He took a puff on his pipe and blew out the smoke before going on. "You just ain't hard enough on your young'uns."

"You've forgotten what it's like," retorted the first man. "All this talk of cars and electric and telephones round here don't help much, neither."

Nellie nearly stopped walking, so badly she wanted to hear the rest of their pointed discussion, but she didn't pause until she'd reached her destination. If men right here in their midst were demanding such things—and she had every reason to suspect they were, despite Ephram's tight-lipped refusal to comment—then surely the bishop would set them all straight. And anyway, why wouldn't a son want to farm with his father? She didn't understand and was quite sure Caleb would never do otherwise as the youngest son in the family. In the Old Order community, the youngest typically inherited the farm.

She thought of Caleb receiving the nearly one hundred acres his father and grandfather had farmed—property that went clear back to his great-grandfather Yoder. Was Caleb itching to claim the land of his ancestors?

Surely he is, she thought. *Just like any son who finds himself on the eve of his father's impending retirement.*

But before Caleb could take on the family farm, he must find himself a bride.

Caleb knew he would remember weeks, maybe months from now, exactly how Nellie Mae Fisher looked as she came walking across the yard toward Deacon Lapp's house. Her face was rosy, like she'd gotten a mite too close to an old cookstove, and a stray slip of hair on her neck made her appear younger than her seventeen years.

Nellie had not been a girl who stuck out in a crowd, at least not until this past summer. As if blossoming overnight, she was suddenly altogether feminine and pretty in a way he couldn't describe. She possessed something more than the curvaceous beauty of some of the girls he'd dated and quickly tired of. The sparkle to her eyes and mystery in her smile made him wonder why he hadn't noticed her before.

He'd gone out to get some fresh air, secretly hoping to encounter Nellie. Instead, he happened upon two men locked in debate. Thankfully the pair were moving now from the interior of the back porch to outside, near the well pump, as their arguing rose to a higher pitch. Unexpectedly three more men marched up, joining the first two as one raised his fist in the air.

"No tellin' where all this will lead." One man's words floated to the sky.

Caleb wanted to spare Nellie the commotion, but she was making a beeline straight for the house. She would have to enter the back doorway and head through the porch to return to the kitchen.

He called to her. "Nellie Mae!"

When her big eyes caught his gaze, her engaging smile spread clear across her face. "Hullo, Caleb," she said right out, not like some girls who seemed nearly afraid of their voices. Of course, he'd expected such composure in a girl capable of running a bakery shop. Surely he could also expect to hear back from her soon regarding his written invitation.

His heart beat more quickly at the thought that, for the first time in more than a year of asking girls to go riding after Singings and such, he couldn't be sure what the answer would be.

"You mind walkin' round the house with me, right quick?" He steered her away from the growing cluster of men.

"Why, sure." She smiled at his request and turned, not waiting for him to smile back. "Did you hear what they were talking 'bout?" she asked.

"Some, jah."

"Well, I didn't like it, not one bit. Did you?" She was straight to the point and it pleased him.

He stopped then, where the Dawdi Haus jutted out from the main house, hiding them well enough. He was glad when she did the same, her eyes squarely on his as she awaited his answer. "There are men who are lookin' for loopholes in the Ordnung," he told her. "Some are willin' to walk away from the beliefs of our forefathers . . . what they laid down as the right way to live and work."

A way of life paid for with the blood of our martyrs . . .

He wouldn't go on; he would spare her too much of his opinion now, alone as they momentarily were in broad daylight.

"Well, I'm altogether sure of one thing," she replied.

"What's that, Nellie Mae?"

"My father will have nothin' of that sort of talk." She did not blink and her pretty, heart-shaped face was mighty sober. "Will yours?"

He grinned at her refreshing frankness. Here was a girl who spoke her mind, not caring to wait first to determine *his* opinion.

"We Yoders are Old Order through and through," he stated.

She nodded and there was a hint of a smile. "Wonderful-good."

They stood there looking at each other. *Has a girl ever intrigued me so?* he wondered.

When Nellie spoke again, he was suddenly aware of her lilac fragrance. "It was nice of you to drop by, Caleb, with your note."

He waited for her response, but she gave no hint of her reply. She merely smiled, turned, and walked away. He watched her head toward the front of the deacon's house, to the seldom-used formal entrance.

That's all?

Never before had a girl treated him so casually—not rudely, but keeping him at an almost measured distance.

When Caleb had waited enough time to prevent people from suspecting he and Nellie Mae had been together, he looped back through the yard and onto the porch, aware only of his great curiosity about Nellie.

Nellie feared her face might be suspiciously rosy as she walked nonchalantly into the house by way of the front door. She retraced her steps in her mind, wondering how she had bumped into Caleb. Was he already outside when she had headed through the porch and down the steps? For the life of her, she could not recall having seen him out there. Had it been an accident, or had he intentionally sought her out? She blushed once more at the thought.

Warning herself to keep her emotions in check, Nellie looked for Nan and Rhoda and found them in the kitchen, still helping Susannah's mother and others redd up.

To think I almost didn't offer to take out the trash today, she thought with a suppressed laugh.

CHAPTER 8

The dawning of Monday's washday was peaceful with Mamma and Rhoda already busying themselves with the laundry. Nellie slipped seven loaves into the belly of the woodstove, wondering why Nan remained in bed at this hour. While her sister slept, Nellie had put her morning to good use making eight pies and ten dozen cookies, mostly chocolate chip.

For a moment, Nellie thought she felt the rumble of a distant train. Pausing from her work, she realized the rumble was instead the sound of the wringer washing machine in the cold cellar below where she stood. If she had a few minutes today sometime during the usual afternoon lull at the bakery shop, she might ask Mamma to tend the store a short time— not breathing a word to Dat, of course. She needed to slip away for some quietude out in the meadow, near the sugar maples, hoping for a glimpse of a deer, rarer these days than she remembered. No doubt the drought had affected them, too.

Strange how wild things and humans can live side by side and yet keep such a distance. She contemplated the mystery of that, and as was often the case lately, her mind made the leap to her deceased sister, fond as she had been of God's creation. *Why hadn't Suzy drawn a line . . . kept herself set apart from the modern world as she'd been taught?*

Nellie shook off the thought. Right or wrong, Suzy had always insisted her friends were wonderful-gut people.

There are good people right here, sister . . . in the hollow.

Nellie shrugged away her opinion and went to check on the cooling cookies. If they were ready to put into her large wicker carrier, she could begin her several trips up the lane to the shop, where she would arrange the day's baked goods and hang the Open sign.

"Another day, another dollar," she muttered, using an expression her father sometimes said in jest. There was more than a grain of truth to the saying.

When she arrived at her shop with the first basket of cookies, someone was already standing outside, waiting for her to open. The woman turned at her arrival—it was Uncle Joseph's wife, Aunt Anna. Uncle Bishop, as she and her sisters sometimes referred to the man of God, certainly loved his sweets.

Anna had come on foot across the cornfield that lay between the families' homes. "Hullo, Nellie Mae," she said right quick. "I saw the light on in your kitchen and decided to pick up some pastries for our trip."

"Oh?" This was the first Nellie had heard they were traveling.

"Joseph says 'tis past due for us to get away for a vacation," Anna explained. "So this afternoon, we're boarding a bus to Iowa . . . Kalona, where I have kinfolk."

"Plain?"

"For the most part."

"Well, come on in." Nellie didn't need to bother with a key, as she never locked the shop; neither did her parents lock the house. She opened the door wide for Anna, who looked awfully glum for someone about to embark on a trip. "I've got plenty of cookies—all nice and warm, too. The pies and such are comin' if you'd care to wait."

Anna shook her head. "Your uncle will be mighty happy with cookies." Anna slowly selected several different kinds—oatmeal raisin, pumpkin, and the bishop's all-time favorite, chocolate chip—almost as if the effort of choosing was too much this morning. Clearly her mind was on other things.

"There'll be no charge," Nellie said when she had carefully wrapped up Anna's requests.

"Aw, Nellie Mae, are ya sure?"

She nodded. "Yous have a wonderful-gut time out where you're goin'."

Anna brightened momentarily. "Denki, we will."

"How long will you be?" Nellie thought to ask.

"'Tis up to the bishop." *And to the Lord God,* Nellie thought she heard Anna murmur with a slight frown on her face.

She watched the gray-haired woman pull her black woolen shawl close around her before heading out the door. Anna made her way toward the desolate cornfield, carefully picking her way among the remaining hard stumps as she moved across the field toward home.

Nellie wondered if Dat knew his elder brother was leaving town for a while. *Why now, for goodness' sake?*

———

When Nellie's Simple Sweets was officially open for the day, Rhoda came to help with customers until she had to leave for her housekeeping job. Nellie was grateful for the assistance, though she wished for some privacy when her friend Rosanna stopped in.

"You're spoilin' us but good, Nellie Mae," Rosanna said after selecting two pies. "These look just delicious."

Nellie slipped away from the counter, delighted to see her again so soon after visiting just last week. "You getting . . . uh, things ready?" she asked, not wanting to say more with Rhoda nearby.

Rosanna nodded. "Oh, goodness, I certainly am. Made an afghan—finished it off early this morning." She whispered, "But I don't have a pattern for baby booties."

"Ah," Nellie said, her voice low. "Walk across the road and see Maryann 'bout that. She'd be glad to help."

"You think so?"

"Well, Maryann's thoughtful that way. And with so many young ones, she prob'ly does have a knitting pattern. No doubt she's making a pair or two herself."

Rosanna touched her arm. "How's your mamma been?"

"Good days and bad."

"'Tis to be expected. Losin' a child is the hardest loss of all." Rosanna smiled weakly. "Word has it . . . well, some of her best friends seem to think she's in need of some peace and quiet."

"Jah, 'spect so." Nellie frowned, glancing out the window. "Aren't we all?"

Rosanna leaned on the display case. "Ach, are you all right, Nellie Mae?"

She didn't want to gossip, but she figured Rosanna had no idea of the bishop's plan to travel to Iowa. "Oh, I'm doin' fine, jah."

"Well, you don't look it, if I may be so bold."

Nellie brushed off her apron and eyed her friend. "What's a-matter with me?"

Rosanna came around behind the counter to her. "Didn't mean any harm. You just don't seem yourself."

"Well, *who*, then?"

To this, they both chuckled. And because she was not about to share any news that might upset either Rosanna or Rhoda, who was surely listening in even though she feigned busyness at the far end of the counter, Nellie kept to herself what she knew of Uncle Bishop and her aunt's trip.

Switching the subject, she asked, "Who else knows?"

"Only Elias and our parents. That's all for now." Rosanna nodded her head toward Rhoda. "So if you don't mind . . ."

"That's fine," Nellie agreed, waving good-bye to Rosanna, who said her farewells and left the shop.

Upon her absence, Rhoda eyed Nellie closely. "Please don't even ask me," Nellie blurted.

"Well, aren't *you* peeved," Rhoda shot back.

Nellie sighed. "I 'spect Mamma has pulled the last of my bread from the oven by now. I'll be back in a bit." Heading out the door, she decided to take the longed-for detour to the meadow, not caring for the moment that doing so might make Rhoda late for her job. *Oh, how I do wish Dat would allow Mamma to mind the store again.*

Lifting her skirt, Nellie ran through the nearby pastureland, all the way out to the vast meadow on the easternmost side of her father's land. *Let Rhoda see what it's like to be inconvenienced for once,* she thought. Her eldest sister had never been one to offer a helping hand—not without Dat's encouragement. Rhoda frequently didn't come home for supper, let alone help to prepare it, and she'd slip out of the house and be gone all day when her sisters and Mamma needed help getting the house ready for Preaching service when their turn to host came around. And if the bakery shop needed a thorough cleaning, Rhoda usually made herself scarce then, too.

No matter Rhoda's tendency to selfishness, Nellie didn't see her getting in over her head the way Suzy had with her English friends. For one, Rhoda didn't seem to have any suitors. No, as far as she knew, Rhoda was getting mighty close to being passed over by the young men in the district—twenty-one was nearly past courting age. Even without a beau, she ought to take baptismal instruction next year and join church.

Someone else hadn't joined church yet, either, although he was much younger than Rhoda. Caleb was holding off, which was interesting, especially the way he'd talked last Sunday. Why hadn't he planned to take the baptismal vow with the rest of the candidates in a few weeks? The day would surely come when she would be doing the same thing herself.

She shivered happily at the memory of speaking with Caleb yesterday. After months of waiting, *she* would be the girl to win Caleb's heart. Or so she hoped.

She couldn't help but smile as she strolled into the woods, suddenly realizing she was farther from home than she'd intended. She relished the idea of having this time to herself and wandered onward, taking her time . . .

breathing in the fresh, clean air, and observing the pretty patterns the filtered sunlight made on the grassy floor below. She whispered Suzy's name,
wondering if the dead could hear what you spoke out into the air. *The Lord
does . . . Uncle Bishop says so.* Yet if that was the case, why then were none
of the prayers offered by the People spoken aloud? Only the bishop or their
preachers ever prayed out loud, and then only at Preaching service.

Her mind wandered back to Suzy, who had so often walked this very
way with her. How had she sneaked away to the world without confiding
in Nellie, when Suzy had so long had a habit of blurting out things better
left unsaid? Until her sister's Rumschpringe, Nellie and Suzy had faithfully
confided everything in each other. Yet in the last year of her life, Suzy had
seemed to turn more to her diary than the anxious ears of her sister.

The diary . . .

Never one to sneak a peek before, Nellie had avoided doing so as Suzy
had grown increasingly secretive, keeping her thoughts hidden in her side
of the dresser.

A single page was all Nellie had allowed herself the day after Suzy
drowned, snapping the diary shut upon reading the words *What have I done
to myself? Honestly, I'm in over my head.*

Nellie Mae tensed at the thought of Suzy possibly about to abandon her
Plain life, on the verge of embracing the world.

Did she die for curiosity's sake?

Nellie would never forget the lengthy admonition the bishop had given
at Suzy's funeral. Uncle Bishop had sounded a clarion call to the young
people that it was time to "consider the consequences" of dying without
having joined church. Nellie had been terrified to think her own dear sister
had died too soon.

Not wanting to submit her parents to further heartache, Nellie had decided to bury the diary and Suzy's many secrets—the evidence spelled out
in Suzy's own hand. Her sister's guarded words and long absences, as well
as her deliberate resistance to Preaching services in her final months, were
burden enough. Yet it appeared that burying Suzy's diary was not enough
to protect the family's reputation. Nellie had noticed strange looks from
some of the more gossipy members of the grapevine, particularly Susannah
Lapp and two of her girl cousins.

The diary's gone forever, she thought, remembering the moonless night
she'd buried it, unable to bring herself to burn it as Suzy had directed. As she
pondered having tearfully dug the hole and tenderly set the plastic-wrapped

diary into the ground, she realized she wasn't sure she could locate its hiding place.

For a moment she regretted burying it at all. Being able to hold Suzy's precious journal—the final words her sister had ever written—might have brought some comfort now.

Why didn't I stash it in the house instead?

She pushed away any lingering second thoughts. *Good riddance . . . a life gone awry should be forgotten. For our sake . . . and for Suzy's.*

Sitting on a fallen tree branch, Nellie bent to tug on the hem of the black apron that covered her feet, her hands now resting flat on the tops of her work shoes. She'd noticed the way the large branch partially blocked the pathway home, overgrown as the faint trail had become.

Birds flew low overhead, the sound of their wings haunting her as she recalled the many times she and Suzy had tramped through these woods. Suzy knew every bird by its color and song, delighting even old-timers with her knowledge. Often they'd watched deer, hiding quietly in the brush and nearly holding their breath so they wouldn't startle them. Suzy had decided a deer's favorite meal consisted of clover flowers or berries from a juniper tree, but never herbs or herbal flowers.

Ach, how Suzy enjoyed nature! Every sound, every sight made Nellie Mae think of her.

When she could contain her sadness no longer, Nellie sobbed into her hands, muting the sound of her broken heart.

CHAPTER 9

Wiping away tears, Nellie Mae stopped at the quiet house to collect the remaining loaves of bread and returned to the shop.

"Where were you?" Rhoda snapped. She'd obviously been fretting.

"I'm sorry, Rhoda," Nellie apologized. "I needed some time away . . . I should've asked."

Rhoda clucked her tongue and turned to fairly fly out the door without another word.

I've done myself no favors with her, Nellie thought sadly.

She noticed a few stray graham cracker crumbs on one of the shelves of the display case and brushed them into her hand. Rhoda didn't keep things the tidy way Nellie liked them, but Nellie recognized it was foolish to expect her sister to see things the same way she did. After all, it wasn't Rhoda's name on the sign outside.

Moving now to inspect the cookie shelves, she counted how many dozen of each kind were left for the day. Plenty of chocolate gobs remained. Some folks called them whoopie pies because children often declared "Whoopie!" when they first tasted the sugary-chocolate concoctions. Nellie smiled, thinking back to her earliest recollection of having enjoyed her grandmother's version. The fat chocolate sandwich cookies were made with cake batter and held together by a thick layer of tempting creamy frosting.

She turned and straightened the floral wall calendar, wishing the shop was less sparsely furnished. Nellie hoped to convince Dat to build or purchase some chairs and tables to set up by the window like she'd seen at other small shops. Certainly there was ample room. She liked the idea of making it possible for those customers who wished to, to linger and visit, perhaps over a cup of tea or coffee.

She had a clear picture in her mind of the way she wanted things to look and be. Apart from these changes, the place was pretty well just as she desired it—well organized, neat, and—except for the crumbs that had escaped Rhoda's attention—clean.

Leave it to me to care 'bout stray crumbs, Nellie thought wryly.

The bell jingled on the shop door, and she looked up to see Rebekah Yoder coming in, all smiles.

"Hullo, Nellie Mae!" Normally ever so prim in a dark green dress and long black shawl, Caleb's older sister was today a sight to behold: A raspberry-colored oven burn marked her graceful forehead, though she didn't seem self-conscious about it. Rebekah's had become a familiar face in the neighborhood in the past few years, since taking a job as a mother's helper to an Amish family a half a mile away. Nan especially had benefited from seeing Rebekah more often. Too bad Nan was home nursing a cold today.

"Nice to see you, Rebekah," Nellie said. "What can I get you?"

Rebekah glanced down at the fringes on her shawl and picked at them a moment before lifting her gaze. "Mamma ran out of time and needs four dozen dinner rolls for a gathering this very evening."

"Four dozen, you say? I can fill that order," Nellie said quickly.

She nodded. "My parents are planning to go over to Preacher Manny's place."

Nellie thought nothing of it, but as she began to bag up the soft white rolls, she wondered if this wasn't yet another meeting about the recent upset in their community—and with Uncle Bishop and his wife gone, too. Were men now allowing their wives to put in their say on the matter?

Rebekah smiled and brushed her hand against the burn on her face as she reached for the rolls. "Denki, Nellie." For a long moment she stood there, gazing at Nellie—almost staring.

Nellie wondered if Rebekah noticed her swollen eyes and abruptly turned to the old-fashioned cash register. "Anything more? Pies? Cookies, maybe?"

"Just the rolls."

Rebekah was beaming now as she handed her a crisp five-dollar bill. "Will you be goin' to Singing next weekend?"

Nellie Mae felt the air go clean out of her. Did Rebekah suspect Caleb was pursuing her? She felt at a loss for words and was actually glad the cash register jammed right then.

"Ach, but there's somethin' wrong with this machine. . . . I need to go and ask Nan." With that, she excused herself, leaving Rebekah standing there without her change.

Nellie hurried toward the house in search of Nan, who always knew how to fix the finicky machine.

When she found her sister in bed sound asleep, her dark hair strewn over her pillow, Nellie didn't have the heart to waken her. It was obvious Nan was in no condition to help today.

Nellie quickly returned to the bakery shop, but she discovered that Rebekah had already gone, leaving behind a note.

Nellie Mae,
   Put the difference on Mamma's credit, if you don't mind. See you next Saturday!

                                                    Fondly,
                                                    Rebekah

Fondly? Nellie laughed.

Surely Caleb's closest-in-age sister knew something of his interest in Nellie, if not his written invitation. She found this quite curious, since dating and courtship were done in complete secret, up until an engaged couple was "published" after Preaching service. At that time the father of the bride-to-be stood up and extended a wedding invitation to all the membership.

Whatever Rebekah's knowledge, Nellie realized she was smiling as she worked with the cash register, which miraculously fixed itself after a few minutes.

Nellie noticed the dwindling batch of chocolate chip cookies and made a mental note to bake more of that kind tomorrow morning.

Wonder if Caleb likes chocolate chip? She giggled, her heart fairly singing now as she glanced again at Rebekah's brief note.

Fondly, indeed!

Caleb worked alongside Ephram Fisher, building a much-needed woodshed. They had been at it since sunup.

What was I thinking, putting a bug in Rebekah's ear? he thought.

Frustrated with himself, Caleb took care not to exert too much force as he pounded each nail. Typically he was in control of his emotions and would not let his annoyance at his own stupidity get in the way of his work. But he felt guilty at having sent his sister over to see Nellie when Rebekah had stopped by after lunch to give several jars of strawberry preserves to Maryann. He'd happened upon the two women discussing his mother's lack of dinner rolls and sent Rebekah to Nellie's to purchase some.

He had merely hoped Rebekah might find a tactful moment to bring up deceased Suzy to Nellie, if the bakery shop wasn't populated with customers. The mysterious circumstances surrounding Suzy's drowning troubled Caleb, who had decided to hold off on his growing interest in Nellie after learning of her sister's death. Whom his family spent time with mattered a great deal to Caleb's father—reputation was everything. Caleb had meant to appease his Daed by finding out the truth about Suzy, along with the rest of Reuben Fisher's family. He'd supposed that Rebekah's friend Nan would have been able to divulge the important information he sought, but it was reasonably clear from Rebekah's subtle prodding that Nan knew precious little about the day of Suzy's fatal accident. Maybe Nellie would reveal more to Rebekah. He only knew he thought it unwise to do the asking himself.

He patted the pocket containing Nellie's letter, glad Rebekah had intercepted the day's mail and thought to bring him the much-anticipated reply. His heart beat more rapidly to think Nellie had said yes, but the problem of his father remained.

Guess one can't blame him. Can't be too careful during these troublesome times when so many are speakin' out against our heritage. These beliefs had defined them for hundreds of years.

Ephram's wife brought out a jug of water. They stopped to take a swig, and Maryann fidgeted as if something urgent was on her mind. When they had drunk their fill, Maryann took back the jug, studying Ephram.

"What is it, Maryann?" asked Ephram.

"Word has it there's a meeting over at Preacher Manny's tonight. Both sides of the debate are comin'."

"That's enough."

"Marrieds are welcome."

"Well, *we* won't be goin'!" Ephram fairly snapped.

The strong response to Maryann's remark startled Caleb. Ephram had always struck him as rather fixed in his opinions, but before now, he'd always seemed fair. Why this sharp tone with his wife? Was Ephram privy to something? Or was it simply that he preferred his wife keep herself out of such discussions?

Ephram was quiet as they finished laying the last few boards on the inside of the building, nailing them into place. The woodshed complete, Ephram gave him a slap of appreciation on the back, and Caleb headed to the barn. He led out his fine horse and hitched it up to the black open carriage his father had purchased for him last year.

Caleb thought again of Nellie's little sister. What was the truth about

Suzy? With rumors still flying, he considered the more pressing question to him: *What's the truth about Nellie Mae?*

He had been lectured more than a few times regarding the importance of "marryin' proper." According to Daed, the apple rarely fell far from the tree. "You're tying the knot with a family, not just the daughter . . . marrying into their reputation. We Yoders won't be linked to wickedness."

For sure and for certain, if Daed had any inkling of his interest in Nellie Mae, he'd be taking him aside and warning him but good. Evidently Reuben Fisher hadn't been able to rein in his youngest girl. Was Nellie Mae born of the same foolishness?

CHAPTER 10

Rhoda and Nan's room was furnished much the same as Nellie's, yet something seemed different about it as she and Rhoda sat talking after supper Wednesday evening. Nan was downstairs, seemingly eager to be out of her room now that she was feeling better, and Rhoda had perched square in the middle of the bed, her feet tucked under her. Loose strands of golden hair poked from beneath her head covering. Nellie sat across the room on the old cane chair beside the window, unable to put her finger on what she sensed. "Something seems amiss here."

Rhoda chuckled and removed her glasses. "Nothing's changed, sister. Or were you noticing my new necklace? See it over there?"

Nellie spotted the long yellow-beaded necklace draped on one end of the mirror. She rose and went to look. "Has Mamma seen it?" Even as she touched it, running her fingers over the firm roundness of the beads, the necklace wasn't the only thing different.

"Mamma poked her head in and frowned."

Nellie gazed at the delicate loveliness of the necklace. *Worldly, for sure. Where did Rhoda get it?*

Here was more evidence that Rhoda's working for Englischers was clearly a mistake, just as Dat had said from the start.

Stepping back, Nellie noted the attractive way Rhoda had looped it over part of the dresser. *Perty as can be.*

She glanced at her sister. "Oh, Rhoda, you're not . . ." She paused.

"I'm not what?"

"Thinkin' of goin' down the path of . . . ?" Nellie stopped, refusing to say Suzy's name. "What I mean is, you're not thinking of goin' fancy, are ya?"

Rhoda's pretty green eyes shone. "Last thing on my mind."

"Why the necklace, then?"

Rhoda's face flushed. "I s'pose hanging it keeps me from wearin' it. Just for show, that's all."

Nellie looked all around the room, still trying to determine what she felt. She went and sat again. "Did you spray something sweet in here?"

"Earlier this mornin'." Rhoda pointed her nose in the air and sniffed. "I guess I do kinda smell it yet."

"Perfume?"

She nodded, grinning. "Want some? I can get you the same thing . . . if you'd like."

Nellie couldn't deny the sweet scent was ever so tempting. "Honestly, that's too strong for me if it lasts all day. I'll stick with my lilac fragrance."

"Suit yourself." Rhoda smoothed her dress, shifting her legs beneath her. "I ran into Susannah Lapp on the way home from work today."

"Oh?" The mention of Susannah's name annoyed Nellie.

"She was full of gossip, more so than usual—said a whole group of folk came to the house last night. Men and their wives, of all things."

Nellie nodded, looking Rhoda square in the face. "I heard from Rebekah Yoder there was a similar meeting the night before at Preacher Manny's. What do you think's goin' on?"

Rhoda reached up to undo her Kapp. Then she began removing the bobby pins, her butter-blond hair cascading down over her shoulders, past her waist. "Seems more folks are demanding tractors and other modern conveniences—enough to form a fairly large group. The meeting at the deacon's was pretty one-sided, as I understand it."

"Which side?"

"Which do ya suppose?" Rhoda shook her hair free. "'Twas the side of the Old Ways . . . as we are now. But the other meeting, the one you mentioned, was open to people from both sides of the issue."

Rhoda surely seemed to be the one in the know.

"Any idea why Dat and Mamma didn't go?" Nellie asked.

Rhoda picked up the hem of her apron and fingered the edge. "I s'pose because they're homebodies . . . like you, Nellie Mae." Her sister gave her a teasing grin.

Nellie sighed. The fact she had only to walk a few steps to work must make her an oddity in Rhoda's eyes. "I daresay there's maybe another reason."

"What's that?" asked Rhoda.

"Dat's ever so settled with the way things are."

Like Caleb's family. The thought comforted Nellie. No matter how many folk betrayed their tradition, her family—and Caleb's—would stand solid and true.

"Sure seems that way," Rhoda said. "But change is coming, and you never know what might happen."

Nellie wanted to tell Rhoda what she knew about the bishop's trip—and how upset Aunt Anna had seemed—but she held her peace. It wasn't her place to say what she presumed, and it was bad enough to hear of two meetings happening behind their backs. If Rhoda didn't already know about Uncle Bishop, the grapevine would tell her soon enough.

———

Nellie Mae settled into her room for the night. She considered writing to her cousins, as the circle letter she'd been expecting had come in the afternoon's mail full of news about who was published to be married last week after Preaching in Bird-in-Hand—Treva had written of the candidates for baptism, as well. Nellie always enjoyed collecting news to add to the letter before sending it along to yet another cousin down in Paradise. The ever-expanding letter would journey on to several others before Treva returned it to Nellie again in another ten days or so. A weekly journal of sorts, circle letters were one of the things Nellie most looked forward to.

This time she had been dismayed to hear from Treva about a group in Bird-in-Hand talking of getting cars and tractors. "Whatever's happening among our people sounds as contagious as the flu," she whispered to herself as she slipped into bed.

Thinking of what she might write back, she deemed it unwise to share the little she knew about the unrest here in Honey Brook. *Maybe I'll wait and reply when things die down a bit.*

She felt somewhat guilty at the prospect of holding up the circle letter—it was no fun when others dawdled—but she wasn't in the mood to write about the ordinary things of her life. And was it really anybody's business what was going on here among the church brethren? Her greatest concern was that such gossip might simply fan the flames of discontent.

If only Rosanna lived nearer. It would have been a relief to talk plainly with her friend, but it was too late in the day for that. Since Elias had found him and Rosanna a nicer house to rent, across from Ephram's, she'd seen less and less of her. At moments like this, she could see how mighty nice it would be to be able to pick up a telephone and call her dearest friend.

Quickly, she dismissed the thought. While some bishops did permit families to install a phone for the purpose of medical emergencies, Nellie could not imagine Uncle Bishop allowing one. No, he and Preachers Lapp and Manny embraced the Old Order as much as any ministers she knew.

Bet Susannah Lapp hasn't ever wished for a phone, Nellie thought. Considering her rival now, Nellie wondered if she dared to flirt a little with Caleb this Saturday night. Unlike most boys who simply invited a girl during the Singing, Caleb had played it safe, planning ahead where Nellie was to meet him afterward. This way no one would likely see them together as a couple. Surely there was a reason for Caleb's desire for such unusual secrecy.

But Nellie wouldn't allow herself to fret over the details of their first date. She could trust Caleb Yoder to know what he was doing, couldn't she? Still, she wondered if his reason had anything to do with Suzy.

———

Thursday evening Rosanna's cousin Kate came striding into the utility porch at the back of the house. With a short knock and a soft "yoo-hoo," she appeared in the kitchen, an enormous smile on her round face. She looked much bigger than last visit, Rosanna thought, trying not to stare at Kate's protruding stomach.

"How are you feelin', cousin?" she asked, quickly offering her a chair.

"Oh, not too bad, really."

"Would ya care for something to drink? A tall glass of fresh milk, maybe? Whatever you'd like."

Kate waved her off as she lowered herself into the chair. A refreshment seemed to be the furthest thing from her mind. "Truth is, Rosanna, I've come to talk about the baby." She fixed her gaze on the table before them. "John and I've been talkin', and *we* think it would be a smart idea to let our baby—yours, really—know who his parents are. Or if it's a girl . . ." Her voice trailed off, and she brought her eyes up to meet Rosanna's.

Rosanna felt her stomach knot up, but she forced a smile. "Why, sure, I think that's fine."

Kate fanned herself, seeming quite relieved. "It's not that we want to have much say-so in his or her life. It's just . . . we think it would be nice for the baby's brothers and sisters to know him, too."

Again Rosanna nodded. "I have no problem with that, Kate. Doubt Elias will, either."

"Well, that's mighty good to know."

"You sure I can't get you something to wet your whistle? You look all in."

Kate's eyes glistened. "Oh, I don't know . . . maybe, jah."

"Well, what's a-matter? You all right?"

Kate nodded bravely, giving a weak smile. "One minute I have such get-up-and-go, and the next, I fizzle out mighty quick. Can't say I've ever felt quite like this with my other babies."

"Ach, maybe you shouldn't have come all this way alone." Rosanna glanced out the window, noting the gray family buggy parked outside. "You want someone to ride back with you?"

"No, no, I'll be fine in a few minutes." Kate breathed in slowly.

Rosanna couldn't help but wonder if Kate's now rosy cheeks had to do with the realization the baby growing within her would know the parents who gave him life. It was a reasonable request.

Elias will surely think so, too.

"The midwife says the baby may be due sooner than we thought," Kate commented as Rosanna poured her some warm peppermint tea.

"Before Christmas would be ever so nice."

"Might be closer to the middle of December, seems."

"Ah, right during wedding season, then," Rosanna said.

"Jah, and what a busy one this will be." Kate went on to say that several nieces and two nephews on both sides of John's and her family were rumored to be getting hitched come late November or early December.

"More couples means more babies." Rosanna smiled. "We'll all be in good company, raisin' our little ones."

The People grew their communities through large families. Ten to fifteen children were not uncommon.

Kate agreed, a knowing look in her eye. "Just think, you'll soon have yourself a wee one to call your own."

Rosanna reached out to touch her cousin's hand, ever so thankful for Kate's generosity, yet hoping her cousin was truly comfortable with the whole idea.

Nellie Mae sat in the corner of the kitchen, behind the table closest to the wall, trying to suppress her envy as she watched Rhoda and Nan sitting on the large rag rug in the center of the room, playing a cozy game of checkers.

I'm always the third wheel anymore, she thought.

That Rhoda and Nan had each other was certain, and just now as Nellie watched them smile furtively before moving their checkers, she truly felt she had no one. *Not even to play checkers with.*

Neither sister had made any effort to reach out to her in her time of loss, though they, too, were in mourning for Suzy.

Redirecting her thoughts, she decided now was as good a time as any to add to the circle letter. No sense inconveniencing those waiting by putting it off. After doing so, she shuffled through her stationery and chose a soft yellow sheet, intending to also write a more personal letter to Treva.

Dear Cousin Treva,

Greetings from Beaver Dam Road . . . and Cousin Nellie Mae.

Have you been out walking much this autumn? I can't resist the nice weather. I'm sure yours is quite similar, although Dat says you can never tell around here. Just look at how odd it was that all our sweet corn—and our neighbors'—was stunted, but yours wasn't. Still strange, I daresay.

It was such fun to hear of the poetry you're reading. I, too, like Emily Dickinson's poems, if they're not too sad. There is enough sorrow without having to read about it, seems to me. My sister Rhoda is reading Pilgrim's Progress and when she's through, I plan to read it, as well. Dat says he read it when he was a teen, so I know he'll approve.

Business is as busy as ever at the bakery shop. It would be awful nice if you and your sisters could come over and see it for yourself sometime. Rhoda and Nan would enjoy seeing you, and while Mamma has recently been in need of some solitude—understandable, considering—she'd no doubt be glad for your company, too.

Lately I've been experimenting with a new cookie recipe, but I haven't put it out in the display case just yet. I want to make sure it's good and tasty first. I haven't decided what to call it, either, but it's chock-full of red, green, and yellow peanut chocolate candies. Mamma says I could call them cheer-you-up cookies because of all the colors. What do you think of that?

The Sunday after next we're having Preaching service at Ephram's, so we'll go over there and help Maryann clean out her corners come Friday. It will be good to have some more time with her and her family again.

I hope you'll write again soon.

Your cousin and friend,
Nellie Mae Fisher

There was so much more Nellie could have written. Next time maybe things would have calmed down to the point she wouldn't have to mention a word about the private "tractor meetings" . . . or that it seemed their bishop had flown the coop.

CHAPTER 11

W hen Nellie spotted Iva Beiler at Singing in a bright cranberry-colored cape dress without even an apron over it, she immediately thought of strawberries and homemade ice cream. Where on earth had Iva gotten the bold, nearly red fabric? Surely not at the yard goods store they all frequented. Was she hoping to catch Caleb's attention?

The sweetness of a lowland musk pervaded the area in the barn just below the haymow. A slight haze of dust hung in the air from the good sweeping the barn floor had doubtless received earlier.

Nellie Mae was glad for the large turnout. *Lots of youth from other districts.* She saw many new faces but not the face she most wanted to see. She certainly didn't want to appear to be looking for Caleb or anyone in particular. That was the way to do things, she'd learned from coming along with Rhoda and Nan for a full year now. A few months back, Rhoda had announced she'd gotten her fill of these gatherings and quit coming. Nan, on the other hand, seemed to live for them, her blue eyes shining like boy-magnets.

Nellie chose to sit with some of the other girls at the far end of the length of narrow wooden tables, content to be where she was. Again, there was no sign of Caleb among the boys on the other side of the tables. Nellie reminded herself there was no need to worry: Caleb was *her* date this night. Oh, the way he'd looked at her last Lord's Day—the inviting twinkle in his hazel eyes, eyes that looked into hers as if he'd been searching for her his whole life.

When at last she saw Caleb across the room, Nellie Mae's heart skipped a beat. He came toward her, finding a place across the table only a short way down from her. In that same moment, Nellie spotted Susannah Lapp, whose eyes fleetingly met hers. One glance of understanding and they saw in each other the potential rivals they were.

Briefly looking once more at Caleb, Nellie remembered sitting with her three sisters in the schoolyard one spring years ago, watching the boys play baseball during afternoon recess. Caleb had been up to bat, and instead of swinging and fooling around at home base like most of the boys did to show off, he had leaned forward with the bat, licking his lips as he awaited the pitch.

Crack! On the very first pitch, the bat had slapped the ball, sending it high into the air, over the top of the boys' outhouse and clear out past the white picket fence into the pastureland beyond. She remembered squealing as Caleb ran around to all the bases, his right foot stamping hard on each one as he flew by, headed for home. Never once had he looked over his shoulder at the outfielder, who was still hunting for the ball. Nellie had pressed her hand over her mouth to stifle her glee, so pleased he'd made the home run.

Presently he grinned across the table at her and then wiped the smile off his face fast. There were oodles more songs before they could talk to each other, assuming Caleb would even want to. The way he'd written to her, planning for her to wait elsewhere for him to pick her up, made her think he might not seek her out here at all, not in front of others. All of that was just fine with her, as long as he appeared later in his buggy to pick her up.

Suddenly feeling a bit shy, Nellie Mae decided to mingle with some of her girl cousins and her sister Nan, far removed from the table where they always sat to sing the usual songs. Surprisingly, someone had brought along a guitar. Instruments were not usually allowed, at least at the Singings meant only for their church district. Was all the fuss about pushing the limits of the Ordnung filtering into the Singings, too?

Dozens of boys gathered around the fellow, and Nellie longed to press in and see the fingers working the strings that made such lovely music. For sure and for certain, something was quite different about this gathering—even though it was much too early in the evening, girls and boys were already pairing off. Some had gone high into the haymow to sit and dangle their feet over the sides, holding hands and laughing.

Her heart beat faster as she wondered if Caleb might sit that close to her tonight in his buggy. While she'd ridden next to several different boys on other nights, none of them had affected her the way Caleb did even now, from the other side of the room.

"Nellie Mae." She turned to see him smiling down at her. "Let's go walkin'."

She nodded, following him, but he slowed to let her walk beside him toward the barn doors, instead of behind like some boys preferred.

"Such a moon." He glanced at her, smiling more freely now as they stepped into the privacy of twilight.

She wanted to say something memorable, but the right words didn't come. It wasn't that she was too timid to speak; she simply wanted every word to count.

"Did you see that guitarist?" he asked. "Came all the way up from Georgetown. My older brother knows of him. Says he's trouble."

"No doubt. Uncle Bishop's gone a few days, and this?" There, she'd said something worthwhile, or so she hoped.

Caleb stopped, his back to the full moon. She couldn't make out his expression in the shadow. "Bishop Joseph's gone? But where?"

Her heart sank. "You didn't know? I figured your father or one of the other menfolk must be helpin' with his livestock." She went on. "Aunt Anna was in the shop Monday to purchase some sweets for their trip. They're out visitin' her relatives in Iowa," she said, telling what little she knew.

Caleb stood silhouetted against the blazing white moon, taller than she'd ever remembered. And silent.

"They're in need of some rest, is all," she offered.

"Well, I hope they have a right good time." He leaned toward her and reached for her hand.

The warm thrill of his touch caught her by surprise, rooting her feet to the soil. She wondered how her hand felt to him—probably all sweaty from nerves, even in this nippy weather—but so far he hadn't let go.

The unmistakable sound of lively guitar music came from across the barnyard.

"My father says it's best to run away from evil, not move toward it."

Caleb surely meant the guitar player in the barn, not their holding hands. Nellie smiled, mighty glad for the shadow cast on them as he led her through the thick willow grove, far from the barn and the devil's music. She wouldn't admit to having been drawn to the pleasing sound . . . wouldn't think of saying anything to make him stop walking with her, his thumb stroking her hand, his arm brushing against hers. She needed to be able to think clearly, to be alert and on her guard all the rest of their time together tonight. No matter her attraction to Caleb, Nellie Mae would not disappoint her mamma by behaving recklessly.

"We'll walk over to that white stake—see it?—then we'll head back," he said, pointing.

"Jah, fine." She had to smile. How confident her voice sounded, nearly fooling even herself.

With the house good and quiet—Betsy busy with her embroidery and the girls all out for the evening—Reuben settled down with two Bibles, the old German family one and the English one. He much preferred sitting in the front room near the open door, but now that fall was in the air, he found himself enjoying the warmth and comfort of Betsy's kitchen.

"Betsy," he said, glancing over at his wife, who sat within the golden ring of light coming from the gas lamp he'd hung over the table.

She looked up from her work. "Jah?"

"I'll be reading the Scriptures now."

She nodded.

She has no inkling what I have in mind. . . .

This night he would read the whole of chapter three in the Gospel of John. Reuben had been downright curious about the passage ever since his visit to Cousin Jonathan's. According to his shunned relative, there was something important—even powerful—to be learned from this section of Scripture. Others too.

He felt a glimmer of guilt as he thumbed through the unfamiliar pages, one mingled with a hint of boldness. Truth be told, he had felt peeved ever since Preacher Manny had laid into him for no understandable cause. Manny knew precisely where he stood on things. Why treat him so?

With all the commotion already going on, what could it hurt for Reuben to read where he wished to in Scripture? He wanted Betsy to hear this, too, halfheartedly though it might well be.

For that reason, he began in English—he would read the same chapter to himself in German later. " 'There was a man of the Pharisees, named Nicodemus, a ruler of the Jews. The same came to Jesus by night, and said unto him, Rabbi, we know that thou art a teacher come from God: for no man can do these miracles that thou doest, except God be with him.' "

He paused, glancing over at Betsy. *Her mind's wandering, for sure.*

He continued. " 'Jesus answered . . . Verily, verily, I say unto thee, except a man be born again, he cannot see the kingdom of God.' "

Right there, that's what Cousin Jonathan talked about: being born again.

Reuben hadn't believed these words were written at all the way his wayward cousin had stated them, yet they were right here before his eyes. Had Betsy heard what he'd just read?

He went on to the next verse, then the next, eager to see what else Scripture had to say. Was this what Jonathan meant by "hungering after the Word of God"? He shrugged off the memory. Leave it to outspoken

Jonathan to say such things. Better for Reuben to do as he was told, to do things the way the People had always done them. Better he should listen to the bishop . . . and close the Good Book right now.

Listen and submit.

But when all was said and done, who was the final authority? Was it God and His Word? Or the bishop and the ministerial brethren?

Reuben struggled with all he had been taught . . . the unique way the Lord God identified the men to lead the People . . . the ordination process by the drawing of lots. All of it.

Can I trust what I know . . . what has always been?

His eyes followed the outline of his wife's ample shape across the room. Her body sagged with exhaustion and grief. Neither of them was getting any younger. Had they missed something altogether important, as Jonathan had suggested? In daring to consider this, was Reuben opening himself up to what was not allowed, letting worldliness creep in? And if he were to memorize these verses, what then? *Would* they spring to life in him as Jonathan had insisted they would?

Puh! He was just offended enough by Preacher Manny's rebuke that he forged ahead. " 'That which is born of the flesh is flesh; and that which is born of the Spirit is spirit. Marvel not that I said unto thee, Ye must be born again.' "

The air seemed to leave him, and he found himself gasping. He read on, silently now. Jesus seemed genuinely surprised that Nicodemus did not know the vital things of which he spoke.

Reuben reread the same verses. Neither had he known the truths Nicodemus had missed. Reuben realized at that moment that somehow he had been kept from the truth due to tradition—following carefully, cautiously, what his forefathers had always done. Never, ever wavering.

If I have told you earthly things, and ye believe not, how shall ye believe, if I tell you of heavenly things?

There it was again. He was as bad off as this Nicodemus fellow. He had not known this at all.

. . . that whosoever believeth in him should not perish, but have everlasting life.

Stunned, Reuben looked at the verse again. Was it truly written so clearly? Yes, he'd made no mistake in the reading. Yet his people did not believe a person could have the assurance of salvation. You had to wait till the Judgment Day to know whether you were heaven bound.

He thought of Suzy and trembled at the thought of her life being snuffed out. He'd lost many nights of sleep over his youngest's death, tormented by the knowledge she had died before making her life vows to the church. Not a soul knew of his dire concern. Not even Betsy, dear woman. He could not consider adding his worries to her own heavy burden of sadness.

He opened his German Bible, the ancient, large book where births and deaths of his ancestors over the generations were recorded. Where he had printed Suzy's date of death with a shaking hand.

Reuben studied each verse from one through fifteen, comparing them to what he'd read in the English version as he balanced both holy books on his knees.

"No wonder some folk want to study on their own, without the bishop present," he muttered.

"What's that you say?" Betsy's question broke into his thoughts.

He stared at her, almost not seeing her at first, so caught up was he in what he'd read.

"The Lord says I will have everlasting life . . . if I but believe." He closed the Bibles and rose from his favorite chair to go stand by the back door, looking out through the summer porch to the pastureland beyond the yard and the small outbuildings.

"Reuben, are you all right, dear?"

He heard his wife's voice, but the haze in his mind was so thick he felt nearly helpless to respond. Not now, while this arrow of light was piercing his soul.

"'That which is born of the Spirit is spirit,'" he whispered, suddenly realizing his actions must be quite perplexing to Betsy. He was behaving strangely, just as she had in the days immediately after their Suzy drowned.

Would his darling daughter burn in hell for her sins as the church taught?

To keep his own pain and fear at a manageable level, he knew he must give Suzy's death and her eternal reward up to the Lord God. Not only once, but again and again for all the remainder of his days.

Maybe this was why his Betsy was so taken with little Emma. Like many of their other grandchildren, James's only daughter had become their sunshine in the midst of deepest sorrow. Surely the Good Lord knew they needed some light in their darkness of loss.

The Good Lord Jesus . . .

Reuben reached for his kerchief and wiped his eyes; then he pushed open the door and headed out into the night without even bothering to pull on his work coat. Out, into the most radiant night he'd witnessed in years.

CHAPTER 12

The moon was a luminous round flare. Below Nellie's feet, small and unseen creatures doubtless scurried in the brush as she peeked through the thicket of trees and shrubs, waiting for Caleb to arrive in his courting carriage. She could still feel his hand over hers as it had been all during their long walk earlier. Really they had talked of little beneath the sky and the willows. The memory stirred in her and she could scarcely wait to see him again.

Will he hold my hand again?

What might it be like to bake his favorite pie or cake . . . serve it to him sitting and smiling at the head of the table? How would she feel knowing he was out digging up, then marketing, their own potatoes, his tobacco crop already cut and stored in the shed, ahead of the frost?

She mused on what their daily chores would be as husband and wife. But no, this was merely their first date; she couldn't be sure if there would be more. All the same, her thoughts turned to the future, pleasant *what ifs* filling her mind while dozens of buggies hurried past her hiding place near the road.

She thought of Nan, who'd asked repeatedly if she was all right, since there was no young man in sight to see Nellie home. Nan, as always, had an invitation to ride long into the night. *I'll walk a bit,* she'd told Nan, not wanting to say more. And, oh, had she walked. A good, long way to this secluded spot previously chosen by Caleb.

Looking up, she could tell the moon had moved only slightly, judging the time by its slide across the sky. Surely Caleb would be along soon.

She reached into her dress pocket, where she kept Suzy's Kapp strings. Some might frown on her decision to snip and cherish the strings, but Nellie took comfort in having these tangible reminders of her sister. These small pieces of Suzy were one way in which the memory of her short life lived on. Little by little now, Nellie found her great sadness was slowly subsiding as she turned toward the good things life had yet to offer. At first, in the days and weeks after Suzy died, she had wished to simply dissolve into the moonlight, disappearing like dew evaporates in the heat of the blazing sun.

Truly she had much to live for . . . much to do before it was her turn to cross the wide Jordan.

She heard a horse and buggy coming, slowing now, and shifted forward to peer through the branches. Surely this was Caleb, yet she must play along with his strange game and be certain before making herself known.

Scanning the overgrown area along the roadside, Caleb reined in the horse, standing now to look for Nellie. It was obvious she'd kept herself from view. *Wunnerbaar-gut*, he thought.

In spite of himself, he had started the evening scrutinizing her, but the more he observed, the more he genuinely liked Nellie. It had been difficult to tear himself away from her to go their separate ways after the Singing, as had been his plan. Even so, he knew it was best to be as discreet as possible, at least until he knew whether he wanted to pursue her. After tonight, once he determined whether there was anything of Suzy in her, he would know what he wanted to do.

Still holding the reins, he halted the horse and lingered without moving. How long before Nellie would emerge from the darkness? Was she here . . . nearby?

Finally, impatient to see her again, Caleb leaped down from the carriage and walked toward the thickest area, where he assumed she was hiding.

On a night so well lit by the moon, he could see nearly everything. The blue-black outline of the elm and oak branches and, if he wasn't mistaken, the shadow of a girl, her head tilted in expectation.

"Nellie?" he said softly.

The girl said nothing.

Was it Nellie standing there?

"It's Caleb," he said more urgently, stepping forward.

Still the girl he could plainly see did not reply.

Then he heard it . . . a small giggle.

He rushed toward the bushes and found himself face-to-face with her, pulling her near before he realized what he was doing. She laughed happily in his arms. "I daresay you're a tease," he whispered.

"And you're not?" She squirmed out of his grasp and stepped back.

He laughed heartily, and his horse whinnied and stomped. "Well, we'd better hurry . . . or we might be walkin' tonight."

He reached for her hand and they scurried toward the black open buggy, all shined up to beat the band, though she might not notice in the darkness. He steadied the horse, glad he'd studded the harness with lots of silver buttons. They caught the moonlight just now as Nellie sprang into the carriage, her face beaming.

Reuben took his time outside, moving along the perimeter of the meadow, the moon illuminating his every step. He had no idea how to pray on his own, to voice his thoughts to the Holy One of Israel. Sure, he'd said all the rote prayers he'd learned as a boy, but he had never cracked open the door of his heart and let God hear what was inside. If the God of Isaac and Jacob had appointed His Son to speak so frankly to a Jewish ruler, what would He be saying to the People today?

Ach, what would He say to me?

Reuben could not shake the remarkable things he'd discovered this evening. To think they'd been there, unmistakably plain, all this time. "Yet I never knew," he murmured.

He had the greatest urge to seek out Cousin Jonathan and tell him about this. Just what *had* happened, anyway? Could he even put his finger on it? "Jah . . . I believe the words of Jesus, the Christ." He lifted his head toward the sky. "O Lord God, almighty One, I believe in your Son as my Savior. May I have the promise of eternal life your friend Nicodemus received?"

As sure as he was Reuben Fisher, he embraced the dawning within his soul. He raised his hands out before him, palms open, fingers spread wide. "Born again . . . by the spirit of the true and living God."

He knelt down in the dirt, asking the Lord God and heavenly Father to receive him into the kingdom. As he did, he pictured Nicodemus doing the same.

He bowed his head low and breathed in the stillness around him, unsure of himself, hoping no one but almighty God was witnessing his gesture of contrition and faith.

In time, he rose and headed toward the house, feeling the need to tell someone. He couldn't begin to describe what he'd experienced out there in the field alone with God. However, he must be careful how he explained it, for if he were to use the wrong words, he could be ousted and shunned like his cousin.

No matter the risk, he must share this with his beloved Betsy. But by the time he opened the door to the kitchen, it appeared he was too late; Betsy had evidently abandoned her embroidery to retire for the night. "Well, now, I s'pose there's tomorrow," he said, disappointed.

Eyeing the Good Book, Reuben went to it and sat down again, opening its pages. Never did he want to forget the splendid words he'd read, so he began to memorize the sayings of his Savior, beginning with the first verse of chapter three.

Haven't our preachers ever read and pondered this chapter? Hasn't the bishop?

Nellie's mamma might have been surprised to know Caleb could hold Nellie's hand and sit smack-dab next to her in his right-fancy courting buggy without attempting to cross any other romantic lines. They'd been riding under the glow of the most beautiful moon she'd ever seen for two hours, yet he had not so much as slipped his arm around her.

Mamma would like this boy, she thought, trying not to smile too broadly.

"You cold, Nellie Mae?" He leaned near.

How could she be cold under several lap robes and with a handsome fellow sitting next to her? "I'm fine," she answered.

"You sure?"

She nodded, wondering if he hoped she might be chilly. By the twinkle in his eye, she was certain she'd guessed right.

They rode without talking for a long stretch, and then he surprised her by mentioning Suzy. "I know it's too late, but I'd like to offer my sympathy."

"It's been terribly hard . . . to say the least." Her throat closed up, and she hoped he wouldn't say more.

"It must be, considerin' the rumors, jah?"

She stiffened. "What do you mean?"

He shrugged awkwardly. "I've heard some talk about . . . well, how she drowned and all."

What on earth?

Her breath came in little catches.

"Some of the People were worried 'bout the company she was keeping."

Surely he'd also heard the sanitized version of Suzy's life that Dat and Mamma had offered. "Her company—you know them?"

Caleb turned his head to look at her. "You haven't heard what's bein' said, Nellie Mae?"

All of a sudden she didn't like his tone. She let go of his hand. "Why are you askin'?"

He seemed to force a smile. "I've wondered, is all."

She let the silence take over. He had no right to question her so; he scarcely knew her.

"What was Suzy like, really?" Caleb seemed to be changing the course of the conversation a bit.

"She was everything you saw." Nellie felt compelled to defend her sister. "I loved her ever so much. She was kind and loving. . . ." She hesitated, realizing that what she wanted to say was more a fib than anything.

Frustrated and fighting the familiar sadness, she began again. "The rumors you've mentioned, well, they're false. Suzy was a good girl." The lie slipped out.

He leaned his head against hers. "I'm sorry, Nellie. Of course they're not true. If you say it, then I know so. I shouldn't have—"

"No, no, it's all right." But it wasn't and she held her breath, trying not to cry. She wanted him to take her home right quick.

"I'm awful sorry," he said, going on to say that his sisters thought a lot of all her sisters, including Suzy. "They talked often of all four of yous."

She sniffled and nodded.

"Sometime, Nellie Mae . . . when you feel you can trust me, can we talk about this again?"

Instead of speaking her mind, she kept her eyes on the lap blankets that covered her folded hands. "I'd rather not," she admitted at last.

"All right, then. Suit yourself," she heard him say as he moved to put some distance between them.

So much for Caleb asking me out again.

Furious at herself for letting him push her into a corner, she wondered if his curiosity was the reason he'd wanted her to go riding in the first place. She hoped not, yet she wasn't naïve.

Have I been duped?

CHAPTER 13

I'll be seein' you, Nellie Mae. . . ."
Caleb's final words echoed in her ears as Nellie lay in bed. Sleep did not come easily. She'd slipped into the house, noticing two Bibles side by side on the kitchen table. She'd wondered about that as she made her way up the steps as quietly as she could, even holding her breath, wishing to make herself lighter on the stairs.

Poking her head into her sisters' room, she had seen Nan was not home and in bed as Rhoda was. This had made her feel better about coming in past two o'clock. Some girls stayed out till nearly dawn, and she'd heard of couples who pulled off to the side of a deserted road, or in a covered bridge, stopping to neck rather than talk. She couldn't help but wonder if Nan was involved in such behavior even now with her beau. Perhaps Nan was close to becoming engaged and published by the minister. If so, all the better, especially if the fellow was whom Nellie suspected: David Stoltzfus, the blacksmith's apprentice.

As for the slumbering Rhoda, Nellie figured she was going to be a *maidel*, which was just fine if that's what the Lord God willed. From what she could tell, Rhoda didn't seem too put out at the prospect.

Tired, she stretched her left hand out to the spot where Suzy had always slept. For as long as she remembered, they'd shared this room—plenty of other things, too, including secrets. Not *all*, though, she thought sorrowfully.

"I still miss you something terrible, Suzy." Nellie pressed her hand firmly into the mattress—never before had she felt this cold in bed. A tremor went up her back, and she supposed she wouldn't feel so chilled if Caleb hadn't probed so hard about her departed sister.

Despite how things had soured, they'd managed to make small talk later, the evening not a complete letdown. Caleb had even asked her to ride with him again next Sunday. Her anger not yet forgotten, she'd thought momentarily of turning him down, except that the young folks were to gather at a

Singing for their own district, which sounded ever so fun. She felt a twinge of sadness at the thought there would likely be no guitar players this time.

Presently she wasn't as upset anymore as simply feeling guilty for not having been plainspoken with Caleb. What would he think if he knew the things she suspected of Suzy? The rumor mill had hastened to convict her sister of many sins. But really, what did anyone know for sure?

Reliving Caleb's earlier comments, she felt even colder. Had the ugly truth managed to surface, even though she'd buried Suzy's diary?

Shaking her head, she defended Suzy in her mind. Whatever rumors Caleb had heard, they couldn't all be true. Maybe *none* of them were. Oh, how she hoped it were so. . . .

Breathing deeply, Nellie Mae slid her hand back toward the warmth of her own body and clasped both hands in a solemn pose for her rote prayers. When she'd finished, a new sense of resolve welled up in her. *I'll let Suzy prove her innocence.* First thing tomorrow, she would head into the woods, even before helping Mamma with breakfast.

Nellie pondered the risk—Suzy's account of her last six months might offer something helpful, or it might present secrets better left unknown. *Is digging up the diary a good idea? Will I regret reading it?*

She rolled over and tried to rest, glad tomorrow was an "off" Sunday—no three-hour Preaching service to sit through. It would be a short night and she despised dragging all day, consumed by thoughts of slumber. There would be plenty of visiting to do tomorrow, too, as the family made their rounds to all her married brothers and their families, starting with Ephram. Then on to Jeremiah and Thomas's place; the twins shared a large divided farmhouse with one side for each brother and his wife and family. Next they'd travel up the road a piece to James's, finishing their day of visits at Benjamin's.

Before Sunday became too busy, Nellie Mae hoped to dig up Suzy's diary and bring it home where it belonged, to the sweet haven of their room, safe at last from the elements of the far-off woods. Somehow, she would prove to herself that she had spoken the truth to Caleb.

Nellie recalled the meadow twinkling with lightning bugs and the sound of crickets filling her ears the deep summer day Suzy had urged her to burn her diary should anything happen to her. At first Nellie had been bewildered. *"What on earth do ya mean?"* she had said at the outlandish request.

"Ach, you know, if I should die young or something," Suzy had replied with a shrug.

Now Nellie thought it odd, wondering if Suzy had been given a forewarning of her own death. Nellie had heard of such things, but she'd never put much stock in them.

Reluctantly Nellie had given her word to her sister, never thinking she'd have occasion to follow through with it.

Staring at the ceiling now, she considered the trek into the woods three months ago and realized she might not remember exactly where she'd hidden Suzy's diary. No particular landmarks came to mind. As distressed as she had been at the time, it was no wonder. Certainly she'd failed to imagine then that she might someday wish to retrieve the journal.

Suddenly Nellie feared Suzy's last words might remain as lost to her as Suzy was.

Getting out of bed, she went to the window and looked out at the land to the west, awash in moonlight. Would she lose a whole night of sleep over Suzy and Caleb, both?

She sighed, staring at the sky. Was Caleb glad they'd gotten better acquainted? Were his toes curled up in anticipation of next Sunday's date, as hers were right now? She laughed at the notion. Caleb was a brawny farmer. If his toes were curling, they were working their way into muddy work boots.

She closed her weary eyes, the moon's light upon her face. *Lord willing, I'll remember where I buried the truth of Suzy's last days.*

The same fervency that had motivated her to conceal the diary propelled her now to find and read her sister's words. For her own sake, Nellie must discover all there was to know.

Even in the gray tint of their semi-darkened room, Betsy could sense something amiss. Reuben was walking up and down the hallway, pacing as though he was either worried sick or too keyed up to relax. Was it good news he contemplated? Or something worrisome? She never could quite tell with Reuben, because normally he concealed his emotions so well.

Just then he entered their room to sit on the chair, moving his hands and looking as if he were praying. Betsy leaned up, unable to sleep much herself. She pushed her loose hair back, the weight of it spilling over one shoulder and her white cotton nightgown.

"You're awful twitchy, dear."

At first he did not respond, but when he did, he kept his face toward the window, its green shade pulled high. "I didn't mean to wake you."

"Oh, you know me . . . a light sleeper, no matter what."

He stood, coming to the bed and placing one hand on the footboard. "Something wonderful-gut's happened, Betsy."

"Oh?"

He nodded his head, moving around to her side of the bed. He reached for her hand, clasping it in both of his. "It's too good to keep to myself." His eyes fairly shone in the dimly lit room.

"I know what we've been missin', love." He leaned down and kissed her cheek, then her lips, lingering there, his fervor so pleasing. "All these years, really."

"Oh, Reuben . . . what is it?" She reached up and linked her arms around his neck.

He kissed her again, leaning into her. "Well, to put it simply . . . I've been born anew."

Alarmed, she felt herself go stiff. She'd heard the passages he had read to her following supper, unmistakably different from the Psalms or Proverbs or other passages from the Old Testament he usually chose. "Best not admit that to anyone else, Reuben."

He pulled her close. "Ach, I'm ever so happy! We must know this salvation together."

She could feel his joy in the strength of his arms, the way his head tipped toward hers, the way he held her so tightly, yet tenderly.

"I want to read all of the Gospel of John with you—I myself have been up reading it through this night." Reuben released her, but his breath was on her face and he held both her hands, bending down to kiss one.

"Can it wait till morning?" She chuckled, taken with his enthusiasm.

"First thing," he said, going around the bed and climbing in next to her. "How fitting that we have the whole day to ourselves."

Betsy didn't know if he meant they would read the Bible instead of visiting their sons and families. Truly, she wanted to hug darling Emma once again! But she also sensed something was mighty different about her husband, talking as openly and excitedly as he was. What would it hurt for her to know more, too?

———

Nellie blinked and slowly awakened, briefly confused. When she was fully alert, she realized from the position of the moon that it was but an hour or so before dawn.

In the cold dimness of her room, she brushed her hair and twisted the sides into a low, thick bun behind her head. She then dressed quickly, choosing her gray choring dress and oldest black apron.

Momentarily poking her head out her bedroom door, she determined the hallway was empty before slipping out and down the stairs, quiet as a feather, as she often did mornings when she arose well before dawn to begin her baking.

She hurried to the summer porch, where Mamma kept their long woolen shawls and heavier coats for work and dress. Sitting on the wooden bench her father had made specifically for donning shoes, she pulled on her work boots and wondered how cold it would be with the sun not rising for another hour. She would do well to bundle up—and quickly, too. "Time's a-wastin'," she told herself, stepping outside into the predawn light.

As she did so she heard muted conversation coming from the road. She turned to see a young woman waving at a black open buggy. Right away Nellie assumed it was Nan bidding her beau a fond good-bye. She pitied her sister for having been out in this nippy weather all the night long—pitied her and envied her, both.

A split second's delay and Nan would see her, and then what would Nellie say? *I'm going digging for Suzy's diary . . . want to come along?*

She turned to head for the barn, but Nan was already calling to her. "Nellie . . . wait!"

"Hullo" was all she could muster when her sister drew near. "You're getting in kinda . . . well, *early* in the morning, jah?"

Nan nodded, touching both hands to her face. "I'm nearly froze." She looked at Nellie Mae. "What on earth are *you* doing just comin' home?"

This was her out if she chose to be deceitful. But Nellie knew better. "Oh, I've been home a good long time already."

"Oh?" Nan eyed her.

"I got in late, but not as late as you." She had no idea what else to say. She surely wasn't going to stand here and chat, not when she needed to move along.

"So you walked all the way home, then . . . after the Singing?"

"No . . ."

"Ah, so you met up with someone." Nan was quick.

Nellie changed the subject, just as any sensible Amish girl might. At this moment, she was particularly thankful for the secretive nature of their dating rituals. "Well, if you hurry, you'll have an hour's rest, at least."

"Jah, 'spect so." Nan suddenly looked all in.

"You all right?" Gently, Nellie touched her sister's arm.

But Nan merely turned away. "I best be getting some sleep." With that she headed for the back door.

Nellie made her way to the barn and selected a shovel that was not too large to lug through the meadow and over to the woods. She hoped Nan wouldn't mention to either Rhoda or Mamma having seen her out here so early. Likely it wouldn't matter to Dat if she was out wandering in the dark, as he was known to do such things, too.

Grabbing the shovel, she spotted a small flashlight and snatched it up, as well. She headed out the back way, through the barnyard, to avoid being caught. She cut across the dewy pastureland, veering north to the treed area, where she tried to recall her steps last June, after Suzy's passing.

She crept along cautiously, aware how easy it would be to stumble in the murkiness. Darkness had never affected her before Suzy's death, but now she felt unusually conscious of the lonely nocturnal hours. She shivered, longing for the warmth of Mamma's kitchen.

In any case, she needed to be back in the house and cleaned up before the rest of the family awoke, ready to go visiting. She enjoyed their no-Preaching Sundays when they went around to each other's homes. Truth be known, here lately, as much as she honored and respected their Plain tradition, Nellie Mae was becoming weary of the church services.

Shining her flashlight around the thicket, she had a sudden notion that she might have dreamed she'd hidden Suzy's journal. Had she been too caught up with grief, only imagining she'd come here?

But no, she recalled carrying the diary beneath her petticoats in a make-shift pouch, created out of quilting scraps. She'd felt she must, at all costs, do her best to respect at least something of Suzy's request. Maybe she had done so, far too well.

Pointing the flashlight at a row of bushes, she sighed. "I can remember endless recipes, but I can't remember where I put Suzy's diary?" *How can this be?*

CHAPTER 14

Before the sun peeked over the eastern ridge, Reuben was up and lighting the tall gas lantern on the dresser. Without a word, he headed downstairs and brought up the King James Bible to read aloud. Betsy lingered in bed, a bit droopy, as she often was at this early hour.

She watched him, the way his eyes were intent upon the words he presently read to her. The lines around his mouth seemed softer in the flickering light, and he removed his glasses partway through the chapter to wipe his eyes.

He looked at her from across the room, tears welling up again. "To think what God's Son did for us—taking our punishment." He covered his mouth for a moment, his emotion apparently too great for words. "Oh, Betsy . . . I want you to share this joy, too . . . this most blessed salvation."

The expression on his face was nearly as convincing as the Scriptures he read, for she had never, ever seen Reuben weep—not at the funeral for Suzy, nor the burial, where they had laid their precious daughter to rest in the People's cemetery. No, Reuben was not one to shed tears at all.

"May I read to you every mornin', love?" he asked, coming around to her side of the bed.

"In secret?"

He sighed and placed his glasses on the bedside table. "Well, I guess that's what I mean. Jah, for now."

For now?

"What about evening prayers? Will you be readin' from this chapter then, too . . . in front of the girls?"

He closed the Bible. "I'll think on that," he said softly. "My prayer is that each of our family will come to know the Savior, as I have."

"Know Him?"

"Jah, love." His face was against hers. "We'll study His ways together."

She sat up, snuggling against him, her head on his chest. "We won't be found out in time?"

"I'm trustin' the Lord God for our future, Betsy. It's His doing, so we must heed the command not to worry." He held her near, as he often did of a morning. But today there was more urgency in the way his arms wrapped around her, as if his embrace alone might convince her to join him in his newfound belief.

If she were honest, she would admit to her husband, dear man that he was, that she was floundering terribly in a mire of sorrow. Perhaps Reuben's keen interest in Scripture—in passages forbidden and otherwise—might be exactly what the Good Lord had in mind for her during this time. If trustworthy Reuben was willing to swim against the current sure to come, certainly it was a good thing for her to consider, as well.

"Let me read the passage for myself." She reached for the book, glad he'd brought up the King James Bible.

"Here, I'll show ya where to start." He thumbed through the pages.

"Denki," she whispered.

"No need to thank me." He turned his face toward the ceiling and closed his eyes. What looked to be a heavenly light shone across her dear one's face. Betsy felt as if she'd seen a glimpse of heaven . . . where she secretly hoped with all of her heart that darling Suzy resided.

Nellie Mae propped the flashlight in the crook of a nearby tree, shining it down at the spot in the ground, her third attempt near the base of the tree she suspected sheltered Suzy's secrets.

How many holes must I dig?

She stopped briefly to catch her breath but then she pressed on, burrowing deep into the soil with the shovel. There had been only a single frost thus far, so the ground was yielding enough. She kept working the spot until she was certain the diary was not to be found there.

She straightened and wiped her face with a hankie, glad she'd remembered to slip it into her pocket; surely her face must be smudged. She stopped to adjust the flashlight and push the shovel into the earth, creating yet another hole.

Daybreak came and Nellie stopped to watch the sun peep over the horizon, its golden light pouring over rolling hills. Despite her frustration, she drank in the sight, surrounded as she was by trees and all of nature. Normally she would be up to her wrists in dough at this hour, too intent on her work to greet the day.

Fondly she recalled now the scent of wildflowers around her feet in early summer. Suzy had commented on the colorful variety when she and Nellie had come walking up here in early June. They'd gone even farther to find the area where as young girls they had planted their favorite red columbine—from the buttercup family—to brighten the spot and attract hummingbirds. Year after year, the five-petaled scarlet flowers had propagated rapidly amid the sun-dappled area.

As a child, Suzy would often return home with a fistful of tiny blossoms, bluebells and columbine mostly. Placing them on the decorative plate on their dresser, instead of in a vase of water like their English neighbors might, she wished for them to dry as they were. *In their perty little dresses*, as she would say. Unfortunately the flowers had never dried the way Suzy had anticipated, but had rather wilted and withered. Yet she'd continued to pick them and take them home, always hoping that one day they might dry *just so.*

The pale blue plate with its floral rim now lay empty on the oak dresser, and Nellie wished for some bluebells to pick in memory of her sister, but the chill of autumn had snatched them away.

She turned her attention back to her search, more concerned than ever about her inability to locate the diary's hiding place.

Why didn't I mark the spot?

Frustrated with herself, she stopped her search and returned to the house. *I won't despair*, she told herself. *Somehow . . . I will remember!*

Back at the house, there was nary a sound. But as she climbed the steps, she overheard her father's voice as he read aloud from the Good Book. Odd as that was, Nellie didn't dare linger at the landing to listen. Instead she hurried to her room, removed her Kapp, and shook out her hair, surprised at the tiny twigs and even the small leaf that fell from her long tresses. Brushing her hair vigorously, she wound it back into the formal bun and pinned her head covering back on. Then she slipped into a better dress for their visiting day.

Heading downstairs again, she briefly visited the washroom to clean the morning's grime from her face. Reassured that no one would now guess at her morning's activities from merely looking at her, she began to lay out the cold cereal, fruit, and juices—there was no cooking or baking to be done on the Lord's Day. It was for that reason Nellie found herself having to do so much catching up early Monday mornings.

She began to slice bananas to top off their cereal and heard laughter, followed by what sounded like weeping. *Mamma?* Instantly she felt heartsick, wishing something could be done to help her mother get through this awful sorrowful time.

Nellie was glad Dat was with her. Her father was more tender with Mamma these days, especially when that sad and faraway look was evident in her mother's eyes. A haunting, troubled look, to be sure.

"Maybe it will help her to be out and about," she said, anticipating today's visits.

After Dat offered the final silent prayer following breakfast, Mamma announced they would not be leaving the house till after the noon meal. No word of explanation was given for this clear departure from their off-Sunday routine.

Nellie Mae did not allow her disappointment to show. Still, it was hard to push aside thoughts of the excitement they typically enjoyed on a day like this. So once the kitchen had been cleared, she went upstairs to ask Rhoda and Nan, now settled in their room, if they wanted to go walking. Without a second thought, Rhoda shook her head, her glasses perched almost at the end of her nose as she studied her crocheting book. Nan yawned and said, "Some other time, Nellie Mae," before climbing forlornly onto their bed.

Nellie dragged her feet back to her room, downcast. She closed her door and sat on the bed, wondering if she might have opportunity to look for the diary another day when there was more time. *Some sun would be helpful, too,* she murmured to herself. Truly, she didn't know when she could get away again, what with her duties at the bakery shop. She knew she should feel guilty for having tramped through the woods, shovel in hand, exerting herself on the Lord's Day, when even sewing and needlework were forbidden. Just now, this rule seemed petty, and she was amazed at her own feelings. How long had she harbored apathy?

She yawned, feeling the effects of precious little sleep. Even so, the hours spent with Caleb were worth any amount of lost rest. She hoped he was like her own father, always so loving and attentive to Mamma.

I want a husband like that.

She propped herself up with several bed pillows, taking from her oak bedside table the weekly newspaper, *The Budget,* which focused on Plain communities. She selected the pages featuring the goings-on in Kalona, Iowa, curious if the journal-style columns might shed some light on what Uncle Bishop and Aunt Anna could be doing there.

Lorena Miller, an Amish scribe from that area, began her column by mentioning the rain, wind, and falling temperatures . . . with frost predicted. She also listed the visitors attending a recent worship service—a Jonas and Fannie Hershberger and the Earl Beechys, all from out of town. Nellie didn't recognize any of those last names.

Lorena also wrote of nightly revival meetings.

Were Uncle Bishop and Aunt Anna aware of such gatherings? Word had it there were similar lively meetings held on Friday and Saturday nights here locally at the Tel Hai tabernacle, an open-air building not far from the road. The place could really draw a crowd, or so she'd heard.

Scanning the paper further, she noticed the first line of a column from Mt. Hope, Ohio. *Best not to tiptoe around what you're yearning for, eyeing it, longing for it . . . or you'll miss your life ahead,* it read.

She wondered if she might not be doing the same thing, marking time while she waited for Caleb. She'd let him see her prickly side—a mistake, probably. Of course, if he had eyes in his head and ears, too, he surely knew she'd always respectfully spoken her mind at school and other places where he'd encountered her.

Sighing, she was too tired to rehash what he might think of her refusal to discuss Suzy's death. Despite their shaky beginnings, he seemed to like her well enough to want more of her company.

A week away . . . an eternity.

Closing the paper, she folded it neatly, still considering the Iowa revival meetings. Who attended such gatherings? And from what did people need to be revived?

She rose and poked her head into the hallway, listening. No voices came from her parents' bedroom, so maybe they'd finished their discussion.

Already weary of being stuck at home, Nellie closed the door and leaned back against it. Why weren't they heading off to visit her brothers and families as they always did before the noon meal? Wouldn't Maryann be putting out cold cuts in expectation?

Too tired to ponder further, she returned to the made bed and lay down to rest on this most disappointing Lord's Day.

"You're quite taken with the Good Book, ain't so, Reuben?" whispered Betsy as they sat on their bedroom loveseat.

Her husband held the Bible reverently on his lap, and she noticed how he caressed it, his big hands moving slowly over the leather. "More than ever before, jah."

She sat, enjoying his presence as always. She couldn't remember their ever lingering this way on any day of the week, let alone a no-Preaching Sunday.

"This book has come alive to me, Betsy." His eyes welled up with tears. "I can't explain it . . . but its words have given me something right here"— he placed his hand on his chest—"something I've needed my whole life."

Moved by his response, she nodded, squeezing his hand. Yet she did not understand what was happening to her strong husband.

He reached for his kerchief. "I wasn't even searchin' for this . . . at least I didn't know it." He wept again openly.

"Ach, Reuben, are you all right?"

He nodded. "Never better, dear one. It's like the Lord God himself came lookin' for me."

And found you, thought Betsy.

CHAPTER 15

James's roomy clapboard house was the third stop on their regular route every other Sunday, and Nellie was overjoyed to see cute little Emma again, late in the afternoon though it was. It seemed Mamma was even happier than usual to see her granddaughter as the girl came running straight to her, wrapping her chubby arms tightly around Mamma's knees.

"Oh, my dear child, I missed you so!" Mamma stooped down to kiss the top of Emma's blond head.

Emma's brothers—one older and two younger—Benny, Jimmy, and Matty—ran to greet their Dawdi Reuben, who hugged them quickly and patted toddler Matty on the head. "Ach, look at yous. You've grown in just one week," he said as all of them jabbered at once in Dutch.

As promised, Emma readily showed her dolly to Nellie and her sisters, though Rhoda and Nan sat a bit aloof over in the corner of the front room. Emma told them the handkerchief doll had been one of Suzy's many creations, her eyes bright as she described her dolly's pretend adventures.

Rhoda perked up some during Emma's telling. But Nan, however, continued in a dismal mood.

Problems with her beau? Nellie wondered. Or was Nan peeved about having to stay put so long at home this morning?

But Emma's antics would not permit Nellie to wonder long.

The girl crawled up on her Mammi's lap. "I have me a secret," Emma whispered, leaning close.

Mamma listened and then pulled back and played at clapping her hand over her mouth. "My goodness, that's just wonderful-gut!"

Rhoda got up to move to a chair closer to Mamma. Removing her shoes, she tucked one pudgy leg under her, perching there like a pumpkin about to roll off. Nan stayed where she and Rhoda had initially sat, appearing almost unaware of the goings-on around her.

As for Nellie, she was mighty curious about Emma's so-called secret, especially when the child slid off Mamma's lap and hurried upstairs. In short order, she was back, carrying a small block of a potholder, three-fourths finished.

"See, Mammi? It's crocheted . . . Mamma taught me how, this very week."

Martha smiled, bobbing her head to confirm it. She sat on her father's old hickory rocker with twenty-month-old Matty sprawled on her lap. "I daresay all I did was show her a few loops and she kept on goin'," Martha said, blue eyes sparkling. "Not to boast a'tall, but she's got a knack."

"Is that right?" Mamma inspected the potholder with its green, blue, and purple strands of variegated yarn, oohing and aahing as she made over Emma's creation. "It's awful perty. Really, 'tis. Maybe you can make a whole bunch of them to give as Christmas presents."

Emma smiled her crooked smile and touched Mamma's arm. "I'll make one for *you*, Mammi Elizabeth."

"I'd like that very much," said Mamma, acting startled upon hearing her formal name.

" 'Cept it won't be a secret now," Emma lisped.

To this, Mamma reached over and cupped Emma's chin with her hand. "You're quite the chatterbox today, ain't so?"

Rhoda laughed softly.

Martha attempted to redirect Mamma's attention away from Emma to towheaded Matty, who was pulling on the hair of one of Emma's ragdolls on Martha's lap. In spite of Matty's adorable grin, Nellie saw it was all Mamma could do to keep her eyes off Emma.

After a while they all sat down together and enjoyed some of Martha's delicious baby pearl tapioca and chocolate chip cookies. Mamma, Martha, and Nellie were clearing the table when Emma tugged on Mamma's skirt and looked up at her. "Aunt Suzy really ain't comin' back ever?"

A frown quickly appeared on Mamma's face. She glanced nervously at Martha.

But there was no time to talk things over, not with Emma within earshot. Mamma smiled ever so kindly. "Our dear Suzy's gone forever, jah. . . ." Her lip trembled and she turned slightly so Emma wouldn't see.

Rhoda quickly diverted Emma's attention, taking her into the smaller sitting room near the front room. Nellie and Nan stayed close to Mamma, comforting her by getting her some hot tea and having her sit at the table awhile.

Later on their drive to the last visit of the day—Benjamin and Ida's place—Nellie couldn't help but notice again how considerate Dat was of

Mamma, asking her if she was all right. Nellie wondered if Emma's question had grieved Dat, too . . . knowing full well that even if it had, he would never speak of it.

————

After she'd completed her baking and helped her sisters and Mamma hang out the wash early Monday morning, Nellie took herself off to the bakery shop. She waited on more English customers than usual, or so it seemed. She didn't mind, as long as they didn't stare, which did happen occasionally—Rosanna observed the same thing, tending her roadside vegetable stand. Nellie preferred the regular Englischers, who were more accustomed to the Plain way she and Nan dressed.

Rhoda had already headed on foot to work at the Kraybills'. So bubbly was she that Nellie wondered if something had happened between yesterday afternoon's visits and this morning.

Nan, on the other hand, remained as *schlimm*—sad—as Nellie had ever seen her. With Rhoda gone for the whole day, Nellie wondered if maybe she might get a chance to hear what was up.

But Nan was slow to assist at the bakery shop, not arriving until midafternoon. By then the place was too swamped with customers for any sisterly talk.

About that time, Rebekah Yoder showed up. "Dat's been draggin' his feet about puttin' down our old buggy mare," she said, seemingly in the mood to chat. "Every time anyone's mentioned it, he's said, 'Ach, there's one more mile in her. A good-natured horse like that's determined to die in the harness.' Anyway, this mornin' he hitched her up and took off to town, going by way of the one-lane bridge on Beaver Dam Road." Rebekah paused for a breath, appearing eager to tell the whole story.

"What happened?" Nellie asked.

The other customers leaned in to listen.

"Well, if the horse didn't collapse right in the middle of the road!"

"That's just awful."

"It was sad, of course, but kind of funny, too, accordin' to Dat." Rebekah shook her head. "There was a long, long line behind Dat's buggy—a whole bunch of buggies, and a good many cars, too. Amish farmers and English drivers both were jumpin' out and askin' what a dead horse was doin' on the road."

"Well, *was* she dead?" asked Nellie.

"Apparently not. A large truck somehow'd got off course and onto the narrow road. When it gave a few loud blasts from its air horn, ach, if the horse didn't leap up on all fours, and they were off again." Rebekah giggled before composing herself, and Nellie laughed, assuming that was the end of the story.

"Turns out Ol' Dolly let out a final shudder on the way home and fell down dead in the middle of the turn lane on Route 322. Poor thing. Probably a heart attack, Dat says."

"Oh, Rebekah . . . what a fright for your father."

"Jah, it was." She sighed. "But he told me he had nobody to blame but himself."

"Good thing no one got hurt."

"Or killed," Rebekah added. " 'Cept the horse, of course."

The cluster of customers began chattering at that, but Rebekah's story had gotten only a halfhearted crinkle of a smile from Nan.

———————

As they closed the shop for the day, Nan took issue with Nellie. "I daresay you overreacted to Rebekah's storytellin'."

"You think so?"

Nan nodded. "Nothin' funny 'bout what she was saying."

"Well, it struck *me* that way."

Nan folded her arms. "You seemed terribly pleased to see Rebekah today. What with the hearsay . . ." She flashed a teasing grin. "I think you must like her brother an awful lot, that's what."

"You don't know that."

"Well, Benjamin's brother-in-law told Becky Glick that he saw what looked to be you and Caleb over in some bushes after Singing, of all things!"

Nellie was stunned. She stopped to stare at her sister. Caleb *had* hugged her in the thicket, but only momentarily. Old Joe Glick's granddaughter—Susannah Lapp's best friend—had made too much of an innocent gesture. Oh, how she despised the grapevine!

"Benjamin's brother-in-law knows nothin' at all, and neither do you," Nellie spouted.

"Well, you did meet up with a boy after Singing. Don't say ya didn't."

"My lips are sealed."

"Jah, and so is your fate."

"You have no idea what you're babblin' about, Nan!" she hollered back. Face red, Nan ran off to the house, slamming the back door.

As much as Nellie wanted to ignore her sister's cutting words, she could not stop thinking about the possibility Susannah had one of Nellie's own brother's kin spying on her. *Susannah must be afraid she's going to lose her chance with Caleb. That's what!*

Nellie followed her sister's lead and went inside, where the smell of one of Mamma's best hot dishes almost cheered her, turkey casserole being a favorite. She hurried to help both Nan and Mamma get the table set and all the serving dishes on the table, trying not to pay Nan any further mind.

Nellie was surprised at the feast, which included baked beans, buttered carrots, and cut corn in addition to a gelatin salad and homemade muffins. Nellie looked at her mother and was heartened to see a healthy blush on her cheeks. *Is she finally feeling better?*

When Dat came in from getting the mules into the barn, he washed up quickly. Rubbing his hands together, he went to get the Good Book down from the tall cupboard at the far end of the kitchen. "We'll be havin' some Scripture reading right after the meal." He took his seat at the head.

Nan and Rhoda exchanged glances as Nan filled the last of the water glasses. She sat down next to Nellie, across from Mamma, who sat in her place to their father's right.

"Let's bow our heads," Dat said. "Our heavenly Father, we ask for your blessings on this food, which we are ever so grateful for . . . just as we are for your dear Son, our Savior, the Lord Jesus Christ. Amen." Instead of praying silently, he had blessed the food aloud.

Nellie had never heard such praying, let alone at the table. She looked first at Mamma, who was beaming at Dat nearly like a schoolgirl. Then she looked at her father, who was getting on with the business of eating, reaching now for the large spoon stuck in the casserole dish.

What on earth was that? Nellie wondered the whole way through the meal.

After they'd finished, Dat resumed his prayerful mood and bowed his head, offering the usual *silent* blessing this time.

Half Amish prayer . . . half not?

Nellie rose to clear the table with Nan's help, telling Mamma and Rhoda to stay seated. As she worked, putting away food and scraping clean the plates while Nan got the water ready for washing, she kept trying to sort out what had just occurred. She'd heard her father pray aloud with her own ears, addressing God as he would someone he knew well.

When at last the kitchen was clean, Dat asked her and her sisters to come and sit at the table, a departure from their usual evening Bible reading, when they were allowed to sit wherever they wished, perhaps even playing checkers or doing something else while he read. Not this night. Dat asked them to listen carefully as he read from passages in the Gospel of John she'd never heard in her life.

The Scriptures told of a man whose name was unfamiliar to her: Nicodemus. Full of questions, he was. *Just as I've been since Suzy passed away,* Nellie thought. She liked this new story from the same old Bible Dat had read from since they were born.

He paused and rested his gaze briefly on them before going on to the next verse. " 'He that believeth on the Son hath everlasting life: and he that believeth not the Son shall not see life; but the wrath of God abideth on him.' "

Nellie found herself fighting back tears. She reached into her pocket and squeezed Suzy's Kapp strings, wanting to ask her father to read the verse again. If only poor Suzy had the everlasting life promised to those who believed on the Son. Was the wrath of God abiding on her?

Not wanting to draw attention to her state of mind, Nellie Mae headed upstairs and closed her door as soon as Dat excused them. She longed to be free of the guilt she carried in her heart, but she had no way of knowing if that was possible.

Her legs felt too weak to hold her, so she knelt beside her bed for the first time ever. Because she didn't know what to say to the Lord God and heavenly Father, so tongue-tied and ashamed was she, Nellie merely wept.

Dat began to make a routine out of reading from the New Testament following breakfast and again after supper. By week's end, he had read them the entire book of John. Nellie had especially enjoyed the story about the woman who'd come for well water and left with something better, her soul satisfied. *The Lord's abundant water . . . life-giving.*

How tantalizing it seemed. Evidently Mamma thought so, too, for Nellie Mae found her reading on her own, right where Dat had placed his long blue bookmark. As relieved as Nellie was to see the rosy glow returning to Mamma's countenance after all these depressing weeks, she was hesitant to discuss this with her mother.

Gladdened, yet perplexed, Nellie prepared for her second date with Caleb, taking extra care in twisting the sides of her hair back into the hair bun, smooth as can be. She scrubbed her face and chose her crispest, whitest

Kapp. Then, waiting till dusk, she slipped out of the house, presumably unnoticed. Nellie was sure Mamma and Nan knew she was going out, but which boy she was seeing was anyone's guess.

Nellie made her way down the road to meet Caleb, wishing Nan hadn't seemed so put out this week at having to help a lot in the shop—peeved at everything, really. "That might change soon with Mamma starting to feel better again," she whispered to herself, eager for the day when her mother would be up to returning to the bakery shop.

———

Caleb had not asked Nellie to wait tonight at any particular spot along Beaver Dam Road, so she made her way near the grassy shoulder, conscious of the somber stillness of every tree. The sky was awash with thin clouds. How fragile they seemed . . . like the way she felt, realizing her words had the power to kill or build her friendship with Caleb.

I best be biting my tongue this time.

She glanced down at her plum-colored dress and fresh black apron, all ironed for the evening. Her black shoes were well polished, too, as if for Preaching.

An open buggy passed by just then, and a few minutes later, another. Each time she kept her head down so as not to be recognized. She did not care for any more gossipy accounts of her doings from Nan.

Niemols—never again!

She puffed in disgust at the audacity of the deacon's daughter, taking the underhanded route by persuading her friend to spy on Nellie—or so she assumed. Of all the nerve; it was exactly like Susannah to behave so. All the same she was not about to allow her aggravation to spoil the evening. She wondered if it would be only a few hours at the Singing, then some riding, and home again. Or would he keep her out all the night long like Nan's beau?

She could only imagine what Caleb had planned. Most of all, she hoped he would not press her anymore about Suzy. She might not be able to restrain her frustration tonight. She would do all she could to keep him talking about more pleasant things.

Spotting his courting buggy, Nellie Mae put on a big smile and waved. His hand went high into the air in a grand return wave, and her heart took flight.

Goodness' sakes . . . I'm done for!

CHAPTER 16

B etsy felt overjoyed to have some time to herself. Reuben had left the house to hitch up the horse and carriage to run an errand over at Ephram's. That gave her plenty of opportunity to read, what with Nellie out with a beau and Rhoda still not back from the Kraybills'. Nan was out taking a walk, or so she'd said.

" 'Who coverest thyself with light as with a garment: who stretchest out the heavens like a curtain. . . . ' " Betsy read where the page had fallen open, which happened to be the Psalms. *Bishop approved,* she thought, and glad of it.

She was compelled to read the entire psalm, curiously taking a close look at God's description of himself as being "clothed with honour and majesty." But it was the reference to light that fascinated her most.

Closing her eyes, Betsy imagined what a covering of light would look like—the heavenly Father's garment, full of goodness and love. She kept her eyes squeezed shut, taking in the picture she saw in her mind's eye.

The Lord God of light and love sent His Son to us . . . for a reason. How happy, even joyful that thought made her husband. Betsy'd never thought of the Scriptures the way Reuben had recently described them.

Life-giving.

She read further, wondering what had prompted Reuben to want to read the Good Book so often . . . and for such long stretches at a time. How had he come upon the chapter he'd read to her last Saturday? Had he purposely searched out new sections to read?

She honestly didn't understand his desire for what he called truth. Their heritage held her fast. Wasn't the truth to be had in the lessons of their forefathers—in their Ordnung?

Opening her eyes, she read the next verse and the next, until she had read the entire chapter—all thirty-five verses. Captivated, she went back, now reading aloud. Pondering each sentence, she felt the urge to move on to Psalm 105, except Nan came running into the house, sniffling.

"Sorry, Mamma . . . I, uh, need to be alone." Nan hurried out of the kitchen and up the stairs.

Ach . . . troubles with a boy, likely.

She would wait a bit, then head up to see if Nan wanted to talk as she sometimes did, although that daughter would hem and haw and never come right out and say what was bothering her. Oh, but Betsy knew. She well remembered her own courting days. All the pain of them . . . and the joy, too.

Returning to the Scripture, she read Psalm 105 through twice, and having done so, she felt torn—both with gladness and an alarming feeling that she had somehow sinned.

Reuben dreaded stopping by Ephram's tonight, scarcely knowing how to conceal his elation at the change in his soul. It had taken him over in the oddest way, making him feel almost like a boy and as light as grain on the threshing floor. The Good News had nothing to do with a set of rules. It was a love story . . . between God and the human race.

He'd reached the point of wanting each of his sons to know this same jubilation that he had already begun to reveal in part to his daughters. Betsy knew all, of course, and he'd already set to praying unceasingly for her to come to the light, just as he had. Clear out of the blue, nearly knocking him between the eyes.

Yet he had not sought it, much like the handful of ministerial brethren back two decades ago whose spiritual eyes were also opened upon reading Scripture. Like him, they had not pursued this path, as it were . . . having believed all along that truth was literally their tradition. Till a week ago Reuben had failed to grasp that this could have occurred without any conscious effort on their part. Would his sons now view him in the same puzzled way?

With some degree of apprehension, Reuben returned sundry tools to Ephram's barn, hoping to avoid seeing his son just yet.

Closing the barn door, Reuben glanced back at the house. Ephram was moving toward him carrying a lantern and his walking stick, his sturdy shoulders seemingly bearing a load that made him old before his time. "Hullo, son!" he called.

"Daed . . . you didn't have to make a special trip over here, and after dark yet."

Reuben waved off the comment. "A nice night, so I saw no reason not to. Besides, tomorrow's goin' to be awful busy."

Ephram leaned on his walking stick. "Someone else dropped by un-expectedly this afternoon."

He waited for Ephram to say more. "Who might that be?"

"A right fancy fella wearin' a tie—Mr. Snavely, he said he was." Ephram pulled a white business card out of his pocket. "Gave me this . . . said I should look him up."

Reuben peered at the card in the lantern's light, noticing the image of a tractor.

"He said something else, too."

Reuben didn't like the way Ephram was frowning. "What's that?"

"He stopped by your place, too . . . talked to Mamm."

This was the first he'd heard of it.

"Mamm didn't mention anything?"

"Nary a word." Reuben chuckled. "You know your mother. She only tells me what she wants me to hear."

Ephram nodded toward the house. "Our women . . ."

Yet Reuben didn't know what to think of this. Betsy had talked with a tractor salesman? How long ago? "I doubt Mr. Snavely got very far talkin' over such things with your mother."

Ephram pushed on his stick again, digging it down, like a stake. "To be frank, Dat, I'll have nothin' at all to do with them tractor folk." He raised his lantern. "If you understand my meaning."

That he did. And good for Ephram. In fact, Reuben would've been right there with him, standing firm in the Old Ways, had he not read the Gospel of John . . . and so many other eye-opening passages, too. For sure and for certain, he'd be taking Ephram's side if heaven hadn't opened the eyes of his understanding about the Ordnung. If it was wrong on some things, who was to say it wasn't wrong on others, too?

"Well, don't know 'bout you, but I'd best be getting home. The air's turnin' chilly," Reuben said, heading toward his horse and buggy.

"So long, Dat."

Reuben stepped into his buggy, anxious to return to Betsy—and to the Good Book. *Jah, eternal life. Such a wonderful-good gift.*

In time, at exactly the right moment, he'd have a sit-down with Ephram.

Caleb had a big talk going, and Nellie was delighted to listen. He was telling her about the hayride next Sunday night after the Singing. "There'll be plenty of goodies to eat and lots of group games and whatnot. Will you go along, Nellie?"

She smiled, knowing the night was young yet. She nodded her head, forgetting he couldn't see her response; nightfall was so complete. Then when she realized he was waiting for an answer, she quickly asked, "Where will it be?"

"Over at the stone house near Mill Road. The deacon's sister's place."

Susannah's aunt!

She groaned inwardly. Would she never escape that girl's scrutiny?

"Sure, I'll go," she replied, nearly grinning at herself.

He surprised her by reaching for her hand. "I'd like to be the one to take you home following . . . all right?"

Why was he asking her so far ahead? Why not pair up at the actual gathering, as was their way? Oh, the flickers of excitement every time he touched her hand!

"Sounds just fine."

From the moment she'd stepped into Caleb's open buggy tonight, she had felt a sense of rightness, as if somehow she was supposed to spend the evening with him. Supposed to enjoy the starry night and the whispers of the dark trees. Something within her urged: *Trust your heart. . . .*

"When do you think you'll join church, Nellie?" The question startled her.

Well, he certainly didn't leave any stone unturned, this boy. Caleb leaned close for a moment, like he wanted her to know he, too, was contemplating making his life vow.

"I haven't thought much 'bout it." That was the truth. "Why're you askin'?"

"Have you considered it?"

"Not yet."

He paused. "Do you plan to put it off?"

"Just bein' honest. It's still early in my Rumschpringe . . . same as it is for you."

He was chuckling now, and she didn't know what to make of it.

"You're laughing at me?" she said.

"A little."

"What for?"

"You're so easy to kid, Nellie." He squeezed her hand.

He thinks I'm gullible. . . .

"When do *you* plan on joining?" She was stepping out of bounds slightly. A girl scarcely ever asked this of a boy, since being baptized into the church was usually followed by a wedding the next month. But he'd put her on the spot, so why not?

"I'll join a year from now—next fall," he stated.

"You know this for sure?"

"Why put off what I plan to do anyway?"

She frowned, glad he couldn't see her expression. No streetlights shone here as they did near the main highway. These back roads he was taking her on were perfect for obscuring facial responses.

Caleb continued. "I'll start baptismal instruction when the time comes. When Deacon Lapp offers classes next summer."

Susannah's father . . .

The silence that followed was one Nellie Mae didn't feel worthy to fill—just as she didn't know how she could possibly kneel before the Lord God and the congregation of the People and say all the things required. Not with all the shame she carried around in her soul.

"We could take the classes together," he suggested.

With all of her heart, she wanted to say yes. *Sure, Caleb, I'll do that with you . . . and I'll be your sweetheart-girl, too.*

"Nellie?" He turned and was mighty close. "I'm askin' you."

The tears came too suddenly to stop them. Wasn't this the very thing she'd wanted . . . for Caleb to show how much he cared?

"Aw, you're cryin'." He reached around her, holding the reins with one hand. "Nellie . . . honey . . . whatever's wrong?"

She couldn't speak, though she wanted to. He must've understood, for he didn't press her further, instead letting her cry on his shoulder, her face against his black woolen coat.

Then almost before she realized it, the horse was pulling the buggy off the road, beneath a towering old tree. He waited for the horse to come to a halt before resting the reins on his knees.

Turning to her, Caleb cupped her face in his hands. "Listen, Nellie . . . you take your time, ya hear? Making the kneeling vow is the most holy thing you'll ever do. The most important, too. No one can tell you when you're ready."

Oh, I might fall too hard for him if he doesn't quit talking like this. She felt the warmth of his breath on her face—his intense, yet tender nearness. She thought he might want to kiss her if only to cheer her up.

Slowly, though, he moved back, his eyes still on her. "We mustn't . . ." He stopped short of saying what she knew he meant.

He likes me more than a bushel and a peck, she thought. Yet as happy as that knowledge made her feel, she had some figuring out to do before she could fully commit to taking the baptismal vow.

In every way, Caleb Yoder seemed to know precisely what he wanted.

CHAPTER 17

B etsy had made several attempts to draw Nan out, to no avail. Her poor daughter merely shook her head, expression gloomy. Truth be told, Nan looked to be pouting, sitting there in her corner of her bedroom.

Somewhat mystified, Betsy studied this pretty girl who was typically full of life. Her delicate features were enhanced by the lovely blue of her big eyes—a striking contrast to her dark brown hair. She'd often thought them a fine combination of Reuben's deep brown hair and her own blue eyes. Nan's looks were the kind to readily attract a boy's attention . . . though it appeared not enough to keep it.

"Looks like you'd rather sit here alone, then?" she said, her final try.

Nan nodded unconvincingly, tears welling up.

Betsy went and stood near her, slipping her arm around Nan's slim shoulders. "You can trust me with whatever's bothering you, dear."

Nan's lower lip quivered. "It just ain't fair, that's all."

Leaning her head atop her daughter's for a moment, Betsy stroked her back, trying to soothe her. "Jah, life may seem ever so unfair at times, no doubting that." She well knew there was no sense in discussing grievances, and she would not inquire about the boy who'd ditched her forlorn Nan. Doing so would hush her girl right up. Why, she'd been much the same way around her own mother, after once being jilted.

Nan sobbed into her hands as though she'd lost nearly everything she'd ever cared about. "Oh, Mamma, I loved this boy . . . I did."

Silently Betsy pulled Nan into her arms.

"And he didn't love me, not like he said." More sniffling.

Better to find out now. Yet she wouldn't dare say such a thing.

She held Nan for a good long time, offering her presence, which, as she remembered when she'd experienced her heartbreak, was all she'd needed from her own mamma.

At long last, when Nan's tears were brushed away and her nose red with the blowing, her daughter surprised her by revealing her beau's change of heart, *after* proposing marriage.

Dishonorable, Betsy decided then and there, battling her ire.

But there was more. Another girl had caught the boy's eye . . . the deacon's niece, as Nan described her. "She took my dear beau away."

"Ain't much dear 'bout him, I daresay."

"Oh, but he was, Mamma. He *was*."

She couldn't bear to see Nan this way, distressed over the worst of the bunch, for sure. Time for Betsy to share something of her own Rumschpringe days.

"Joshua was my first beau ever," she began, hoping to get Nan's mind off her obvious melancholy. "He was everything I thought I wanted and much, much more. . . ."

Their parents were downright strict about when Joshua and Elizabeth could do their courting—Sunday night Singings only. Betsy was "awful young," or so her mother thought initially, pleading with her father that just because Betsy'd turned sixteen, the expected age to begin courting, she wasn't ready to be dating yet. But tradition won out over her mother's insistence, and her father permitted her to start going to the various youth activities, where she met Joshua Stoltzfus, the best-looking boy in the whole church district.

They dated for nearly six months, marking each and every month's anniversary with intense emotion and promises of love. But, alas, when a new family moved into the area, renting a farmhouse from Englischers that was already wired for electricity, Joshua offered to help uninstall it. While doing so, he met and fell in love with the second of their six daughters.

"In the end, though, I was ever so glad it happened thataway," Betsy admitted.

"Why, Mamma?" Nan said.

"Well, think of it . . . what if Josh hadn't gotten his swivel neck straightened out before we got married? What then?"

Nan blinked her weepy eyes. "I s'pose, for one thing, I would never have been born."

Betsy chuckled. "You can say that again." She sighed at the memory. "I lost track of Joshua and his family some years after they moved to the Finger Lakes area of New York to help some of their elderly relatives. I heard later that he and his wife never had any children at all."

"Oh, I'm so glad you didn't end up with that boy," Nan was saying, a peek of a smile appearing. "You would have been unhappy all of your days without all of us, Mamma."

"'Tis true." She kissed Nan's forehead. "I say, be glad this beau of yours left when he did. Count your blessings, dear. All right?"

Nan was nodding. "When you put it that way, jah, I can see things . . . for what they are." She brushed away a solitary tear. "Or were."

"That's my girl." Betsy patted Nan's hand and went to stand in the doorway.

Smiling, Nan replied, "It was good of you to dredge up your past like that for me."

"Ach, our little secret. How's that?"

Nan's smile was complete this time. "Jah, our secret."

With that, Betsy made her way down the hall to Nellie's room. There, she leaned on the doorjamb, thinking now of Suzy and her Rumschpringe. Her mind still played tricks on her at times, because if she hadn't known better, she would have thought she'd just seen Suzy hurrying down the hall and into this very room . . . her waist-length hair, the color of corn silk, floating behind her.

But she's gone for good, she reminded herself, moving to the antique dresser and staring down at the small blue plate, remembering the notes Suzy and Nellie had left for each other there. *Roses are red, violets are blue, wildflowers are best, and so are you!* Suzy had once written to Nellie.

Going and sitting on Suzy's side of the bed, she felt glad to be able to help Nan through her heartache. *If only the brethren would agree to push back the Rumschpringe till the youth were older . . . some of this heartache might well be avoided.*

Betsy wanted to protect all of her girls for as long as possible. Nearly all the women her age said the same about their daughters. So it was. Most had grown up by experiencing both the heartbreak and the delight of dating. Sadly, there was very little in between.

Caleb felt sure he was lost, though he'd traveled this way at least once before. But no, he must have blocked out the memory of *that* night completely. He wouldn't let the chuckle that came just then escape his lips, however, for neither did he want to dwell on that particular date, nor did he wish to explain to Nellie Mae why he was suddenly so amused. Now this girl sitting next to him was as sweet as the cherry pie she baked. She was much too good to lose—he sensed it as clearly as he knew he'd taken a wrong turn somewhere several miles back.

He'd known the horse fences and expanse of cornfields along the road back yonder. But nothing at all looked familiar now, although it was difficult to see much in the murky night, what with the moon hiding behind a thick covering of high clouds. Even so, he had earlier recognized Preacher Manny's house and Preacher Lapp's spread of land, too . . . and Bishop Joseph's, evidently gone out west for some peace of mind. It was no wonder the bishop had a hankering for time away. According to the grapevine, several meetings a week were happening, the dissenters taking advantage of the bishop's absence.

A pair of ring-necked pheasants scuttled along the low-lying brush, across the roadside gully. Caleb steadied the reins and watched as the twosome began to rise almost vertically, a loud whirring in their wings. He was now certain he did not recognize a single landmark, though he knew by the stars he was heading east, away from Nellie's father's house. The farther away they went, the longer it would take to return. He was mighty content to ride onward with Nellie snuggled next to him, close enough for him to feel the warmth of her arm on his, their hands intertwined beneath the heavy lap robe.

"Have you ever thought you knew where you were headin' only to find out you really had no idea?" he asked her.

"Well, you could take that two ways." She sat up straight, releasing her hand from his and stretching a bit.

"I don't have the slightest notion where we are."

She laughed softly. Her gentle laughter was like the rippling music in the mill creek near where he'd met her on their first date, the destination he'd contemplated taking her yet tonight. It seemed to suggest she almost enjoyed the prospect of wandering together.

He felt emboldened. "Jah, I admit it—we're lost."

"We could go back and try to find where it was we lost our way."

He chuckled. "But how's that any fun? Don't you want to keep going and find out where we're headed . . . eventually?"

"If you've got all night, I s'pose."

"All the time in the world."

They both laughed at that and he leaned against her arm, wishing her hand was available now. He decided to wait till later, at the millstream, to hold her hand again . . . assuming they ever found their way back. And if they didn't, well, they'd simply ride all the way to Delaware. They'd bump into a major highway somewhere along the way.

The thought of riding aimlessly into the night with Nellie to talk to was as delicious a thought as his mother's schnitz pie. How was it he had missed her all this time? It was as if he'd just met Nellie, even though they had grown up in the same community.

He had courted several girls for short periods of time over the past year. Only one had he deemed worthy to take to the lovely, secluded setting behind the mill, but in the end even she had been too eager for words of love, and he had held back, more hesitant as time went by.

Nellie, for her part, was unpredictable, sometimes warm toward him and other times almost distant, as if she were testing the waters. Even so, conversation between them generally came easily, which again was a change from the other girls he had courted. He'd been quick to discover he had not loved any of them. Caleb was waiting for the girl with the missing puzzle piece that matched his heart perfectly. Was Nellie that girl? To think she'd been here all along, awaiting his notice.

"Are you warm enough?" he asked. The bricks he'd heated before heading over to Beaver Dam Road to fetch Nellie had not held their warmth as he'd hoped. But maybe that had more to do with the strength of the cold and not the short time the bricks had been in the fire.

"I'm fine, Caleb. How 'bout you?"

"My toes are a smidgen cold, that's all," he said. *So are my hands,* he thought, reaching for his gloves tucked under the seat and putting them on. He would be practical, as he usually was. *Practicality reigns,* his father had always said in regard to women, though his father had courted and married a girl far different from Nellie. *His choice . . . we all choose.*

Seeing a cluster of lights up ahead, he decided to turn soon, and coming upon an extra-wide intersection, he maneuvered the horse into the fan-shaped turn, mindful not to tip over the buggy—something he'd done upon first receiving it from his father. *Won't make that mistake twice.*

Now they were heading northwest. Caleb directed his horse to gallop, speeding up the ride. He didn't want Nellie to be too tired before they stopped at the spot he'd chosen . . . if they found it. The question was how she would respond to what he had in mind.

Had it not been for her sister's untimely death, Nellie might be more outgoing, perhaps. He understood her grief, for it had not been too many years since his young nephew had fallen to his death inside a silo. Weeks had passed before Caleb could begin to think of much beyond Henry's accident.

We can't wish our loved ones back. Suzy's early death was God's plan for her, he thought. The same went for young Henry.

Caleb had decided not to bring up Suzy at all tonight—not unless Nellie herself happened to. So far, that seemed unlikely, especially since he suspected her tears earlier were related to that sister.

He reached to open his glove compartment, removing a tin box containing more than a half dozen cookies, fresh this afternoon from his mother's oven. "Would you like a treat? Mamm's peanut butter cookies."

She accepted one. "Your mother must enjoy bakin', too."

"It would seem so. Every time I head into the kitchen, she's opening the oven door, pushing something in or taking something out."

"Sounds like me in the early morning. Of course, my customers like having a variety of choices. I keep a running list of their favorites."

He was engrossed by Nellie's talk of baking and running a business on her father's property.

"Have you ever run out of pastries?"

"Sometimes, if a customer places an unusually large order, but I generally don't run low till late in the afternoon."

"So you estimate everything that will sell in one day's time, then?"

"Oh sure. But the best part of the work is all the fun I have talkin' with customers."

"How many are English?" Secretly he wondered how comfortable she was with worldly folk.

"Well, there are the regulars from up and down the road. Whenever they have company or folks droppin' by, they bring them over and go hog wild in my shop."

He loved the way she expressed herself so clearly. Nothing timid about Nellie, and she was not only interesting, but ever so appealing to look at, too. Apprehension reared its head, and Caleb could hear Daed's words now—should Daed ever put two and two together and realize his youngest was seeing Suzy Fisher's sister. *You're courtin' Nellie Mae, sister to that lost soul? Ach, Caleb, use your head . . . don't let me down. We're Yoder men, staunch followers of das Alt Gebrauch—the Old Ways.*

He hoped the rumors about Suzy would blow over before his father could speak such harsh words to him. Anxious to get his mind on more pleasant things, he asked Nellie, "What's your favorite cookie?"

"To eat or to bake?"

"There's a difference?"

"Why, sure. I enjoy baking lots of cookies, especially my thin sand tarts, but I much prefer biting into a thicker cookie."

"Jah, substance in a cookie's a fine trait." He offered another peanut butter cookie from his stash. *Come to think of it, substance aptly describes Nellie, too.*

"What's *your* favorite, Caleb?"

"Chocolate chip first and peanut butter second."

She let out a giggle.

"What's so funny?"

"You." She was still laughing.

"Let's see . . . I'm funny because I answered your question?"

"No, because you're so thorough." She smiled at him. "You're quite funny."

"No one's ever said that before."

"It's a very nice thing, believe me."

"If you say so, it must be." He would not restrain himself any longer. He slipped his arm around her. "*You're* ever so good, Nellie Mae."

She briefly leaned her head on his shoulder.

"We're no longer lost, I see," he said, recognizing a signpost now. "Would you like to walk awhile?"

"I wore extra socks, just in case."

"So did I," he admitted, finding it encouraging that she'd planned to be out with him a long time on this, their second date of what he hoped would be many.

CHAPTER 18

W hen Reuben confronted her, Betsy was reluctant to acknowledge that a sales representative had dropped by ten days ago. "The man was here but a few minutes," she reassured him.

"When were you goin' to tell me?"

"Wasn't . . . I s'pose."

He shook his head and smiled at her. "Well, ain't you the case?"

"What did Ephram tell you, anyways?" She was curious, having heard a bit of gossip from her daughters-in-law at a recent quilting. According to Martha, there was a growing group among them who favored using tractors.

Reuben scratched his long beard. "Ephram's not at all interested in fancy farm equipment, if that's what you're worried about."

"Not worried, no. Just wonderin'." She finished brushing her hip-length hair, noticing in her small dresser mirror the streaks of gray intermingled with the flaxen . . . and the ever-widening middle part. Goodness, she had been pulling a comb down that part for nigh unto forty-eight years now, next birthday come July. "I am awful tired," she said.

"Before you sleep, let me pray for you," Reuben said.

"Whatever for?"

He inhaled slowly, his eyes solemn. "Aw, now."

She felt immediately sorry and stretched out her hand. "Reuben . . ."

"That's all right, love. I'll be prayin' for ya on my own."

She knew he would, because she'd awakened in the night to him kneeling at the bed, hands folded, lips moving in the lantern light. Not wanting to disturb him, she'd tiptoed around him, heading down to their one and only indoor bathroom. It was as if Reuben took the verse to "pray without ceasing" literally.

Truly, Betsy didn't know how to view what was happening. It seemed all encompassing—either he had his nose in the Good Book or his nose pressed into his hands as he prayed. Highly unusual, she was ever so sure. She guessed if she contemplated God's Word long enough, she might give herself over to it, too, and get herself into the hot water her husband surely was headed for. For now she felt too drained of energy to walk such a road herself.

With talk of Reuben's parents moving as soon as next month into the Dawdi Haus next door, Reuben would have more than his share of work to tend to. *And less time for reading and praying.* . . . Doubtless his father would intervene, as well, if Noah Fisher realized what Reuben was daily studying.

Her husband *had* become ever so considerate since memorizing Scripture, doting on her now more than ever. There was no question Reuben's devotion for his God had filled him to the point it was spilling over to her.

Just so the brethren don't come round asking questions once he starts sharing Scriptures with our sons. . . .

She thought of Rhoda, Nan, and Nellie, having observed their reactions to the twice-daily readings and their father's expressive table blessing before the meal. None of them had said anything, but if it continued, Nellie would likely be saying something—and not any too kindly, knowing that one.

Betsy pushed her pillow beneath her head, seeking a comfortable position. Nellie was out with a beau again tonight, she was quite sure. Looking over at Reuben, still leaning against the side of the bed in prayer, she wondered if she ought to ask him to remember both Nan and Nellie in beseeching the Lord God and heavenly Father this night. One for a shattered heart . . . the other for strength for whatever was to come.

The long ravine toward the old gristmill—now a knittery—was nearly too dark to walk through. Nellie picked her way over the uneven ground near the bank of the millrace, glad for Caleb's foresight in bringing a flashlight. So far she was enjoying herself, yet in her happiness she felt a touch of sadness, too.

Regardless of time's passage, she struggled some with the notion of enjoying herself at all. Nellie contemplated the peculiar feeling, wondering why she felt guilty to be getting on with her life. Was this a common thing for people who'd lost loved ones?

Neither Rhoda nor Nan had voiced any such thing. But now Mamma . . . she might understand.

Nellie wanted to fully delight in Caleb's attention; he had long been the boy she'd dreamed of. There were times when she felt completely at home with him. At other times, she felt less relaxed with him than with other boys. Was she bracing herself for future questions about Suzy? More likely she was nervous about the lie she'd told him. If, indeed, it was a lie, which she must find out somehow.

She breathed in the cold air and held it. *Enough of that thinking.* Then, letting the air *whoosh* back out, she wanted to pinch herself. Was it too good to be true the way Caleb looked at her? Would she ever awaken from this wonderful-good dream?

When he pointed his flashlight to shine directly on her path, Nellie Mae was brought out of her reverie. Oh, how she wanted this night to last and last. Such a romantic setting, one Caleb must have picked just for her.

He laughed softly. "It's so beautiful—private, too. My sisters and brothers and I sometimes ice skate on the pond, over yonder." He asked where she and her sisters liked to skate, and she mentioned the pond not far from their house. He nodded and said, "I'd like to bring you back here when it's sunny. I think you'll come to like this place as much as I do."

She wouldn't ponder whether he'd brought other girls walking here in this secluded area. Not when he was seemingly quite content to be with her now.

He reached for her hand and once again she thrilled to his touch. *Will this always excite me so?* Careful to guide her and keep her from slipping, Caleb shone his flashlight as a guiding beacon.

Soon they came upon a lively stream and stopped to listen to its murmuring as it spilled over rocks, making its way south below them. Nellie wished for a moon—the surrounding trees and shrubs suddenly seemed ominous and too black. She shivered, fearful.

"What is it, Nellie?"

"I . . . uh, it's awful dark out . . . is all."

They were deep in a dense covering of trees, the stream nearly at their feet. "I'm here with you. Don't be afraid."

She held tightly to his hand. "Honestly, I was never scared of the dark . . . well, before . . ."

"Before Suzy drowned?" His question came without warning.

She looked up at him, overwhelmed, and shrugged, afraid another discussion about Suzy might begin.

"I can see why you'd feel thataway." He led her toward the millstream, making no further comments about Suzy to her surprise and relief.

Then he leaned down to place the flashlight on the ground, pointing it toward the water. Straightening, he turned to her, a smile on his face. "I want to ask you something, Nellie."

She held her breath.

"Will you be my girl? Will you go for steady with me?"

All during their lengthy ride tonight, she'd considered what it would be like to be without Caleb, as before . . . her heartfelt longing to know him. She did not want to return to those days.

"Will you, Nellie Mae?"

Only one answer formed on her lips. "Jah, Caleb . . . I will."

He leaned forward and planted a kiss on her cheek, then let out a whoop and a holler.

She laughed out loud, his delight mingling with her own.

All the way back to the horse and buggy and on the long ride home, too, she considered that she knew for the first time what Mamma had meant. *You'll know when the right boy comes along. . . .*

Nellie Mae's heart sang and her toes wiggled as the buggy flew through the wee hours. Caleb Yoder was going to court her, and in due time, she would become his bride. Nothing could possibly stand in their way.

CHAPTER 19

⸻

Nellie sensed an air of anticipation in Mary Glick's house on Thursday morning. The place was abuzz with chatter and delicious treats as she, Mamma, and Nan arrived for the quilting bee, eager to stitch together a wedding-ring quilt for a new bride-to-be. Though the girl wasn't related to Nellie, she was one of Rosanna's many first cousins, and Nellie looked forward to seeing her dearest friend here today, too.

Standing in the tidy kitchen to warm her hands near the stove, Nellie overheard Susannah Lapp's mother talking about their bishop. "He's under the weather out there in Kalona. I daresay he and Anna've been gone a mite too long, jah?"

"Sure seems so" came the reply. "Next thing he'll be stuck out there, being ill 'n' all."

Susannah's mother sighed loudly. "Time he gets home again."

Uncle Bishop must surely be perturbed to have to remain so far away, Nellie thought. *Or is he lingering on purpose?* She moved away, lest she give in to the temptation to eavesdrop—a fault she disliked in others.

Mary Glick's front room was filled with a large quilting frame and twelve chairs set up around it. There were six piles of fabric stacked on the wooden settee, neatly folded and sorted by color. "Looks like there's another quilt in the plannin', too," Nellie remarked to Nan, who was more pleasant and cheery today than she had been in a good while.

"Wonder when they'll start doing the piecework." Nan inspected the brightest colors, choosing a bold plum color and holding it up. "What would I look like in a dress made out of this shade of purple?" She held it under her chin. "What do you think?"

The image of Iva Beiler at the last Singing flickered through Nellie's mind. "Why, it'd look plain worldly, wouldn't it?"

"Amishwomen in Holmes County wear cape dresses of this color," Nan said. "And even brighter colors, too."

"How do ya know?"

"From my circle letter."

Nellie found it odd that Nan should write to someone so far away. "Who in your letters is from there?"

"No one." Nan was still fingering the radiant fabric as if she was coveting it. "One of my friends in Paradise seems to know all about the doings out in Berlin and Sugar Creek. That's all."

Nellie nodded. Funny how the grapevine worked—it had a way of piping in the tartest hearsay . . . and the sweetest. But the words coming from right behind her now were more surprising than sour or syrupy.

"I've just found out the most exciting news," Kate Beiler's mother, Rachel Stoltzfus, was saying. "My daughter Kate is carrying twins."

"Ach, really?" said her friend.

Rachel was beaming. "Who would've thought?"

"Twins?" Nellie murmured, eyeing Rachel. Was Kate's mother aware of the arrangement her daughter had made with Rosanna?

Nellie Mae couldn't help but think now of Kate's having shown early. And here lately she'd looked as if the baby was coming any day instead of close to Christmas. Nellie craned her neck, looking for Rosanna, who still had not arrived. When Nellie asked, neither Nan nor Mamma had seen her.

The fact Rachel had ceased talking about the babies and did not say a peep about Kate and Rosanna's agreement made Nellie wonder if Rachel knew anything more.

Has Kate informed her mamma?

Soon they all sat down, and Nellie saved a spot for Rosanna, who, according to her mother, was most definitely on her way. A small scrap of somewhat mismatched fabric was peeking out between two others right in front of Nellie. Only a few of the older women kept this tradition alive; Mary, for one, liked to have a slight imperfection in every quilt.

When a full hour passed with no sign of Rosanna, Nellie presumed she wouldn't be coming after all.

Is she home sewing up double of everything? Or is she so stunned about twins, she'd rather stay put? Nellie truly hoped Rosanna was all right.

As much as she was fond of babies, she couldn't begin to imagine what it would mean to care for two newborns at once. Of course Mamma knew all about that, having had Thomas and Jeremiah first off.

She wondered what Rosanna would do with twins instead of a single baby. Kate, too—would she change her mind? Surely she wouldn't split up the babies between the two families. Even so, Nellie had heard of such a thing—parents who couldn't provide for their triplet babies dividing them among the mother's other siblings.

Raising them like cousins.

Nellie tried her best to focus on making the tiny quilting stitches expected of her, but her hand shook as she contemplated dear Rosanna's possible response to such news.

If she even knows yet. . . .

Rosanna listened with both ears, unable to edge in a word as Kate sat across the kitchen table, eyes glistening. "Listen," she finally managed to slip in, "I'll take all the wee babes you want to give."

Kate's eyes grew wide and solemn. "Honestly?" She brushed away her tears. "You have no idea what you're sayin', Rosanna."

"Oh, but I do." Rosanna knew she could care for twins. In all truth, she'd care for as many as God saw fit to give her. "I'm ever so glad you stopped by, cousin. You almost missed me."

"Jah, there's a quilting, and I'm sorry to keep you from it."

"No worry."

Rosanna noticed how Kate cradled her stomach. How must it feel to carry two babies?

"All right, then," said Kate. "It's settled."

They went on to talk of booties and blankets and all the many items of clothing the little ones would be needing. Rosanna mentioned having made one afghan so far; there was ample yarn to make another. "I have plenty of time to get ready, Kate. Don't fret."

Kate sighed, looking toward the window. "I don't know what John will say . . . if they're both boys."

"You haven't discussed that with your husband?"

"Oh jah. He just hasn't decided what we oughta do, well, 'bout you and Elias getting both of them."

Rosanna felt as if the wind had been knocked out of her. *What's Kate saying?*

"I know what we talked about, but—"

"Well, I just don't understand," Rosanna interrupted, terribly confused. Her cousin seemed befuddled. Was this unique to expectant mothers or had the news of twins somehow addled her? She couldn't recall Kate behaving like this before—wavering back and forth. No, Kate had always been one to make up her mind and stick to it.

"We'll talk it over more, John and I." Kate rose slowly and headed for the door.

Rosanna choked down her emotions and followed her waddling cousin out the back door and down the walkway. "Take good care now, ya hear?"

Kate nodded.

"Come over anytime."

"I'll visit again . . . help you sew up some baby clothes." Kate waved, a half smile on her face.

"That'd be fine." Rosanna's heart sank as she wondered how many more times Kate would second-guess her offer.

Reuben never even heard Preacher Manny open the barn door and step inside. He was busy pitching hay to the mules when he looked up and saw the preacher there.

"Well, you almost scared the wits out of me," Reuben said, trying not to let on how jolting it was.

"I called out to you more than once. Didn't ya hear me?"

"No." Then Reuben noticed that Preacher Manny seemed more shaken than he was gruff—as white as if he'd had himself a nightmare.

"Reuben . . . I don't know who to tell this to," Manny began.

Leaning on his pitchfork, Reuben observed a twitch in Manny's jaw. "What's a-matter, Preacher? You got troubles with your hay crimper again?"

"Naw, ain't that." Manny grimaced, rubbing the back of his neck.

"You got yourself some pain? I say get your wife to rub that hot oil on your back and shoulders again."

Manny removed his felt hat. His bangs were smashed flat against his forehead, and he seemed terribly restless, even troubled. "It's not a pain in my neck, though it could turn out to be."

"You all right?"

"In a bit of a quandary, really." He hemmed and hawed. Looking at Reuben, he asked, "Is there someplace we can go and talk?"

"Well, I—"

"I want to speak as a cousin and a friend . . . leavin' the preacher part behind for now."

Reuben was immediately concerned. He hoped this wasn't more talk about which farm equipment to allow in their Ordnung next month when they would vote on additions and such. By the look of Manny's sober expression, Reuben couldn't begin to guess what was up unless it was something of that magnitude. "Why, sure . . . let's walk out to the woods a ways." He poked his hayfork down into the loose pile.

"No need callin' attention, jah?" Manny added quickly, falling in step.

As they walked, Manny explained that he had begun regularly reading the Good Book, poring over it, as it were. He hesitated before adding, "I don't know any other way to say this, but a light's turned on in me."

Reuben felt a shiver of recognition . . . and excitement. Emboldened, he asked, "Where were you readin', Manny?"

He turned and looked hard at Reuben. "You mean to say you ain't goin' to ask me what I was doin' reading and studying thataway?"

"Nope." Reuben was itching to tell his relative what he himself had done, hoping that maybe Manny had also uncovered some previously unknown kernels of truth.

A smile spread across the older man's face. "Well, now, Reuben Fisher, what're you sayin' to me?"

"Just that I believe I understand, Preacher . . . er . . . cousin." He took a gulp of a breath. "You see, I know exactly what you mean by that light goin' on."

Manny stopped walking. "Ach, can it be?" His words came slow and solemn. He was nearly gawking now as he looked Reuben over but good.

Reuben couldn't keep his grin in check.

"Well, then, you must be saved, too. Ain't ya?"

Reuben wanted to fess up with everything in him, though he knew there would be no turning back. "Jah, and I read the whole book of John, mind you. Ever look closely at chapter three?" He didn't know why, but he was whispering now, when he wanted to holler it out.

Manny blinked his big eyes. "I believe God directed me to talk to you, Reuben. Jah, I believe He did."

Reuben listened, comprehending. "I'm mighty glad ya did."

"I, too, read that chapter . . . and then the entire Gospel of John." Manny was grinning himself.

Reuben clasped his arm. "It's so good to know we're brothers in this."

Then Manny began to tell about his most recent circle letter, which shared that a half dozen preachers across the country—"including out in Ohio, too"—believed the eyes of their understanding had been opened. "All in a short space of time."

"Really? Must be some sort of awakening, then."

Manny's face lit up. "Bishops are havin' dreams of the Lord with outstretched hands, showing them His pierced hands and feet. 'For you I died so that you might have eternal life,' He's telling them. Others are being drawn to the Scripture, devouring it like starving men."

Reuben nodded. "That's me."

"What about us havin' a Bible study? For anyone who'd like to attend."

"Well, I don't have to tell ya what the bishop will say."

"Bishop's gone . . . and may not be back for some time is what I hear."

Reuben still felt they should make an attempt to get a sanctioned gathering. "Whether or not we have his blessing is one thing—"

"We'll never get it, Reuben."

"You goin' to write him and ask permission, or should I?"

Manny shook his head. "It's a waste of time for me to try."

Reuben could see where this was going. "Well, since Joseph's my elder brother, I s'pose . . ."

Manny nodded, smiling. "Jah, that's just what I was thinking."

He's mighty glad to be off the hook, thought Reuben, wondering how to explain to Bishop Joseph their desire to study Scripture.

CHAPTER 20

Nellie struggled with a feeling of distress all that next Friday morning after the quilting as she pondered the goings-on in the house. What had caused her father to develop his strange obsession with the Bible? They read twice each day as a family now, but then Dat spent several more hours reading and studying on his own, hurrying through his chores to do so.

Peculiar . . . and worrisome.

She wanted to talk with Mamma about both that and Dat's fancy praying, but she couldn't bring herself to raise the topic. Oddly, her mother seemed to be in compliance. Mamma was known for often speaking up, yet in such a gentle way that Dat could never scold her for being less than meek.

She recalled the night Dat had first read from John to them—how vulnerable she'd felt kneeling at her bed, weeping into her hands. It was impossible to forget her longing at that moment . . . how she'd wished for the Lord God to soothe, even mend, her guilty heart. Like a young child in need of loving help.

Nellie forced her thoughts back to taking note of the varieties of muffins, whole wheat rolls, and cupcakes already dwindling fast this morning. She began to count the dozens of cookies.

Hearing a car pull into the lane, she looked up to see a group of five women enter the shop. "We saw your cute little sign out front," said one.

"Hope you don't mind if we come in," said another.

"Make yourselves at home," Nellie Mae replied.

"Do you sell to non-Amish?" a third woman asked, the tallest and youngest-looking of the bunch.

"Everyone's welcome," said Nellie.

A redheaded woman who looked to be in her thirties was the first to order, requesting a half dozen of Nellie's morning glory muffins. The Englischer got to talking about recipes with her three friends while Nellie filled the order.

"Will that be all for you today?" Nellie asked.

She raised her eyes to Nellie's. "Actually, I was wondering where I might get my hands on some authentic recipes."

Nellie smiled. "Well, if it's Amish recipes you're after, I have plenty in my noggin." She tapped at her temple. "What would you like—hot dishes, baked goods . . . desserts?"

The woman brightened. "A general question first—do you use shortening or butter for your cakes and sweet breads?"

"Well, that depends on what we have on hand," Nellie answered. "There are times when I use lard, too."

The redhead was now eyeing the sticky buns, tapping on the glass counter with her long pink fingernails. "And do you use store-bought flour or grind your own?"

"Oh, either's fine," Nellie said. "We don't mind going to the grocery store for things, but we like to make do with food off the land." She paused to determine their interest before continuing. "Each family puts up about a thousand jars of vegetables, fruit, and preserves every year at the harvest."

"What about your delightful language?" the oldest-looking woman in the group asked. "Is there any way to learn it?"

Nellie shrugged. "Outsiders call it Pennsylvania Dutch, but it's not Dutch at all. It's a folk rendering of German—not written anywhere that I know of."

"Not even your Bible?" one piped up.

"Ach, that's in either High German or English." Nellie felt like a pincushion all of a sudden. Surely these were the most openly curious Englischers she'd ever met.

"Would you mind if I asked about your faith?" the youngest-looking woman said.

My what?

Nellie felt trapped. She'd never had such a conversation, and she wished with all her heart Nan would hurry up and come running.

"Or are your . . . uh, ways based on—"

"Pamela, no . . . that's not what you want to say." A previously silent woman was talking as though Nellie weren't standing right there.

"Aw, don't mind her," the first woman said to Nellie, linking her arm through Pamela's.

Nellie stared past the Englischers, looking out the window. *Where are you, Nan, when I need you?*

"I'm sorry," Pamela said. "I didn't mean to embarrass you, miss."

Nellie tried to think of something to say or do to change the subject, but nothing came. Finally she said, "Well, jah, we have our beliefs . . . our ways, passed down from generation to generation." Nellie figured Dat might have had a more suitable answer. Or would his interest in soaking up the long sentences in the Good Book make his answers to Englischers too free?

How soon before his fondness for Scripture reaches the wrong person's ears? She clenched her jaw, hoping Caleb's father might never, ever hear of it.

"Really . . . I want to apologize." It was the redhead again. "We didn't mean to be rude."

Nellie forced a smile. "Not to worry." She accepted the money for the muffins, thankful for a working cash register today. "Is there anything else I can do for you?" she managed to say. "A written recipe, perhaps?"

The redhead nodded, and Nellie began to write down the ingredients and instructions for her sweet bread—a coffee cake recipe from her great-grandmother.

The women thanked her repeatedly, and then the others took turns ordering cookies and other goodies. When they'd paid and made their way back to their fancy red car, Nellie sighed with relief.

Not much time later, she noticed Dawdi and Mammi Fisher entering the drive in their enclosed family buggy. She assumed they wanted to talk with Mamma about getting settled into the Dawdi Haus—leaving behind the farmhouse over on Plank Road, where they'd lived since Dat received this house after marrying Mamma. Nellie was looking forward to having her father's parents closer, especially Mammi Hannah, known for her stories about their family and its doings through the years. All the Fisher women would benefit from having Mammi living under the same roof, so to speak—especially Mamma.

But Nellie's present concern was finding time to rescue Suzy's diary from the woodland soil before winter's onset. Almost two weeks had gone by since she had first made her search, and thus far no other opportunity to look had presented itself. Her responsibility to run the bakery shop and always be on hand for her customers left her with virtually no time of her own. That, coupled with the frustration of not remembering the diary's exact location, worried her.

Will I ever find it?

Nellie Mae glanced up to see the crimson red car creeping back up the driveway. Pamela stepped out, returning to the shop. "I nearly forgot—do you have shoofly pie?" she asked.

"Sure." Nellie picked up one of the two pies remaining and showed it off as if it were one of her offspring. "We make the wet-bottom kind here," she said.

"Sounds perfect." Then Pamela asked, seeming a bit shy, "Would you happen to know the ingredients offhand?"

"I'm happy to jot them down for you." Nellie waited for the woman to pull out a tablet from her small brown pocketbook.

"It's ever so easy, really," Nellie told her after writing the recipe. "Nothing more than eggs, corn syrup, baking soda, and boiling water for the filling. Do you make quite a lot from scratch?" she asked.

"I can hardly stay out of my kitchen." The Englischer laughed and motioned toward the wet-bottom shoofly pie. "I'll purchase that one, please."

Nellie placed it in a white box and taped the lid shut. "Anything else?"

"That'll do it. Thanks!"

"Enjoy the pie," Nellie called, happy that her supply was dwindling. She would need to get up extra early to make sure she had plenty of choices for customers tomorrow.

So, no trip to the woods for at least another day.

Pamela paused at the door, and Nellie had to smile. *Now what?*

"Do you happen to know where we can get a buggy ride?" the woman asked.

Nellie thought about that, fairly sure they were expecting to pay for the experience. "Can't say I know of anyone."

The woman's disappointment momentarily registered before her expression brightened again. "Well, thanks anyway. Have a nice day!"

"Same to you!" Nellie said. Only when Pamela was on her way did Nellie allow her pent-up laughter to escape. *Goodness, such a curious sort!*

When Nan had finished her indoor chores, she carried the mail out to Nellie. "Here's a letter for you, sister," she said. Nellie noted it was the circle letter she'd been expecting from Cousin Treva.

"Did you get one, too?" asked Nellie, thinking a letter would further improve Nan's frame of mind.

Nan shook her head, eyes downcast. "I don't 'spect to, neither."

"Aw, Nan . . . I'm sorry. Really, I am."

"You don't have to be sorry. It's my *dumm* fault."

Nellie's heart went out to her sister. "I'm a good listener, ain't so?"

"Well, maybe you are. Still, I don't want to talk 'bout it." Unexpectedly Nan turned and departed for the house.

When will she ever let me in?

Then Nellie realized Nan must've misunderstood, thinking she was asking about her former beau. *And now I've peeved her. . . .*

Nellie stepped back behind the counter. Since there were no customers, she opened the envelope and pulled out the six handwritten pages.

Dear Cousins,

Hello from New Holland! I hope you are all doing well. We've been canning up a storm here, and some are already doing a lot of quilting for the wedding season.

Something more's happening over here, too, and not the usual goings-on. I can't begin to explain it, but there are groups of folk getting together on no-Preaching Sundays for a sort of Sunday school. A handful of people are even having Bible studies of an evening—or so my sister says. She's been going rather regularly. So far, the bishops don't seem to mind. Either that or they don't know yet.

"Oh, but they will," Nellie muttered to herself. It was impossible to keep something like this quiet.

She read on, finding it interesting that a number of others were as preoccupied with the Good Book as her father.

When she'd finished the first letter, she was reluctant to move on to the others and Cousin Treva's. She felt as though she might be ill as she sat down to let all this sift into her mind.

What's it mean?

Surely her father wasn't caught up in this gathering storm, was he?

She hoped not. It wasn't for the sake of the People she felt that way—a selfish motive ruled her entirely. She must shield her deepening relationship with Caleb with every ounce she had.

Heading out of her shop, Nellie Mae stood outside and breathed in the brisk autumn air. A scuttle of wind came up then and she shivered, wishing she'd slipped on her woolen shawl. She watched the leaves swirl at her feet and sensed an ominous feeling much like the one Dat had expressed when the corn quit growing nearly overnight.

In the distance a long V-shaped pattern of Canada geese dotted the sky. She had always wondered what sort of coded messages they sent to each other to create such precise flight formations. Did every bird know exactly where to fly in the lineup? Did the Lord God direct them from on high? If it *was* a divine thing, did that same Creator God care about the course of her life? And Dat's?

She shuddered to think what might befall their family if either Nan or Rhoda began talking about Scripture to friends or cousins, locally and otherwise. No worry of Mamma saying anything. And, of course, Nellie sure wouldn't think of sharing about her father's odd behavior, not even with dearest Rosanna.

No, the brethren must never know. . . .

CHAPTER 21

————

Nellie found it excruciating to sit in the cluster of girls during Sunday night's hayride. Surrounded by so many—Susannah Lapp and Becky Glick included—Nellie was able to catch only an occasional glance from Caleb. She pretended not to care that they were separated for the long and bumpy ride, preferring to think ahead to their time together later.

Susannah was awful *bapplich*—chatty—as she eyed the bunched-up boys on their end of the hay wagon. No doubt she sought Caleb's attention. A few minutes later, Susannah actually dared to call over her shoulder, "Ain't that right, Caleb Yoder?" before bursting into a rainbow smile directed at him.

Nan, too, was smiling to beat the band, which was surprising because she had been withdrawn and nearly sullen again since Friday. Nellie couldn't begin to fathom what had put the sunshine on Nan's face, but the clouds were surely gone tonight as she whispered with Caleb's sister Rebekah. So caught up were they in private talk, it was impossible for Nellie to speak with her own sister.

Taking a quick survey of the boys, Nellie wondered if Nan was over her former beau and already sweet on someone new. Knowing Nan, though, that seemed unlikely. Nan was not known to be fickle, but she hadn't weathered well the storm of splitting up—twice it had happened already. Yet, given time, Nan would surely find another suitor in their crowd. Certainly there was no shortage of boys, and Nan had plenty of admirers among them.

The night was nippy with a damp breeze. Some of the girls were shivering even though they sat shoulder to shoulder, while the boys were talkative and, in some cases, louder than usual.

With Nan talking with Rebekah, and Susannah the obvious center of attention, encircled as she was by a dozen or so other girls, Nellie felt some-what alone. Knowing it was simply for now, she rather enjoyed it, relishing the thought of her upcoming buggy ride with Caleb.

Looking at the stars, she began to count them silently. The fainter ones at first, all across the expanse of sky, then the more brilliant ones—intense white sprinkles against the black backdrop of space.

Quite relaxed at present, she leaned against a soft mound of hay, lost in the enormity of the sky above. She felt small and insignificant and remembered one late summertime night when she and Suzy had slipped out of the house. They'd gone into the meadow, trying to find the exact middle of the field, where they lay in the thickest patch of sweet clover. On the verge of adolescence, they began to count stars, soaking up the serenity of the night. Suzy lost count after two hundred or so, but Nellie reached four hundred, maybe because her eyesight was sharper than her sister's.

Sighing now, Nellie adjusted her head covering, making sure it hadn't gone cockeyed or gotten stuck with hay. That had happened to her once before on one of her first hayrides last fall, a time when she'd had no real interest in any of the boys on board. Tonight, though, it was hard not to think of Caleb, whose furtive glances delighted her heart and made her think foolish, romantic thoughts.

Nellie tried to keep her smile in check. What *was* it about Caleb—his whole face appeared to light up when he looked at her.

She and Suzy had occasionally talked about their opinions on boys and love. Nellie remembered one particular afternoon right after the New Year, six months before Suzy died. The two of them had closed themselves away on a dismal and cold afternoon, cozy and comfortable under the old quilts piled on their bed.

Suzy'd had a room-spinning headache, including nausea. Nellie could hardly tend the bakery shop, hating the thought of Suzy sick and all alone. Finally she'd pleaded with Mamma to let her spend some time with Suzy, promising not to catch whatever it was her sister had.

As she'd slipped under the quilts beside Suzy, her sister had moaned, opening her eyes. "Ach, now I won't be able to meet my friends tonight," Suzy had whispered. "Not with this awful headache."

"Meet who?" Nellie had wondered if she meant a group of more progressive Amish youth.

Suzy squeezed her eyes shut against the pain. "Oh, Nellie, I've gotta tell you something . . . my greatest secret."

Bracing herself, Nellie covered her head with the top quilt, but Suzy promptly sighed and changed her mind. "Maybe I'd better be tellin' my diary instead."

"Ach," Nellie said, emerging from the quilt covering, "I'm listening, honest I am."

By then, though, Suzy seemed put out. She went silent on her, a far cry from the way she usually behaved, always chattering and living to the full, pushing the light at both ends of the day.

To think such an energetic, jovial girl had died at dusk, her lungs filling up with lake water at the moment of sunset. Had Nellie kept Suzy from boating that day, Suzy would still be alive and sitting right here beside her, leaning back in the hay, saying she'd given up on counting stars.

Oh, Suzy . . . will I soon know your great secret? The whole truth about you?

Breathing in the splendor of the night, Nellie thought back again to the night she'd buried the diary. Suddenly she recalled a detail she'd forgotten.

There had been a honeysuckle bush sending out a glorious, sweet aroma nearby. Its scent had registered even as the fading sunlight had made blurry prisms of her tears.

Pushing her hands into the straw, she sat straight up, her mouth gaping open. She might have said something right out into the cold air had she not remembered she was riding with thirty or more teenagers on the hay wagon.

I know where I buried Suzy's journal!

Caleb sat in the far corner of the hay wagon, as close to the edge as he could get, dangling his legs as the road passed beneath his feet. He'd worn his older brother's shoes, embarrassed of his own, so thin were the soles. His father had asked him to make do for yet another month, "till the snow flies," and he'd agreed. Where Daed was concerned, he was agreeable to a fault.

The rumble of the wagon wheels shot right into his hips, but Caleb didn't mind. He was used to the jolts of wagons and farm equipment . . . of life in general. But now things were going to be mighty different—here he turned to cast a fleeting look at his darling. Already Nellie Mae was precisely that to him. As soon as they turned eighteen next year, he would love and cherish her till death. Then he would claim the land that was rightfully his, and his parents, who were ready to be free of the toils of farming, could move into the larger Dawdi Haus, while Mamm's parents would move to the smaller built-on addition. He and Nellie would enjoy life together as husband and wife in the big farmhouse, smack-dab in the middle of the two older generations. There he would do his best to ease her sorrow and brighten her day, and they would live and love and create their family as the Good Lord saw fit.

Caleb twisted a piece of straw between his thumb and pointer finger, staring at it, then sliding it between his teeth. He looked out across the field, aware of the silence beyond. Somewhere out in the dimming twilight was a stillness he longed for. Here on the rowdy wagon there was no place to be alone with his girl. He yearned to have Nellie in his arms, but lest his passion get the best of him, he must refrain. His older brother had not heeded that inner warning and was forced to marry before he was ready, premature fatherhood thrust upon him. The family secret had been well kept, and it had served as a powerful warning to Caleb and his siblings. To be sure, there were honorable and less than honorable boys among them . . . even riding now on this wagon. The same thing was certain of the girls.

Suzy Fisher came again to mind, but he dismissed her immediately. Nellie had assured him Suzy was innocent of the sins attributed to her by the rumor mill.

Caleb removed his felt hat and ran his hand through his hair. Courtship, as he saw it, was training ground for the union of man and woman under God. Regardless of the tales of Suzy's Rumschpringe—whatever the whole of it—he loved Nellie.

Caleb tossed his piece of hay straight out as he'd pitched paper airplanes at classmates in the one-room schoolhouse over on Churchtown Road, where students were both English and Amish. The worldly and the set-apart learning together.

He sighed. The reputation of his future bride and her family was utterly vital, at least to his father.

Right or wrong, Nellie's my girl, he thought. *I'll worry about Daed later.*

Caleb was more talkative than usual this evening, and Nellie was intrigued by his stories of horses, especially his mention of Amish selling some breeds to racetracks down in Florida. "Can ya imagine such a thing?" he asked, appearing to stifle a laugh. "You wouldn't think of paying money to see one of those races, would ya?"

"More sensible ways to spend money, seems to me."

He nodded. "Jah. Yet there *are* Plain folk who deal in that. Daed says it's wrong."

"I s'pose mine would say the same." As closely connected to the world of horses as Dat was, Nellie'd never heard her father speak of this. To many of the men his age, horse races meant one thing: a big waste of money. Betting and gambling were of the devil.

They headed straight for the millstream behind the old stone millhouse, going to sit on a wrought-iron bench not too far from the creek bank. "It's so perty here," she said, still feeling a bit awkward at first when alone with Caleb. Even though she longed to talk and laugh with him, the initial moments together took some getting used to, particularly after the hubbub of a youth gathering. They wanted to be near each other so badly but were both trying to balance that desire with propriety.

"Our place, jah?" He slipped his arm around her.

She nodded, glad to lean her head on his shoulder.

Caleb talked of the weather, wondering if there would be any much-needed rain before winter's snows. Then he brought up the hog-butchering frolic the Saturday afternoon after next at his uncle's house. "'Tis over near Cains, a little south of here. Several families are donating meat to the ministerial brethren. I'm goin' to help hang the large hams and shoulders. Are you goin'?"

She sat up straighter. "Um . . . s'pose I could."

"What, Nellie? You don't like watchin' the slaughtering?"

She cringed. "It's the smell I can't abide."

He chuckled, "Well, some of my brothers will cut out the intestines and wash them so that *you* can stuff 'em and make sausage." He was clearly amused.

"I wouldn't mind helpin' grind meat, maybe. But better get someone else to stuff the sausage."

He laughed softly. "I don't know too many Plain folk who are squeamish 'bout that."

She had to laugh, too. "Guess I'm better suited to workin' with flours and spices and such." She looked at him; even by the dim light of the moon, his eyes seemed to twinkle.

"Mind if we walk a bit?"

She agreed and he reached for her hand as they strolled through the black trees along the creek bank, their feet making soft padding sounds on the soil.

————————

Hours later, after Caleb's fond *"Gut Nacht!"* at the end of her lane, Nellie felt almost too tired to put one foot in front of the other—they'd walked and talked that much. But deep within, where Mamma said the soul of a person resided, she was skipping with delight. Caleb had been ever so thoughtful again, making it known he wanted her by his side for all the upcoming youth get-togethers. She had herself a true beau.

One who will never break my heart. Not like Nan's.

She thought again of Nan and how happy she had been tonight. Was it because of Rebekah's friendship? Between Rebekah and Rhoda, Nan had her share of confidantes. Nellie wished her older sisters might sometimes include her, in spite of the age difference. Now that Rosanna was preparing for a baby—*twins!*—Nellie felt even more alone. Of course, she had Caleb, but it was a completely different sort of sharing than one did with a sister or a girlfriend.

Noticing a light in her parents' bedroom, she was stunned to think her father was still up reading. With that in mind, she crept all the way back around the barn, lest she cause a racket and send her father outside.

There, just inside and hanging on the high hook, Nellie Mae spotted Dat's lantern, essential for her late-night task. Tomorrow's duties would start in a few hours, with all the extra baking required after their Lord's Day and the washing to be hung out on the line.

No time to waste . . .

CHAPTER 22

Reuben had started writing the letter to the bishop more times than he cared to count, the crumpled-up pages of lined paper lying like popcorn balls on the bedroom floor. Remarkably, Betsy had slept through it, dear wife that she was.

I'm putting my family in jeopardy, he thought. *We'll be lumped in with those wanting tractors!*

Going to the window, Reuben stretched his arms. Was he doing the right thing by writing to the weary man of God? Word had it his brother had fallen ill out in Iowa. *What kind of man am I, putting this on him, too?*

Certainly in the eyes of the Lord he was doing right by requesting the Bible studies. Pleasing God was Reuben's focus now. He would gladly give all he had to follow Him.

My aging parents are coming to live in a house with their soon-to-be shunned son. He swallowed hard, blinking back the tears that threatened his sight. How had Cousin Jonathan and his family survived thus far? His sons, all farmers, held as firmly as their father to their newfound belief. Yet Jonathan's parents and grandparents were strongly opposed, as staunch in tradition as most older relatives were expected to be. Still, when a man chose to wholly follow the Lord, as Jonathan had, the family often followed close behind. Reuben had seen this before among the People.

He had much to ponder. Going out in the hallway to pace the floor from one end of the long corridor and back, he could hear daughter Rhoda snoring softly as he moved past her room. Nellie Mae, on the other hand, didn't seem to have returned from the evening's event. Evidently she was still with a beau.

He smiled, recalling his own courtship of dear Betsy. Like a sunrise, she'd appeared in his life. He still remembered the pleasure of seeing her eyes light up for him that first time.

I'm a blessed man, Lord. And I ask you this night for yet another blessing. . . .

Without intending to cause a ruckus, Reuben planned to sit down with his father and lay out what he'd learned about salvation by grace. After nearly a lifetime of believing you worked your way to heaven, Reuben now knew the Bible's position on the matter. Naturally there would be plenty of room for the Plain way of doing things, so well ingrained now, but Betsy and the girls, at least, must accept the whole of the gospel, too. He prayed it would be soon.

What his Daed might say would make no difference to Reuben's path, but his father would have a choice to make: His parents could reside here in the Dawdi Haus as expected, or they might prefer to live with one of Reuben's other siblings who would remain in this church district, after the dust settled.

What will my sons choose to follow? What of their wives and children?

He thought again of young Emma, so much like their Suzy at that age. Would she grow up to know the Savior? Would any of his precious grandchildren?

These questions occupied his mind, taunting Reuben as he wore out the rug.

It was pointless to try to sleep after nearly an hour of staring at the window in his room, watching for the first hint of dawn. Any rest eluded Caleb. So he rose, dressed, and went on foot a ways, traveling a mile or so east. He had to walk off his pent-up energy, though he would be dog-tired at first light. Time to put his interest in Nellie Mae into some logical perspective. Yet how could he hope to accomplish that by walking to her house and standing out in the trees along the road? Caleb looked up at the many windows under the eaves, wondering which one belonged to her. In order to shine his flashlight on the right window, he must know . . . should the day come to ask Nellie Mae to marry him.

He knew there were young people in other church districts farther north who practiced bed courtship—*Bundel.* Here it was frowned upon, although he'd heard enough stories to know some of the older folk had practiced bundling—grandparents and the like. Some of them were now the same outspoken elders who were trying to hold the line against tractors and other worldly pressures.

What *was* acceptable for an engaged couple was a visit to the girl's bedroom, where, in most cases, she had a small couch in the far corner. He'd never seen a girl's room, except his sisters' at home. Most likely, Nellie's was especially neat, just as she was. It would smell mighty nice, too, no doubt.

Nellie had confided in him earlier tonight that she and Suzy had shared nearly everything as sisters, including their room. This revelation had him even more curious than before. That and another offhand comment from one of Susannah Lapp's friends.

He hoped Nellie Mae was quite certain about her sister's behavior. Suzy was even mentioned in passing among the local boys.

Truth be told, Caleb was attracted to Reuben Fisher's third daughter like a parched man to cold spring water. Not only was he fond of Nellie, he wanted to shorten the time between their dates. He wished the seasons would fly, too, bringing next year's baptismal Sunday around right quick—and, not long after that, his and Nellie's wedding day, Lord willing. He could envision Nellie baking her delicious pastries in his own mother's kitchen, greeting him with her endearing smile, and holding their little ones someday, too.

I'll write her a letter, Caleb decided, knowing his father would advise him to slow down—and right quick.

The tree stump made an ideal lampstand. Lowering the heavy lantern onto it, Nellie was glad for the wide swath of light the oil lamp provided. The right honeysuckle bush had been relatively easy to locate, thanks to the ancient stump next to it. The pyramid-shaped sweetgum tree, its leaves showing traces of the purple-red it soon would be, was the other familiar landmark.

As she dug, Nellie thought of Caleb, wondering what he would think of her up here doing man's work. He might be impressed at her strength, though she was not even half as strong as any of her five brothers. *Course, he'd be mighty curious 'bout what I'm up to.*

She kept reliving their date. How would she possibly wait another whole week before laying eyes on him? She wondered if it would be too forward to write a note—make a little card for him, maybe. Yet if she let herself express the things she was eager to say, she might embarrass herself.

No, best not to pick up a pen at all.

Nellie's shovel bumped into the dirt-caked plastic she'd wrapped around the diary. Quickly she leaned down to retrieve it from its earthy hiding place. Gently brushing away the soil, she unwrapped the book and wiped it with the hem of her apron.

She clung to the journal, relieved to see it remained in good condition. "Suzy . . . oh, dear sister. What people are saying 'bout you."

A sudden fear welled up as she contemplated what might be revealed within these pages. Suzy had recorded her honest thoughts, surely never thinking someone other than herself would be reading them, even someone who loved her dearly. Nellie was the sole protector of Suzy's intimate reflections . . . of her dreams. Perhaps of her sins, too. Here between the hard covers of her sister's journal was the disclosure of what had pulled a good Amish girl toward the world.

Dare I read it?

Still gripping the diary, Nellie reached for the lantern, suddenly aware of the dancing shadows, the way the light, adequate for digging, now played insufficiently against the darkness . . . the predawn gloom. She lowered her hand and shivered as uncontrollably as she had at hearing that Suzy's life had been snuffed out. Hugging the diary, she felt grateful for its recovery and somehow closer to her dead sister. Then, making a pouch from her apron, she carefully tied the book into the fabric. Reaching again for the lantern, Nellie Mae slung the shovel over her shoulder before picking her way through the woods, the fatigue of having been up all night—and the weight of what she might soon discover—creeping into her bones.

The attic extended the entire length of the house. Given that Betsy hadn't mounted the creaky steps in months, she decided to organize a bit, her other morning work caught up for a while.

Time to chase away some dust bunnies.

Reuben was out training his new colts, giving them commands on the track behind the barn, and the girls were working in the bakery shop or, as was the case with Rhoda, for their English neighbors. So Betsy headed to the attic to redd up, hoping to locate several older quilts that might prove useful with Reuben's parents coming to live there. Of course, her mother-in-law, Hannah, would bring a good many quilts of her own, but with the cold of winter on its way, one could never have too many.

Mammi Fisher's multicolored antique quilts were of exceptional quality, especially the sixteen-patch quilt, with its bold reds, purples, and deep blues, handed down from the 1880s on the Fisher side—Reuben's grandmother's handiwork. Suzy had once spent several days with Mammi Hannah taking in the stories behind the quilts, the quilting frolics, and the womenfolk who had gathered to make them.

Betsy had not forgotten the bright-eyed wonder on Suzy's face upon returning home. "I saw me some wonderful-gut stitchin', Mamma!"

Suzy . . . my little quilter.

She gave in to her tears, there on the narrow attic steps. She leaned her head on the wooden railing, sobbing. More recently she had not allowed herself to be overtaken with grief, although her husband likely thought otherwise. Why else would he continue to be so worried as to steer her clear of the bakery shop, where she might break down at hearing condolences offered by loyal customers? More than likely that was why Reuben had put the nix on her helping Nellie.

Drying her eyes with her apron, Betsy made her way to the landing and into the large attic room. She laid down her feather duster and surveyed the place. Over in the far corner, she spotted the old family trunk and lifted the lid wide. She peered into the depths of her collection of heirloom quilts, astonished to see an envelope with *To Mamma* printed on it in Suzy's hand.

"My, my, what's this?" She reached for the envelope, and for a moment she merely held it. "For goodness' sakes," she whispered, choking down more tears.

Looking on the back, she saw that her youngest had written, *Just another little note from me to you. Love, Suzy.*

"Was she planning to give this to me and forgot where she hid it?" Betsy said into the dim light.

It made no sense . . . unless Suzy had placed yet another note somewhere—something she'd enjoyed doing. Still, why would Suzy leave it in the quilt collection, as though hoping Betsy might find it?

She couldn't bring herself to open it, and she set the envelope aside while selecting two large quilts for winter, deciding she would ask Reuben to take them downstairs later. She then began straightening stacked boxes, making sure the lids were fastened tight. Several old chests needed dusting and she took care of that right quick, also tackling the cobwebs near the dormer windows.

When she was satisfied things were more orderly, she returned to the quilt trunk. Eyeing Suzy's note, she stood there, overwhelmed at this unexpected gesture of love. She felt a strange chill, as if she might be coming down with something. One of Suzy's favorite places to play as a child, besides outdoors, had been this very spot high in the house. Betsy sighed, remembering the way her youngest had liked to hide here with a book or some needlework. Or her diary.

Even as young as five, Suzy could be found up here chattering to her faceless dolls, all of them lined up on a trunk or chest, making each speak by changing the sound of her own voice.

Betsy stared at the envelope, lip quivering now, thinking of all the evenings sixteen-year-old Suzy had left the supper table ever so quick. *Why'd you go and run off like that? I scarcely ever knew where you were.*

She thought of Rhoda, who went off now quite as often herself. Same thing seemed to be happening with her, only Betsy knew where she was most of the time—at least she thought so.

"Ach, go on, open it," Betsy told herself. She needed a dose of courage this minute, despite yearning to hear Suzy's voice in the words she'd written. *When did she pen this?*

Betsy reached for the envelope and opened it.

Dear Mamma,

Look under the bottom quilt in this trunk to find a surprise . . . an early birthday present.

Lots of love,
Suzy

Betsy smiled. "What's she got under there?" she muttered, leaning down to lift one quilt out after another. She smelled it even before she'd spotted the small purple pillow, its seams handsewn with tiny, even stitches. Betsy realized it was one of Suzy's special sachet pillows filled with lavender, marjoram, and crushed cloves. Suzy had named her clever creation a "headache pillow," something she had kindly made for several sisters-in-law during their pregnancies.

And also this one, for me. . . .

Kneeling before the wooden trunk, Betsy pressed her nose into the face-sized pillow and wept. *Suzy was always doing such thoughtful things. Our little darling.*

After a time, Betsy rose and began to replace each handmade quilt, mindful to keep them wrapped in heavy tissue paper for protection. Then, closing the lid, she sat down, staring first at the lovely pillow, and then at the note.

A verse she'd secretly memorized came to mind. *For God sent not his Son into the world to condemn the world; but that the world through him might be saved.*

The meaning was ever so clear—the Lord would not have condemned Suzy to hell if she had belonged to Him.

If . . .

Sitting there, she recalled other verses Reuben had requested that she read, verses he himself was committing to memory. She had carefully done so, often many times over. She was deeply sad—sorry even—about the way she'd lived so long in the dark, thinking the hard work she did for her family and community might give her a better chance of heaven someday.

I could only hope before . . . now I can know.

"But, oh, dear Suzy. . . ." She sighed, wishing the Lord God had brought this spiritual light to her Reuben before that dreadful June day. She was torn, not knowing what to think about all of it—or much of anything she'd been taught.

Bowing her head, Betsy prayed, "O Lord, I want to be counted as your child." She pressed Suzy's note against her heart. "Take my sins far from me. I want to follow your Son, Jesus, no matter what it means for Reuben and me. Or for our family."

Just please let me see Suzy again . . . someday.

CHAPTER 23

———

From the moment Rosanna arrived at Maryann Fisher's house, she felt on edge. Both the Fisher toddlers were crying—wailing, really—and dishes were piled high in the sink. She didn't know why she was so *naerfich* today. She assumed it had started with Cousin Kate's visit Thursday—all the talk of the twins and Kate's seeming reticence. It had permeated Rosanna's dreams since. Didn't every mother long for twins? Elias was excited about the possibility of sons. Of course, there was the unspoken concern, for him, that Kate's babies might turn out to be daughters. Every Amishman wanted boys, and as many as possible, but Rosanna secretly longed for a little girl.

Now that she was here, she reached for sniffling Katie, attempting to soothe her cries, swabbing the runny nose with her own embroidered hankie, making sure she did not wipe the child's tender nose on the side with stitching. "There, there, honey-girl," she whispered, rubbing the curve of her lower back and feeling the small spine.

One day I'll do the same to quiet my own children. . . .

"You're so good to help," Maryann said from across the table, balancing even smaller Becky on her right knee, jiggling her up and down as she rolled out dough for three pie crusts. "As soon as I get these pies in the oven, I'll sit and chat."

"Oh, I don't mean to take up your time," Rosanna said quickly. "I'm simply here for a bootie pattern, if you have one."

"You must be knittin' some for your cousin Kate's wee ones, jah?"

Rosanna nodded, feeling peculiar not telling Maryann the full reason for why she wanted the patterns.

Nellie's sister-in-law's face was a rosy pink now, and perspiration was evident on her forehead. Her disheveled light brown hair looked as if it needed a good washing. Even a solid brushing would help.

Will I look this schtruwwlich *as a mamma?* Rosanna wondered, recalling how admiring her husband was of her. She would not want to dampen Elias's enthusiasm, so to speak. It would take some doing, but she hoped to remain attractive for her darling even with twin babies to care for.

Maryann placed the dough in three pie plates and pinched the sides all around. She glanced up at Rosanna, her countenance serious. "I'm worried 'bout our bishop," she said softly. "Imagine the good man being so sick so far away and all."

"He's still under the weather?"

"Jah, word is he's too ill to travel."

Rosanna noticed the angst in Maryann's eyes. "I hadn't realized 'twas that serious."

"So I'm told . . . but I don't know much. Only what Ephram says."

Rosanna was not very fond of Nellie Mae's staid big brother. "How'd he hear?"

Maryann frowned. "Well, I really shouldn't say."

Rosanna nodded without prodding further. She understood that tone and look.

Maryann put Becky down to play with her sister and some empty spools for thread. She slid the pies into the belly of the cookstove. "Now, then, you're here for some bootie patterns?"

"Jah." But as Maryann hurried out of the room, leaving her with Becky and Katie, Rosanna suddenly felt concerned. She had an irresistible desire to ask the Lord God to help their bishop, older man that he was. Some of Elias's friends in another church had made such prayers, and she thought it a wonderful-good idea to beseech the Lord for protection and care. And, in this case, for the bishop's healing.

So she bowed her head and prayed silently, trusting their heavenly Father to hear and answer. When she was done, the little girls were still sitting near her feet, babbling and laughing, draping the strung-together spools on each other's arms.

Rosanna daydreamed, wondering what her life might be like in two short months. As a mother, she was ever so sure she would be praying daily for her children, just as she had for the bishop. Even if secretly.

Slipping the loop of the rope over the colt's sleek neck, Reuben led it around the training track. Glancing up, he noticed that one of the martin birdhouses high on a post near the back of the house was listing to one side. He'd have to fix that before spring.

As a boy Reuben had helped his father build many a martin birdhouse;

the six-sided "apartment style" was the most popular among their family and neighbors. They'd given them away as gifts, although Reuben knew some Amish who built them for profit nowadays. His father had also placed several such birdhouses strategically around this very house to keep unwanted insects at bay. The whole family had watched the male martins with their blue-black feathers—gleaming almost purple in full sunlight—arrive in the spring, followed later by the gray, pale-bellied females.

Reuben's favorite thing as a curious child was to watch all the tiny beaks poke out of the many holes on the birdhouses he'd helped make. What fun it was to see the new hatchlings eventually fly away.

Once, he and his father had banded a new bird to calculate its lifespan. They'd observed the same bird return for seven consecutive years, which his father had thought might be something of a record. Since that time, Reuben had read of purple martins living to be even nine or ten years old.

Nine or ten years old . . . about the age Suzy was when she helped me build several birdhouses. "Course, that was before she decided she liked boys better than birds," he said ruefully.

Reuben clucked to the colt and watched as it picked up its gait, the memory of working beside his daughter giving him pause. It had been too long since he'd shared the tradition of making birdhouses with a child. He'd tinkered with the idea of making an extra-large birdhouse with his grandson Benny, James's oldest. Perhaps after the harvest and the wedding season there would be time.

An ambitious project for a six-year-old, but doable with some help.

If his parents decided to go ahead with moving back to their original home place, he might just include his aging father in the birdhouse-making task. And if James joined them to help saw or sand or paint, there would be four generations of Fishers working side by side.

Coming full circle.

Leading the colt around the track a final time, Reuben contemplated the coming Lord's Day, which might be the last peaceful one they'd have around here. Preacher Manny had informed him last night that Bishop Joseph was seriously ill and that Reuben should refrain from writing to ask permission to hold Bible studies until their leader was better. Reuben felt stricken at the news, because he'd already sent the request to the bishop, inviting him and others of the ministerial brethren to join with Manny and himself. Reuben had figured there was no reason to exclude anyone, even though he doubted they would participate. On the contrary, they'd

be appalled to think one of the preachers was involved, as well as Reuben,
a member in good standing.

"The timing is in God's hands," Manny had said, taking the news of Reuben's letter well.

Manny must think my request could worsen my brother's health, Reuben
thought now. *How sick is Joseph?*

He stared at the side of the barn a stone's throw from the training track,
noticing a few places where the sun had beaten hard on the west side. He
would see to it that either Ephram or one of the twins got it painted and
right quick. It wouldn't do to go into winter with any of the siding peeling,
what with the harsh weather the almanac forecasted. While they were at
it, one of his sons could right the birdhouse, too. He wasn't quite as spry as
he used to be on a ladder.

It came to him that his sons might not be as ready to help as in the past
once they heard of their father's newfound belief. *This great salvation has
the power to unite or divide us all. . . .*

Reuben began to pray as he led the colt, asking the Lord to protect his
close-knit family. "Bring all of them safely within the fold of your grace."
He sighed, mopping his brow with his hand. "And may we not lose another
one for eternity, O God." His voice thickened as he thought again of Suzy.

Inhaling deeply now, he added a prayer for the bishop, both for renewed
health . . . and for an understanding heart.

Betsy and Nan chopped piles of carrots, celery, new potatoes, and onions
to make a beef stew for the noon meal. "How's Nellie Mae doin' out there
today?" Betsy asked, glancing out the window at the bakery shop.

Nan shrugged. "Lots of customers for the middle of the week, I'd say."

"More than usual?"

"Seems so." Nan scooped up a handful of carrot chunks and dropped
them into the black kettle. "Must be autumn's in the air."

"Jah, the tourists flock in from all over, seems."

"Some from as far away as London, Rhoda says."

Rhoda knows of this? Betsy felt somewhat surprised that Rhoda should
be privy to the comings and goings of such fancy people. "Your sister hears
these things from the Englischers she works for?"

Nan blushed, nodding. "Jah . . . and Nellie and I both hear a-plenty from
the shop's English customers, too, Mamma."

Betsy straightened. "Ach, I'm afraid of that."

Nan left the counter and went to the sink, washing her hands quickly. Her daughter often put a quick end to conversation whenever Betsy came close to touching on anything to do with Rhoda and her work outside the home. More and more young Plain women were eager to make money, cleaning for Englischers or working as nannies, but Betsy had a mother's concern that permitting such things endangered the Old Ways. Betsy wanted to ask Nan if she, too, was thinking along the lines of getting a job, but she didn't feel up to hearing the potential reply. What would be would naturally come; there wasn't much stopping the young people once they got something in their heads.

At least Nan seems mighty interested in good Amish boys, Betsy reassured herself. She had higher hopes in that regard for Nan's future than Rhoda's. At least, she *had.* Now she honestly didn't know how this daughter was doing.

"I don't think you have a lot to worry 'bout where Rhoda's concerned," Nan said suddenly, interrupting her thoughts.

"Why do you say that?"

" 'Cause I believe I know her."

"She's not too taken by the world; is that what you mean?"

"Not like Suzy was. . . ." Nan's eyes grew wide and she covered her mouth. "Ach, Mamma, I'm ever so sorry. I didn't mean to bring up Suzy. Truly I didn't."

Betsy had wept enough for one day. She turned to head for the sink to wash her hands, hoping Nan hadn't seen her tears spring up.

"Nellie's sufferin' something awful, too . . . over, well, you know." Nan's voice quivered.

Betsy nodded her head, the lump in her throat nearly bursting. "We'll all suffer for a long, long time, I daresay."

Nan sighed. "You and Nellie most of all."

Betsy leaned her head on Nan's shoulder as her daughter placed a gentle hand on her back. "Nellie's got to be in terrible pain, really." She didn't go on to say what she was thinking. Fact was, the two girls had been inseparable from the time Nellie had first attempted to hold her sister—Nellie had been nearly a baby herself at eleven months old. The pair had been much like twins, being so close in age.

"Honestly . . . I think Nellie's reading something of Suzy's," Nan whispered.

"Oh?"

"Jah, I wouldn't be surprised if it's her diary." Nan looked sheepish.

"You're sure?"

"Jah, looked like Suzy's little diary to me." Nan moved to the counter again to chop the last of the potatoes.

Startled, Betsy considered whether Nan knew what she was talking about. Pushing the thought aside, Betsy dried her hands and set to working again. "Time you got back out and helped your sister," she said at last.

Nan chuckled. She finished quickly with the potatoes and hurried over to the sink to clean up once again.

Betsy was glad to have the stew ready to go onto the fire. "Thank you, Nan. I love all my girls . . . ever so much."

Nan smiled. "I know you do, Mamma. I know." With that she was off to assist at Nellie's Simple Sweets.

That one sure knows how to get me stirred up, Betsy thought, wondering again whether what Nan said was true. She'd known Suzy had kept a diary, but it hadn't occurred to her it might still be around.

Betsy thought again of the note Suzy had left for her. What else had her youngest written before she died?

CHAPTER 24

After supper and Dat's evening Scripture reading, Nellie shut her bedroom door and pulled the diary from its hiding place in her side table drawer, under several Sunday hankies. Then, settling onto her bed, she tucked her legs beneath her and set the book in her lap, running her hand along its cover before opening the diary.

I figured I couldn't hold out till my birthday, so I bought this journal with some money I received for Christmas. Now that I'm nearly sixteen, I want to remember everything that happens to me. Especially the boys I meet once I'm old enough to go to Singings and whatnot all.

Nellie smiled, torn between the satisfaction of hearing Suzy's perkiness in the words she'd written and missing her even more because of it. Suzy's writing was tiny and precise, like Suzy herself.

Sighing, Nellie began reading again.

Today is New Year's 1966. I will faithfully write each day no matter how busy I get doing chores with Mamma, or Dat, who needs me to help curry the colts and tend to the chickens. Of course, there is always baking to be done for Nellie, as well, which I like best, because I love Nellie Mae so. She's the dearest person I know, except for Mamma.

When I've got time, I like sewing, too—and embroidering. Right now I'm stitching some pillow slips secretly for gifts, and I have some tatting started. Doilies will make nice surprises for my sisters' hope chests. A hopeless chest, really, as far as Rhoda goes. I'm laughing a little as I write, which ain't so nice, is it? And now I'm talking to myself! I just don't understand why a boy hasn't invited her driving after Singing or frolics—she's always home long before either Nan or Nellie Mae. Rhoda's as pleasant as the day is long, and right pretty in her own way. She's a good cook, too, so she'd make a fine wife. It's the strangest thing that no one else seems to think so.

Nellie paused, dreading to read Suzy's private thoughts further. She rose and went to the dresser, picking up the blue plate. "This feels like a betrayal," Nellie whispered, her heart pounding ever so hard. "Should I continue?"

After a while, she returned to the diary and began to read the third page.

I remember hearing the snowplow before ever laying eyes on it. Awful noisy it was, grumbling up the road behind me, making a clean sweep ahead. In more ways than one I need a clear path, too.

But finding that path seems nearly impossible. . . .

The sky was a shining arc of cloudless blue and the roadway was piled with snow on both sides, forming a wide tunnel. Suzy didn't mind whether the snow was knee-deep or plowed here on the road; she was having herself an adventure, headed to see her new friends this brisk January day. A *wonderful-gut way to begin the year!* she decided.

Congratulating herself on being sly enough to slip away from the house following afternoon chores, Suzy picked up her pace. She wanted to be where she'd promised to meet her friends at the appointed time, so she clomped over the snow-packed road all the way to the intersection of Route 10 and Beaver Dam Road. She caught herself grinning because Jay Hess, so blond and good-looking, would be driving today, or so she had been told by several of his school friends. She'd seen him around school two years ago when she was still young enough to attend—the People didn't go past eighth grade—but had never given him a second glance. That had changed when seventeen-year-old Jay spotted her walking in the square at Honey Brook before Christmas, enjoying her freedom and the fancy decorations. He'd asked her if she wanted to go for a ride in his car, and Suzy had smiled and accepted, eager for some excitement.

Today they were all going to that same square to mill around and have some ice cream, since school had let out for the day for Jay and his friends. Dat would find her easy way with Englischers another argument for why Amish pupils would do well to attend their own schools, no doubt. *A life set apart.* She'd heard this said so much she was tired of it. Tired, too, of being expected to grow up "in the faith." In short, Suzy was ready for some modern living, like some other Amish youth her age, though mostly it was the boys who pushed the limits. Boys got away with things girls could never get by with, like driving cars and hiding them from their parents.

Suzy often wondered why her older brothers had never strayed from the

People. Or had they just kept it hushed up once they decided in favor of the church?

But no, she was mighty sure Benjamin, James, and Ephram hadn't sown wild oats. It was harder to know about the twins, because Jeremiah and Thomas were so much older, going on thirty now. Even so, they'd married before twenty, as had all her brothers. *Following the example of our parents by wedding young.*

Suzy knew she was being lured away from the Plain life by her own longing for freedom. She was reaching for a little heaven on earth, sowing her wild oats and hoping for crop failure, as some Plain boys would say.

Truth was she liked Jay and his friends—both the girls and the boys. Not a single one looked at her askance because she wore humble garb and pulled her hair back in a tight bun. They accepted her completely.

Darlene Landis and Trudy Zimmerman were the most interesting of the girls. Jay had whispered to Suzy they were "only friends," but when one day she'd heard Trudy talking to another girl about wanting Jay to kiss her again, Suzy'd gasped outright before she could stop herself. Even knowing that, she was curious about Jay and his ultra-casual way—what she supposed some called a "devil may care" attitude. If getting to know him meant associating with Trudy or anyone else he might have kissed, then so be it. She was not about to give up this chance.

Gingerly now she made her way over the thick coating of snow, slipping occasionally as she went. Enjoying the brisk air and the sun on her face, she looked toward the woods south of the road. Trees flocked with light snow glistened in the late afternoon sun. She assumed the majority of school kids had hoped yesterday for a snow day today, but Suzy was thankful the weather hadn't spoiled their plans.

Presently she stood waiting at the junction of Route 10 and the road she lived on, glad for some wind shelter. Scooting up close to the wide trunk of an old oak, she wondered how long she might have to wait for Jay and his buddies. Assuming he would be along any minute, she breathed the icy air into her lungs and slowly exhaled.

She began to shiver but not from being too cold. Waiting there, Suzy felt the edge of the precipice on which she'd been balancing. She could nearly see it before her as she leaned over as far as she could—and then some—knowing there was no safety net at the bottom should she fall. Neither Dat nor Mamma would approve of her plans today—Nellie, neither. Nor would they have wanted her going anywhere with Jay's friend Dennis

Brackbill, as she had for the past two weekends. Two long dates—two too many. Dennis was a fun-loving clown, but he had been reckless in his driving, even though she was in the car. *No regard for a girl's safety,* she thought.

Like Jay, Dennis had been her schoolmate before she was forced to leave and work with her mamma on the farm, as dictated by the Old Ways. The local school wasn't the best place to make friends with boys, her parents would surely say if they knew. But they didn't know, and they never would if she handled things right. Now if only Jay had remembered. . . .

Nellie closed the diary. She stared at the page, not sure she could bear to read any further. For the past couple of days, she'd glanced through the diary, reading stray lines here and there—accounts of quilting bees and walks with girl cousins—but until tonight she hadn't found anything out of the ordinary. Nothing at all like what Nellie had just read—at the start of the diary, no less.

How long had Suzy's interest in Jay or Dennis—or Darlene and Trudy— lasted?

Nellie wished she'd left the diary buried in the woods, but she'd started this troubling journey and now she must see it through, returning to it another day.

How on earth did I miss seeing this brazen side of Suzy?

———

When Nellie awoke earlier than usual Thursday, she felt ready to read more of Suzy's diary, but when she sought to do so, Nan stopped by. As much as Nellie longed for more interaction with her sisters, she couldn't help but wonder why Nan had to poke her head in the door. It was as if she suspected something.

Has Nan been spying on me?

Nellie tried her best to think back. Hadn't she been discreet enough, closing the bedroom door and sitting with her back to it as she had?

"Is it me, or are you up too early?" Nan asked, coming by yet again in her long white cotton nightgown. She hadn't taken time yet to slip on her bathrobe, and her hair was still uncombed.

Nellie was not amused and quite glad she'd kept Suzy's diary hidden from view just now. "The question is, why are *you* up three hours before breakfast today?" she asked. "You plannin' to help me bake some pies?"

Nan grimaced. "Couldn't sleep anymore, is all."

Nellie didn't know what to say to that. Nan had always slept longer and deeper than anyone she knew. Nan had once announced at the breakfast table that she wished she might sleep in longer of a morning, to which Dat had nearly choked on his coffee.

When Nellie offered nothing more, Nan padded back to her room. Nellie waited till the door to Rhoda and Nan's room clicked shut. She heard their bed creak and assumed Nan had slipped back in for an added forty winks. She had little time left to read before she must begin the day's baking, so Nellie quickly found her ending spot from yesterday.

Suzy's written account took Nellie back to February and March of last winter, the time of year when their lives revolved around visiting family, butchering, and farm sales. Even the public schools closed for the latter, since teachers realized that a number of Plain and English students were involved in the auctions' social aspects.

All the while, Nellie's beloved sister had yearned after darkness, becoming ever more caught up in the world. . . .

For Suzy, every spare moment these days was spent with Jay Hess and his "clique," as those outside his group referred to the six students who went nearly everywhere together. Suzy had gladly gone with them to the movies, to bowling alleys, and even several times to a dance hall. Wherever Jay chose to go, Suzy aimed to be right by his side, soaking up his modern life like a dry sponge.

She remembered how light-headed she'd felt the first time she'd puffed on Jay's half-smoked cigarette, his face close to hers, as if he longed to somehow be a part of her first smoke. They'd laughed at her momentary dizziness and he'd kissed her later, long and lingering. In a few days she'd adapted, eager to have a full smoke of her own when with Jay. He was on her mind all the time now as she cooked and cleaned with Mamma. In her free time, she artfully drew his name and wished she were still in school waiting for him after the bell.

Dat would more than have my hide if he knew.

Anxious to maintain her secret, Suzy promised herself not to become too keen on Jay's smokes; nor would she drink more than two beers at once. For his part Jay never suggested she bring a change of clothes when they went out, something she viewed as a sign of his affection—he liked her enough to be seen with a Plain girl, of all things. Besides, there were others like her. Suzy wasn't alone in her search for a way out of the dead-end street she'd been born on.

The two other Amish girls who ran around with Englischers never dressed Plain when they did so—they let their hair down, too, and even cut and styled it. Both had downright shallow boyfriends who probably would have preferred to date a nice English girl if they could have gotten any of the fancy girls interested in them. At least, that was how Suzy looked at it.

Jay was better. He liked her as she was . . . though that was not how she planned to remain.

By late March, he wanted to spend more and more time alone with her. They drove the back roads, frequently pulling over to park. Together in the private darkness of his car, they talked and drank and laughed till Suzy cried, tarrying longer each time.

How alive Suzy felt with Jay, alarmingly so. The whole world halted in its tracks when she was with him. He admitted the same thing to her in so many words. *"You're my baby girl,"* he would say and reach for her, holding her so tight she believed he would never let her go.

When it came time for sowing alfalfa in her father's wheat field, Jay seemed put off by her absence. "You shouldn't have to do boys' work," he said at first. Soon, though, he was more relaxed about her chores, telling her all was well. "I'll wait for you, Suzy. You do what you have to, to please your family."

She warmed to his words as she had from the start. Fact was he could get her to see things his way just by the smooth way he suggested them, though she hadn't done all the things some schoolgirls succumbed to in the name of love. Still, she knew she was treading on dangerous ground, ever so close to getting the cart before the pony.

It wasn't that Suzy didn't trust herself to be able to keep resisting Jay. What worried her more than possibly giving in was the emptiness she felt, in spite of the thrill. Was this all she was willing to trade her wholesome, dreary life for? She'd longed for freedom from the heaviness she felt living Plain . . . bound to eventually dying that way, too, if nothing changed. Bored with life, she yearned for more than her roots could possibly offer.

But the more she reached for what she expected would fill her up, the more drained Suzy felt. All the same she simply could not go backward to the repression that had driven her away from her family and their beliefs, in search of light and love. The Old Ways were less appealing than ever.

Jay managed to get her talking about eloping one night after they'd fogged up his car windows but good. She told him she loved him, adding that she was interested in running away with him if he wanted. Just that quick, he changed the subject, muttering something about attending vocational school or a community college next year.

"You don't really want to get married yet, do you?" she challenged him.

"Why sure, baby. You'll see." But he had new excuses for her nearly every time they saw each other.

In early April when the tobacco farmers were sowing seeds in their sterilized tobacco beds, Suzy helped her parents and sisters plant potatoes. She had begun to chew gum nearly round the clock at home, pushing in a fresh stick every half hour or so in an effort to cover the smell of cigarettes. She chewed so many packs of gum, it was as though she were addicted to that, too.

Gum, cigarettes, and Jay Hess . . . but not in that order.

Nellie slammed the diary shut. She felt unclean, like she ought to bathe. *Poor Suzy . . . all mixed up, looking for acceptance far from the People.* She thought back to Suzy's wild days, stunned by her own naïveté—how little she as a sister had suspected. When Suzy's clothing had smelled a smidgen like cigarette smoke, Nellie never dreamed her own sister was the one smoking. To think drinking and necking—with an outsider, no less—were also to be counted among her dear sister's sins.

"Ach, why'd she feel the need to run fast with the world?" For the life of her, Nellie Mae couldn't begin to grasp that she'd shared this very room—and nearly everything of her own life and dreams—with Suzy, never once guessing her sister was so *ferhoodled.*

She stared at the diary. "This would not just break Mamma's heart . . . it might make her sick," she whispered.

Tears spilled down her cheeks. *You fooled me, Suzy! I thought you were merely childish, not this.*

"I trusted you. I thought I knew you."

The truth she had so desperately sought was too shameful to accept. Nellie slid from her bed and crumpled into a heap on the floor, burying her face in her hands and sobbing louder than she'd ever meant to.

CHAPTER 25

E arly Friday morning, Betsy knocked on Nellie's door, asking to come in. Nellie mumbled a yes and rubbed her sleepy eyes, looking up from her snug spot in her big bed, as her mother entered. Betsy was struck by the fact the bed looked too large without Suzy in it.

She'd heard Nellie burst out crying early yesterday morning but felt she should wait a day, at least, before approaching her about it. She knew all too well that sometimes grieving people preferred to be alone. "Are you all right, dear?"

Nellie Mae nodded. "Are *you*, Mamma? You're up awful early."

Betsy couldn't help but smile. *Nellie, ever thoughtful* . . . "I heard you cryin' yesterday," she said.

"Oh jah . . . that."

"We all miss her terribly," she said.

Nellie sighed and rolled over, covering her head with the quilt and saying no more.

"I'll help with your baking today," offered Betsy, but Nellie only grunted slightly in response.

Closing the door gently, Betsy wondered if Nan was right about Nellie's reading Suzy's diary. If so, it didn't seem like such a good idea for Nellie Mae in her susceptible state. *Seems like a lesson in futility, really.*

Nevertheless, Betsy could not deny her own curiosity about Suzy's Rumschpringe.

———

As Betsy and Reuben dressed for the day, she knew it was time to tell her husband of her prayer in the attic—she'd waited too long as it was. She had been hesitant, wanting to keep it to herself, so foreign the experience was to her. She couldn't help but wonder how she and Reuben would find their way together as new believers.

She finished placing her Kapp on her head and went to him, reaching for his big callused hands. "Reuben, I must tell you that I understand what you feel when readin' the Good Book."

His eyes met hers. "You do?"

She could hardly go on. "I believe . . . just as you do," she whispered. "I couldn't put it off . . . didn't want to wait any longer to receive this blessed salvation."

His smile spread clear across his ruddy face, prematurely wrinkled from long hours in the sun. "Ach, this is the best news, Betsy." He wrapped his arms around her, enfolding her.

"I'm ever so glad you got me thinkin' . . . I best be catchin' up with you, love."

Reuben laughed heartily and leaned down to kiss her cheek. "Our eyes have been opened wide by the grace of our Lord." He beamed into her face. "I daresay there may be more than we know."

"What will happen to us all?" Betsy asked.

"We'll simply go about our business and family, trusting God to make the way clear and straight before us."

"Will we leave the church?"

He frowned momentarily. "All the present upheaval in our midst . . . I say we bide our time, wait till things calm down some before pulling up roots."

"It's not like we're ashamed. . . ."

"Not at all, Betsy. What makes you say that?"

"We could simply leave the church and face up to the Bann. Look at Cousin Jonathan and almost the whole of his family . . . all of them shunned."

"'Tis mighty disheartening to think of us—all the People—treatin' him so."

"Seems we're kinder to outsiders who burn down our barns and run over our buggies with their cars—never pressing charges—than we are to our own." Her words caught in her throat.

"Forgiveness is the expected way." He picked up the Bible on their dresser. " 'Tween you and me, Betsy, I've never fully embraced our shunning practices. I've got private opinions 'bout that."

"Oh?"

"Our boys know this. The twins are more inclined to see eye to eye with me, but Ephram's downright outspoken against my views." Reuben looked at the floor and then raised his eyes to meet hers. "We cut off our own folk . . . and for what? Too short a haircut on a man . . . too wide or narrow a hat brim, for goodness' sake? What difference does any of that make in the eyes of the Lord?"

"Ach, Reuben, I never knew this of you."

"Well, I take issue with some of our rules, puttin' it mildly. But I've held my peace for this long, love. Time I began declaring what I believe to someone, starting with you. Upholding the rules of the Ordnung is not vital to salvation."

Betsy turned toward the window, watching the horses grazing in the distant paddock, the early-morning sun making their hides shine. "We've been taught all our lives that it's not God's will for folk to get together to study the Bible . . . but I honestly feel the need for it."

Reuben agreed. "I've been talkin' with Preacher Manny about this very thing."

She gasped. "Your cousin Manny knows of this?"

He took her hand and sat with her on the loveseat near the window, sharing all he had discussed with both Manny and Cousin Jonathan. "No matter whether we get the bishop's approval—and we won't—we'll start up a Bible study right here ourselves."

Reuben was a man of surprises, for sure and for certain. She felt more love for him than ever before . . . knowing he'd gently yet consistently shown her the truth. To think she was God's child, just as her husband was—this man who had led her to drink of the living water, like the woman drawing well water in the biblical town of Samaria.

"I can hardly keep from tellin' our girls what's happened," she said softly.

Reuben grinned. "We can tell our family together."

"All of them?"

"What's to lose?"

She touched his hand. "Oh, my dearest love . . . just about everything. Look at Cousin Jonathan and his family." Pausing, her eyes rested on her dear husband. "Jonathan lives among the People, yet he and his family are alone in their beliefs."

Reuben shook his head. "Jonathan won't be alone for long."

A heavy silence ensued as Betsy pondered all that her husband had shared.

At breakfast Betsy offered to help her husband mow hay, since last evening Reuben had announced this would be a "good, clear day for it."

By late that morning, the hay was out drying in the sun. Her husband had indeed chosen a fine day—sunny yet cool enough to make hard labor comfortable.

All during the noon meal, whenever Reuben looked her way, he was smiling. His eyes simply danced with joy.

Nan got up to serve the dessert she'd made, urging them to stay put.

Betsy noticed again how empty their long table looked most of the time now, what with the boys grown . . . and Suzy gone. But she was determined to look at life differently. Instead of dwelling on what she didn't have, she wanted to embrace what she did have, and to the full. Since yielding her life to God, she felt a stirring within.

Is God helping me find hope amid my grief?

She glanced at Nellie Mae, who looked utterly miserable, her eyes tired and downcast as though she was trying hard not to let her distress show. Betsy's heart went out to her.

Nan was more talkative than usual, mentioning several of the morning's customers at the shop. Much as Betsy enjoyed hearing her describe the regulars, she hoped they weren't becoming too important in Nan's mind. She mustn't fall into the curiosity that had surely pulled Suzy down.

Rhoda began talking about the many tall martin birdhouses in the Kraybills' yard.

"Like we have," Betsy said, finding this tidbit interesting.

"Well, Mrs. Kraybill's about as Plain as you can get and still be English," Nan said.

"What do you mean, dear one?" Betsy asked.

"She cooks from scratch like we do," Nan said, glancing at Rhoda, who was nodding. "And she sews the children's clothing, too."

"Most by hand," Rhoda piped up.

"Now, that is surprisin'," Betsy admitted.

"She's even tried making her own paper—imagine that!" Nan laughed softly.

Betsy smiled at her daughters and at Reuben, who looked to be about ready to pop his suspenders. Twice during the meal he'd actually winked at her. Once he reached for her hand and covered it with his own, squeezing it quickly before letting go.

So great a secret we share, she thought, looking fondly at her daughters. *O Lord, please show your narrow path to our dear girls. . . .*

Nellie Mae didn't want to stare, but she couldn't help but notice the affectionate exchanges between Dat and Mamma during the meal. What was going on between them? With all she'd learned of Suzy's life, she felt still more troubled by Dat's incessant Scripture reading. No matter that his waywardness pulled him in a different direction than Suzy's—it failed to follow their tradition just the same.

She hadn't even considered opening Suzy's diary this morning before getting out of bed. No, she wanted to rest her mind, hoping to erase the troubling visions her keen imagination provided. Her once-innocent sister had willingly dabbled in sin, and because of what? Simple boredom with the Plain life?

The very notion angered Nellie, and she hoped what she felt was more on the side of righteous indignation than resentment. There was no point in allowing anger over the revelation of Suzy's iniquity to cause her to sin, as well. Thankfully she was not the ultimate judge.

Unable to sit still and hide her feelings a moment longer, Nellie rose abruptly from the table. "Who wants ice cream with Nan's cake?" she asked.

Nan frowned, obviously not pleased at Nellie's attempt to usurp her role of server. Rhoda's mouth gaped open, and she appeared ready to reprimand Nellie. Of course, she had every right to, being older.

"Girls, please sit down, the both of yous," Dat said, surprising Nellie and obviously Mamma, too, who wore a concerned look on her sweet face.

"I've got something on my mind," he continued when Nellie and Nan had taken their seats. "Something that will change the direction of our lives."

Suzy's shenanigans lingered in Nellie's mind in spite of her father's words. What possibly could alter her life more than what she'd already discovered? "Your mamma and I have accepted all the teachings of Jesus." Dat's face turned solemn as he spoke the words, and Nellie's stomach clenched. "We want to know more, to study the New Testament with others who are saved, as we are."

Rhoda raised her eyebrows, and Nan turned white.

"Saved?" Nan blurted out.

Nellie gulped, immediately thinking of Caleb. *Ach no, not that!*

CHAPTER 26

Nellie felt as though she were drifting, her mind pulling her backward to Dat's frightening announcement . . . and forward, into the future, which seemed less clear than ever. She tried her best to get her bearings in the midst of a steady stream of customers all Friday afternoon. But her attempt to remain rooted in the here and now was futile.

It seemed inevitable that the People would band together against this notion of Dat's and follow the bishop on the matter of salvation. Declaring it as a completed act was ever so prideful, or so they were taught. Yet the way her father talked, one of their own preachers wanted to have meetings to study the Bible with as many families as were interested.

Dat had quoted the verse "as for me and my house, we will serve the Lord" as his prayer for his family. Naturally he would desire his offspring to follow him in his beliefs, although it would be a real miracle if all five of her brothers abandoned their baptismal vows for this. Ephram, for one, was headstrong—and firmly tied to the Old Ways. So was Benjamin. Wasn't the Ordnung supposed to be obeyed, without exception?

Ach, how can Dat expect us to follow in this?

Between customers, Nellie stepped outdoors to soak in some of the sunshine and promptly developed a headache. A tightness wrapped around her head, like a wide rubber band pressing on her brain. Still, she lingered outside, inhaling the spicy fragrance of midautumn. The sky shone as if newly washed.

Suzy's first missed autumn . . .

Nellie spotted several sugar maples, their leaves turning to reddish orange at the edges. She took heart in the promise of blazing splendor soon to come.

Her thoughts turned to Mamma. No good thing could come of handing over the diary to her mother or anyone else. And Nellie knew she should not have given in to such impulsive crying yesterday.

Watching a car filled with more customers pull into the lane, she realized suddenly that their English neighbors, or even some of the People, surely must have bumped into Suzy last spring in town during her wild times. She would have been difficult to miss, spending time with such a crowd in her Plain attire.

Suzy did nothing at all to conceal her rebellion. How far did word spread?

Nellie feared that this, coupled with Dat's announcement at the dinner table, was merely the beginning of their sorrows. "So the rumors were true," she said to herself.

Do I dare admit this to Caleb?

Nellie couldn't help but think the life Suzy had lived—as well as the one Dat seemed determined to live—could doom her chances with her beau.

Betsy had never dreamed she would do such a thing as violate the privacy of a daughter's bedroom. Yet she felt convinced this search for Suzy's diary was justifiable. Even so, she hadn't decided how she would explain the deed to Nellie Mae. In some strange way, Suzy's writings struck her as Nellie's rightful possession.

She had sensed something change in Nellie nearly overnight. Her daughter appeared terribly depressed, and it worried Betsy no end. She felt the tension in her neck and shoulders as she relived the heartbreaking sound of her Nellie-girl crying her eyes out.

Betsy stood at the threshold and scanned Nellie's room—the bed, the dresser, the large rag rug. *Am I strong enough for this? Do I really want to read Suzy's account of things?*

Betsy knew what to look for because she'd seen Suzy writing in her little book . . . her head tilted down close to the page, hand fisted around a stubby pencil. Oh, but the very memory triggered pain—an intense one at that. *Do I need to know whose influence our Suzy was under?*

She wondered where Nellie Mae might keep such a book of secrets . . . and why Nellie herself had felt the urge to learn more about Suzy's rebellion.

Going to sit on the bed quilt, Betsy touched the small table where Suzy had set the lantern at night. Betsy recalled the many times she herself had sat in this very spot, soothing Suzy's feverish brow with her hand or bringing a homemade chicken corn soup to either daughter when she took ill. Her heart felt a pang at the memory of Nellie Mae and Suzy sitting on the bed, dangling their short legs as they hugged each other, giggling over their little-girl secrets.

This room holds so many memories. She rose and went to the dresser, seeing an unfinished circle letter lying there. She picked up the small hand mirror and frowned into it, aware of new lines in her face—all the not-so-subtle changes created by the sadness around her mouth and eyes.

Setting the mirror down, she wanted more than anything to know what would have caused Nellie Mae to weep here, in this room.

Both Nellie and I want answers, evidently, she thought. Even Reuben had so many unanswered questions; he just hadn't voiced them, at least not to her.

Betsy walked back to the bed and gently lifted both pillows, glancing beneath them. Moaning softly without meaning to, she worried she might be walking over Nellie Mae's still raw emotions if she pressed forward. It wasn't like her to trample on the trust of her daughters. Nellie might be horrified to know her mamma was snooping about while she was out closing up the bakery shop for the day.

Such a hardworking girl she is.

Fluffing the pillows and smoothing the coverlet quilt, Betsy eyed the bedside table yet again. *Would Nellie bother to hide the diary? Or simply keep it nearby?*

When she opened the drawer of the small table, the air went out of her for a moment. Slowly she reached for it, lifting Suzy's journal to her lips and pressing it there for ever so long, like clasping a gem to her heart.

It was enough to merely feel the book in her hands, against her cheek. "Oh, Suzy, I wish I might've helped keep you innocent. . . ."

She placed the diary back in the drawer. She was not as upset with herself for intruding on Nellie's special bond with her sister as she was sorrowful for a life lost for all eternity.

Lingering there, her eyes fixed on the diary, Betsy decided not to read a single page unless Nellie offered it. *Otherwise, I might lose her, as well.*

Caleb lifted the reins and clicked his tongue. *Four months ago this week, Suzy Fisher drowned,* he thought. *How's Nellie Mae taking the terrible anniversary?*

The hay wagon jolted forward, and he remembered precisely where he'd stood in the tobacco-drying barn when the astonishing news had reached his ears. *A group of carefree Englischers drove to the lake at Marsh Creek State Park for a day of fun. None was wearing a life jacket. One Amish girl drowned. . . .*

For days he'd walked in circles, concerned for the girl who'd stolen his heart in a single glance, realizing his pursuit of her would have to be pushed back. He'd thought at the time that it didn't matter what you'd done up till the point of your death—when your number was up, that was that.

Yet deep inside, where he squelched the more difficult questions, Suzy's death was to him like a night without a single star. Venus snuffed out, never to shine like the white jewel it was.

His gaze roamed over the alfalfa field. He had always enjoyed the way the breeze rippled through it in waves. All the many acres surrounding him called to his sense of beauty . . . and pride. To think this fine spread would someday be his. He was ready to claim his inheritance, even though it would be yet another year before he could do so, Nellie Mae by his side. Daed had said at breakfast that any day now they'd sit down and talk over the plan for the farm's transition to Caleb. He couldn't imagine being more grateful for the gift that was to be his. For this reason alone, he would always defer to his father, including him in the day-to-day management of the farm. Daed and Mamm would be well cared for. He'd see to that.

He chuckled outright. His hope of writing Nellie Mae a letter had not been acted on as the busy week wore on. No time had surfaced to sit privately in the kitchen, what with Mamm and his sisters hovering. Besides, he saw more wisdom in directly telling Nellie Mae the things in his heart. *Jah, all the things . . .*

He looked forward to the day when he could make her his bride . . . but first things first; he had yet to pinpoint the location of her bedroom window, for when the big day arrived. Of course he could learn it by merely waiting around after letting Nellie out by the road tomorrow, following the hog-butchering frolic—watch to see which window lit up. *A good plan.*

Caleb thought how ridiculous he must look out here in the middle of the field with the mule team and a big grin on his face.

Daed will think I'm a man in love . . . or a fool.

Reuben rode fast after an early dinner Saturday, passing Ephram's place as he headed toward his firstborn sons. Jeremiah and Thomas would hear from him today about God's plan for man's salvation, as stated in the Good Book.

Although he had been praying for this encounter for a while, he asked now for divine wisdom and the right words to say.

Thomas and Jeremiah were the best starting place among his grown children, because if he could persuade them to get involved in Bible study, they would more than likely encourage their younger brothers to follow in their footsteps.

Reuben's heart sang with praises as he rode toward the sunset, making his way along Beaver Dam Road, then turning south on Plank Road. God had already worked a miracle by turning Betsy's heart toward Him so swiftly—Manny's, too. He noted a few dozen feathered stragglers perched high on a telephone wire. When all was said and done, how many of the People would heed Preacher Manny and pursue saving grace? He couldn't help but wonder how he'd feel if he and Cousin Jonathan were the only ones sticking their necks out; he was mighty thankful they had Manny to look to for direction.

He thought of Bishop Joseph, concerned about his older brother's health. Would he respond soon to his and Manny's request? Perhaps having a minister conducting the studies would somehow suffice. He could only hope for a yea.

All in God's hands . . .

Spotting his sons' big farmhouse on the left, he slowed the horse, seeing his eldest sons putting away the sickle-bar hay mower. So they'd been making hay today, too. *The apple doesn't fall far from the tree.*

Though eager to share those things Reuben wished he'd known years ago, he took his time turning into the drive. He marveled at the brilliant orange, gold, and white mums in the flower beds in front of the porch and running alongside the house; nearly the same color arrangement as Betsy's own flower garden. Esther and Fannie—Thomas's and Jeremiah's wives—were known to work well together, painstakingly planning the color scheme. A laughing good time they always had, especially with their daughters alongside.

O Lord, help us keep our closeness as a family in spite of the upheaval ahead.

"That wasn't so bad, now, was it, Nellie?" asked Caleb as they rode away from the hog butchering.

Nellie had to admit she'd enjoyed herself, thanks in no small part to Rhoda. Her eldest sister had chosen to work alongside her, mixing seasonings into the sausage, while Nan spent her time with Rebekah Yoder, helping grind the meat.

For a change, Rhoda didn't seem like a stranger, thought Nellie, happy for some time with her.

She leaned close to Caleb presently, her hand in his. "Thank goodness for that good, stiff breeze . . . it cleared out the awful smell."

"You and your smells."

"Must run in the family," she said, thinking of Suzy's famously sensitive nose—quick to savor a lovely fragrance, swift to wrinkle at a foul one.

"Aw, love, maybe that's partly why you enjoy bakin' so much—all the wonderful-gut scents."

Love? Her heart sped up. *Dat calls Mamma that!*

He let go of her hand and slipped his arm around her. "Come here closer."

"Closer?" A giggle burst out. "That's just about impossible, Caleb."

He kissed her cheek. "Well, now, it won't have to be like this forever."

He's thinking of marriage, surely he is!

He leaned his head on top of hers. "You're my girl, Nellie Mae. Don't forget."

She sighed, fully content to be riding into the twilight with him. She didn't want to ruin the special moment, but she felt she ought to be forthright about the things happening with her parents, and the sooner the better. *Better he doesn't hear more tittle-tattle 'bout our family from the grapevine.*

"Um, Caleb, mind if we talk frankly?"

"Why sure. What's on your mind?"

She took a breath for courage, hoping what she had to say wouldn't create a wedge between them.

"My father's taken a shinin' . . . well, to studying." That was all she could get out at first.

"You had me uneasy there for a minute. I thought you were goin' to bring up all the tractor talk." He turned to look at her.

"Jah, but Dat has no interest in goin' fancy. What he's mighty interested in is the Good Book." She continued, her heart in her throat. "He's waitin' on word from Uncle Bishop to see if he and Preacher Manny can hold meetings on the no-Preaching Sundays."

"What for?"

"Bible study."

Caleb fell silent.

He's displeased. She could almost hear the beating of her own anxious heart in the quiet.

"I've heard of Amish in other districts wanting this," he said at last. "But I can't imagine our bishop allowing it. It's not in keeping with the Old Ways."

"Seems so." She sighed sadly. "What do you think will come of this, Caleb?"

He squeezed her hand. "No matter what, you and I won't be affected by it. Will we?"

She loved Caleb and wanted to say it right then, but now wasn't the time. Such a profession of devotion must come from him first. "I hope not," she said softly.

Truth was, Dat's determination to have the entire family follow his beliefs could pose a problem. She dearly hoped Caleb's and her relationship would not suffer as a result.

CHAPTER 27

———

This was a day of wonders, the way Reuben saw it. Not only had his twins eagerly joined ranks with him, but James and Benjamin, as well—his youngest son a bit more hesitant—agreed to unite in learning Scripture at the meetings Preacher Manny planned. They'd also voiced keen interest in tractors and electricity, but Reuben hoped that was not the motivation for his four sons' ready agreement. Still, he was anything but ignorant.

It was Ephram who would have to see the light, in good time, he told himself as he made his way toward his father's place. Ephram had refused to hear him out, as Reuben had supposed he might; his son had not wanted to make any trouble with the bishop. Reuben could only pray that his father would not greet this unexpected news the selfsame way. For certain, he felt as nervous as a young boy just now.

Mamm ushered him into the front room, where Daed was reading *The Budget.* Reuben sat down across from him, praying silently for wisdom.

"How's Betsy?" asked Daed right off.

Reuben guessed his reason for asking. "Well, she's surely missin' Suzy yet." He paused. "We all are."

"'Tis God's doin', and we must accept it as His plan." Daed hung his head for a moment. "Mighty hard to understand why she'd go off with worldly folk, though."

"Daed . . ." Reuben didn't want to get his father worked up before he'd even begun. "I came to talk 'bout other things."

"Oh?"

Reuben leaned forward. "I want you to hear this from me . . . from your son who loves you and respects all you've done for me." He paused briefly. "You and Mamm, well, you brought me up in the fear of the Lord God. I appreciate that. But there's more to God's ways."

"What're ya sayin', son?"

He stopped, weighing the moment, then continued. "I'm a believer, Daed—saved by the blood of the Lord Jesus Christ."

Daed rose swiftly, his face nearly ashen. "*Nee*—no, Reuben! This is the last thing I want to be hearin' from you." He walked away, stopping to stare out the window, his back to Reuben.

"Hear me out, Daed. I want to explain what I've learned . . . all that God is teachin' me through Scripture." Reuben went to his father and placed a hand on his shoulder.

"Get out of my sight!" Daed spun around, frowning. A glint of a tear was in his eye. "Be gone!"

Reuben did not want to risk upsetting him further, though he would have welcomed a conversation without such turmoil on Daed's part.

How did I expect him to respond? Reuben wondered, stopping to kiss his trembling, bewildered mother on the cheek before heading out the back door.

———

Long after supper and spoken evening prayers, Reuben sat with Betsy in their bedroom. "Ephram flat-out rejected the idea of attendin' any Bible study, just as I supposed," he told her. "Said he didn't want to make trouble with the bishop, which is understandable."

"That one has always clung to the Old Ways . . . much like our Nellie Mae seems to be doin'. She's come right out and said she's opposed to anything involving change," Betsy remarked.

"I pray she'll come around in time," Reuben said, glad for this moment with Betsy. He needed her comforting presence after such a day. "At least Nan's showing some interest, but Rhoda's a harder one to read. Do ya think she'll embrace the gospel?"

Betsy shrugged. "Still findin' her bearings, I daresay," she said.

"Seems so." He reached for her hand. "Let's pray for the Lord to lead all our dear ones to Him."

She nodded, tears welling up. "*Jah*, pray I will."

Reuben held her hand, looking down at their intertwined fingers. "We've been through some awful hard things, love." He paused, attempting to stay composed. "I hate to say it, but the days and months ahead could be ever so trying."

Betsy's eyes filled with tears. "Don't know how I'll manage. Yet somehow . . ." She tightened her lips. "*Jah*, somehow we will."

"We've placed our trust in our Savior . . . and I'll do everything I can to spare you more pain." Reuben didn't go into what he foresaw in the near future, but just the same, he sensed it was coming. Like a bolt out of the sky, lightning would strike and divide the People smack down the middle.

———

The first sign of serious trouble came in the form of a reply letter from Bishop Joseph the Tuesday nearly two weeks after Reuben had sent his request. It seemed his brother's health had taken a swift turn for the better, and he and Anna were heading home right quick. *Just so you know—Preacher Manny, too—it cannot be God's will for any of you to come together to study that way, preacher or no preacher*, the bishop wrote. *Folk who do don't stay Amish. I've seen it time and again. . . .*

Reuben's courage wavered briefly as he read the short and pointed note. So that was that: His brother had denied them. Reuben had expected as much, but there had remained a small spark of hope.

Reuben knew precisely what would happen if he and Manny forged ahead, disregarding the bishop's wishes. Reuben had heard of families elsewhere who had held Bible studies and were found out, never having asked permission. Eventually, if they refused to "come under" the Ordnung, a six-week probationary shun was slapped on them. If that didn't teach them, then they were shunned for life. The only way to get back into the church and the brethren's good graces was to repent and say you were back on the straight and narrow.

The Gospel was divisive; no questioning that. In some cases in Scripture, following God severed offspring from parents, and spouses from each other. Abram of old, for one, had followed the Lord God out of his father's house and country, forever away from his kindred.

Am I willing to obey God at any cost?

Forcing air out of the side of his mouth, he decided that the minute his hay was raked for baling, he would go and talk things over with Preacher Manny, who was also in danger of being ousted if he crossed this line.

Yet to stand still is to go backward, Reuben realized.

———

Nellie exercised patience at the cash register while their English neighbors, Mrs. Landis and her daughter, Joy, chattered on and on right at closing time. Tired from being on her feet, Nellie was anxious to sit at Mamma's supper table and enjoy the juicy ham she knew was roasting.

Mrs. Landis swept back a strand of raven-black hair—noticeably dyed—into her neatly flipped shoulder-length hairdo. "Joy tells me her cousin Darlene knew your sister Suzy from school," the woman said, startling Nellie Mae. "Quite well, in fact."

"Oh?" Nellie's throat pinched up. *What does she know?*

The woman's daughter blushed quickly and shook her head. "Mom, *please* don't bring that up."

That silenced Mrs. Landis, and after the two of them had left the shop, Nellie pondered what could have been on Joy's mind. But her curiosity was not enough to make her crack open Suzy's diary again. No, she would not open *that* wound tonight. She was much too tired to contemplate the further transgressions of her sister. Was her lifelessness, even melancholy, due to what she'd discovered through Suzy's words, or was she coming down with something? She had been known to absorb tension in a way that made her ill. *Come to think of it, is that what happened to Uncle Bishop?*

What on earth will he think when he finally returns? she wondered, what with Dat—a stalwart church member—making prideful talk of being "saved." What would their bishop do about that?

Going to the shop door, she stood on her tiptoes and turned the Open sign around to Closed.

Oh, how she wished she could take comfort in Rosanna's company. She wondered how things were for her friend as she readied her household for the coming babies. *Won't she have fun with two to care for!*

Nellie thought ahead to what it might be like to hold a baby of her own . . . hers and Caleb's. She smiled in spite of herself. She and her beau planned to ride over to the millstream this coming Sunday afternoon in broad daylight—Caleb's suggestion.

He's getting mighty bold. Nellie laughed softly, pulling the door shut before heading toward the house.

Supper was set out—pork chops, fried potatoes and onions, and buttered lima beans, with a small dish of chowchow. Rosanna had taken great care to prepare a fine hot meal for her husband.

Before they could begin eating, though, she quickly showed Elias the matching reversible cradle quilts she had been making for the babies. One side featured a pattern in pastel pinks and green, the other one in blue and lavender. "That way if we have two boys, or two girls, or one of each, we'll be just fine," she said, putting them away before she sat down.

Elias frowned at the head of the table. "Two girls, you say?"

She nodded, hoping her husband wasn't opposed to the idea of daughters. "These are to be our firstborn, Rosanna."

"Jah."

"For pity's sake, do we want girls, really . . . if we have a say-so?" His frown grew deeper.

"Well, I figure if we can't ever have any babies of our own, then why on earth not take what we're given? Besides, the more the better." There—she'd said at last what she had been wanting to say for days.

Elias rose abruptly. "Why not wait and decide when your cousins' babies are born? See what they turn out to be."

"Wait till they're born? But, Elias—"

"No, you ain't listenin'." He stood with both hands on the back of the chair. "I aim to have a son. At least one."

She didn't understand what was bothering him so. Surely the possibility of their raising two girls wasn't all there was to it.

He marched to the back of the house, where she heard him muttering out in the summer porch. She knew better than to go to him. He obviously was trying to hold his peace about something. Elias was not a man who would usually quibble, and initially he had appeared as grateful as she for Kate's offer—maybe even more so. But the past few weeks had been a trial for him.

Was it the slim harvest? Even with less of a hay crop to bring in than usual, he was beyond tired. They all were, working from sunup to sundown.

Lord, won't you bless my husband . . . give him peace?

She didn't know what had come over her, thinking a prayer like that. Maybe she'd secretly visited Jonathan Fisher's place one time too many. Dear shunned Linda was a fountain of information on canning pureed food for babies, though Rosanna'd never once let it be known that all the questions she was asking were for herself.

So much to learn . . . and Linda is ever so prayerful.

As far as she knew, Cousin Kate had not yet told anyone that she planned to give her babies away. *How will the womenfolk react, especially with twins? Everybody loves two little ones in a baby buggy, side by side.*

Sighing, Rosanna ate the delicious meal alone, not happy about the idea of sitting here while Elias fumed. *Will he settle down tonight long enough to eat supper?*

Surely his hearty appetite would bring him back to the table.

Jah, he'll return in a few minutes. Then, when he's filled up, he'll tell me what's really troubling him.

Caleb headed toward the barn to check on the bedding straw for the animals, particularly for the new calf. He whistled a tune he'd heard in town, a snappy melody he'd liked immediately. His Mennonite cousin Christian

Yoder had told him it was a "jingle" often used on radio stations right before the news or a sports report. Of course, not having been around radios much, Caleb wasn't aware of such things. The tunes Cousin Christian liked to whistle were as foreign to Caleb as the worldly jingle he found himself whistling repeatedly tonight.

The young calf seemed to like the sound as Caleb moved into the pen with her and petted her soft coat. He gave her more straw, pushing it around to even it out, and was getting ready to return to the house when he heard his father talking to someone up in the upper level of the two-story barn.

Not one to eavesdrop, he almost headed out of the barn, but the topic of conversation swayed him. A man whose voice Caleb could not place was talking about someone who'd served out his conscientious objector status in Civilian Public Service years before. While doing so, the young man had been introduced to lively prayer meetings and Bible studies. "He even started watchin' television," the man said, sounding indignant. "Well, if this here fella didn't start second-guessin' the absence of a tractor in his father's fields and the lack of electricity flowing through the house, mind you."

"I've heard similar tales," Caleb's father replied. "Too much mixing with Englischers 'most always comes to a bad end."

"No doubt of that, David. And same thing can happen when the youth start attendin' gatherings where the Good Book's discussed every which way. A march starts toward this enticing new path—a new order, some call it—and you hear every excuse under the sun for changing the Old Ways. 'Tis harder to turn your back on 'thus saith the Lord' than on 'thus saith the church,' some say. You just watch, David, if it don't come to that here . . . that tabernacle nearby's invitin' trouble."

Caleb realized he was holding his breath. He slowly exhaled, waiting to hear what Daed might say. "We were all young once, so I can't be talkin' against the youth. But to go against the Ordnung as a baptized church member? There's just no excuse for crossin' *that* line."

"I say it's Uncle Sam's fault all this got started," the unfamiliar man replied. "Far as I can tell, trouble reared up when he forced our hand and made us serve our time, even though we were conscientious objectors."

"Jah, look where that got us." Daed huffed loudly, and Caleb darted out of the barn while he had his chance. He felt terribly guilty for listening in as he had, but with Nellie Mae's family stepping so close to this same dangerous edge, he was anxious to know all he could.

CHAPTER 28

S weet breads and anything made with pumpkin were the most-requested items at Nellie's Simple Sweets now that they were into deep October. The demand for such goodies moist with pumpkin always rose near Halloween, though Nellie Mae never cared to acknowledge the day. While the practice of trick-or-treating mystified her, Nellie found the idea of dressing in costume to be most curious—she especially couldn't picture grown-ups dressing like storybook characters or favorite animals the way neighbor Diana Cooper described.

She expected the market for harvest-time desserts to last well into November and the start of the wedding season. Keeping up with the ever-increasing orders was so much of a chore for both Nellie and Nan that Mamma sometimes helped with the baking. Nellie could scarcely keep count of the quantity of pumpkin whoopee pies she was making between her dates with Caleb. They aimed to see each other every few days now that the silos were full.

Twice this week, Caleb had surprised her with thoughtful notes, none marked with a return address. Unable to wait until Sunday afternoon after all, Caleb had taken her driving last night to their spot near the picturesque stone mill. There they had huddled against the cold on the wrought-iron bench, sitting so close they could have squeezed into Caleb's heavy woolen coat if they'd tried. They had wandered up and down the creek after a time, walking over to the millrace and back, talking and trying to keep warm by moving alongside its gurgling waters.

Nellie had noticed how Caleb reached for her hand almost absentmindedly. *Like I'm a comfortable part of him somehow.*

There had been moments during last night's conversation, though, when Caleb had seemed tentative, as if holding back something important, although she wouldn't think of pressing him. He would tell her when he was ready, and until then she must simply swallow her fears that it concerned her parents, who were planning an upcoming meeting at Preacher

Manny's . . . minus the blessing of Uncle Bishop. Might Caleb have heard of that?

She did not understand her parents' decision, but it was not her place to question. Dat and Mamma had made their promise to the church and to the Lord God long ago—who was *she* to remind them? According to Caleb himself, as well as her customers in the bakery shop, there were plenty of people who were still holding firm to tradition.

Here lately, she was glad she hadn't been born a boy and therefore more privy to the bishop's fury as his will clashed with those pushing for change. She'd heard Dat and Preacher Manny describe it in just that way as they talked openly yesterday morning while drinking coffee in Mamma's kitchen. They had not pretended to talk of other things when Nellie came to fetch a batch of pumpkin sticky buns for Mrs. Kraybill.

"Listen, Manny, the lines have been drawn and erased and redrawn near endless times over the years," Dat had let fly from his lips. *"Don't you see the contradictions?"*

Preacher Manny had wholeheartedly agreed, which was evidently part of the reason the two of them remained so determined to begin their Bible-study meetings, starting on this next no-Preaching Sunday. To Nellie the whole thing sounded dangerously as though they were not only questioning the Ordnung but outright refusing to obey the bishop, too.

Setting themselves up as God . . .

Nellie shivered and glanced around the shop, taking inventory of her bakery items. Being out all hours last night had sapped her energy today for sure . . . though she wouldn't have minded the weariness if things were more settled at home. She couldn't begin to fathom why Dat and Preacher Manny would want to willfully go against the grain, so to speak.

Elias held Rosanna in his arms on this first no-Preaching Sunday in November, and as they relaxed, waiting for the morning sunrise, he spoke. "It's not so important that we get boys or girls or one of each, dear," he said. "Tell ya the truth, I'm still hopin' we'll have some of our own."

She cherished his nearness, relieved to know at last what had been troubling him. "Jah, doctors aren't always right . . . and we're still young, too."

"Lots of years ahead to keep tryin' for a little woodchopper." He stroked her long, thick hair. "Was it almost four years ago we got hitched?"

"I'm not a bit sorry for not waitin' longer, are you?"

He kissed her again, lingering this time. "Who'd be sorry to have such a pretty wife?"

She smiled. Elias had a way of saying the right things at the right time. "Well, maybe, Lord willin', we'll have us a baby someday. But won't it be fun having two wee ones here, right quick? Special delivery in a way."

"Not soon enough for you, that's for sure." Elias grinned in the dim light.

"Well, since twins tend to come early, it's a good thing we're all ready with the cradles and whatnot."

He leaned up on his elbow, looking down at her with adoring eyes. "We'll fill this old house with lots of little ones, jah?"

She hoped so, partly to please Elias. Truth be known, she would rather have a baby in her arms than most anything. But for now, Elias was cradling her in his, drawing her ever so near. His lips found hers again, and Rosanna was heedless to the dawn as it crept under the window shade and spilled light over their bed quilt. Not even the rooster's crowing succeeded in getting the two of them to rise and shine.

With a sense of joy mixed with trepidation, Reuben rode up with Betsy to Preacher Manny's farmhouse. Bishop Joseph had returned from Iowa mighty upset, far beyond the proverbial righteous indignation. Now Manny was under a watch for the Bann by his own ministerial brethren. They had warned him that he would be brought before the membership if he did not cease his activities.

But Manny had made his stand—he was immovable. To some extent it was Manny's doggedness to "push forward with God's calling" that had brought them here today.

Reuben paused at the back stoop with his Bible. "O Lord, go before us," he whispered, noticing seven buggies parked off to the side.

"The People are hungry, looks like to me," Betsy said softly as they made their way into the preacher's roomy kitchen.

By now a dozen or so folk were seated on folding chairs in the next room, rather than the long wooden benches common to Preaching services. Many had their Bibles open on their laps, ready for Preacher Manny to begin. Among them were Reuben's own four sons, Ephram being the only one missing.

Spotting his cousin in the corner of the kitchen, Reuben hurried to his side. "Manny, are you ready?"

The preacher's eyes were bloodshot. "I was up most of the night prayin'," Manny said, wearing his best white shirt and black broadfall trousers. "Will you offer a few words before I say what the Lord has put on my heart?"

Reuben flinched. "You want me to speak?" He shook his head. "I'm no preacher, mind you."

Manny gripped his arm. "I said nothing about preachin', Reuben. Just talk some about what God's been showing you in His Word."

"Well, I s'pose . . ."

Manny leaned closer. "Nothin' at all hard about it. The power that raised up God's Son from the dead lives right there in you." Manny pointed to Reuben's heart. "Remember that."

Straightaway Reuben breathed easier. Putting it that way, sure, he could tell the group how God was working in him. Standing in the threshold between the kitchen and the large sitting room, he recognized several more of his own kin, including Cousin Jonathan and his wife, Linda. These hearty souls were his brothers and sisters in the family of God.

I can do this, he decided. *With the Lord's help.*

Preacher Manny stood before them, cheerfully welcoming each person. Then he bowed his head for a prayer of blessing, encouraging all of them to open their hearts "to the tender witness of the Father's presence in our midst."

This was a far cry from what they were accustomed to hearing in prayer of a Sunday, and for this wonderful-good start to the meeting, Reuben was thankful. He and Betsy sat close to the front, in one accord, sharing the Good Book when Manny read from the verses that had transformed his life in the past weeks. The reading was powerful to Reuben, as well as to others, some of whom were sniffling. Tears spilled down his own Betsy's cheeks. *They're starving for this, just as I am*, Reuben observed, his heart filling at the very thought.

CHAPTER 29

O n the day before they were to move Reuben's parents into the Dawdi
Haus next door, Betsy had an unexpected visitor.

Heavy snow had fallen in the night, a good six inches by the looks of
it. A gray November haze sagged over dormant fields like a dark blanket,
making it difficult to see.

Betsy was both surprised and concerned when she heard a horse neigh-
ing in the lane. She hurried out to see Reuben's mother making her way
toward the back door. "Well, hullo. What brings you on such a Wednesday?"
asked Betsy.

Hannah leaned on the crook of her cane, all bundled up in her heaviest
woolen coat. *"Wie geht's?"*

Betsy hurried down the shoveled walkway and took Hannah's arm to
lead the dear woman up the steps and into the house. "You want something
hot to drink?" she asked.

"That'd warm me up a bit, jah."

"You came all this way by yourself?"

"Me, myself, and the horse." Hannah smiled momentarily as she lowered
herself into Reuben's rocker with a groan.

Betsy couldn't help wondering why she'd risk traveling alone. "How
were the roads?"

"Just terrible." Suddenly Hannah's eyes were bright with tears. "Ach,
Betsy, we best be talkin'."

The poor woman looked so completely distraught, Betsy assumed someone had died.

On edge now, she pulled one of the chairs away from the table and settled
in beside Hannah. "What is it, Mamm?" She reached out to touch her arm.

"Oh, Betsy, word has it that you and Reuben . . ." Hannah stopped,
hanging her head. Her shoulders trembled. "Oh, goodness me."

"What 'bout Reuben and me?"

Hannah slowly raised her head. "Ain't you with that bunch who's plannin' to jump the fence? Over there at Preacher Manny's?"

Betsy said, "Now, Mamma, we're all sincere . . . all of us growin' in the Lord together."

"You'll grow right out of the Amish, then . . ." Hannah lowered her gaze, shaking her head. She began to rock in the chair. "Movin' far away from the church of your baptism. It's just as Noah said."

"Oh, Mamm, don't be sad. I've never felt so happy . . . truly."

Hannah reached into her dress sleeve and pulled out a folded hankie, dabbing her eyes. "You'll be shunned if this keeps up."

Betsy knew as much. She and Reuben were waiting for the deacon to come knocking any day with a warning.

"I hate to say it, but I doubt we'll be movin' in here with you and Reuben after all."

All the plans they'd made—everything was set in motion to bring Noah and Hannah under the covering of this house. "No . . . no, yous mustn't change your mind on that."

"Ain't for me to say." Hannah wept openly. "And you neither."

Getting up, Betsy went to boil some water, having forgotten to put the kettle on. *Well, we ain't shunned yet!*

"Our attending Preacher Manny's meeting last Sunday doesn't have to affect you and Noah." Betsy realized she was pleading. Hannah was as stubborn as Reuben and his brothers had always been. Being a saved man hadn't changed Reuben's tenacity, and she knew what he'd say about his mother's visit.

When the teakettle whistled, she poured the boiling water into her pretty yellow teapot for brewing. Then she went to sit again with Hannah. "It would be wonderful-good if you came to hear what we're learnin'," Betsy suggested. "I never thought I'd be sayin' such a thing, but there's so much that's been . . . well, kept from us, it seems." There. She'd said right out what was on her mind.

"We'll be doin' no such a thing," Hannah said, her eyes flashing. "And looks to me like we're gettin' *naryets*—nowhere—on this."

"Reuben said believin' was likely to bring a separation"—and here she touched her heart—"but I was ever so hopeful . . ." She couldn't finish, lest she weep.

Hannah rocked harder in the chair, gripping both of its arms, her lips pursed. "Let's say no more on this for now. I'll have that tea, Betsy."

She rose and went to pour the tea, putting a little extra sugar in Hannah's cup for good measure. Then she took the matching teacup and saucer to her, gently placing them in her wrinkled hands. "Here you are, Mamm."

Hannah accepted it, had herself a sip, and blinked her eyes at Betsy. "Speaking of partings, have you heard what Kate Beiler's plannin' to do?"

Betsy shook her head. She found it interesting that Hannah had so quickly abandoned her dispute. "What 'bout Kate?"

"The strangest thing, really." Hannah frowned deeply. "She's going to give her babies to Elias and Rosanna, but it's all hush-hush."

Betsy was stunned and almost asked Hannah if she was sure . . . if she wasn't mixed-up, as she sometimes could be.

"Seems your Nellie Mae has known of this for some time. Rosanna told her, as I understand it from Kate's midwife, Ruth Glick."

My girls and their secrets . . .

"Nellie hasn't said a word."

"Well, Ruth thinks the twins will be comin' sooner than was first thought."

Dear, dear Rosanna, keeping wee ones all bundled up in this cold. "Guess Rosanna will be ever so happy. Sure has had a time of it, jah?"

Hannah nodded, drinking some more tea before answering. "I daresay Elias will be sleepin' in the spare room some."

To this both women smiled.

"Poor man has no idea what he's in for," Hannah stated flatly.

"Do you know why on earth Kate would give her babies away like this?"

"Kate loves her cousin is all I know. Like I said, it's a secret . . . not even Rachel knows."

"Kate's own mamma doesn't?" Betsy shook her head. "That's mighty surprisin', ain't so? Best we be keepin' word to ourselves, then." Betsy didn't want to think of Rachel's possibly hearing such news from someone other than Kate. Truly, the midwife should know better than to be speaking of it to others.

Hannah nodded. "When the news is out, some will take it in stride; others will be flabbergasted." Hannah wiped her eyes with her hankie again. "I say it's just the nicest thing, truth be told. Rosanna's getting her heart's desire, two wee, perty babes."

Betsy had to agree with pretty, because every one of Kate's brood was just that—as fine-looking as any children she'd ever seen, including her own. "Such a generous thing to do, jah?"

Hannah drank the rest of her tea, pausing to look over her cup at Betsy.

"Wonder if the babies will know who their real parents are." Her hand trembled.

"That'd be a good thing, given they're all cousins."

But Hannah thought differently. "Those poor young'uns wouldn't know who to mind, though, would they?"

Betsy hadn't thought of that. She couldn't imagine what Rosanna might face if that were so. "I hope all goes well, but I could never do what Kate's doin'. And I'd be nearly beside myself if any of my children were to hand off my grandchildren to someone else!"

Hannah nodded slowly, finally agreeing with something Betsy had said. They talked about less contentious things for a while—the next quilting bee and how many weddings were coming up this week.

"Would you like a quick visit with Nan and Nellie Mae?" Betsy looked out the window. Unless someone had arrived on foot, there didn't appear to be a single customer at the bakery shop.

"Sure I would." Hannah brightened significantly.

"I'll go and call them."

Unexpectedly, Hannah remarked, "If her sisters don't mean to be on hand, your Nellie's goin' to look mighty lonesome during Preachin' next Sunday, I daresay."

At the comment Betsy stopped in her tracks as she was heading out to get her shawl. Turning to stare at Hannah, she wondered why she'd brought this up. "Why would ya say this, Mamm?"

Hannah ignored the question. "I daresay sensible Nellie Mae's goin' to marry herself an Old Order fella, and you and Reuben won't even be welcome at the wedding."

Betsy had heard all she cared to. "Well, for goodness' sakes."

"Now you be thinkin' good and long 'bout this, Betsy. You and Reuben need to consider what you're givin' up." Hannah had scooted herself to the edge of the rocking chair. "You think on it real hard, ya hear?"

Betsy bit her tongue and hurried to get her wrap. Stepping into the cold, she realized she had been thoroughly reprimanded and humiliated by her mother-in-law. In the past she would have given the woman what for, but today she decided to offer the utmost kindness to Hannah and prayed to that end, making her way to the bakery shop.

Nellie saw Mamma approaching the bakery shop around the time she'd told Nan they ought to slip away to see why Mammi Fisher had come on such bad roads. Now here was Mamma hurrying into the shop door, her face redder than it ought to be from the short jaunt.

"Girls, your grandmother's eager to see you." Mamma put on a smile. "Go down and see her once."

Nan nearly ran for her shawl and out the door, but Nellie paused. "Why on earth . . . today of all miserable days?"

"For a visit." Betsy turned away.

"You're upset, ain't so?" Nellie went to her.

Mamma breathed visibly. "Your Dat said things like this would happen. I never dreamed . . ."

Nellie leaned her head against her mother's. "What did Mammi say?"

"She and Dawdi won't be movin' back here. We're as good as shunned."

Nellie struggled with the lump that threatened to close her throat. She felt frightened to think of such a thing happening to her parents . . . to their family as a whole, as would likely be the case. "Is there no stoppin' this?" she whispered.

Mamma shook her head, clearly trying to keep her composure. "Go visit with Mammi now."

Nellie nodded, willing to obey her mother on this account. But unbaptized though she was, she wouldn't think of abandoning the Old Ways—not for the world, nor for Dat's faith.

CHAPTER 30

S now fell in thick, fluffy flakes as Nellie Mae closed up the bakery shop
that Wednesday. She had a hankering for a walk, and since she'd already
enjoyed a short visit with Mammi Fisher earlier, she bypassed the house
and headed toward the road for a breather, ready for some time alone. She
could see through the window that Mamma and Mammi still looked to be
hashing things out in the kitchen.

Mamma's all fired up, she thought, taking in the sight of waning maples
outlined against the frosty curtain of snowflakes. *Dawdi and Mammi refuse
to move here. If that don't beat all!*

Nellie pulled her shawl more tightly around her, against the chilling air.
She wondered how many folk would be affected by the commotion in their
midst. How far would the disagreement over the rules of the Ordnung spread?

Putting that out of her mind, she breathed in the refreshing frostiness of
the late afternoon, watching the heavy snow and remembering the many
times she and Suzy had caught snowflakes on their tongues. Such wonderful-
gut growing-up years.

The account of Suzy's slide into sin still gnawed at Nellie, keeping her
awake at night. She hadn't decided whether to bury the diary again or
completely destroy it, but she was going to do something. She couldn't
risk anyone else in their family reading about Suzy's disgraceful behavior.

Mrs. Landis's comment about Joy's cousin Darlene and Suzy came back
to her just then, haunting her.

Suzy's past is nobody's worry now. Even so, it was dreadful to know others
remained all too aware of her younger sister's wicked behavior.

She forced her thoughts back to Mammi Fisher and her grandparents'
sudden decision not to live here. Had Dawdi sent her to confront Mamma?

Nellie pushed through the snow, moving faster as her head cleared. She
had not heard yet this week from Caleb, even though he had written three
letters to her last week. The weather being this cold, they hadn't seen each
other for seven days, despite their original plan to go to the millstream

together last no-Preaching Sunday. She missed him, wondering when their special night might come. When would they talk quietly in her room while sitting on the little loveseat? Cousin Jonathan's father and brother were well-known in the area for upholstering these beautiful pieces of courting furniture with their delicate oak arms and legs.

Smiling momentarily, she wondered what she would have done if Caleb's flashlight had shone on her window while Suzy was still alive and sleeping soundly in the room. She supposed she might have asked her sister to sleep in the spare room for that particular night. The way she'd heard it from Maryann and her other sisters-in-law, most girls could sense when their beau intended to propose.

Caleb loves me. What's keeping him from asking me to be his bride?

She'd had fears that Caleb was upset at what she'd told him about Dat's keen interest in the Good Book. More than likely, he knew of her parents' connections to Preacher Manny by now. It seemed nearly everyone was aware who had attended the meeting last Sunday.

And who hadn't.

Lately she felt nearly frayed, loving Caleb yet wanting to obey her father in his leanings, as she'd been taught to do. Rhoda and Nan were planning to join their parents and older brothers at Preacher Manny's house come this Sunday. A bold and foolhardy move, holding a meeting on the actual day of Preaching, of all things!

As for Nellie, she planned to walk alone to Preaching service, where she assumed Uncle Bishop would give the main sermon—his first since returning.

What will Caleb's family think if I show up by myself?

Even though courtship was usually to be kept confidential until the planned marriage was announced, Nellie was fairly sure that at least Rebekah had an inkling Caleb was seeing her. That girl didn't seem to be one to miss anything.

Up ahead the roof of a tobacco drying barn glistened thanks to an ample layer of snow, and she was struck by how picturesque it was, though she must have seen the same barn hundreds of times.

She continued walking briskly, the dense cold penetrating her bones. When she sighed, her breath nearly froze in midair, and she wished she'd worn a scarf to wrap around her face.

A good half mile later, she spotted Rhoda's distinct silhouette coming up the road's shoulder. She called "hullo," glad she'd stumbled upon her. Even though they lived in the same house, recently she'd scarcely spoken two words to her oldest sister. "Hullo!" she called again.

"Nellie Mae . . . where're ya goin'?" Rhoda crossed the road toward her.

"Just needed some fresh air."

"Well, you've picked icy air." Rhoda laughed.

Nellie smiled. "You must be workin' a lot these days."

Rhoda hugged herself, rubbing her mittened hands against her arms. "It seems best, well, to be away from the house as much as possible here lately."

"Are you really goin' to Preacher Manny's with Dat and Mamma?" asked Nellie.

"Only out of respect for Dat. Aren't you?" Rhoda asked.

"Can't."

"Must be you've got yourself a beau, then?"

Rhoda sounded like Nan had some weeks back. Nellie wouldn't be tricked, however; she would not say a word about Caleb.

"Well, do you?"

"Look, Rhoda, I don't ask you 'bout your friends or what you do away from home, do I?"

Rhoda shrugged. "I'd tell ya. Ask one question you're dyin' to know."

"All right." The air stung Nellie's lungs. "Why's it so important to work away from home . . . for Englischers, of all things?"

"That's two. I said only one," Rhoda snipped.

Looking at her, Nellie was shocked at Rhoda's sassy, even worldly response. She flinched, shying away. "Never mind, I guess."

"Aw, come now, Nellie Mae. What's wrong with you?"

With me? Nellie stared.

Rhoda sighed. "Dat's sure been ferhoodled lately."

"Ach, now you're bein' rude."

"Well, you and I know better than to say we're *saved*. I'm surprised Mamma's putting up with it, even sayin' she believes such things, too. What's happening to our family, anyway?"

"I s'pose I could ask you the same, Rhoda. Seems you're gone an awful lot."

Rhoda's eyes flashed her frustration. "I like workin' . . . making some money, is all."

"Savin' up for something?"

"Maybe so." Rhoda gazed at her. "But it ain't for what you might think."

Nellie Mae had no idea what she meant. "Well, I didn't mean to pry."

Rhoda huffed, walking past her. "I'll see you back at the house, sister," she called. "Don't stay out too long, or you'll catch a cold and miss goin' to your precious Preachin' come Sunday."

Nellie sputtered, her breath turning to ice crystals before her. *She's just dying for electric, no doubt.*

Walking faster, she felt terribly annoyed. "Who does she think she is, livin' a double standard?"

Just ahead a buggy was swiftly heading this way, through the shroud of snow and fog. "Hullo, Nellie Mae!" came a familiar voice.

She recognized the woman in the buggy as the midwife—Mary Glick's granddaughter Ruth. "You look to be in a hurry," Nellie called to her.

"Kate Beiler's wee ones are a-comin'!"

So soon? Turning, she watched the enclosed gray buggy as it sped by. "Ach, Rosanna. Today's your blessed day." She wished she might run and catch up with the carriage to ride straight to her dearest friend, but the horse had already galloped past.

Nellie stood there in amazement. "I hope Kate's—and Rosanna's—babies come healthy and ever so safe."

She rushed back to the house to divulge the startling news, glad she'd have something worth writing to Cousin Treva and the others in their circle letter. Out of breath, she spotted Mammi's buggy still parked near the back door.

Maybe I can borrow it to run over to Kate's, where Rosanna surely will be.

But when she arrived inside mere moments after Rhoda, Mamma was tending to Mammi Fisher, laying a wet cloth on her forehead and soothing her with her gentle hands and voice. Rhoda knelt at her feet.

"What's happened?" Nellie rushed to the rocking chair, shocked at how red and stricken Mammi's face was.

"Will one of yous ride for the doctor?" asked Mamma.

Nan brought another damp cloth. "What's wrong with Mammi?"

"She nearly collapsed," Mamma explained. "Limp as a dishrag now."

"I'll go for the doctor." Nellie turned and ran for the back door, throwing on her winter things. She was glad a horse and carriage were already hitched as she hopped inside and picked up the reins.

All the talk of shunning . . . no wonder Mammi's ill, she thought, feeling sick herself as she headed toward a completely different destination than Kate and Rosanna's tiny babies.

———

Having alerted the doctor, Nellie dashed back down the steps outside the doctor's cottagelike office, anxious to return to Mammi's side. She watched the doctor's car speed out from behind the building and turned to see Mrs. Landis coming up the walkway, her arm in a sling. "Hullo, neighbor," she said to the older woman. "What did you do to yourself?"

"Oh, it's so embarrassing, really. I fell on the sidewalk in front of my own house. I'm just heading in for a follow-up appointment," Mrs. Landis told her. Then she lowered her voice. "I'm so glad I ran into you, Nellie Mae. My daughter was terribly self-conscious at your shop, you must know."

"Oh?" Nellie fidgeted, eager to be off, but she was polite and listened.

"Fact is, your sister Suzy saved my niece Darlene's life. Suzy made all the difference to a girl who was sinking fast."

Saved her life? "Your niece . . . did she get into a bad crowd?" Nellie felt she was sticking her neck out by asking, but she had to know.

"Oh, mercy, yes! But Suzy kindly helped Darlene see the error of her ways."

Thunderstruck, Nellie had almost forgotten why she was standing there. "Ach . . . I'm awful sorry to have to run off, but my grandmother's ill. The doctor's already on his way over to our place."

"Well, I hope she's all right," Mrs. Landis offered. "I'll be sure to say a prayer for her."

Nellie thanked her and waved good-bye as she raced down the walkway. *My sister must've fooled Mrs. Landis but good. What's she mean by saying Suzy helped Darlene?*

Nellie was mighty sure—Mrs. Landis had the wrong Suzy.

CHAPTER 31

By the time Nellie arrived back at the house with the horse and buggy, the country doctor's car was already parked in the lane. Swiftly she tied the horse and hurried indoors, relieved to find Dawdi Fisher there, as well as Dat.

Dawdi Noah leaned over Mammi. "Poor, poor, dear," he said as he fanned her. All of them were hovering until the doctor shooed everyone into the front room so he could take her blood pressure and try to determine if she'd had a stroke.

Anxious, yet relieved to see Mammi more coherent now, Nellie headed to her room for some quiet. Observing her grandmother so incapacitated at first had been frightening. She would stay put until the doctor was finished with his examination.

Her worry for Mammi alternated with her curiosity about the twin babies Rosanna would soon hold in her arms. Of course, it was too dark to venture over there now. Besides, the midwife at John and Kate Beiler's place might be saying the selfsame thing as the doctor here, scooting everyone out till the babies came. She could only hope and pray the wee ones were strong enough, being born so early.

With troublesome thoughts swirling in her head, she decided to add to the circle letter. This time of year, once the harvest was in, the circle letters fairly flew back and forth, and her cousins would be expecting news.

Finding the lined stationery in her dresser drawer, Nellie Mae felt a strong need to narrate her day, to keep her mind occupied.

Picking up her best pen, she began to write.

Dear Cousins,

Hello from Honey Brook.

There is so much to tell you, starting with the most wonderful news: Kate Beiler's twins are soon to be born—I haven't heard if they have actually come today, but the midwife fairly flew past me when I was taking a walk a while ago. I'll give you the firm details in my next letter. All right?

We've other interesting news here, too. Our bishop is back from a long vacation in Iowa. His trip wound up being longer than planned due to an illness, but I hear he's healthier now.

My sister-in-law Maryann's baby will be the next one to arrive, at least for our family. Of course, there are oodles of little ones on the way. And, oh goodness, all the weddings! Mamma said we've been invited to three on a single day next week. Not sure which one they'll pick, but it'll surely be fun.

She paused in her writing, wondering which weddings Caleb and his family might attend. If Caleb happened to be at the same one as she and her sisters and parents, would she end up at the feast table across from him, maybe?

Sighing, Nellie contemplated the pleasure of seeing Caleb at an all-day wedding celebration now that they were truly a couple. But that wasn't the kind of thing she would share with Cousin Treva and the others who would receive this letter.

Thinking again of her very sick Mammi, Nellie struggled to remain upbeat—she didn't want to spoil the tone of the letter. After a moment, she resumed her writing, apologizing for bearing the sad news about Mammi Fisher. *We're still awaiting the doctor's word as to what she's suffering from.* She added a few more lines before signing off, asking Treva and the others to please keep the letters coming "nice and fast." Then she folded the letter.

With Mammi's health still weighing heavily in her mind, Nellie Mae slipped the folded letter into the drawer of the small bedside table. Pausing there at the sight of Suzy's diary, she reached in and picked up the book, terribly aware of the guilt that yet lay hidden inside her—the anger, too, which made her impulsively lift the bed mattress at one end and shove in Suzy's diary.

There. That's where it stays till I burn it up.

She straightened the quilt coverlet and headed out of the room to see how Mammi was doing.

The labor was intense for her cousin, and Rosanna cringed each time Kate stirred from rest to moan. Rosanna sat in the corner of Kate and John's large bedroom, not close enough to see the babies crown and be birthed, as she was hesitant about being present at all. Yet Kate had insisted she be in the room once word had reached Rosanna that the babies were most likely coming today. Ephram had received a call on the community telephone

up the road from Rosanna and Elias's place, and Maryann had rushed over
to deliver the news. Upon hearing it, Rosanna had offered nary a word of
explanation, other than to say her cousin surely needed her help.

When will Kate reveal her plan for her babies? Rosanna wondered. Perhaps
her cousin had decided it best to wait until the babies were actually born.

Several times Kate's cries jarred Rosanna so much that she held her
breath, feeling more and more as if she, too, were a part of the birthing
process. As if in some strange way, she were the babies' mother, too.

O Lord, please help them to arrive safely. . . .

Kate moaned again, and Rosanna's heart went out to her suffering cousin.
She would stay by Kate's side as long as it took, waiting patiently for the
twins' birth.

Reuben hadn't seen so many folk in his house since before James and
Benjamin had married and moved away. More were on hand than could
possibly be of help, yet he was grateful for their presence, a sign of their
care and concern for his mother. Presently, he attempted to occupy his
father's attention even as his mother was seriously ailing, but it was nearly
impossible to keep Noah Fisher away from his bride of over sixty years. How
thankful Reuben was that he'd fetched his Daed right quick after arriving
home and learning of Mammi's condition.

Reuben struggled with the lump in his throat as Daed checked in with
the doctor for probably the tenth time this hour, getting reports every few
minutes. At last the doctor determined his mother should not be moved—at
least not tonight. With Mammi ordered to bed rest, his parents would stay in
the downstairs bedroom whether they liked fellowshipping with "Preacher
Manny's bunch" or not.

Reuben helped the doctor get his mother into the spare room and settled
on the edge of the bed. She was more coherent now and the color had
returned to her face. The doctor had administered a diuretic to lower her
blood pressure, as well as a medication to open her blood vessels, assuring
them that, in time and with rest, she would recover.

Betsy, ever thoughtful and kind, helped dress Reuben's mother, offering
one of her own nightgowns. Once she had settled her under the covers, she
left Mamm alone with Dat, who remained there all during supper.

After the trying events of the day, Reuben was eager to retire early for the
night and told Betsy so. He would not tell her, however, of his encounter
with outspoken Ephram this afternoon, because it would only serve to upset

her more. Ephram had been awful hotheaded, saying some mighty hurtful things. *"Best be cuttin' the cord with Preacher Manny and come back where ya belong,"* his son had spouted off, a deep frown of condemnation on his ruddy face. *"You're embarrassing your family . . . bein' the focus of community criticism 'n' all."*

No doubt Ephram's anger and disappointment had compelled him to say the disrespectful, even harsh, words. Yet Reuben had heard nearly the same from a whole group of men in Bishop Joseph's barn, armed with spiteful threats. Preacher Lapp himself had put pressure on Reuben to sever his ties with Preacher Manny and return to the fellowship of the brethren. But that hadn't smarted as much as his intimidating remark—*"We'll starve you out if you're not careful, Reuben Fisher!"*

Never had Reuben thought someone's beliefs could cause so much loathing. He'd headed home to seek refuge, only to find his mother suffering the aftereffects of an apparent stroke.

What he needed most was Betsy's tender touch on his brow, the loving way she had of caressing his cares away. Reuben went around extinguishing the gas lamps and then took Betsy by the hand to lead her upstairs.

"Oh, he's so tiny," Rosanna said as Ruth Glick, the midwife, placed Kate's son into her arms. She fought back tears, wanting to clearly see his wee red face, so wrinkled and sweet.

"Say hullo to your first son," Kate said weakly between more labor pains—the second baby was coming fast.

Rosanna was surprised at how very light he felt in her arms. Nearly as tiny as a baby doll. Oh, the joy of cradling him so near! And to think a sister or brother was on the way.

Soon her attention turned back to dear Kate, who was clearly struggling harder with this second birth. By the time the blanketed baby boy was replaced with an even smaller infant girl, Kate was unable to control her mournful cries, which shortly became muffled shrieks of pain.

Something's terribly wrong, thought Rosanna, wanting to shield the infant in her arms and to ease her poor, dear cousin's pain.

———

Rosanna did her best to keep her emotions in check as she held Kate's hand. Her cousin reclined slightly in the backseat of the English neighbors' car, groaning and gripping her abdomen. John was at her side, while

Rosanna and Ruth Glick each held one of the babies. Rosanna wasn't even sure which twin snuggled in the crook of her arm; they looked that much alike. But as rosy-faced as the babies were, they were too early and small, and their lungs might have difficulty with breathing. The hospital would keep them in an incubator for some days—possibly longer.

This was not as disappointing as it was worrisome, but Rosanna would not borrow more anxiety than she was already experiencing, what with Kate bearing such enormous pain next to her.

Kate's neighbors had kindly offered to drive all of them, including help-ful Ruth Glick. Such a crowd for one vehicle! On a day like this, Rosanna was thankful for the speed and warmth of the car as it raced toward the hospital. Anything to spare Kate's life.

I wish there was a way to alert Elias, thought Rosanna. She would like for him to join her at the hospital somehow, to meet their perfect children. Probably he sensed something was up, what with her still being away at this late hour.

Are other couples as closely connected? she wondered.

Outside, the shadowy landscape and occasional lights seemed to liter-ally fly by . . . she'd never gone so fast in her life. Goodness, but she could scarcely focus her eyes on the lit houses and other cars. Was this what it was like to be fancy?

She'd heard tell of a group of folk meeting over at Preacher Manny's house and wondered if all of them would be driving cars next thing. Tractors, surely, as that was all *es Gschwetz*—the talk. She wondered if Elias might not have been upset at supper a couple weeks ago about all that ruckus, more than worried about not getting a boy.

Well, he's got himself a son after all . . . and I've got me a daughter.

Now if the doctors could just help Kate . . . and get these little ones to a healthier weight, Rosanna and Elias could bring them home to the snug oak cradles Elias's father had made. Then, and only then, would all be well.

CHAPTER 32

An hour before dawn, Nellie Mae rose and dressed to do all the baking for the day. When the last five pumpkin pies were out of the oven and cooling, she began mixing the eggs and milk for scrambled eggs for everyone.

In spite of Dawdi's protests, Mammi Fisher walked slowly from the bedroom to the kitchen table with the help of her cane. Looking much better this morning, she seemed terribly reluctant to sit at the same table with all of them, even though they were kin and had bedded her down for the night. This struck Nellie as ridiculous, but she had no desire to laugh. Who was her grandmother to arbitrarily slap the Bann on *all* of them, for pity's sake?

Dawdi was less inclined to hover today, Nellie noticed, and he and Dat slipped out to the barn together following breakfast, probably for a man-to-man talk.

Rhoda and Mamma began to wash and dry the breakfast dishes as Mammi headed back to the bedroom for some more rest. Nan politely offered to tend to the bakery shop so Nellie could go and see if she could help out at Kate's. Nellie could hardly wait to set eyes on the babies, so she took the pony and cart over to Beilers', glad for her sister's easygoing manner today.

The pony cart shifted and skittled over the snow, and she wished she'd brought Dat's old sleigh instead. Even so, the cold tranquility was soothing, just as her walk had been yesterday—prior to having words with Rhoda. She shook her head, wondering when Rhoda had become so direct.

Like Mammi Fisher was with Mamma . . .

When Nellie arrived at the Beilers', she was stunned not to see a single buggy parked in the yard. She wouldn't jump to conclusions, but she couldn't help but think Kate might have needed some medical help birthing the twins.

Curiously, she peeked in the back door and saw Kate's niece Lizzy playing with two of the younger children.

"Come in," Lizzy called at her knock, meeting her at the door. "If you're lookin' for Kate, she and the babies went to the hospital last night."

"Are the twins all right?"

Lizzy grinned. "Ach, though ever so tiny . . . a boy and a girl."

Oh joy, one of each!

"Did Rosanna King happen to stop by, do you know?" asked Nellie.

A warm smile spread across Lizzy's face. "Oh my, did she ever. Rosanna said the midwife handed the first twin—the boy—right into her arms nearly the second he was born."

Nellie felt like crying. "That's so dear, ain't?" She assumed Lizzy knew why Rosanna had been on hand for the births.

Nodding, Lizzy agreed. "Kate's the one they're most worried about, I guess."

"Oh no. What's a-matter?"

"All I know is she needed to get to the hospital along with the babies, and right quick."

"Well, it's a good thing you're here," she told Lizzy.

One of Kate's toddlers howled in the kitchen behind them. "I'd better get back to bein' a mother's helper," said Lizzy. "Come again, if you want."

Nellie said good-bye and returned to the pony cart. The hospital was much too far for this colt, even though it was one of Dat's best trained. Had she brought the enclosed family buggy she might have considered making the trip to town. Besides, it was treacherous on the roads, especially with all the traffic and impatient Englischers.

Somewhat disappointed, Nellie headed home, wishing she could offer something besides the rote prayer that now sprang to mind.

———

The rooster's sharp crowing nudged Nellie Mae awake at the break of dawn, and she jumped out of bed, having overslept this Lord's Day.

Mamma was waiting in the kitchen, already laying out fruit and cold cereal, her expression as gray as dusk. "Dat and I would like you to come along with us to Preacher Manny's."

"I'd rather go to Preachin', really." Nellie disliked standing up to Mamma this way, torn between loyalty to her family and love for her beau.

"Well, remember you live under the covering of your father, dear."

Nellie wasn't surprised at Mamma's words. After all, a young woman her age was expected to follow the rules of her father's house without question.

Mamma stood behind Dat's chair at the head of the table, her eyes softening, as if she might be thinking that maybe, just maybe, Nellie had found a beau. "I hope we won't be divided on Sundays . . . you, Dat, and me on the opposite sides of the fence, ya know?" she said sadly.

But she and Dat have moved away from the right side, thought Nellie. *I haven't gone anywhere.*

Without saying more, Mamma turned quickly to make her way out to the summer porch to don her work coat—going to feed the chickens, no doubt.

Feeling glum, Nellie moved to the window. *Oh, the weight Mamma must carry, and now I'm adding to her sorrow.*

Later, after washing and dressing, Nellie was met with a cool response from Nan, who glared at her when they passed in the hall. None of her usually cheerful, "How'd ya sleep?" or *"Gut Mariye*, Nellie Mae!" Nan must've had an earful from Rhoda, for certain.

She felt terribly alone as she left the house to make the long trip on foot to Caleb's uncle's house for Preaching service, glad for her warm snow boots and knitted mittens. Just as her grandparents had refused to live with them because of her parents' beliefs, Nellie was turning down her parents by striking out on her own today, following her heart. *And the tradition of the People*, she thought as she slipped along the snow-packed road.

I'll look ever so odd, sitting alone without Mamma and my sisters, she realized. Odd . . . and a magnet for attention, which she despised.

She hadn't walked but half a mile when Ephram and Maryann, with their children huddled near, came along and stopped the horse and sleigh for her. "Hullo, Nellie Mae! Want a ride?" It was Maryann, looking ever so sympathetic.

Nellie got on board, and chubby Katie crawled over to snuggle on her lap.

"Such a perty Lord's Day, jah?" Maryann said, turning to look at Nellie, but her sad eyes and lifted brow seemed to say, *Sorry you're all alone today. . . .*

Filing into the house with Maryann and her little ones, Nellie felt nearly as conspicuous as if she'd been by herself. She noticed that John and Kate Beiler were absent, and she hoped Kate was improving quickly and that the babies were all right, too. All told, there were several dozen folk missing, and she assumed most were over at Preacher Manny's and not at the hospital with the Beilers. Even Nellie's own grandparents were absent, though on doctor's orders. *Dear, dear Mammi*, she thought, hoping her grandmother would remain on bed rest for a while as suggested. *She'll be fine if she does.*

Fine physically, but what about otherwise? How can Mammi and Dawdi reject their son and family?

The service began, and Nellie Mae sang every song, as she always did; however, she was conscious of the tightness in her throat during silent prayer, when they knelt at the wooden benches. And she was ever so conscious of Caleb . . . and his family. What must they be thinking?

After the first sermon, offered by Preacher Lapp, the bishop rose and began to speak in more conversational tones than she'd ever heard at a Preaching service. He even read the Scriptures in English rather than High German so everyone could understand. She realized at once why he had chosen to do so as he read from the third chapter of Colossians: " 'And let the peace of God rule in your hearts . . . ye are called in one body. . . . ' " He went on to build his sermon on that text, admonishing them to avoid disunity and to steer clear of those claiming "a strange belief."

Nellie found it interesting that the entire sermon was, in fact, pointing fingers at Preacher Manny and his group. The bishop's stern words—"those who uphold such a way of thinking put on a treacherous kind of pride . . . as unto death"—echoed in her memory all through the common meal.

Settling in at the table with Ephram and Maryann, she felt as if all eyes were on her. Some of the older folk went so far as to extend their concern to her, coming up and inquiring of Mammi Fisher, which dispelled some of the tension.

But the awkwardness returned when Maryann took the children off to the washroom, leaving Nellie alone with her obviously brooding brother.

"Dat's mighty foolish, I have to say. I pity you, havin' to live at home."

She wouldn't agree with him, so vicious were his words. "Looks like our grandparents won't be stayin' with us, after all."

"Well, it's Dat's fault, don't you know?"

"Nothin' either of us can do." She looked at him. "Is there?"

He ignored her. "Dawdi Fisher's havin' to move all the way back to Bird-in-Hand, mind you." Shaking his head, he mumbled something she couldn't make out. Was he cussing under his breath?

"Look on the bright side," she said softly. "They're goin' where they'll fit in."

"Puh! They belong in Honey Brook—not clean over there, where we have to go so far out of our way to visit and whatnot."

"So it's an inconvenience, is that it?"

Now it was his turn to pale at her remark.

"You're not thinkin' of Dawdi and Mammi at all."

"Just like Dat ain't thinking 'bout all the trouble he's in," he shot back. "Or 'bout how all this affects us."

So he's peeved because what Dat does reflects poorly on him.

"By the way," Ephram added quickly, "I'm mighty glad to see you here, toein' the line, Nellie Mae."

You sure have an interesting way of showing it, she thought, ever so glad when Aunt Anna Fisher came over and sat next to her. Anna asked about the possibility of Nellie's helping with kitchen cleanup at one of the upcoming weddings, and Nellie was quick to agree. All the same, secretly she hoped this wedding wouldn't be one that Caleb and his family might attend. If so, she would not be able to see him much at all.

When Aunt Anna rose and moved to another part of the long table, Nellie noticed her brother had disappeared. She sighed with relief, well aware of her own floundering feelings this day . . . something akin to swimming up a stream, the current so strong it threatened to drag her under.

She considered Preacher Manny, her own relative, of all things—the man of God's choosing for the People. She felt terribly frustrated, suddenly wondering if she shouldn't hear him out. After all, he had been appointed by God, so what did it mean that he was moving away from his original calling? Here where so many were still honoring their life vow to God and the church.

Preacher Manny was partly the reason her parents had abandoned the church of their childhood and hers. Where was she expected to take her kneeling vow to the People now? Where was she to make her marriage promises someday, to become a good Amish wife to her dear Caleb?

Right here, she told herself. *I'm staying put.*

She was about to help clear tables when Caleb's father stormed toward her, wearing what looked to be an out-and-out scowl. She turned to glance behind her, certain he was heading for someone else.

She was just getting up when he surprised her by speaking to her. "Nellie Mae, mind if I sit with you a minute?"

It was highly unusual for a married man to talk with a single, unrelated young woman. At the request, her neck felt too warm and her heart thumped much too hard. And Caleb . . . where was he?

"Nellie Mae," he began, "I'm mighty curious—where might your parents be today? Your family, as a whole?"

She wanted to remind him of Ephram's family and their presence here, but she felt terribly awkward speaking up to this man.

"My father's . . ." If she finished by telling the truth, she might not see Caleb again, and she was fairly sure that's where this conversation was leading. Oh, she wanted to search out her darling with her eyes. Where was he?

"Nellie?" David Yoder leaned forward, expression sober. "Has your father joined up with Preacher Manny?"

She looked at him, afraid she might burst out crying.

"Would it trouble you to ask Dat instead?" It took all she had, but she'd said precisely what she wanted to—what she *had* to. She must put him off somehow. Would this suffice?

"Well, Nellie Mae Fisher, I believe I'm talkin' to you here and now."

She could not keep her tears in check any longer. Just when her lip began to quiver and she felt as though she might either rise and say something out of order—either that or bawl like a child—just then, Caleb appeared at the back of the room, coming her way.

Ach, thank the Good Lord!

Fearless, as if he'd encountered such confrontations himself, Caleb walked right up to the table and stood to his father's left. "Nellie? I'd like to have a word with you."

He's as forthright as his father. Yet she knew without a doubt he was rescuing her, and she loved him all the more for it.

"Daed," he said, turning to face him, "Nellie Mae's comin' with me for a while."

She wanted to laugh—oh, she wanted to clap. This beau of hers, wasn't he the best? She knew she'd follow him no matter where he led her today, which turned out to be clear to the end of the cornfield and beyond, to the high bluffs overlooking Honey Brook. It was a spot she'd always loved, and there she stood, hand in hand with Caleb . . . then swiftly she was in his arms.

"You are one brave girl," Caleb whispered in her ear before kissing her forehead.

"I was so . . . speechless," she admitted.

He nodded, his forehead pressed against hers, seemingly already aware of the line of questioning his father had taken with her. "Don't feel put upon, Nellie Mae. Please don't."

Well, she *had,* but no longer, not with Caleb's kind and comforting manner. Goodness, she believed she could go through most anything with him by her side . . . with his encouragement. She could tell by his admiring glances and the squeeze of his hand that he adored her all the more for choosing the Old Ways today. And him.

But eventually Nellie had to return home and endure the disapproving glances of her family, knowing Dat would give her a good talking to sooner or later. Suddenly, waiting a full year to wed Caleb seemed much too long.

CHAPTER 33

All Dat could talk about upon arriving home was Preacher Manny's meeting . . . how it had nearly doubled in size this Lord's Day. "What will it be like by next Sunday, with word spreading as it is?" he wondered aloud. Mamma was simply glowing. As for Rhoda and Nan, they seemed to have been won over by a single visit.

The four of them chattered excitedly at the supper table, but Nellie did not feel too left out—not with Caleb's support. She would not embrace the "strange belief" Uncle Bishop had hammered against for two full hours in his sermon.

With the family's topic of talk seemingly limited to one thing, nightfall couldn't come soon enough to suit her, and Nellie slipped away to her room. On the way, she spotted Rhoda and Nan in their own room, their heads bent low over Dat's King James Bible. For this further proof of their companionship, Nellie was envious. Wasn't it bad enough to lose Suzy? Now must she also lose the remainder of her family . . . and to a foreign faith, at that?

She lay down to rest, clinging to the hope of having some good fellowship with Maryann once again—and Rosanna, too, when the new babies were safely home. Perhaps she would spend time with Kate once she was completely well again. She didn't see much chance of enjoying that with Ephram, as it didn't seem to matter which side of the fence you were on with him. Either way, she could not seem to please *that* brother!

She turned on her side in an attempt to get more comfortable, willing herself not to think about Caleb's father's approaching her. She took solace from the fact she would soon put an end to Suzy's dark secrets . . . tomorrow, after she closed the shop for the day, she would destroy the diary.

Suzy's wicked life will never touch another soul. . . .

Washday dawned mighty quick, and since Mamma was in bed and under the weather, the time-consuming chore fell to Nan and Nellie, because

Rhoda had to leave for work earlier than usual. Rhoda didn't say why, which annoyed Nellie, what with having to juggle the washing and the larger-than-normal amounts of baking.

Down in the cellar, Nan talked to Nellie of wishing for an electric washing machine—"maybe even a dryer, too, someday. Lots of folks at yesterday's meeting said such things matter little in the eyes of God." Nellie sighed inwardly and was mighty sure this sister had missed out by not being present for the bishop's warning yesterday at Preaching. *Goodness—seems she's already set on goin' fancy.*

As kindly as was possible, she put up with Nan's evident enthusiasm for modern conveniences, paying closer attention when Nan said she saw "two new groups rising among those at Manny's gathering."

"What do you mean?"

"Just what I said." Nan pushed more clothes into the gas-powered wringer washer. "There's one group that's mostly concerned about knowledge of salvation, like Dat. And there's another group wanting to own tractors and cars and other useful things."

"What's Preacher Manny think of all this?" Nellie had assumed Preacher Manny's splinter group would be consumed with Bible study, like her parents were—not the yearning for fancy things like Nan indicated.

"I don't know exactly," Nan admitted. "He talked only about Scripture, really."

"Can you imagine Dat ever drivin' a car?" Nellie had to ask.

Nan shook her head. "Never."

"But he could fall prey to the other group eventually—like the Beachy Amish—and desire those things, ain't so?"

Nan laughed a little. "Mamma will keep that from happening, don't ya know?"

Nellie agreed that was probably true.

"I've heard some talk of Dat's cousin Jonathan bein' interested in cars," Nan added.

"Does he own one yet?"

"He will soon, I 'spect . . . according to the grapevine. Doubtless he'll have himself electric next and a tractor with rubber tires, too. Why not, when he's already shunned."

Nan went on. "You should go to Preacher Manny's with us and see for yourself, Nellie Mae. I think you'd be surprised, just maybe."

She stiffened. "I'm not interested in turnin' my back on the Old Ways."

"Ach . . . the Old Ways." Nan chuckled. "Just imagine not havin' to hang all these clothes on the line, and on such a frosty day, too." With that she flounced upstairs with another wet load, leaving Nellie to ponder every speck of their conversation. If nothing else, she was glad Nan was at least speaking to her again.

———

Rosanna sat in the hospital waiting room, exerting some degree of patience as she awaited further word on Cousin Kate's condition. Being the only Amishperson in the room made her feel like a pea out of its pod, yet she was determined to see Kate. Unfortunately, she didn't know precisely how to go about requesting a visit, what with so much hustle and bustle in the hallways as doctors and nurses came and went.

After a time, she rose and searched for what looked like an information desk to ask about her cousin.

"Are you related to Mrs. Beiler?" the woman asked, recognition in her eyes.

It's the head covering, no doubt.

"I'm her first cousin," Rosanna replied.

The woman paused, nodding and glancing down at a list of names. "Mrs. Beiler's one popular woman, or so it seems. She's had a total of nine cousins visit her already."

Rosanna didn't see how she was going to convince her that she, too, was a cousin. She might have turned to leave without seeing Kate at all, if Aunt Rachel hadn't walked toward her at that moment. Rachel came up and slipped her arm around Rosanna's waist, leading her down the hall. "Are they keepin' you from Kate?" she asked.

"Not sure, really." Rosanna paused. "Is she goin' to be all right?"

"Well, she's terribly weak . . . they're watchin' her closely. She lost an awful lot of blood. You haven't heard?"

Rosanna shook her head. "I'm so sorry to learn of it. Will she be able to go home soon?" She didn't dare ask about the twins, because she wasn't sure if Aunt Rachel even knew yet that her grandbabies were going to be raised by Rosanna.

"Jah . . . soon." Rachel gazed seriously at her, then whispered, "Ach, Rosanna, I think what Kate's doin' is downright peculiar, 'tween you and me. I just yesterday heard from John what he and Kate decided to do for you and

Elias." Her aunt seemed a bit put out; then her eyes brightened some. "Even so, it seems the twins will know who their first Dat and Mamma are, jah?"

Rosanna recalled that awkward conversation and nodded her head. "That's what Kate wants."

Aunt Rachel touched her hand. "I'll be wantin' to see my grandyoung'uns quite a lot, I'm sure you know."

Rosanna agreed, feeling sorry for Rachel, who was only now getting used to the idea of her flesh-and-blood grandbabies going home with someone else. "You can come see them anytime. In fact, I'll be happy for the extra help."

Rachel smiled suddenly. "Oh, you'll have all kinds of help, trust me."

"Denki," whispered Rosanna, grateful Rachel seemed accepting of the plan. "Thank you ever so much."

———

Nellie was grateful when Nan stopped by the shop midmorning with the last of the baked goods, even going so far as to help unload them into the display. Once her sister left to start cooking the noontime meal for Mamma, however, Nellie took great care to rearrange the gingerbread and oatmeal cakes. "I'm a fussbudget," she muttered, knowing it was ever so true.

Going around the front of the display case, she stepped back, pretending to be a potential customer, surveying the place. Just then, dark-haired Joy Landis entered. Nellie was surprised to see her on a school day. "Hullo," she said. "Can I help you?"

The girl smiled shyly, and Nellie caught sight of the tiny American flags on her earlobes. Nellie must have stared too long at her earrings, because Joy reached up to touch one ear and asked, "Do you like these, Nellie Mae?"

Nellie felt her cheeks flush red and forced a smile. "Jah, they're perty."

"I'm wearing them because it's Veterans Day. We're off school today."

Nellie vaguely remembered having a day's break on a November Monday back when she was a student. The teacher had told her the holiday was to honor soldiers who'd fought in America's wars, so it wasn't one a peace-loving Amish girl was likely to recall.

Joy suddenly seemed awkward, looking away as if perhaps she had something on her mind but didn't know how to express it.

"Care for a sample?" Nellie offered, thinking that might be what she wanted.

"No . . . but thanks anyway." Joy strolled nearer the display case, eyeing several kinds of cookies.

Nellie went around the counter to stand and wait, wishing she could think of something to say to fill the silence. She thought of bringing up Joy's cousin Darlene, wondering how she was doing *this* school year, but then felt she had no business inquiring.

Just when she thought Joy was going to stare a hole in the peanut blossoms, she looked up, meeting Nellie's gaze. "I'm not here to buy anything today but because I promised my mother I'd set the record straight."

Listening, Nellie did not move an inch.

"I know some people around town thought your sister was a wild one, but Suzy helped a whole bunch of kids from school. I'm not kidding."

Nellie studied her. "Why are you sayin' this?"

Joy looked over her shoulder at the car parked outside. "My mother didn't think you believed her."

"Why should I?" Nellie's words slid out too quickly. Joy would surely know by this that Nellie assumed her own dead sister was as wayward as gossip had her.

"You thought she was a rebel?" asked Joy.

Nellie couldn't admit this to an Englischer. "Ach, I didn't say that."

"Well, just so you know, Suzy was the best thing that ever happened to Darlene." Then, without saying good-bye, Joy turned and left the shop.

Nellie watched the slender girl slip into her mother's car. It was obvious Joy had been coerced into coming here, and Nellie felt sorry for her. Yet she was glad, too, that Joy had found the courage.

"Goodness' sakes," Nellie Mae murmured aloud, rather stunned. "I guess it's time to read the rest of your diary, Suzy . . . ain't so?"

CHAPTER 34

Nellie Mae raised the bed mattress and tugged on Suzy's diary. She would give it one more look, hoping to find something good in her sister's story. Even so, she dreaded wading through more of the muck and mire of Suzy's Rumschpringe.

Flipping through the pages, well past the spot where she'd given up before, Nellie began to read again, hoping to find something good this time.

Today I spotted a weasel's footprints in the mud along the stream on the other side of the road. Of course I had to follow them. Such natural things are so appealing. Honestly, it's like there are two of me. . . .

Suzy's work boots squished in the moist soil along the creek as she followed the footprints, wondering where they might lead. She had wandered away from the house, wishing Nellie might come exploring with her, but there were customers, so Suzy didn't bother to ask. She followed the weasel's footprints all the way through the expanse of field adjacent to the neighbors' land.

As she did so, she pondered the weasel-like way Jay Hess had behaved in recent weeks. She had not seen this side of him before—a spoiled child throwing a tantrum . . . and all because he couldn't have his way with her.

To top things off, she'd happened upon some clean-cut boys passing out invitations to a "lively meeting," as they called it. Truly a temptation it was, especially since the invitation came from the tall blond boy, Christian Yoder. His face reminded her of someone, though she couldn't place who. She supposed if he hadn't been so nice and talkative, she might not have accepted.

Naturally she knew better than to tell Jay of her Friday evening plans, lest he fly into a rage as he did if she so much as looked at another fellow. She'd wished he'd play by some of his own rules, since *he* flirted with other girls till the cows came home. She surprised herself by looking forward to an evening without him.

When that Friday evening arrived, Suzy slipped away after supper to the meeting, taking the pony cart. There were lots of young people—English and Plain—in attendance. Not many were in Amish dress like she was.

She'd noticed before merely in passing how pretty the Tel Hai camp-grounds were. The cedarwood tabernacle building, with its open sides, drew her as she walked in behind a group of distinctly Mennonite girls, their hair combed straight back and topped by their cup-shaped, pleated white head coverings.

The music was as lively as Christian had said it would be—and inspiring. A young evangelist wearing a black suit shared God's words, fervently urging repentance. Hundreds were present, including many couples and families sitting in lawn chairs—even buggies parked along the road so their occupants could listen in. Folk were transfixed by the sober words coming from the young minister, and many wiped their eyes, brushing back tears.

Suzy sat upright, captivated by the passion emanating from the preacher behind the wooden pulpit positioned in the center of the long platform. She was amazed to see dozens of weeping people rushing to the timber altar at the end of the sermon . . . and so many teenagers gripping hands, leading friends to the front.

Suzy couldn't miss Christian in his yellow shirt. He sat nearby with three other young men, all apparently without girlfriends. None of them responded to the call at the altar, so Suzy assumed they were already among the "saved." Christian held his Bible open to share with the boy seated next to him, occasionally bowing his head in prayer as the evangelist addressed the group kneeling at the front.

With a name like Christian, he must be from a Plain background, she guessed, but his loud shirt indicated otherwise. *Unless he's as unruly as I am.* But she doubted a wayward boy would be promoting an event like this—a church service in a lovely, peaceful setting like none she'd ever been to.

The evangelist left the pulpit to walk back and forth. "Listen to the Bible: 'These things have I written unto you that believe on the name of the Son of God; that ye may know that ye have eternal life, and that ye may believe on the name of the Son of God.' Notice the words 'that ye may know.' "

I want to know.

Suzy thought of her boyfriend—his reckless behavior, the wild friends she and Jay ran with. Then she thought of her family, steeped in tradition. Were they *all* lost, as this preacher declared? What did the Good Book really say?

She clenched her hands, repressing her desire to get up and walk to the front, rejecting what the evangelist called "the convicting power of God." With tears threatening to spill down her cheeks, she rose and slipped out the back.

The next day, she wandered off to the wooded area beyond the paddock after chores, watching for springtime birds.

Everywhere she looked, she saw God's handiwork. The truth of His creation surrounded her; even the cross-shaped limbs on the oldest oak tree reminded her of the young minister's sermon. *"Nailed to a tree, the Savior died for you. Because of His life sacrifice, you can have salvation in His name."*

She thought again of the tearstained faces of the young people rushing to the altar, their obvious relief and joy after they prayed with the evangelist. Maybe the boyish preacher really did know what he was talking about.

Although she'd always sensed it, Suzy saw a fundamental order in the woods this day, from the tallest, most stately tree to the smallest woodland mouse.

Order is everywhere, she thought, spotting a grouping of tulip poplars, or whitewood trees, as Dat called them. Their highest branches swept together in one direction, and they made the maples and oaks seem small.

Why, God even directs the smallest sprout in and out of dormancy, she thought as she walked, embracing the beauty and grateful to have heard such wonderful-good news of God's love. The words of the young preacher persisted in her memory. *"Read for yourself—don't take my word for it,"* he'd said.

Wavering back and forth, Suzy struggled, knowing she was at a crossroads. Either she could continue down her present path with Jay and his friends, or she could grab hold of the Savior's hand and come out of the darkness.

She longed to know this Jesus the preacher had talked about. Her whole life, she'd never heard such things.

Jay caught up with Suzy on Tuesday when she was running errands in town. He asked where she'd kept herself on Friday night and why she hadn't shown up at the appointed spot. She invited him to come along with her to hear "something truly good" but stopped short of saying it was a church gathering, hoping to win him over by telling about the exciting music.

When he asked where this cool place was, she said east of Route 10 on Beaver Dam Road. He must have put it together, because he sneered and said, "You must think I'm stupid, Suzy. I wouldn't be caught dead with a bunch of fanatics."

"Then you won't be seein' *me* anymore!" She turned on her heel and started to leave.

At that Jay began to ridicule her fiercely, gouging her with every conceivable slur. She had never expected this kind of treatment from someone who had once claimed to love her. Now she doubted he had ever cared for her at all.

When later Darlene asked if she'd broken it off with Jay, Suzy admitted she had. As much as she wanted to have a boyfriend, the tug toward the rustic tabernacle was stronger.

As the week wore on, Suzy sneaked peeks at Dat's English Bible, folding slips of paper into it to mark her place—especially in the New Testament, where her father wouldn't see them. She found several of the verses the evangelist had referred to and copied them carefully in her diary. She was eager to learn more, but her loss of Jay was in the back of her mind. She thought of all the pieces of her heart she'd given him, wishing she could do most anything to have them back.

While Suzy wanted to share her loss with her closest sister, she didn't tell Nellie what was happening, fearful Nellie wouldn't understand—not when the boy involved was English. And not when her heart was being pulled in a new, equally forbidden direction . . . away from what she'd always been taught.

How she wished her family had more religious understanding. As far as she could tell, they merely lived in accordance with the teachings of their ancestors. Sure, Dat and Mamma took the family to Preaching every other Sunday, but it felt to Suzy that they were simply putting in their three hours. There was no talk of a relationship with God's Son, no urgency toward Christ. No, the way they were going, bound by the rules of the church and the bishop, nothing apart from a divine miracle could save her family.

They're lost to tradition.

That second Friday evening at the tabernacle, Suzy was one of the first to walk "the sinner's aisle." Even though the minister was older this time, and possibly wiser, the message was the same. "God's promise of salvation can be trusted," he stated. "It is clear—'Verily, I say unto you, He that heareth my word, and believeth on him that sent me, hath everlasting life, and shall not come into condemnation; but is passed from death unto life.' "

No condemnation . . . She wept, thinking of this. *Lord Jesus, I trust in you as my Savior today*, Suzy prayed from her heart. She rose from the altar with tears on her face.

The very next day she set out to share her new faith with her English friends, inviting Darlene to go to the Honey Brook Restaurant to have ice cream. Darlene immediately agreed—a surprise, since she typically had been reluctant to spend any time at all with those she called "goody-goodies."

"You're not happy with the way your life's goin', are ya?" she asked Darlene.

Tears sprang to her friend's eyes.

"Won't you come with me to the meetings?" Suzy asked.

"I can't."

"You won't be sorry," she urged. "Just this once?"

Darlene shook her head. "I'm into things you can't begin to know about."

"Well, I don't have to . . . and God already does."

They talked together till their ice cream was nearly soup. Even though Darlene had refused her invitation, Suzy prayed she might change her mind.

At the next revival meeting, Christian Yoder noticed Suzy and went to sit with her. They got to talking, and it turned out he was Rebekah Yoder's second cousin, Christian's family having left the Amish decades ago. Soon Suzy had met his siblings—all boys—and their friends, finding fulfillment in the wholesome company of this brand-new group.

As her life began its compelling new chapter, Suzy spent quite a lot of time praying, asking God to bring her family to salvation. "Whatever it takes for them to come to you, Lord, I am willin'." She longed for her family to experience this rebirth, and she made a point of praying nightly for them over in James's former bedroom, the most secluded spot in the house.

A few weeks later, Darlene stopped her on the street. "Do you have time for a soda?" she asked. Suzy nodded, and when they'd settled into a booth at the restaurant, Darlene broke down and revealed how hopeless her life was. "I've been watching you lately, Suzy, and . . . whatever you've got, I want it," she admitted.

Suzy could hardly walk for flying. God was already answering her prayers!

She even had a new boyfriend—Christian's brother Zachary. Zach's goal in life was to make it to the mission field, an idea that appealed greatly to Suzy.

It was Zach's idea for their entire group to go out row boating on Saturday afternoon, June ninth. Suzy decided it would be the perfect opportunity for Nellie Mae to meet the Yoder brothers. Truly, she had no reason to be ashamed of this circle of friends.

When Suzy invited Nellie to go along, asking on behalf of Christian, she was surprised at her sister's strong disinterest. Nellie was obviously put out, even defensive toward the suggestion, and Suzy wondered if perhaps her sister had a beau she didn't know about. They argued about Suzy's plans, Nellie huffing about the room, saying, "It doesn't look right for you to be runnin' with a group of mostly boys—and Englischers, too—for pity's sake! What are you thinkin', Suzy?"

"But the boys are all brothers, and there'll be girls along, too. I thought it was kind of Zach's brother to offer to pair up with you. It would be just as friends. He's ever so nice . . . his name's Christian, and he certainly is that."

"I don't accept blind dates," Nellie replied, frowning. "'Specially not with worldly boys."

Suzy had known it was rather optimistic to hope Nellie might join them, but she'd honestly hoped—and prayed—her sister might say yes. She was completely taken with the idea of getting her sister out on the water, surrounded by her believer-friends. After all, Jesus had taught His disciples in a boat out on the Sea of Galilee, hadn't He? Honestly, she felt called to this day.

If only Nellie Mae hadn't gone and spoiled things by being ever so stubborn!

Nellie rose, the diary clasped tightly to her chest. She didn't know what to think, yet the tears flowed all the same. *Suzy ran wild for a time but found something far better in the very strange beliefs our own bishop preaches against,* she thought.

It was impossible to disregard Suzy's zeal. And to think that God had seemed to answer Suzy's constant prayers for Dat and Mamma . . . why, nearly the whole family looked to be headed down that selfsame path.

Whatever it takes, Lord, Suzy had prayed.

Nellie stopped for a moment and looked at the diary in her hands. Had Suzy unknowingly offered up her own life for her family? Was such a thing even possible?

Lo and behold . . . she knew. Dat's and Mamma's grief over Suzy's death had opened their hearts wide. They had feared the worst possible loss—everlasting punishment for their youngest. If what Dat and Mamma believed was right, then Suzy was with the Lord. *Oh, to think . . .*

Nellie moved to the window, opening to the last page of the diary. She brushed her tears away so she could see the words, the final writings of a girl who had fallen in love with God's Son.

> *I wish Nellie and I hadn't fought this morning. I wish she would change her mind and go along with Zach and me and the others. She wouldn't have liked Jay and his friends, I know that. But my new brothers and sisters, so to speak? There's no question she would be ever so fond of them.*
>
> *Maybe someday she'll meet the Yoders . . . in God's good time.*
>
> *Ach, but I love Nellie Mae. She's simply acting like a big sister, trying to keep me safe—always worried about appearances, and all.*
>
> *So it's all right. I forgive Nellie, dear sister of mine.*

Nellie cried, unable to stop the tears. "Oh, Suzy, how I wish now I'd gone. I didn't know it was so important to you, that these weren't the reckless Englischers the grapevine whispered about." Her shoulders shook as regret once again engulfed her. "I'll never understand why you went boating in such deep waters without a life jacket. . . . I would've made sure you had one."

Nellie threw herself on the bed and wept, with every sob slowly releasing the guilt that had bound her. Suzy's precious, life-giving words echoed in her mind: *It's all right. I forgive Nellie. . . .*

CHAPTER 35

A t first light Tuesday, Bishop Joseph held a meeting in the barn between those who were "causing a nuisance" and a group of men who supported the Old Ways. He'd spread the word the day before, and no matter their opinion, Reuben noted the men of the community had complied by showing up.

The scene unfolding before him was more cantankerous than any he'd experienced, including the meeting some years earlier, when the church district had divided after growing too large to accommodate house meetings. There had been a heated squabble that day, too, what with people wanting to go with this or that relative or friend.

Yet that was almost comical compared to this, he thought, looking at the now thirty or so men lined up along one side. If Reuben hadn't known which of them belonged to Manny's group, he might've spotted the believers by their meek demeanor and the tractor-lovers by their set expressions and arms over their chests, as if ready for combat. The bishop's stern bunch were generally the eldest among them, and some looked downright befuddled as they tugged on their long beards.

The bishop began by making a declaration. "Some of yous are here because your wives want electric and you want a car to drive. Others want to do missions work overseas or win your neighbors to a new gospel." He paused to inhale audibly, as if he were making a point with his very breath. "All of you dissenters are less than satisfied with the way things have always been. Don't say this ain't so!"

Reuben saw the fire in his older brother's eyes and wondered how he could ever salvage his relationship with Joseph after these weeks of infighting.

When the bishop was finished, he allowed discussion. First one spoke, then another, in an orderly fashion, until Old Joe Glick aligned himself with Preacher Manny. All of a sudden Reuben's father spoke out sharply against them, his face growing so red that several men on his side had to restrain him. Even at this early-morning hour, the uproar had been ignited.

211

Reuben couldn't have gotten a word in edgeways if he'd wanted to. He would've liked to defend his cousin Manny, and he would also have liked to see his eldest brother have a tender heart toward the Lord Jesus.

A sudden flutter of wings startled him and the others, and their gaze followed to the wooden rafters, where two phoebes flew round and round, as though frantically searching for a way out.

"Well, lookee there." Preacher Manny pointed upward. "Those birds are like me . . . like some of the rest of you, too. They feel as trapped as if they were in a silo—can't find the door."

"*Himmel*, there 'tis!" hollered one, pointing to the barn doors as guffaws erupted.

"Jah, be gone . . . get thee behind me, Satan!" said another, thrashing his black hat.

Manny attempted to still the crowd. "Come now, brethren—"

At this, the bishop waved his arms. He bowed his head, working his jaw while the crowd silenced. When he raised his eyes and spoke at last, his words were barely audible. "Does it not matter, beloved, that you are in danger of losin' your very souls?"

Unexpectedly Reuben thought of Suzy. He leaned his head back to look at the long rafters supporting the barn above, wondering when the phoebes had flown away. And to where?

The bishop continued. "You leave me no choice but to—"

"You're goin' to shun us all?" asked a man smack-dab next to Preacher Manny. "Then we'll take the whole of our families with us!"

A roar of support filled the room.

Reuben locked his knees. There was no way out . . . not the way this was going. They were devouring each other.

The bishop stepped forward. "But you're not taking *all* your family. Many of them are already alienated from you. Will you trade the fellowship of your extended family for tractors and cars?"

The roar faded.

The bishop turned to Preacher Manny. "Will you abandon your grandsons for an arrogant gospel?"

Reuben shuddered. *Arrogant?*

David Yoder placed his hand on the bishop's shoulder, eyes blazing. "Look how you're divided amongst yourselves. For this you'll abandon the tradition of our ancestors? For this you'll risk losin' your families?" He fairly growled. "As for me and my house, we will choose the Lord."

Reuben's face burned with resentment. Choosing tradition was not choosing God. To Reuben's dismay, the crowd of men began to argue loudly again.

At last the bishop stepped forward, his hands raised high.

A hush spread over the barn as he went around, pointing to each man to inquire of his decision. After the first man, the bishop literally began to take roll, asking for a "yea" or "nay" on upholding the Ordnung. Some clearly felt put on the spot, and Reuben, for one, disliked his brother's approach.

When Joseph came at last to Reuben, his jaw quivered. "Where do you stand, brother?"

Reuben fixed his eyes on the bishop. "The Ordnung is not the way to salvation. I say 'no.' "

His older brother nodded, jerking his head. "Well, then. We have a split down the middle . . . nearly fifty-fifty."

Once more bedlam erupted in the barn.

After several attempts to regain control, the bishop merely shook his head. In dismay he turned and headed for the barn door, yet the arguing continued.

That's it, Reuben thought. *We're as good as excommunicated!*

He'd prayed before arriving today, asking God to give him insight and the wisdom to make a suggestion to the bishop at the right moment, if indeed the time came. He stepped forward now, calling for peace. "My brother— our bishop—needs a reprieve." He waited for them to turn to look at him before adding, "Don't you see we're gettin' nowhere?"

"We'll have the way of our forefathers," David Yoder shouted.

Cheers backed him up.

"Let's be respectful 'bout this, brethren—for the sake of our families and our heritage, if not for the Lord God almighty." With that Reuben left to find Joseph.

When he found him in the woodshed, the bishop was pacing. "Bishop Joseph," he said. "My brother by blood and under God, may I have a word?"

The bishop looked his way, eyes moist. "What is it, Reuben?"

"I appeal to all that is good and right. Not only are families rending asunder, but the conflict is eatin' all of us in this community alive." He stopped, praying silently, then went on. "If I might be so bold, a wide-scale shunning may not be the answer. It was never meant to be used in this way, was it?"

Joseph frowned.

"The best chance for those who are in error to see the light—if indeed we're in error—isn't to shun us, but to keep lines of communication open, jah?"

"What do you suggest?"

The man of God is inquiring of me? "Why not encourage harmony . . . so desired amongst us?" Reuben said.

The bishop's eyes were kind; the fire was tamed.

"While in prayer the past weeks," Reuben continued, "the Lord revealed a plan to me. I've told no one . . . 'cept now I'm tellin' you. Why not offer a peaceable parting? Let each man choose his path, under God, for his own family."

"Sounds like the children of Israel—every man doin' what is right in his own eyes."

Reuben should've seen that coming.

The bishop stood tall, his jaw set. He squinted at an uncut log, then he picked up his ax and flung it deep into the piece of wood, where it stayed. "I've got loose rocks to haul out of my fields today—work to be done. Come. I need to finish what's been started."

The men immediately ceased their talking when the bishop walked into the barn with Reuben at his side. Reuben joined his cousins Jonathan and Preacher Manny, not knowing what the outcome would be.

His elder brother straightened, his mouth a thin line. "Those of you who insist on following your own way unto perdition, so be it. If you're askin' for my say-so to abandon the beliefs of your fathers and the Lord God and heavenly Father who brought our ancestors out of martyrdom, then you have three months to choose your side without penalty of the Bann. Either go or stay—leave the Old or embrace the faith of your fathers. If you wait longer than the ninety days, you'll be shunned. Now, I wash my hands of this."

Bewildered, yet thankful, Reuben hurried home to Betsy and breakfast. *'Tis nearly a miracle. . . .*

Over a breakfast of fried eggs, German link sausage, waffles, and black coffee, Reuben shared the bishop's surprising announcement with Betsy and the girls. His wife said little, but he could tell by her raised eyebrows that she was as shocked as he was.

Nellie spoke up, though. "It's about time for all this to settle down, ain't so?"

That's the truth, he thought, truly relieved. Now he could continue to have good fellowship with Ephram and others, including his parents, who were scheduled to move to Bird-in-Hand tomorrow. He'd offered to help with his parents' relocation, but the way things had gone with Mamm's last visit here, Reuben's younger brother thought it best to "leave things be."

His thoughts turned to the upcoming Sunday meeting, and he felt energized whenever he pondered hearing the teachings of the Good Book with like-minded souls.

Now that their path was clearer, Reuben anticipated a call at some point for the ordination of a second minister in addition to Preacher Manny. And years down the road there might be need for a bishop, as well. For now, odd as it might be, his brother would no doubt continue to oversee them.

Silently, he offered a prayer of thanksgiving for God's prompting him to propose a peaceable schism. Who'd ever heard of such a thing? But the bishop had heeded, and for that there was much cause for praise.

CHAPTER 36

Nellie was both intrigued and nervous about going to Preacher Manny's house the Lord's Day following the bishop's declaration. Suzy's diary had awakened in her an intense curiosity, and she intended to find out more about the reason for her sister's devotion to her faith.

Dat said not a word, but Mamma smiled and nodded when Nellie followed Rhoda and Nan into the horse-drawn sleigh. The day was brisk and dark clouds threatened flurries, yet Nellie had an air of anticipation as they rode over the snow-packed roads already heavily rutted by steel buggy wheels.

Arriving at Manny's, she noticed right away the fifteen or so gray family buggies lining the side yard. It felt odd not to file in after the men and boys, as the womenfolk usually did. In other ways, though, the house-church gathering was less like the informal Bible study she'd imagined it to be, and more like an Old Order service, with the men and boys sitting on the right, and the women, young children, and babies on the left.

Preacher Manny's words and the verses he read and explained in the packed-out house moved Nellie to tears as she sat between Mamma and Nan.

Do I feel like Suzy did . . . her first visit to the tabernacle?

The singing was hearty—two songs from memory from the *Ausbund*, their old songbook, and another she'd heard only at one of the more lively Sunday Singings—"What a Friend We Have in Jesus."

Preacher Manny mentioned briefly the coming church split, advising those present to search their hearts for their future. Most likely the group would eventually become a new order—a designation Nellie had never heard before. "Each man and each woman must make this a matter of prayer."

Each woman? Now, Nellie found that interesting.

Certainly Suzy had embraced salvation for herself, not waiting for a man—the brethren or her future husband—to impart it to her. The road of Suzy's life had curved, then turned again.

Nellie Mae tried to look about her discreetly, aware of Ephram's and

Maryann's absence. Dat must be feeling it even more so, with his family incomplete here in this meeting place. As for herself, Nellie yearned more for Caleb's presence. What would he think of hearing Scripture passages "read in context," as Preacher Manny made a point to say. She wished, too, that Caleb could witness the enthusiasm springing from their minister as he instructed them, his face shining like a lighthouse beacon.

The longer the meeting lasted, the more Nellie understood why these people sought to experience God's grace, something she'd failed to comprehend before reading Suzy's diary. She confessed to herself that she wished to know something like it with Caleb; such a blending of hearts would be the icing on the cake for their relationship. *And for our future*, she thought.

And yet Nellie wanted to know whether giving herself over to this still-foreign belief was the only way to know the grace her dear sister—and parents—seemed to have found. *Is this for me?*

When it came time to pray, they turned and knelt at their chairs as was their usual custom, but Preacher Manny led them aloud. Dare she learn how to pray like this, just as Dat prayed—not to receive answers so much as to reveal her heart?

Hesitant as she was about appearing to turn away from what she had been taught, Nellie Mae wanted to know more. It was impossible not to sense the joy of this gathering. Caleb should see it for himself.

She would write to Caleb this afternoon and invite him to attend with her next Lord's Day.

———

Caleb was not surprised to see a letter from Nellie Mae in the mailbox Tuesday afternoon, but he was astonished at her bold request.

Dear Caleb,

Will you consider going to Preacher Manny's for church next Sunday? I want to know your honest opinion. . . .

Caleb could not believe his eyes. What had happened to the girl who'd assured him of her faithfulness to the Old Order? How could she be interested in Preacher Manny's rebellious talk?

His temples throbbed. Reading the letter again, he noticed she'd signed it, *With love, Nellie Mae*. Seeing that, he took hope.

Our love is still alive, he assured himself, determined to talk her out of this impulsive idea.

He stuffed the letter into his pants pocket and returned to the barn, recalling their walk to the bluffs behind his uncle's farmhouse, after Daed had confronted Nellie Mae at the common meal. How was it possible for her to open her mind to change when she had been so strong in her stance that day? Hadn't she vowed her loyalty?

If Daed gets wind of this . . .

Caleb scarcely knew how to persuade his father of the depth of his love for Nellie . . . the rightness of his choice. It was a rare departure from the norm for a son to confide such matters, but his father had obviously figured out whom he was seeing—thanks to Rebekah, probably. "I shouldn't need to defend my preference for a mate," he muttered, heading out to the far pasture to tend to the cattle's water.

He must see Nellie, and before next Sunday. No doubt she had anticipated some resistance from him. Perhaps she'd hoped he would mull over the letter and acquiesce, if only for a single Sunday.

Caleb couldn't begin to read her mind. Even so, he knew one thing: He would follow the mandates of the Ordnung at any cost . . . and once he had talked sense into Nellie, he was sure she would, too.

———

Nellie Mae still smelled the sweetness of the bakery as she hurried up the steps to her room. Tuesdays were exceptionally good days for selling pastries. Most people did their washing on Mondays around here—English folk included—making Tuesday the more popular day to get out and purchase goodies from Nellie's Simple Sweets.

Lighting the lantern, she happily settled into her room for the night. She began to take her hair down and brush it, thinking of Caleb. Her letter had surely arrived at her darling's by now, and she could only guess what he'd thought. The sad truth of the matter was that the planned split of the People was tremendously complicated, especially with her father and Caleb's going separate ways. Yet Uncle Bishop seemed to think it for the best, even though he was relinquishing his power by handing over the ultimate decision to the heads of households.

Dear Uncle, he must be relieved in a way. She would not want to be in his shoes, nor her aunt Anna's. The sanctioned split could not possibly go well. Already she'd heard from the grapevine that some were beginning to behave like sheep needing a shepherd. *Cars are an awful big enticement,* she thought.

She was glad Uncle Bishop was allowing people ninety days to make up their minds. *Will Caleb and his family cross over, too?*

The barbed manner in which Caleb's father had recently approached her seemed to make the likelihood of his ever leaving the Old Order extremely slim. All Nellie Mae could do was hope for a truly peaceful resolution in spite of Caleb's and her misery.

———

Nellie Mae had curled up in bed, snug in her warm cotton nightgown, yet unable to sleep. Having retired earlier than the rest of the house, she stared at the ceiling, not counting sheep but days.

What would Suzy have thought of all this?

She opened the drawer next to her. Suzy's Kapp strings lay in her diary as a bookmark of sorts. Nellie had wanted to mark the spot where Suzy's life had made a turn for the better. *Is she with the Lord because someone invited her to hear another side to things? Could it be?*

She wondered about that and pictured Caleb sitting alongside Dat and her brothers, all in a row at Manny's meeting. What would happen if he came?

Still imagining the scene, she fell into a deep sleep.

Some time later, she happened to hear a *tick-tick* on her windowpane.

Sitting up, she thought she saw a flicker of light, too.

Am I dreaming?

Heart in her throat, Nellie Mae scurried to the window and looked out. There, standing in the snow below, was Caleb, shining his flashlight into her eyes.

Ach, is this the night? Has he come to propose?

She unlocked the window, raised it, and poked her head out. "I'll be down in a minute," she whispered. "Will you meet me at the back door?"

Caleb turned off his flashlight just that quick, and she hurried to shut out the frigid air, pushing down hard on the window frame. "Oh, goodness . . . what'll I do?"

Nearly in a panic, she stumbled about, lighting the lantern and snatching up her white bathrobe and slippers—but no, she couldn't go down in her nightclothes. What was she thinking?

Lickety-split, she changed into her Sunday best and brushed her long hair, pushing it back over her shoulders. Only family members were supposed to see it hanging free of her bun and Kapp, but she'd already kept Caleb waiting long enough. Suddenly she laughed softly, realizing that Caleb would see her like this for many years to come. *I'm going to be his bride, for goodness' sake!*

After taking a moment to make her bed, Nellie snatched up the lantern, carrying it down the long staircase, glad for the solitude of the hour. She considered Maryann's emphatic remark—that the girl always knew, supposedly, when this night had arrived. *She* hadn't had the slightest inkling, or had she somehow missed it at the last cider-making frolic?

More fully awake now, she began to worry that Caleb might have been disturbed by her letter. Put out, even.

But he's here! What does it mean?

Tiptoeing across the kitchen floor, Nellie Mae hurried to the summer porch, eager to lead her beau to her room, where they would sit on the pretty loveseat, holding hands as he spoke tender words of love.

Nellie held the lantern high as she went to the back door, smiling her welcome. "Oh, Caleb . . . it's so good to see you!"

"You, too, Nellie Mae." He seemed surprised at her hair . . . first looking, then not looking. He rubbed his hands together, his cheeks rosy red, his eyes meeting hers.

"Come in and get warm," she offered. "We can talk in my room, if you want."

His face darkened, his eyes serious. "Nellie, I'm not here for that. . . ."

She felt her mouth drop. "All right," she said.

He's not going to ask me to marry him.

"We need to talk, Nellie Mae."

She paused. "Where?" She glanced over her shoulder. The kitchen was vacant and dark.

"Best not be wakin' up your Dat." Caleb glanced at her again, and his gaze admiringly followed the length of her hair. "Can you bundle up and go ridin'? I brought some heavy lap robes . . . and some hot bricks."

She forced a sad little smile. He waited for her to roll her hair into a makeshift bun so she could push it into her black winter bonnet. Then she donned her heaviest coat and other winter clothing, all the while her heart sinking.

What will he say?

They pulled out of the lane slowly, without speaking. Then, once they were out on the main road, Caleb began to talk. "I read your letter, Nellie."

He reached for her hand, but his glove felt stiff against her mittens. "Don't you understand what this means . . . what you're asking?"

She swallowed hard. "Jah, but the meeting was ever so interesting. Nothing like what I s'posed."

"It's foolishness, that's what! Heresy—the things Preacher Manny's teaching." His voice was earnest, pleading.

She felt as if she might literally sink into the seat. She'd believed the same thing before reading Suzy's diary, but now she did not wish to swiftly dismiss the teachings that had transformed her sister's life. "But, Caleb, if you could just hear what I heard . . . if you could just help me understand."

"I don't need to go. I know what's bein' said."

She sighed. "You're judgin' by what others say? Ach, the rumor mill will be the death of us."

"Now, Nellie . . . love."

She was torn between the submissive way she'd been taught to speak to a man, and what she felt she must say. "Won't you hear Preacher Manny out, Caleb? Just this once?"

Once was all it took for Suzy.

He turned to face her, still holding her hand. "I woke you up tonight for a reason. I'm here to ask you to cling fast to the Old Ways." His voice grew stronger, ringing through the darkness. "I trusted you when you said Suzy was a good girl, no matter the rumors, and I've pursued you knowin' my Daed's concerns. I stood up for you with my father, Nellie—told him you're the kind of woman he should welcome as a daughter-in-law."

She was silent. She *had* insisted to Caleb the rumors about Suzy were false, but that was before she'd discovered everything about her sister. "I told you the truth about Suzy," she protested. "She wasn't a wayward girl when she died . . . she was—"

"I want you to turn from this nonsense, Nellie. The sooner the better."

"Have you closed up your mind . . . your heart, then?"

"My heart is for *you*, Nellie Mae. I want you to be my bride. Marry me next year, after baptism."

Marry me?

The words she'd longed to hear, yet he'd spoken them in the midst of an argument. Even so, how could she refuse him? She couldn't hold back the tears. "I love you, too, Caleb. Honest, I do. And I *want* to marry you . . . but . . ." She couldn't go on.

"Jah, we love each other," he replied. "That's why I'm here, to protect you . . . to keep you from makin' the biggest mistake of your life."

"I'm not sure I see it that way." She brushed away her tears. "Can't you just go and hear for yourself?"

He shook his head. "I know what I believe."

"Jah, tradition. Plain and simple."

"I'm not goin' to a silly meeting."

"You're diggin' in your heels like an obstinate mule, Caleb Yoder."

"Call me whatever you like, but it won't change my mind."

"Your ears are closed tight, ain't so? You don't want to know more than what we've always believed." She sighed. "Well, I'd like to know if there's more than that—if God's own truth's behind what Manny's preaching."

He let go of her hand and leaned forward, the reins draped over the lap robe. "Nellie, it all boils down to this: My father would disown me if I left the church for this newfangled whatever it is. I'd have no way to make a living . . . for us. I'd lose everything. The land, my immediate family. Daed's respect."

"Well . . . you'd have *us*. We'd find a way somehow. Love can win out, jah?" she offered tentatively, yet the words sounded hollow even to her. She touched his arm. "Your land's mighty important, sure it is. But how can land mean more to you than our life together?" Her voice shook with both sadness and frustration.

"I could ask the same of you. How can my goin' to a meeting mean more to you than my reputation with my father . . . or the life we planned?" He leaned back, regarding her, his eyes softer now. He turned then to stare straight ahead and was quiet for a good, long time. "I've heard you out, Nellie. Now I'll say what I must. I've never cared for a girl like I do for you." He looked at her again, the muscles of his face quivering. "I wish we hadn't fought . . . honest to goodness."

"I'm sorry, too."

He drew her into his embrace. "I'm fearful, love. I'm afraid of what could become of us."

"It's not enough that we love each other?"

He closed his eyes, blowing out a breath. "I think I'd best take you home now."

"Jah, 'tis best," Nellie Mae agreed. Quarreling had gotten them nowhere.

CHAPTER 37

The wind rose up in the night, bringing with it freezing rain and snow. The wedding season was off to a bitter start.

Nellie gladly fulfilled her promise to Aunt Anna to help in the kitchen at the wedding she'd mentioned, filling up the week before it with as much work as daylight would allow. Neither her path nor her family's crossed with Caleb's at any of the all-day wedding celebrations Dat and Mamma chose to attend on the first Tuesday and Thursday, days set aside for weddings. For that she was truly sad.

She did see Caleb at the weekend cider-making frolic, his furtive gaze meeting hers. He seemed as willing to invite her to ride into the night as previously, but he did not care to hear her talk about the upcoming New Order youth gatherings. Already, a small group of youth had formed, thanks to the decision of many families to immediately accept the bishop's offer. Nan had decided to attend tonight's initial gathering, and for the first time, Nellie had found herself on her own, without any sisters at a frolic.

Nellie was aware of a small sorrow growing within as she wondered how she and Caleb could ever truly unite as man and wife when everyone around them seemed bent on division. She had been wholly honest with him and now must attempt to trust the Lord God for the outcome as Suzy might have. Yet she found herself increasingly given to silence, lest their relationship continue to be strained. Truly, there was simply too much at stake.

Rosanna took care not to slip on the crusty ice along the sidewalk as she carried baby Rosie toward the waiting vehicle. Elias offered his free arm to her, cradling tiny Eli in the other.

"We've got ourselves a Mennonite taxi service." He smiled at her.

"Jah, I see that."

"I wanted their first ride home to be nice and warm for our son and daughter," he added as they walked. "They seem a mite too fragile for this cold, if ya ask me."

"The doctors said they're both perfectly healthy—strong, too. Bet it won't be long before you're chasing after that son of ours." Rosanna gave him a loving glance. "You must be mighty happy about your boy."

"Well, I daresay I would've settled for two girls, seein' that perty smile on your face just now, love."

"Aw, Elias." She didn't let on that she'd nearly held her breath for Kate to birth a boy. "Thank the Good Lord."

"Jah, you can say that again."

The driver stepped out to assist them into the cozy van, and Rosanna carefully slid inside, next to her beaming husband. Leaning down to kiss Rosie's rosebud face, Rosanna felt her heart fill with a love that went beyond any she had known . . . and was content.

———

On the first day of December, Nellie awakened to a landscape of white, the sky as colorless as the ground. The horse fence and every tree in sight— even the side of the barn—were completely covered with snow due to a blistering Nor'easter.

Nellie hurried to dress and ran downstairs to help Mamma and her sisters with breakfast.

"Just think, you get a day off from bakin'," Mamma greeted her, smiling.

"I sure won't be goin' to work in this weather," Rhoda said woefully.

"Oh, but the Kraybills will understand once they look out their windows," Mamma said, trying to cheer her up.

"Jah, I'll say. We're downright snowbound," Dat declared, and they all laughed at that, gathering around the table when it was time to eat.

During the meal of scrambled eggs, ham, and fruit, Nellie excused herself and scurried upstairs to retrieve Suzy's diary. *This is the perfect time*, she thought, opening her drawer.

She turned the book to the page that had changed her thinking about Suzy. For sure and for certain, there were oodles of pages chronicling Suzy's sins, but the joy lay in where her search had brought her.

Nellie returned to the kitchen and approached the head of the table. Taking a deep breath, she said, "Suzy believed like you do, Dat."

Dat leaned forward, spilling his coffee.

"What?" Mamm gasped.

"It's all here . . . in her diary. She wanted each of us to know the Lord she loved."

Not trusting her voice, she handed the book to Dat where he sat. "Will ya read this page?" she whispered.

Dat's eyes held hers in question. Appearing reassured that she was earnest, he nodded and began to read silently.

Nellie Mae returned to her spot at the table and sipped some orange juice. Watching his lips move, she could not keep her eyes off her father's astonished face. Soon tears flowed down his cheeks.

Mamma frowned, looking at Nellie.

When Dat finished reading, he handed the diary to Mamma. His face radiated pure joy.

Mamma started to read, as well, and soon reached for Dat's hand. "Suzy's prayers were answered," she said reverently. "Her faith . . . and God's great mercy brought us to our knees, ain't so, Reuben?"

Dat, who evidently still hadn't quite found his voice, managed to whisper, "'Twas Suzy, all right . . . and our dear Lord."

Then Nan asked to see the diary, followed by Rhoda. Nan's eyes filled with tears, and Rhoda shook her head in wonder.

Mamma could hold back her happiness no longer. "Oh, glory be! Our Suzy's safe . . . not lost forever as we'd supposed."

"She's with the Lord," Dat said, blinking back tears.

They joined hands around the table as Dat thanked the living God "for this best news of all."

———

Reuben left the kitchen the minute the meal was done and went to the barn to be alone with his thoughts. He moved in and around the horses, paying special attention to the young ones, all the while pondering the surprising revelation in Suzy's diary.

He leaned down to stroke the mane of his favorite foal. "God was watchin' over my little girl all those months," he muttered as though talking directly to the colt. "Now, what do you think of that?"

Embracing the hush of the barn, Reuben walked to the back, facing north toward the vast whiteness of the pastureland concealed by heavy snow. In awe of the stark beauty, he thanked God for His care of Suzy. "I will not doubt you, O Lord . . . I know I can trust you to watch over all of my family," he prayed. "Each and every one."

———

Rosanna was as tired as she'd ever been after the first week home with the twins. She sat on the bed, brushing her long hair, talking with Elias about their babies—the holding, changing, bonding, and feeding—all of it precious to her. "Did ya ever think we'd be so busy?" she asked. "Some call it a double blessing 'cause we waited so long and got ourselves two." She smiled at that.

When Elias didn't respond, she looked over her shoulder. He was sound asleep, still wearing his choring clothes, his mouth hanging wide open. And he was lying on top of the quilt, of all things . . . holding Eli in his arms. The infant's tiny face was peeking out of the handmade blanket, the pink side of the quilt out by mistake.

She tiptoed around the bed and stood there admiring this wonderful man who'd agreed to become a father to someone else's children. Gently she covered him with a spare blanket before wandering out to the next room, a small sitting room where they'd placed the homemade cradles. *Nice and close by . . .*

Leaning over, she looked into the tiny peach-face of dear Rosie, who was in all truth both her cousin and her daughter, just as Eli was. The faint smiles during sleep, the smallest hands she'd ever seen, all curled up in tiny fists . . . the sweet, milky smell on their breath. . . . oh, how she loved them!

"You did this most wonderful thing for Elias and me, O Father in heaven. I couldn't be more thankful," she whispered.

She'd heard from Linda Fisher that Preacher Manny prayed as though he were talking to a friend face-to-face. Elias had no idea she'd spent any time with Nellie Mae's cousin this past week since the babies' release from the hospital. Linda was the sole reason Rosanna had kept up with the washing and the cooking—there were never enough hours in the day. Linda had encouraged her to read the Good Book, too, when she had a chance. "*Start with the gospel of John,*" she'd suggested.

Rosanna returned to the bedroom, thinking how odd it was that none of the nurses, nor the doctor in charge, had been aware that Kate's babies were to become hers and Elias's. She wondered if it had been kept mum for legal reasons.

After all, what were the laws of the world to them—two cousins in complete agreement, and with the bishop's blessing, too? In the midst of folk leaving helter-skelter for a so-called new order, the bishop surely had wisdom from above . . . or so Rosanna hoped.

Immediately she felt distressed for having second-guessed the man of God. Bishop Joseph was the divine appointment for the People. *Ach, for certain.*

Presently she blew out the lantern and slipped quietly into bed so as not to waken either Elias or Eli. There were precious few hours before the babies would be crying for nourishment.

They'll never be this small again, she thought, glad they were thriving in her care.

O dear Lord, help us bring these wee ones up in your grace and loving ways. And may we be ever mindful of your salvation, full and free. . . .

CHAPTER 38

The snow stayed on the ground for nearly a week, and then a Chinook wind blew in—a snow-eater, Dat liked to call it—to the surprise of everyone.

Nellie was in dire need of a brisk walk, and since it was the afternoon of the Lord's Day, there was nothing to keep her tethered home or to the shop. Feeling out of sorts and missing Caleb, she turned in the direction of White Horse Mill on Cambridge Road.

Our special place, she thought of the secluded area behind the old stone mill.

She didn't know why she was struggling so, but since their disagreement, whenever she considered Caleb's and her love, she felt a peculiar inner tug. She wished she could talk to someone, but no one knew how serious Caleb was about her. Or how much Nellie cared for him.

Truth was, she felt alone, and she found herself talking aloud, as if the air, or God, might have something to say on the subject. "Honestly, I know what I want . . . it's Caleb for my husband. He says I'm the girl for him—the one he wants to marry, but how can that ever be?"

Since Caleb was the youngest son in his family, the land would normally fall to him; but if provoked, his father could easily decide to give Caleb's bequest to his next-older son. She contemplated Caleb's life without the land he longed for. He would be miserable . . . might even blame her for his loss of it.

The fluttering of a crow caught her attention, and she thought of Suzy, whose favorite bird had always been the reddish brown veery—a shy, even elusive bird often seen in the woodlands near their house. It flew far away in late September, but no one knew where it journeyed for the winter.

Just as none of us knew where Suzy was all those months she was running with Jay and his friends.

Nellie sometimes thought of going to search out Suzy's Mennonite friends, as she assumed they were. She even wondered if talking with Zachary and

Christian Yoder and the others who'd gone with Suzy to the lake might provide her with some final answers.

Looking about her, she realized she'd lost track of where she was. She spotted the wrought-iron bench where she and Caleb had sat and talked so many times and headed toward it.

Can our love survive the church split? she wondered, knowing there already had been a vast parting of the ways for so many. Thankfully her own family had suffered little in comparison to others—there would be no shunning to keep them from spending time with Ephram and Maryann and their children, and they could still visit with Uncle Bishop and the many people who would surely remain in the original church.

If Caleb and his family came over to the New Order side *after* the ninety days the bishop had allowed for decision making, how sad for them. But no, Nellie Mae wouldn't allow herself to think that way. She must live a joyful life, all the while knowing if she converted, she'd be saying good-bye to Caleb . . . and if she remained, she would say good-bye to Suzy's gospel.

Pausing to sit on the bench, she closed her eyes. There was something sweet in the air, or was it the fresh smell of December after a bitter cold snap? Beneath the dampness of the creek bank, the promise of spring was buried deep within the soil. But the sweetness she sensed wasn't that found in the earth. Perhaps it came from knowing spring would come again, no matter how far off it now seemed.

Maybe our corn will reach its full height next summer. . . .

It was getting cold and Nellie hadn't planned to come this far at the outset of her walk. She thought she might end up crying if she lingered here in this place.

She rose, wanting to go have one last look at the mill creek. Walking to the bank, she leaned against the cold trunk of a tree.

A rustling sound . . . then a familiar voice.

"Nellie Mae, is that you?"

She turned and saw Caleb coming down from the frozen pond. "Hullo," she said, her heart in her throat.

Had she spoken his name aloud? She wasn't sure.

"Nellie, what're you doin' here?" His eyes were bright at the sight of her.

She laughed. "I should ask you that."

"So we're both here spontaneously," Caleb remarked.

They looked at each other awkwardly, almost as if they'd just met, so surprised were they.

"Would ya like to walk with me?" he asked at last.

Without waiting for her to respond, Caleb reached for her hand and they strolled together, like old times . . . re-experiencing the delight of first love.

Yet she knew as well as he that things were different. Preacher Manny had said in a sermon that the Word of God was as powerful as a two-edged sword. Were they about to witness this divisiveness firsthand?

"I couldn't stop thinking 'bout this place . . . wanted to walk along the millstream again," Caleb confessed.

She listened, enjoying the sound of his voice, the way his eyes twinkled when he smiled. "It's perty here, that's for sure. Even on a cold day."

"We sure picked a fine place, jah?"

She smiled at him. "You picked it, Caleb . . . remember?"

"I certainly do." He paused as though considering what he wanted to say next. "I must tell you something, Nellie. Something I despise saying."

She braced herself.

"My father forbids me to take you as my bride. He said so earlier today." Caleb shook his head, his eyes fixed on the ground. "He'll withhold his land and all he's promised me if I marry you, Nellie."

A fury rose in her, and she wanted to declare his father unfair. But that was false—David Yoder had every right. It was his land to give, and he *did* have other sons already married and walking in the way of the Old Order church.

"What will you do?" she asked, not sure she could bear to hear the answer.

He was silent for a time, clearly frustrated. "We must do as my father demands and part ways."

Ach, no . . .

She stopped walking to face him and study his dear face, his hairline, the way his eyebrows framed his beautiful eyes. "Are you goin' to—"

"Make it appear so," he added. "Till I can think this through."

"You've spoken up to your father on this?" It was forward, but she had to know.

"More than once. Believe me, it's not the wisest thing to do."

She understood. There were a good many stern fathers and grandfathers amongst the People, some harsher than others, but most unyielding all the same.

Unexpectedly Caleb reached for her, pulling her toward him. "I can't think of losin' you. I won't."

She pressed her lips together to make them stop trembling and willed herself not to cry. "I would never do this to my son or daughter, would you?"

He reached to lift her chin, his face ever so near. "We cannot be seen together . . . ever. Even though we might attend the same Singings and whatnot, I won't take you out ridin' afterward—not because I don't want to. Do you understand, love? Rebekah, who's always been fond of you, will now surely become a spy for Daed."

Nellie nodded, the lump in her throat nearly choking her so that she could not speak.

"Nothing will stand between us. I'll see to that . . . somehow." He pressed his forehead to hers, lingering ever so near. "We'll find a way, I promise."

"I pray so" was all she could bring herself to say.

Caleb kissed her cheek tenderly, holding her hand till her fingers slipped away.

Honor thy father and thy mother, she thought as she walked toward Beaver Dam Road alone, wondering how following that arduous commandment could yield a blessing of long life. The way Nellie Mae felt now, she couldn't imagine wanting to live to a ripe old age without her beloved by her side.

EPILOGUE

—

I dreamt of Suzy last night, at long last. She came walking toward me in a meadow of red columbines and bluebells, wearing a purple cape dress and white church apron. She was as radiant as a bride, and in the dream I thought she must be wearing her spotless heavenly robe, her tears over her misdeeds all wiped away.

Dat says Suzy's gone to Jesus, and I think of it every morning as I rise to greet a new day, wondering if it is true.

As for Mamma, she's ever so busy passing on her new faith. She and little Emma were doing a bit of stitching this morning when I left the house to go to the bakery shop. Emma was curled up on Mamma's lap, leaning on the kitchen table while my mother showed her how to do a simple cross-stitch on a pillow slip. I had to stop and listen when Mamma said, "You know Aunt Suzy's in heaven."

Emma looked up from her embroidery square and blinked her big eyes. "What's she doin' there?"

"Oh, all kinds of wonderful-good things, I 'spect."

"Like what?"

"Spendin' time with the Lord Jesus, for one," said Mamma.

"God's Son?"

"That's right . . . let me tell you more 'bout Him." Mamma's voice went on, but I had to leave.

Seems in this house, there is much talk of "the Savior." In all truth, my parents speak of Jesus quite a lot, which is very different from what I heard all of my growing-up years. I guess they think some of us have a lot of catching up to do, myself included, though I'm ever so guarded in my curiosity. How can I be otherwise?

Nan, surprisingly, is warming up to me; we've been distant for so long. Her heart must still be broken, though she won't come right out and say so. I sometimes see the pain in her eyes, just as I see my own in the small hand mirror on my dresser.

I've decided not to part with Suzy's Kapp strings. I've been slipping them into my dress pocket again. At times I think it's peculiar to keep them at my fingertips, an ever-present reminder, but they bring more comfort than sadness nowadays. Mamma would probably not care at all if she knew.

Besides, Mamma showed me something of Suzy's that she, too, sometimes carries with her. A small pillow, stitched as finely as any I've seen—one made to alleviate headaches, of all things.

Dat says he knows now why so many of our crops failed last summer. He believes we were supposed to learn something important about trusting God. It was a message of hope to look to in the time of struggle. He says it's as if our heavenly Father were saying, *Look to me, even amid your uncertainty and loss—whether crops or loved ones—I am here, calling you to my joy and peace.*

In spite of my bewilderment over Caleb's father's demand, I am hopeful as I go about the duties of my life, knowing love can win out in even the worst of circumstances. Of all the stories Dat reads from the Good Book, the best example of great love is God's Son, seems to me. To think He would give up all of heaven to meet us here—to court us, wooing our hearts. Such a surprising thing, really.

Mamma says the best part is we will never be separated from that love, neither here nor over yonder. She figures Suzy must know that already—she says she can't imagine what Suzy's experiencing. So now when I think of my departed sister, I try to think like Mamma does, with jubilation and maybe a bit of envy.

Soon it will be Christmas Day, and this year will mark a special celebration of the Lord's birthday round here. Sometime before then, I'm going to settle in my mind what happened on Suzy's final day on earth. I want to thank her good friends, too, for looking after my wayward sister, helping to rescue her from the evils of the world.

Sometimes I wonder if I ought to visit the tabernacle come summer, if for no other reason than to honor my close sisterly connection to Suzy. Ach, but I hope my reticence won't keep me from meeting Zachary and his brother. I've already avoided them once, not accepting the chance to go boating with them that dreadful day. I was selfish, not wanting to spoil my chances with Caleb by being linked to his English cousin. In the end, though, I paid a terrible price for not going—yet if I can follow through and find them, what will *this* meeting cost me?

No matter what the days ahead may hold, I will keep baking the goodies my customers crave, extending kindness and good deeds to all I meet. And somehow, I hope the Lord God will watch over Caleb and me, even though our future looks mighty bleak. After all, the peaceable parting offered to the People by the bishop was a true miracle.

Why can't Caleb and I be a miracle, too?

ACKNOWLEDGMENTS

While doing research for this series, I learned of two schisms that occurred among the Old Order Amish in 1966, a time of great upheaval . . . and saving grace. And the mercy of one Amish bishop.

Much gratitude to my cousins Jake and Ruth Bare for their careful research, as well as to those from whom they received valuable information and memories.

Many thanks to my wonderful editorial team—David Horton, Julie Klassen, and Rochelle Glöege—and everyone at Bethany House who helps make my writing journey a joyful one.

Loving appreciation to my husband, Dave, for his terrific plotting advice, to Carolene Robinson for her medical expertise, to Barbara Birch for her excellent proofreading, to each of my Lancaster County research assistants, and to my partners in prayer in various places.

Above all, my deep thankfulness to our heavenly Father, who guides me in all my ways.

The Forbidden

To John and Ada Reba Bachman,

my dear uncle and aunt.

With love and greatest gratitude.

PROLOGUE

Winter 1967

I dreamed of Suzy last night. In the dream, it was deep winter and heavy snow fell as we walked to the barn to feed the calvies . . . little sisters once again. The whistle of a distant train, its sad, haunting sound, hung in the dense, cold air as it echoed through our cornfield. Yet why was the corn still tall and thriving in the dead of January?

All of this was crammed into a dream that lasted only a few minutes at most. My friend Rosanna King says dreams are like that, tantalizing you with a mixture of puzzling things that don't make a whit of sense.

Even so, I awakened with the knowledge that I must be moving beyond my initial grief. *Jah*, I long to see Suzy again, to talk with her and feel her gentle breath on my hair as she sleeps, sharing our old childhood bed. Sharing our lives, too. But something has changed in me. Maybe it helps to know that *Dat* and Mamma believe Suzy's in heaven, even though she died before she could join church. So terribly bewildering, as this idea goes against the grain of everything we've always believed.

Following her death, I didn't dream very often of my sister, though I'd wanted to. Now it's like going from a drought to a torrential rain. The floodgates have opened and she and I are together nearly every night as young girls . . . as if the Lord God is permitting a divine comforter to fall over me.

I daresay it is a comfort I sorely need, what with the six-month anniversary of Suzy's death having come and gone—December ninth, which my oldest sister, Rhoda, says was not long after Pearl Harbor Day. Another sad anniversary—the start of a world war decades ago. *Ach*, such strife between our country and another, and now a terrible clash is going on in a place called Vietnam, according to Rhoda.

She brings up the oddest things relating to the modern world. I see the look of surprise in Mamma's eyes nearly every night at supper. Dat is more stoic, slowly running his fingers up and down his black suspenders as he quietly takes in Rhoda's remarks. My sister Nan's disapproval is evident in the jut of her chin and the way her blue eyes dim as Rhoda chatters about the foreign things she's learning while working for the Kraybills, our English neighbors who live half a mile away on the narrow, wooded section of Beaver Dam Road. She works every weekday, snow or not, and sometimes on Saturdays. At times I wonder if she'd be willing to work Sundays, too, given the chance.

Rhoda's not the only one working extra hard these days. Dat has been busy, as well. The bakery shop—called Nellie's Simple Sweets—will soon be home to three cozy sets of tables and chairs, about the size of those in the ice-cream parlors *Englischers* frequent. Three customers will be able to sit at each round table, and if some want to squeeze in, then four. Oh, such gossip that will fly. I must be careful lest I hear things not meant for my ears, especially from fancy customers.

Mamma's returned to working with me just recently. Nan still helps some, too, but only when things get real busy. Otherwise, it is my mother and me tending the store and, oh, the interesting tales she tells of bygone days—like a tomato-growing contest she won as a girl by supporting the tomato with a hammock of netting, and raising pigs with her younger brother. Like *Mammi* Hannah Fisher, Mamma has a knack for describing past doings.

My beau, Caleb Yoder, has only dropped by the bakery once, but he won't be doing that at all now—not if he wants to receive his inheritance of nearly a hundred acres of farmland. His father has forbidden him to court me, but Caleb has promised we'll see each other secretly . . . somehow.

Already three weeks have passed since he revealed the startling news and we held each other before parting ways. Ach, but it feels like forever. There was no word from him during Christmas, so he's abiding by his father's wishes. No matter this temporary silence, I trust him to know what to do to gain his *Daed*'s approval of me. Surely word has reached David Yoder's ear that I have not gone to Preacher Manny's church a second time—nor do I intend to. I'm not walking the "saved" path that has enticed a good many families in our church district already.

My staying put has caused an awful rift in the house, especially on Preaching Sundays when my family and I go our separate ways. I to the old church, and my parents and Rhoda and Nan to the new.

Plenty of folk are at odds on this issue. There is even a growing division amongst those in the new church—some have still stronger leanings toward the world, desiring electricity and cars, of all things. My parents won't hear of that, so we continue to drive horse and buggy and bring out the gas lamps and lanterns at dusk.

There's a hankering for light on both sides of the fence. For some this breaking away has required a quick decision, as Uncle Bishop has decreed a ninety-day grace period on excommunication and shunning for folk who want to leave the old church and join the new. The incentive is mighty strong for those already baptized into the Old Order church, since there are only a few short weeks to decide for or against the tradition of our ancestors. A right sobering thought.

Knowing that this new way was Suzy's belief makes it strangely appealing. But as curious as I am, I won't risk my future with Caleb Yoder, even though I am still in *Rumschpringe*—a running-around time sanctioned by the People. The old church is where I belong, with my beau. Dear Dat and Mamma don't realize I've already decided against embracing their faith— Caleb and I would stand no chance if I were to be baptized into the New Order. How can I think of doing so, when marrying him is my very best hope for happiness?

CHAPTER 1

Nellie Mae Fisher loaded her newly baked goods onto the long sleigh and covered them with a lightweight tarp before tying everything down securely. She slipped her outer bonnet over her *Kapp* and breathed lightly as she pulled the sleigh through the backyard, toward the bakery shop behind her father's farmhouse. The January air was frosty, and she pushed the woolen scarf into place to protect her nose.

The expanse of land beyond Nellie's Simple Sweets lay buried beneath a blanket of snow, the unfruitful cornfield of last summer now as white and perfect as any neighboring field. A ridge of tall trees to the west stood stark and forklike against the sky, and only a handful of stray leaves still clung to the maples near the barnyard. Closer in, a few scraggly remnants of cornstalks remained, their reedy stems silhouetted brown against the snow.

Our first Christmas and New Year's . . . without Suzy.

Nellie Mae sighed, struck by the way the sky seemed to hold back the daylight behind a barricade of gray-white clouds, hoarding it away, depriving the earth of direct sunlight. She'd heard her father compare the icy ground to iron, telling Mamma quietly that even death itself was not as hard as a field of frozen ground. With recent heavy snows and continuous arctic air, Nellie was certainly glad to have rescued Suzy's diary from the earth well before this cold, long month.

There had been times as children when she and Suzy would wade through waist-deep snow, unbeknownst to Mamma, who would've had a thing or two to say about it had she known. They'd longed for summer's glow during the dark months of the year, just as Rhoda and Nan had. All four sisters had used this selfsame sleigh over the years, pushing through the snow on foot, in search of spring's greenery. Even the sight of dull green lichen on a tree trunk gave cause for rejoicing.

Oh, for spring to hurry!

Nellie opened the door to the snug shop and began unloading the sleigh of the day's inventory of goodies. Immediately, though, she sensed something was amiss, and when she moved behind the counter, there was nineteen-year-old Nan crouched with her best friend, Rebekah Yoder, Caleb's older sister. They rose, streaks of tears on each girl's face, and Nan quickly sputtered, "Ach, but it's just so unfair."

Confused, Nellie shook her head. "What is?"

"Rebekah's father . . . well . . ." Nan glanced at her friend, who was clearly as upset as she.

Instantly Nellie knew why the pair had been hiding.

Rebekah dabbed her face with a handkerchief. "I'm not supposed to be here," she admitted and sighed loudly. "What with the split between the People, my father's not in favor of certain friendships."

Certain friendships?

Unable to divulge her own predicament, Nellie simply nodded as Rebekah revealed that her plight was "all the family's, truly." She didn't go on to explain what that meant, but Nellie presumed she was speaking for herself and her brother Caleb, as well as Rebekah's mother, who until these past few months had often given Nellie's mamma rides to and from quilting bees.

Nan suddenly reached for Nellie's hand. "Would it be all right, do ya think, if Rebekah and I met here sometimes to visit?" Nan's eyes were pleading.

Nellie forced a smile. *Will I get myself in further trouble with David Yoder, harboring Caleb's sister?*

Nan groaned. "Oh, I don't understand why this has to be."

Rebekah's face was taut with worry. "Me neither."

"Even the bishop said no one's to be shunned for followin' Preacher Manny and the new church," Nan reminded.

"Well, you don't know my father, then," Rebekah said. "He'll shun if he wants to."

Nellie's spirits sank like a fallen cake.

"Come." Nan reached for Rebekah's hand and led her toward the door.

Nellie watched them go, not knowing who had her sympathy more—Nan and Rebekah, who were most likely scheming about future ways to visit—or her beau, Caleb.

She turned on the gas-run space heater in the far corner and then removed her coat, scarf, and mittens. Rubbing her hands together, she waited for heat to fill the place. As she did, she walked to the window and stared out at the wintry landscape. *Why didn't Caleb send word during Christmas?*

"How much longer till he gets his father to see the light?" she blurted into the stillness.

Deep within her, she feared Caleb's longing for his birthright. One hundred acres of fine farmland was nothing to sneeze at, and his father's land was ever so important to him. To her, as well, for it would provide their livelihood as Caleb cared for her needs and those of their future children. He had worried something awful about this when they'd met unexpectedly at the millstream—their last time together. She'd heard in his voice then the hunger for his inheritance. Soon she would know where things stood. After all, Caleb was a man of his word. He'd asked her to marry him and she had happily agreed, but that was before his father had demanded they part ways.

Why should David Yoder keep Rebekah and Nan apart, too?

Having witnessed Rebekah's misery, she worried that David Yoder had more sway over his son and daughter than she'd first believed. What with Rebekah busy working as a mother's helper for another Amish family, she had less opportunity to be influenced by the world than Nellie's sister Rhoda did working at the Kraybills' fancy house. No, Rebekah would most likely join the old church and stay in the fold, just as Nellie would when the time came. Doing so meant Rebekah would also eventually comply with her father's wishes and choose a different best friend, which would hurt Nan terribly.

Turning, Nellie took visual inventory of her baked goods—an ample supply of cookies, cakes, pies, and sticky buns. The bleak reality was that there had been few customers willing to brave the temperatures this week. She'd thought of asking Dat if she ought to close up during the coldest weeks as some shops did in Intercourse Village, although many of those were not Amish owned. Yet Nellie had hesitated to ask—her family needed the extra income from the bakery more than ever this year, due to last summer's drought.

"Right now we look as good as closed," she murmured, eyeing the road and the lack of customers. It was safe to head to the barn to see how Dat's new tables and chairs were coming along.

On her way, she noticed Nan and Rebekah now walking side by side toward Beaver Dam Road, Rebekah's hands gesturing as she talked spiritedly.

Rebekah knows her own mind. At twenty, she would be marrying before long—if not next fall, then the following year. As far as Nellie knew, Rebekah had no serious beau, though, of course, that didn't mean anything. Courting was done secretly, and most couples kept mum.

Glancing over her shoulder, she looked back again at Caleb's sister, graceful and tall even next to willowy Nan. Nellie couldn't help but wonder what the two girls were cooking up, the way they leaned toward each other. For now, at least, their tears had turned to laughter.

Nellie opened the barn door and headed to the area opposite the stable. Her father had carved out a corner there for his business records and occasional woodworking handiwork.

His back was to her as he appeared to scrutinize one of the chair legs, his nose nearly touching the oak. "Hullo, Dat," she said quietly so as not to startle him.

He turned quickly. "Nellie Mae?"

"Not many customers yet . . . well, none at all, really. Thought I'd drop in." She paused, aware of his pleasant smile. "Just curious to have a look-see." She pointed at the unfinished chair.

"Two tables are done, but, well, I'm a bit behind on the chairs, as you see." He set the chair down. "You discouraged 'bout the winter months, with so few customers?"

"The pies sit, is all."

He nodded slightly. "Seems winter's got sharper teeth this year, jah?"

She couldn't remember such a long cold snap. "I daresay we'll be eatin' more of those baked goods ourselves if . . ." She didn't finish. No need to say what Dat knew.

It wasn't merely the cold that kept folks away. Here lately they were seeing fewer of the families who held steadfast to the teachings of her father's older brother, Bishop Joseph. *Uncle Bishop* Nellie had always called him—a term both of endearment and reverence. Though the bishop himself had instructed the People not to shun one another because of the church rift, the truth of the matter was clear in the dropping number of customers at Nellie's Simple Sweets. Never had it been so quiet.

Nellie wondered if she'd have to start working for worldly folk, as Rhoda did, upsetting her father even more. Doing so would bring in extra money and help make up the difference for the family in the long run, though it would further jeopardize her chances with Caleb.

"Saw David Yoder's girl over here," Dat spoke up.

Nellie nodded, unwilling to say anything.

"Seems odd, ain't?"

"Jah." She sensed his meaning.

"We'll reap what we sow . . . sooner or later."

She inhaled slowly. "'Spect so."

Dat winced openly. "It's a new day in many ways, and there's no tellin' folk what to do. You and I both know that."

She said not a word, for she was unsure now what he was referring to. She suspected he might've had his ears filled with David Yoder's disapproval of Preacher Manny's teaching on "salvation through grace." More than likely that was a big part of it.

Sighing, she figured if Dat suspected Caleb's father of keeping her and Caleb apart, he'd be all for encouraging them to continue courting. Dat was like that. When it came to love—the kind you married for—she was sure he would err on the side of the couple's choice.

"Like I said, people will embrace what they long for, Nellie Mae."

She caught the perceptive glint in her father's eye. *He knows I have a beau.* . . .

CHAPTER 2

R osanna King wasn't surprised to see Kate Beiler around midmorning on Friday. Her cousin had been faithfully coming once a day to supplement the twins' formula following their release from the hospital five weeks earlier.

Kate liked to coo at the babies, kissing the tops of their fuzzy little heads. Since New Year's, Rosanna had noticed Kate was visiting more often than simply to be a wet nurse. But today she looked tired, and Rosanna wondered if she might stay for only a short time.

Making a beeline for tiny Eli, Kate picked him up from the playpen. "Ach, look at you." She stroked his rosy cheek. "You're catchin' up to your sister, seems to me." She held him out a ways, moving him up and down, as if weighing him in a scale of sorts.

"He's eating right good," Rosanna spoke up.

"Every four hours or so . . . like the nurse at the hospital said?"

"Jah, and if one baby doesn't awaken and cry for nourishment, the other does, and soon they're both up. They're well fed, I'd say."

Kate turned back to Eli, who was bundled in one of the crocheted blankets Rosanna had made.

Meanwhile Rosanna reached for Rosie, whose soft fists were moving for her open mouth. "You need some love, too, jah?" Cuddling Eli's twin, she walked the length of the kitchen, pondering her feelings. Why was it every time Kate arrived, she felt like declaring, "The babies are mine, too"?

Lest her brooding show on her face, Rosanna sat down at the table and smiled down at Rosie. It was clearly time for the babies' feeding, and she ought to be glad for the break in the near-endless bottle-feeding routine. There were instances when she had to resort to propping up a bottle for one twin while holding the other. When that happened, she'd burp the one before switching babies for the second half of the four ounces of formula.

Helpful as Elias tried to be, her dear husband obviously had more on his mind than assisting with the twins, although it was plain he was partial to baby Eli.

Truly, Rosanna was getting plenty of motherhood training with her double blessings, both of them precious gifts from the Lord. She glanced over at Kate, still cradling little Eli in her arms, and pushed away the peculiar thoughts that beset her today.

No need to worry. . . .

She lifted Rosie to her face, burrowing her nose into her warm, sweet neck. "You ready for somethin' to eat?" she whispered, loving the smell, the feel of her.

"You go ahead and take care of Rosie while I tend to Eli here," Kate directed. "Not sure I'm up to feeding them both today."

Rosanna felt some surprise at this, though she knew it was time for Kate to be done nursing the twins altogether. In all truth, she had been looking forward to this day.

Eli let out a howl and Kate began to undo the bodice of her cape dress. "Mamma's here," she muttered, never looking Rosanna's way as she offered her breast.

Rosanna's heart caught in her throat. *Maybe Kate's not the best choice for a wet nurse.*

Now Rosie was *rutsching,* nuzzling for nourishment in earnest. Put out with Kate for her comment to Eli and for always placing his needs before Rosie's, Rosanna stood to warm her daughter's bottle, swaying back and forth and making soothing sounds as she did so.

She recalled Kate's unexpected decision to nurse the twins after their birth. Kate had never conferred with her cousin about this, though Rosanna had assumed she wanted to give the premature babies a good start. Despite her intentions, the recovering Kate hadn't had enough milk to keep up with the minimum six feedings a day per baby, so after a week, she'd nursed each of them only once daily, returning to the hospital for the feedings after being discharged herself. With the debt of gratitude Rosanna felt she owed her cousin, she had been quickly persuaded that Kate should continue to supplement the babies' formula until they were two months old. What she hadn't realized was how awkward the arrangement would be. *For both of us, probably.*

As she nursed Eli, Kate cooed softly. Then she addressed Rosanna from over her shoulder. "I hear your husband's been spending a lot of time with Reuben Fisher."

"Jah, Reuben—and others—have been a big help to Elias."

"No, I don't mean helpin' round the farm." Kate frowned. "Your Elias and Reuben are talkin' Scripture, that's what."

For the life of her, Rosanna did not recall Elias mentioning any such discussions with Reuben Fisher or anyone else, although Nellie Mae's father often assisted her husband in mixing feed and unloading it from the silo. "Are ya sure 'bout this, Kate?"

"Well now, I wouldn't make it up."

Suddenly she felt all done in. "Who Elias chooses to work with ain't my business."

Or yours . . .

Kate's eyes widened. "You must not understand. I meant—"

Nodding, Rosanna softened her tone. "Well, I believe I do."

"You're sayin' you don't mind if Elias is listenin' to wrongful teaching?"

"If the bishop's not troubled by it, then who are we to—"

"No!" Kate shook her head. She removed Eli from her breast and put him on her shoulder, rubbing his back. "Flash conversions, Rosanna . . . that's what's going on here. Folk are getting emotionally caught up, talking 'bout prideful things like a close relationship with God. It ain't right."

Secretly Rosanna hoped her husband *was* drawn to the teachings she'd been hearing herself from Linda Fisher. To her, they seemed wonderful-good—not wrongful at all.

Without saying more, she carried Rosie to the rocking chair in the corner of the kitchen, putting some distance between herself and Kate. Rosie lurched forward when presented with the bottle, and Rosanna enjoyed her nearness as she rocked gently, caressing the baby's downy soft hair.

Watching Rosie, she wondered if there was a way to bring milk into her own breasts. She'd heard of it, though perhaps it amounted to an old wives' tale—or something requiring a Lancaster doctor, maybe. *What would it take?*

Kate's voice startled her. "Don't fool yourself about the bishop, cousin. He's mighty troubled . . . yet bein' ever so lenient where Manny and Reuben—well, the whole lot of them—are concerned." Kate coaxed a resounding burp from Eli, then another, and promptly put him on her other breast. "You must not be keepin' up with things."

I'm too busy for the grapevine. If there was something Elias wanted her to be aware of, Rosanna knew he'd tell her come nightfall, when he was so dear to her once the twins were settled into their cradles. Elias was like that, always eager to share with her the things on his mind while they nestled in each other's arms. Eager in other ways, too.

Nellie Mae took care to redd up the bakery shop following a not-so-busy Friday afternoon—less than a handful of customers the whole day. She counted the money and placed it in her pocket, thinking she'd like to slip away to the millpond behind the old White Horse Mill to ice skate. She and Caleb had gone there twice as a courting couple, so perhaps she might catch at least a glimpse of him. She hadn't forgotten seeing him the last time she'd been there—most surprising and ever so nice, till they'd had to say good-bye.

Earlier she'd run to the mailbox, as she had every day for the past few weeks, hoping for a letter. Caleb could easily write her without anyone's knowing if he just left off the return address.

Unless he's ill.

The thought had not crossed her mind before now, although she hadn't seen Caleb at any of the youth gatherings associated with Christmas. She hadn't seen him in church on the Sunday two days before Christmas, either, but that didn't mean he hadn't been there. The house of worship—Deacon Lapp's farmhouse—was so packed full of folk she might simply have missed him.

"Maybe Caleb *is* under the weather." She knew of several families who'd suffered from the flu in the past days.

Glancing around the bakery shop, she eyed the area where she envisioned putting the tables and chairs. If customers could linger and talk, they might purchase more goodies.

She wondered if she shouldn't add sandwiches or homemade soups to the selection of items printed on the small blackboard on the wall behind the counter. But with the nix on their family by many devoted to the Old Ways now that Dat and Mamma and her sisters were attending the new church, Nellie might not get to realize her hopes of that. Besides, most folk wanted to eat next to their own fireplace on a bitterly cold day. Who could blame them?

She turned off the portable gas heater and headed for the door. Leaning into the wind, she picked her way across the snow-covered ground, aware that a substantial amount of ice lay beneath. Friday nights were skating nights at the millpond. If she could just get out of washing dishes later, she would bundle up and go.

With renewed anticipation, Nellie Mae stepped into the house and removed her boots, coat, and scarf. She fairly flung off her mittens, suppressing her giggles as she sent them flying across the summer porch.

If Caleb and I can bump into each other once, why not again?

Delighted at the prospect, Nellie made her way into the warm kitchen for supper.

CHAPTER 3

———

Nellie's muscles were already stiff from the biting cold, yet she pushed onward. When she rounded the bend on Cambridge Road, she spotted Rebekah Yoder and several of her sisters there. Her heart leapt.

If they're here, surely Caleb is, too.

Merrily she dashed across the snowy banks along the millpond, near the area where she and Caleb had once walked hand in hand. She had never been afraid of the ice, not even in late winter when the pond would begin to thaw in places. She'd always assumed she'd have more sense than to fall in.

Thinking suddenly of Suzy, Nellie realized she hadn't followed through with her hope to find out more about what had happened the day her sister had drowned. Even though the busy days of Christmas had come and gone, she'd had no desire to go in search of Zach and Christian Yoder, two Mennonite brothers who had befriended Suzy. Nevertheless, she was still quite curious to talk to anyone who'd been with her sister on that terrible June day.

Pushing that sad thought aside, she took note of the dozen or more young people presently skating and continued to look for Caleb as she put on her skates. She dared not ask Rebekah or her sisters about him. She would mind her own business and glide out onto the large pond to skate.

The first star of the evening appeared like a pulsing dot of white light. Nellie was so taken with the icy splendor around her, she scarcely even saw Susannah Lapp until she nearly collided with her. Susannah squealed and narrowly missed falling, and Nellie skated hard to the right, trying to maintain her balance.

Ach, not her!

Quickly she chided herself. No reason to view Susannah as a threat any longer. *Caleb's father is my greatest fear now.*

Nellie made another pass around the pond, this time carefully skirting the others. But the longer Nellie stayed, the colder she would be by the time she departed for home. Again she pondered Caleb's whereabouts, and a little panic flitted through her mind: Surely he was not avoiding her.

Still she remained, determined to be on hand in case he happened to arrive late. After all, it was a perfect night for skating, and no doubt he would think so, too. The ice was hard and slick, its formerly rough surface swept smooth by the wind.

A night meant for a girl and her beau . . .

She was gaining speed again, waving and smiling at Rebekah Yoder, when she thought she saw someone standing dark and rigid against the trees on the banks of the millpond, across the way. Was it Caleb?

Not wanting to stare, Nellie forced herself onward, heart pounding with anticipation.

Elias didn't mention Reuben Fisher at all while Rosanna lay in the crook of his arm. She waited and wondered as she thought back to the peculiar things Cousin Kate had voiced with such conviction. Were they true?

Elias *did* have something interesting to talk about between kisses. Maryann Fisher, who lived across the way with her husband, Ephram, had been home alone when her labor pangs began. Elias had stopped by to deliver some tools for Ephram, who'd gone to the town of Cains on an errand.

"Honestly, I thought I might have to help deliver Maryann's baby while her four young ones looked on."

"Oh, Elias . . . what on earth?"

"Well, I was able to send the oldest boy up the road to the community phone booth—thank the Good Lord for that—and the midwife came just in time."

Rosanna shook her head. "Poor Maryann, she must have been terribly frightened."

"On the contrary . . . said she'd be fine if I would watch her littlest ones, Katie and Becky."

Rosanna couldn't help but giggle. "You must be countin' your blessings 'bout now."

He chuckled. "S'posin' if I can deliver calves, I can help bring a baby into the world." He paused, pulling her closer. "But watching them toddlers of Maryann's and keepin' them out of trouble . . . now, that's another story yet."

Rosanna smiled up at Elias, who quit his laughing and looked at her with a familiar glint of yearning. "Let's not be talkin' of Ephram's new baby, love," he said softly, his face very near.

Let's not talk at all. She wrapped her arms around his neck, impatient for more of his kisses.

The shadowy figure was a man, but not one young enough to be Caleb, Nellie decided as she cast another furtive glance. He inched his way toward the pond, and she could not tell if he was watching any skater in particular. Even so, the man was clearly observing them, and his presence made her uneasy.

Who is it?

She wondered if other skaters had noticed the man. It was obvious from his appearance he was Amish. Otherwise, Nellie would have been even more concerned.

She sped twice more around the pond before stopping to wait for Rebekah on the side nearest the trees. When Rebekah spotted her and waved, heading that way, Nellie motioned her over. "Don't look now, but there's a man standing there . . . watching us."

Rebekah dug in the blades of her skates, spraying ice as she came to a stop. "Oh jah, I know." She laughed softly. "It's my father, come to take us home . . . when we're ready."

Nellie felt silly. "Seeing a man there scared me." She paused. "Well, just a little."

"I'm not surprised." Rebekah acted a bit sheepish. "He's overseein' us, I'm guessin'."

Giving a quick squeeze of her hand, Rebekah headed off around the pond again, catching up with her sisters.

Nellie Mae was now so cold her toes were numb. *I should head home.* She clumped to the bank, where she leaned against a tree to remove her skates, wishing for the wrought-iron bench where she and Caleb had sat and talked, his strong arms around her when she began to shiver.

But the bench was on the other side of the millstream, and she dared not try and climb down to it, not when her feet felt like clubs. She wondered if her toes were frostbitten and attempted to wiggle them beneath her thick socks as she worked on her snow boots. Then she took the long way around the stream to a footbridge, moving toward the road.

Forcing her feet forward, she looked up at the sky and at the many stars of the Milky Way, pondering the fact that while a good many of Caleb's family were present this night, he was nowhere in sight.

Squeezing her eyes tight, she fought back tears. *I miss you so much, Caleb.*

After a time, she heard the *clip-clop* of a horse and buggy slowing down behind her.

"Nellie Mae!" Rebekah Yoder called. "Come, get in the buggy with us."

Fatigued, she had not the strength, nor the gumption, to refuse. She turned and hobbled to the carriage. "*Denki*, ever so much."

"Ach, Nellie, you're limping." Rebekah helped her inside.

"Did you hurt your foot skating?" one of Rebekah's sisters asked from the back as Nellie settled into the front seat next to Rebekah.

David Yoder spoke up before Nellie could respond. "She's a farm girl— she'll be fine." He kept his gaze toward the road.

Is he picking me up so Caleb can't?

"I'm ever so thankful for the ride," she managed to say, not sure how she would ever have made it home with the feeling all but gone from her feet.

Rebekah reached under the heavy woolen lap robe and squeezed her hand. "I did something like this once . . . skated too long and nearly lost a toe."

"What'd you do?"

"Soaked my foot in cool water . . . let it warm gradually." She paused, glancing at her father. "Your mamma will know what to do."

Jah. Bet she'd chuckle if she knew why I went in the first place.

Then, a moment before they crossed the one-lane bridge on Beaver Dam Road, Rebekah leaned over to whisper, "I'll be tellin' Caleb I saw you."

Nellie Mae let out a gasp, her breath twirling into the air. *No question about it. She knows. . . .*

Barely missing a beat, Nellie whispered back, "I'll tell Nan I saw you, too."

CHAPTER 4

———

R osanna awakened to Eli's cries early Saturday morning. Pulling on her old chenille robe, she glanced at Elias, in deep slumber.

How does he sleep through such howling?

Hurrying now to the sitting room-turned-nursery, she bent down to pick up Eli. More than Rosie, he was typically impatient to be fed, especially after the midnight hour. She looked at peaceful Rosie and was again surprised that anyone, infant or father alike, could sleep through such hearty cries.

She gripped the stair railing with her free hand, wishing at times like this they might consider moving to the large bedroom on the first floor. Of course, that would mean having the babies sleep in the same room as they, something Elias would not want even at this tender age. She also cherished their time of lovemaking, especially this night. She'd felt quite vulnerable and ever so put out at Kate for calling herself mamma to little Eli. Couldn't her cousin guess how Rosanna might feel about that?

Downstairs, she warmed Eli's bottle, and when it was ready she watched as he worked his cheeks and lips. Later, when he was burped sufficiently and asleep in her arms, she climbed the stairs. Still groggy, she tucked him into his cradle, only to rouse Rosie to feed her next. Tired as she was, Rosanna treasured these nighttime feedings. *Just the babies and me . . . and the dear Savior.*

Rosie nestled her wee face into Rosanna's bosom, which again made her wish she could suckle both babies—not just Eli, as Kate had chosen to do today. Swiftly she removed the second small bottle from the gas-powered refrigerator, shaking it before placing the bottle into a pan of water and turning on the gas stove. Elias had been wise to replace the old woodstove before the twins had come home.

"*Ballemol*—soon," she promised Rosie as she kept an eye on the stove, making sure the bottle didn't get too warm. Rosie burrowed her head into her once more. *Oh, dear little one.* She wondered whether Eli and Rosie would ever fully bond with her, with her cousin constantly coming around. Did they sense, on some subconscious level, who Kate was?

When the bottle of formula was warm enough, Rosanna sat in the rocking chair, facing the window and looking at the moon—a wide fingernail in the heavens. And she prayed, asking God questions she hoped He might see fit to answer. Their good neighbor Linda sometimes expressed herself in such a way in prayer. Linda had invited her and Elias to attend a "new group" with her and her husband, Jonathan, some Sunday, and although Rosanna was intrigued, she was reluctant to mention it to Elias. But if her husband was discussing Scripture with Reuben Fisher, as Kate reported, maybe Elias wouldn't mind if his wife started praying out loud.

Sighing, she thrilled to the intimacy between her and the daughter she had longed for as Rosie began to relax. "You're my own little darlin'," she whispered. "You and your brother . . ."

Thinking of the day ahead and of missing quilting bees and work frolics, Rosanna did not regret being sequestered in her home with two adorable babies. Presently it seemed she had no need for human interaction beyond that with her husband and children, though there was no chance they'd be left to themselves. The twins' maternal grandmother, Rachel Stoltzfus, had initially come nearly as often as Kate herself, but her interest had seemingly faded in the past few days. Rosanna wondered if Kate's keen attention might diminish over time, as well, particularly once she was no longer acting as a wet nurse.

Feeling guilty at the thought, Rosanna allowed a short prayer to form on her lips. "Lord, help me to be generous with these little ones . . . so graciously given."

———

Betsy Fisher overheard her daughters talking in Nellie Mae's room prior to Saturday breakfast. They had never before congregated there, at least not that Betsy recalled. Yet they were certainly there now and talking quite loudly, too—loud enough for her to make out every word.

Rhoda's sharp voice rose above the others. "You really ought to go again, Nellie Mae. You seem to think you're better than the rest of us—standin' your ground thataway!"

"What way?" asked Nellie. "That ain't fair to say."

"Sure it is," said Nan. "Rhoda can speak her mind—it's 'bout time someone did."

Nellie fell silent.

"Jah, you should come along on Sundays," Nan said, her tone more gentle. "Why not?"

"I know you'd like me to join you, sisters," Nellie answered, her words less defensive. "But I like followin' the way we were all taught to follow since we were babes. Why's that wrong now?"

"Well, there's nothin' at all wrong with that if you like livin' without electric and cars and whatnot," Rhoda said, worrying Betsy.

"Seems to me you're chasin' after the world, not Scripture," Nellie spoke up.

Betsy touched the small sachet pillow Suzy had made for her—the headache pillow was often tucked inside one of her pockets—and walked toward the door of Nellie's room, her hand poised to knock. More than anything she wanted to put a stop to the senseless conversation. She'd had no idea how interested Rhoda seemed to be in fancy things, other than the necklaces dangling over her side of the dresser of late. Was Nan leaning the same way?

She sighed, folding her hands now. She yearned for her children to know the Savior, not fuss over living in a house with or without electricity. She'd hoped they would catch that insight from Preacher Manny's sermons, or from the Sunday school the new church was talking of starting up soon. The thought gladdened her heart, for she prayed daily that more souls would come to understand the saving grace of the Lord Jesus, bishop's deadline or no.

The girls were talking again, but the conversation had veered away from Preacher Manny's Sunday meetings to the upcoming Singings and other youth-related activities planned for those in the New Order. Feeling awkward about listening in, Betsy knocked on the door.

Nellie appeared, looking well rested, her big brown eyes brighter than usual. "Mornin', Mamma."

"Anyone hungry for breakfast?"

That got a quick response from Rhoda, who rushed past her and down the stairs. Nan followed close behind, but not before giving Nellie Mae a sidelong glance.

Nellie remained, going to sit on her bed. Betsy said no more and simply headed toward the stairs, wanting to give her pensive daughter the room she needed.

Rhoda entered Mamma's kitchen ahead of her sister. Being she was not scheduled to work today, she would attempt to help as much as possible in her father's house . . . her home for the time being. Today she would simply go through the motions again, just as she'd done since first starting to work for Mrs. Kraybill. Preparing breakfast *there* was a joy, what with such appealing and thoroughly modern appliances. Mamma and her sisters would surely succumb, too, if they had the opportunity to see such wonderful-good things as blenders and electric mixers in action.

Jah, they're missing out something awful.

Her thoughts swirled back to yesterday, when Mrs. Kraybill had caught her paging through one of the several family picture albums. Rhoda had closed it right quick, apologizing, but the still-youthful Mrs. Kraybill had not been at all displeased and had even encouraged her to "enjoy whatever you see." Rhoda had relished the look of kindness and even pleasure on her employer's sympathetic face. That moment she turned a corner in her thinking about what she'd always been told was sinful.

What would Mamma think? Rhoda was torn between wanting to shield her parents from her longings and moving forward with her secret plans.

Truth be told, she was itching to immerse herself as much as possible in the Kraybills' wonderfully enticing world—full of not just fancy items but lovely ones. Rhoda craved beauty; she craved travel, too. She dreamed of owning a car and of seeing the country someday, especially the ocean. Other than pinching her pennies, which she was quite happy to do, it might not take much effort at all to realize her dream.

First chance she got Monday, she'd have another look at the Kraybills' newspaper to see how much money a used car might cost her. She didn't feel comfortable going to a used car lot by herself to look around, like some boys in their Rumschpringe were known to do, but she could easily read the classified ads. Who knows? If she had enough gumption to ask, perhaps sometime Mrs. Kraybill would take her car shopping.

Monday's the day after Preaching, Rhoda thought, not knowing why she should plan such outright wickedness after the goodness of the Lord's Day. When did willful disobedience ever pay off?

She shuddered, thinking of Preacher Manny's urgent calls to the youth for repentance . . . and Suzy's drowning came to mind. No matter what Nellie Mae had shown them in Suzy's diary about her surprising turnaround, Rhoda still assumed the Lord God had allowed her youngest sister's death. Might her own disobedience come to a similar bad end?

Rhoda shrugged. With so many opinions about which way was right flying around Honey Brook, it was up to her to find her own way. Right now that meant letting her enthusiasm for experiencing what she'd been deprived of all these years guide her. *No, I'm not at all ready to join the old nor the new church, neither one.*

Part of Rhoda's hope was to catch a man, fancy or otherwise. *A shiny blue—or even green—car might do the trick,* she thought. Hiding her yearning for a beau had not been easy, but she'd managed to conceal from Mamma and her sisters her dire disappointment at being passed over at Singings and other gatherings. What good were such finicky fellows? She would gladly leave them in the dust and make her own future. She refused to die a *Maidel*.

She pictured herself driving along dressed fancy, her long, uncovered hair flowing in the breeze. She'd find herself some pretty new glasses, too, though she would not stoop to wearing those sleeveless tent dresses or silly-looking halter-top blouses she'd seen in the catalogs on Mrs. Kraybill's coffee table.

She laughed with glee at the Rhoda of her imagination, a Rhoda who would not remain lonely for long. Fact was, if she made the jump soon, she could be married within the year.

Still, I must keep my plan a secret, Rhoda thought. *And I best be careful. . . .*

CHAPTER 5

C hristian Yoder had a powerful sense that someone was hovering near his bed. He lifted his head and saw his younger brother, Zach, leaning on the footboard, his shape visible by the light of the moon streaming into their shared bedroom.

"Zach?" He paused. "What's up?"

The room was weighty with silence.

Chris sat up and swung his legs over the side of the bed. His bare feet touched the floor. "Man, it's cold in here."

Zach made a gesture in the dim light. "Sorry. Didn't mean to wake you." He reached up to his bulletin board to straighten a five-by-seven photograph of Suzy Fisher, an enlargement of the only snapshot he had of her. The picture had gone up the week after her untimely death. "I . . . couldn't sleep."

It was hard to see his brother like this. Until last year, most people would have described Zach as an incurable optimist. "Don't worry about it. I'm awake," said Chris.

Still standing by the bulletin board with its mementos and news clippings, Zach shook his head. "She's with the Lord, right? Isn't that what we believe?"

Chris sat quietly. He understood Zach's grief. Suzy was his brother's first love, and there had been something remarkably special about her, beyond being interesting and full of life.

Or was it Zach's guilt, knowing they were partially responsible for Suzy's death? The guilt dug at Chris's soul, too. She had several sisters, if he remembered correctly, including Nellie Mae, the sister Suzy had talked about most often. It had been his idea to ask Suzy's close sister along that day, an offer she'd refused.

How devastated Nellie Mae—the whole family—must have been. Must *still* be. Great as the gulf was between their way of life and his, he'd wanted to express his utter sorrow and somehow . . . apologize. As if that would make a difference.

"Suzy is more alive than we are . . . don't forget that," Chris said.

"Yeah." Zach wandered from the window back to his bed, where he sat staring out at the moonlight. "I guess we'd better get some sleep." His eyes looked hollow.

Suzy's death had affected everything—even Zach's spiritual life. Not to say he was struggling in his faith, but he'd been shaken to the core, just as Chris had been. Their whole family had felt the loss; they'd all been so fond of the freckle-faced Amish girl with wheat-colored hair.

"Ever think of going back out to the lake?" Chris hadn't planned to say that.

But Zach nodded slowly. "Maybe we should sometime. When do you want to go?"

Chris already regretted making the suggestion, but he couldn't back out now, not with Zach agreeing to it. "Next weekend's good. Too much going on today at church."

Zach glanced at the bulletin board once again, then at Chris. "Sure, guess I can wait."

"Hey, it's already the Lord's Day . . . lighten up." Chris threw his pillow across the room, but Zach ducked.

———

Reuben Fisher waited for church to begin, killing time in the raw air. He noticed Benjamin, one of his five married sons, hurrying his way.

"'Mornin'," said Benjamin, ankle-deep in snow. "Seems your cousin Jonathan Fisher's bought himself a used car. A '65 Rambler Marlin—a two-door fastback."

"Ach, but you know a mite too much 'bout this here car business, son."

Benjamin poked at the snow with his black boot. "Honestly, I wouldn't mind gettin' me a good-lookin' car like that. Perty beige color."

Reuben shook his head. Were the New Order meetings merely leading to this? He glanced across the way at his eldest sons—twins Thomas and Jeremiah, both in Sunday black—and wondered how long before they would start such talk. "How is it you're privy to Jonathan's purchase?"

Benjamin brightened. "Saw the car myself while I was over there helpin' in his barn. It's a dandy, I daresay."

Reuben swallowed hard. "A car is the last thing I need . . . or want." Fact was, he'd heard tell of others roaming around used-car lots, asking English neighbors for advice and whatnot. All of them wasting time running helter-skelter.

"What we've got is a split within a split, seems to me." Benjamin moved toward the back of the house. "How many will there be, when all's said and done?"

Reuben recognized the truth in his words and was worried about his own family, and not merely his married sons. Even Rhoda was giving him cause for concern, since she was the only unmarried daughter outside the protection of his roof, spending more time at her employers' place than she did at home anymore.

He paused to take in the landscape, white and crisp. Winter was a time for resting the land, but his body needed some rest, too, thanks to several new foals here lately and three older horses in need of veterinary attention. Come to think of it, his brain could use something of a respite, as well. He pondered now several recent lengthy discussions he'd had with Elias King, just twenty-four. Young, for certain, but what a good head on his shoulders. The young man seemed hungry to talk of the Lord, but not in the way one might expect of a staunch Amishman. Clearly, Elias was searching, much as Reuben himself had been. Longing for the meat of the Word, as Preacher Manny sometimes referred to spiritual sustenance.

Just then Reuben caught sight of his cousin Manny—the Lord's appointed—coming up the lane with his family, all of them waving now, squeezed into the enclosed gray buggy.

"Lord, bless him abundantly for stickin' his neck out," he whispered, waiting to greet Manny and grip his firm hand yet again.

What's Manny think of all the car talk?

Preacher Manny was not a judgmental sort, though he liked to follow the rules. He had not lightly dismissed the teachings of the *Ordnung* on salvation, and he was putting much care and thought into the new ordinance being discussed now. Soon they'd all be back to square one on that as the new church worked to incorporate God's Word, their primary guidebook for living, into the new Ordnung. Meanwhile, those yearning for cars and electricity were already joining up with a nearby Beachy group, whose church met at a separate meetinghouse instead of in houses, and where services were held in English, of all things.

Nellie Mae huddled under her quilts, staring at the bedroom ceiling. *When have I ever been so ill?* She found it ironic that she'd wondered if Caleb was sick, and now here she was, too feverish to get out of bed.

She closed her eyes, well aware she was the only one home on this particular Sunday. For the fast-dwindling Old Order group, today remained a no-Preaching Lord's Day. Her family, of course, had made their way to Manny's church after Mamma had once again invited Nellie to join them. Even if she'd wanted to, there was no way she could go today.

Honestly she was so weak she couldn't think of getting up early to bake tomorrow, as she always did on washday before helping Mamma and Nan with the laundry.

Maybe none of the regulars would notice if the bakery shop was closed. She felt sure she would still be lying there flat on her back come morning, so hot was her brow . . . and nauseated her stomach.

Is it the flu? Or did I eat something bad?

Oh, she wished Mamma had stayed home to warm up some chicken broth or brew a pot of chamomile tea. In her haze of intermittent discomfort and rest, Nellie missed Caleb even more.

When she did at last fall into fitful slumber, she dreamed they were walking along the millstream, only she was on one side and he was on the other, the water rushing between them.

Caleb was telling her she was old enough to make a stand for or against the old church . . . and her family. "What will *you* do, Nellie?" he asked.

She wanted to say that while she was an obedient daughter, she was also ready to be out from under the control of her father. Ready, too, to make a life with her husband someday soon.

"You know how much I despise conflict," she managed to say in her dream.

"Well, who doesn't? Anyway, you haven't said which side you'll be on, if things heat up."

Her mouth felt dry. "You think it'll come to that?"

"Oh jah, there'll be a battle. I'm sure of it." Then he asked again, "Whose side, love?"

In her dream, she hoped it wouldn't mean having to choose. Such things created horrid complications between siblings, parents and grown children, close friends. . . . She'd heard plenty of reports about families here and there leaving the Amish community for the Mennonites and other Plain groups. Yet even in the midst of her very mixed-up dream, Nellie seemed to know that this battle had already taken place, and she was simply reliving the church split that now divided so many.

When she awakened, the anxiety the dream had stirred up lingered, and she hoped Caleb might never goad her in such a manner in real life. She curled tightly into a ball beneath Mammi Fisher's warm winter quilts and pushed the awful dream far, far away.

A while later, thirsty and wishing to know the hour, Nellie crept out of bed and down the stairs, then limped dizzily toward the kitchen. After managing to pour a glass of water, she propped herself up with her arms on the counter and squinted up at the day clock. *Nearly time for Preaching to come to a close*, she thought as she eyed the clock's blurry face.

Her head ached with the effort and Nellie moaned. She should have spoken up and given Mamma a clearer explanation as to why she was staying home. Her family might find it a bit too coincidental that she had begged off attending their church yet again. Certainly Rhoda had seemed to view her resistance to their invitation with some disdain.

Serves me right, their abandoning me, she thought ruefully, slowly heading back toward the stairs.

Then, glancing out at the snow-covered fields and yard, she noticed a tall black shape moving down the road. Inching nearer the window, Nellie tried her best to make out who was there. Could it be she was sleepwalking and merely dreaming?

She leaned on the windowsill, almost too feeble to stand. The man headed straight to their mailbox and stopped in front of it. "What on earth?" she muttered, frowning as she watched.

A wave of nausea forced Nellie back to the stairs, and she pulled herself up step by step, gripping the railing, until she came at last to the landing at the top, where she fell into a heap on the floor. There was no way she could get out to the mailbox to look inside . . . not in her sick state. The best she could do was edge down the hall and climb back into bed, hoping Dat and Mamma wouldn't tarry at the common meal following church. Hoping, too, that if Caleb *had* risked placing something in the mailbox for her, her family would remain none the wiser.

If, indeed, it was Caleb at all. . . .

CHAPTER 6

L ong before dawn Monday, Nan surprised Nellie by coming in and sitting on the bed. "You never woke up for supper last night," Nan whispered. "Mamma tried to nudge you awake several times."

Nellie stretched her legs beneath the quilts, achy all over. "Ach, I slept ever so hard . . . yet I'm still all in."

Nan touched Nellie's forehead. "I'd say you've got a fever."

"Can you . . . would you mind puttin' a sign on the bakery shop?"

"Why sure. But you stay put, all right?" Nan smiled sympathetically. "Seems you've got the old-fashioned flu."

Nellie's head throbbed. "Much too early for you to be up, ain't?"

"Don't worry over me. You're the one burnin' up." Nan rose slowly. "I'll get a cool washcloth for your forehead."

Closing her eyes, she felt relieved that Nan wanted to take care of her. As much as she desired to get up and bake and go about her regular Monday routine, she simply could not.

Hours later, when she'd awakened again and daylight had come, she heard voices downstairs. Was it her lively niece Emma with her mamma and younger siblings? Normally Nellie would hate to miss a morning's fun with her five-year-old niece and her two younger brothers, Jimmy and Matty. Six-year-old Benny, now a first-grader, would be at school.

Soon Nan brought in another cold cloth to replace the warm one, and Nellie tentatively sipped the cup of lukewarm chamomile tea, sweetened with honey.

"This'll do ya good . . . not too hot to spike your fever." Nan's voice was as gentle as Mamma's might have been . . . or Suzy's.

"Kind of you." Nellie lifted her eyes to Nan, whose blue eyes were ever so bright. Her sometimes-distant sister was being unusually attentive. Whatever the reason for the change, Nellie Mae was grateful.

"Martha's downstairs with the children," Nan said, confirming Nellie's earlier hunch. "Here for a quick visit."

"I'd hate for any of them to get this flu."

Nan agreed. "We'll keep the little ones downstairs, but I'll be checkin' on you in a bit."

"Denki, sister." Nellie offered her best smile.

Nan left the room, leaving the door ajar.

Once, when Betsy Fisher was in her teens, she'd gone walking along one of the back roads, only to be knocked down by the thunderous boom of a low-flying jet plane. She recalled the sensation of being stunned by the sound and sight of the enormous plane even now as she held her granddaughter Emma on her lap while sitting at the kitchen table. This time, though, the shock had reverberated from a few simple words.

"We're looking into buying a tractor." Had her daughter-in-law really said such a thing?

But clearly she had, and Martha went on to add that her husband, James, and his younger brother, Benjamin, had recently hired a driver to take them into town to talk to a contractor about installing electricity in both their houses.

Ach, what a big can of worms we've opened. Betsy was appalled, knowing even more was sure to come.

Her head spun with the realization that yet another group had obviously exploded forth from Manny's New Order church, this one bent on all things modern. For sure and for certain, the Beachys were much too fancy for her liking.

She suddenly realized she must have been holding Emma too tightly, because the little sweetie protested and slid off her lap. She felt stricken, similar to the way her eardrums had been assaulted years before, although presently it was her sense of right and wrong that was being shaken. Betsy had lived long enough to know that when certain things were set in motion, one simply could not stop the coming change.

Before Cousin Kate was to arrive for the babies' midmorning feeding, Rosanna wanted to prepare two loaves of bread to bake. She'd missed kneading bread dough, missed the feel of the flour between her fingers. There'd been precious little time for either baking or quilting—her two fondest interests—since Eli and Rosie had arrived. Even so, she cherished her time with her babies, holding them longer than necessary, spoiling them at every turn. Oh, the joy of cradling such snuggly wee ones close to her heart, where she had longed for them as dearly as any birth mother.

No wonder Kate offered to be an occasional wet nurse, she thought. *How could anyone resist such adorable children?*

It nagged at her, though, that Eli was Kate's obvious favorite. Rosanna brushed away her frustration and began to measure the sifted flour. Then, setting it aside, she combined the shortening, salt, sugar, and boiling water, mixing them together till the shortening was dissolved. At last she was ready to add a mixture of yeast, sugar, and warm water and thoroughly blend all the ingredients in her largest bowl.

She thought of her mother, deceased now for many years. Oh, what she wouldn't give to have Mamma here, helping to nurture Eli and Rosie, offering loving advice on everything from feeding schedules to how to burp Rosie when she seemed so tense and colicky, tucking her tiny knees up close to her tummy.

She remembered how elated she and Elias had been at the babies' birth—how much more would her mother have delighted in having these unexpected grandchildren, Rosanna's blood cousins. She'd spent hours studying the set of their eyes and the shape of their earlobes, seeking any resemblance to herself and her many brothers . . . longing for even the slightest connection.

She continued working the dough, adding the remaining flour until the mixture was soft and no longer sticky. Now she would let it rise for a couple hours or so.

Moving into the front room, she sat for a time, enjoying the quiet before Kate's arrival, knowing it would soon come to an end. *Maybe today's visit will be more comfortable for all of us.* With that hope in mind, Rosanna began to talk to the Lord, her very own Savior, according to the Good Book. She had Linda Fisher to thank for opening her eyes to this most priceless truth.

It was past ten o'clock when Reuben finished rubbing liniment on several of his older horses' legs. He thought ahead to writing out detailed feeding regimens for his growing colts as he moseyed out to the road to mail a feed payment. Observing the graying sky, he wished for the piece of blue over toward the south to spread this way. The days had been too long dreary. Some steady sunshine would undoubtedly lift the spirits.

Having son James's wife and little ones visit there that morning might be precisely what he needed, though he knew Betsy would enjoy the visit, as well. Thankfully his wife didn't seem so much blue anymore as mighty busy. And a busy person—as opposed to a busybody—was a wonderful-good thing.

Truth was, he was miffed at Cousin Jonathan, getting this whole car-buying thing started. The man who'd been the first among them to talk openly of salvation was now a believer with a car, of all things.

Just what was Jonathan thinking? Didn't he know others would follow? The idea of his own cousin driving a car gave Reuben the heebie-jeebies as he lifted the flag and opened the mailbox. He would have slid his envelope right in but stopped when he noticed a piece of mail already inside. *Has the postman arrived?* He looked down the road a ways, to the neighbors' mailbox. Their flag was still up.

That's odd.

Reuben pulled the envelope out before placing his own letter in the box. He saw what looked to be a personally delivered letter to Nellie Mae. *C. Yoder* was boldly written in the corner, yet there was no return address.

David's boy's courtin' our Nellie?

The idea peeved him. David Yoder was one of the most outspoken, bull-headed men he knew, and although Reuben had shown kindness toward those in his former church, he struggled now with the notion that Caleb might be pursuing Nellie Mae. Surely Caleb hadn't bargained on the letter's being discovered by anyone but Nellie, her being home alone yesterday for no-Preaching Sunday.

He glanced again at the lackluster sky. Disheartened, he decided to let Betsy be the one to deliver the letter to Nellie Mae, tempted as he was to destroy it or return it to the boy. Still, he would not fall prey to David's own tactics. He'd heard from Deacon Lapp himself that David was encouraging an arrangement between one of the deacon's daughters and Caleb, all to the end of keeping the youngest Yoder boy firmly planted in the old church.

Seems David might be a bit late, Reuben thought wryly.

CHAPTER 7

<hr/>

"I hope you and Rhoda don't get this awful bug," Nellie said softly. Nan had come upstairs again after Martha and the children left, and Nellie was glad for the company. The silence of the house now was a stark contrast to the playful noises of her little niece and nephews.

"Ah, well, the flu's missed me the past several years," Nan was quick to say. "I'm ever so lucky, really."

Nellie looked at her slender brunette sister—so obedient and loyal to attend Preacher Manny's services with Dat and Mamma. "Don't you mean you're blessed, not lucky?"

Nan cast a sideways glance. "You must've heard that at the new church, jah?"

"Prob'ly." Now that she thought of it, she had heard it on the one Sunday she'd succumbed and gone.

"If you ever want to borrow our Bible—Rhoda's and mine—just say so." Nan smiled pleasantly. "It's ever so interesting to read for oneself, truly 'tis."

Nellie had often wished she understood the Scriptures read in High German at Preaching service. "In English, is it?"

"Jah. Dat says sometimes it's best to read a verse several times. Let it sink in, ya know."

"Never heard it put thataway."

Nan sighed fitfully and looked toward the window. "There's much that I'm learnin'." She was silent for a moment and a tear trickled down her cheek. Swiftly she brushed it away. "Ach, I'm sorry."

Nellie's heart sank. "Nothin' to be sorry for." Nellie wanted to add, *We're sisters, after all . . . you can tell me what's troubling you,* but she merely reached for Nan's hand.

"I read the Good Book for more than just to learn what's written there," Nan whispered through more tears.

Nellie listened, holding her breath, not wanting this moment of sharing to slip away.

"My heart's in little pieces." Nan pulled a hankie from beneath her

272

narrow sleeve. "Mamma knows . . . but I've never told another soul. Not even Rhoda."

"Aw, Nan."

"Dave Stoltzfus was everything I loved in a beau, Nellie Mae. Everything . . ." Nan wept openly.

"You cared deeply" was all Nellie could offer without crying herself. This was the first she'd heard the name of the boy who had wounded her sister so.

Nan bobbed her head, her face all pinched up. "I mostly read the psalms. King David endured much sadness, too, yet he could sing praises to Jehovah God in spite of it."

Nellie had never heard the verses Nan spoke of. "I'm glad you're finding some solace."

At this Nan seemed unable to speak, and she looked down at Nellie, whose heart was warmed by this demonstration of tenderness from the sister who'd always preferred Rhoda.

Nellie woke with a start and saw Mamma standing near the bed.

Slowly Mamma sat, an envelope in her hand. "I didn't mean to waken you, dear." She tilted her head, concern in her eyes. "Your Dat brought this in . . . for you."

She'd nearly forgotten about having seen someone near their mailbox earlier . . . yesterday, was it? The indistinct man by the road had become lost in a tangle of confusing dreams to the point Nellie'd felt sure she'd imagined him. "Ach, what's this?"

Mamma said nothing, though she remained. After a lengthy moment, she asked, "How are you feelin' now? Has your fever broken?"

Nellie shook her head. Oh, what she wouldn't give to be free of the fierce heat in her body. She felt hot all over, even to her own touch. Yet despite the fever, she felt an uncontrollable chill and could not get warm. Even now she had to will herself to relax so her muscles wouldn't lock up and become so tense she shivered all the more. She craved a reprieve from the sickness that had plagued her since Saturday night.

Has it been only two days?

Mamma changed the wet cloth on her forehead and had her sip more tepid tea with honey. Then, laying a hand on Nellie's brow, she bowed her own head, lips moving silently.

Nellie felt comforted, yet uneasy, as she wondered if Preacher Manny taught this sort of praying. Truly, she seemed to be learning newfangled things without even attending his gatherings. But she was touched by Mamma's gesture and hoped the prayer might indeed restore her to health sooner.

When Mamma was finished, she opened her eyes. "I pray that the power of the living God will raise you up once again."

Nellie found herself nodding, although she doubted the Lord God and heavenly Father wished to be bothered with such a small request.

Mamma lifted the cool cloth and leaned down to kiss her forehead before departing the room. Then, and only then, did Nellie dare to lift the envelope to her eyes. The letter was indeed from Caleb.

Despite being so ill, her heart skipped with joy, and she quickly opened the sealed envelope.

My dearest Nellie,

I haven't forgotten you, not for a single minute! Christmas was terrible, not seeing you. And for that I'm awful sorry.

I feel like a bird in a locked cage. And confess that I'm sinning to carry this letter to your mailbox today, Sunday, January 13th, by pretending to have the flu, which is sadly going around. So while my family is out visiting, I'm "sick" in my bed—well, I'll soon be out walking to your house, darling Nellie.

If ever there was a girl for me, it's you. The times when I think of you, even dream of you, are more than I can count. I hope you don't think poorly of me, leaving you without the company of a beau for even a while. For certain I despised doing so.

And now here it is nearly mid-January already, and I still have not solved our dilemma. Daed has demanded that I shun you and your family, yet I yearn to talk with you and be near you once more.

You musn't fear for our future, my dear, dear Nellie. I will know very soon what must be done so that we can be together.

> *With all my love,*
> *Caleb Yoder*

Hands trembling, though no longer from fever, Nellie folded the envelope in half and slipped the letter beneath her pillow. *Oh, Caleb, you risked so much to deliver this. How could I have doubted you?*

She hadn't forgotten his endearing words, the way he held her at the millstream as he kissed her face, though never her lips. To wait was their unspoken courting promise.

Sliding her warm hand beneath the cool pillow, Nellie touched his letter, wishing she might find a way to get word back to him.

While Rhoda dusted the Kraybills' front room, their cat pushed against her leg. Back arched high, he let out a resounding *meow*.

"Ach, you're hungry, is that it?"

Pebbles meowed again. This pet was always looking for a handout.

He followed her across the entryway, then through the formal sitting room, with its high wooden mantel and matching gold overstuffed chairs, and into the kitchen. Opening the bag of kitty chow, Rhoda filled Pebbles's dish and checked his water bowl, too.

Standing there, she watched the black-and-white cat nibble away at his dinner, knowing her father would never allow something as frivolous as keeping a pet indoors. Then, eager to get back to work, she returned to the living room, as Mrs. Kraybill referred to their cozy and well-furnished front room. Rhoda straightened the coffee table, trying not to glance at the magazines stacked neatly there, especially one periodical that seemed to have strayed from Mr. Kraybill's study—*Car and Driver* magazine. She'd noticed the new issue had appeared last week. Her parents would be chagrined if they knew she was coveting the cars featured within the shiny pages, yet she couldn't deny to herself that she was ever so weary of horse-and-buggy travel.

Like some of the church boys surely must be.

Several from the old church had purchased cars and hidden them far from their fathers' houses, sowing disobedience before eventually becoming baptized church members. Some of those same fellows had given her the cold shoulder at Sunday night Singings. Not caring to admit it, even to herself, Rhoda realized she was on a path to show them just what they'd missed.

Even so, she would wait to investigate the pages of the most current car magazine until she knew she was truly alone here—till Mrs. Kraybill, wearing a wine-colored suit and black heels, left for her ladies' auxiliary meeting in New Holland. She glanced at the clock. *How much longer must I wait?* she thought.

Of course, she was expected to thoroughly clean the first floor today, but midafternoon Mrs. Kraybill allowed time for her to enjoy another break, complete with tea and cookies—the latter frequently purchased from Nellie's Simple Sweets.

Rhoda was less interested in the goodies here lately, as she desired to drop a few pounds. She felt sure that a trimmer figure and a pretty car were just the ticket to getting herself a husband.

CHAPTER 8

Nellie Mae felt better when she awakened Wednesday morning. Though her fever had suddenly broken yesterday, Mamma and Nan had covered for her at the shop, baking fewer items than normal, since customers were only trickling in anyway.

Nellie soaked up the compassion offered by her next-older sister, who smiled warmly across the breakfast table as she passed the food directly to her.

Later, after the table was cleared and Rhoda was off to work, Nan washed the dishes while Mamma dried, with both insisting that Nellie simply sit and sip tea at the table.

But it was after Mamma had left the room to go upstairs and have a "devotional time" with Dat that Nan sat down beside her. "Rebekah Yoder was here for another visit," she whispered.

"When?" asked Nellie.

"Yesterday, when you were still in bed." Nan looked troubled. "She told me something awful surprising. Said her mother heard that someone ran an ad in the *Lancaster New Era* to advertise Nellie's Simple Sweets."

"What? You're sure?"

"That's what she said. Seems her mamma was ever so outspoken 'bout it, saying it sounded just like 'them Fishers' to do something that worldly."

Nellie was horrified to think Caleb's mother would talk about their family like that. "Well, who would've done such a thing?"

"Only one I can think of." Nan glanced toward the doorway. "My guess is Rhoda."

Nellie laughed. "But why?"

"Seeing some of the old church folks droppin' off as customers since the split . . . well, it's bothered Rhoda somethin' awful." Nan paused. "Probably she's tryin' to help, is all."

"Ever so nice, really, when you think 'bout it."

Nan agreed. " 'Specially since she's been rather aloof here lately." She took a sip of tea. "You know what else?"

Nellie listened as she pushed her teacup and saucer away.

"Rebekah said she thinks the ad's a wonderful-good idea. She says we'll get more Englischers than we'll know what to do with."

Nellie groaned. "If that happens, how will we keep up?"

"Wait and see. No need to borrow more worry." Nan was grinning to beat the band. "I'll help ya more, Nellie Mae, and Mamma will, too."

"Dat's nearly finished with the tables and chairs," Nellie reminded her. "Maybe that's why Rhoda would pay to publicize the bakery shop—do ya think so?"

"Who's to say? Knowin' her, she might simply have an interest in bringing in more fancy folk." She sighed. "She sure seems to like the Kraybills' house a lot."

Better than ours . . .

Nan rested her face in her hands, her elbows on the table. "I daresay things'll start lookin' up round here."

"For you, too, Nan?"

"In some ways, maybe." Again Nan looked toward the doorway, as if to make sure Mamma was out of earshot. "I'm ready to forgive . . . to overlook my former beau's foolishness. But I can't say I'm ready to put aside my anger toward Rebekah's father. He's got no right keepin' friends apart."

That's the truth! Nellie thought.

"You'd think David Yoder would listen to Uncle Bishop, of all things. He seems so bent on following the old church, it really makes no sense that he won't follow the bishop's bidding 'bout not shunning." Nan rolled her eyes.

Nellie agreed and rose, carrying her cup, saucer, and spoon over to the sink. "Oh, how good it feels to be stronger again. Can't remember the last time I was so sick."

"Well, thank the Good Lord for health . . . and Mamma for her prayers," Nan said.

Nellie didn't share how Mamma had placed her hand on Nellie's forehead while she had prayed right over her. Nan probably knew something about that sort of praying now, too. For sure and for certain, this family was changing—and mighty fast. And if Rhoda had indeed placed the newspaper ad, their older sister seemed bent on heading in a direction of her own choosing.

Chris Yoder stood in the doorway, waiting for his class of boys to arrive. The Wednesday night group had doubled in size since he had begun teaching.

Two of the most outgoing boys had invited school friends the same age, and the new kids simply kept coming, bringing along even more friends.

He walked to the windows and leaned back against the sill, regarding the classroom. He and Zach had given the place a fresh coat of eggshell-colored paint this fall, replacing the former gray. Chris had also purchased a chalkboard with his own money.

He prayed for the impressionable young lives God allowed him to shape each week, whispering their names to the Father. One boy particularly concerned him—Billy Zercher—a loner with dark circles under his wide blue eyes.

"Help me reach him. . . ."

Chris knew he was probably too impatient for results. With high school graduation just around the bend, he was eager to get on with life in general, as well as ready for the divine call. His father had always said it was better to be a moving vessel than a stagnant one . . . waiting for something big to happen. And big was what Chris wanted. Outside grocery stores and along the sidewalk at the local public schools, he and his brothers had passed out tracts containing invitations to revival meetings at Tel Hai campground. While their efforts were met with modest success, he hoped for something even more fruitful, something that might reach more than the two or three stragglers who found their way to the meetings. If he had his way, he would work tirelessly to stamp out the recent "God is dead" nonsense heralded by *Time* magazine and others.

As for his future livelihood, his father's landscaping business was definitely an option. Chris knew the ropes—the appropriate, careful way to handle tree roots during transplanting and the like. He'd effortlessly memorized every perennial unique to this locale. He knew their watering needs, how deep the roots went, and which were blooming plants and which were not.

Lately, though, he longed for something with eternal meaning, some kind of full-time ministry. Hopefully he'd figure that out while attending Bible college in Harrisonburg, Virginia, next fall.

Chris wasn't the only one with grandiose dreams. He knew Zach had his heart set on ministry, too, and had even been praying for his life mate with that in mind, asking for a girl who loved God with all her heart, mind, and spirit. When he met Suzy Fisher, Zach had believed that his future bride *had* been revealed, if perhaps a tad too early. Their next-older brother, along with their dad, had tried to dissuade Zach from falling too hard, too fast . . . especially for an Amish girl.

Chris, on the other hand, had never encountered any girl who turned his head. But Zach was sure he'd found a special love early in life and had confided as much to Chris. He'd decided to ask Suzy to go steady the afternoon of their outing to Marsh Creek State Park. And then in one terrible instant, Suzy was gone, swallowed up by the vast lake.

Chris and Zach had immediately jumped into action, as had their three older brothers, leaving their horrified dates alone in the other rowboats. At first, Chris's terror kept him from filling his lungs with adequate air to dive farther down.

But finally, on his third dive, Chris managed to dive deep enough to swim up with Suzy. Too late—her lungs were already full, her body limp.

She never knew Zach thought that *God had brought them together. . . .*

Chris believed in God's sovereignty, as did all four of his brothers. Their parents had drilled it into them as youngsters. To think Suzy, so new to their Mennonite church, might have become his sister-in-law had she lived. But now it troubled him to know that Zach was unable to shake the memory of Suzy standing up—then teetering—in the rowboat, her long dress billowing as she lost her balance and plunged overboard. He suffered frequent nightmares, thrashing in his bed across the room he shared with Chris. The dreams and flashbacks kept him on edge all day, and his grades had plummeted.

Even Chris had struggled to concentrate after last June's accident. He recalled going through the motions at the nursery, alongside his dad. When the opening for a Wednesday night youth leader had come, he'd gladly accepted.

The Lord knew I needed this class. . . .

Moving away from the window, he scattered extra Bibles on the large, round table before scanning his note cards once more. But his thoughts stubbornly returned to Suzy Fisher's conversion and sudden death.

To think she might have died in her sins.

He thanked the Lord again for causing their paths to cross, for preparing Suzy's heart to receive Him. He prayed, too, that somehow Suzy's death would not be in vain.

The group of boys rushed into the classroom with a bustle of talk. Quickly they took their seats, forming a circle of eight energetic third- and fourth-graders. Chris hurried to sit at the table with them, wanting to be on their level, like an older brother. "You guys ready for the sword drill?" he asked.

There was a sudden flurry as those who hadn't brought Bibles snatched up the ones in the center of the table. Thumbs poised over the gilded edges, they waited, eyes bright.

"Galatians 6:2," Chris announced.

"Bear ye one another's burdens, and so fulfill the law of Christ," one boy belted out, not bothering to search for it.

"No fair!" another boy piped up.

"Isn't this a *sword drill*, not a memory verse drill?" asked Billy Zercher.

Chris looked at Billy in surprise. "You're right." He smiled. "Want to pick a Scripture?"

Billy turned shy, eyes blinking. He lowered his head and fell silent.

"Let me!" came the chorus of voices.

Chris glanced at Billy. *I won't give up on him. And not on Zach, either . . .*

CHAPTER 9

The moment had come.

His countenance absolutely serious, Daed sat Caleb down Wednesday night and began to outline the future, beginning with his expectations for the initial division of farming and dairy responsibilities, next moving on to the eventual land transfer. "Son, I want you to be in charge of everything—plowing, planting, and working the land, overseeing livestock. For a while, of course, you can rely on your older brothers for some help with that, just as I do now." He ran his thumbs beneath the length of his black suspenders before delving into more detail.

Anxious as he had been for this day to come, Caleb paid mighty close attention. *My birthright, at last!*

After a time, Daed leaned back in his chair and seemed to appraise him. Caleb met his father's gaze, uncomfortable under the unexpected scrutiny.

"Listen, Caleb, I'm proud of you for breakin' things off with that girl of yours. That is, I assume you have."

His father's words filled him with resentment, but he managed to maintain eye contact.

"Don't think I haven't noticed you're not attendin' Singings and whatnot."

Caleb clenched his jaw, saying nothing.

"Now's the time to find a befitting wife. Don't let the grass grow under your feet." His father added, "A deal's a deal. I'll sign the deed over when you've found yourself a suitable bride."

"Suitable?" Nellie Mae was the most suitable bride he could imagine. "Why not Nellie Mae? She hasn't joined Preacher Manny's church, Daed. She's staying Old Order. You'll see for yourself next fall when we're both baptized."

His father grunted. "Way I see it, girls tend to follow their mammas even after marriage. It's a good thing you've let her go."

Caleb opened his mouth to respond but changed his mind. It certainly wasn't Nellie's fault Reuben Fisher had abandoned *das Alt Gebrauch*—the

Old Ways—getting caught up in his preacher cousin's dangerous way of thinking about things like studying Scripture. Why should Caleb have to abandon his affection for Nellie Mae because of his father's opposition to Reuben's keen interest in all of that?

Daed continued. "You could marry any number of girls in our church district . . . Deacon Lapp's daughter, for one."

"Susannah?"

Daed's eyes brightened. "She's a strong one—a hard worker. Mighty pretty, too. Even prettier than the Fisher girl." Daed pointed his finger at him. "What I'm saying is, I expect you to marry a respectable girl from one of the families in our church. It's the only way to get your land." By this his father meant no one would do from among either the "saved by grace" folk or those splintering off further yet. Caleb had heard that several of the so-called tractor enthusiasts were already dialing up folk on telephones installed *inside* their houses, no less.

Judging by Daed's flushed face, now was not the time to press further, risking his ire. No, his father was much too caught up in this split, drawing fine lines for his family about who was and was not fit for association. Caleb had wondered if his sister Rebekah wasn't given a similar ultimatum. Yesterday he'd overheard quarreling between the usually calm Rebekah and Daed, and Rebekah had burst out crying, saying she was going to visit her best friend, Nan. "And no one will stop me!"

Clearly he wasn't the only one put out with his father's bias against the Fishers, though it appeared Rebekah was more headstrong than he.

Or so Daed assumes . . .

Daed didn't bother to dismiss him but simply rose and ambled out to the utility room. Caleb couldn't forget this was the same man who had nine years ago railroaded Abe, his older brother, forcing him to marry his pregnant girlfriend. But Caleb's situation was nothing like that of the too-amorous Abe.

Still, he shuddered to think how swiftly he could be pulled into a ferocious tug-of-war between the inheritance he was raised to and darling Nellie Mae. Fact was, all could be avoided if his father saw for himself that Nellie Mae was wholly faithful to the Old Order. If only Daed would just give it time.

———

Word spread about the newspaper ad for Nellie's Simple Sweets like dandelions gone to seed in summer. Betsy's sister-in-law Anna, the bishop's wife, took it upon herself at the sewing frolic on Thursday morning to point out that it was "just a sinnin' shame" for the Fishers to stoop to such a deed. She said it right to Betsy, who was taken aback.

"Well, it's not Reuben's or my doing," Betsy replied.

"Whose, then?"

"I don't know." No one in the house even read the daily paper put out by Englischers. The only paper they subscribed to was *The Budget,* a Plain publication from Sugarcreek, Ohio, that chronicled the week's activities.

"I daresay some folk will do anything for extra money." Rachel Stoltzfus put in her two cents as if she hadn't heard Betsy at all.

"Had nothin' to do with it, I tell ya." Betsy turned away, peering down at her sewing. This morning's group numbered eight other women, including her own daughters-in-law Esther and Fannie—wives to Thomas and Jeremiah.

Always one to offer a kind word, Esther spoke up on her behalf. "Now, why would ya think such a thing of *Mamm?*"

Rachel harrumphed, keeping her head down, her eyes fixed on a torn seam on her husband's shirt. All of them were mending various items of clothing, gathering for the fun of it as they did several times a year. But today's frolic was proving not to be much fun for Betsy, and she decided to go about her business, stitching up the hem on her oldest dress, hoping to get another month or two's wear.

"Ask your mamma if she's purposely stirring up trouble by bringin' more English customers into the neighborhood," Rachel prodded again.

It was daughter-in-law Fannie's turn to retort. "Listen, Rachel, you can speak directly to Mamma—for goodness' sake, she's right there across the table!"

"Jah, and you can't say yous don't rely on outsiders for feed and grain and suchlike," Esther pointed out, momentarily setting her work aside to look at Rachel.

"Feed salesmen ain't exactly outsiders," Anna said, re-entering the conversation.

"True," said Betsy, "they're *Mennischte*—Mennonite."

"But tractor salesmen, what 'bout them?" Rachel shot back.

Now Betsy was really peeved. "I have nothin' at all to do with them."

"Oh, but others here do . . . and you know right who you are, too!" Rachel rose quickly, marching to the back of the house, where a small washroom had been added on, similar to Reuben's addition on the Fishers' own house.

Silence reigned while Rachel was absent, though Betsy felt like spouting off but good. She was being sorely tested here in her sister-in-law's house, but she was holding her peace all the same, just as she had the day Reuben's mother had lambasted her. Of course, that had been a different matter altogether.

Well, maybe not so different, come to think of it.

All these insinuations from Rachel and even Anna were directly related to the tension between the church groups. Three of them now—Old Order, New Order, and the Beachys. Truth be told, it was rather surprising that the bishop's wife would have included womenfolk from all three groups at today's work frolic.

Got to give her some credit for making an effort at unity, Betsy mused.

She recalled Preacher Manny's sermon last Sunday on having a brand-new life. Manny had said the Lord would not force His life upon anyone against his or her will. One's will played a big part in coming or not coming to Calvary's cross. That, and the divine calling—the inward drawing and wooing, much as in courtship the lover pursued the beloved. Might Anna and the bishop eventually be drawn to salvation? Might Rachel, too? Betsy faithfully prayed so, just as she trusted for others in her community still in bondage to tradition.

Less than one month before changing churches means certain shunning!

Rosanna wished to goodness Cousin Kate had gone to the sewing frolic instead of staying so long after nursing Eli this morning. That her cousin had entirely given up on nursing Rosie seemed odd, though it was time now for Cousin Kate to be done nursing both babies.

Rosanna's anticipation had nothing to do with keeping Kate away from the babies. But Kate was not at all herself, and her behavior was setting Rosanna on edge. Was it postpartum blues? Plenty of women suffered during the months following a birth, and she, of all people, wanted to be understanding and compassionate. Even so, it jarred her when Kate completely ignored her gentle question about when she planned to stop nursing Eli.

Rosanna tried again. "Two months have come and gone, cousin. Elias and I have appreciated your help, but I'm sure ya have better things to do with your time than make daily visits here."

Even after this, Kate seemingly refused to look Rosanna in the eye. Instead she leaned over Eli, stroking the dimpled arm that peeked from beneath his blanket.

"Such a handsome one, he is," Kate murmured. "So like his father."

Rosanna shuddered at the comment. How would Kate feel in her place? Leaning hard against the doorframe, she tried to see things from Kate's perspective—how very difficult this must be, giving her babies away. She couldn't begin to imagine it.

"Look how his right eyebrow arches ever so slightly," Kate said, tracing it with her pointer finger.

"I've noticed, too."

Then Kate touched her own eyebrow, as if comparing.

Rosanna had to glance away. She could not abide her cousin's coming here any longer.

Inching back toward the kitchen, she wondered if Kate was taking any herbs known to help alleviate depression. Maybe she should simply go through her cupboard and offer Kate some blessed thistle or evening primrose oil to brew for tea. She knew, as many of the womenfolk did, that these would not interfere with nursing. *Though I wouldn't mind that coming to an end.*

Suddenly Kate burst into tears in the next room. "Oh, my precious *Boppli.*" She rose from the rocking chair, waking tiny Eli. Then, wandering to the front room, she carried him over her shoulder, stroking his back while he blinked his little eyes at Rosanna.

Ach, is she having a breakdown? Or does she really have so little regard for my wishes?

Then and there, Rosanna decided she'd definitely go to the next quilting frolic, or maybe go visiting and take the babies along. *Let Kate come to call and simply not find us here!*

———

Nellie Mae suppressed a squeal of delight when she went to pick up the mail before returning to the shop after the noon meal Thursday. Caleb's name and return address were printed in the corner of an envelope for all to see.

Another letter so soon . . . how bold of him!

She ran across the snowy yard to the front porch, where she sat, in spite of the cold, to read the letter from her beloved.

Dearest Nellie,

I've missed you more than I dare to write. I must see you again. Let's meet secretly at our special place.

*I will come on foot this Friday following supper. Hopefully it won't be
too cold for you. Bundle up, all right?*

Counting the hours.

> *Yours always,*
>
> *Caleb Yoder*

She pressed the letter to her lips. He cared deeply for her—that much
was clear. He had again risked being found out with yet another letter. Of
course, there was nothing for him to fear *here*, for her parents were not
holding an inheritance over her head.

No, Nellie was free to see whomever she wished . . . to marry Caleb,
for that matter. Obviously Dat and Mamma wanted her to join them in
their beliefs, but they had not expressed any conditions about whom their
daughters might marry.

Even so, Nellie worried for Caleb . . . for them. What would he do if his
father refused to change his mind and allow him to court her?

Will Caleb love me enough to bid the farm good-bye?

Nellie knew that Caleb's love for his birthright lay less in the land than
in what it meant for his future family. Caleb was not selfish in desiring it.
Rather, he showed himself to be prudent and reliable, and for that she loved
him all the more. But she could not tell him so before Friday, because she
did not dare to write a letter back.

Tomorrow I'll see him!

CHAPTER 10

F riday evening Nellie managed to leave the house only after helping in the kitchen, making small talk with Mamma and Nan. It was imperative, to her thinking, to lend a hand, since Rhoda hadn't yet arrived home, something that was becoming the norm. Nellie stayed as long as she could, risking being late for meeting Caleb.

Had her heart ever pounded this hard before? She hurried now along the snowy road to meet her beau, the air of excitement within more noticeable to her than the bitter cold.

Soon, very soon, we'll be together!

She wished she might have thought to hitch up the horse and buggy. Maybe, just maybe, Caleb was counting on her doing so, though he hadn't suggested it in his sweet letter. Still, she had plenty of layers on and would fare well on foot for a good couple of hours or so, if necessary.

As she picked her way along the road, she longed to lay eyes on Caleb—to see him, talk to him, and listen to the news he had to share with her. To think they had been apart for more than a month. How long would it be till they'd see each other again, after tonight? She would not allow herself to think that way. It was far better to live for this precious moment and be thankful for what time they did have together.

When she rounded the bend of the old mill, she looked everywhere, eager for a glimpse of him. A few couples were already skating on the pond, and their occasional laughter wafted across the millrace to where she stood. She hoped Caleb hadn't brought his skates, since she hadn't carried hers. Feeling awkward, even conspicuous, she scanned the area for signs of her beau, in case he'd decided to wait for her off the road.

She squinted through the trees, looking, but when he did not arrive, she circled the stone mill to check the other side. He might have decided to be careful and hide from prying eyes. She hoped she hadn't misunderstood his letter or arrived too late. Had she lingered too long after supper?

She spied the wrought-iron bench where they'd sat together. The bench seemed to her now a symbol of their courtship, the place where they had shared their first words of endearment and where she had accepted his tender affection. She smiled, recalling the way his gentle kisses had created feathery tickles in her stomach.

Caleb's fondness for her was evident in the genuinely respectful manner in which he conveyed his love, unlike some boys who pushed the limits. Truly her beau was nothing less than a gentleman.

Turning to face the road, Nellie peered into the twilight, longing for Caleb. *Where are you, love?*

Though he disliked admitting to harboring any pride, Reuben took pleasure in not being easily *ferhoodled*. In fact, he was nearly always composed and had refused to be drawn into the too-frequent church debates of late. A good many arguments were flying back and forth between the three Honey Brook Amish groups, despite the bishop's attempt to keep the peace.

This evening he'd slipped out to visit with his son Ephram. The problem, as Reuben saw it, was that Ephram and Maryann had but a few weeks left till the *Bann* threatened any baptized adults who chose to leave the old church. Where would that leave Ephram if he decided to join Reuben and Betsy in the new church *after* the grace period was up? While either group of new church folk would surely welcome him, Ephram and his family would be shunned from the old fellowship, many of whose members were blood relatives. If that came about, Ephram's livelihood would suffer, just as his father's presently did. *Bann or no Bann, there's no denying times are tough.*

Now that Reuben had arrived, he found himself pacing, nervous. "'Tis high time we got things out in the open, son," he said after greeting Ephram.

"I'll never see things your way, Dat." His son leaned against the wall, arms folded over his thick chest. "Save your breath, I say."

Reuben shook his head. "I've held my peace long enough," he said. "I've been praying for ya, son."

"Like I said, Dat, best be savin' your breath."

His heart's closed up. . . .

Lifting his eyes to the rafters, Reuben recalled how unbendable his bishop brother Joseph had been earlier today. Fact was, Ephram and the bishop saw eye to eye—their thinking as skewed as Reuben's had been for all the years of his life, till now.

"Someone's been running a newspaper ad for Nellie Mae's bakery shop in the English paper," Ephram said, abruptly changing the subject. "The grapevine's swinging wide and far about it, wonderin' if it'll show up in next week's papers, too."

"Well, what on earth?"

Ephram's eyes narrowed. "You mean you had nothing to do with it?"

"Why should I?"

"I just thought—"

"That's where you got yourself in trouble, son. You're jumping to conclusions, when you ought to be askin'." Reuben forced a laugh.

"I'm askin' *now*."

"Folks wrongly assume things all the time. But what's it matter if you or anyone else thinks I placed an ad?"

Ephram's expression turned to one of astonishment. "Matters a whole lot if you're set on bringin' in more and more outside folk to Nellie's bakery shop. Looks bad, like you're too anxious for the fancy."

"Ain't my doin', that's for certain."

"Maybe so, but you've been turnin' the other way for as long as Nellie's run that shop, ain't so?"

Reuben could scarcely believe the tone his son was taking with him. He refused to defend his decision to allow the bakery shop to Ephram or anyone else—plenty of Old Order families had roadside vegetable stands and the like. No, right now he was beginning to feel like walking straight out of Ephram's barn, lest he fall into temptation and put his hands on his brawny son's shoulders and shake him good. The grapevine was indeed ever present, but the way folk interpreted what they heard from the rumor mill was the real problem.

"Nellie's Simple Sweets does our family more good than harm," he said at last. "And I've never had cause to question the way your sister handles things. You should have the sense to know she'd no more place an ad than I would."

After a terse good-bye, Reuben hurried to the buggy, more aware now of the cold. "A body shouldn't be out in this for long," he muttered to the horse.

He arrived home to Betsy, who was anxious to discuss Nellie Mae. "She's been gone awhile—on foot, no less." She looked up, her embroidery balanced on her lap.

"Meeting a beau, no doubt." He glanced at the kitchen clock.

"Not just any fella, I don't think."

He knew as much. And the worst of it was knowing Caleb Yoder was not likely to shift toward the New Order—not the way his father was shooting off his mouth amongst the old church brethren. If Nellie Mae married Caleb . . . well, it meant a worrisome situation.

"We'll lose her," he whispered. "She'll submit to her beau's way of thinkin'."

Betsy frowned.

"And just when I'd hoped she might be leanin' toward salvation." He remembered her momentary tenderness after she'd gone with them to hear Preacher Manny that once.

"Let God do His work in His way, love." She reached for him.

He bussed her cheek. "You're right 'bout that." He wouldn't admit it, for surely his wife suspected it already, but he'd gladly help the Lord along, and right quick, too, where their children were concerned.

Betsy picked up her embroidery hoop. If Reuben wasn't mistaken, she was repeating a Scripture verse as she worked.

He hadn't removed his coat, since he'd intended to check on his horses. His boots left prints in the icy snow as he trudged toward the barn, where he looked in on the new foals first. When he was satisfied they each had enough bedding straw, he went to the small corner of the barn where he kept files on his horses' breeding records, as well as their veterinary appointments. It was there also that he had put in a good many hours crafting the round tables and chairs for Nellie's bakery shop.

Perching on his work stool, Reuben thought again of the grapevine. "Nonsense is right," he muttered, tracing a circle in the sawdust on the workbench. He cared not one iota who might've paid for the ad. As for bringing it up to Betsy, he'd let her mention it. No sense making a big to-do.

Going to inspect one of the completed chairs, he ran his hand over its smooth seat, then the straight slats on the back. He would be finished by Monday, perhaps at just the right time, too, since Nellie Mae was well enough to tend the store again.

Let the Englischers come. . . .

An enclosed black buggy appeared in the near distance, and Nellie's heart sank. *Puh*—no way could it be Caleb. Yet she lingered in the brush, beginning to shiver. Surely Caleb would have an explanation as to why he was this late, if he came at all.

She had heeded his suggestion and worn two sets of long johns, donning her heaviest sweater and warmest black coat over her dress and apron. She guessed she was a sight to see, surely having expanded a few inches in girth.

She observed the horse and carriage as it slowed. Lo and behold, it came to a complete halt. Suddenly there he was—Caleb, leaping off the buggy! He paused momentarily, evidently searching the area.

She stepped out into the clearing. *Goodness, he is here.* She placed her hand over her heart as it fluttered with joy. "Caleb," she whispered.

He let out a stifled whoop and began running through the snow, straight to her. "Nellie Mae!"

Ach, Caleb . . . She struggled to keep her composure at the sight of her beau, her love.

His arms opened for her and she fell into him, welcoming his crushing embrace. "Oh, I missed you so," she whispered into his long woolen coat.

He pressed his cheek against hers. "Oh, Nellie, honey . . . your face is like ice." He leaned back to look into her eyes; then he happily hugged her again. He seemed reluctant to release her, but he reached for her hand and led her toward the buggy. "Come, let's get you warmed up."

As they walked, he explained that he'd taken the extra time to go to a cousin's and plead to borrow his new carriage. "I figured we'd be frozen sticks otherwise. There should be enough heavy lap robes to keep you cozy, love."

Love . . .

Oh, the sound of his voice.

The thought of warmth, after having been so very cold, as well as of having this private time with him, made Nellie hurry to match Caleb's stride.

"We've got ourselves a family buggy." He chuckled.

"Jah, I see that."

"It's not for courtin', but it'll keep us much warmer."

She laughed as he literally lifted her into his cousin's carriage.

Oh joy!

CHAPTER 11

O nce settled in the buggy, Nellie realized just how chilled she was, especially her fingers and toes. As soon as the horse pulled forward onto the road, Caleb let go of the reins and began to warm her hands by rubbing each finger, one at a time, between his own hands, next kissing the tips of them.

She laughed softly as he did so rather comically. "Oh, you silly," she whispered, leaning against his arm.

"No sillier than you." He had taken great care to wrap her in the woolen lap robes. "My cousin'll be glad we put these to good use."

"He's got himself quite a nice buggy." She eyed the dashboard.

"Nice is right. Cousin Aaron purchased a dilapidated family buggy back when he first got married, so he's needed a new one for a while. He wasn't too keen on partin' with this fine one, even for one night. I had to beg, which is why I took so long."

"Maybe he suspects what you wanted it for."

He smiled and picked up the reins. "Well, he had his share of forbidden loves, too."

"Ach, really?"

Caleb explained that Aaron had never been of the Old Order Amish but rather one of the "team Mennonites," who drove black buggies—close cousins to their way of life. "But Aaron dated some progressive Amish girls, I'm told, and sneaked around doin' so."

Like us tonight.

The carriage moved down the road with a gentle jostle, and Nellie wondered if Cousin Aaron might be one to betray Caleb, though she didn't want to mention it.

"How've you been, Nellie Mae?"

"Oh, all right."

"No . . . really," he urged. "Catch me up on what I've missed."

They'd never sat together so privately like this, sheltered from both the elements and observers. The carriage was a marked change from Caleb's open courting buggy. The dimness of its interior felt strangely intimate, and Nellie felt self-conscious, although she would have welcomed Caleb's presence in any circumstance.

"Well, let's see. I'll start with Christmas. My brothers and their families all spent the day, and my nieces and nephews took turns stringing popcorn near the cookstove. Emma, Mamma's favorite—no secret, I daresay—was awful cute, reciting a poem she'd learned from my brother Ephram's oldest boy. I clapped when Emma finished, and Rhoda said I should quit teachin' her to be vain." As soon as Nellie uttered the words, she felt ashamed.

"Rhoda's got a lip on her, then?"

She wanted to make quick amends, for she was not one to speak against her family. "Well, she was prob'ly right," Nellie added.

"Aw, honey . . . it's okay to say what you feel."

His response made her wonder if there were things he, too, would like to share about a family member, namely his father. But she wouldn't bring up that sore topic. "How was Christmas at your house?" she asked.

He leaned back, nestling her in the bend of his arm before answering. "Worst ever . . . without you." He leaned closer. "Next year, just think, we'll be man and wife."

Nellie blushed, glad for the darkness, but she wondered how on earth he would ever get his father's blessing. *If he's sure it will happen, I should simply relax and quit worrying.*

"I'll convince Daed that we belong together, you'll see." He paused. "I say we tie the knot right away in November, all right?"

Happily she nodded, surprised he was suddenly so open with her when things had seemed quite bleak before. Had something changed? "When the time is closer, I'll talk it over with Mamma. She'll want two weeks to get things ready, I'm thinkin'."

He agreed, lingering near. "I think often of you bein' close like this, Nellie Mae. Think of it all the time."

She sighed, letting herself rest in his arms. Just knowing he had found a way for them to be married was mighty encouraging.

He kissed her cheek. "I love you."

She kissed him back, a mite closer to his lips than she'd intended—a daring thing, but she wasn't one bit sorry. "I love you, too."

He reached around her and drew her startlingly close, and the lap robe slipped off. "Oh, goodness, look what we've done."

"We? *You* did that!" She could hardly stop giggling.

Leaning over, he pulled the thick blankets back onto her lap, letting her tuck the edges in once again, keeping both of his hands on the reins now.

They rode for some minutes in total silence, although Nellie was stifling another laugh. She might have let it free if Caleb hadn't spoken. "My father and I talked about my future this week—went over every detail of the land transfer." He was quiet for a moment before adding, "Honestly, I believe Daed will relent where you're concerned . . . in due time."

"Such good news, Caleb." She found his demeanor surprising. Something had radically changed between David Yoder and his son—something Caleb wasn't telling her.

"We might not see each other much, or at all, in the meantime. Do you understand?"

Having experienced how delightful it was to be with him again tonight after being apart just over a month, Nellie would gladly wait for him. She would make the days pass by keeping busy with chores and all the baking required of her. The busy life of running a bakery shop would certainly be a comfort.

Yet even as she looked ahead to a life with Caleb, Nellie worried that, despite her beloved's reassurances, his father would be the one to have the last word. She hoped with all her heart that Caleb was not sadly mistaken.

Betsy had a sinking feeling as she lay in bed, wide awake. She couldn't shake the notion that something was amiss. Her eldest daughter had not returned home from work yet—if, indeed, Rhoda had been there at all. It was close to ten o'clock already, as she could tell by the position of the nearly three-quarters moon that shone beneath the window shade.

She'd noticed a fifth necklace today on Rhoda's side of the dresser she shared with Nan. The growing collection doubtless marked a growing interest in the world, as well.

Nellie Mae, on the other hand, was as Plain as Betsy was and always would be—or so it appeared. Since one was not privy to another's heart, how was it possible to fully know, even about her own daughters?

She'd heard from Esther and Fannie—who, like her, both attended the New Order church—that Jonathan and Linda Fisher had joined the Beachys, just as her own son James and daughter-in-law Martha had. Would the fancier, more progressive group divide yet again? *Everyone's splitting away, it seems.*

And what might Bishop Joseph think of all this? His doing away with any shunning for a full three months might have backfired in some ways, causing this air of leniency.

Betsy slipped out of bed, aware of Reuben's deep breathing, his arm flung over his head. The dear man worked the bulk of each day outdoors, from before dawn to as late as after supper, feeding, grooming, and exercising his horses, training them over time to become accustomed to reins and bridles and harnesses.

She did not begrudge Reuben these moments of needed rest. Going to the window, Betsy moved the shade slightly to peer out at the moon-whitened snow and trees.

Dear Lord, please look after Rhoda this night. I fear she is far from you. And please put your arms of love around my hurting Nan. Send her a kind and loving man to wed. As for Nellie Mae, I trust you'll watch over her wherever she may be. Cover each of my children and grandchildren with your grace, goodness, and your love. I ask this in Jesus' name. Amen.

Rhoda guessed her clothes surely reeked of cigarette smoke. She had been sitting at a booth in the Honey Brook Restaurant since well past the supper hour, having gotten a ride to town with Mr. Kraybill, who'd run an errand. She'd felt she might simply burst if she didn't get away and do something completely different—even daring—for a change. Impulsive as this outing seemed, Rhoda wanted a quiet place to browse the latest car ads in the newspaper, somewhere far from the prying eyes of her family.

Suddenly, though, she had no idea how she would be getting herself back home.

Silly of me not to plan ahead, she decided now that the place looked to be emptying.

She'd met the nicest folk here tonight, some more talkative than others. Yet her mind had remained fixed on her task, and she had pored over the ad section of the newspaper Mrs. Kraybill had kindly allowed her to take from the house. Presently Rhoda circled the ads that piqued her interest, though was disappointed to see most were well over two thousand dollars—at least the most recent models were. She couldn't imagine spending even that.

Rhoda regretted having saved only four hundred fifty dollars in the past three months. *Too many frivolous purchases.* Still, she thought she could handle payments, assuming she had enough to put down on a car loan.

A brown "fully loaded" 1963 Rambler caught her eye, as did a red 1965

Rambler convertible, impractical as it was, and a blue 1960 Falcon. The thought of a black 1964 Imperial sedan inexplicably brought to mind her brother Benjamin's courting buggy, long since traded in for a family carriage.

Rhoda sighed. Truth was, she hadn't the slightest idea how to go about purchasing a car, unless she got some credit. But who would lend her the money?

Will the Kraybills continue to hire me to keep house? A big consideration. Dat had always said never to count your chickens before they're hatched. She wondered how far into the future she could hope to be employed within walking distance of her father's house.

Returning her attention to the paper, she spread out the several pages. She reveled in trying to decode the ad for each car.

Eventually she felt someone's gaze and glanced up to see a nice-looking man, his deep blue eyes seeming to inquire of her.

"Excuse me, miss. I happened to notice you sitting here alone."

She nodded, feeling terribly awkward. What a sight she must be—the only young woman in the whole place wearing a cape dress and a head covering. He must be wondering what she was doing circling car ads so eagerly.

"I'm lookin' for a nice, well, a used car," she explained. *The perfect car . . .*

He was not a waiter, she realized when he asked hesitantly if he might help. "May I join you?"

She looked around. "Are ya askin' to sit with me?"

"Only if I can be of help, miss."

"Rhoda," she was quick to say. "And do sit, if you'd like."

He introduced himself as Glenn Miller, named after some band that had made a debut in New York City the year he was born. He was surprisingly friendly and chatty—polite, too. Possibly he was curious about her Plain attire just as others had seemed to be, yet everyone she'd visited with this evening had been exceedingly gracious.

Rhoda realized it was her turn to say more about herself, so she mentioned that her father bred and raised horses. "We've got a bakery shop on the premises, too. Seems an ad's even been runnin' in the Lancaster paper 'bout it."

Glenn repeatedly blinked his blue eyes. "I'm sorry, Miss Rhoda . . . I guess I don't follow."

She felt ever so silly. "No, maybe it's me that should be sorry. I'm surely speakin' out of turn, jah?"

"I wouldn't say that." He winked at her and she blushed immediately.

"You go ahead and speak however you wish." He flashed another smile. "Now, which cars have your interest?"

She didn't think she ought to say—suddenly she felt all ferhoodled, sitting in an English restaurant with such a fine-looking man. Was it a good or bad sign that he kept smiling at her? In truth she had no idea who this Glenn fellow was.

"Well, I oughta be gettin' home," she said softly, wondering why she had announced that. By implication, she'd pretended to know how she was getting home, when she certainly had no idea.

"You got your horse and buggy out back?" Glenn glanced out the window. Rhoda could see by the streetlights that it was beginning to snow again.

"Not this time," she admitted, lowering her head.

"You need a lift, don't you, little lady?"

Little? This was the first she'd heard that since she was maybe ten or so. From then on she'd grown to become pleasingly plump, although perhaps chubbier than most fellows cared for. Most, except for Glenn here, who was now reaching across the table for her hand with the most endearing look. "I'd be honored to take you wherever you want to go, Miss Rhoda."

She hesitated. Should she let this strange man touch her hand?

Rhoda had never been told she was or wasn't a good judge of character, so when Mr. Glenn Miller, with his appealing smile and crisply ironed white shirt and handsome knit sweater vest, asked her yet again if she wanted a ride, Rhoda actually considered saying yes. She felt sure that if she looked hard enough into his clear eyes—the windows to his soul, as Mamma said—she would know whether it was prudent to accept his kind offer.

CHAPTER 12

———

Rhoda was not so much alarmed as she was tired when Glenn pulled his car over onto the shoulder and slowed to a stop. She'd done the selfsame thing with the horse and buggy when she'd lost her way. She and her newfound friend—an Englischer, of all things—were apparently lost somewhere in Chester County, well beyond Beaver Dam Road. She wished for a map to guide them back to Route 340, but she didn't dare mention it. Glenn had talked nearly nonstop since they'd left the restaurant, describing a number of bossy women in his life, as he put it. Several at work . . . two younger sisters and suchlike . . . but not a word about a girlfriend.

She was determined to show him by sitting demurely in the front seat that she was not the bossy type. No, Rhoda was satisfied to wait for him to decide what to do about their having gone astray. At least they hadn't run out of gasoline, like she'd heard happened occasionally to others. On such a clear and brilliant moonlit night, surely they would find Dat's house in due time.

A thin cloud passed over the moon, and Rhoda gazed at the vastness of the dark sky, filled with jewel-like stars. They reminded her of the several necklaces she'd purchased so spontaneously. *My weakness*, she thought, realizing she'd have to curb that impulse if she was to have enough to make car payments.

She turned her attention to the man behind the steering wheel. Glenn seemed to be in no hurry to discover where they'd gone off the beaten path. More eager to get home now, she asked, "Are you thinking we should retrace our steps?"

"Not just yet."

She felt tense suddenly . . . and irritated.

"We'll turn back soon enough," he said.

Trying not to sigh too loudly, Rhoda guessed Glenn merely needed to sit there and talk awhile longer.

Nellie felt fully contented while riding over the back roads in Caleb's borrowed carriage. She relaxed as he rambled, talking now of his Yoder relatives who'd left the Old Ways decades ago. "I scarcely know them, but they're close with my cousin Aaron and his family."

"Oh?"

"Their grandparents made the mistake Preacher Manny and so many are makin' even now."

He means my parents, too.

"Turning away from the Ordnung?" she asked.

"Well, more than that. Not only did they leave the church, but they skipped over a few of the more conservative churches, makin' a beeline for the Mennonites."

"Who do ya mean?"

He paused.

Had her question caused him distress, asking about this branch of his family tree, no longer in the fold? "It's all right, Caleb. I don't have to know, really."

"Well, I daresay you oughta . . ." He reached for her hand. "I 'spect their leavin' the People influenced your Suzy away from the church . . . which led to her death."

"What?" Startled, she looked at him.

"I recently heard that several of my own cousins were with Suzy the day she drowned. Dreadful news."

Nellie wouldn't admit already knowing as much from Suzy herself. "She was with a whole group of young people that day," she pointed out.

"Oh, there were plenty there, all right. But my own kin would never have been present had their grandparents remained in the old church. Don't ya see, Nellie, everything has its consequence? You choose where you'll go, what you'll do. Everything affects everything else."

His words seemed important, even insightful. "This troubles you, ain't so?" she said.

"I can see the future. Ours." His words were barely audible. "If we don't exercise our will—"

"Over your father's?" she interrupted. "Oh, Caleb . . . this seems very hard."

"I'll find a way for Daed to accept you." He kissed her hand. "I must."

He leaned his head against hers as though they were molded in thought. Deeply upset, he was, and no wonder. Their future, their love, was entwined with strife.

She choked back tears. "Sometimes I see a boat in my mind . . . like the rowboat Suzy fell out of," she began. "Dat, Mamma, my family—all of them—are in it, leavin' me behind for a distant shore. I feel that if I don't catch that boat somehow, I'll be stuck on the other side forever. It worries me somethin' awful, to tell you the truth."

He squeezed her hand. "Your heart's tender toward your family, is all."

Hearing his care, the gentleness in his voice, Nellie began to sob. "Don't you see? If I keep refusin' to go to church with Mamma and Dat, I'll miss out on knowing more 'bout Suzy's faith. Yet if I join the new church and you remain in the old, we'll never have a chance to wed." She wept into her hands.

"Oh, Nellie. Don't cry . . . don't."

Caleb fell silent. More than anything, Nellie hated the thought of being divided from either him or her family. Yet she could not help but notice the excitement her parents and Nan now had for Sunday Preaching and evening Scripture reading.

Caleb's voice broke into her thoughts. "Nellie, we mustn't lose each other. Not for anyone or anything."

She wished she could clearly see his dear countenance . . . his hazel eyes. "I must sound all mixed-up to you, and believe me, I am sometimes."

"Well, you don't need to be confused. Just remain in the Old Ways, where you belong."

She breathed in the icy air. "I hope you understand why I worry so." She stopped for a moment, hesitating. "God's Word—that's what Dat calls the Bible—changed everything for the better for Suzy. And now for Dat and Mamma, too. So many of my family." She wiped her tears.

"Aw, Nellie Mae . . ." But his voice trailed off as he lifted the reins and held them firmly.

"The tabernacle over at the Tel Hai campground played a big part in Suzy's life last spring."

Caleb let out a low groan. "She had no business there."

"But she went all the same."

"You've never told me this, love." He slipped his arm around her. "You'll get all this salvation talk out of your system, sooner or later."

Nellie was still. Bewildered as Caleb no doubt was at her admission, she believed that if he loved her, he would understand.

A fleeting thought nagged at her, and she shuddered to think she might lose her beau forever. Pushing her fear aside, Nellie yielded to his loving embrace.

Rhoda leaned against the car door as Glenn Miller continued to talk a blue streak. Several times now he'd reached beneath his seat to bring a small bottle up to his lips. This being her first experience with anything like a real date, she wondered how Nan and Nellie Mae managed to stay out all hours. She was in no way accustomed to being up so late, and she was second-guessing her decision to allow this stranger to drive her home.

"I'll take you car shopping if you'd like," Glenn offered, reaching for her hand. "How about it? Tomorrow?"

She pondered her response, not sure she wanted him holding her hand right now. "I have chores with my mamma after work."

A frown crossed his brow and he squeezed her hand. "Now, honey-bunch, you've surely got yourself a host of sisters. One of them can cover for you this once."

He slid across the front seat toward her, and she became aware of his dreadful breath. Why, it smelled like the moonshine some of the wilder church boys brewed and brought along to Singings, unbeknownst to the brethren.

What'll I do?

Her free hand fidgeted near the door. Why should she have such conflicting feelings when she'd yearned so long for a man to give her the time of day?

Glenn's arm was around her shoulder now as he inched closer. His reeking breath annoyed her.

But even as Rhoda leaned away, he asked if he could see her again. "Why not tomorrow evening? I'll pick you up wherever you say." He stroked her cheek slowly with the back of his hand.

She clenched her jaw. *What if he tries to kiss me?* She had always assumed her first kiss would be ever so special, saved for her husband after the preacher said they were joined as man and wife, "under God."

"I have chores after work," she repeated, hoping her words wouldn't provoke an angry reaction.

Glancing at the door, she noted the handle. She didn't think the door was locked, but she was already leaning so hard against it she doubted she could get it open. Even if she did, wasn't it a terrible idea to leave the car's warmth on a night like this?

I could freeze to death.

"Let me take you to look for cars tomorrow. I know the best used-car lot. You'll have your pick of the place." He raised her hand to his mouth, his lips brushing her knuckles. "Aw, honey, you know you want to."

"I . . . I'd rather you didn't do that."

He ignored her request. "I can help you, Rhoda. Take time with you . . . teach you . . . things."

"You mean hunt for a car?" She pulled her hand away.

"That, too."

The slur of his words put the fear of the Lord God in her. "Glenn, please—"

"Oh, you're *asking* me now, are you? Well, sure, honey. You say *please* mighty nice, don't you?" He leaned in and kissed her cheek before she could stop him.

Tilting her head against the ice-cold window, she said, "No!" She spoke the single word loudly—louder than she'd ever raised her voice to anyone.

"Rhoda, my little girl . . . you can't mean it. You're so pretty, honey. You're just the sweetest thing I've—"

"Let me go!"

Scrambling quickly, Rhoda managed to get out of the way as she yanked on the handle. The door flew open and she leapt out. Glenn toppled partway out, too. She didn't stop to look back to see if he pulled himself back into the car or was now making chase.

Rhoda ran as hard as the coyotes in the nearby woods. Soon her lungs burned from the fierce cold, but she struggled to keep up the pace, certain from the position of the moon that she was heading west.

Surely I'll reach a crossroads somewhere.

She heard no sound of pursuit behind her, but her noisy panting and the crunch of her own feet on the snow-packed road could easily block out all else. To think that what had for a while seemed so exciting and enjoyable now had her running for her life. A few unwelcome kisses might not kill her, but they would certainly spoil everything she hoped for . . . and put a blight on her, for sure.

Ahead a light flickered. With new energy, she forced her legs still faster and ran toward a distant farmhouse, her heart pounding hard against her rib cage.

Suddenly she heard the sound of a car motor coming up alongside her on the road. She dared not look over her shoulder lest she accidentally plunge off into the uneven snow. Terrified, Rhoda willed herself to press forward as the car drew ever closer, slowing as it came.

CHAPTER 13

R hoda spied an open gate at the end of the long lane leading to the farmhouse. Quickly she dashed up the drive. The car had stopped out by the road. Was it Glenn's?

Oh, she wished she'd never darkened the door of that restaurant. What had she been thinking, asking Mr. Kraybill to drop her off there?

She ran up the porch steps, rapping hard on the front door, glancing over her shoulder to see if Glenn was indeed in pursuit of her.

A tall young man wearing a navy blue bathrobe appeared in the doorway, eyes squinting against the light. He peered at her sleepily. "Hello?"

"S-someone's . . . followin' me," she sputtered.

The man looked past her and she froze with fear. What if he didn't let her inside?

"Teresa, come quick!" he called over his shoulder. A woman, presumably his wife, rushed into the front room as he opened the door to Rhoda, who swiftly stepped inside. "Call the police," he instructed Teresa.

"*Nee*—no! Just let me stay here . . . till it's safe." Rhoda turned to look out the window, and her heart dropped at the sight of Glenn but a few yards from the porch. "Ach! Don't let him in, whatever ya do. Oh, please don't."

"Come!" Teresa reached for her hand and led her back into the kitchen. "You'll be safe here, I assure you."

The blond, soft-spoken woman couldn't have been more than twenty-five or so, Rhoda guessed, but her lack of terror was remarkable. Her eyes radiated a calm strength that reminded Rhoda of Mamma.

A loud exchange commenced at the front door, and Rhoda trembled as she covered her ears to block out the angry, slurred words of the man she'd thought was a newfound friend.

You'll be safe here, the young woman sitting next to her at the table had promised. This same woman was folding her hands in prayer.

Say your prayer aloud, Rhoda thought suddenly, removing her hands from her ears, curious to hear what this unruffled woman might be asking the Lord God.

In a few minutes the front door closed and she heard the husband set the lock. Then he made his way to the kitchen, where he stood next to his seated wife. Teresa looked up from her praying.

"I'm going to take this intoxicated man to his house. He has no business driving." He looked kindly at Rhoda. "Are you all right, miss?"

"Now I am."

"If you'd like a ride someplace, I'll be glad to drive you when I return."

She nodded. "Denki ever so much."

His gaze indicated his bewilderment—why had she, an Amish girl, been chased down by such a man?

Rhoda felt obliged to explain why she'd found herself in a predicament that justified interrupting the couple's sleep. She gave a quick summary, stopping short of admitting her interest in the stranger. "It was a rather stupid thing to do, I realize now. Thank goodness you were home."

"We're glad to help," Teresa said when Rhoda stopped to catch her breath. "By the way, we're Timothy and Teresa Eisenberger."

"And I'm Rhoda . . . Rhoda Fisher."

Teresa rose to boil water for tea as Timothy excused himself to drive Glenn home. "The Lord sent you to us, I believe," Teresa said softly to Rhoda as she removed two teacups and saucers from the nearby cupboard.

Rhoda had heard of divine guidance at Preacher Manny's meetings, but she'd never thought of it as a reality.

"God leads us in our distress." Teresa took out a box of chamomile tea. "I've experienced it firsthand."

Jah, distress it was, Rhoda silently agreed as she offered to help with the tea. She couldn't believe her foolishness in having needlessly put herself in harm's way. The thought crossed her mind that if God had truly directed her here, then she ought to pay closer attention to Preacher Manny's sermons from now on.

It's the least I can do.

Betsy heard Nellie Mae's bed creak and was relieved her daughter was home at last. Breathing a prayer, she was determined to set aside her frustration over Caleb Yoder's pursuit of her youngest. She had overheard his mother say in passing at a work frolic that her husband planned to have Caleb take over the family land as soon as he was wed. Betsy was smart enough to know the Yoder farmland was tied to Caleb's staying in the Old Ways. A stern man like David Yoder would have it no other way.

Tomorrow being the Lord's Day, Nellie and the rest of the family would undoubtedly go their separate ways, as had sadly become the norm. Nellie had made it plain she was not interested in joining them for worship.

Sighing, Betsy rolled over. She looked at Reuben, sound asleep. It was highly unusual for him not to be already awake and nuzzling her neck. Had he awakened in the night, walking the hallway to pray over the family as he often did?

She sat up and pushed a bed pillow behind her, leaning against the headboard to await the sunrise. Her thoughts wandered from Nellie to Rhoda, who'd only recently returned home in a stranger's car, of all dreadful things. Had her eldest daughter fallen in with a fast crowd, like Suzy? She'd seen the driver who had dropped Rhoda off, definitely an Englischer. The young man had accompanied Rhoda all the way to the back door.

She must trust in the Lord's care more fully. With that in mind, she turned her thoughts to Reuben's parents, Noah and Hannah, wishing she and Reuben might make a trip to Bird-in-Hand. Perhaps tomorrow, after the common meal? It was high time they visited, or they might appear to be distancing themselves.

Betsy leaned forward, lifting her long, heavy hair and letting it fall behind her. No need for their family to slip out of reach just because they no longer saw eye to eye. They were kin, after all, and she missed seeing her mother-in-law and hearing her stories at quilting bees. How was Hannah feeling since her minor stroke?

Glancing again at the sleeping Reuben, she wondered how he, too, was dealing with the painful rift. He and Noah had always been close.

She rose to turn on the gas lamp and then picked up the Bible from the small table next to the bed, opening to the book of Proverbs. Preacher Manny had said it was a good idea to make a point of reading a proverb each day. *It'll change your life.*

So much to absorb, really. Betsy had been largely unacquainted with the knowledge in God's Word for so long, she wanted to glean as much as possible from every reading. She was glad for this quiet moment while Reuben lingered in his slumber.

Even as she began to write, there was a stirring within Rosanna. She had stayed up instead of returning to bed after the twins' early morning feeding.

Now was as good a time as any to jot down instructions for making blessed thistle tea. One of her aunts had claimed it worked miracles for her own struggle with baby blues.

Pour 1 cup boiling water over 1 1/2 to 2 grams of crushed blessed thistle. Steep for twelve minutes. Drink one cup 2 to 3 times per day, before meals.

"Maybe Kate'll try this," she muttered to herself, sitting in the kitchen as the day began. She hoped it would settle her cousin.

She folded the small paper with the tea-making directions on it and set it squarely beneath the cookie jar. Pleased with herself, she prepared to bake bread for the noon meal. In no time now Elias would be up and dressed, looking forward to having a quiet breakfast before he headed outside for another day of helping the next farmer over with repair work on some bridles. Later he planned to go to a farm auction near Smoketown.

"If I'm quick, maybe I can make sticky buns, too," she said, liking the idea of filling up the kitchen with the delicious cinnamon scent.

Maybe I can even offer some to Cousin Kate this morning . . . along with her tea, of course!

Elias would find that amusing. He would lean his head back and laugh heartily before taking her in his arms to kiss her.

Rosanna smiled. Elias would have every right to chuckle. *Anything to cure peculiar Kate!*

Rhoda breathed deeply, stretching as she opened her eyes. *Thank goodness I'm home . . . and safe.* She glanced over at Nan, who was still sleeping, despite a thin ray of sunshine peeking beneath the green shade. She considered what might have been, but she did not allow herself to linger on that; the memory of last night still caused her turmoil.

Hadn't she wanted a peek into the world of fancy men and cars? Cars she could take, but fellows like Glenn Miller she could do without.

Even so, how did a girl tell a good apple from a rotten one? Fact was, Glenn had fooled her but good.

She got up and tiptoed to the window and lifted the shade a bit, careful not to awaken Nan. What had happened last night seemed like a bad dream now that she was secure in Dat's house, having shared the comfort of the bed with her younger sister. Why had she placed herself in such jeopardy?

Nan must never know about Glenn, she resolved.

Rhoda looked out at the sky, clearing to the east as the dawn penetrated the dreary gray. A ray of hope, perhaps?

Turning, she stared at the pretty necklaces she'd collected and strung along her side of the dresser mirror. Was it wrong to feed her fancy desires in this manner?

Brushing aside her musing, Rhoda went to the row of wooden wall pegs and reached for her bathrobe. She slipped it on and headed downstairs to the washroom, where her father had gone to the trouble of putting indoor plumbing in their house. Even so, the small bathroom was nothing compared to the thoroughly modern, even glamorous *two* at the Kraybills' house.

She closed the door and ran the water for her second bath in less than twenty-four hours, preparing to wash away the memory of Glenn—his offensive breath on her neck and face, his arms around her. . . .

Rhoda shuddered. Had he planned to lose his way all along, tricking her by saying they were lost? Was he like some of the church boys who whispered sweet nothings, hoping to get a girl to let her hair down before her wedding night? She'd heard some terrible stories from Nan, especially, about a handful of young men in their church district—well, their former one. She honestly didn't know much about the new church's youth, because she'd refused thus far to attend any gatherings. She was tired of being overlooked by Amish fellows, even though her sisters and Mamma all had told her she was plenty pretty.

As had Curly Sam Zook, five long years ago. But though that was an eternity past now, she couldn't forget how he'd held her hand and said the nicest things out behind the barn one cold night, only to break her heart a month later. Like Nan's beau had done not so long ago.

She shivered anew, thinking what a *Dummkopp* she'd been with both Sam and Glenn. No way would she let such a thing happen again. *I won't be anybody's fool!*

"One day I'll have me a fine automobile and a nice young man, too," Rhoda promised herself while staring into the small mirror over the sink. She slid her glasses up the bridge of her nose and then opened the mirrored medicine cabinet, looking for an aspirin to alleviate her headache. But the aspirin bottle was empty.

Frustrated, she was determined to get a bottle of her own and put it in one of the drawers in the room she shared with Nan. Stepping into the warm bath, Rhoda wondered why it was suddenly so important that her things belong solely to her, just like her future.

CHAPTER 14

B efore Saturday breakfast, while Reuben was pulling on his work trousers, Betsy brought up the daily ad for Nellie's Simple Sweets. "I've seen it with my own eyes—just ain't befitting us at all." She stood near the loveseat at the window, holding the very paper.

"Why do ya say that, love?"

"Because it isn't. Honestly, I see no reason why Rhoda would do such a thing."

He stopped dressing, suspenders pulled midway up. "You know for sure she did?"

"Nan assumes it, and since they're ever so close, I guess she should know."

He found Betsy's conclusion flimsy. Just because Nan said Rhoda placed the ad, why should Betsy blindly believe it? Nan had been known to misinterpret things in the past. But he refused to point that out. If more customers came to Nellie's bakery shop because of the ads, then the tables and chairs he'd made might come in real handy.

"Why not simply ask Rhoda?" he suggested.

"Jah, I will."

"Well, *gut.*" Reuben had more on his mind than Betsy's notions. For one, he was still put out with Ephram—Bishop Joseph, too. Not only had he butted heads with his son, but his frustration over his conversation with his older brother—revered as the man of God—continued to escalate in his mind.

He combed his oily hair, wishing it were closer to bathing time tonight, when he would wash for the Preaching service over at Cousin Manny's place. Presently Bishop Joseph was overseeing both Manny's New Order church and the Old Order group, as well as trying to persuade those who were still inclined toward the Beachys to say no to cars and telephones.

As for himself, Reuben had no inclination toward the Beachys, though he relished the idea of bathing more often. *A right pleasant thing.*

"What do ya say we go 'n' visit your parents after church tomorrow?" Betsy suggested as he put away the comb.

He missed chewing the fat with his father. "Jah, a good idea, indeed."

Heading downstairs, he wished that whoever was tying up the washroom would hurry so he could get in there and shave his upper lip. He chuckled to himself as he waited near the door. Sure seemed you could never have enough of most anything, no matter how much of it you already had. But if cleanliness was next to godliness . . . he was ready to take a dip in the bathtub each and every day.

He heard what sounded like Rhoda in there muttering to herself. Abandoning the idea of waiting, Reuben headed for the kitchen and wondered what was keeping Betsy, impatient now for his first cup of coffee and a cinnamon bun or two.

From the moment they arrived at Marsh Creek State Park on Saturday, Chris Yoder knew it was a mistake. Yet Zach insisted they stay, getting out of the car nearly before Chris set the brake. Zach stood stiffly near the front fender, eyes fixed on the enormous lake.

It was late morning and the sky was as dismal as any January day Chris could recall. Everything from the lake to the boat launch was gray and solidly blanketed with ice and snow.

"If you don't want to stay—" Chris suggested, not sure of his own voice.

"No, we're here now," Zach interrupted, heading for the lake without inviting Chris to tag along.

Yeah, we're here, all right. Chris clumped through the deep snow, eyeing the lake—more than five hundred acres fed by a nearby watershed.

Today was a bleak contrast to the clear and balmy June afternoon the last time they'd come. He would never have imagined Zach would want to take him up on driving out here. Winter had stolen what little remained of its summer allure.

Turning, he saw Zach walking gingerly on the ice. Chris hoped it was good and thick. After months of frigid weather, he assumed so. He watched Zach make the labored trek toward the middle of the lake.

Where Suzy died.

But as Zach trudged onward, Chris breathed a prayer that it might be a healing time. *Somehow.*

Zach folded his hands momentarily as he went, either praying or talking to himself, his lips moving. Occasionally he looked toward the sky, then back at the frozen surface.

Shifting his muffler to cover more of his face, Chris headed toward the area where Suzy had fallen overboard and drowned. He recalled how perfect the day had been when the whole bunch of them had piled into several rowboats, bringing Suzy along for the first time. One of their older brothers had pointed out how the sunlight looked like diamonds bobbing on the water's surface that afternoon. Some of the guys began to row harder, showing off a bit for Suzy and several other girls from church who were with their three older brothers in two more boats. Once they were well toward the center of the lake, Zach suggested they drift awhile, having in mind a quiet moment to present a gold bracelet to Suzy.

Chris hadn't intended to stare, but it had been hard not to watch their infectious smiles as Zach had placed the delicate bracelet on her small wrist.

Moved by the memory, Chris shook his head. He forced air through his pursed lips, looking again at Zach in the distance. *Why does God spare some and not others?* Sure, God was sovereign. To seek to understand the whys was not as important as putting one's complete trust in God's will. He'd learned this from his parents, observing the way they chose not to fret over the challenges that came their way. They believed Suzy's death would prove to be part of the "all things" found in Romans chapter eight, verse twenty-eight—that some good might ultimately come from her death.

All the same, Chris's private questions plagued him, especially because he saw such a discrepancy between prayers that were obviously answered and those that were not. He'd heard a sermon after Suzy died about letting waiting times be trusting times as one sorted out the complications of life. Difficult as it was, especially for Zach, they both attempted to be patient, waiting for God's timing in helping them—as well as Suzy's family, who were often in their prayers—through this tragedy.

Pushing forward, he managed to catch up with Zach, who had clipped across the lake at a surprising pace. Chris stood next to him as they absorbed the silence, interrupted only by the calls of a few hardy winter birds. Chris could almost guess what Zach's thoughts might be, for his own weighed heavily.

"I promised myself I'd never come back," Zach admitted.

Chris understood. This was new ground for them. Besides losing Suzy, nothing truly dreadful had ever happened to them or their family.

Zach continued. "Just thinking . . . this is the last place Suzy was before . . ." He stared at the spot, and his shoulders heaved.

Chris clapped a hand on Zach's shoulder. "It's tough, I know." He sighed, fighting the lump in his throat.

"All of us should've worn life jackets." Zach's words were a desperate whisper.

What were we thinking?

After a time, Zach motioned to leave. "Let's get out of here."

Chris was ready, too.

They crossed the lake, heading back toward the parking area, where some rowboats were stacked near the shore. "I can't remember which boat we took," Zach said. "When Suzy fell . . ."

He squatted beside the upturned boats, their bows held off the ground by a metal rack. Reaching over, he fingered the state-park identification numbers. "I doubt the office would have a record of which boats we rented that day."

"Probably not."

Zach shook his head. "Man, they all look the same." He started to get up, then dropped back to his knees. "Wait a minute. What's this?"

Chris wouldn't have bothered to look, except Zach was staring hard. *Surely he doesn't think . . .*

"Could it be?" Zach said, brushing away the excess snow.

Chris peered closer. He saw what appeared to be a glint of gold in a clump of frozen leaves and other debris.

"See it? Right there." Zach pointed.

"Could be anything."

"I think it's her bracelet."

Chris wasn't convinced. Suzy's bracelet was most likely at the bottom of the lake.

"It must've slipped off her wrist when she fell."

Highly unlikely. Chris hoped his brother wasn't setting himself up for disappointment.

"We need something to pry this loose." Zach looked around. "Anything in the trunk we can use?"

"Not that I know of."

"We'll have to come back with a hatchet or something to cut it free."

Come back? That was more than Chris had bargained for. "Come on, let's go."

On the drive home, Zach reminded Chris of the Scripture verse he'd had inscribed on the bracelet. "Her favorite. Remember?"

Chris nodded.

"Just think, her whole family probably knows what she believed," he said unexpectedly. "Suzy wrote in a diary every day, you know."

"No kidding?"

Zach nodded, breaking into a faint smile. "She didn't want to forget a single thing. It was all so new and wonderful to her."

Although it was good to see the sparkle in Zach's eyes again, Chris was alarmed at his brother's new obsession. And by the time they reached home, Zach was convinced he had indeed discovered the bracelet. "I have to know for sure," he muttered, determined to get back to the park before anything could happen to it.

Chris knew Zach well enough to realize there was no stopping him once he fixed his mind on something. His zeal for God was rivaled only by his feelings for Suzy Fisher, and evidently his passion to connect with anything related to her wasn't about to let up. No, the trip to the lake hadn't helped to heal Zach at all. If anything, his brother was more troubled than ever.

CHAPTER 15

Nellie was thrilled about the prospect of a visit to *Dawdi* and Mammi Fisher's, as Dat announced at breakfast Sunday. They would leave the minute they all returned from Preaching. "We'll see how Mammi Hannah's doin'," Mamma added with a smile.

Nellie hoped, if time permitted, she might also have the chance to slip away and see Cousin Treva. Perhaps she could finally persuade Treva and her sisters to come visit sometime and have a look around the bakery shop.

Her father eyed Nellie conspicuously as she ate her cold cereal and fruit. The way he looked at her evidenced his growing concern over her, living under his roof and holding firm to the Old Ways.

As soon as the dishes were dried and put away, she hurried to the washroom to scrub her face carefully, knowing Caleb would surely be looking her way this Lord's Day. Not that he didn't every other Preaching service, but since their recent reunion, she felt even closer to him, longing for their wedding day.

Will Caleb succeed with his father? Nellie intended to do all she could to make sure David Yoder saw no reason to find further fault with her.

Closing the door behind her, she reached for a fresh washcloth. No need to stew. She drew the water and applied the homemade soap, pushing away thoughts of church baptism. Dat undoubtedly had that in mind. Choosing Caleb and the Old Ways over her parents' faith was the hardest choice of all.

When it came time for the womenfolk to form a line outside Ephram's farmhouse, Nellie was happy to see Rebekah Yoder waving to her. Caleb's sister, her fair hair shiny and clean, slipped in beside her.

"How're you?" Nellie wondered if Rebekah had any inkling of Caleb's disobedience—or their secret meeting.

"Oh, fine. Did ya walk clear over?"

"Jah, but I should've hitched up the sleigh, I s'pose. Bein' it's just me . . ." She didn't explain further, but surely Rebekah understood.

"Been wishin' I could get away to visit Nan again," Rebekah whispered. "Doesn't seem right, not seein' her."

"Same with missin' nearly half the People, jah? So many have jumped the fence."

Rebekah agreed. "Must be they're afraid to wait too long. I've heard some say they might as well get it over with before the Bann's a threat—just go ahead and make the leap." She frowned, glancing over her shoulder. " 'Tween you and me, I'm awful curious 'bout the new church, Nellie Mae." Her hand was on Nellie's arm now. "Don't breathe a word, all right?"

"You're thinkin' of visiting Preacher Manny's?"

Rebekah leaned close. "If I can find a way, I'd like to go next week," she whispered behind her hand.

Taking care not to react, Nellie was curious what Caleb's sister had in mind, but she'd have to wait till after the common meal—if Rebekah was willing to talk further. Meanwhile, she quieted herself, preparing to be most reverent as the line moved forward toward the temporary house of worship. As she did, she reached into her coat pocket and felt the strings from Suzy's Kapp, a constant reminder of her dear sister. The strings seemed oddly out of place here.

Was Suzy wiser than all of us?

Seeing sweet Nellie made Caleb miss her already, not knowing when he might make another escape from Daed's house. He didn't want Nellie to become impatient or to lose heart because he was staying home from Singings and such.

He placed his black felt hat on the long wooden bench near the stairs and took his seat next to his father and older married brothers. He bowed his head when his father did and folded his hands. The three-hour meeting stretched before him in his mind, and he struggled to keep his thoughts on the Lord God and heavenly Father. Truth was, his recent date with Nellie Mae was continually before him. When could he possibly arrange to see her again? Each time they shared made him yearn even more for the next meeting, and the next. *The way of love*, he thought. When you met the girl you wanted for your bride, you pursued her . . . moved heaven and earth to be with her.

Opening his eyes, he turned his attention to the front of the large room, where he noticed Ephram Fisher, Nellie's older brother, standing there in his black frock coat. He and his wife, Maryann, had themselves another little one, although Caleb hadn't laid eyes on the baby yet. Some women stayed home longer with their infants than others.

One thing seemed definite: Ephram had not budged one inch since the church split late last fall. Ephram's four brothers were nowhere in sight, however, and Caleb assumed they'd followed their father, as had Rhoda and Nan. Mighty enticing, the newfangled ways. He himself fought against the desire for a tractor, knowing how much easier it would make farming.

There were times when Caleb worried that if something didn't happen soon, Nellie also might succumb to the urgings of her parents and the New Order. He could lose her forever.

I won't let that happen.

Rosanna settled onto a bench at the back of the room, close to the kitchen. She'd tiptoed inside with Essie, her sister-in-law, who sat next to her, helping with the babies. Rosanna had purposely chosen to hold Eli during the Preaching service. He nestled against her during the first long hymn from the *Ausbund* while Rosie slept soundly in Essie's ample arms.

Other than to Elias, Rosanna had not breathed a word of Cousin Kate's obvious preference for Eli, nor her insistence on continuing to act as a wet nurse. Wondering what Essie might think if she knew, Rosanna joined in the singing of the second hymn, the *Loblied,* as the People awaited the bishop and two preachers. It would be several more minutes before Bishop Joseph returned with the other ministers from upstairs, where they were deciding which of them should have the first sermon and who would preach the lengthier main sermon. She secretly hoped their bishop might be the one to offer the second sermon today, since at times she sensed something deeper in his messages. Perhaps that was merely because he was the eldest man of God in their midst.

Kate Beiler glanced back at Rosanna. *Oh no, is she thinking of changing seats?* Very soon the introductory sermon—the *Anfang*—would begin and there'd be no moving about. Rosanna held her breath, suddenly realizing she'd forgotten to bring along the herbal tea brewing instructions for Kate.

Eli made a soft little sound in his sleep. Oh, the sweet way his wee hands fell across his rising chest . . . the long, long eyelashes. *Such a beautiful child.*

Looking up, she half expected to see Kate staring back, jealous as all get out—certainly she seemed that. But Kate sat straight now, face forward, as she should be. Still, it was painfully obvious Kate was behaving strangely toward her and the babies. Even Elias had privately voiced his concerns to

Rosanna. After all, they had only the bishop's blessing on their raising Eli and Rosie, not a fancy judge's decree. Was it enough?

After the common meal, Caleb slipped outdoors in hopes of seeing Nellie, who'd left for the outhouse a few minutes before. His mind was alive with ideas and he wanted to reassure her not to give up hope. He was convinced that if she was still on this side of the fence after the practice of the Bann was resumed, it would definitely sway his father.

If he was quick, he might catch her on the way back to the house. *Even a few stolen moments would be worth the risk.*

The cold was brutal as the sun splayed blinding light across the snow-laden field. He shielded his eyes, looking for Nellie, not daring to call out for her with several other foolhardy folk milling about, braving the chill.

He shivered. He hated feeling as if he were doing something wrong by tailing Nellie Mae on the Lord's Day. Was it so terrible to want to be with the girl you loved . . . even though in his case, doing so meant willful defiance?

Waiting near the barn door, he was caught off guard when Daed called to him from near the corncrib, waving in a high arc. "Caleb! Over here, son!"

Looking toward the path that led to the outhouse, he glimpsed Nellie walking his way. *Puh, such ill timing!* His heart sank.

Did Cousin Aaron snitch on me?

Caleb scuffed his boots against the barn's threshold and then strode out into the snow, his neck tingling as he crossed paths with his sweetheart. He dared not so much as glance Nellie's way, however, keeping his eyes trained on the father whose will seemed fixed on bending his own.

CHAPTER 16

Nellie stood in the shadow of her brother's barn, observing Caleb and his father talking up yonder. She couldn't help but wonder what David Yoder was saying so dramatically, but lest her presence add fuel to the fire, she waited where she couldn't be seen if either Caleb or his father happened to look her way.

How could his father continue to treat Caleb's feelings with such disregard? She watched them, David Yoder's breath rising in a straight line from his black winter hat. Caleb, however, was strangely silent.

Nellie would have worked her way around the side of the barn to continue watching, but right then, Rebekah emerged from inside. "Ach, you scared me half to death," she said when Rebekah reached for her mittened hands and pulled her back into the barn.

"I *have* to talk to you." Rebekah's eyes were watering. Was she crying, or was it from the fierce cold?

"You all right?"

Rebekah nodded, leading her toward the milking stanchions, the smell of livestock thick in the closed-up space. "I've already told ya what I want to do." She looked over her shoulder.

"Won't you be in terrible trouble with your father?" Nellie asked.

"I won't wait any longer to see Manny's church for myself," Rebekah whispered.

"Do you think you can really get away next Sunday?" Nellie recalled what Rebekah had told her before Preaching.

"I'm goin' to try."

"Does Nan know? Do my parents?"

"You're the first I've told."

Nellie was stunned. "Are ya ever so sure, Rebekah?" There was no telling what consequences might befall Caleb's sister if she was found out.

Rebekah nodded. "So will you tell Nan . . . hush-hush?" At Nellie's nod, she sighed as though a great burden was lifting. "I'll wait along the road, if your parents won't mind pickin' me up."

What'll David Yoder say when she's not at home next Sunday?

"I must do this . . ." Looking down, Rebekah blinked. "Even if I'm . . . disowned, or worse."

Ach, what could be worse?

"Be prayin' for me, all right?" Rebekah gripped Nellie's hands again.

Nellie was startled by this turn in their conversation. She hadn't the slightest inkling what to say, nor did she know how to go about sharing any of this with Nan.

Just then they heard the sound of heavy boots on the cement beneath the strewn hay.

Ephram, maybe?

The girls ducked down, and Nellie Mae held her breath for a long time before she exhaled slowly, too aware of her own heart's pounding. "Who was that?" she whispered after a time.

"Sounded like Caleb. His walk—I'd know it most anywhere."

Nellie had seen him outside earlier, looking as if he'd spotted her but didn't want to let on—not with his father calling to him.

"Ach, Nellie, my brother's head over heels for you," Rebekah said softly, "in case you don't already know."

Nellie's heart fluttered at Rebekah's admission, but with Caleb going behind his father's back in order to see her, she wasn't about to let on that she felt the same about him. If he was working on a way for them to be together without jeopardizing his birthright, then woe unto her to mess things up.

"We best be goin'." She glanced around them at the dozens of milk cows waving their tails above the manure ditch.

"I'll go first." Rebekah smiled sweetly before slipping away.

When Nellie rose, she spied the top of a man's black hat. Was it her beau, hoping for an opportunity to talk secretly?

Not at all sure of herself, she walked slowly, assuming that if Caleb was there waiting, he would call to her to tell her not to leave.

She was pushing the barn door open when a man's voice rang out.

"Nellie Mae Fisher!"

She froze in her tracks.

Caleb's father? She turned and there he stood, his face glowering and red. His black felt hat was tipped forward, nearly concealing his eyes.

"You stay far away from my son, do ya hear?" David Yoder demanded.

Has someone spied on me and Caleb? Who?

Without thinking, Nellie bolted directly out the barn door and ran all the way to the shelter of Ephram's house.

Caleb was downright furious. To think he'd been caught merely darting outside to see Nellie Mae. His hands shook with frustration as he hitched his courting carriage to his horse. He was in the mood to do something crazy—like have a wild buggy race. If only this were any other day but Sunday. He had to blow his stack somehow . . . somewhere.

Worse yet, Daed had threatened to go find Nellie. First, though, his father had raised his voice to Caleb, saying he suspected him of sneaking around with Nellie Mae all along—something Caleb had done only once.

Now his father was threatening to cut him off if he did it again . . . and he was requiring Caleb to promptly make amends or be disinherited immediately. His father's way of having him do this—his demand—struck Caleb as utterly ridiculous.

Caleb rubbed his hand across his face. He could hardly believe he was considering doing his father's bidding. Yet what choice did he have?

It wasn't such a difficult demand to fulfill, really. And it would buy him more time. Susannah Lapp was, after all, a treat for the eyes. Why not satisfy his father's unreasonable order and spend a little time with her? Nellie wouldn't have to know. Now that they were no longer able to regularly see each other, she appeared less interested in going to the old church's Singings. And if she did find out, he could simply explain himself. After all, he'd be doing it for Nellie Mae . . . to preserve any hope of a future together.

He'd do *anything* to be with his beloved, and now his father's blessing was tied to Caleb's agreeing to see Susannah—just once.

Clucking his tongue, he hastened the horse, glad for the openness of his courting buggy. He wished Nellie were there, just the two of them. *Later . . .*

For now, he must prove to his father that neither Susannah nor any other girl held any interest for him. Maddening as it was, there was no getting around the fact Daed held the reins of his life. His father's land was everything . . . he must have it; otherwise he could offer nothing to his bride. Nellie deserved everything he had to bring to their marriage and much more.

Unnerved, Nellie stayed around to help with the kitchen cleanup, prickles of uneasiness plaguing her. She stopped drying dishes to talk with Maryann, who asked her to hold the new baby—a darling girl named Sadie—while

Maryann hurried upstairs to tend to young Becky and Katie, putting them down for a nap. So convenient since Preaching service had been held there at her own home.

Never had Nellie enjoyed gazing into a baby's tiny face so much. *Will Caleb's and my babies be as pretty?* she wondered, then silently chastised herself, wishing also for inner beauty for each of her children . . . some sweet day.

Even after her sister-in-law returned to the kitchen, Nellie continued holding Sadie, fondly admiring her newest niece's soft hands and face. Oh, she could just hold this little one all day and never get a speck of work done. Sadie's company was a balm after the alarming run-in with David Yoder.

Cousin Kate and her family followed Rosanna and Elias all the way home, never bothering to ask if it was a convenient time for her to visit. She hopped out of the Beilers' family buggy when Elias pulled up to the back door, leaving her six young children and husband, John, as she scurried up the snowy walkway on Rosanna's heels.

The gentle shifting of the buggy had lulled both babies to sleep in Rosanna's arms. She couldn't think of anything more pleasant than a nice long nap, but Cousin Kate's unwelcome presence made that impossible for her now. Kate stepped in close, face glowing as she eyed Eli, still in Rosanna's arms. Rosanna longed for Elias to come and rescue her, but he was unhitching the horse and buggy in the barn . . . obviously keeping his distance.

Without a word, Kate took Eli from Rosanna the moment she'd shed her coat. She carried him into the front room, cooing into his ear, acting for all the world as if this were her home rather than Rosanna's. Suddenly Kate began to cry. No, it sounded like she was out and out sobbing.

"Well, for goodness' sake," whispered Rosanna, handing Rosie to Elias when he stepped into the kitchen. What could be done to soothe her cousin's wounded heart?

Elias shrugged and marched toward the back door, peering out as if wondering whether he should go solicit John's help.

He muttered something under his breath before coming over to whisper, "If things get out of hand, come get me." Then he lifted Rosie to his shoulder, taking her upstairs and leaving Rosanna to console Kate.

She supposed it was a good idea to simply let her cousin cry it out. Kate was bawling now, and Eli's irritated wails blended with her keening.

This just ain't right. Rosanna paced the kitchen, stewing up a storm. Was it possible to hold her tongue any longer on this Lord's Day?

She went to the window and looked out. Kate's husband was also pacing out there in the snow, talking occasionally to the children, who were piled into the back of the buggy as they waited. No doubt they were all wondering how much longer Kate would be, and why Elias would let them sit in the cold like this.

"What a knotty problem," she said right out, gripping the shade at the window and firmly pulling it down.

By now, Elias was surely resting upstairs, like she wanted to be.

The cries from the front room continued, and Rosanna knew she must speak up. Heading through the sitting area and into the front room, she stood over her cousin—this woman who'd done the unthinkable for her and Elias. "What is it you want?" she asked softly. "What will make you happy again?"

"I don't know," Kate said as Eli continued to howl, his arms and fists shaking. "Here, you take him."

Rosanna pulled all of her will together and took her son calmly. "Your husband's weary of waitin', I daresay."

"Jah, I s'pose I best be goin'." Kate wiped her eyes and rose.

"Before you leave, I have something for you." Rosanna headed to the kitchen, swaying as she went to soothe poor Eli. She took the instructions for the blessed thistle tea from beneath the cookie jar.

Kate accepted the card without ever looking at it. She kissed Eli's hand before heading for the back door, and Rosanna did not feel obliged to see her out.

By the time Nellie Mae arrived home, she discovered an empty house. She'd completely forgotten about Dat's plans to visit Dawdi and Mammi Fisher.

Going to the kitchen table, she spied an apologetic note in Mamma's quick scrawl, declaring they'd "waited and waited" for her, but Dat had urged them on so that they could return before dark.

"Phooey!" She poured some milk and took a chocolate chip cookie out of the jar to soothe herself. "How'd I forget?" Yet even as she voiced it, she knew the answer: The events at Preaching, first with Rebekah and then David Yoder, had been most distracting.

Heading upstairs, she passed Rhoda and Nan's bedroom. Immediately she backtracked and went to sit on their bed, pondering what all of them might be doing right now in Bird-in-Hand. Were they laughing and listening to

Mammi Hannah's tellin's? Enjoying her famous apple pie with gobs of real whipped cream?

Nellie wished Dat might have been content to wait a bit longer before leaving. Was this his way of making a point to her? Was this how life would be once the whole family joined the New Order?

Feeling truly left out, she stood to inspect Rhoda's necklaces. Curiously she reached up to touch the only long golden pendant, which she'd never seen before. Running her fingers lightly over the chain, she wondered if the gold was real. If so, where had Rhoda gotten it? Surely not as a gift from a beau. Or was an Englischer interested in her out there in the world of the fancy Kraybills? Was that why she had come in late this past Friday night?

"Oh, to return to simpler days." Nellie placed the necklace back on the mirror and went to stand at the window, staring at oodles of snow in all directions. Soon, very soon, the bishop would reinstate the Bann, and where would that leave them? Which side of the fence would Rhoda be on by that time? And Nan? Was she leaning toward joining up with the tractor and car folk?

According to Dat, giving up one's will for the sake of God's was the key to salvation. The prospect sounded very hard, if not impossible, yet could she be truly content otherwise?

Without a doubt, Nellie knew she wanted to marry Caleb. How could she possibly be happy without her beloved? She didn't want Preacher Manny's church to dictate the future to her differently, or to force her to choose between her dearest love and Suzy's Savior.

CHAPTER 17

The silo behind Dawdi and Mammi Fisher's glittered like highly polished silver, but sunbeams lacked warmth on this harshly cold Lord's Day afternoon. Even so Rhoda stood outside, watching Nan fling dried bread crumbs on the snow for the birds, chirping quite like a winter bird herself.

They'd both bundled up to wait while Dat and Mamma talked privately with their grandparents indoors. Rhoda figured what was up; it was obvious Dawdi wasn't so keen on living clear over here in Bird-in-Hand when most of his immediate family was back in Honey Brook. Dat likely saw this as another opportunity to discuss the new church with his parents—it seemed to Rhoda that anymore he was always seeking to recruit folk into Manny's fold.

The minute they arrived home, she would talk to Mamma about having her own space in the house. She craved more privacy and freedom, even though her first real attempt to satisfy the latter had backfired. Of course, she hadn't given Glenn Miller a second thought in a romantic sense since running away from his clutches. What a hard lesson indeed, and one she would not repeat.

She and Nan were nearly as frozen as icicles when Dat finally began to hitch up the family carriage to the horse. Rhoda realized again how tired she was of traveling so pitifully slow. *Twenty-five minutes by car*, she thought. There were plenty of things she had become weary of—a wood-warmed house, the same dull evening chores, endless Bible reading, and an early bedtime. She'd seen the way Mr. and Mrs. Kraybill lived, with their toasty warm central heating, a fine compact radio in the kitchen . . . and a nice-sized color television in what they called their living room, where they actually spent most of their leisure time. Nothing like the front room where her family went only to shiver the evening away, far from the woodstove and the warmth of Mamma's big kitchen, the place they usually gathered. No, their *front room* was not the family's gathering place at all, but merely the room located at the front of the house. As such, it was used primarily for setting up large quilting frames and—when it was their turn—to hold the congregation for Preaching.

Lately word had it that the tractor and car folk had already located a meetinghouse in which to worship, splitting the original splinter group down the middle. But the New Order, as Preacher Manny called his group, would continue to turn their front rooms and kitchens into temporary houses of worship.

She heard Mamma saying her good-byes to Mammi, the two of them hugging as Dat and Dawdi shook hands amicably. *Good. Maybe Dawdi will return to Honey Brook.*

She found out differently on the ride home. Fact was, Dawdi and Mammi had no intention of moving in with them on Beaver Dam Road, not as long as their family was "cluttering up" their minds with the "wrongful message" being spread far and wide by Preacher Manny—no matter that he was Dat's first cousin.

Rhoda gathered all of this from the things Dat and Mamma said in snippets to each other, as if they'd managed to forget Rhoda and Nan were sitting in the seat behind them, fully able to read between the lines. It was quite clear what had transpired while Nan was out feeding the birds and Rhoda was bored silly.

The painfully slow *clip-clop* of the horse made Rhoda more determined than ever to buy a faster means of transportation—and escape—even if doing so meant plunging herself into great debt.

Elias turned to face her as Rosanna lay down to rest, and he began to discuss Kate. "What do ya think your cousin was doin' coming here right after she saw the babies at Preaching? Didn't ya say she'd nursed Eli there?"

"Well, you didn't make matters any better," Rosanna replied softly. "You could've gone outside to talk to John."

"What good would that've done?"

She wanted to cry. Ferhoodled Kate had messed everything up, and Rosanna could scarcely bear it.

Elias fell silent, and she had the thorny sense she'd overstepped her bounds. Immediately she was sorry.

She knew him well . . . he was undoubtedly rehearsing what had occurred earlier. *Why hadn't he intervened with Cousin Kate, sending her home?*

He closed his eyes and sighed. "Ach, Rosanna . . ." Then he rolled over, away from her.

"Doesn't matter, really. Kate's gone now," she whispered. "Just rest, love."

He lay still, hardly breathing, and she assumed he'd fallen back to sleep. She ought to do the same if she was to be wide awake enough for suppertime and tending to the babies' needs, as well as being good company for Elias later.

Rhoda stood in the doorway of James's former bedroom first thing Monday morning. Oh, the things she could do with a spot like this!

Stepping boldly inside, she eyed the double bed, with its pretty oak head and footboard, pieces made by her father when James was only a boy. Mamma would be suspicious of her when she asked—*if* she had the courage. Yesterday had not presented an opportunity, but today, this very day, she would request the move.

Touching the lovely bed quilt, she noted the striking purple, red, and navy blue Bars pattern, delicately double stitched by Mammi Hannah long before James was even born—before Mamma was married, too. Mammi Fisher, along with Mamma and her sisters, had kept this family warm for many years with many layers of quilts.

Smiling, Rhoda hoped against hope Mamma would agree. Making this empty room—presently kept for overnight guests—her own was but the first of two things she wanted, and wanted badly. She'd take steps toward the second today, when she went with Mrs. Kraybill to look at used cars after work.

Mamma startled her, mop in hand, and Rhoda stepped aside. "Oh, sorry."

"No . . . no, that's all right." Mamma glowered. "How would you like to dry mop and dust this room?" She squinted. "Seems you've got some time on your hands."

"Honestly, I best be goin'."

Mamma pressed the mop to the wide-plank floor. "Guess you'd rather clean an Englischer's house."

There was a surprising sting in Mamma's words, but Rhoda refused to react. She headed down the hallway to her room with Nan. So much for talking to Mamma about James's room.

Later, she poked her head into Nellie's bedroom and said, "We missed you yesterday at Mammi's."

Nellie nodded. "I lost track of time, is all."

"Well, it's too bad, 'cause it would've been nice to have you along." Pausing, she sighed. "How long before we get over there again, ya know?"

"I know, and I feel just awful 'bout it—not seein' our grandparents and all." Nellie put down her brush, her rich brown hair flung over her shoulder and draped like a thick curtain down to her waist.

Rhoda hesitated for a moment, then said, "Seems you and I have something in common."

"Oh?"

Slowly she nodded. "Jah, you're far removed from this family, so to speak, just as I am."

Nellie Mae looked befuddled. She resumed her hair brushing and turned to face the window. "The church split's caused plenty of problems, I'll say that."

Rhoda saw the flicker of pain on Nellie's face. "I don't suppose you'd let me see Suzy's diary."

Nellie frowned. "What for?"

"She was my sister, too."

"Why now?"

"I'd just like to read it, that's all." Rhoda wouldn't stoop to pleading.

Nellie set down her hairbrush. "Best not."

Rhoda had figured as much and left the room. Sometime when Nellie was sleeping, she would simply borrow it. . . .

At breakfast, when Rosanna passed the basket of muffins to Elias, he surprised her by saying, "I heard you prayin' this morning, love."

She started. "Oh. Didn't realize—"

"And you've been studyin' Scripture, too."

Had he seen the Bible lying open, or the list of verses Linda Fisher had written down?

She held her breath while he paused, looking at his callused hands.

"I've been thinkin'," he began. "We ought to at least look into Preacher Manny's group. See what it's all about."

Hope filled her. "Really?"

"I've talked to a few of the tractor folk, too."

She heard the excitement in his voice and feared he might want to bypass the New Order flock, the group most interesting to her. Biting her lip, she wanted to word her question carefully, so as not to sound critical. "Is it the farm equipment that has your interest?"

"I won't deny it would be a great help, what with so many years before little Eli can work alongside me," he replied. "But it's more than that. I've been talkin' to Reuben Fisher. Ach, the things he's shown me in Scripture—wonderful-gut things, Rosanna . . . things I've never heard before. Well, I want to learn more, too." He looked at her. "I hope this doesn't scare you."

Oh, how she loved him. "I've been more than curious, too . . . wanting to know more—wanting to know the Lord God truly as Linda Fisher does. I've felt this way for some time, Elias."

He reached for her hand. "I thought as much."

"You aren't angry with me, then?"

He rose and kissed her cheek. "I'm hopeful, love. I want Eli and Rosie to study God's Word—not just follow the ordinance. To hear Reuben talk of Suzy, the comfort of knowing she's with her Savior, that they'll see her again someday . . . I want that for all of us. For our family."

"We are a family now, ain't so?" She glanced over at the playpen, where the twins slept side by side.

Nodding, he smiled. "We always were, but now all the more, with God's gift of these two little ones."

Nellie smiled, unable to suppress her glee as a whole group of customers left the bakery shop for their cars. "Oh, Mamma, what's happenin' to bring in so many folk? And scarcely anyone Plain."

Her mother leaned on the display counter, looking ever so pretty in her green cape dress, her hair somewhat looser than usual around the sides of her round face. "Must be that ad someone put in the paper, is my guess." Mamma stifled a chuckle. "I asked Rhoda 'bout it, but it wasn't her."

Nellie shook her head. "'Tis a mystery."

"I should say."

Looking over the remaining cookies, bread, rolls, and coffee cake, Nellie worried they might actually run out of baked goods. "Well, if the ad brought those Englischers, then prob'ly there'll be more, jah?" She hoped so, since they had much catching up to do in the way of income.

"No question in my mind why they came." Mamma threw away the pieces of paper where she'd totaled up the sales amounts for each of the last twenty-five or more patrons. "I've never laid eyes on any of those ladies before, have you?"

"They're new to me, jah." Nellie noticed another car pulling into their lane. "Looks like more, too . . . a right steady flow."

"Dat will be prancin' with joy." Mamma pressed her hands to her face. "Ach, I don't know when I've had such a fine time."

Pleased as she was about the increase in business, Nellie was glad for the slight lull in customers, so they could catch their breath. She expected she'd have only a short time to talk with Mamma about the things on her heart. Perhaps while they cleaned up the noontime dishes there would be additional time . . . if Nan was off somewhere else, maybe. Otherwise, she'd have to wait till afternoon. By then surely they'd have run out of the day's offerings and have to post the Closed sign on the door.

Such a good problem to have, Nellie thought, wondering again just who'd placed the newspaper ad.

CHAPTER 18

Betsy glanced through the bakery shop window, delighted to see daughter-in-law Martha arrive for yet another visit with her three littlest ones in tow. The unexpected sight of her beloved granddaughter running through the snow toward the bakery shop took her by surprise. Dear Emma looked so like a young Suzy. Betsy's heart tugged ever so hard, and here just when she'd begun to feel some better.

"Oh, Nellie—Emma's come to visit!" she announced over her shoulder and rushed to the shop door.

Nellie Mae dutifully remained behind the counter, helping customers while Betsy ran out into the cold, arms flung wide. Emma fairly flew to her, wrapping her little arms around Betsy's neck and squeezing ever so tight.

"Mammi Betsy, I missed ya!" Emma said, her plentiful kisses raining on Betsy's face.

"Emma, darling, let your brothers have a hug now, too, please," said Martha, who was carrying a very bright-eyed and smiling two-year-old Matty.

Jimmy, three and a half, clumped forward in black boots too big for his feet, squealing, "Mammi, Mammi!"

Betsy released Emma and received Jimmy's hug, then kissed him on his chubby red cheeks. She was quite aware of Emma, who stood beside her all the while. "Go and get warmed up in the house." She shooed Martha along. "I'll be down later. Nellie Mae and I've got our hands full today."

"Business is pickin' up?" Martha patted Matty's head as he giggled, now reaching his arms out to Betsy, who gladly took him and gave him a sound kiss.

She nodded. "Never busier. Nan's making a nice big pot of chili for the noon meal . . . so yous can stay and eat with us, maybe?" She nearly held her breath, waiting for Martha's head to bob in agreement. Then she waved and leaned down to give Emma another kiss on her sweet cheek before hurrying back into the bakery shop, where Nellie Mae looked red in the face.

Betsy hurried around to the other side of the counter to help the next two women in line, with the more outspoken woman paying for both orders. She watched Emma run to catch up with her mamma outside, trying not to smile too broadly when Emma turned and looked back toward the bakery shop before she reached the walkway leading to the back door.

Bless her heart!

Oh, but it was hard to keep her mind on the work. Thankfully, they'd all be eating dinner soon, enjoying some of Nellie Mae's moist corn bread, and Emma would plant herself right next to Betsy at the table.

Sighing, she counted change for the two women, grateful they and all the others had come on such a nippy day.

When the bakery shop cleared out a bit, she touched Nellie's hand. "You doin' all right?"

"Why, Mamma?"

"Well, ya looked tuckered out earlier."

Nellie nodded. "Don't know when I've ever had so much goin' at once." She glanced toward the windows and took a deep breath. "Mamma, I've been wanting to talk to you. . . ."

Betsy's heart fluttered. *What about?*

"You're just so happy since, well . . . since you and Dat started goin' to the new church." Nellie fidgeted with the keys on the cash register. "No, I guess it's more than that—it's your joy. Honestly, Mamma." Her lower lip quivered.

"Oh, honey-girl." She slipped her arm around Nellie's slender waist. "Come, now."

"No, you *are* happy, Mamma. Your eyes are a-shinin' all the time."

"Ain't my doin,' dear one." She measured her words. "The change came right in here, thanks to the Lord." Patting her heart, she hoped that maybe Nellie was hungering after the things that had brought light and life to her and Reuben.

Nellie Mae's eyes filled with tears. "You prayed for me . . . when I was ever so sick. Remember?"

Oh, she remembered, all right.

Eyes pleading, Nellie asked, "Will ya keep prayin', Mamma?"

Her heart nearly broke at this from her girl who'd seesawed about the New Order. It appeared Nellie was more curious again. Could it be Nan's doing? She'd noticed that daughter had devoted much more attention to Nellie this past week. "Why, sure I will."

A car pulled into the lane, inched up to the bakery shop, and parked. Four more English customers got out, heading toward them.

"Remember, you're always welcome to attend Preachin' with us," Betsy said, frustrated that this important conversation must come to a premature end. When might she and Nellie Mae ever again talk so freely?

More than a dozen crows flew over the road directly in her line of vision as Rosanna drove the enclosed family buggy with baby Eli snuggled in one arm. The birds looked exceptionally large and black against the starkness of the white snow, and their *cawing* sounded menacing. Rosanna held the reins with her free hand, glad to have left Rosie at the neighbors', not wanting to risk taking both babies in the carriage by herself for even this short drive.

She had begun to suffer a bad case of cabin fever. Hopefully the ten-minute trip to see Linda Fisher would suffice for getting some fresh air on this most beautiful, yet cold, Monday morning. She'd hung the washing right early while the twins conveniently slept. She smiled at the memory of rushing back and forth to check on them, not wanting to leave them alone for more than a few minutes, even though they were snug in the cradles Elias had brought down to the warm kitchen first thing in the morning. What's more, he had helped by giving Eli his early morning bottle before heading off to a nearby farm sale.

She began to hum a church song, hoping Eli would continue to sleep till they arrived at Linda's. Church songs and church itself were less interesting these days; it was Elias's curiosity in the newly formed New Order group that had her most excited. Preacher Manny's flock attended services every Sunday—the "off" Sundays were for Sunday school—setting the People all abuzz.

How strange it would seem to go each and every Lord's Day. Rosanna supposed they could get used to going so often. *Especially if the sermon and Scripture readings are understandable.*

Not wanting to hurry the horse, she embraced the thrill of their future—so many possibilities. Surely the winds of change had begun to blow already, with Elias on the verge of jumping the fence . . . or at least seriously thinking about it. And even though it seemed like a wonderful-good thing to do, she feared how her father and her extended family might take such news. At least making the leap before the bishop declared the return of the Bann meant they could continue to enjoy fellowship with their family and friends in the old church.

Looking into the tiny face of her son, she whispered, "Your pop wants you to know all the good things found in God's holy Word. You and your sister both." She kissed his peachy cheek. Rosanna would leave it to Elias to decide if such things as tractors, electricity, and telephones were for them.

No matter which new path her love might choose, the future seemed ever so bright to Rosanna as she pulled up to the Fisher home.

Linda greeted her at the back door. "Come in, come in!"

Rosanna moved into the warm kitchen with Eli, who'd mercifully slept during the buggy ride.

"Well, this is a welcome surprise!" Linda began to flutter about to put some cookies on the table.

"Can't stay long . . . must be gettin' back to Rosie." Rosanna explained why she hadn't attempted to bring both babies.

"I can imagine it would be difficult to travel alone with them both, at least till they're old enough to sit up." Linda stopped her preparations to make over Eli, who was peeking at her with one open eye as he slowly roused. "He's a handsome boy, that one."

Rosanna lifted him onto her shoulder. "He'll be hungry here 'fore too long."

"You should sit down and have something for your sweet tooth while you have the chance." Linda put a pot of water on to boil and returned to the table, sitting across from Rosanna.

They talked of the cold weather and all the snow, of the farm auctions, and how many folk had already scattered churchwise.

"Jonathan's downright pleased 'bout seeing so many converts." Linda's big brown eyes sparkled. "I daresay you've heard as much."

It was interesting to hear Linda talk like this—about grace and electricity mixed into one convenient package. "Jah, we've heard, and between you and me, Elias said at breakfast just this morning that he'd like to visit Manny's church. 'Course, he also talked about tractors, so he might be leaning toward the Beachys. He could surely use a tractor's help in the fields."

"A tractor?" Linda was smiling. "Well, wait'll ya see Jonathan's new car. It's a beauty."

It was so odd hearing this from Linda, although the grapevine had already heralded the news. "Where's it now?"

Getting up, Linda looked out the window. "He's out taking his driving test—hired a man to teach him, can ya believe it?"

"I declare." Rosanna laughed softly, repositioning Eli on her lap. "This one might like helping his daddy on a tractor when he's a little bigger. Ain't so, darlin'?"

Linda looked her way, smiling at Eli. "Some of the farmers up the road plan to take their boys along, come spring. One farmer even paid extra for air-conditioning in the cab. Now, what do ya think of that?"

"Ach, really?"

Suddenly there was a commotion in the lane, and when Rosanna looked, she saw Linda's husband sliding up toward the barn door in his automobile, narrowly missing it as the brakes caught at the last minute.

"Such a time to be out driving, jah?" Linda rushed to the back door and outside, leaving Rosanna to sit with Eli in her arms.

"What's the world comin' to?" she whispered. "Cars and all the new-fangled whatnot."

Even so, she was mighty curious.

"Dat's lookin' to buy a car, Mammi Betsy," confided Emma in whispered tones before they sat down to the noon meal.

Nan glanced over at them from the stove, where she was stirring the chili, and Nellie Mae's eyebrows shot up. Betsy was thankful Reuben hadn't come inside yet for dinner.

"Now, Emma," Martha said quickly, eyeing Betsy. "Your Dat's only talking 'bout it—nothin's for sure."

Oh, but it won't be long, thought Betsy sadly. Wanting to change the subject, she asked Emma, "What new sewing project have you started since Christmas?"

But the child was not to be dissuaded. "We'll be able to go ever so fast then, ain't so, Mammi?" Her big blue eyes fairly danced.

Jimmy started to frolic about the kitchen like a very fast horse, and Martha, quite flummoxed, turned her attention to Matty, on her lap.

Nellie Mae made a suggestion. "Here, Emma, put this basket on the table for me."

Emma nodded and carefully carried the large wicker basket of corn bread over to the table. "There," she said, gently setting it down. "What else can I do?"

Apparently glad she'd succeeded in getting Emma's attention, Nellie looked over at Betsy, smiling. "Put all the napkins around, too." She showed Emma how to fold them in half, placing the first one under the fork on the left side of the plate. "Do this for each fork, jah?"

Emma set about doing as Nellie asked, any further talk of automobiles evidently forgotten.

Later, when Reuben was washed up and sitting at the head of the table, he bowed his head and prayed longer than usual. Betsy wondered if the content of the audible prayer was for Martha's benefit, as Reuben undoubtedly had already heard of James's plan to purchase a car. Maybe that was why he ended the prayer with "And, Lord, keep us—all of us—ever mindful of the narrow way that leads to life everlasting. Amen."

The light filtered through the side window of the enclosed family carriage as Rosanna headed home. Ever so glad she'd made time in her busy day to see Linda, she shifted Eli in her arms. He had been perfectly placid and sweet all during both the carriage ride there and during the visit.

She stopped to pick up Rosie at the next farm over and decided it was safe to let the horse lead them home, the reins draped loosely across her lap blanket as she held both babies near.

Upon her arrival, she got Eli and Rosie settled inside the house in their playpen. She was glad to see Elias coming for dinner, willing and ready to help with unhitching the horse for her and leading it to the barn.

One less thing to do, she thought, rushing to reheat the chicken corn chowder she'd made on Saturday. Now all she needed was to put some dinner rolls on the table with several kinds of jams, and Elias would be smiling.

Fast as a wink, she took off her coat and went to wash her hands at the sink, where she spotted a note with her name printed on it in bold letters.

Dear Cousin Rosanna,

I stopped by to nurse Eli today and you were gone! How can you possibly think it's safe to take Eli and Rosie in the carriage by yourself? Or did you have help, maybe? I certainly hope you had that much sense!

Well, I'll see you later today, if I can get away. This is such an inconvenience to me, I daresay, your being away from the house and all.

Till later,
Your cousin,
Kate Beiler

It was Martha who took charge of stacking the dirty dishes and gathering up the silverware with a little help from Emma. Nellie was pleased to see her sister-in-law again, happy she'd come by to have a meal with them now that Nellie was well enough to join in the visit. Meanwhile, Mamma was in a hurry to get back to the bakery shop, rushing off to wash her hands and face in the washroom "right quick."

The more she pondered it, the more fascinated Nellie was by the recent change in her mother. Initially worried sick about Mamma's grief-stricken state in the weeks and months after Suzy died, Nellie could see how near-jubilant she was now. Momentarily, perhaps all of them had lost their way, but truly for Mamma, *her* life had changed, apparently for the better. She'd begun to refer to this life journey as a "gift of grace" even while living in the midst of great grief, and Nellie doubted the change had come because she'd pulled herself up by her own bootstraps. No, Mamma's joy came from an intangible source beyond anything Nellie had known.

"Nellie Mae," Dat said before leaving to return to his woodshop. "The new tables and chairs will be ready later this afternoon. Maybe I could bring them over after you close?"

"That'd be ever so nice."

"Just in time, too." He said it with a twinkle in his eye.

"Ain't that the truth!"

Nellie stepped outdoors as Martha got the children bundled up and settled into the carriage with some help from Dat. Emma carried on with extra kisses for her Mammi and a wave for Nellie Mae.

Turning her attention back to the bakery shop as they drove away, Nellie was anxious to see how many customers might come yet today.

Did I bake enough?

She wasn't sure, really, though they'd soon know. She looked forward to seeing firsthand how inviting her father's tables and chairs made their corner of the shop. She hoped the women who frequented Nellie's Simple Sweets—both the new customers and the regulars—might stay longer to visit . . . and open their pocketbooks and spend more while doing so.

Pleased as pie, she waited for Mamma to return from her good-byes, thinking they might resume their previous discussion, if time allowed.

She considered Mamma's words and her invitation to church. She knew what her parents longed for. Except for Ephram and Maryann, she was supposedly the last to come to her senses. But all the confusion of folk splitting off from the old church and becoming even more broad-minded, getting cars—like James and Martha were talking of doing—made Nellie even more sure that the Old Ways were best . . . at least for her and Caleb.

Yet she couldn't dismiss her curiosity about the transformation in Mamma's life, especially. *Much like Suzy herself changed*, she thought suddenly.

One thing she would never understand, however, was the desire to own or drive a car. What was James thinking? Nellie shook her head. She'd ridden in automobiles enough to know she preferred to leave the driving to the Mennonite folk her father occasionally hired. Besides, Nellie saw no need to go so fast or so far. Life wasn't meant to be lived that way, was it?

CHAPTER 19

Nellie made a complete circle in the bakery shop, admiring the way the small alcove and window across from the display counter made for a cheery spot on a sunny day, thanks to Dat's beautifully made tables and chairs. With twelve places for customers to sit and nibble, the shop was the perfect spot to visit with friends.

For now, Nellie Mae was the only one who sat there, grateful her father had taken the time and care to do this thoughtful thing for her and her customers. On a slow day, Nellie and Mamma could even sit down themselves to relax, enjoying a cup of cocoa and a bite of cookie, perhaps. Of course, a day like today kept both of them on their feet.

Nellie daydreamed of Caleb during the short lulls in business. She envisioned him coming up the lane on foot or in his fine black open buggy, just to see her. On different terms . . . in a different time, he might have done so. What a lovely thing it would be if the schism had never happened, if the People had continued in the Old Ways as they had for more than three hundred years. She could scarcely imagine what it might be like for Caleb to court her as he wished, even though that, too, would have been in secret, as was their custom.

But now theirs was a desperate sort of secrecy, their courtship completely forbidden. Was that what made them all the more determined to be together? She hoped that wasn't the case, for if true, it seemed to diminish their love.

Nellie dismissed the idea. They loved each other deeply. Sometimes, if she were to admit it, she even loved Caleb fiercely. She would do almost anything to be with him. She knew her own heart, which beat with Caleb's name. Surely his did the same for her.

Just then, the small bell on the door jingled loudly. She jumped, startled. Turning, she was surprised to see Nan jostling inside, all wrapped up in one of Mamma's heavy woolen shawls, her own black outer bonnet on her head.

"Hullo, Nellie . . . I hope I'm not intruding." Nan looked around. "You alone?"

"Jah."

"Well, do ya mind?" She sat down. "I . . . wanted to see the chairs. Dat said they were all set in place." Nan ran her hands over the backs of the finely sanded oak chairs, her face solemn as could be.

"Sit for a while."

Nan looked somewhat relieved.

They were quiet for a time, relishing the silence. Then Nan said, "I'm takin' a big step come midsummer. I wanted you to know directly from me."

"What's that?" She couldn't imagine what her sister wanted to say.

"I'm goin' to take baptism instruction—to join the new church."

"Preacher Manny's?"

Nan nodded and smiled. "Jah, the Lord God's helping me set aside any longing for modern conveniences. I've been thinking 'bout it for a while now and I believe He's calling me to do this."

Nellie felt surprise at the earnest tone in Nan's voice; she'd never known her to be so serious about such matters.

"Won't ya think on it, too, sister?"

For so long she'd yearned for this sort of sharing . . . this special closeness with another sister—the way she and Suzy had always been together. "Does anyone else know?"

Nan blinked back tears as she slowly shook her head. "I thought of tellin' Rhoda first, but 'tween you and me, I fear we're losing her to the world. I can only pray that our oldest sister does not fall prey to the fancy."

"She must find her own way—"

Nan looked pained. "No, I don't believe that. Not at all."

"What do you mean?"

"Just that Rhoda *is* following her own will, desiring her own way. Left to her plans, she could fall into sin. I'm ever so worried." Moving her hand over the tabletop, Nan sighed. "I won't be joinin' church to go through the motions, Nellie Mae."

Did Nan have more to tell? Had she perhaps found herself a new beau already? Joining church usually signaled a wedding.

"I've found what Mamma has . . . and Dat . . . in the Lord Jesus."

Nan reached for her hand across the table, palm up. "Ach, I haven't been a very caring sister, Nellie Mae. I'll be changin' all of that, believe me. You'll not be grieving alone anymore."

"Oh, but . . ." Now it was she who could not keep back the tears.

"I love you, Nellie."

Nellie nodded, accepting her dear sister's hand. "And I love you, too." She looked at their clasped hands. "There is something I promised to tell you. Something your closest friend asked me yesterday to share with you."

"Rebekah?"

"She has made an equally difficult decision. Well . . ." She paused. "Possibly more so."

Nan frowned, her radiant expression suddenly clouded. "Is Rebekah all right?"

"I'm thinking so. She asked if she could ride along with you, Dat, Mamma . . . and Rhoda to church next Sunday."

Nan clapped her hands, leaned back, and made a little whooping sound before quickly composing herself. "Ach, what news! Did ya tell her she could?"

"Well, there wasn't much to say, really. She seemed to have pondered it at length and said she'd be out on the road on foot, and if Dat wouldn't mind, he could stop and pick her up."

Nan covered her mouth. "Oh . . . she'll be in such straits with her father, jah?"

"I brought that up, but Rebekah was unwavering." She paused. Such a good time she was having here with Nan as dusk settled in around them. "You can be proud, even *thankful*, to have such a strong-willed friend, I daresay."

"And you're not equally strong willed, Nellie?" Nan's comment threw her off guard. "Surely you're still seein' Caleb, despite his father's—"

"Nan . . . you silly, we're talking 'bout Rebekah—of her interest in your church, nothin' more."

Nan giggled, and with that Nellie rose, torn between what she wanted to revel in and knowing what she must do to protect her beloved.

A single glance at Nan, still sitting, led Nellie to wonder if she ought to have shared openly with this sister who seemingly desired to make amends. *Jah, I should have.* But the moment had passed, so she slipped into her coat and bid Nan good-bye, pulling the door shut behind her.

The lights strung high over the car lot nearly blinded Rhoda as she stepped out of Mrs. Kraybill's gray-and-white Buick Electra, with its white sidewall tires. She'd seen the term "loaded" and wondered if Mrs. Kraybill's comfortable car would be considered that.

She'd fantasized about what she wanted in a car, and this evening she might just lay eyes on it. Mrs. Kraybill, looking pert in her rimless glasses and woolen hat and tweed coat, had asked on the drive there what price range she'd had in mind. Rhoda told her precisely what she could afford. "No higher, and I'd rather spend less."

Glancing around now, she admired the neat rows of cars, looking for all the world like some kind of fancy crop. The lot was light and bright and thankfully quite devoid of customers. Someone had plowed the area so people could easily walk without slipping in the snow.

Soon, a man dressed in a long gray overcoat and matching hat walked across the lot to them and politely extended his hand. "Good evening, ladies. I'm Guy Hagel," he greeted them. "Any chance I can help you find the car of your dreams? I'd like to make tonight worth your trip."

Rhoda immediately liked him. Mr. Hagel was both well-mannered and considerate, walking clear around the lot with them, pointing out the features of each car and offering to let them take first one and then another "for a spin," in spite of the snowy streets.

"Now, here's something really special—a sixty-one Chrysler New Yorker in a striking dubonnet red color. Took it as a trade-in just last week." He waved his hand toward a bright wine-colored two-door with rear fins—a mite too flashy for Rhoda's tastes.

Rhoda spoke up. "Thanks for your help, but we're just seein' what's here." At this Mr. Hagel looked dubious, and with a bit of embarrassment she realized she did not appear to be someone who would be in the market for a car.

"If you don't mind, my friend and I will keep looking for a while," Mrs. Kraybill added, relieving the awkward moment. "We'll certainly let you know if we need any assistance."

They continued to wander rows of Buicks of all kinds—convertibles, Rivieras, LeSabres . . . and even several Electras like Mrs. Kraybill's. Black and white seemed to be quite popular, as were a soft gray, a pale blue, a tan, and a sort of turquoise green. But it was not so much the color that appealed to Rhoda as the entire package.

They took their time, with Mr. Hagel allowing them to sit in the cold interiors of three different cars, all as nice as could be. So nice, in fact, the cars were beginning to run together in Rhoda's memory. How would she ever narrow it down to one?

"We'd best be headin' home," she said quietly while Mrs. Kraybill sat in the driver's seat of an especially eye-catching coupe, admiring its plush upholstery and chrome-accented dashboard.

By then Mr. Hagel had excused himself to meet another customer, and

Rhoda could hear him repeating much the same words he'd said to them earlier.

"Well, what do you think?" asked Mrs. Kraybill, her black-gloved hands still on the steering wheel. "Do you have your eye on one in particular?"

"They're all so perty, ain't?"

Mrs. Kraybill smiled. "They truly are . . . especially *those* fetching machines." She laughed heartily, pointing to the convertibles next to them.

"Jah."

"It's getting too cold to be out, dear. Shall we call it a night?"

Rhoda agreed, torn between wanting a car right away and wanting to be able to actually drive it. "Could we come back tomorrow in the daylight?"

Mrs. Kraybill agreed that was a good idea, and she offered to teach Rhoda how to drive. "However, you'll need a learner's permit first."

"Oh?"

"I'll take you to get one soon, if you like. First you'll need to study for the written test. I can pick up a copy of the *Pennsylvania Driver's Manual* the next time I'm in town."

Though her mind was now reeling with the decision ahead and all she had to learn, Rhoda was determined to do whatever it took to get what she wanted. *To think of being forever finished with horses and buggies!*

More than an hour later, Rhoda bowed her head while Dat offered a tedious prayer, followed by an equally lengthy Scripture reading. Tonight the passage was from the first chapter of 1 Peter. Dat read a verse about souls being purified by obedience several times . . . and something about a pure heart, too. She didn't feel he was singling anyone out in doing so, but he *was* clearly urging their attention on that particular verse.

He'd be furious if he knew where I went tonight.

She wanted to make sure her father—both of her parents, really—was unaware of her car purchase till it was too late for him to intervene. Not like some of her older brothers who actually sought out Dat's advice beforehand. Nan had reported that their own brother James was interested in buying a car, too. She assumed it wouldn't be long before the oldest boys—Thomas and Jeremiah—would also have one each. Or maybe they'd share one between them. They seemed to like to do that sort of thing, living as they did in a large farmhouse, split in half by a center hallway. One side for Thomas and his wife and children, the other side for Jeremiah and his.

After evening Bible reading and prayers were finished, Rhoda waited around, hoping to talk to Mamma. When the time came, she said, "I'd like to move into James's old bedroom."

Immediately it was apparent Mamma wasn't keen on the idea, shaking her head right quick. "Nee." She frowned. "There's no need, Rhoda. You and Nan are just fine together in your present room."

Well, that was that. No one in her right mind would think of arguing with Mamma. Rhoda knew she was stuck, exactly as she feared she might be if she didn't hurry and set her plan in motion to purchase a car—and net a fine husband.

More than anything, Nellie longed to write a letter to Caleb, but that was out of the question. She sat on her bed, several pillows supporting her back, and tapped her pen on the stationery, frustrated that Caleb could send *her* a letter, but she could never reply. Their situation felt as lopsided as all get-out, and she pushed away her resentment toward David Yoder.

Puh, my future father-in-law!

Wondering if Caleb might also be thinking of her now, she leaned against the headboard, considering their love. Could it survive the expected separation?

The Lord willing, Nellie surprisingly found herself thinking. Suzy had often written that in her diary, following her conversion.

Would it take God's intervention for them to marry? She really didn't want to think that way. Such thoughts of divine miracles and interventions were appealing, but they went against the teachings of the Old Ways she and Caleb believed.

Writing the date, *Monday, January 21*, Nellie sighed. If she couldn't write her thoughts to Caleb, then what about a nice long letter to Cousin Treva? They'd become good pen pals over the past year, occasionally enjoying personal letters while still sending much of their news in circle letters. Tonight, though, Nellie sought a more personal way to express herself.

Dear Cousin Treva,

Hello from Honey Brook on a very chilly day. Is it equally cold there, I wonder?

Well, my family traveled to your neck of the woods yesterday afternoon and—can you believe it—I missed the trip! I got to holding Ephram

and Maryann's pretty new baby, Sadie, and it was like time just stopped.
Honestly, have you ever experienced such a thing? I did not want to give
that baby back, nohow.

I felt like such a silly, not getting home in time to go with my family to
Bird-in-Hand, especially when I might've been able to visit you, as well as
Dawdi and Mammi Fisher. Such a Dummkopp I am!

I'm telling on myself, jah? Anyway, I'm hoping you'll come for a visit
when things warm up a bit—maybe the next Sister's Day, if you're able.
If you want to, you and one or more of your sisters could spend the night
in the spare bedroom next to mine. We have two more guest bedrooms
downstairs, off the front room . . . and, of course, the Dawdi Haus. That
remains empty, even though I know Dat would like to persuade Dawdi and
Mammi Fisher to reconsider moving here.

Thinking of that, lots of changes have happened in our district. Nearly
half of the Old Order folk have now gone to the New Order or the Beachys.
How many are still in the old church there? Do you see Dawdi and Mammi
Fisher at Preaching service?

Well, write when you can. I always enjoy hearing from you.
Hope the new year is off to a good start.

> *Your cousin and friend,*
> *Nellie Mae Fisher*

Personal letter though it was, she didn't think of writing even a hint
about her brother James's fascination with cars—no need to hand that off
to the rumor mill. Such embarrassing news flew through the community
mighty fast.

Much like the never-ending guessing about who's pairing up.

Despite couples' attempts at secrecy, parents and grandparents whispered
amongst themselves. It was a known fact that most mothers of the bride
had more than an inkling about the groom's identity prior to the couple's
intention to marry being announced at church each fall.

Folding the letter, Nellie thought again of Caleb, wondering how to get
word to him from time to time. Maybe that was not what the Lord God
intended for them. Maybe she was supposed to bide her time—*their* time,
since Caleb, too, had his hands tied. Thing was, she had no idea what was
going on between him and his father, no idea what good thing was being
accomplished, if any, by their painful separation. She felt totally in the dark.
Still, she clung to the hope that if she stayed true to the Old Order long

enough—proving herself faithful—David Yoder would eventually change his mind about her and allow Caleb's and her marriage.

I must trust that all will be well. . . .

When the house was still and everyone was deep in slumber, Rhoda found the flashlight she kept under her side of the bed for emergencies. She slipped out from under the quilts and into the cold hall, shining the light on the floor. Going to Nellie's room, she tilted the light inside, reluctant to shine it on the bed lest she awaken her younger sister.

Once she'd determined that Nellie Mae was indeed asleep, she turned off the light and knelt on the floor, keeping her head low so as not to be seen if Nellie should awaken. Opening the drawer to the bedside table, she reached inside.

Empty.

She moved her hand all the way to the back of the drawer, wondering if it had slid over to the left side, perhaps. But still she found nothing, even though Rhoda had once seen Nellie stash the diary in there when Rhoda had walked in on her reading it.

Where'd she hide it?

Picking up the flashlight, she managed to crawl out of the room, not wanting to take unnecessary risks by searching further. It was mighty clear Nellie had moved the diary, suspecting Rhoda or someone else would try to snatch it away.

Must be some big secrets in there.

Heading back to bed, Rhoda felt rather defeated. First by Mamma's resounding denial, and now by Nellie's silent rebuff.

CHAPTER 20

I t was hard at times to remember just how close she had been to Suzy, although it had not even been a year since her sister's death. Nellie's dreams of her sister only added to the confusion as the dreams and the memories joined together like the pieces of a quilt. Except what remained was not something whole at all, but rather wispy fragments.

Snuggling now beneath several layers of Double Nine-Patch quilts, she wished she had the nerve to ask the Lord God to keep her from dreaming. She needed a reprieve. A good solid night of sleep would be much appreciated.

As she lay there, knowing it was nearly time to begin Tuesday's baking, she wondered if she ought to let Nan in on her secret. She felt bad about shutting her out yesterday, when they'd shared such a sweet moment together alone in the bakery shop. And then if she hadn't gone and spoiled things!

She must seek out Nan and open her heart to her, trusting that her sister would keep this confirmation of Caleb's and her forbidden relationship in strict confidence.

Nellie pushed back the quilt and sat up, yawning and hoping she would be doing the right thing by her beau.

Today is the day! Rhoda thought as she left the house that morning, bundled up with so many layers she could scarcely move, heading to work at the Kraybills'. If she and her father were on better footing, she might've asked to borrow the buggy, but that would have tied up his transportation all day long. Besides, she had no business asking—not considering what she looked forward to doing this very day.

Over the noon hour, Mrs. Kraybill planned to drive her to the nearby bank preferred by the Plain, where she'd fill out the necessary loan paperwork. The thought gave her the willies. If all went well, they would head back to the car lot and make her purchase. Rhoda could hardly wait.

She realized it was premature to purchase a car, but she wanted what she wanted and was tired of being denied. Now was the time to make the leap into the world. Then, once all this snow was gone from the ground, she'd have herself some driving lessons.

Meanwhile, Rhoda would hide her secret out behind the Kraybills' house, where Dat could not be privy to her deed.

Betsy knew one thing for sure—January held the power to signal the first hints of springtime. Most people would look at her with surprise if she dared say it, but she knew it was true firsthand.

So busy was she in the bakery shop with Nellie Mae there was scarcely time to say three words to her daughter. But she was breathing silent prayers for her dear girl in response to Nellie's request. Once things settled down a bit and there was even the slightest letup in the continuous stream of customers, she would tell her what she'd discovered in the cold cellar.

Meanwhile, she was taken aback by Nellie's bold question to a customer, a middle-aged woman wearing a loud red woolen coat and white knit scarf and gloves to match. "If you don't mind . . . did ya happen to see a newspaper ad 'bout the bakery, ma'am?"

The woman smiled and shook her head. "No, I actually heard about this place from my neighbor here." She turned to the younger brunette standing nearby. "But *she* saw the ad in yesterday's paper."

The ad's still running? Who on earth would spend that kind of money?

Betsy was quite surprised at the revelation but said nothing, simply glancing at her Nellie-girl. She knew better than to ask, "What on earth?" That never worked with this daughter. Come to think of it, it didn't work with Rhoda, either. And that one, well, she was up to something for sure. Betsy had seen it in her steady, determined gaze that morning at breakfast. *Jah, Rhoda has her secrets, no doubt about that.*

Nan, bless her heart, had resumed the work of cleaning house and cooking nearly all the meals, now that Betsy was helping Nellie Mae in the bakery shop once again. Nan much preferred the quiet of the house, or so it seemed. Was it a way to mourn the loss of her beau?

Opening the display case and removing two pies, Betsy personally was glad to be working alongside Nellie Mae. *So good of Reuben to allow it,* she thought, grateful he, too, was past the very worst grief. Sometimes Betsy awakened with tears on her face, not remembering ever weeping. Silent tears of loss and of deep joy, as well. Their youngest was with the Lord.

For that reason, September, the season of great salvation for this house, would always be for Betsy the most wonderful-good month of all.

To think it began with my dear Reuben.

Glancing out the window, she noted the low-lying clouds. Winter days were too short, and even this early in the day, sunshine fought to get through the gray haze. *Like the light trying to shine forth in the heart of a rebellious soul.*

She sensed such in Rhoda and could only pray, because confronting her had never worked in the past. Now she wished she had listened to Reuben from the outset; they'd made a serious error in allowing their eldest daughter to work away from home.

"Mamma . . . look, we're runnin' out of pies." Nellie disrupted her reverie. "Yesterday it was cookies, today it's pies."

Betsy smiled, motioning for Nellie to come and sit with her, since it looked as though there might be time to catch their breath.

Nellie commented how thankful she was for her father's contribution of these sturdy, even pretty, oak tables and chairs. Betsy, too, enjoyed having a place to sit and rest a bit, and they could easily see from this vantage point if customers were driving up the lane.

"I've been prayin' for you." She looked right at Nellie Mae, who inhaled slowly and nodded.

"I want to do the right thing, Mamma. Truly, I do."

"And you will . . . the Lord will lead ya." Betsy folded her hands.

Nellie was silent. Then she said, "I sometimes wonder what might've happened if Suzy'd lived a full life. Would she have stayed Amish, do ya think?"

"She may not have been as conservative as Dat and I are . . . but once Plain, always Plain." Betsy smiled. Folks said it was ever so hard to get the Old Ways out of the soul if you were raised in them.

They sat quietly for a time. Then, eager to share what was mighty close to bursting forth, Betsy began. "Yesterday I happened to go to the cold cellar to fetch two jars of peach jam for supper. Guess what I found in the potato storage rack? Sprouting potatoes. Both the red and white potatoes are just a-springin' to life already."

Nellie listened, glassy-eyed, obviously daydreaming.

"Beyond a doubt, the buds have begun to rise . . . and all this in the cool darkness." She sighed. "Of course, we don't count on using *those* potatoes to see us through the winter, but for cuttin' apart, an eye for each section, to plant when the ground is thawed."

"All this is happenin' in the dark," Nellie said flatly. "When everything else seems dead . . . or is."

Betsy smiled. "Jah. On one of the darkest of days comes the first hint of life. 'Tis that way for everything . . . even potatoes." She wanted to reach over and pat Nellie's hand, because all of a sudden her daughter looked to be quite taken with the comparison. But Betsy remained still, letting her remarks sift into her daughter's mind.

————

Nan surprised Nellie by coming to help carry the few leftover baked goods back down to the house so they wouldn't freeze overnight. Actually, Nan urged Mamma to go ahead of them and leave the work to her. While alone with her sister now, Nellie took the opportunity to apologize. "I was snooty yesterday afternoon, and I'm sorry." She added, "I'd like you to come to my room tonight, after evening prayers. Will ya?"

A flicker crossed Nan's eyes and then she offered a warm smile. "Oh, Nellie Mae . . . I wondered if you'd ever ask."

"I want to tell you something very dear to me."

Now I have to keep my word.

Nan looked both surprised and pleased. "I can't wait. Oh, sister, you have no idea!" With this, Nan kissed her face.

"Well, if you feel as lonely as I do sometimes, then I *do* know." Nellie set about gathering up the last pie and a few assorted cookies, unable to squelch her own smile.

Am I wise to tell her my secret? she wondered, but she pressed on with the chore at hand, refusing to second-guess her resolve.

During supper, Dat talked of the cold having turned a corner and become dangerously severe. He glanced outside now and then at the heaviness of the snow as it fell silently, covering the earth with yet another layer of white.

Then, during a dessert of pie and cookies, the focus of his comments took a marked turn, and he leaned forward, looking directly at Rhoda. Nellie flinched, wondering what now.

"Rhoda, it's come to my ears that you've committed a most disobedient deed."

At the accusation, Rhoda's eyes turned a stony gray. She pushed away her plate of pumpkin pie, her frown as deep and as harsh as the cold beyond the kitchen walls.

Dat did not beat around the bush about the reliability of his source. "Your brother James spilled the beans 'bout your car." His eyes tapered into stern slits. "He saw you at the car lot this afternoon."

Like-minded souls those two—James and Rhoda, Nellie thought. *Dat must have gone over to try to talk sense to James today, only to find this out!*

"So, then, under God, I ask you, Rhoda, where is your heart in all this?"

Rhoda raised her eyes, her expression moving quickly from embarrassment to anger and suddenly to bitterness. "Am I not of age, Daed?"

Nellie was struck by Rhoda's use of the more formal address of their father. *Daed* was the word Caleb used to refer to *his* father.

"Are you not living under my roof, under my authority, daughter? And don't you eat my food? Enjoy the warmth of this house . . . the fellowship of this family?"

Squirming, Nellie held her breath. Rhoda was treading on dangerous ground, and everyone at the table, including Mamma, awaited her respectful response.

"My heart just ain't here." Rhoda rose from the table. "I'm leavin'—tomorrow, first thing."

Mamma gasped. "Rhoda . . . no!"

"Let her be." Dat touched Mamma's arm.

Rhoda left the table and the room, her feet pounding fast on the stairs. It was all Nellie could do not to run after her and beg her to think hard before carrying out what she'd so daringly declared.

———

Nellie's original plan to tell Nan about Caleb took a backseat to their worries about Rhoda later that night. Mamma's lip had quivered all through Bible reading, and Nellie wished something could be done to smooth things over with their oldest sister. "What'll she do out there in the world, anyway?" Nellie sat on the bed, leaning against the headboard, while Nan sat facing her, her back against the footboard.

"Well, 'tween you and me, I don't see Dat backin' down," Nan said. "I'm worried she'll do what she says and leave tomorrow."

"And then what?"

Nan shook her head sadly. "She may never darken the door of this house again."

"Why do you thing that?"

" 'Cause she's so headstrong."

"You oughta be spendin' time with her." Nellie felt bad saying this on the first night Nan had come to talk. *So ill-timed, really . . . like most things these days.*

"I'll go over there in a minute, but you had something you wanted to share with me, jah?"

"It best be waitin'," she said, thinking only of Rhoda.

Nan studied her. "You sure?"

"If Rhoda goes ahead with what she's threatened, we'll be losin' another sister."

Nan agreed. "I'll see what I can do." With that, she climbed off the bed, saying good night and leaving Nellie to wonder what Nan might say to take the stinger out of Rhoda. And if she did convince Rhoda to change her mind, would Dat change his, too?

By sheer coincidence, Caleb had seen Susannah Lapp at a farm sale that morning, though not for more than a few seconds. She'd arrived with her mother, bringing a hamper of food to her deacon father for the noon meal.

He had offered a tentative smile when their eyes met. In all truth, he'd felt deceitful doing so, but he'd hoped a smile might be enough to set up the possibility of a longer encounter at the upcoming Singing. *No sense putting it off.*

Now, ready for bed, he leaned on the windowsill, looking at the inky black sky, recalling the way the dense atmosphere had added to the depth of color, making the sky appear flaming red at sundown, hours ago. He had been on his way out to the barn to check the livestock—his responsibility—when he'd noticed it. He was glad to do whatever he could to prove to his father and grandfather that he was up to the task of taking on this large operation. Willing and ready, minus one small piece of the future—a bride.

Well, he was on his way to fixing that. Once he could honorably report back, man to man, that the deacon's daughter was of no romantic interest whatsoever, Caleb understood he'd be at liberty to pursue the young woman he truly loved. All it would take to finally obtain his farmland was doing things his father's way.

Sunday's the day. . . .

Putting out the gas lamp, he climbed under the bedcovers, leaning his head back on his crossed arms. He felt a peculiar rush of excitement at the thought of seeing Susannah again—excitement that quickly turned to mortification, even though she had been as pretty as ever today when he'd bumped into her. He knew his heart belonged to Nellie Mae and to her alone.

Susannah is the only path to Nellie Mae, he reminded himself.

CHAPTER 21

R osanna King was up and pacing the floor in the wee hours Wednesday morning, but not with a babe in arms. She simply could not rest, let alone fall asleep. Not with what Cousin Kate had pulled last night before supper. She'd arrived with three of her youngest ones to see "their baby brother and sister," as she put it, propping Rosie in her blanket on the lap of her two-year-old.

Elias had frowned all the while, evidently expecting Rosanna to put her foot down. They'd had words again after she'd fed and tucked in the twins, who continued to sleep soundly now.

The growing tension between herself and Elias gnawed at her. How she resented Kate's coming to visit for more than the agreed-upon midmorning feeding—and she'd worn out her welcome with even that. It was time someone put a stop to it and mighty fast, lest next time Rosanna stoop to sinning and spew fiery words at Kate.

Fuming now as she relived the intrusive visit, Rosanna went to look in on her sweet babies. *Kate's undermining my mothering. Slowly but surely.*

She felt nearly desperate, wishing she could confide in the bishop's wife, Anna, or in one of the preacher's wives, since her own dear mamma was long deceased. Perhaps Nellie's mother would have some wisdom to offer. Sighing, she knew she and Elias needed help with this mess. The empathy she had repeatedly attempted to show her cousin was dwindling fast.

Oh, how Rosanna had longed for a child, and now she loved these babies to pieces. Her family was at Kate's mercy, and things had gone awry faster than either Elias or she could ever have imagined. Truth was, Kate's visits were starting to feel like something completely different from how they had started out.

Something frighteningly different.

Tossing on his robe, Chris Yoder slipped quietly down the stairs and slumped into a chair at the kitchen table. He couldn't sleep—not with

Zach in bed on the other side of the room, talking on and on about Suzy's bracelet. His brother had even tried to convince Chris to drive him back to the state park after school instead of waiting for the weekend. He wanted that frozen bit of gold from the ice near the lake, and he wanted it now. Chris had firmly refused; he didn't have time on school nights. Besides, that shiny gold object encased in ice wasn't going anywhere, and it was most likely not the bracelet, anyway.

But not a single line of reasoning seemed to faze Zach—he was single-minded. He must have Suzy's bracelet.

Chris ran his hands through his hair, making it stand up. He worried that Zach seemed in danger of losing his sense of reason. His brother's grief was spiraling off into something weird.

Struck with how helpless he felt, he began to pray. "Father in heaven, I ask for divine comfort for Zach, in Jesus' name. Let your light spring to life in his heart and mind. Soothe his pain, and help me be the brother and friend he needs to walk along this hard path. Guide me and let me know when to silently support him and when to offer words of comfort. I'll thank you for it. Amen."

Leaning his head into his hands, he remembered an evangelist at the Tel Hai campground who said that when you extend yourself to those who are suffering, you find out who you truly are. You discover yourself . . . what you're made of.

He decided he needed to be more patient and understanding with his brother. Here he was complaining to himself, wishing Zach would snap out of it. But he hadn't ever experienced firsthand what Zach was dealing with. He'd never loved a girl that way. Nor had he called upon the Lord for his life mate, fasting and praying for days like Zach had. How quickly the answer had appeared to come . . . only to be taken away!

God's ways are always higher than ours. Knowing full well that his parents had prayed since his birth for the young woman who would someday become his wife, just as they had for each of their sons, Chris realized he'd never once prayed that way.

What am I waiting for?

He felt convicted suddenly. Compelled by it, he bowed his head again, this time with deep gratitude for God's ongoing providence. He didn't ask for his future bride to be outwardly pretty, as Suzy Fisher had been, but he did ask that she be a partner in whatever ministry he would eventually be called to. "Protect her from sin and harm . . . and may she not be discouraged in seeking your will for her life, Lord . . . wherever she may be. These things I pray in the name of Jesus. Amen."

———————

"I never thought my own brother would tell my secret!" Rhoda bemoaned her state to Mrs. Kraybill that morning. She told how she'd bundled up earlier to trudge through knee-deep snow to the very same brother's house before dawn. "I startled James and Martha but good."

"And why was that, may I ask?"

Rhoda fought the urge to weep. "I asked to move in over there—they've got two spare rooms off the sunroom downstairs."

Mrs. Kraybill frowned and tapped her well-manicured fingernails on the table. "I assume you've given this some thought, Rhoda?"

"All night long I pondered it."

To think Mamma, Nan, and Nellie Mae were all witnesses to Dat's words . . . and mine, she thought ruefully, reliving the suppertime feud.

"Mamma made a noble attempt at breakfast . . . asked me to apologize to my father." She stirred sugar into her black coffee. "But I haven't changed my mind. Honestly, I'm more than ready to start over somewhere new."

"Well, I do hope you'll continue working here—for us." Mrs. Kraybill searched Rhoda's eyes. "You have a car payment now, remember."

She remembered, all right. It was the main reason she hadn't asked to stay with the Kraybills, even for a short time. She needed pay, not free room and board. "I'm rather strapped now, ain't so?"

Nevertheless, she was fond of her beautiful car—a black-and-white four-door Buick LeSabre with under thirty thousand miles on it. It was fully loaded with whitewall tires, a 335 Wildcat engine—whatever that was—power steering and power brakes, and a radio. "The works," Guy Hagel had told her.

Mrs. Kraybill smiled kindly. "You're a determined young woman, Rhoda. I believe you'll do well in your new life."

It was time to spread her wings, anyway, regardless of Dat's probing words. Maybe the car purchase was exactly what she'd needed to propel her away.

"Would you mind ever so much helping me move my things to James and Martha's?" she asked. "I'd be very grateful."

"I'm happy to help." Mrs. Kraybill rose to pour herself more coffee. "I do have to ask you—are you still thinking of keeping your car here?"

Rhoda nodded. Was Mrs. Kraybill concerned she could encounter trouble with Dat somehow? "Don't worry 'bout my father comin' over here and giving you a tongue-lashing. That won't happen, I promise you."

Mrs. Kraybill appeared relieved.

I'm old enough to make up my mind, Rhoda thought, rising to clear the cups and saucers off the table. *No matter how hard Nan tried to talk me out of leaving last night. And no matter how sad Mamma and Nellie Mae looked at the breakfast table!*

———

The snow had stopped altogether by midafternoon, and Rhoda was pleased Mrs. Kraybill consented to go home with her, having left her two preschool-aged children with the neighbors. The eldest was headed to a friend's house after school. They were picking up two suitcases full of Rhoda's clothing and personal belongings, including her necklaces, which left the bureau mirror looking mighty bare.

She was relieved that Nellie Mae and Mamma remained out in the bakery shop, not coming inside for a last-ditch effort to keep her home. Even so, Nan came running upstairs, tears glistening in her eyes. She stood out in the hallway with her hands clasped, staring in at their room.

"If you find more of my things, just box 'em up, Nan," Rhoda said, hating to be so pointed. Nan didn't deserve to be treated this way, but if Rhoda appeared any other way but deceptively strong, she would surely break down and start crying herself.

Mrs. Kraybill carried down the first suitcase, leaving her alone with Nan, who leaned forlornly against the doorjamb. "Listen, I just don't fit here anymore, and I'm tired of hiding the real me. I'm going to the new church now—with the tractor folks, I've decided." Rhoda exhaled forcefully. "Nellie Mae doesn't see eye to eye with our parents, either, but they are a lot more patient with her. . . ."

"Oh, I think Nellie will come around in time."

"Well, I won't. Give up my perty car for a horse and buggy? Not on your life!"

"Rhoda, please." Nan touched her arm.

"No. I've had it with livin' like this. I'm not cut out for the Plain life. I have to get out or suffocate!"

Nan sniffled, her sobs coming in little gulps. But that didn't keep Rhoda from reaching for the remaining suitcase and marching past her dearest sister, right down the stairs.

Nellie comforted Mamma as they stood at the bakery shop window, observing Rhoda and their English neighbor load the last suitcase. "She's really leaving. I'd hoped she'd change her mind." Nellie's throat ached.

"Me too." Mamma reached for her hand. "I should have let her move into James's old room like she wanted."

"This isn't your fault, Mamma."

"Still, I'm takin' this much too hard, I fear."

"Oh, Mamma, no. You love Rhoda—we all do. She's making a mistake, that's certain. Of course you feel ever so bad." She led Mamma away from the window.

All Nellie and Mamma could do was pretend not to wince at the sounds of Mrs. Kraybill closing the trunk of her car and the slamming of two car doors—shutting them out.

Reuben stood near the window in the haymow, leaning forward to watch his eldest daughter making the worst mistake of her life. He wished he might retract last night's statements, yet he felt strong in his stance. Rhoda needed to find where she fit into the family of God, certainly, but she also needed to be less bullheaded.

Will she learn anything worthwhile out there with Englischers?

Betsy had made a point earlier this morning before they'd ever gotten out of bed. *"You're doin' to Rhoda just what your parents did to you . . . and all over a difference of opinion."*

So his wife was put out with him, too.

Betsy's right. He removed his black hat and held it over his chest—over his heart—as Mrs. Kraybill pulled her car forward and turned around, heading down toward the road.

God be with you, little girl. . . . Flee to anner Satt Leit—*the other kind of people—if you must.*

He prayed it might prove to be beneficial in the long run. After all, the apostle Paul had relinquished the degenerate man over to the devil for the salvation of his soul.

Reuben moved away from the window and pulled himself together. It wouldn't do for the feed salesman, expected any minute now, to see him all broken up like this.

———

At half past nine Friday, the twins were back in their playpen for their morning nap. Rosanna was well occupied with bread baking and dinner making, thinking of Elias as she worked. Her husband had been extra kind this morning at breakfast, holding his son and going out of his way to make over both babies, which had started the day on a sweet note.

Seeing his gentle way with the twins made her long to be in his arms again. Instead, she'd made his favorite breakfast of German sausage, three fried eggs, and blueberry pancakes. He always took his coffee strong, with only a spot of cream, but oodles of sugar.

They'd talked congenially, all forgiven. The only thing Elias had to say with any connection to Cousin Kate was that he'd noticed she had cut back on her multiple visits, giving them a reprieve of sorts. Here it was already Friday morning and she'd dropped down to one daily visit since Tuesday. "What the world?" Elias had asked, chuckling.

She'd told him about giving Kate the instructions for making blessed thistle tea—*"just the thing for Kate's baby blues."* Again, he had laughed heartily, and they'd both assumed the herbal tea was doing its job.

"Hopefully," she muttered to herself, rolling out whole-wheat dough for a large beef potpie. She best be getting it in the oven before long or Elias would be twiddling his thumbs when the time came to sit down to eat the main meal of the day.

Carefully she lifted the dough from the counter, pressing the top crust over the beef and home-canned vegetables before poking holes in the top with a table fork.

Glad the snow had ceased falling yesterday, Rosanna yearned for a long, brisk walk, though that was not possible just yet. Still, she thought ahead to the day when Eli and Rosie would be able to walk along and keep up with her on a mild winter's day. *And come summers, too.*

She imagined all the fun the twins would have growing up here—little Eli helping Elias tend to the animals and working the land together as father and son. Such a wonderful-good team they'd be. She would have herself a grand time teaching Rosie to bake breads and pies, passing along everything she knew about quilting and sewing and tatting and cross-stitching to her darling little girl.

Oh, such fun!

Stooping to open the oven, she slid the potpie inside, wishing dear Mamma could see her now. Was she looking down from on high? *Safe and sound in the arms of the Lord God . . .*

Thinking on this, all of a sudden she missed holding her wee babies and went to the next room to look in on them. She cherished watching them sleep or drink from their bottles. Fortunately, they had become quite attached to the latter, especially Rosie, since Cousin Kate had ceased nursing her.

Hearing a muffled noise outside, her heart sank. Cousin Kate had arrived . . . right on time.

She put on a smile and hurried to the back door to greet her cousin, who had little blond, blue-eyed Rachel with her again, seemingly as happy as ever to see Rosanna. Kate gave her a quick hug. "I'm feelin' ever so good today. How 'bout you, Rosanna?"

Kate chattered on about her morning—the baking she'd already done, with some help from niece Lizzy, who was old enough to act as a regular mother's helper and who baby-sat the younger children each morning when Kate came to nurse Eli. Rosanna had been wondering how Kate was keeping up at home.

Sitting down with two-year-old Rachel on her lap, Kate seemed calmer than on previous visits. Curious, Rosanna asked, "Did you happen to try that tea recipe?"

Kate said she had, offering a smile. "I've been drinkin' it several times a day, as a matter of fact . . . awful nice of you."

They talked about various kinds of herbal teas and how they were reported to help what ailed you. Rosanna actually found herself enjoying this visit, mostly because Kate hadn't rushed into the other room and focused her attention on the babies, or purposely awakened them. It was ever so nice to sit and talk together, like they had long before the twins were born.

Soon they were all three sipping hot cocoa, little Rachel blowing softly on hers while sitting up close to the table on Kate's lap.

So far, it was almost as if Eli and Rosie were of no interest to Kate today, for she said not a word about them. Surprised, Rosanna wondered if she was going to simply ignore the fact that the twin babies were napping in the next room.

It was Rachel who asked in her tiny voice, after the hot cocoa was finished, "See *Bobblin*, Mamma?" Rosanna's imagination flew to Eli and Rosie's second birthday. She assumed Rosie might look a lot like little Rachel, who was now wriggling to get off Kate's lap, wanting to have a "look-see" at the babies.

Kate rose with her daughter and carried her to the doorway. Then she turned and asked, "Is it all right, Rosanna?"

Before Rosanna could think to say not to awaken the babies *this time*, she agreed. "Why sure . . . show her the twins." But she needn't have worried, for Kate merely held Rachel up to look at them.

"Babies sleepin'," Rachel whispered, holding her pointer finger up to her mouth. "Shh," she said in such a darling way, Rosanna nearly forgot the previously upsetting visits.

Kate straightened and headed back to the kitchen with Rachel still in her arms. "When do ya plan to go to a quilting bee next?"

Rosanna wanted to go soon if the weather cooperated. Her neighbor to the east had offered to baby-sit at least one of the twins so she could handle the reins on the buggy whenever she wanted to get out of the house. "Where's the next one to be?"

"At Esther Fisher's."

"That'd be right nice."

Kate eyed her for a moment. Then, looking away, she added, "Might be best if you don't go a-quiltin' with the New Order womenfolk, though."

"Oh?"

Kate put her daughter down to toddle about. "Bishop Joseph ain't exactly putting his foot down about it, askin' for separate work frolics just yet. But even so . . ."

"Jah, once the ninety days is past . . . what then?" Rosanna sighed. "Hard to know what'll happen."

"Well, one of two things, I daresay. Folk will either be in or out." Kate's gaze was scrutinizing.

"In" meaning the old church, thought Rosanna wryly.

Long after Cousin Kate and Rachel left, she pondered the peculiar change in Kate's demeanor, especially toward the babies. More than anything, she'd wanted to urge Kate to keep drinking more of the blessed thistle tea before she left, but thought better of it.

CHAPTER 22

O n Saturday Chris Yoder reluctantly drove his brother to Marsh Creek State Park as promised. With their dad's camping hatchet on the floorboard, Zach was determined to dig up whatever had frozen into the ice and debris under the rowboats.

All week Zach had talked of little else other than cutting the shiny thing loose, obsessed with the idea of retrieving it.

Chris was sorry he'd ever suggested going to the lake in the first place. If Chris had *his* way, they would simply wait for Mother Nature to do her work in a few short months during the spring thaw.

But Zach was not at all interested in waiting.

"Do you ever wonder where heaven is?" Zach asked suddenly. He was staring out the car window. "Up from our planet . . . or out from the solar system on the other side of the sun or something?"

He'd never even considered it.

Chris didn't answer, but Zach continued anyway. "Heaven's closer now. . . ."

Because of Suzy, thought Chris.

"She went too soon—I feel cheated, you know?"

He figured Zach would feel this way, and most likely for a long time, too. Chris didn't say what he was thinking—that there would come a day when his brother would love again. "Yeah. I'm not surprised."

Chris pulled the car into a parking spot near the rowboats. He turned and put his arm on the back of the seat, leaning toward his brother. "Listen, I can't possibly know what you're feeling, Zach. And I can't imagine the pain you live with, either." He glanced at the lake. "I wish we'd insisted on safety that day. . . ."

Zach nodded. "Yeah. Pure stupidity."

"Well, I bear the responsibility. I know that."

"No, we're all guilty . . . we should've known Suzy couldn't swim. She never had a chance." Zach pushed his door open and climbed out.

Chris got out on his side and quickened his pace to catch up:

Armed with the hatchet, Zach strode to the boats and knelt on the ground. "Hey, it's still here!"

He chopped away at a small cube of ice-encrusted snow and debris, the glint of gold at its center. "Let's get this home and thaw it out."

Zach was more intense than Chris had ever seen him, cradling the chunk of ice and snow like a trophy. He carefully set it in an old cooler in the trunk, and they drove back home.

Together they entered the house quietly, hoping not to run into their mother. Zach carried the cooler upstairs. Chris followed behind him, unwinding his scarf as he trudged up the stairs.

He found Zach in the bathroom, running water over the block of ice. "You could just wait—it would melt on its own."

Zach paid him no mind, intent on his mission.

Chris hung around, hoping Zach wouldn't be devastated to find an earring or coin or something of even lesser value stuck in there.

Someone turned on a radio downstairs. "Close the door," Zach whispered tersely. "Lock it!" He looked pale now, desperate.

Chris frowned momentarily, worried. What if he *was* right and this whole thing turned out to be nothing?

He shuddered at the memory—Suzy Fisher sitting in the rowboat, her white prayer cap strings floating in the breeze as she and Zach rowed to the middle of the lake. . . .

"Look!" Zach said now, gently extracting something from the small remaining hunk of ice. "Here it is." He turned off the water and held up the gold bracelet.

Chris leaned closer to inspect it. He could hardly believe it—the very bracelet Zach had purchased for Suzy, the etched Scripture verse still visible.

"See? I told you!" Zach dangled it triumphantly.

"Better keep it down. Mom'll wonder what's going on."

Zach slipped the bracelet into his pants pocket and told Chris to go and keep Mom occupied while he cleaned the dirt and leaves from the sink. Chris didn't like being his brother's conspirator in this weird project but reluctantly complied.

Downstairs, he found Mom in the kitchen, taking a rare coffee break with her latest issue of *Good Housekeeping*. She offered to make him a sandwich, but he told her he was glad to make his own. While he leaned into the refrigerator and pulled out ingredients, she asked, "How's Zach doing, do you think?"

Chris hesitated. Part of him wanted to unload everything, all his worries about Zach's obsessions with Suzy, her photograph, and now the bracelet. But he didn't want to worry their mother, who had enough to be concerned about with three older sons away at college.

"Zach's a little better, I think."

"I offered to buy him a scrapbook for all his mementos of Suzy—the photo, the revival meeting flyer you were handing out when you met her, the newspaper clippings. But he's really defensive about that bulletin board of his."

"I know." Chris stacked roast beef, Swiss cheese, and lettuce between two pieces of bread.

"How long has it been now?" Mom asked.

Chris sighed, his appetite suddenly gone. "Seven months." *Seven long months.* How long would it be until Zach was himself again?

In the backseat of Jonathan Fisher's Rambler Marlin, Rhoda began to doubt her resolve. Her brother James was behind the wheel and Cousin Jonathan sat in the passenger seat beside him, issuing nonstop instructions and advice as if he'd had a license all his life. Feeling the wheels slide across the icy road once more—and her stomach slide, too—Rhoda wished she had waited to ride with a more experienced driver.

It was James who'd egged her on, saying it would be good for her to ride along while Jonathan gave him driving instruction. James had applied for his permit even before purchasing a car, so he was one step ahead of her— legally able to practice with a licensed driver. All Rhoda could do in the backseat was grab the door handle and hang on for dear life.

"That's right. Now tap the brakes gradually. Never slam them on a slick road, or—"

Too late. Seeing the T-intersection ahead, James had already hit the brakes, and the car spun around. Rhoda cried out and gripped the seat in front of her, sure they were about to crash. Instead, the car straightened and rammed nose first into the pile of plowed snow at the edge of the road, cushioning their stop. Rhoda felt queasy and wondered if this was how it felt to spin around in one of those carnival rides she'd seen at the Lancaster County fair.

James tried to back the car out of the snow, but the wheels squealed and spun.

Jonathan put on his hat. "I'll get out and push." He let himself out and positioned himself on one side of the car, leaning down with hands against the hood. He pushed and James gave it gas, but still the wheels spun. Giving up, Jonathan motioned to James. "Come and push on the other side. We'll need to get 'er rocking. Rhoda, you'll have to take the wheel."

Rhoda was startled. "What? No. I don't—"

"You won't be driving. Just hold the wheel and push on the gas pedal when I tell you."

Rhoda couldn't believe it. This was not at all how she had imagined her first time "driving" a car. Feeling shaky, she climbed out of the back and slid into the driver's seat. She checked the rearview mirror. The Kraybills' yard was behind her across the intersection. She could see the snowman and small fort the children had built earlier in the week. She was relieved the family was not home to witness this scene and that no other cars—or carriages—were approaching.

She rolled down the window to better hear Jonathan as James took up his position on the other side of the vehicle. Both men began pushing in rhythm.

"When I tell you, give it a little gas, Rhoda," Jonathan called. "Not too hard."

"Jah . . ." Rhoda answered. But she had never pushed a gas pedal before. How would she know how hard to press it?

"Okay, push!"

Rhoda did, but the car stuttered to a halt. She'd hit the brake pedal instead.

"Sorry!"

She saw Jonathan shake his head and James roll his eyes. *Hey, I wasn't the one who got us stuck in the snowbank!* This time, she'd be ready. She checked the rearview mirror again and then glanced down, lifting her hems slightly and poising her right boot directly over the gas pedal. Again, the men pushed.

"All right . . . now!"

Rhoda pressed—hard. The car lurched away from the men and flew backward across the road. She heard James grunt. Saw a blur as James fell face first into the snow. She whipped her head up to look in the rearview mirror . . . just as the car plowed into the Kraybills' yard. She had only a second to glimpse the snowman—jaunty hat, carrot nose, and coal smile—before she flattened him.

The car shuddered to a stop as Rhoda found the brake. She squeezed her eyes shut, humiliated. Her first time behind the wheel, and she already had her first fatality. She shook her head. She would definitely wait until spring to learn to drive.

Reuben felt a certain weariness on this Lord's Day morning, which was accompanied by more than a few aches and pains, the result of fighting an exceptionally spirited horse that had protested yesterday's first-time hitching. His knees ached when he pulled himself out of bed. Later, when hailed by Nan's best friend, Rebekah Yoder, his back pained him so much he nearly lost his balance while stepping down from the buggy.

Nan had only just mentioned that Rebekah was to meet them along the road, "for church." Sure enough if David's daughter wasn't standing along the roadside, wearing snow boots, her black winter bonnet, and all wrapped up in layers, waiting.

Now, here's an enthusiastic soul, he marveled.

Rebekah quickly got settled into the carriage amidst joyful greetings from Nan, who seemed especially glad to see her friend, with Rhoda living at James and Martha's—or so the grapevine had it.

All of them yearning for the world . . .

Picking up the reins, he considered what an upheaval Rebekah's going to church with them would cause for David Yoder's household. He considered his own family's present disruption—Rhoda's having left in a huff—which had more than added to Betsy's pain of loss. *Dear wife of mine . . .*

The two girls chattered happily in the second seat, talking in low tones. He leaned toward Betsy and whispered, "David Yoder might come a-callin'."

"I was thinkin' the selfsame thing."

"Nothing to fear, love." He reached for her gloved hand. "God is at work."

She smiled sweetly, flashing her pretty blue eyes.

When they arrived at the host family's farm and the *hostler* boys had unhitched the horse and led it to the stable, Reuben got himself situated in the house meeting, mighty pleased to see Elias King sitting in his frock coat a few rows away. He'd thought Elias was leaning toward the tractor folk, but so far, apparently not.

Curious, he gave a discreet glance toward the kitchen area, where the nursing mothers congregated, and there was Rosanna sitting with Nan and Rebekah, who each held an infant. *Rosanna and Elias's twins,* he thought. Fatherhood was a heavy responsibility, Reuben knew, one that made a man more aware of his need for divine guidance. Reuben prayed that even today the Lord would call Elias to repent and open his heart to the Lord and Savior.

Betsy sat near the front of the large room, where the wall partitions had been removed, making a spacious enough area to accommodate the growing number of members.

Already, a good many of the youth had indicated they planned to join church come fall, after baptism instruction next summer, as she knew Nan would. And now it looked as though Rebekah Yoder, of all people, had an interest, as well.

Betsy was happy to see both Rosanna and Elias King in attendance. Rosanna especially appeared to be listening intently to all Preacher Manny was saying, her eyes fixed on his face. And later, when Elias went forward to surrender his life to God, tears streamed down Rosanna's cheeks. Tears filled Betsy's eyes, as well. How she wished she might see her own Nellie Mae heed the call one day.

Soon . . . very soon, they'll all have to make up their minds.

Betsy bowed her head and prayed silently. Along with Nellie Mae, Rhoda topped her mental list for prayer—poor, mixed-up girl. Surely she would tire quickly of the world.

She thought again of Nellie Mae's heartfelt request for prayer. *May Nellie find you as her Lord and Savior in your way and in your time. In Jesus' name. Amen.*

────────

A new snowstorm began to squall around noon, blotting out the edges of the barren cornfield and nearly obliterating Nellie's view of the barn and woodshed from her spot at the kitchen window. Sighing, she hoped Dat, Mamma, and Nan would arrive safely home from the New Order Preaching service. She fixed herself a light meal using cold cuts and some pickled beets and hard-boiled eggs, because it was the Lord's Day. She had never questioned the unspoken rule of no cooking or baking on Sunday, simply taking it in her stride. As an avid baker, she believed the first day of the week was something of a fast day for her, since she was giving up that domestic task most dear to her.

Sitting alone at the table, she looked over at Suzy's vacant spot, left so even when the whole family came together to eat, out of respect for her sister's life . . . and her death.

"It's hard to believe you're gone sometimes," she whispered. "The truth of it is slowly dawning on me, though."

Considering her losses, Nellie contemplated Caleb and the evening's Singing. If she chose to attend, she faced the prospect of going alone and having to drive herself back home. Caleb wouldn't ask her out tonight—nor any night for ever so long, she realized anew.

She fidgeted, thinking about going through the whole winter long, and possibly the springtime, too, without Caleb near. How she missed him!

No sense even bothering to go to any of the youth gatherings, Nellie decided. She would simply stay home and keep Mamma good company.

Rhoda was thankful to ride home from the Beachy church with James and Martha and the children instead of having to walk, what with the blowing snow already creating near-blizzard conditions. Balancing Jimmy on her knee in the front seat, next to Martha, who held Matty, she stared out the window. The wind was so fierce it seemed to lash the color right out of the sky. The stone walls along the roadside were nearly impossible to make out.

She thought again of her Buick, getting snowed on over at the Kraybills'. *So good of them to let me keep it there.*

Had she been less impulsive, she wouldn't have made the jump to getting the car before the license, somewhat equivalent to getting the cart before the horse. Even so, she had what she wanted now. Come summer, she could drive a whole carload of folk to the Beachy meetinghouse.

Rhoda liked the idea of a separate church building, as opposed to the same old approach to things—turning the first level of a house into one enormous room and cramming in two hundred grown-ups and oodles of babies and children.

To her way of thinking, it made perfect sense to live in your home and attend Preaching in a separate church building. It wasn't that she appreciated the sermon or the prayers and hymns any more—none of that was terribly important to her. Her mind had been on the several good-looking young men sitting over on the right side. She knew which ones were married and which weren't based on whether or not they wore a beard. Courting-age men were clean-shaven and sat with others their age, rather than next to their fathers—not at all different from both the old church and the New Order, come to think of it.

Won't I be something? Rhoda thought, anxious for winter to roll into spring. Anxious, too, to drop a few more pounds. Then she'd show the fellows what they'd missed!

Nellie watched from the front room window, choking back tears as she kept looking for Dat's buggy. The afternoon snow was so heavy, she could hardly see the road. Strangely, she felt the urge to pray for her family's safety. In silence, she asked the Lord God to guide the horse home if Dat had any difficulty directing with the reins in these white-out conditions.

Recalling Dat sometimes concluded his spoken prayers with a grateful addition, she said right out, "And I'll thank you, Lord. Amen."

She sat on the wide windowsill, reaching into her pocket for Suzy's Kapp strings. Holding them up to the frosty window, she caressed them. "Oh, Suzy . . . you'd prob'ly giggle if you knew I kept these."

Clutching the long, ribbonlike ties, she held them against her heart and wept. It had been quite some time since she'd felt so helpless to stop the flow of tears. Missing Suzy and not finding much solace at all in her prayer, Nellie rose and went to the next-door Dawdi Haus, going from one east-facing window to another, her heart in her throat. She wouldn't let herself think that something dreadful had happened to her family. In due time, Nellie returned to the kitchen of the main house to make some hot tea, hoping to get her mind on other things.

Opening the cupboard where Mamma kept her many herbal teas, Nellie pulled down a package of chamomile leaves. She glanced out the window yet again as the wind shook the house. Then she set about adding logs to the woodstove and brewing some nice hot tea in an attempt to calm herself.

By the time Mamma walked in the back door, Nellie had already drunk three cups of tea, waiting for the herb to take effect. In her relief, Nellie was taken by surprise at the sight of Caleb's sister coming in the door along with Nan, snowflakes dusting her shoulders and black candlesnuffer hat.

Well, for goodness' sake! Given the weather, she had not expected Rebekah to follow through with her plan to attend Manny's church, though Nellie was glad for another opportunity to see her again so soon. Rebekah and Nan sat down at the table for some tea, as well, after removing their coats, scarves, and boots and laying them out near the stove to dry.

Dat stood with his back to it. "The Lord saw fit to spare us out in that storm," he remarked. "I daresay only by His providence did we make it home."

Mamma nodded, going to run water over her cold hands. "Thank the dear Lord."

Nan and Rebekah were talking quietly, and Nellie heard bits and pieces of their conversation without intending to. Rebekah revealed to Nan that she'd slipped out of the house early that morning, not having said a word about her plans.

"You mean your parents don't know where you are?" Nan asked softly, her blue eyes wide.

"I didn't tell them."

"Nee, you don't mean it!"

"Well, I'd never have gotten out of the house today, otherwise."

Nan nodded. "I s'pose."

"No supposing 'bout it—I'd be sittin' at home today."

Nan glanced over at Nellie. "If the snow stops, would ya want to go with us to the Singing?"

She knew better than to ask which one. Undoubtedly Nan was referring to the new church group. Her sister wasn't about to stop inviting Nellie to the various youth functions sanctioned by Preacher Manny. "Well, not this time."

"Oh, Nellie Mae . . . that's what you always say. Won't you give it a chance?" Nan pleaded.

"Jah, come with us to the Singing," Rebekah chimed in. "Please?"

Nellie had no intention of succumbing to their pleading. "I'll drop you two off, how's that?"

"Sure, if the weather improves," Nan reminded.

She'd momentarily forgotten about the storm, so intrigued was she by Rebekah's being there against her father's wishes. *Ever so risky to go out in this.*

Pouring more tea, Nellie was struck by Rebekah's brave stand against her father's position on Preacher Manny's group.

Will Caleb be as tenacious . . . for our love?

CHAPTER 23

Caleb opened his eyes to the coming twilight. He'd fallen asleep in the haymow after going up there to consider his plan for that night's Singing, supposing travel was even possible. The insidious cold had awakened him, and he wriggled through the hay hole, dropping down to the stable area below.

Outside, the wind and snow had ceased, though the impending dusk signaled suppertime—and very soon the Singing. Caleb wanted to make it clear to his father where he was headed, not wanting to put any suspicions into Daed's mind about Nellie Mae this night.

Despite the strange, nearly tangible calm that now prevailed, the temperature was still bitter cold enough to keep some of the youth from showing up. He couldn't help wondering if Nellie might venture out. If not, this certainly would be the best time to seek out Susannah and invite her riding afterward . . . if she came, that is. *Best be getting on with what I must do—the sooner the better.*

When Mamm called everyone for supper, Caleb hurried to wash up before taking his place at the trestle table. Tomorrow at breakfast, he would be ready to speak up to his father about his intention to marry Reuben Fisher's daughter next November. He hoped Daed wouldn't insist he seek out Susannah Lapp more than one time.

Daed walked to the table and pulled out his chair. He stood there, his hand clenched on the back of the chair. "Rebekah's still among the missin'?"

Mamm nodded. "Haven't seen hide nor hair of her since breakfast."

Daed looked at the rest of them lining both sides of the table. "What 'bout any of yous? Did ya see her leave the house earlier?"

Caleb and his siblings shook their heads.

"Run off, maybe?" Daed's flippant response surprised Caleb.

Mamm grimaced and made a point of folding her hands to wait for the silent prayer. The fact that she uncharacteristically revealed her emotions demonstrated how put out she was at Rebekah, who knew better than not to say where she was heading—especially on the Lord's Day.

"Oh, I wouldn't worry," said Caleb's older sister Leah. "She's prob'ly over at one cousin's or 'nother."

"No doubt," offered Emmie, another sister. "Hopefully she's out of this cold."

Caleb didn't know what to think of Daed's taut expression and furrowed brow. His father clearly suspected something intolerable, and Caleb hoped for Rebekah's sake that she could give an acceptable explanation.

Nellie was more than happy to take her sister and Rebekah Yoder to the barn Singing, two miles away. She delighted in Nan's obvious excitement, knowing how much it meant for her and Rebekah to spend the day together. But there had been no mention as to how the night would end. Would Rebekah simply let a boy from the new church take her out riding and then back to her father's house? If she was somehow caught with a boy from Preacher Manny's group, wouldn't she be met with even further disapproval from her father?

None of that had been discussed within Nellie's earshot, but Nellie knew both girls were sensible enough to have a plan. Still, because of Caleb's father's tendency toward annoyance, she hoped Rebekah knew what she was getting into. *Sure glad it's not me*, she thought.

Rebekah's voice broke the stillness as they slowly made their way through the ice and snow. "I have to thank you both for welcoming me so kindly."

"Any time," said Nan. "Ain't that so, Nellie Mae?"

She glanced at the two of them sitting to her left on the front seat of Dat's enclosed buggy. "Awful nice you could visit Nan's church today."

"Well, you oughta try it sometime, too," Rebekah said. "Honestly, I think you'd like it."

"Oh, Nellie's already been there." Nan gave a little laugh.

Nellie had to smile at their constant efforts to convert her. *Doesn't Rebekah know what would happen to Caleb and me if I went back?*

"My father won't know what to think when he hears I've visited 'that brazen bunch,' " Rebekah announced.

"Brazen?" Nan was aghast.

"Oh jah—and far worse."

Nan covered her ears playfully. "I can't bear to hear more."

Rebekah sighed. "I don't know how I'll make it through what's ahead of me tomorrow mornin'. . . ."

"You'll catch it but good," Nan said sadly.

"I can only imagine. . . ."

"Well, if you ever need a place—"

"If it comes to that," Nellie broke in, thinking what a big to-do it would be if Rebekah ended up staying with them. *One more black mark against the Fishers.*

Nan was the one who sighed now. "Jah, I s'pose. I just wish there wasn't such tension among the People. It's terrible."

"Can't be helped, I daresay," Rebekah said. "I believe I've found what I've been needin'—what I've been looking for."

"You too?" asked Nellie. Out of the corner of her eye, she saw Rebekah nod her head.

"I've never felt such peace," Rebekah admitted. "I want to go again next Sunday."

"Fine with me," Nan said. "And I'm sure Dat and Mamma won't mind one bit, either."

"Well, we'll see if my parents even let me out of the house!" Rebekah sat up straighter. "If I tell them where I've been, that is."

Sounds like poor Caleb!

The golden light from Preacher Manny's farmhouse windows beamed a welcome, and Nellie reined the horse into the driveway, aware of several cars parked along the side.

"Looks like some of the Beachys are here, too," Nan said. "We'll have a good crowd."

"Your father wouldn't hear of you buyin' a car, now, would he, Nan?" asked Rebekah.

"*Nix kumm raus*—nothing doin'.""

"I thought as much." Rebekah turned and thanked Nellie for bringing them, asking her yet again if she wouldn't consider staying. "It'd be fun— something different, for sure."

"*Denki*, but not this time."

"Well, *another* time, maybe?" Nan piped up.

"Go on, both of you." Nellie laughed and held the reins steadily as they climbed down from the buggy and waved back at her, heading toward the light of the two-story barn.

Have yourselves some fun . . . before the axe falls, she thought, hoping Rebekah's risk would be worth the pain of David Yoder's displeasure.

Tugging the reins, Caleb steered the horse into the lane leading to the barn, glancing at the empty spot next to him where Nellie Mae had sat before tonight. He groaned inwardly.

For a moment, he hoped Susannah Lapp might, indeed, have stayed home on this miserable night. But if that was the case, he would have to wait yet another two weeks to accomplish what his father had demanded.

Jumping down from the open buggy, he was glad he'd worn boots, since the snow was midcalf where he tied up the horse to the fence post. He glanced at the sky, noting the moon's brightness.

To light the way, he thought, wishing he might have borrowed Cousin Aaron's covered carriage so as not to be readily seen with Susannah. *So as not to be found out by dearest Nellie.*

When the time was right, he would explain everything to Nellie. He hoped that she would be understanding.

Caleb entered the barn, noticing right away that only a few boys had shown up thus far—odd to see far more girls than boys present. Undoubtedly some of the fellows would be taking two or more sisters home instead of pairing up.

The weather was but one factor in the low attendance. Truly, he suspected the Singing at Preacher Manny's had drawn some of the Old Order teens away, though Susannah wouldn't be one of them.

A fleeting thought crossed his mind, and he wondered if his "missing" sister might be over with the New Order youth, looking for new courting options, maybe. Daed would lock her up, and mighty fast, if she were so bold-faced. Besides, he couldn't imagine Rebekah doing such a thing.

Moseying over to stand with the other young men, he was filled with sudden trepidation when he spotted Susannah Lapp in a cluster of girls, laughing and obviously the center of attention. She wore her blond hair looser in front than he'd ever noticed before, although it was still pulled back into a bun. Even so, the look was suggestive for a deacon's daughter.

Nevertheless, he found the style to be quite appealing, although he refused to stare, lest anyone notice and think he was flirting.

Looking around for Nellie Mae, he already viewed himself as a betrayer. Yet he must follow through with his father's bidding. As the Lord commanded Judas—what you must do, do quickly.

Part of him hoped to goodness Nellie might quickly appear in the barn door, arriving with some of her cousins. That would surely save him. But the more the boys stood around joking and laughing, passing the time till they were to sit down and begin the actual singing part of the evening, the less likely it seemed Nellie would brave the weather. Even if she did come, they could do no more than trade smiles because of their necessary parting. *Soon to come to a happy end, after tonight,* he thought.

A band of moonlight shone through the uppermost barn window, high in the rafters. Caleb managed to make his way to the long table to sit on the boys' side, not wanting to be situated directly across from Susannah. It was best if she didn't catch him looking her way more than, say, once or twice during the course of the songs. It would make things easier in the long run.

During the second hymn a few more girls trickled in, taking their seats among the other young women. Still no sight of Nellie Mae, however.

Recalling the first time he'd ever driven her home, he could scarcely continue singing. She had been so sweet that night . . . so trusting of him, letting him talk a blue streak while listening like a good wife—er, sweetheart—should. She had taken his heart by surprise in every way.

Then, suddenly . . . if Susannah wasn't looking directly at him this minute. He glanced away, nearly embarrassed, before remembering that he should probably look back at her.

She's even more forward than I thought. . . .

The songs carried them through the next hour or so and then the pairing up began. Quite by accident, Caleb literally bumped into Susannah before he was ready, although Susannah, wide-eyed and all smiles, didn't seem to find it a surprise at all. No, he sensed she'd planned it right down to the second.

All the same, he walked with her toward the side of the barn, where the couples liked to either sit or stand, talking until it was time to go riding.

"How're you doin', Susannah?"

"Ever so nice to see ya here tonight, Caleb Yoder."

He knew she meant it was nice seeing him here *alone*, but he forced himself not to recoil at her flirting. She was, after all, right pretty, and it wasn't a hardship to listen to her talk, her face aglow with his attention.

"Is your . . . well, is Nellie Mae around?"

"You mean is she comin' tonight?"

She nodded ever so sheepishly at first and then her expression changed. "Might be too cold for her, jah?" She batted her pretty blue eyes. Honestly, the girl was flirting up a storm, and Caleb was seized with a desire to run.

She planted herself near him, leaning ever closer as she talked about one frivolous thing after another. All the while he could think only of Nellie Mae and how *she* shaped her words and ideas. The things she enjoyed discussing with him were so much more interesting, and he always felt he was talking with a friend, if not an equal.

He listened politely to Susannah, forcing an occasional smile.

Susannah was babbling about the Fishers now—something about Nellie's bakery shop. "All the fancy folk over there have no doubt put a wedge 'tween the two of you, jah?"

Well, it sure hadn't helped matters any, that was certain. His parents were livid about the whole notion of Nellie catering to Englischers. In fact, he wasn't so keen on it himself.

"No doubt your father is disturbed 'bout Nellie's little bakery shop. But really, Caleb, I don't blame Nellie one bit. She wants to help support her family, jah?"

Caleb's face grew warm.

Susannah touched his arm, walking backward slowly, toward the hay bales, as if she wanted him to follow. For the moment, he did. She stood close enough for him to smell her perfume.

"Of course, I don't blame your father, either. After all, we need to uphold the traditions of our forefathers, ya know, not follow after the world."

He shrugged, ready for this conversation to end. He'd heard enough. Then it struck him hard. Why *was* Susannah so interested in talking about Nellie's bakery shop?

"Aw, Susannah, Nellie's not responsible for any wrongdoing." He observed her closely. "Nobody knows who placed the newspaper ad."

Her face looked innocent. She was smiling a broad, full smile that stretched clear across her heart-shaped face. But her eyes revealed something else.

"Susannah?"

She folded her delicate hands, her eyes brightening as her eyebrows rose. "Jah, Caleb?"

"Do *you* know who placed that ad?"

In the split second before her face fell, Caleb saw it again. Deception.

"Why . . . Caleb. Why would I?"

Their eyes locked, and she gave him a knowing wink.

Caleb grabbed her arm. "You did it, didn't you, Susannah? You took out the ad for Nellie's Simple Sweets!"

She opened her mouth to protest but stopped. Glancing down at his grip, she smiled. "You have such strong hands, Caleb. And I do like strong men." Immediately he released her. "So you admit it, then?"

Her eyelashes fluttered again. "Ask yourself why Nellie Mae didn't simply close up the shop when all those Englischers started linin' up. In her heart, she's leanin' toward the fancy, Caleb, and you know it." She touched his arm lightly. "Might as well face it: Nellie Mae Fisher will never, *ever* be able to please your father."

Caleb was stunned at what lengths this girl was willing to go to stir up trouble for Nellie and her family. "Nellie and me—that's none of your concern!" With that, he turned away, intending to leave Susannah standing alone.

Just that quick, he raised his gaze and spied Nellie Mae standing near the door, her brown eyes piercing his.

His brain was scrambled; his beloved had arrived late. What had she observed? How long had she been there? He groaned, wanting to talk to her, to set her mind at ease.

Oh, Nellie, it's not what you think. . . .

Fast as a flicker, she turned her back, as if to shun him. Then, making a beeline for the barn door, she hurried into the night.

Walking toward the other side of the barn, he wanted to run after her but hesitated, his father's battle cry ringing in his ears. The hay bales seemed to taunt him as young couples blurred alongside them in his vision.

No!

With all that was in him, he had to right this wrong with Nellie . . . not caring what the grapevine might trumpet back to his father's ears. In the whole world, there was only one girl for him, and Nellie had to believe that. *Now,* lest she trust what her eyes had witnessed and not what was truth.

Images of what Nellie might have seen raced through his mind—Susannah and himself over in the corner so privately. The brazen girl had touched him more than once, and as if in a dance of sorts, she'd followed each time he'd stepped away.

Caleb winced.

Even though it would mean disobeying his father once again, he knew he could not break Nellie's heart. He must pursue her.

Not caring what Susannah or anyone else thought, he jogged across the wide-plank boards. He dashed out the barn door into the bitter night, looking to the right and left. But he had waited too long. There went the Fisher carriage, moving rapidly away on the snowy roads.

Himmel . . . He was disgusted with himself. *You are a fool, Caleb Yoder.*

CHAPTER 24

The white spray of moonlight on newfallen snow could not have been more untimely. Nellie longed for the concealment of darkness as she rushed home with the horse and carriage.

Caleb's flirting with Susannah? What on earth?

She'd deliberated coming to the Singing at all after taking Nan and Rebekah clear to the other side of Lilly Road. But then, not wanting to spend the evening at home, with Rhoda gone to James and Martha's, she'd decided in favor of the Old Order Singing. Slipping in ever so late, her eyes had searched for Caleb. Oh, the pain in her heart when she had finally seen him over in the corner with Susannah, all privatelike.

She wanted to cry; she wanted to holler, too. She didn't know which feeling to express, because she simply could not understand what she'd witnessed. For sure and for certain, Caleb and Susannah had looked like a courting couple!

She tried to remember precisely what she'd observed—the interplay of flirtatious glances, not just Susannah's, but Caleb's, too. She hadn't known for sure how to interpret the dreadful scene, but Caleb had looked mighty guilty when his eyes had met hers.

She'd never before had any reason to distrust him. Yet there he'd been with Susannah . . . why? Had he thought this a good night to cozy up to the deacon's daughter, since it must have appeared that Nellie wasn't coming? Had he been seeing Susannah all along?

No, surely not. How could she think such a thing of her darling?

Then she realized it must have been Susannah's doing; the girl had always made her interest in Caleb perfectly plain. Yet as Nellie fretted and fumed, she didn't want to think that way about it, either, presuming Caleb to be vulnerable to Susannah's wiles.

Like Samson and Delilah . . .

Nellie tried to shrug off the comparison, only to begin to weep so hard she could hardly see her way home.

Caleb rode all over creation, alone in his courting buggy, wishing there was a way to smooth things over with Nellie immediately. Even so, he knew he deserved to feel the way he did. Nellie had fled from the barn, surely believing he'd been caught red-handed. She probably thought little of him now . . . and rightly so.

He drove aimlessly, his mind on Nellie and her sweetness, wondering what it would be like to kiss her soft lips someday . . . if he'd ever have the chance.

Caleb finally arrived home. He eyed the tobacco shed, his worry-sick mind wandering. Although he'd never mentioned it to his father, he thought it wise to tear down the dilapidated outbuilding and build a new one. Daed's approach to it—or at least what he'd done in the past—was to buttress the whole thing, basically propping it up so it wouldn't fall down.

His father and grandfather before him had always raised tobacco. There had been some talk against growing the crop lately, though. Tongues wagged and word got around mighty fast when it was a preacher who was declaring it a sin to raise tobacco. Surprisingly enough, a good number of farmers were in agreement with the outspoken Preacher Manny.

He heard some commotion behind him as a courting buggy pulled up to the front of the house, over near the mailbox. He was far enough into the lane to be somewhat disguised, he knew, and a quick glance over his shoulder told him it was his long-lost sister, saying good-bye to a beau. Had she been with him all day?

She was obviously interested in the fellow, for she stood near the buggy, looking up at him as they talked. Then he jumped down and walked her partway to the house.

After Rebekah had gone inside, Caleb let the harness slide down his horse and then heaved it off. Taking his time unhitching the buggy, he pondered his sister's desertion for the day, so unlike her.

Where *had* Rebekah gone? It was none of his business, really, yet he wondered how she had managed to stay safe and warm on this brutally cold day. Now that he was stabling his horse, he realized how near frozen he was himself. Rebekah could not have spent the day out in this.

He made his way through the stable area and pushed the barn door open. Heading across the way, he heard the crunch of snow beneath his boots, glad he'd worn an extra pair of woolen socks. As he entered the back door, he heard voices—Daed's and Rebekah's. This was no time to emerge from the utility room.

"I know where you've been!"

Caleb was stunned at the sting in his father's voice.

Total silence from Rebekah.

"You never think before you act, do you, daughter?"

Caleb cowered, concealing his presence.

"If you were out where I think you were, you ain't welcome in this house!"

Wisely Rebekah remained silent. *As a lamb brought to slaughter . . .*

"Did you attend the New Order church today?" came the angry inquiry.

"I will not lie, Daed."

Caleb slumped.

A crack—the sound of his father's fist slamming against the table, the one he'd made decades before. Surely this blow had split the wood.

Caleb could see there was no talking to Daed tonight about his own decision. No, he would bow out, and quickly, hoping for a reasonable discussion at a later time.

"Get out!" Daed shouted. "I do not want to see the likes of you."

No! Caleb wanted to defend his sister, but once again he felt trapped beneath his father's dominion . . . and his desire to protect any future with Nellie Mae.

What will Rebekah do?

"Jah, I was disobedient," his sister said meekly. "But I choose to follow my Lord Jesus Christ."

"Then begone from my sight!"

Caleb heard sniffling, then sobs, as Rebekah dashed up the stairs to pack a bag in submission to their father's unreasonable punishment.

I won't let her flee alone into the night, he decided, slipping out the door to hitch up his poor tired horse yet again.

Nellie's tears were nearly dry by the time she arrived home. She unhitched the carriage from the horse and left the enclosed buggy near the barn for Dat to tend to in the morning. Refusing to give Caleb another thought, she led their best driving horse into the stable.

Once inside, she hurried to her room, where she sat for the longest time, unable to move.

She heard a creak in the rafters and finally removed her heavy bonnet. Then she reverently removed her Kapp and slowly prepared for bed, slipping into a fresh nightgown. Oh, how she wished the sights of this evening could be shed as easily as her clothes. Now that she was home, she wondered if Nan was back from the New Order gathering. She longed to share her heartache with someone, and Nan was the most natural choice.

Moving silently down the hall, she stopped at what had always been Rhoda and Nan's bedroom. *So many changes lately*, she thought, poking her head in the door.

Seeing her sister already tucked into bed and thinking what a comfort it would be to simply slip in next to her, Nellie did just that. She was careful not to lean too hard into the mattress on Rhoda's former side so as not to awaken her sister. The warmth from Nan's slumbering body soothed her as she settled herself beneath the heavy layer of blankets and quilts.

Then, lying as still as could be, she realized she could not sleep. The image of Caleb's handsome face rose up in the darkness—the light in his eyes as he'd talked to Susannah . . . the set of his lips, his whole body in alignment with hers, or so it seemed. Would she ever be able to erase the vision of her beloved talking so intently with Susannah? Standing so close . . .

Every breath she took was filled with missing him. Yet he'd deceived her so. She groaned inwardly, struggling to hold herself together in the bed where her older sisters had often talked late into the night, before Rhoda got the ridiculous urge to chase after the fancy.

Nellie recalled the fervent hope in Rebekah's face—and the upturn of her determined mouth—as she departed for the Singing tonight. What would come of Rebekah's departure from the Old Order for a full day was yet to be known.

She's fortunate to have such a faithful friend in Nan.

Nellie slid her hand toward her sleeping sister, stopping when her fingertips touched the edge of Nan's gown, spread out against the flannel bed sheet.

The hope of sharing her heartbreak with Nan faded with each of her sister's rhythmic breaths, and Nellie missed Suzy more than ever.

Rebekah's sadness resonated with Caleb's own this night. He sensed it in his sister's slumped posture as she sat next to him in the carriage, even though she showed no other outward sign of grief. As far as he could tell, her resolve was remarkably intact as they made their way to the Fishers'.

"You sure Nellie's . . . er, Nan's house is where you want to stay tonight?"

She was quick to nod. "Ever so sure." Her teeth chattered.

He endured the frigid temperature as best he could, dreading the return ride, chilled as he was to the bone. But Caleb felt he deserved whatever punishment the elements meted out. Hadn't he broken Nellie's heart tonight?

That he hadn't done so intentionally offered no consolation. To think he was heading right now to her father's house, to shine his flashlight on her window as he had done once before, this time to get her attention for his outcast sister's sake.

He gripped the reins and tried to will away what had transpired earlier at the Singing—the searing pain in Nellie's pretty eyes.

"You feelin' awkward 'bout this? Taking me to the enemy, so to speak?" Rebekah glanced his way.

"No." He wouldn't let on precisely how awkward the whole situation was.

"Seems kinda odd, really. And Nan's goin' to be surprised, I daresay."

He considered that. "Well, maybe not."

"S'pose you're right." After all, Rebekah had spent the entire day with the Fishers. Surely Nan could guess what Daed's response to that might be.

"Did the whole Fisher family attend the new church?" he asked, not wanting to come right out and inquire after Nellie Mae's whereabouts.

"All but Nellie."

So there it was. His sweetheart was being true to the Old Ways . . . and to him.

But now? What would happen between them? Would she accept his explanation, once given?

He couldn't allow himself to ponder that now. Truth be told, he must first see to it that Rebekah was safely settled for the night—take on the responsibility of a good brother, something Daed had unknowingly handed off to him. He shook his head at the memory of their father's permitting things to escalate out of hand. As far as Caleb was concerned, it was Daed's fault that Rebekah was out on her ear tonight.

Rebekah was still in her running-around years, not having joined the church yet, so why should she be punished for visiting Preacher Manny's church?

None of this made a lick of sense.

At last they reached the end of the Fishers' drive, where he left the horse and buggy, his sister still perched inside. Caleb crept up the lane and shone his flashlight high onto Nellie's window. He waited, holding the light there, wondering how long it would be before he might attract her attention.

He waited with no response. He thought of knocking, but he didn't want to wake Nellie's parents, who had no doubt been asleep for hours.

Again he shined the light, leaving it poised there. Then, when Nellie did not appear, he moved the flashlight around in circles, still shining its white beam on the glass. When even that failed to bring her to the window, he rotated the light back and forth between the two west-facing windows.

Perhaps she was ignoring him. He certainly couldn't blame her for that. Fact was, she had not so much as peeked out from behind the shade to see who was standing down in the snow, shivering beneath his long johns and heaviest wool coat.

"Caleb!" called his sister from the road. "I'm terribly cold."

I'll try one more thing before I wake the whole house. Quickly, he turned off the flashlight and leaned down to scoop up a small bit of snow. Then, rolling it even smaller, he tossed it lightly so as not to make a loud thud.

He waited, growing more concerned for his sister as the seconds ticked past. Twice more he threw a snowball.

Could it be that Nellie had decided to give him a taste of his own medicine and ridden home with someone else? Caleb dismissed the niggling thought. Not his Nellie. Even so, where was she, if not sound asleep in her bed?

Nan started and rolled over, apparently surprised to encounter Nellie lying there next to her, wide awake. "I didn't mean to scare you. I simply couldn't be alone." Nellie sighed, wanting to open her heart to her sister. Yet she hesitated, wondering if she should unburden her woes when Nan was still smarting from her recent breakup.

"I'm glad you're here." Nan inched closer. "What's wrong, Nellie?"

"Caleb's betrayed me," Nellie said softly.

"Oh, dear sister . . ."

Then the misery of her discovery began to pour out of her like a dam breaking apart. She told Nan everything, beginning with the secret meetings at the old mill, walks along the millstream, Caleb's letters, their forbidden love. "We've willfully disobeyed his father, just as you and Rebekah have." She struggled to speak. "And now . . . this . . . with Susannah."

Nan reached over and cupped Nellie's cheek with her hand. "I'm ever so sorry, Nellie. Truly I am."

"After all the planning—for our future together—he ups and does this baffling thing." Nellie could not hold back her tears. "I never would've believed it if I hadn't seen it with my own eyes. Oh, Nan, it was like he's held a torch for her all this time." She wept so hard, the bed shook. "How could I not have known?"

She thought of the times she'd seen Susannah flirt with Caleb or attempt to during youth gatherings—one hayride in particular, she recalled. And there had been plenty of other times, too. But she had never noted any interest from Caleb toward Susannah—till now.

"Oh . . . it hurts so bad." She clung to Nan, certain her broken heart would never mend.

"Nellie . . . Nellie." Her sister held her as she wept, saying no more, soothing her by stroking her hair.

"Caleb?" Rebekah's voice was laced with worry. It sounded as if she was about to cry.

He hurried back toward the buggy, thankful for the traction of his boots against the hardened snow. "I can't raise anyone. I'm terribly sorry." He leaned against the horse, hugging him for warmth. "Come here, Rebekah." He must not let his sister get so chilled that she became ill. That, on top of being ousted from home, was a trial she should not have to bear.

"This is . . . just awful," she said.

"Don't cry. Your tears will freeze to your face."

She wiped them with her mittened hand.

"I guess we'll just have to knock," he said.

"What if I simply slipped inside?" Rebekah glanced toward the farmhouse. "I know right where Nan's room is. . . . I could go up there . . . try not to startle her."

"Would you be welcome, do ya think?"

She nodded, trembling now as he pressed her against the horse, sandwiching her between himself and the steed. "Nan wouldn't want me to freeze to death."

"Nor would Daed." The words escaped him. Surely their father would not wish for Rebekah to suffer. Why *had* he abandoned her? Had he no concern for his own flesh and blood this bitter night? Caleb could not imagine treating a son or daughter this way.

"Come, sister, I'll walk you to the house."

Rebekah reached for his arm, and he felt the weight of her, though she was ever so slight.

Stepping quietly into Reuben Fisher's enclosed back porch, Caleb felt like an intruder in more ways than one. But getting out of the elements for a few moments was essential now.

"I'll do my best to keep in touch," Caleb whispered. "Somehow we must."

Rebekah only nodded.

Once his sister had stepped into the kitchen and out of sight, he contemplated Nellie's whereabouts once again, hoping she was not still riding around in this cold.

Nellie Mae was a sensible girl. Certainly she was not one to get revenge. She would have headed directly home after their brief encounter at the barn Singing. Doubtless she was here in this house and so deep in slumber—hopefully not weeping—that she hadn't noticed his flashlight on her window.

Caleb consoled himself with that and let himself out of the house as quietly as he'd entered a few minutes before.

A sudden sound in the hallway made Nellie's ears perk up. She strained to listen, and then there was nothing. "Did ya hear that?" she asked Nan.

"It's late . . . could it be Rhoda comin' back?"

"Rhoda's long gone, I daresay," Nellie replied.

More creaking came from outside the bedroom door. Then they heard, "Nan . . . it's me, Rebekah." This brought Nellie and Nan straight up in bed.

"What the world?" Nan leapt onto the cold wooden floor. "Come in. Ach . . . are you all right?"

Caleb's sister sniffled as she entered. "Daed's done kicked me out."

"Oh, you poor girl!" Nan gave her a quick hug.

"My brother Caleb brought me here."

Caleb went home without riding with Susannah?

"I thought I might stay here for—"

"Stay as long as need be," Nan said, still hovering near Rebekah.

Nellie leaned her arms on her knees, astonished at Rebekah's late-night appearance and moved at Nan's loving concern for her friend.

Rebekah sat on the edge of the bed. "I'll try 'n' find somewhere else to stay after tomorrow, though, so you won't be stuck with me."

"Puh, don't be silly. You're welcome here," Nan insisted.

Nellie had an idea and she said it right out, thinking Rebekah might wish for solace from her stressful night and for the comfort of friends, as well. "Nan, let's untuck the bed sheets and lie sideways across this bed . . . you know, like you, Rhoda, Suzy, and I used to."

"When we were just girls?" said Nan.

"Jah, when we were ever so little." She sighed at the thought of the changes the years had brought . . . each broken heart there.

Without another word, they did precisely that, pulling the bedclothes off quickly to remake the bed horizontally. Nellie went to her room to get a third pillow. Then they all crawled into the bed and curled up—Nan and Nellie at the head and foot of the bed, with forlorn Rebekah between them.

CHAPTER 25

———

I'm behind on my washing." Rosanna bemoaned the fact as her cousin came in the back door Monday morning.

"Well, here, let me help," Cousin Kate said, reaching for baby Eli.

Grateful, Rosanna hurried downstairs to complete the task of doing the laundry. She'd begun with two loads of the babies' clothes and was now sorting Elias's trousers and long-sleeved colored shirts. She put the clothes into the old wringer washer powered by a small gasoline motor.

Soon she made her way up the stairs and discovered Kate in the front room, swaying slowly as she held Eli, talking quietlike. Rosie, too, was awake now and crying in the playpen, and since it was nearly time for the next feeding, Rosanna went to the kitchen to pick her up. Despite Kate's offer of assistance, Rosanna sensed a real sadness in her cousin—her cheeks drooped and her eyes were swollen. Had she been crying?

Kate didn't return with Eli to the kitchen as Rosanna wished she might. Instead she sat in the rocking chair in the front room and opened her dress to nurse him within view of Rosanna, two rooms away.

Rosanna squelched the lump in her throat. Kate was again willfully ignoring her request that she adhere to the original plan and stop nursing either baby at two months of age, a date that had passed nearly a month ago. She might break down if she didn't keep herself in check—either that or storm in there and tell her cousin what she really thought for once.

Not wanting baby Rosie to sense her frustration, Rosanna breathed deeply and asked the Lord for patience, praying the way Preacher Manny had taught them yesterday at the worship service. Thinking of the wonderful-good gathering, the joyful sermon, and Elias's conversion, she already missed the fellowship of those who'd come to hear the Word of God and were eager to do it. She truly hoped Elias was in favor of returning next Sunday . . . and the next. If so, they'd be joining that church next spring, after council meeting and a day of fasting. Rosanna was so thankful to the Lord for calling her husband as He had her.

Doing her best not to stare at Kate with Eli, she prepared Rosie's bottle, gazing into her darling face all the while. Rosie blinked up innocently at her, her big eyes ever so trusting. "You're hungry, aren't ya, sweetie?" She kissed Rosie's ivory forehead. "Won't be long now, I promise."

All of a sudden the emotions she'd been masking since Kate arrived began to shift from deep in her heart to her throat and now, this minute, to the tip of her tongue. If she didn't hurry and get Rosie's bottle ready, she might not be able to see due to her tears.

Why does Kate torment me so?

She moved to stand in the doorway between the kitchen and the small sitting area, watching Kate rocking and cooing. But Eli was hers now. *Hers.* How dare Kate come here and disrupt things—incite near rage in her?

Returning to the kitchen, she covered her eyes so as to shut out the cozy sight in the front room. But she found herself moving forward, heading toward Kate while Rosie rutsched against her own bosom.

Rosanna marched into the front room, stopping smack-dab in the center of the large braided rug, glaring at Kate with Eli at her breast. She gasped, then muttered, "I . . . you . . ."

Kate looked up and smiled. "You all right?"

"Not one bit!"

Quickly her cousin's smile faded into a frown. "What's a-matter, cousin? You not feelin' so well?"

That too.

"Here, pull up a chair." Kate motioned to the corner and the old cane chair Elias had recently redone. "Sit with me . . . I want to talk to you."

Rosanna pulled the chair over, surprised at herself for being this compliant when all she really wanted was to snatch her son from this cruel woman. Even so, she sat and lifted Rosie onto her shoulder, patting her back and willing herself to remain calm and listen to Kate.

"John and I were talkin' this morning, early . . . before breakfast."

Rosie squirmed.

"We're concerned." Kate paused. "If you continue goin' to the new church, well, more than likely, Eli will make his kneeling vow to *that* church." Kate looked down at Eli, stroking his hair.

Rosanna was confused. "What're you sayin'?"

Kate shifted Eli to her shoulder and rubbed his back, waiting for the burps, which came quickly in a series of two . . . then a softer third.

"John wants our children to remain in the Old Order, where they be-long . . . where you and Elias ought to stay," Kate said, her voice trembling.

Rosanna held Rosie close, fear rushing through her.

"And . . . 'specially Eli." Kate kissed the top of his head. "We worry what might happen if the lot, the divine ordination, were to fall on him when he's grown."

Rosanna was all befuddled. So the divine appointment was of concern suddenly because of her and Elias's visit to Preacher Manny's church? Was that it?

"I say, if God appoints Eli for His service, then who are we to question?" Rosanna choked back a breath.

"That's why John and I want our son raised up in the Old Ways . . . in case the Lord chooses him to be a man of God."

"You're most worried 'bout Eli, then?"

Kate nodded slowly, deliberately.

"Rosie here doesn't matter?" Rosanna cuddled her daughter near.

"Why, sure . . ." Kate said unconvincingly.

"Well, she could end up a preacher's wife . . . we just don't know." Kate's favoritism angered her, but Rosanna chose to push it aside. "So it seems you know where we went yesterday."

"Ain't a secret, that's for sure."

"Elias and I didn't intend to hide it."

Kate sighed loudly, guiding Eli to latch on to her other breast. "How could we have known this was goin' to happen?"

"The church split?"

"Jah, back when we promised the babies . . ."

Rosanna sucked in her air too quickly and had to cough. "Well, I hope you don't regret it."

Rosie began to whimper, and it was time to get the bottle out of the hot water, lest it be too warm for her tender mouth. Rosanna made her way to the kitchen, unable to think. Kate seemed truly sorry she'd given up Eli and Rosie. On the other hand, was this merely because of the baby blues? Maybe Kate needed more herbal tea. *Blessed thistle . . . do I have any on hand?*

Beset by the smell of scorched baby formula, she placed Rosie in the playpen and rushed to the cookstove. Using a potholder, she plucked the boiling hot bottle out of the pan and placed it in the sink. Clearly the formula was unsalvageable.

"It's my fault for listenin' to that woman babble on," she whispered. She poured it out and went to prepare another bottle for wailing Rosie.

Her daughter's cries pierced the silence that had gripped the house, creating even further agitation in Rosanna as she shushed and gently jostled her. She moved from one window in the kitchen to the next, looking out at the icy coating on the sheep fences running in neat, boxlike patterns across the snowy grazing land, and the silvery garlands on the few evergreens up near the crest of the hill, by the woods.

"It's all right," she repeated, knowing the words were meant not only for Rosie but for herself.

Once the bottle was warm, Rosanna sat with Rosie suckling hard. She rocked in Elias's favorite rocking chair, aware of the relative quiet—the void left by Rosie's wails as she was soothed with warm nourishment.

Yet Rosanna's fury still raged within, increasing when she heard Kate declare to Eli in the front room, "You must grow up in the fear of the Lord God . . . on the right side of the fence."

Rosanna shuddered and steeled herself, looking into Rosie's contented eyes. She mustn't let her frustration get out of hand.

Surely Kate would settle down as she always did. One thing or another had upset her ever since the twins had come to live here. Perhaps it *had* been a good idea for Kate to continue on as Eli's wet nurse, soothing herself some, as well as baby Eli.

Rosanna prayed silently for wisdom—no need for Kate to confront her about speaking her prayer aloud. Bad enough the grapevine had delivered the news of her and Elias's attendance at Manny's church to the Beilers' ears, although she was not sorry. She couldn't imagine them returning to the old church now, not after Elias's heartfelt repentance.

She caressed Rosie's hair, soft and wispy as corn silk, recalling her first miscarriage . . . the bleeding, then cramping pain, followed by a constant dull ache low in her back. It was not the physical symptoms that had caused the greatest suffering; rather, it was the knowledge of losing what she'd longed for, the wee one growing beneath her heart.

Her bottle finished, Rosie relaxed, but Rosanna knew she must be burped or she'd suffer colic pain later. "Let's get some of that gas up," she whispered, moving her forward to a sitting position and pressing gently on her little tummy while patting Rosie's back. She realized as she did so that her anger had subsided. She did not know how this could be, unless the Spirit of God—as Preacher Manny had referred to the Holy Spirit yesterday in his sermon—had removed her resentment.

Truth be known, she was relieved to be free of it. She got up and held Rosie against her shoulder, going downstairs to check on the laundry. She'd left a wicker basket lined with soft baby blankets there because she always seemed to have one twin or the other in her arms when doing the washing.

Today was no different, so she placed Rosie inside, knowing she'd be only a short time running the clothes through the wringer. She talked to Rosie as she worked, delighting in her gurgles and the cute way she made tight fists of her hands.

"You're a happy little one, jah?" Her heart was so full of love for Rosie and her twin brother. She marveled at how both of them could raise their heads momentarily when she put them on their tummies. They were growing stronger each day.

The wringer got stuck and Rosanna had to open it and start over with a pair of trousers, glad for Rosie's patience.

Finally she finished and, reaching down to bring Rosie up to her face, kissed her. "Now Mamma's ready to get ya to sleep." She nuzzled her and headed for the stairs.

In the kitchen, she went to the cupboard, found some herbal tea to offer Kate, and set the teakettle on the stove. Then, settling down in the rocker, Rosanna sighed and leaned her head back, closing her eyes for a moment and reminiscing about the days when she and Elias were still waiting for a child . . . Kate and John's baby.

Rosie started in her arms, and Rosanna glanced down at her perfect rosebud mouth. A mule brayed in the distance, and the steady ticking of the day clock came from the sitting room. Other than that, peace prevailed.

Then she realized how quiet things seemed. The creaking had ceased in the front room, where Kate was also rocking. Rosanna bit her lip, refusing to ponder further Kate's pointed talk about the old church versus the new.

Sighing, she rose and carried Rosie to the playpen. Once she was tucked in, Rosanna looked into the front room. The rocker was empty.

Must be upstairs in the nursery for a diaper change, Rosanna thought and decided not to follow Kate, who was adept at such things, having six children of her own. Eight, if you counted— She caught herself, believing that Kate's twins were, indeed, her very own. In every way that was important, Eli and Rosie were her dear ones, connected by both blood and love.

Returning to the kitchen, she started some cookie dough, hungry for chocolate chip oatmeal. She glanced out the window as she worked. "What the world?"

Dashing to the back door, she looked out. Kate's horse and buggy were no longer parked in the driveway. Her gasp caught in her throat.

Swiftly Rosanna ran to the foot of the stairs. "Kate?" Then her voice rose to a shout. "Kate!"

Only silence. That and the beating of her own heart, louder and louder in her ears.

Kate left without sayin' good-bye? "Why . . . why?"

Oh, but she knew. She knew as the wrenching pain hit her soul—the same pain she had known when her babies had died in that special place near to her heart. *Dear Lord, no.*

Rosanna flew up the stairs. Panic rising and tears streaming, she ran frantically from room to room. There was no sign of precious Eli. Even the afghans and quilts and things she'd lovingly made for him . . . gone.

CHAPTER 26

Rosanna raced from the house to the barn, not bothering to put on a coat. "Elias!" she called as she ran. "Elias!" He would know what to do. He would rescue Eli, would rescue them all. . . .

"Elias, come quick!" No answering call. She threw open the barn door and dashed in, but there was no sign of him or the family buggy, either. Glimpsing the hay in the barn, she remembered: Elias had taken the buggy and gone to help a neighbor fork hay. *Himmel . . . no.*

Only then did she feel the icy cold reach her overheated skin. What to do? How to find help? For the first time in her life, Rosanna wished she owned a telephone.

She left the barn and searched the yard, the driveway, and the road beyond—as empty as her arms. The wind gusted and she thought she heard a cry. Had Rosie awakened? A new panic filled her. Kate hadn't come back for Rosie, too, had she? Fear fueled her, and she hurried back across the yard and into the house. Lungs heaving, she found Rosie, still asleep in the playpen. Safe.

Oh, Lord in heaven, keep Eli safe, too. Rosanna prayed no harm would befall him, especially out on these snowy roads, with mad Kate at the reins.

Leaning over the playpen, she laid her trembling hand on Rosie's soft head. She needed to touch her. "I'm sorry, little one," she whispered. "I'm sorry I didn't watch over your brother more closely. I didn't know . . . I never thought . . ." Her tears fell unchecked. "I'm so sorry."

What was Kate thinking, leaving with Eli? Like a kidnapping, really, right out from under her nose.

Trying to keep her mind and body occupied, Rosanna paced the full length of the house, from the front room—eyeing the rocker where Kate had sat with Eli—all the way back to the utility room, where Elias's work boots and their winter things were neatly stored.

When she could bear it no longer, Rosanna returned to the side of the playpen holding Rosie so that she could keep her eye on her wee daughter. As if something dreadful could happen to make her vanish, too.

She reached in again and this time touched Rosie's tiny fist, crying quietly, not wanting to wake her darling girl.

Oh, Kate . . . how could you do such a terrible thing?

She thought of Elias, knowing he was more tender toward Eli, and it made her weep all the more. Why hadn't she suspected what Kate was up to—hadn't she nearly spelled it out there in the front room, with all the grim talk about the New Order?

Holding her middle, she peered out the frosty windows. How could Kate possibly keep Eli warm out there?

Lest she make herself sick worrying, Rosanna straightened her apron and sat in the rocker. She began to pour out her heart to the Lord, beseeching almighty God for protection and care for both Eli and Kate . . . and a double portion of grace for poor Elias, who loved Eli with his whole heart.

Betsy Fisher could no longer quell her yearning to visit Rhoda, to reassure herself that Rhoda was indeed all right. Since Rebekah Yoder was with them today, helping out in the bakery shop, Betsy thought she could be gone for an hour or two without leaving Nellie shorthanded. Knowing it was Rhoda's monthly morning off, Betsy decided to take a chance that she might find her at James and Martha's.

Betsy drove the family carriage along the edge of the road, the old buggy bouncing and jerking over the hardened ruts of packed snow. When Elias and Rosanna's house came into view, she thought of Nellie's friend, suddenly the mother of twins. She remembered her own firstborn sons—twins Thomas and Jeremiah—and felt a pinch of nostalgic longing to hold a baby in her arms again.

Why not stop in and visit Rosanna? she thought. The sudden urge took her by surprise. *No. You're headed for Rhoda's. Don't want to be gone all day . . .*

She decided she'd come another time and clucked her tongue to prod the horse to go faster. But again, she felt she ought to stop. Was the Spirit of the Lord prompting her? Did Rosanna need some advice about caring for two at once? Some help, just maybe?

Betsy pulled on the reins and turned the horse into the Kings' driveway.

She tied up the horse and walked onto the porch, only to hear weeping before she even reached the door. *What's this?*

Knocking, she called, "Rosanna? It's Betsy Fisher. Are you all right?"

The door opened and there Rosanna stood, her face a startling mixture of red blotches and gray pallor, her eyes wild and teary, her prayer Kapp askew.

"Oh, Mrs. Fisher! I thought you might be Kate come to her senses."

Rosanna sobbed and turned away from the door, leaving it open for Betsy without inviting her in. Betsy followed anyway, a terrible dread balling up inside her.

The kitchen counter was a mess. Mixing bowls, open canisters, and flour were strewn all around.

"You didn't pass Elias on the road, did you?" Rosanna asked desperately.

Betsy shook her head. "Rosanna, what is it? What's happened?"

Rosanna stared bleakly out the kitchen window. "Kate has taken Eli from me. Took him right from the house."

Betsy gasped, moving toward the table, leaning on it. "You mean she snuck him out? Just left with him?"

Rosanna nodded, fresh tears on her cheeks.

Betsy was stunned. *What a wretched thing!*

"I don't know what to do!" Rosanna wailed. "Elias is off somewhere with the buggy."

"Did Kate say anything? Leave a note?"

"No. She walked out with Eli while I was down in the basement. I should have known. I should have watched over him better. Maybe I'm not a fit mother . . . maybe that's why—"

"Nonsense, Rosanna. You're a perfectly loving mother. This is Kate's fault, not yours. How long ago did she leave?"

"More than an hour ago. Poor Eli! I hope she got him home safely. At least I assume she went home. Where else would she go? You don't think she would do anything crazy, do you?"

As if kidnapping her own flesh and blood isn't crazy? "Shh . . . Kate may be mixed-up, but she would never do anything to harm Eli," said Betsy. *Lord, let it be so!*

"I'm so frightened," Rosanna said.

Betsy remembered how God had nudged her to stop here at this very time. "I'm going to pray for you, Rosanna. For you and Kate and Eli, too. All right?"

"Oh yes! Please . . ."

Betsy took the younger woman's hand right there in the kitchen and beseeched the Lord out loud to watch over every member of the family and bring a peaceful solution to this most hurtful of acts. "Oh, Lord, calm this mother's heart, I pray. Give her your peace. Help us trust you with our lives and the lives of our children. . . ." Betsy thought of Rhoda, whom she worried over and longed to see. Could she trust the Lord for her children, just as she had prayed for Rosanna?

Betsy sped home, dismissing her plan to see Rhoda. Leaving the horse and carriage in the yard, she jumped down and ran into the barn. There, she found Reuben tending to one of his colts.

"Reuben! The most terrible thing has happened. . . ." She repeated all that Rosanna had told her.

"Rosanna is completely heartbroken," she concluded.

Reuben shook his head. "Kate can't be thinkin' clearly. Does John know what's going on, I wonder?"

"Who's to know? But to do such a thing to Eli and Rosie! The Good Lord makes a strong bond linking twins. I've heard it—seen it, too—many a time. Think of our own Thomas and Jeremiah. Why, they're grown men and still they can't seem to be apart from each other."

Reuben nodded, chewing his lip.

"And think of Rosanna . . . and Elias. They've longed for a child, and now to have this happen." *They even named the babies after each other!* Betsy thought.

Nellie burst into the barn. "Mamm, are you all right? I saw you leave the horse and run—"

"Oh, Nellie. It's Rosanna. Kate's taken baby Eli back."

Her daughter looked stricken. "Ach no! When?"

"Only a few hours ago. Elias may not even know yet."

"Poor Rosanna!" Nellie turned pleading eyes toward her father. "Dat, isn't there something you can do?"

Reuben pulled on his beard, shaking his head doubtfully. "I don't know. I suppose I can go to John, see if I can talk to him and Kate. Might not be till tomorrow, though—I've got a man arriving from Ohio to look at horses this afternoon."

"Oh, thank you, Reuben!" Betsy said. "I told Rosanna I was sure you would help."

"Don't thank me, Betsy. I fear there's little I can do. We had *all* better pray."

Betsy nodded and breathed a prayer right then and there. *Please, dear Lord. Help Kate come to her senses!*

Rhoda reclined on Mrs. Kraybill's luxurious sofa, reading the entire article on weight loss from start to finish, glad to be alone a while. Mrs. Kraybill had come to pick her up for a half day of work, then promised to go over the *Pennsylvania Driver's Manual*. Meanwhile, with the youngest daughter playing quietly in her room, Rhoda and Pebbles the cat were the only ones downstairs.

Rhoda liked the Kraybill home for more than its niceties. She was fairly content living with James and Martha, helping with the cleaning and tending to her niece and nephews. But after being surrounded by all the bustle and noise of her brother's house, she enjoyed the relative quiet of the Kraybills'.

Stretching out on the long tufted sofa, Rhoda closed the magazine and imagined how trim she could be in a matter of weeks if she stuck to her plan. Could she do it? Oh, she dearly loved to eat. Ever since Suzy's death, she had found such solace in eating—especially sweets, which the article said was the worst possible fare for a person like her, already in need of a serious change in her diet.

She daydreamed about what sort of handsome fellow might come along to court her. Would he find her pretty in every way? What about her beautiful car?

There were several good-looking boys at the Beachy meetinghouse. She supposed if she continued attending and began going to the various youth activities, she might just get to know one or two of them.

She rose and headed to the kitchen to peer out the window at her LeSabre, parked in the snow. Having the black-and-white beauty within sight made her as happy as tasting one of Nellie's shoofly pies. Truth was, she dreamed of the day when she could take it for a spin. After her ill-fated "driving lesson" with James and cousin Jonathan, she realized she had a great deal to learn. But she loved having the car near, a symbol of the direction her life was taking.

Soon, very soon, she would drive wherever she wanted to go, thanks to Mrs. Kraybill, James, and Jonathan—they'd all offered to give her the instruction needed to put her in the driver's seat.

Come the spring thaw, she thought, eager for ice-free roads.

Right now, though, she had more on her mind than obtaining her license. The Kraybills' unmarried nephew, Ken, was coming to supper next Sunday night. Mrs. Kraybill had invited Rhoda, as well—insisted upon it, really. But Rhoda felt odd about it, even though Mrs. Kraybill said that this was not to be a "blind date," whatever that was.

Rhoda would think about it and hope to lose a few more pounds before then, maybe. *What if I didn't wear my Plain dress and apron, for once?*

Rosie simply would not stop crying, no matter what comfort Rosanna gave her. She wailed as if her heart were breaking, her little tongue curled back in the wide opening of her mouth. The more Rosanna walked her and rubbed her back—even offering an additional warm bottle—the more inconsolable Rosie seemed.

Her crying made Rosanna want to be strong for her precious baby daughter, but it was nigh to impossible to swallow back her own sobs.

When Elias arrived at last, she fell into his arms, weeping as she held Rosie near. "Kate's taken our Eli away."

Such a look of shock came to his dear face. "What do ya mean, Rosanna?"

She explained the sequence of the day, beginning with all the talk of the Old Ways and the word that had obviously traveled about the New Order church service they'd attended. "Kate—well, John, too—they want Eli raised in the old church."

Misery masked his features. "Well, we shouldn't be surprised. They're prob'ly upset at us."

"Kate said as much."

He pulled on his beard. "Rosanna . . . love, where were you when this happened?"

Her heart stopped. "Down in the cellar, doin' the washing . . . with Rosie."

"And where was Kate?"

"With Eli, in the front room : . . nursing him."

He shook his head slowly. "You've been through this before . . . you should've put a stop to it."

She nodded her head, covering her trembling lips.

Then Elias took Rosie from her. "No . . . no, I'm sorry. You aren't to blame." Gently he led her to the table, where he pulled out a chair for her. "I'll head right over there . . . as soon as Rosie here settles down." Their little daughter was snuggling close to Elias now.

She surely senses his strength. . . .

And in a few short minutes, Rosie was sound asleep.

"What about your dinner, love?"

"Food is the last thing on my mind."

"Oh, Elias . . . what're we goin' to do?"

"We'll trust the Good Lord. What else is there?" His eyes softened. "How long ago did Kate leave?"

She told him, and he kissed her cheek and laid Rosie down in her playpen. Then he turned toward the back door with another wave over his shoulder. Oh, how weary she felt. Too fatigued to get up and see him out.

Instead of eating anything herself, she glanced at the now sleeping Rosie and went to the back door to lock it—something she'd never done before in this house, nor in any other. Quite unnecessary amongst the People. Nevertheless it was essential, this day, for her own sanity.

She rushed downstairs to check on the clothes hanging in the cellar— far warmer than outside, where they'd surely freeze. The clothes remained quite soggy, so most likely the makeshift clothesline would be laden with her family's clothing come tomorrow.

Good thing Elias has an extra shirt and trousers.

She touched Eli's tiny sleeping gowns and booties and wept again. If God had called Cousin Kate to give up Eli and Rosie, how was it possible she'd changed her mind?

CHAPTER 27

C hris Yoder was ecstatic Monday afternoon when he saw the 97 percent on his calculus test. The teacher tapped him on the shoulder as he returned to his desk from distributing the exams. "Fine work, Mr. Yoder."

Truth was, he'd hardly cracked open the textbook, but thanks to what he assumed were his genes, he was a natural in all things related to mathematics. His father had noticed this ability early on, which was one of the reasons why he was a shoo-in to run the family's landscaping business if he wanted, keeping the books.

Yes, numbers Chris could understand, but Zach was another matter. His greatest concern at present was his younger brother's seeming inability to get over his obsession with Suzy Fisher. And now he had something new to be preoccupied with—the gold bracelet they'd found at the lake. He'd spent hours yesterday lying on his bed, arm outstretched, staring at the bracelet, letting it dangle as it caught the sunlight. *Strange,* thought Chris, and he was worried enough to pause right there and silently ask God to help Zach.

He'd tried to talk Zach out of keeping the bracelet. Why not give it away to someone, as a gift? After all, it had a terrific Scripture inscribed on it, one that Suzy had chosen herself. Zach had told her he wanted to purchase something special, asking her for a life-changing verse. Her favorite.

Life-changing is right, Chris thought, recalling his brother's excited talk about the gift last June, and seeing Suzy's delight when Zach had placed it on her wrist that terrible Saturday.

Now the bracelet was back, and Chris feared his brother would spend a lifetime gazing at this sad reminder of the first love Zach had embraced fully—and still did.

Caleb located his father in the barn, knowing it was best to get a discussion started . . . not let things just hang and fester. He knew he was taking a big risk, what with Rebekah being told to leave home last night.

He found Daed spreading straw on the floor, and immediately Caleb was handed a rake to help. He set to work, realizing now was not going to be the time after all. His father's scowl was hardly an invitation to begin the much-needed conversation, so he raked for the next hour, finishing the chore while Daed oiled the harnesses.

Later, around four o'clock, when they were spraying the cows' teats in preparation for milking, he said, "I'd like to talk to you, Daed."

His father's head bobbed up. "What's on your mind, son?"

Caleb swallowed, consciously raising himself to his full stature. "I did your bidding."

"What's that?"

"Susannah Lapp. I made a point of seeing her at the Singing last night." He resisted the memory of Nellie's observing them. "Frankly, she's of no interest to me, Daed."

Now it was his father who straightened, putting a hand on the rump of the Holstein. "You speak nonsense, Caleb. Any young man would find her . . . completely appealing."

"She's beautiful, I'll give you that." He would not continue with this line of talk. "This may not be what you want to hear, but I hope to be marryin' someone else come next fall."

A knowing look passed between them. Typically this announcement would be met with congratulations, marriage being the prerequisite for Caleb's receiving the land.

Daed exhaled forcefully. "Thought by now you would've put *that* girl out of your mind."

Caleb paused, stunned at Daed's disregard. "Nellie Mae's who I want for my bride."

"Well, then, you ain't thinking straight."

Caleb held back lest he speak disrespectfully.

"How can ya dare to think she's the one for you?"

"I love her."

His father scoffed, making a sweeping gesture. "Love, you say? So you'd give up our plans—your future here?"

Caleb crouched down to wash the next cow's udder. He hadn't said anything of the kind. He was not interested in giving up the chance to provide well for his bride and their children someday. He didn't know all the ins and outs of this sticky situation, but he *did* know that Nellie Mae would be a wonderful-good wife, and he cared deeply for her.

"I love Nellie Mae," he repeated. This was the most awkward discussion ever. His father had no right to even know whom he was seeing, let alone his intended—at least not until closer to the wedding season, nearly ten months away yet.

"I forbid you to marry a Fisher!"

Fury rose in Caleb's chest, and he stood up. "I best be goin'." He rushed toward the barn door.

"Caleb . . . son!"

It went against everything Caleb knew to be respectful and good, but he ignored his father and strode straight to the house, leaving the milking wholly to him.

As Nellie, Nan, and Rebekah closed up the bakery shop for the day, they talked about the "sad, sad story" Mamma had relayed to Nellie, who couldn't imagine how her friend Rosanna must be feeling.

"You'd think Kate would've had more sense," said Rebekah as she wiped down the display case.

"Taking one twin, you mean?" Nan asked.

Rebekah nodded. "That and giving the babies away in the first place."

"Jah . . . seems strange, ain't?"

Nellie spoke up. "Well, the way I understand it, the Lord God supposedly impressed on John and Kate to give their twins to the Kings. I don't understand all that, but it seems some folk tend to hear from God more than others."

"Well, I can't imagine the heavenly Father directing Kate to take back her son now," Nan said. "Such a cruel thing."

Silently Nellie agreed. She couldn't help but wonder whether Jehovah God was indeed responsible for the initial decision. And, if so, what about Kate's change of heart *now*? Nellie herself had always feared something like this might happen, though she had never voiced it to Rosanna, not wanting to spoil her friend's excitement over the babies.

As Nellie pondered this, she refused to fret about the fact that Caleb's own sister was right now in their home, redding up her bakery shop, of all things. According to Rebekah, her brother had brought her here late last night in the wee hours. So it was Caleb who'd done the good deed for his outcast sister, in spite of David Yoder's having sent her away—such a willful thing for her beau to do, considering he was already on shaky footing at home.

As he is with me.

But no, she could not dwell much on Caleb, or she would feel as despairing as she had following their brief encounter at the barn Singing last night. She did not want to relive that scene with her beau and Susannah looking so cozy together.

Nellie fixed her thoughts instead on dear Rosanna, whom she wanted to visit and comfort as soon as she could get away.

Half asleep, Rosanna held Rosie while sitting in the rocker in the kitchen, expecting Elias any minute. Her husband had been gone much too long for her liking, though she'd had plenty of time to practice her praying—talking aloud to God.

She glanced at her sleeping daughter, who'd struggled yet again after her bottle, refusing to give in to sleep. Could Rosie sense her twin brother wasn't there?

Getting up, she placed Rosie in the playpen, gently tucking her blanket around her and looking fondly at Eli's matching one. Running her hand over it, she wanted to trust the Lord God to return her son to them somehow. Today? Tomorrow?

She fought a battle of wills—what she knew she wanted, and what God had allowed. Was this His sovereign will? She'd been taught her whole life not to question His doing. But with all of her heart she wanted Eli back. Even so, if Elias did not succeed in getting Kate to change her mind, Rosanna must not allow herself to be bitter. At all costs, they must show Kate the love of the Lord. *Somehow.*

When Elias finally returned, he was red in the face—whether from his encounter with the Beilers or from the cold wind, Rosanna wasn't sure.

Rosanna said little as she warmed up his supper. She hurried to get the food on the table, sitting with him, watching him eat. He prayed an extra-long prayer of thanksgiving, both for the food and for "every good and blessed gift."

Before he began to eat, he said thoughtfully, "I spoke at length with John, who certainly supports Kate's taking Eli. They both feel it's necessary to have their son raised under the Ordnung."

She listened, taking in his every word.

"I had a mighty good opportunity to talk about our recent experience at the new church, 'bout seeking a relationship with God's Son. But John washed his hands of it, said he wants nothin' to do with such things."

"Rosie . . . what'll happen to her?" She held her breath.

"They'll let us keep her without a fight. That's what they said."

Rosanna let out a whoosh of air. "They don't mind if Rosie's raised in the more progressive church?"

"I guess they're hopin' she'll marry an Old Order boy, when the time comes. Honestly, I think they just assume the new church will lose its steam eventually, and those who've left will come to their senses and return. I don't see that happening, though."

She didn't, either. The groundswell was strong. Freedom to worship, to study Scripture—well, it was too powerful to stop.

Elias pulled his suspenders, looking at her. "But the way things are with Kate, I guess we can't count on anything."

"You mean she could go even more ferhoodled and come take Rosie away, too?"

"As John kept sayin', 'Things are different now.' "

Something she could not contain rose up in her. "It's wrong, Elias! Wrong as anything! Eli and Rosie must grow up *together*." Shaking now, she described Rosie's crying nearly all afternoon as if her little heart was aware of the separation. "I won't stand by and let Kate do this!"

"I know how you feel, but getting worked up won't help." His gaze lingered on her. Then slowly, deliberately, he put his hands to his face and covered his eyes for the longest time. He, too, was weeping.

"Aw, Elias . . . love. You want your son back, same as I do."

He nodded, his face still buried in his burly hands. "Jah, more than I dare say."

CHAPTER 28

A fter supper, while Nellie, Nan, and Rebekah were redding up the dishes, Nan asked Rebekah, "So, did you like helpin' out at Nellie's Simple Sweets?"

Rebekah nodded, drying a platter before handing it to Nellie to put away. "The Englischers are so friendly and chatty, jah? I was surprised how many asked for recipes."

"And I don't mind," Nellie said. "Here lately we're getting all kinds of new folk in the shop. Repeat customers, too." She hoped she wasn't boasting.

"Oh! About that," said Rebekah. "I almost forgot! You'll never guess who's responsible for all the fancy folk makin' a path to your door."

Nellie exchanged glances with Nan.

"Who?" asked Nan.

"Susannah Lapp."

Nan's mouth fell open. "You don't mean it."

Rebekah nodded. "It's true. Caleb mentioned it last night. She all but admitted she's been spending her egg money on newspaper ads. Appears she's intent on stirring up the staunchest Old Order folk."

Nellie was befuddled. "Why on earth?"

"Well, finally. One mystery solved!" Nan said, laughing. "What a schemer."

Nellie didn't feel any too kindly toward Susannah for the boost in sales. It seemed clear the girl was trying to build a wedge between herself and Caleb. And after last night, she'd accomplished it, too.

"Well, her plan didn't work exactly as she hoped, now, did it?" Nan went on more gently, perhaps recalling what Nellie had confided. "The ads have helped more than the tittle-tattle hurt us."

Nellie wasn't so sure. Truth was, she found Susannah's trick to be downright conniving, in spite of the beneficial influx of customers.

Wait a minute . . . could that be what Caleb was talking to Susannah about at yesterday's Singing?

Without even a glance out the window, Caleb knew there was a racket in the barn. It sounded like the driving horses had gotten out—galloping off—and he dashed outside to investigate, leaving *The Budget* behind on the kitchen table.

Caleb checked the barn and confirmed his suspicion, then went promptly to search for the horses in the deep pinewood, hoping to use the newly fallen snow to his best advantage by following the fresh horseshoe prints.

Something had obviously spooked the spirited horses, and he hoped they might soon be noticed by another farmer. He'd known of horses sprinting off into the cold and, having a mind of their own, being found dead in the snow the next day. For this reason he persevered, continuing his search through the knee-high snow, wishing he'd taken time to at least put on an extra layer of socks.

What caused them to run off in this weather? Eventually he turned back toward the house, where his father stood out on the front porch, waiting.

"I couldn't catch 'em," he called. "What do you want me to do?"

"You should've thought of that before leaving the stable door open, son."

So he *hadn't* latched the gate. . . .

But it was not the runaway horses that his father wanted to address as he headed down the steps and around the side of the house to the back door. "Come with me, Caleb."

He followed his father inside to the kitchen, where Mamm was pushing wood into the belly of the old cookstove. He was told to "sit awhile," and he did, though not at his usual spot at the table. Instead he purposely sat at the foot, down where Rebekah had always sat.

"What's on your mind, Daed?" He was taking the lead, an impertinent thing to do.

"Your sister Rebekah." Stopping for a second, Daed looked at Mamm. "Your mother and I want to know where you took her last night."

He's asking only now?

Caleb inhaled. "Rebekah wanted to go to the Fishers' . . . so that's where she is." He wouldn't reveal that she'd slipped into the house unknown to anyone. Surely Nan and Nellie welcomed her with open arms.

Mamm sat to the right of Daed, her hair a bit unkempt as it sometimes was this late in the day. Her eyes seemed all washed out, almost gray where there was usually color, and the wrinkles in her face were deeper than he remembered, settling hard on her laugh lines. "Was she . . ." Mamm paused, reaching up her sleeve for a handkerchief. "Was Rebekah terribly upset?"

He nodded slowly.

"Weeping, I s'pose?" Mamm's lower lip quivered uncontrollably.

"No . . . not that."

She stared at the tablecloth, tears spilling over the knobs of her cheeks. It was obvious how worried Mamm was—and how angry Daed was, too.

"She'll be fine over there with Nan . . . and Nellie Mae," he added, thinking of the letter he must write to Nellie. He had hoped the conversation with Daed would have made their predicament less dire, enabling him to offer her some word of hope along with his woeful attempt to explain.

"That's the last place you should've taken her, son."

"Where, then? It was awful late," he protested. "And so cold . . ."

Daed shook his head emphatically. "Reuben Fisher's house was not the place, and you know it. That's two misdeeds in less than a day's time."

Caleb cringed, chafing under his father's rebuke. He was glad when Daed headed upstairs to retire for the night, Mamm following dutifully behind. Caleb poured himself a glass of milk, downing it quickly. As he set the glass on the counter, he was amazed to hear the muted sounds of wayward horses galloping on the snow-packed lane, heading toward the barnyard.

"They're back!" Caleb dashed outside to thank their neighbor to the south, who had driven them in, then made sure the horses had no gashes or scrapes. When he was satisfied they were in good shape, he muttered his own disgust at his second transgression, as Daed had declared it, and latched the barn door, this time double-checking.

As soon as Nellie finished setting up the display case Tuesday morning, she left Nan and Rebekah in charge of Nellie's Simple Sweets and rode over to see Rosanna.

Entering the King home, she unloaded her baked goods onto the kitchen table and then threw her arms around Rosanna. Her friend seemed to have shrunk since Nellie had last seen her. Teary-eyed and frightened, Rosanna looked young and lost, and Nellie suddenly felt the older of the two, though Rosanna was nearly four years her senior.

"I am so sorry, Rosanna. Awful sorry," Nellie said softly. "Mamma's completely aghast at Kate's behavior. And Dat, too."

"We shouldn't hold anything against her." Rosanna helped Nellie off with her heaviest coat and two scarves. "Kate's not herself."

"How are you and Elias holding up?"

She shrugged. "It still doesn't seem real. I keep thinking I'll turn around and there he'll be, in the playpen."

"Kate hasn't changed her mind, then?"

Rosanna shook her head. "Elias went over there yesterday afternoon, but . . ." She bit her lip, unable to continue.

Tears filled Nellie's eyes and she squeezed her friend's hand.

Rosanna turned to warm a bottle for Rosie, and Nellie offered to feed her. Holding the little one in her arms near the corner stove, Nellie relished Rosie's sweetness as she took her bottle. Smiling, she glanced up from Rosie's face and saw the heartbroken look in Rosanna's eyes.

She could imagine how quickly one grew attached to a baby like Rosie. *What a loss!* She was tempted to remind Rosanna that it wasn't as if she'd never see Eli again—she wasn't losing him to death the way her family had Suzy. But Nellie thought better of it.

"I don't see how we can go on this way, without our baby boy." Rosanna's words tore at Nellie's heart. "Surely, the Lord will bring Eli back to us. . . ."

Nellie didn't know what to say.

Rosie had slowed her anxious sucking now, eyes mighty droopy, and she began to succumb to sleep.

Rosanna took Rosie from her, going to lay her down in the playpen. When she returned, Nellie gave her another long hug.

"I hope your son comes home to you very soon," she whispered.

"Thank you, Nellie Mae." Rosanna smiled through her tears. "From your lips to God's ear."

CHAPTER 29

Following Tuesday supper, Reuben headed to John and Kate Beiler's, wishing he'd had an opportunity to do so when Betsy had first told of the dismaying news. Yesterday's horse buyer had remained into the evening, staying on for supper after purchasing several fine Morgans. Thankful as Reuben was for the business, his mind had been elsewhere. Oh, but goodness, he felt someone ought to have a man-to-man talk with John, even though John was known to have a will like a wolf trap.

Reuben couldn't help but wonder if John had been influenced solely by Kate. Or was there more to it?

Navigating the horse along the icy roads, he wondered about his own son James, out learning to drive a fancy car in such treacherous conditions. How awful spoiled a body could become in short order—so much comfort on four wheels—especially on a miserable night like this.

Holding the reins with both hands now, Reuben rode past one farm after another. It was a bright yet freezing night. Following the area's recent heavy snows, livestock were safely stabled in all the farms up and down Beaver Dam Road. Passing Deacon Lapp's place, it looked to him as if the deacon's pasture gates and horse fences were nearly buried in white drifts.

He could see in his mind the deacon swaying from side to side as he walked, something like a grandfather clock. The kind and hardworking man had survived several farming accidents over the years. Despite the many changes of the past months, Reuben still considered the former ministerial brethren as his own, even though he assumed that eventually his brother would cease to oversee the New Order group.

Old things are passed away . . . all things are become new. Thankful for that Scriptural promise, he clucked his tongue to spur the horse along, wishing the Amish brotherhood might eventually see the light of divine grace.

In God's own way . . . and time.

Now that he was out alone in the darkness, Reuben realized he hadn't eaten his fill, and he was sorry he'd refused the tasty coconut cream pie. It certainly had tempted him, but he'd excused himself, pushing away from the fine turkey and stuffing dinner—practically a holiday feast, thanks to dear Betsy. But the wonderful-good pie was all Nellie's doing.

Seeing John Beiler's house, he made the turn into the driveway and wondered how the conversation might go. It wasn't his place to tell John and Kate what to do, but he'd come on Betsy's persuasion, and, well, here he was. Too late to turn back now.

Won't the bishop have something to say about Kate's wicked deed? He'd heard his elder brother had permitted John and Kate to give their babies to the Kings in the first place.

Reuben contemplated the man of God who had been wise enough to suspend the Bann for nearly three months, though that time was rapidly coming to a close. Nearly everyone had marked the date in red on their calendars—February eleventh. Well, everyone safely settled in the new churches had.

But tonight it wasn't so much the church split on Reuben's heart as two little babies being pulled apart from each other . . . and the family raising them.

Unbelievable.

He'd suffered enough loss for the rest of his life, with Suzy's drowning the worst blow of all. But what about Elias and Rosanna . . . all the unborn babies they had lost, only to come to this? Wasn't anyone willing to speak on their behalf? This went much deeper than two women squabbling over babies, he felt certain. The way Betsy had described it, Rosanna could have Eli back, but only if she renounced her interest in the New Order church.

But she hadn't, and now he had appointed himself to defend Elias King, brand-new convert that he was.

One by one, people are coming to Christ. . . .

Hastily Reuben tied up his horse, glancing at the old stone farmhouse where the Beilers resided. With a prayer on his lips, he walked to the back door.

Caleb slid his long legs under the desk in his room, tuckered out from single-handedly unloading more than three tons of hay for a neighbor whose supply was running low due to last summer's drought. Tomorrow would bring more of the same. He leaned back in the sturdy chair, relaxing at last.

He eyed the pulled-down green window shades that blocked the moon's white radiance. The shades were like the shadows on his soul. Never before had he felt so hemmed in there, in the very place he stood to inherit, assuming he bowed to Daed's demands. Caleb thought he had done so—had jeopardized his relationship with Nellie in doing it—but the end result was not to his father's liking.

Did Daed think Susannah could actually beguile me . . . change my mind about Nellie Mae? If so, what sort of man would I be? And what sort of husband?

He felt ensnared, trapped by his father's impossible expectations, yet unwilling to abandon his love for Nellie. His frustration gnawed at him. *I have to find a way to make this work!*

But first things first. Picking up his pen, Caleb began to write to his sweetheart.

Dear Nellie Mae,

I hope you're all right, even though by the looks of your sad eyes Sunday night I fear you aren't. Frankly, neither am I. To think I might lose you because of this ridiculous deed . . . well, I simply can't stand by and let you think the worst of me.

Truth be told, I went against my better judgment. My father insisted I spend time with Susannah Lapp, hoping I would regard her as a future bride. Now, I realize you have merely my word on this, but what I'm telling you is true.

Talking once with Susannah was the only way for me to say I'd obeyed my father's bidding, something I was anxious to be done with. Then you came into the barn and saw us together, when she and I were already in disagreement, to put it mildly. That girl is more trouble than I ever suspected.

I want nothing more than to see you again, Nellie. Will you meet me at our special place this Saturday night?

I'll bring my courting buggy, so we can at least ride a bit. Please hear me out. Won't you give me a second chance?

Until then.

> *With all my love,*
> *Caleb Yoder*

Satisfied he had explained things adequately to his darling, he slid the letter into his bureau drawer to mail later.

Mamma appeared absolutely chagrined at the news of who'd placed the ad. "Susannah, you say? Why, that schemer!"

"Nan thought so, too." Nellie cut generous wedges of coconut cream pie for Mamma, Rebekah, and Nan as they gathered around the table. Dat was out paying someone a visit.

"Sure would be nice to have Rhoda home," said Nan, changing the subject. Nellie and Mamma muttered their agreement.

"It was your sister I'd set out to see yesterday when I felt impressed to stop in and visit Rosanna instead," Mamma mentioned. She didn't bring up again the heartbreak Rosanna was enduring, yet Nellie knew it was on all of their minds.

They sat quietly, savoring their pie for a while before Rebekah said, "It's been awful nice of you to let me stay here for the time being."

"Won't your father ask you to return home?" Nellie asked gently. Was David Yoder so hard as to forbid his daughter to ever come home?

"I doubt it." Rebekah took another bite of pie, her face serious.

"Well, girls," Mamma said, "let's not forget God does impossible things. He's surely at work in your father's heart, jah?" Mamma's eyes were suddenly bright with tears. "You're welcome to stay with us as long as you wish, Rebekah dear."

Rebekah reached for Mamma's hand. "Will ya remember my family in your prayers? I'd be so grateful," she said, surprising Nellie—Nan, too, apparently, because her eyes looked like big blue buttons.

"How about right now?" Mamma opened a hand to Nan, as well, and Nellie slowly put hers out, too. They all bowed heads. "Our heavenly Father, will you look over our broken hearts—each one—and mend and heal those who are in need of mercy? Please give your grace to Rebekah. Watch over her parents and her brothers and sisters and their families . . . and give her peace this night."

Mamma paused as if to keep from breaking down, releasing Nellie's hand to blow her nose. Nan and Rebekah kept their eyes closed, evidently waiting for the amen, which was only slightly delayed by Mamma's addition of "poor Rosanna and Elias" to her prayer, as well as "dear Rhoda." When she said Rhoda's name, her voice cracked.

Nellie wondered what Rebekah thought of such fervency, but Caleb's sister seemed unfazed and actually inquired about what Mamma thought was the "best way to pray."

"Anyone can talk to God," Mamma explained, looking at Nellie now— "like you would to a close friend or family member." Mamma was undoubtedly hoping to win her over yet.

Sighing, Nellie wondered if she shouldn't get Suzy's diary out of hiding again. She'd felt so tenderhearted after reading the last third of it. Suddenly she recalled Rhoda's request for it. She'd refused, afraid of what Rhoda would think after reading of Suzy's wild months in the world. But with Rhoda gone, Nellie wondered whether it might have done her oldest sister some good to see Suzy's path to transformation. If Rhoda had read the journal through to its sweet end, maybe she'd still be here with them now.

She looked at Mamma, who had endured such painful losses in the past year. Presently her mother was talking about "trusting in our Savior, even when people around us disappoint."

"Sometimes it's terribly hard, though." Rebekah sniffled.

"Well, sure it is. But it's not so much how we manage to get through the hard things as it is being willing to cling to God's promises while we're gettin' there, ya know?"

Nellie was surprised at the way her mother described things. She couldn't deny being somewhat curious about her parents' loyalty to their newfound faith . . . a faith shared by Nan and Rebekah. *Elias and Rosanna, too.* And to think the Kings' choosing the New Order had taken little Eli from them and put him back in Kate's arms!

When Reuben knocked on the Beilers' back door, he was quickly met by John, who did not usher him inside with his formerly cheerful welcome. Rather, he gave a single nod and stepped aside awkwardly to let Reuben pass.

Immediately it was clear Eli was the center of attention that evening. A doting Kate held him, surrounded by all the children.

Reuben's heart sank but he didn't dare let on. As pleasant as the scene before him was, he could think only of grieving Rosanna King. How was he to broach that thorny subject over the soft buzz of voices?

Kate tenderly kissed Eli's cheek, and the two youngest children leaned in on either side of the rocking chair, kissing him, too. John moved to his wife's side, leaving Reuben to merely observe.

For a moment he almost forgot why he'd come, but Eli began to cry as if he was downright hungry. The oldest girls shushed and made over him, but nothing seemed to work. "What do ya think's wrong?" asked the older of the two. "He just ate, and he's wearin' a fresh diaper."

The domestic peace broken, John finally turned his attention back to Reuben. "What's brought you out on such a wintry night?"

Normally by now Reuben would have been offered a seat at the table and a slice of pie, but there was no sign of hospitality from either John or Kate, and Reuben felt increasingly disconcerted.

Lord, please keep a rein on my temper. Help me to know how to bring up Kate's heartless deed.

Just then someone pounded on the back door, and John hurried to see who it was.

There stood Elias King, his face ashen. "Hullo, John . . . Reuben." Elias's expression registered surprise.

"Elias . . . good to see ya." Reuben's throat tightened up. He felt for this fine young man; it was obvious Elias had come to beg for the child's return, as awkward as it seemed.

Kate rose and wordlessly walked out of the room with Eli, who was still wailing. All six children followed, like ducklings scurrying after their mamma.

When John waved them toward the table, Elias eased himself onto the bench, pain on his face. He folded his hands on the table and eyed Reuben. "I'm glad you're here," he said. "You're witness to the things I mean to say." He then directed his gaze at John.

"Elias, you won't be changin' our minds, no matter how many times you come over here." John reached for his coffee.

"Now, wait a minute," Reuben spoke up. "Look at this man. Hear him out, for pity's sake."

John's posture stiffened. "Eli is my son."

"That he is, though I feel as though he is mine, too." Elias took in a long breath and offered a thin smile before becoming more solemn. "But hear me out. A baby girl is cryin' without end for her brother, over yonder." He glanced toward the window. "And my wife's pining for Eli, too."

"Eli will be raised here," John stated. "With God-fearin' people."

"We *are* God-fearing people, John. And in the fear of the Lord, you gave Rosanna and me a son . . . and a daughter. They belong together."

John's neck and face were red, although thus far he appeared stubbornly in control of himself. "My son belongs with us, here, where he will grow up in the Old Ways."

"What Eli needs is to grow up knowin' the saving grace of the Lord," Elias stated, his voice firm but calm.

The tension in the air was palpable. It was agonizing to watch this exchange over a single baby—a man-child. It seemed to Reuben there was no satisfying either person, and he again beseeched the living God for aid.

A flickering thought crossed his mind that a third party was needed, someone to guide them in the right direction. *In the same direction.* "Bishop Joseph should decide," Reuben said suddenly.

"No, I've already made up my mind. I won't allow my boy to be raised by folk professin' an alien gospel."

"But surely you trust the bishop? The wisdom of the Old Order?"

John looked at Reuben, as did Elias. A mutual hope filled both men's eyes. "If that's what it'll take," John said, and Elias nodded in agreement.

"Then I'll speak to my brother on your behalf."

Surprisingly, John reached over to shake Reuben's hand as all three men stood.

"I'll let Rosanna know," Elias said gratefully to Reuben as he made his way toward the back door.

"And I'll tell Kate," said John with confidence.

Reuben bid John good-night and headed home to Betsy. He wondered if what he'd proposed had been divinely dropped into his heart, perhaps. *I'd dread to be in the bishop's shoes!*

Rosanna had been walking the floor with fussy Rosie for more than an hour, not understanding how such a tired baby could simply refuse to give in to sleep. So she held her near, talking softly during the short intervals when Rosie would let up to catch a breath, only to begin howling again. Rosanna tried humming, cajoling, rubbing her back, her tummy—everything that had always helped in the past, but to no avail.

When Elias finally arrived home, she was ever so glad. He took Rosie from her, kissing her little forehead, then the top of her head. Even so, she continued to cry.

"What do you s'pose is wrong?"

"Could it be she senses Eli is gone?"

She'd considered that earlier. "Could be, jah. We'll simply give her more attention . . . till her brother's home again."

Elias's face sagged; he must have been dead tired. But she knew it was more than that.

"Kate might not bring Eli back, Rosanna. You must know this."

"No . . . no, let's not think that way."

"Well, the decision's not ours anymore. Nor is it John and Kate's."

"What do you mean?"

He paused as Rosie gave in to sleep. "Where Eli should grow up is the bishop's choice to make now," he told Rosanna, who followed when he carried Rosie upstairs to her cradle.

"But no! Bishop Joseph will surely rule in their favor." She began to cry.

He reached for her, tenderly pulling her into his arms. "Come here."

She felt the strength of him, the great affection he had for her, in the gentle brush of his lips against her cheek and then her mouth. "Oh, Elias . . . I've worried so."

He took her hand, leading her to their room. "We must trust God for Eli's future. Not a speck of worry will change a thing."

She agreed, trying to focus on her darling as he sat on the bed, drawing her to him.

"You're so perty, love."

She forced a smile as she sat next to him, his arms around her now. His kisses were ever so light, comforting her, if only for this moment.

"I love you, Mrs. King." He often said this somewhat comically during their most intimate moments, but tonight his tone was wholly serious. "Let me ease your sadness . . . for now." He cupped Rosanna's chin as his kisses grew more fervent. Their tears of joy and sadness mingled as they comforted each other with their love.

CHAPTER 30

By nine o'clock Wednesday morning, the bakery shop was filled to capacity and abuzz with fancy talk. Nellie was glad for the extra help as Mamma served up warm muffins and sticky buns oozing with icing and glazed sugar.

Nan and Rebekah periodically delivered more freshly baked goodies to the bakery shop from the kitchen at the house. Soon, though, the most requested items on the "menu" were hot coffee and cocoa, which were plenty easy to make on the hot plate Dat had rigged up to a small gas-powered generator.

Next thing, he'll want to put in an oven, Nellie thought with a smile. More and more of the People were having electricity installed, along with phones—her own brother James and family were among the latter. So far, though, there was no talk of such happening under Dat's roof. Nellie was secretly glad, although there was no reason now to worry over whether Caleb and his family approved of them—not after what she'd witnessed last Sunday evening. She truly wanted to look on the bright side of things, as Mamma often encouraged her children to do, but she was consciously bracing herself for a breakup letter from Caleb.

Several regulars were sitting at the table farthest away, where Miss Bachman was indulging in her usual treat—peanut butter fudge—saying nothing else could quite compare. Laughter cascaded from the middle table, where all four chairs were occupied, as was also the case at the first. Twelve customers in all, and every one having a wonderful-good morning together.

Nellie refused to puff up with pride, but she was delighted to see the pleasure they took in enjoying her creations. Oh, she wished she could bottle up some of this happiness and carry it over to Rosanna. If Kate Beiler hadn't seen the light and returned Eli by now, there was surely great sorrow in the Kings' house again today. Sadness seemed to abound in any number of hearts here lately, including poor, displaced Rebekah's.

Even so, David Yoder's loss is Nan's and my gain, she thought, glad they could receive Rebekah during her plight. Spending so much time with Caleb's dearest sister was an unexpected gift.

Sudden hilarity sprang from the second table as a customer told of putting up elderberries for the first time. "I made such a mess. I kept finding purple stains on tea towels and my clothes for months," the woman confessed.

More ladies chimed in about harvesting and canning "like Plain folk."

Nellie headed to the door to meet Nan, who was arriving with yet another basket of cookies—hopefully snickerdoodles and chocolate chip.

"Word has it twin babies were separated near here," one woman said rather loudly, nearly stopping Nellie in her tracks. "The baby boy was taken from his adoptive mother by the biological mom, no less."

"I heard that, too," said Miss Bachman. "Evidently the birth mother changed her mind and took the boy back."

"How awful!" exclaimed another woman.

Nellie felt awkward eavesdropping and was glad for the momentary distraction Nan provided. "Would you mind tending the store with Mamma, following the noon meal?" Nellie asked as they worked side by side behind the counter to unload the basket.

"I'll have plenty of time, jah." Nan explained that Rebekah had gone on foot to her job as a mother's helper for the Amish family less than a mile away.

"What do you think'll happen with her?" Nellie asked.

Nan looked sober. "You know David Yoder as well as anybody."

Nodding, Nellie Mae squeezed her sister's hand, grateful she'd confided her woes to Nan earlier.

Nan returned to the house to put the finishing touches on dinner when the crowd of customers emptied out, closer to the noon hour. Nellie Mae was happy to have a few moments alone with Mamma.

Smoothing her apron, Mamma slipped her hand into her pocket, pulling out two Kapp strings. "I found these on the floor in the cellar, near the wringer washer."

Ever so sheepish, Nellie was reluctant to own up. "What on earth?"

"You snipped 'em off your sister's Kapp, ain't?"

So Mamma knew already. "Jah." She braced herself for the reprimand. "That's my doing."

"Oh, Nellie Mae, you loved Suzy so. Here, keep them close to your heart, or wherever you'd like."

Wiping tears, she put the Kapp strings safely in her own dress pocket. She would be more careful with them, not wanting to raise eyebrows with Nan or Dat . . . or even Rebekah. "Denki, Mamma," she whispered, reaching to embrace her. "Denki, ever so much."

———

When Chris and Zach arrived home from school, Zach headed up to their room while Chris made his way to the kitchen. He found his dad sitting at the table, listening to the radio and drinking a cup of coffee.

"Where's Mom?" Chris set down his books and opened the old Frigidaire.

"We're out of milk." Dad glanced toward the stairwell. "Zach barely said a word to me. Everything okay?"

Chris closed the refrigerator, empty-handed, and sat heavily in the chair across from his father. *He knows Zach's still taking Suzy's loss hard. . . .*

Neither spoke for a while. Finally Dad set his coffee cup on the saucer. "Things any better these days?"

"Sometimes," Chris hedged. "Sometimes not."

Dad took another sip of coffee. "Your mother's quite worried. She thinks maybe Zach should see our pastor."

Chris nodded. "He'll be okay."

"Do the two of you . . . talk about it?"

"Now and then." Chris shrugged. "Hasn't helped much, though."

His father smiled. "I've attempted a few conversations, but Zach seems so closed."

"He's always been . . . oh, I don't know."

"Independent?" his father chuckled. "And stubborn?" Another moment passed as he drained his cup. Then he got up and went to the sink. Coming back, he placed his hand on Chris's shoulder. "Listen, the two of you have always been close. More than anything, you've been the best for him, Chris."

"His faith is strong."

"I don't doubt that."

Dad headed toward the back door and turned. "He'll pull out, stronger than before. I'm praying that way."

"Yeah." *I hope Zach gets past the worst soon.*

A half hour later, Chris was still sitting at the table, thinking . . . praying. Zach came wandering down just as he was about to head upstairs to change into sweats.

"Wondered what happened to you." Zach pulled some ice cream from the freezer. "Want some?"

Chris gestured toward the seat his father had vacated.

"What?"

"I've been thinking . . . about Suzy Fisher."

Zach dipped into the half-gallon container. "That's my job." He scooped ice cream into a bowl. "Last call. Double fudge dip."

"Seriously, Zach."

Frowning now, Zach sat down.

Chris took a deep breath. "I need to play older brother for a sec."

Zach groaned. "Not this again."

Not wanting to start off on the wrong foot, he paused. Then, he said, "We're all starting to worry about you."

"Who? Dad? Worry about what?"

Chris sighed. This wasn't going so well. He rubbed his chin. "Look, Zach . . . do we really believe the Good News?"

"C'mon, Chris."

"I mean, sometimes we act like what we believe doesn't hold up in a world where suffering's real. Like the Gospel works as long as things are going well, you know?"

Zach's frown deepened, his jaw clenched. "But you weren't in love with her, Chris."

Chris felt the familiar tension between them. He thought of Suzy's picture, the one Zach continually stared at. "Suzy was a simple Amish girl, right? How do you think she'd feel about that big photo hanging on your bulletin board?"

Zach nodded, glancing out the window. "She wasn't going to stay Amish."

"Maybe not. But it's like you've created a shrine or something."

"I just don't want to forget her."

Chris leaned toward his brother and Zach looked away. "Did it ever occur to you that pictures are forbidden by Amish *because* they can become like idols?" Chris locked eyes with his brother. "Maybe you've done that with Suzy."

Zach clenched his teeth again. "I feel *guilty*, okay? That's not going to go away. She was a lousy swimmer, Chris. We messed up."

Chris swallowed hard. "Yeah, I know."

"Well, then—what do you want from me?"

"To do what we ask others to do."

"What?"

"To accept God's forgiveness."

Zach blew out a breath and looked down, shaking his head. At last he nodded, tears falling freely. "All right. I get it. And I'm trying, okay? I'm trying. . . ."

Chris cuffed his brother's wrist. "Well, don't try so hard, goof. Stop fighting it. Let God work it out."

"I need more time," Zach whispered, swallowing. "It's not easy."

"Take all the time you need, but don't shut me out. And don't push Mom and Dad away, either."

Zach sniffed, wiping his eyes. A long moment passed until a trace of a smile crossed his lips. "You know, you can be really annoying sometimes."

Chris grinned. "'Cuz I'm right?"

"No, 'cuz you're annoying."

"It's my birthright, you know. The older brother thing?"

Zach sighed again, his smile fading. "Okay. I'll take the picture down."

Chris nodded. "Hey, I just want my brother back."

Staring hard at his ice cream, Zach said softly, "It's hard to feel forgiven."

"I know, man. I know."

Zach finished eating and then the two of them trudged up the stairs. Chris carried no illusions. Things weren't going to change overnight, but for the first time in a long time, he sensed a glimmer of hope. The old Zach was definitely not gone for good.

Nellie Mae visited Rosanna again that afternoon and could tell her friend hadn't slept much, if at all. Her eyes were swollen and red, and the apples of her cheeks were puffy, too.

Rosanna helped Nellie off with her coat. Then Nellie embraced Rosanna and encouraged her to sit down.

Rosanna complied, sitting in one of the chairs near the stove. "Elias went over there again last night. Your father, too, I understand . . ." Her voice was weary.

Nellie nodded.

"Kate and John won't change their minds. We're going to wait and see what the bishop says now."

They sat quietly for a few minutes while Nellie got warmed up. She didn't want to hold tiny Rosie with such cold hands. Besides, Rosie was sound asleep, and Rosanna was saying how she'd struggled to get her settled since Monday morning, when Kate had left with Eli.

"It's not like her," Rosanna said. "Could it be she senses my grief?"

"Guess she might." *I sure do,* Nellie thought sadly.

"You know I lost babies before, Nellie Mae . . . before they were even born. But this . . ." She sniffled. "Oh, this is the hardest thing, havin' a babe taken away after he's been in my arms for nearly two months."

Nellie's eyes filled with tears, and she reached over and squeezed Rosanna's hand. Then she said, "And to hear Mamma's stories about Thomas and Jeremiah—twins are ever so close. Could be Rosie misses Eli, too."

"Jah, I think so. Growin' in the womb together must make them closer than other siblings."

Nellie remembered all the talk among the English customers earlier. "Some folk say it's unhealthy to separate twins." The words slipped out before she could stop them.

"Oh, I believe I know as much." Rosanna glanced toward the playpen, which was just out of reach of the woodstove. "You don't have to tell me Rosie's missin' Eli, in her own way. Either that, or she's got one fierce case of colic."

It felt so good to spend time with Rosanna two days in a row, like they had as girls. Under different circumstances, of course, they would be working on a quilt or sewing dresses and aprons all afternoon. She didn't dare ask if Rosanna had a quilt in the frame, or if the frame was even set up. She knew better. Lately Rosanna's time had been wholly spent tending to Eli and Rosie.

Nellie had an idea. "I'll make supper for you and Elias, if you'd like to go up and rest a bit."

Rosanna brightened. "Oh, would ya?"

"Whatever I can do to help."

Rosanna smiled, nodding. She showed her where Rosie's next bottle was kept in the refrigerator. "The formula is all ready. Just shake it up a bit and warm it on the stove if she wakes up."

"I'll look after Rosie. Not to worry." Shooing her dear friend off for a nap, Nellie watched her amble over to the stairs and climb them slowly. *She's clearly exhausted.*

If her coming could provide Rosanna even a small respite, Nellie was ever so glad.

———

When Nellie returned home from Rosanna's that evening, Nan and Rebekah were curled up near the cookstove, reading the Bible Nan and

Rhoda had purchased some time ago. Nan encouraged Nellie to join them, but Nellie declined, using as her excuse the recent circle letter. Then, when she had finished updating her cousins on recent happenings, she wrote a private letter to Cousin Treva, as well, hoping to mail both at the same time.

That done, she looked up and found solace in observing Dat and Mamma, their heads together as they read Scripture, like two lovebirds. Dat still read aloud to all of them every night, but increasingly he and Mamma took extra time to study further.

At moments like this, Nellie missed Rhoda the most. Things were out of kilter here without her oldest sister. It seemed strange knowing Rhoda was staying at James and Martha's, though Nellie was glad Rhoda was living with family, even if that family had "fallen into the world," as Dat complained.

She hoped the rumor mill was mistaken and that James hadn't bought a car like Rhoda had. *If Caleb's heard there are two cars in the Fisher family, no wonder he's pursuing Susannah!*

CHAPTER 31

———

By midmorning the next day, the fertile farmland, long since buried beneath more than a foot of snow, looked hemmed in by heavy clouds. Nellie Mae pulled on long johns beneath her dress and wore boots and several layers for the jaunt out to get the day's mail. She breathed ever so lightly on the walk back to the house so that her lungs wouldn't ache with the below-zero temperatures.

When will all this ice and snow begin to thaw?

Spring would arrive eventually, but a thaw in the attitudes of the People seemed less likely. The impending fate of many still hung in the balance, and they all knew what was coming. Would the split succeed in destroying the unity of families and the community despite Uncle Bishop's decision to temporarily stay the Bann?

Nellie glanced through the letters as she carried the thick stack of mail toward the house. Her heart leapt up, then sank nearly as fast when she saw Caleb's handwriting. A sad little groan escaped her. Was he writing to break things off? She must hasten to read this, not waiting as she sometimes had before, wanting to savor his words of devotion.

She looked to see if Mamma might need her at the bakery shop. For a change customers were scarce, so she went to the house and tugged off her boots. Still wearing her coat and scarf, she ran up to her room and closed the door before opening the letter. She scanned it quickly and was relieved to see it was a letter of explanation.

So the encounter with Susannah Lapp had been a requirement of his father's? What sort of man demanded such things, especially when aware of his son's love for another?

Despite Caleb's attempt to explain, she couldn't dismiss the troubling realization that her beau would do nearly anything for his father's land. He'd taken a terrible chance with their love, even though things must not have gone well with Susannah or he would have invited her to ride home. Instead it was Caleb's sister Rebekah by his side following the Singing that night, not the flirtatious Susannah.

420

She read the telling line again: *Talking once with Susannah was the only way for me to say I'd obeyed my father's bidding, something I was anxious to be done with.*

As skeptical as she felt about Caleb's motives, she tried not to cry. She'd spent enough time weeping over Caleb Yoder; loving someone so deeply seemed to involve pain. *Just look at Nan's mess with her former beau.*

For sure and for certain, love and falling into it could bring a profound measure of sorrow. Who could argue that? *Except maybe Mamma, who got the pick of the crop with Dat.*

Nellie refolded the bewildering letter and placed it under the mattress, alongside Suzy's diary, and went downstairs to don her boots. Making her way back to the bakery shop, she was hesitant about her decision. She felt as bleak as could be, thinking about the wedge Caleb had created between them—all in the name of obedience to his father. She continued to deliberate. Should she give Caleb another chance? Was their love strong enough to weather this gale?

She must stop second-guessing and make up her mind. *Jah, maybe it's a gut idea to hear him out.* Once again she would brave the wretched cold to meet her beau, though this time her enthusiasm would not help to keep her warm.

Rhoda enjoyed Mrs. Kraybill's attempt to suppress her laughter. "Well? What do you think?" Turning around twice, Rhoda stopped and stood still. She was modeling a chocolate brown midi-skirt, ginger-colored fashion boots, and a gold satin long-sleeved blouse with a fitted deep chocolate velveteen vest—the most striking outfit she'd ever seen. Rhoda had purchased it only yesterday in Lancaster, on the square at Watt and Shand's Department Store, after deeming it the perfect look for this Sunday night at the Kraybills' beautiful home—the night she was to meet Ken.

The enterprising store clerk had also tried to steer her in the direction of the makeup counter, saying how very "mod" false eyelashes were now, to which Rhoda thought the ones the Lord God had given her were thick enough. It was easy to see that the clerk herself had false lashes pasted on her own eyes, because a glob of glue showed on her eyelid. Rhoda had barely managed to keep from smirking. *Mod indeed!* That was one mistake she could easily avoid making.

"I suppose from your turning around repeatedly, you're hoping I'll say I like it, is that it?" Mrs. Kraybill smiled and touched the fabric of Rhoda's soft sleeve.

"You're teasin' me?" Rhoda asked, suddenly less sure of her purchase.

Mrs. Kraybill stepped back. "Rhoda Fisher, you are quite stylish. Our nephew will be pleased . . . and that *is* your desired goal, isn't it?"

Rhoda blushed uncontrollably. She wouldn't come right out and admit to wanting to look pretty—fancy, too. But she knew the cut of this outfit hid a multitude of pounds while emphasizing her best features, and that was more her objective than anything. "I don't want to embarrass myself . . . is all."

"Oh, Rhoda, you surely don't worry about that, do you?"

"Well, I don't really fit in round here with your family. I'm like a kernel off its cob."

The way her words tumbled out made Mrs. Kraybill smile yet again, and soon Rhoda's own silly laugh was mixed with her employer's wholehearted amusement. Such a good time they were having!

Mrs. Kraybill motioned for her to sit on the living room sofa. "You're lovely as you are, Rhoda, even when you dress Plain. Never forget to be yourself. No need to mimic anyone else."

Mrs. Kraybill must not sense how dissatisfied Rhoda was with her weight, her looks, and her life in particular. All that aside, she wouldn't pump for more compliments, which only made her feel more self-conscious.

Folding her arms, Mrs. Kraybill continued to regard Rhoda, obviously pleased with the skirt, blouse, and vest combination. "If you wear that or your regular Amish attire—either one—you'll be fine. It's your decision alone."

Rhoda felt wonderful-good, hearing that. There weren't many areas of life where she had been encouraged to show such confidence, especially by another woman. Mrs. Kraybill's remarks were foreign to be sure. The women she knew best, Mamma included, curtailed all inclinations toward independent thinking.

"I'll wear this outfit, then." With a flair, she adjusted her glasses. "Maybe I'll take off my Kapp and get some new eyewear, too."

"So it's settled."

"Thanks for givin' me your opinion," Rhoda said, glad she'd asked. James would soon return to take her over to his place, where Martha could use her help with the children.

Rhoda considered how Mamma had trained her in the ways of submission and total respect for authority. Beachy Amish though she now was, Martha's daughter, Emma, would be raised in a similar, though less strict, fashion. Plain girls grew up to become compliant young women, knowing nothing else.

Why must I crave something different, then?

Even though Martha was becoming more progressive with each passing day, Rhoda knew exactly what both Martha and Mamma would think of her fetching outfit and bold plan to snag a man. She knew . . . and cringed.

Between brushing down the foals—growing before his eyes—and forking hay to freshen the stall bedding, Reuben managed to slip away to pay a quick visit to his brother Bishop Joseph.

He found him slumped over with sleep in his chair near the woodstove, his big German Bible lying open on his lap. The bishop looked up when Reuben was led into the kitchen by Joseph's eldest granddaughter, who quickly made herself scarce. She headed into the front room, returning to the quilting frame, where she sat with Anna.

He waited as Joseph made an excuse for reading the Good Book in the middle of the day. "And not studying it, mind you," the bishop said before closing it. "What brings you out in such inclement weather?"

Reuben pulled up a chair—no sense stalling. "S'pose you're aware of the Beilers' change of mind and heart 'bout their youngest son, Eli—one of the twins they gave to the Kings."

Joseph narrowed his already-squinting gaze behind his spectacles. "Heard as much."

"Then you must know Kate's taken Eli back?"

Joseph nodded slowly.

Reuben sighed, not sure he was getting anywhere with his brother, whose eyes appeared to long for the remaining forty winks. "I was over talkin' with John about it the other day when Elias showed up, beside himself. In the end I spent some time with both of them, and finally I suggested bringing this matter to you."

"I see." His brother looked as serious as Reuben had ever seen him.

"Rosanna's in deep mournin' for the baby boy she was all set to raise, and Kate's equally set on keepin' him. As for Elias, I witnessed his sorrow myself."

"I gave my blessing for the Beilers to give up their children months ago, jah?"

"Must've taken some deliberating on your part, Bishop," he offered.

Joseph rose and walked to the sink for a glass of water. "Seems you're talking now 'bout the present time . . . and the future."

"The present is fraught with sadness and pain for Elias and Rosanna."

Joseph turned, holding his tumbler of water. "And the future of the children?"

"That's why I'm here . . . hopin' you might have some wisdom in the matter. The People are torn. Not just over the church split, but a good many are takin' sides concerning the twins, too." He shook his head.

"Siblings bein' raised in different families?"

"At least for the time bein'."

Joseph scratched his gray head. "Till when?"

"Until you intervene in this tomfoolery. John and Elias are in agreement on that. They'll do your bidding, seems."

Joseph shrugged, smacking his lips. "Very well. I'll meet with 'em next week."

Reuben hated to question his bishop brother. "That long?"

"I say, leave plenty of time for it to work itself out."

Again he felt obliged to speak up. "A whole week will seem like an eternity to Rosanna."

"And to the wee twins?"

Reuben hadn't quite looked at it that way, but he supposed that was also true. He nodded. "Seems there's great sorrow in the little ones' hearts. Both of them."

Joseph bunched up his wrinkled forehead into a deep, searing scowl. He tugged hard on his beard, the length of it seeming to grow. "Mighty prickly situation, I'll say that."

Not wanting to press the issue, Reuben chose not to ask yet again for an earlier meeting. His brother was known to rule on the side of mercy and usually had a sensible approach to the conflicts amongst them. They'd simply have to wait. "So next week it is," Reuben stated.

Joseph gave a quick head bob. "Jah. Tell them I'll see to it then."

He thanked Joseph and hurried out the back door. Hopefully he'd gained some ground for both families, though he couldn't begin to guess how Bishop Joseph would decide.

'Tis not for us to know the times and the seasons, nor the hearts of men . . . but to simply trust.

During the ride home Reuben prayed for a satisfactory and pleasing outcome for both parties, one that would allow Eli and Rosie to grow up as siblings, not as cousins. But what Reuben prayed most of all was for them to come to know their Savior, however the Lord willed it.

CHAPTER 32

Her father was out hitching up the family carriage to the horse on Saturday evening as Nellie made her way out the back door after supper. Not wanting to be noticed, she hurried down the lane toward Beaver Dam Road.

"Where ya headed, Nellie Mae?" Dat called after her.

"Oh, just out for a bit."

"Why not ride with me, then?" he offered. "I'm heading over to visit Elias King. That the direction you're going?"

Altogether baffled, she accepted, welcoming the chance to be warmer when she arrived at the stone mill. "Denki, that'd be right nice."

He tightened the girth and checked the straps. Once he was seated and holding the reins, he said, "Hop in, Nellie."

She'd never felt so awkward before, riding alone with her father on the night meant for pairing up with a beau.

"This here cloud cover's goin' to bring us more snow," Dat said, making conversation.

"Can't say I'm eager for more."

"Me neither, tellin' the truth." They rode for a distance and then he added, "Weatherman says there's a change comin', starting tomorrow."

"Really?" Nellie was surprised her father would be privy to such news.

"Heard it over at James's."

She tensed up. "My brother's got himself a radio?"

Dat seemed reluctant to talk more on the subject. "Appears he's facing in the wrong direction, least for now. No telling if he'll keep heading thataway. He's just itchin' to be somewhere he's never been." Dat sighed. "Make sense?"

"I think so." She assumed her father was saying James wasn't solidly on the wrong path, only toying with it. "There are some who have to find out for themselves that what they've been missin' ain't what they want."

Dat turned to her, smiling. "That's exactly what I mean, Nellie Mae."

No wonder Mamma found Dat so interesting. With her many siblings, Nellie had rarely gotten time with him all to herself.

"I have to say there's plenty of hope to go around." He leaned forward, looking up at the sky.

She didn't say more, and neither did Dat. His last words merely floated between them.

Hope . . .

Soon, when Elias's drive came into view, Dat stopped on the road and offered to let her out there. She got out and waved at him, thankful he hadn't asked where she was heading. With no moon to guide her, she was glad the old mill was only a short distance away.

Nellie spied the back of Caleb's open buggy as she made the bend in the road and experienced again the torrent of sadness she'd felt at seeing him with Susannah Lapp. There he was, waiting for her, parked around the corner from the mill.

She willed herself not to cry and kept walking. She would not make a fool of herself running to him, though she was hungry for his embrace, longing for the good Caleb she knew and loved.

"Nellie Mae . . . over here," he called, stepping down from his courting buggy. He must've heard her boots on the snow.

"I see you, Caleb!"

He moved swiftly toward her. "I'm so glad you came." He wrapped his arms tightly around her.

After a time, she stepped away.

"Ach, you've been walkin' a long ways." He reached for her hand and led her to the buggy. Then, lifting her up like a doll, he settled her in his buggy and hopped up to join her.

"I was fortunate to get a ride with my father." She explained that Dat was going to visit Elias King. "Such a sad story *that* is."

"But the Kings made a poor choice, ain't?"

Nellie bristled. She recalled comforting Rosanna. " 'Tis true Elias has moved away from the Ordnung. That's made John and Kate furious."

"S'pose it's understandable."

This night was starting out on the wrong foot. Why had he continued in this vein when his letter had indicated he wanted to patch things up?

"I'd say a promise is a promise . . . and it must be kept." She'd said what she truly thought about the Beilers' offering their twins to Elias and Rosanna—what she thought about Caleb, too.

She stuck her neck out even further. "Along the same lines, how am I to understand what you and Susannah Lapp were doin' together last Sunday night?"

"Nellie Mae . . . honey, surely you read my letter." He slipped his arm around her. "That's why you're here, jah?"

"I'm here 'cause I want you to tell me how you could go back on your word, being with another girl. We're betrothed, Caleb."

"I told you . . ." He paused. "If I could do it all over again, I'd stand up to Daed and not seek out Susannah."

She stared at him, not yet sure whether to believe him.

"Susannah's nothin' but trouble," he said.

"I'd hate to think where you'd be if you *had* defied your father."

"Out on my ear, like Rebekah." He looked at her. "And I'd lose the land."

"And where would you go if your father kicked you out?"

He was silent for a time. Then he sighed loudly. "I don't know. Maybe Mamma's folks—they have a vacant Dawdi Haus."

She couldn't see his eyes, nor all of his face. His reply made her wonder. Was he merely throwing out an option to sound persuasive?

Fact was, she had no way of knowing, because he had already *made* the choice to follow his father's bidding. He'd flirted with Susannah, trying to . . . what? But no, Nellie wouldn't ask what he'd had in mind, or what his father had hoped might come of the encounter. Too painful.

Caleb broke the stillness, reaching around her to pull her close. "Ya sure you're warm enough? You're shiverin' so. I'd hate for you to get sick again. What if we stopped off and got warmed up at my grandparents' place? I could show you the Dawdi Haus I'm talkin' about."

"Ach . . . I don't know, Caleb."

"It's where my Daed's parents will move once you and I are married. Mamma's folk live in the main house . . . so the Dawdi Haus is empty."

"Empty?"

"Jah. There's even a second smaller addition built on to that one, too . . . both vacant, though only for the time being. Someday it'll be all filled up with our aging relatives—yours and mine."

She'd seen as many as four additions attached to a farmhouse, all graduated in size, so this was no surprise. It was his suggestion about spending time there that surprised her.

"Well, are you sure it's all right?" she asked.

"What better place to pass the time on a freezin' cold night? Courting in an open buggy in the dead of winter is downright silly, don't ya think?"

She heartily agreed, beginning to shiver already.

"No one'll know," he said. "If that's what you're worried 'bout."

Before she could challenge him further, he added, "It's not as if we haven't been alone before. As a courting couple, we could even spend time in your bedroom, too."

Nellie was well aware of that—she had a special courting loveseat for just such an occasion—but she wasn't sure why he was so quick to mention the latter now. All the same, he was quite right. No matter where they went, they'd be alone, so why not take shelter from the cold beside a nice fire?

A golden light streamed from Rosanna's kitchen as Reuben lifted the woolen blanket off his driving horse, preparing to head home. He would never forget the look of innocent anticipation on both Elias's and Rosanna's faces. He'd offered a brief prayer for them, asking God to protect and keep the young twins safe, as well. Elias had offered his own request for "wisdom from above" at the tail end, which gave Reuben hope. The youthful couple had grown in the knowledge of the Lord in a very short time, and already they were being tested beyond what Reuben himself thought he might be able to bear.

He and his Betsy had never had trouble conceiving or birthing their nine children. There was something particularly tragic about having your first son offered under the guise of a heaven-sent gift, only to have him stolen away.

Martha had asked Rhoda to read a selection from *Uncle Arthur's Bedtime Stories* to Emma and Matty while Benny and Jimmy were having a shared bath. Feeling quite obliged to her brother and sister-in-law for offering her a place to stay, Rhoda was eager to do whatever she could to ease Martha's nearly endless duties. Tonight Emma and Matty were clean and cozy in their nightclothes, ready for *Aendi* Rhoda to read the "Susie and the Scissors" story.

Matty curled up next to her on the bed while Emma sat nearby, legs crossed beneath her long cotton nightgown and bathrobe. Midway through the story, Matty decided he wanted Mamma reading instead, and soon Emma was mimicking him. "Mamma, Mamma . . ." Rhoda realized she was a poor substitute for their mother.

"How about I sing a song?" Rhoda asked.

"Sing 'bout Jesus," Emma suggested, smiling.

Rhoda didn't know what sort of songs she meant. "You sing one, sweetie."

"*Yesus liebt mich* . . ." Emma sang in her childish voice, Matty joining in as best he could. When they'd finished, Emma grinned and looked her full in the face. "'Tis true, ain't so?"

Rhoda scarcely knew what to say. Till now, she hadn't thought of Jesus loving her. The preacher at the meetinghouse talked that way to be sure, but Rhoda had never thought of it so casually.

Martha appeared in the doorway and came to kiss the children, signaling bedtime. Rhoda likewise said good-night and kissed their soft foreheads and said, "Don't let the bedbugs bite."

"If they do . . . squeeze 'em tight." Martha chuckled.

Rhoda had to smile as she looked over her shoulder at them before closing the door. Such cute little ones. Now it was her turn to bathe, but she wanted to share tomorrow's plans with Martha first, so she followed her down the hall, pausing at Martha and James's bedroom door. "Do ya mind if I come in?"

"Sure, Rhoda."

"Mind if I close the door, too?"

Martha's face brightened. "Ah, secrets?"

"Not really." But she thought again. "Jah, I guess 'tis." She began to tell about Ken Kraybill and her supper plans for tomorrow night. "What do ya think?"

"Sounds like you're inchin' away from the People mighty quick, jah?"

That she was, and with little remorse.

"My mother always said you should only date the kind of man you'd want to marry." Martha went to sit near the foot of the bed.

"I can see the benefit of that," Rhoda said.

"So what would ya want with an English fella?"

"He ain't Amish, that's what." Her words probably sounded brazen.

Martha scrutinized her. "You're ready to leave the Plain life behind?"

"'Tis a puzzle." Rhoda sighed. "Some days I think I am. Others, no."

Martha had a big talk on. "I s'pose you'll discover some good out there in the world—look at us, we've got ourselves a radio . . . and a car, for goodness' sake. James says we can spread the Gospel better because of it—gives us a way to see more believers and whatnot, too."

"So are ya saying you're staying Plain, even though in some ways ya ain't?"

"We're set apart but keen on traveling to church more than twice a month. With a car, we'll get to the meetinghouse more quickly, maybe pick up others along the way. To us it's simply a better buggy, not somethin' to take pride in."

"It's all so confusing," admitted Rhoda.

"The way James sees it, it's hard to say you know you're saved and still be Amish."

"You'll dress Plain but drive a car and dial up folk on a telephone, ya mean?"

"Why not?"

Rhoda thought on that. It sure seemed like Martha had this figured out. If only she herself could be just as certain.

Nellie felt awkward, even shy, as Caleb led her into the darkened house, pushing the door open for her and swiftly closing it behind him. He leaned back against it, gently pulling her into his arms. "Come here, love. . . ."

They scarcely moved as their eyes grew accustomed to the dimness, even though if she were to admit it, she kept her own mostly closed. In spite of herself, in spite of all that had happened—all the forces that threatened to keep them apart—she savored how wonderfully near he was. Her broken heart seemed to mend in his reassuring embrace, and she pushed away the memory of all the sad hours after last Sunday's scare, hoping . . . wishing what she'd seen with Susannah Lapp was a bad dream.

"I'm sorry," he whispered against her ear. "Forgive me?"

Could she? She felt herself starting to cry.

"I had a choice, and I made the wrong one, I know now." He caressed her face with the back of his hand. "I didn't need to talk with Susannah to know she's not who I want."

Nellie could scarcely speak for her tears. "I wish to believe ya . . . I do."

"I'll make it up to you, love."

"Jah, I forgive you." She wiped away her tears.

He nodded. She could see him faintly in what little light reflected from the snow outside. The black silhouette of the barn, where he'd put his courting buggy and unhitched horse, filled much of the view through the back window of the Dawdi Haus.

"You're sure this is a good idea . . . being here, Caleb?"

He kissed her cheek, then the tip of her nose. "We're together now. Someday soon we'll always be."

Should she give in to his ardent affection and simply enjoy his near-ness—this almost too-special closeness?

"I love you, Nellie Mae." He pulled her still closer.

An unfamiliar, nearly delirious feeling swept over her. It was probably wrong to yield, but, oh, she wanted to. "My Caleb . . ." She wrapped her arms around his neck.

He kissed her hairline, bumping back her Kapp in his enthusiasm. "I was scared I'd lost you."

Nellie tried to breathe, her face against his. Something clicked in her, like an alarm somewhere in the distance. Their fondness for each other was far too powerful to be given much rein. They shouldn't linger here in this tantalizing seclusion. Slowly, consciously, she pulled back, holding him at arm's length. "We . . . shouldn't stay. . . ."

"Why not?"

She inched back. Being this close to Caleb made her all ferhoodled. "I think we'd best be goin', truly."

"Let's just talk awhile. Come, I'll build a fire."

Even without the woodstove fired up, the kitchen of this snug Dawdi Haus was far warmer than Caleb's open carriage. She shivered at the thought of returning to the elements for the long ride home.

"What is it?" He gently tugged her back to him. "Are you frightened?"

"A little, jah."

"There's nothing to fear. I promise." He led her through the darkness of the small kitchen to the equally cozy sitting area, where an upholstered settee was positioned near a black stove.

She let him kiss her hand, unsure how long he planned for them to remain. "Caleb . . . I . . ."

He pressed his finger on her lips. "You're worrying needlessly. Let's just enjoy this evening."

She longed to do exactly that . . . but without realizing it, she'd stepped away from him.

Caleb pursued her. "Just pretend we're riding in my courting buggy, Nellie Mae . . . how 'bout that?" He kissed her cheek. "Can you think of our time here like that?"

Can I? This setting was far different than a ride in his open buggy, or even sitting beside him on the wrought-iron bench by the millstream. Anybody knew that.

This time Caleb trembled as he held her near, and her only thought was how much she liked being this close to him.

"Jah . . . I can," Nellie said at last, her worry fading as she surrendered again to his tender embrace.

CHAPTER 33

The settee was nearly too small for the two of them, yet she and Caleb had been whispering for nearly an hour now, reveling in the warmth of the fire and each other. Her feet were tucked beneath her and she leaned on his chest.

After a time, she stretched her legs and went to stand closer to the woodstove. "I like this little house. It's perfect for two, jah?"

"Well, too small for the family we'll have someday."

He was right, of course—she wanted as many babies as the Good Lord saw fit to give them.

Caleb patted the settee. "Come sit with me again, Nellie Mae."

She found her way back to him in the firelight, and he reached for her hand. Snuggling again, they talked for a while longer of the family they longed to have someday. Then Caleb gently caressed her face. "You're ever so lovely. I can't imagine a prettier wife. . . ." He paused, reaching up to touch her Kapp, letting his hand rest there momentarily. "Would you think poorly of me if I asked you to take your hair down, love?"

Nellie was startled. Wasn't it enough that they'd hugged so intimately? "I've seen it down before, remember?"

She did recall the night he'd seen it unwound, long and flowing. The night she'd rushed to the door, sure he'd come to ask her to marry him in the privacy of her room. She had been robbed of that special time. They both had.

Unexpectedly, she thought of Susannah. Wouldn't *she* do Caleb's bidding if the tables were turned? A jealous fury rose in her at a vision of Susannah reaching for Caleb.

Slowly reaching up, she removed her head covering, slipping it off with ease. Then she began to slide the hair pins out, one by one.

Caleb leaned over and, before she could respond, his hands mingled with hers, as together they undid her long, thick hair.

He turned her face to him, and he cupped her face in his hands. His touch took her breath away. Was he going to lip-kiss her, their first real kiss?

432

"You're mine, Nellie Mae, no matter what my father says."

Nellie fought her senses. The distant alarm she'd sensed earlier had returned. What she knew was right—what Mamma had taught her—clashed against what she wanted to do with all of her heart. Suzy had written about feeling the same way in her diary, including a Scripture about despising what was evil and clinging to the good.

But Caleb was miles different from other boys. She believed that much even as his hand slid down the full length of her hair. "I can't count the times I've imagined this moment, Nellie."

She raised her face to him.

He ran his thumbs lightly over her eyebrows before leaning near to kiss her lips softly. Lingering there, he backed away for a moment, looking longingly into her eyes. Then his lips found hers again with such fervency she felt dizzy. But she did not wince or move away, delighting in this new thrill.

"Nellie . . . we'll be together soon. Married. I promise."

She nodded slowly and then leaned forward and kissed him back.

"Oh, love . . ." Caleb's voice was husky as he rose to put out the gas lamp.

Still nestled in Caleb's arms, Nellie Mae fought hard the sleep that threatened to overtake her. Caleb had already succumbed, his head back against the settee, his chest rising and falling slowly.

Nellie had always thought she'd wait to lip-kiss till after she'd said her wedding vows, but the warmth of the room and the tempting privacy here, in this tranquil place, were more than she'd bargained for.

Glancing again at Caleb, she slipped her hand into his limp one. How long should she let him sleep before they headed back into the blistering cold? She must not stay out all night; nor did she want to worry Mamma, most of all.

Nellie wished she might pin up her hair again, for she felt worldly with it cascading all over her, caught between her back and the settee and Caleb's shoulder. Yet lest she awaken him too soon, she decided to let her hair remain long and flowing, trapped between her desire to fully embrace this night and the reality of the passing hours.

No longer able to keep her eyes open, Nellie eventually gave in to the heaviness behind them. *Just for a few minutes,* she told herself.

"Wake up, Caleb! Wake up, I say!"

Someone was shaking him, and when he opened his eyes, Caleb looked into the glowering face of his grandfather.

"*Du muscht mir here!* Hearken to me!"

Gradually he became aware of his surroundings—the Dawdi Haus . . . and Nellie Mae asleep on his shoulder. And his grandfather, who was staring at Nellie, too, with her lovely hair strewn over her shoulders.

Caleb sat up quickly.

"I'll be havin' a word with ya, son. Upstairs."

Caleb rose without speaking, first releasing Nellie, who must also have slept through much of the night on the settee. The old stove was now as cold as it had been warm earlier. Nervously he followed up the narrow steps. Without a doubt, he would catch what for.

Were the private hours alone with his beloved worth the tongue-lashing he was sure to receive? As Dawdi closed the door to the front bedroom, Caleb was suddenly concerned for Nellie Mae, who was all alone now. Would Mammi go in and speak straight to her, too?

Her hair being down is an abomination.

He recalled how responsive Nellie had been last evening. How, once he'd assured her there was nothing to fear, she had seemingly enjoyed his touch, leaning toward him as they kissed. But there was plenty to fear, he knew. *What have I done?*

Wide awake now, he sat down on the cane chair as Dawdi instructed. "Listen here, Caleb, if I were your father, I'd be out and out *angscht*—concerned."

Eyes cast down, he nodded. He knew better than to speak too soon, if at all. He must wait till Dawdi had his say and only then offer an apology. He had to do something to keep this mum, though. *What a foolish thing . . . not counting the cost beforehand.* Nellie was far more prudent than he—she'd asked repeatedly if they were taking unnecessary risks, and her fears had been proven true. For putting her in such a bad light, he was most sorry.

"You ain't turning out to be like your big brother Abe, are ya?" Dawdi bellowed.

At the mention of Abe's name, Caleb blanched. Abe was the family's black sheep, as his father had called him for a full year following—that and so much worse. No, Caleb was nothing like that brother.

"I'm waitin' for your answer, Caleb." Dawdi's eyes were black as stones.

"My intentions toward Nellie Mae have nothin' to do with Abe's mistake." Caleb swallowed his dread and considered how shallow his defense would sound. After all, his grandfather had found the two of them asleep together.

"Well, my guess is that you'll be marryin' this girl, jah?"

"This year."

"The sooner the better, ain't that right?" Dawdi's eyes narrowed, growing more solemn. "I'll let you in on a secret, Caleb. What you feel for Nellie Mae has nothin' at all to do with marriage or a future together. Not commitment, neither."

Inwardly, Caleb disagreed. He loved holding Nellie in his arms, kissing her—he'd scarcely been able to stop. She was to be his bride, after all.

Dawdi rose and stood in the window, his outline dark in the predawn light. "You like this girl a lot, that's apparent. But if you love her, you'll make sure she's pure on your weddin' night."

Caleb cringed. This Dawdi was more plainspoken than his own father, who had never talked about the birds and the bees or suchlike. "We did not sin as you believe," he spoke up.

Dawdi made a vague gesture in the dim light. "I don't mean to run this into the ground, but hear me out. The first kiss opens the door. You begin to crave more kissin' and whatnot, and soon you yearn to have all of her." His brow furrowed as he pulled on his long gray beard.

Dawdi walked toward him, paused, frowning, and sat down again. "There's more, Caleb."

He shifted in his seat. When would this stream of criticism cease?

"That's Reuben Fisher's daughter downstairs, jah?"

Caleb felt goose bumps down his back. "Jah, Nellie Mae is Reuben's."

A deafening silence, then—"I think you know your father's stand on courting a girl from Preacher Manny's bunch."

"Jah, I do."

"Yet you deliberately spent the night with her?" Dawdi harrumphed. "How do you think your father will react to this?"

My *father?* He stood up to protest. "I promise you, Dawdi, this will never happen again."

His grandfather rose, eyes glaring. "That is for certain, and your father will see to it."

Caleb groaned. "But, Dawdi . . ."

"How could you risk your land for a girl from the Fisher family? Haven't you heard the stories—how Suzy died in the arms of an Englischer?"

Caleb dropped his gaze.

"Your inheritance hangs in the balance. Don't be a fool." Dawdi eyed him, his meaning all too clear to Caleb.

Too stunned to speak, Caleb left the room.

Downstairs, he found Nellie weeping, her hair wound up in a makeshift bun, eyes red and swollen. Mammi sat erect in a wooden chair.

Because he'd brought all of this upon her, Caleb fought the lump in his throat as he helped her into her long woolen coat. Mammi gave them both a sour look as he ushered Nellie Mae out of the front room and toward the back door without another word.

Nellie could not speak for her embarrassment, not only for herself but for the dreadful things Caleb's grandfather had presumed of them. Pressing her lips together to keep from crying, she shivered in the morning cold as she recalled the shouting concerning Abe Yoder, Caleb's oldest married brother. Had Abe pushed the sacred boundaries as a youth? If so, to think David Yoder and his family had kept that secret till now.

Her thoughts whirled as Caleb hurried the horse, recalling how he'd shown such grave concern over Suzy's sowing wild oats . . . over *her* suspected indiscretions—mere hearsay at the time. Yet, all the while, he'd been privy to his own brother's very real sin.

It appeared no one was good enough. No matter how hard she strived, it was impossible to completely measure up. Preacher Manny had said so quite clearly the time she'd gone to the New Order church, adding that God's Son did for us what we couldn't do for ourselves.

With the way she'd longed for Caleb last night, Nellie was a sinner, too. She'd wanted him enough to prematurely push past the courtship boundaries, letting down her hair.

Even so, she mustn't fret over what might come of her and Caleb's recklessness. She'd made a poor choice, and now she must live with the consequences. She and Caleb had set themselves up for being found out, and that's exactly what had transpired.

She shouldn't have allowed her jealousy over Susannah Lapp to fuel her vulnerability. Yet she had no excuse. Nellie knew that she, and not Susannah, was responsible for her actions.

Knowing the truth as she did, she could easily let herself be disgusted with Caleb and his family. She thought of Caleb's brother Abe and found herself grinding her teeth. The Yoders were the biggest hypocrites she'd ever known!

Presently Caleb's breathing was rapid, as fast as when suddenly they'd pushed apart last night, ceasing their kissing. But he also wore a look of both determination and frustration, one she had not witnessed before.

Truly, they were equally at fault. After all, hadn't she encouraged his affection . . . giving hers so gladly?

Her emotions flew back and forth between love and sheer disappointment—with Caleb and with herself. She sat straight as a board as the horse galloped all the way back to Beaver Dam Road, coming to a halt at the end of her lane.

"When the dust settles, we must talk." Caleb jumped out of the buggy and came around to help her down.

She needed no help and wished to go inside quickly. Nonetheless, he pulled her up close and, before she could object, kissed her soundly on the lips. Nothing like the sweet yet passionate kisses earlier, this kiss felt reckless, even possessive. Slipping free, she stepped back and appraised her beau. "It was impossible not to hear what your Dawdi said 'bout your brother Abe."

He looked her square in the eyes. "This doesn't change anything for us, does it?"

She stared past him to the pale horizon. There was precious little time before her father would make his way to the barn. Mamma would be getting up, too, setting the table for breakfast.

I spent all night with Caleb, and now it is the Lord's Day.

"Next time, we'll play it smart and stay at the millstream," he said quietly.

She looked back at the house, relieved the windows were still dark. "Next time? *What* next time? Didn't you hear your Dawdi?"

"Oh, Nellie, have I wronged you so?" He reached for her hand.

"We can't take back what we've already given." She felt as guilty as if she'd lost her virtue. "Our first kisses will never be new again." She whimpered in his arms, her face pressed against the harsh weave of his wool coat.

"No matter what Dawdi said, I can't be sorry for what we've shared, Nellie Mae. I just can't."

She understood that. Oh, how she did! She loved him desperately, yet she was more afraid than ever for their future.

"I best be goin'." Nellie made a move toward the door, but Caleb quickly seized her shoulders, turning her around.

"Nellie, wait . . ." He sighed loudly. "We may have gotten a bit carried away. I'm sorry for that."

"So am I." She turned and walked toward the house.

"This doesn't change my love for you." Caleb's words hung in the air like frost clinging hard to a tree.

Nellie whispered his name with each snowy step . . . as guilt engulfed her.

CHAPTER 34

N ellie plodded out to the carriage bright and early to squeeze in along with Dat, Mamma, Nan, and Rebekah. This day she would be counted among those missing from the old church.

As dreadful as she felt over last night, she tried to dismiss Caleb from her thoughts while the buggy headed into the sun. All down the shimmering road, she wondered if the remorse she carried in her heart showed on her face. She'd peered into the small hand mirror in her room, searching for the slightest hint, fearing the People would suspect what she'd done.

A single moment had the power to alter one's life, Mama had once told her. She'd thought the same of Suzy's reckless living—her sister had learned of the perils of first love the hard way. Sometimes such affection was as short-lived as the morning dew. Mamma had always said it was old love—*long* love—that was best in the end.

Presently Mamma was commenting on how much warmer it was today than it had been for weeks.

Dat spoke up. "Months, it seems."

Sitting behind her parents, Nellie tuned out the occasional remarks from Nan and Rebekah next to her, wishing for solitude. She was nearly too tired to sit up.

The fields were dazzling white as far as she could see. Thanks to the unexpected sunshine, the day was brighter in all respects—a welcome change from the many gray weeks.

Nan and Rebekah continued their pleasant prattle, and Nellie went deep within herself, where the truth hurt most. She'd thought more highly of herself than she ought. She was all puffed up, as Dat would say—filled with the pride of life, *her* life . . . thinking she could withstand temptation and putting herself right in the middle of it last night. She had tempted Caleb and herself, believing she was invulnerable to sin. According to Suzy's diary—which she'd opened and read part of again this morning—it was far better to be repentant than to continually try to be good enough . . . on her own strength.

Nellie in that moment realized why she'd attempted to be good and failed: She'd wanted to do things her way. *That's pride, pure and simple*, Suzy had scrawled across the top of one diary page, when considering her desire to forge her own path.

Nellie and her younger sister had quite a lot in common.

Caleb stood outside the preacher's farmhouse, dog tired. He looked around, aware that Nellie Mae was not present. Had he offended her beyond her ability to forgive him? Certainly she'd not been herself when he'd taken her home before dawn—and no wonder. He could kick himself now for setting them up for his grandfather's accusations.

Today, following the common meal, Dawdi would seek out Daed and the hammer would drop. It was not possible to brace himself for a calamitous response from his father, but he would not hesitate to say that Nellie and he were actually innocent, no matter how things may have looked to Dawdi.

Looking now at Abe, where his brother stood in the lineup of men waiting to go into the house for worship, he noticed the set of his jaw. Was Abe always this solemn on the Lord's Day? Or was he merely reverent, and nothing more? Not till today had Caleb paid much mind to Abe, who already had five children and another on the way. Was he content with his lot in life, without an inheritance?

I must get Daed to hear me out, he thought. *If only I can get him to see the light . . . that Nellie Mae is still Old Order through and through.*

It was foolish, perhaps, to hope, but after last night, Caleb was convinced he must have Nellie Mae for his bride at any cost.

In spite of a lack of appetite, Caleb forced himself to eat. He kept his eye on his grandfather in mute dread as the older man set down his coffee and rose unsteadily to his feet. Caleb watched over the rim of his own cup as Dawdi lumbered across the room with grim determination. Standing before Caleb's father, Dawdi tilted his head to the side, beckoning Caleb to follow. At least the whole room wouldn't be privy to the confrontation to come.

Realizing it was futile to avoid the impending clash, Caleb rose from the bench and followed his father and grandfather out of the room, pausing only long enough to squeeze his mother's hand as he passed.

In the utility room, he pulled on his coat. From the small window, he glimpsed his father and grandfather already in the yard, their breath rising and mingling over their heads at the heated force of their words. There was no mistaking the reddening of Daed's cheeks above his beard.

Caleb sighed and headed out to meet his fate.

His grandfather passed him on his way back toward the warmth of the house, his expression worrisome, though regretful nonetheless. Daed remained several yards off, hands on his hips.

"Son," his father began, "I would not have believed it if your own grandfather hadn't told me. Did I not forbid you to see that Fisher girl? That's bad enough. But to carry on with her in your Dawdi's house? What kind of—"

"We did nothing wrong."

"All night, with her hair down—not wrong? What kind of son have I raised? And you wanted me to believe you loved this girl, respected her?!"

"I do, Daed, I plan to—"

"Were you hoping to force my hand? Well, you're dreadfully mistaken if you think I would give you my land, my life's blood, just so you can have your way with that loose girl!"

"Daed, please—"

"Do you reckon me ignorant? Just because you are—thinking with your body instead of your brain! New church indeed—a woman up to Eve's old tricks, if you ask me!"

"I don't deny I was foolish to take her to the Dawdi Haus. But that was my doing. On my word, Nellie is as innocent today as she ever was."

"And how can that be?"

"It's my fault, Daed, not hers. I bear the full responsibility."

"Indeed you will, Caleb. A mighty heavy price you'll pay. I demand you abandon your relationship with Reuben's daughter and repent . . . to me. Then, and only then, will I consider handing over my land. Meanwhile, you have a single hour to pack your things and get out of my house."

The words—and the cold calculation in which they were delivered—were a knife to his soul. He assumed his father would be angry, but he hadn't expected this. Nor had Caleb expected to feel his father's rejection so deeply. Still, this man was his Daed, his pillar and strength since boyhood. How could it not hurt to be condemned so mercilessly?

Since it was such a sunny, nearly balmy day, Rebekah suggested she visit the Old Order Amish family where she helped each week with the little ones. Nan offered to take her and invited Nellie Mae along. "Let's get some fresh air."

Even though Nellie had gone on the long ride to church, she jumped at the chance to ride with Nan and her friend. She felt disconnected and anxious for companionship.

It turned out Rebekah was invited to stay with the family, who offered to come by the Fishers' later for her things. Nan and Nellie rode back home together, talking for a while about Rebekah's eagerness to influence all of her old church friends toward saving grace. "She views livin' with them as a way to witness . . . hopin' to lead them to the Lord."

Nellie Mae hardly knew what to think. Caleb's sister had become a zealous soul in only a short time, a transformation she'd also observed in both Dat and Mamma, as well as in Nan. "God's Word has amazing power to divide and to heal," Preacher Manny had said that very morning. "Allow it to renew your mind . . . and your heart." He'd quoted a Scripture, too, one she'd never heard. *"Let this mind be in you, which was also in Christ Jesus."*

Renew her heart? Would that remove the sting of her guilt?

I can be forgiven, she thought. *Made clean—like new?*

Looking out at the stark black trees as she rode, Nellie knew her goose was cooked, and by her own hand—just as Caleb's was, only for a different reason. If she continued to soothe her conscience by going to the new church, which had pleased her family today, then Caleb would not want to court her.

How will he ever convince his father to relent now?

Deacon Lapp's house came into view as they rounded a bend, and she saw Susannah outside with several of her sisters, playing with their dogs. Nellie's heart sank at the sight of her.

Nan looked over at Nellie from the driver's seat. "You're so quiet all of a sudden."

"S'pose I am."

"Was ist letz?—What's the matter?"

Nellie hesitated to tell Nan all that had transpired in the past twenty-four hours, yet here was Nan, wanting to chat, her face reflecting genuine concern.

Nellie took a breath, hoping she wasn't handing off a burden to Nan. "Did you ever let your hair down for a beau? Ever even think of it?"

"Why *would* I?" Nan was staring at her. "Why'd ya ask such a thing?"

"Just wonderin'."

"Well, I know some girls who do. But from what I've heard, it ain't such a good idea. Leads to . . . well, worse things."

Quickly Nellie changed the subject to Rhoda, and thankfully Nan latched on to that. "Should we stop over at James's to visit? You miss her as much as I do, I'm sure," Nellie Mae said.

"More than she prob'ly realizes."

"We could drop in right quick."

"Not today," Nan said.

Nellie paused. "Surely she's sorry she left, wouldn't you think?"

Nan sighed and urged the horse onward. "She seemed bent on leaving, and we haven't seen her since."

A wave of renewed sadness swept over Nellie. "We can only hope she gets her fill of the fancy . . . and soon," she replied.

It was a bit chilly in the Kraybills' formal dining room, and Rhoda was glad to be offered some tea. When it was served, piping hot, the steam floated above the dainty cup. She tried to hold it just so, the way she'd seen Mrs. Kraybill do. Mr. Kraybill, on the other hand, was having black coffee, as was Ken Kraybill, their blue-eyed nephew. His eyes weren't the only appealing thing about him as he sat tall in his chair across from her, frequently singling her out with his friendly gaze.

The tea gradually warmed her, and when it came time for Mrs. Kraybill to serve her homemade strawberry cheesecake pie, Rhoda noticed both Ken and Mr. Kraybill waited until Mrs. Kraybill picked up her small fork—the only one left at each place setting—before reaching for theirs.

She felt rather ignorant, though relieved at having managed to somehow make it through the meal this far. The multiple forks and spoons on either side of the lovely china plates, the neatly pressed white linen napkins, and the crystal vase of flowers that graced the center of the table—all of it was a wholly new experience.

Even knowing when to speak was a challenge. She'd taken small bites, like Nan and Nellie Mae always did, to make sure it didn't take long to quickly chew and swallow before replying when someone spoke to her. Thankfully the food was just delicious, all made from scratch, as she knew Mrs. Kraybill enjoyed doing.

Self-conscious in her outfit, despite Mrs. Kraybill's—and even Martha's—assurances that she looked very nice, Rhoda had to remind herself to breathe. Especially when she looked up only slightly to ask for the sugar and felt Ken's eyes on her. Did he think she looked like a Plain girl masquerading in an Englischer's getup? Or did he even know she was Amish?

Thank goodness for Mr. Kraybill, who had carried the conversation nearly the entire meal. Presently it was Mrs. Kraybill who was telling an amusing story about having gone to the pantry and realizing one of the children had removed most of the labels on the soup cans. They'd had what she called "mystery meals" for weeks on end.

Ken chuckled, and Rhoda watched the corners of his mouth turn up, accentuating his handsome features.

Rhoda took another little bite of the pie and was reaching for her teacup when Ken addressed her. "Have you lived in this area long?"

"My whole life."

Mrs. Kraybill intervened. "Rhoda's father raises horses not far from here."

Not a peep about her Amish background. Was that purposely left out? Try as she might, Rhoda did not recall Mrs. Kraybill ever saying that Ken was aware of her being Plain. But now that she was here, flaunting fine and fancy clothes and a loose, English-style bun, she guessed it might not be such a good idea to come right out and spoil things—not with the admiring way Ken looked at her.

Pushing away the memory of another Englischer's gaze, she asked, "How long have you lived in Strasburg?"

"Nearly three years. My family lived and farmed in the Georgetown area, southeast of Strasburg, where I grew up." He paused to take a sip of his coffee before continuing. "I purchased an old house listed on the National Registry of Historical Buildings, right on Main Street. It's something of a real-estate investment. I live on the third story and rent out the first and second floors."

"Like a bed and breakfast?" Rhoda blushed, realizing he probably was not a cook, unless he hired someone to do that.

His smile lingered and she had to look away. "Interesting you mentioned that, because I've thought I might want to go that route someday."

She wondered suddenly if he was looking for a cook, perhaps. But no, surely that was not why he was sitting here at the Kraybills' candlelit table. His presence was, after all, Mrs. Kraybill's doing, or so Rhoda assumed.

"Shall we move somewhere more comfortable?" Mrs. Kraybill asked, getting up.

Rhoda rose as well, reaching for her plate and the teacup, thinking she would help by carrying them into the kitchen.

"Leave everything on the table," instructed Mrs. Kraybill in a near whisper.

The adjournment into the front room, or living room as Mrs. Kraybill was fond of calling it, was more relaxing for the three of them than it was for Rhoda, who was seated next to Ken on the sofa.

Glancing occasionally at Mrs. Kraybill, who seemed very pleased with herself, Rhoda put two and two together. Here was a young man who looked to be in his mid- to late-twenties, yet with possibly no prospects for a wife. Had he, too, been passed over for some reason? She studied Mrs. Kraybill's demeanor, wondering.

The talk turned from Ken's favorite movie star, Sean Connery—whoever that was—to Mr. Kraybill's obvious concern over the cost of the war in Vietnam. "Over twenty-five billion dollars a year. Imagine that!" he said with a fierce frown.

Well, Rhoda certainly couldn't begin to. She wasn't even certain how to write a number that big, let alone comprehend how it might otherwise be spent. Mr. Kraybill obviously had no such difficulty himself as he sat with one leg balanced on his other knee. "Really," he said, leaning forward as if to emphasize his next point, "this war has become too personal for LBJ."

Rhoda listened carefully, concerned that Ken might think she was a bump on a log. She'd heard the president referred to by his initials before, but she didn't know enough about politics to express an opinion.

Just now she felt like a fish flopping on dry land. How might she ever fit in with fancy folk, really? It was one thing to work for them, but to socialize? She must start reading the newspaper more carefully, during her morning break. More interaction with English folk was key if she truly wanted to be part of their world.

When it came time for the Kraybills to put their children to bed, Rhoda and Ken found themselves alone. Unexpectedly, he asked if he might call her sometime, and she felt terribly shy. He seemed very gentlemanlike— nothing like the dreadful Glenn Miller—and Rhoda thought it might be nice to spend more time with him. *Another way to get better acquainted with the English world.* Demurely, she nodded and smiled before giving him James and Martha's new phone number.

"I'll look forward to it." Ken smiled a most pleasant smile.

"So will I," she replied, glad she hadn't said "jah."

CHAPTER 35

A ll six of them, including babies Eli and Rosie, were situated in the bishop's front room Wednesday afternoon. The two couples faced each other, Rosanna cradling Rosie as she sat beside Elias, and Kate holding Eli, next to John.

Bishop Joseph stood before them, all in black, except his white shirt. He explained to them the purpose of the meeting, his expression grave. Swallowing hard, Rosanna could hardly keep her eyes off little Eli, sound asleep in Kate's arms. Oh, but if he hadn't grown in the past week! She longed to hold him again, to breathe in his sweet baby scent, but she refused a single tear, determined to keep a sober face, no matter what might result from this most awkward and difficult gathering.

"Are the four of you in unity?" the bishop asked.

John and Kate shook their heads no.

"Elias and Rosanna?"

"We pray only for God's will." Elias's voice was steadfast.

"The outcome, then, is not your concern?" asked the bishop, singling out Elias.

"We desire what is best for these little ones" was his confident reply, and Rosanna regarded him with a healthy dose of pride.

"And you, John? What is your answer to that?"

John's face turned red. "This here's my son, and Rosanna has our daughter . . . over there with her." He breathed slowly and Kate momentarily put a hand on his arm. "We'll be raisin' the twins as cousins, if you see fit, Bishop. 'Tis how we look at it."

Everything within Rosanna began to churn. "No . . ." The word slipped out before she could stop it. She looked to Elias for support, groaning inwardly.

"My wife thinks of Eli as her own—we both do. We love him just as we love Rosie and intend to follow through with our agreement to raise them both." Elias looked across at Kate. "You've broken your cousin's heart, Kate. Truly you have."

The bishop cleared his throat. "No stone throwing, Elias."

A strike against them; the air went out of Rosanna. Bishop was leaning toward the Beilers, it seemed.

"Kate, you'll have your say-so now." The bishop gestured to her.

"Eli's the fruit of my womb. He belongs in the church of his forefathers."

"Jah, growin' up in the Old Ways," John spoke up. "We can't think of our son learnin' heresy!"

Elias rose to his feet. "Did not the Son of Man come to show us the way to the Father? Aren't we all sinners, in need of redemption? You call that heresy, to be counted among the saved?"

John leapt from his chair. "Our son should be shielded from the lies of Satan. Declarin' you're saved? That's the worst of it!"

"And Rosie?" The bishop stepped forward. "Is it right for *her* to know and embrace such teachings?" He eyed John and Elias. Making a motion toward the chairs, he said, "Please sit."

Both men took their seats. The room became hushed once again.

The bishop shook his head. "No amount of reasoning will solve this knotty problem. I see it as being a bone of contention all the days of these youngsters' lives . . . and yours." He scrutinized each couple.

Rosanna prayed silently, trembling within and without. *Show mercy, dear Lord . . . give us your grace.*

Bishop Joseph continued, "There will be no end to the strife 'tween your families." Alternating his gaze between the couples, he pulled on his long beard. "I'll leave the four of you to have one last chance to hash this out. When I return, I want you *cousins* to have come to a reasonable solution." Turning, the bishop left the room.

Rosanna looked down at darling Rosie—her tuft of light brown hair was so thin and silky. Somehow she managed to rest peacefully amidst this storm of wills.

Elias sat stiffly, tension emanating as he spoke suddenly. "John and Kate, don't you see what we bear . . . the pain we have lived with these few days without Eli? We love that little boy dearly." Elias paused as if trying to maintain his grip on his emotions. "His sister Rosie has been cryin' all week without him next to her in the playpen. Multiply that by all the years ahead . . . it ain't right."

The silence was broken only by Eli's quick gurgle as he moved in his sleep.

"Kate, won't you take pity on your cousin? On Rosie?" Elias asked.

"We've said our piece," John replied. "You've made a poor choice, leaving the church of your baptism . . . and we're takin' back our gift."

Kate spoke up. "Out of the kindness of our hearts, we'll allow you to keep Rosie as your own. That's more than fair."

"Aw, Kate," Elias said, his voice quavering. "Can't ya see? That's awful wrong."

The bishop returned, wearing a deep frown. "Is there no resolution, then?"

"We've offered Rosie, but they want both babies," John told the bishop.

"Well, then. I have no choice but to rule in this unspeakable situation." The man of God straightened to his full height.

Rosanna noticed the room brighten as unexpected sunshine streamed in from behind a cloud, filling the front windows with light. They'd gathered in this large room many times over the years for Preaching, blending their voices in one accord with their kinfolk . . . including John and Kate.

"The Lord God created these young ones as unique and separate people, yet they are bound fast by unseen cords." Going to Eli first, the bishop touched his head, lingering there. Then he moved across to Rosanna and placed his hand on sleeping Rosie's head.

Kate scowled at Rosanna, who remained silent.

Looking helplessly at her husband, Rosanna held back her tears. *All the happy days and years ahead . . .*

Then, though her heart was breaking, she could no longer keep still. "Bishop?"

He looked at her tenderly, his eyes filled with understanding, as if he knew what she was compelled to say. "Speak your piece, Rosanna King," he urged her.

"Ach, the babies shouldn't be torn apart." Her chin trembled. "Eli and Rosie must grow up as brother and sister, as the Lord God created them in their mother's womb."

"Rosanna . . ." Elias touched her arm. "Love . . ."

She dared not look at her dear husband or she might lose heart. Continuing, she said, "I believe it is better for John and Kate to raise both babies." With that, she rose and carried Rosie to John and placed her in his arms, blanket and all. Then, faltering as she went, Rosanna returned to Elias, who took her hand as she sat down again without saying more.

The bishop wiped his own tears. For more than a minute, silence reigned. "You, Rosanna, are a true and faithful mother," he pronounced. "I pray you might birth many-a wee babe, should the Lord God see fit."

Ashen, Elias looked at her. But there was no protest in him as they stood in unison and made their way through the kitchen toward the back door, neither looking back.

Dear Lord, please give me strength, thought Rosanna, suppressing a flood of tears till she was safely in the carriage.

Much to Nellie Mae's delight, the sun was making a steady reappearance, and the glossy white acres stretched out to touch the brilliant blue of the sky. She had been hankering for a walk all morning, so when Nan offered to stay at the bakery shop with Mamma, Nellie stepped out for some air.

I feel much lighter without all those layers. Making her way toward the one-lane bridge, she headed east on the narrow strip of road. It wouldn't be long till the creek was running free. She smiled at the memory of splashing its waters on her face one long-ago spring morning at Suzy's suggestion. How surprised she'd been at dipping her hands into its cold—like liquid ice. Suzy had delighted in its freshness, claiming, "It wakes a body up clean to the quick."

She hadn't been walking for more than fifteen minutes when a car came toward her and slowed to a crawl. A man who looked about her age rolled down his window. "Excuse me, miss . . . you must live around here. I think I'm lost."

She hadn't had much contact with English men, so she was leery of going near the car. Even so, she stopped.

"I'm trying to locate a particular Amish family," he went on. "I've already counted more than a dozen Fishers on the mailboxes. Like looking for a needle—"

"In a haystack?"

He laughed merrily, his gaze softening.

"Which Fishers?" she asked, keeping to her side of the road.

"They had a daughter Suzy, who drowned last year."

The air went out of her. Surely she was staring at this stranger. What could this be about? she wondered. "Suzy was my younger sister," she admitted ever so slowly.

His eyes registered momentary sadness. "Then . . . you must be Nellie Mae."

She nodded, wondering how he knew.

He opened the door and stepped out. "I'm Christian Yoder . . . my younger brother, Zachary, was your sister's boyfriend."

Startled, she noted a slight resemblance to Caleb as he drew near. How long ago was it that she'd determined to search for Suzy's friends, and here one of them was smiling at her?

"This is a surprise," she managed to say.

"It sure is—all those Fishers, and I run into you."

He was taller than Dat, and his hair looked nearly golden in the sunlight. In a burst of memory, she recalled Suzy saying this brother had invited her rowboating the day she'd drowned.

Christian reached into his jacket and pulled out a photograph. "Zach wanted Suzy's closest sister to have this. That's you, I guess." Slowly he handed it to her, as if uncertain whether she'd take it.

She gasped to see Suzy's familiar freckles, warm smile, and pretty blue eyes looking back at her. Behind her sister, sunbeams danced on the water of a lake. Tears sprang to Nellie's eyes. "Oh, *Denki*, it's wonderful-*gut* to see Suzy again." She brushed back her tears.

"I realize your loss is still raw for you . . . for all of your family." He paused, glancing down at his feet in the snow before lifting his gaze again. "Suzy talked of you often, Nellie Mae."

A little sob escaped her. "Ach, I'm ever so sorry. . . ."

"Don't apologize. I can't imagine losing Zach or any of my brothers." He dug into his jacket pocket again. "Here's something else." He held out a gold bracelet. "Zach gave this to Suzy not long before . . ." His voice trailed off.

Nellie stared at the bracelet. "Suzy must have loved it."

"My brother was going to ask her to go steady that day." Christian hesitated momentarily. "Zach's young, but he loved her. Everyone noticed the special something they had. An amazing pair . . . they would have been great in marriage someday . . . in ministry, too."

"Ministry?"

He nodded. "Yeah. Zach loves to preach, and Suzy was encouraging him in that direction."

Suzy was in love with a preacher?

She listened, soaking up every word. Again, she studied the bracelet, noting its inscription: *Not by works of righteousness but by His mercy He saved us.*

"Based on the first verse Suzy ever memorized," Christian explained.

She couldn't believe he was offering the bracelet. "Doesn't your brother want to keep it?"

"Not anymore. The bracelet's for you or your family."

"Thank you ever so much." She didn't know what more to say, though she cherished both gifts. She found herself looking at the forbidden picture again, knowing she would treasure it most of all. A far better reminder of Suzy than her Kapp strings!

"It's nice to finally meet you, Nellie Mae Fisher," Christian said, smiling a little.

She felt nearly too embarrassed to speak, yet she knew he was only being friendly. "Will you tell Zach how much this means to me?"

He smiled again. "I'll do it. He'll be glad to hear you liked them." He leaned slightly forward. "Please extend our condolences to the rest of your family, especially from Zach."

"So kind of you . . ."

He seemed reluctant to leave, or at least she sensed as much. "Were you heading somewhere?" he asked.

"No," she said quickly, lest he offer her a ride. "Just out getting some sun."

He nodded, gave a half wave, and headed back to his car.

Nellie turned, walking swiftly as she carried Suzy's bracelet and picture. As Christian Yoder's tan car pulled away, she dared to raise her eyes to follow it all the way down the road, toward Route 10, till it became a shiny dot in the distance.

CHAPTER 36

U pon their return from the bishop's, Rosanna washed away her tears and dried her face. She asked Elias to help her set up her quilting frame, determined to return to making quilts for sale, just as before. Keeping her hands as busy as possible was the best way to keep from breaking down and weeping. Her two sisters-in-law might not be interested in helping anymore, now that she and Elias were attending the new church. But Elias reminded her that the Lord both gives and takes away, and His name was to be praised, no matter.

Before today, she'd feared how their jumping the fence might affect extended family relationships. Yet despite the hard events of this morning, peace prevailed in her heart. Who besides the Lord could possibly know the future?

Returning without the twins to this house, the place where she and Elias had intended to raise Eli and Rosie, was the second most difficult thing she'd done today. The first was placing precious Rosie in John Beiler's arms. Now she must relinquish the babies in every way, praying for the strength to do so . . . and for the ability to forgive.

The loving gift Kate offered me is gone.

Unable to hold back her tears, Rosanna folded up the playpen in the sitting room. At least her darlings were together, and she and Elias would surround them daily with prayer.

Caleb counted his possessions, glad at least to own a good, spirited driving horse and the courting carriage his father had given him back when he'd turned sixteen. He had gathered his few personal belongings and carried them into the Dawdi Haus where he and Nellie Mae had spent their blissful, forbidden hours. Banished by his father, he would live there, laboring for his maternal grandfather.

Daed planned to drop by at the end of the week, to talk man to man. His father seemed certain Caleb would come to his senses by then, as he put it. Yet as long as it meant giving up Nellie Mae, Caleb was unwilling to relent.

Eyeing the little house she had liked so much, he began to unpack. He could kick himself for the mess he'd made. He *did* respect and love Nellie Mae, even though both his Daed and his Dawdi doubted it. A few kisses were nothing to be embarrassed about, were they? He hadn't thought so until he'd seen in Nellie's eyes the weight of guilt she carried. Given enough time, he would make it all up to her, just as he promised. For now, though, he must work off his debt of sin here, knowing that when he'd saved up enough money, he could make his next move.

The strange encounter with Christian Yoder stood out in Nellie's mind as she went about her daily routine, baking enough pastries to supply the increasing demand. Although the ad had disappeared, a host of customers were still coming, especially since the weather was more promising. Any leisure moments were spent reading the Bible Nan had offered to her weeks earlier. Nellie also found herself rereading the final sections of Suzy's diary.

While she knew better than to reveal the picture of Suzy to anyone else, the gold bracelet could not be kept a secret. She'd shown it first to Mamma, who had merely looked at it, not making much over it, except for the inscribed verse. Nan, too, cared little about jewelry, though she touched it gently. Nellie was glad to have it, placing it carefully on the dainty blue dish on her dresser—the cherished gift from Suzy so long ago. Each time she walked past, she remembered what Christian had said about the verse being Suzy's favorite.

Not by works of righteousness . . .

Could she rest in God's love and not continually blame herself for being too affectionate with Caleb? She'd tried for days to assuage her guilt, rationalizing their intimate behavior, but each time she came up short, feeling even more disgraceful. Giving away even a single kiss had been too much.

Reuben glanced toward the bakery shop, noticing Nellie Mae's Closed sign hanging on the door. For some odd reason, no one had bothered to get the mail earlier, so he lumbered through the snow, the scent of woodsmoke in the afternoon air.

Out on the road, he opened the mailbox, spotting a single envelope inside addressed to him.

The name and address of the sender was nowhere to be seen. *Well, what the world?*

Tearing open the envelope, he began to read.

Dear Mr. Fisher,

My name is Zachary Yoder, and I've waited too long to send this. I'm writing to ask your forgiveness.

I know you only through your daughter Suzy. We dated for a short time late last spring, and I was with her when she drowned. She wasn't wearing a life jacket, and I bear the blame for that.

I hope it helps to know Suzy was happy that day. She loved you and talked so fondly of her family. I don't know how you might feel about this, but she was a new Christian, having just found a relationship with her Savior, Jesus Christ. I hope this news brings you some comfort.

Every morning I pray for you and for your family.

I will miss Suzy for the rest of my life.

Most sincerely,
Zachary Yoder

Tears sprang to Reuben's eyes as he stared in wonder at the short letter. So this Zachary fellow was a believer, too, just like their Suzy. . . .

He folded the letter, somewhat curious about the young man who'd written it. Thoughtful as the gesture was, he decided then and there not to share this note of apology with Betsy, fearing it might stir up her grief.

————

Sunday morning, Nellie was the first one ready after Dat, who'd gone out to hitch the carriage to their best driving horse. At church, when Preacher Manny quoted the verse etched on Suzy's bracelet as his sermon text, she let out an involuntary gasp. All during the preaching, she felt a familiar tug, wanting to bow her head in prayer. She recalled having felt the same way the first time she'd attended here. Oh, the strong urge to confess each and every one of her sins!

She listened intently as Preacher Manny went on to speak out against "worldly things" before the final prayer. "There are some who would push the limits. Such things may have their place, but not here." She assumed he was attempting to separate the chaff from the wheat, those who fancied the modern from those who desired only the Gospel, as he'd mentioned in today's message to the People.

Folk were eager to discuss the sermon during the common meal—the usual old church menu of bread, butter, jelly, cheese, red beet eggs, pickles, coffee, and many pies. Nellie found some things to be comfortingly similar.

By the time they returned home, Nellie was even more tender toward the Lord and the words she'd heard this day. It was impossible now to ignore what she knew to be true.

Without telling Mamma where she was heading, Nellie hurried to the barn, where she slipped inside her father's woodworking shop and closed the door. It was a well-isolated spot on the Lord's Day, and she briefly wondered about the Nazareth shop where Jesus had worked as a carpenter.

Standing near the table saw, she gazed out through the windows to the sky. It wouldn't be too many more weeks before she would help Mamma and Nan clean out their corners, from the attic all the way down to the cold cellar, with its many shelves for hundreds of canned goods and jams. Dat, for his part, would rake out the lawns and plow and cultivate the fields, preparing for another season of growth . . . and harvest. Spring would soon bring new life for all the People of Honey Brook.

Sighing now, she thought how quickly the grace period had come and gone. Tomorrow the Bann began anew, but that was not her concern. Wholly ready to follow in Suzy's footsteps, Nellie knelt in the sawdust and released the burden she'd carried inside, as well as her guilt over Caleb. She offered them up to the Lord God, whose will and gift of grace she'd rejected far too long. "O dear Lord," she began, "will you receive me as I am, with my black heart a-tickin' ever so hard just now? Please wash me as clean as new snow." She paused, thinking of Caleb. "Will you also call my beau? May he take your hand, just as I am now. . . ."

Jehovah God had led her—nearly all of her family, really—to this wondrous place of peace. Feeling spotless and clean, Nellie Mae rose and hurried to the house.

———

Before sunset on Sunday, Caleb headed to the Fishers' home. He steered his horse into the lane with a bit of trepidation, having violated courting custom, coming here to Nellie's father's house. When he'd tied up the mare, he walked to the back of the house and knocked soundly on the door.

As he waited, he considered his plight. *So much at stake now* . . .

Moments passed, and he heard the sound of rustling from inside. Then the door opened, and there stood Nellie, wearing her blue *for good* dress. In the dying sun, she looked radiant, until her eyes met his.

"Ach, Caleb?" Nellie looked shocked. "What are you doin' here?"

He said quietly, "Is there someplace we can talk?"

Glancing over her shoulder, she hesitated. "Uh, wait here." Then she disappeared inside.

His heart was pounding as he waited. She seemed startled to see him, and he sensed her uneasiness. The intimacy of last weekend was exacting a heavy price from both of them. To think all of this could have been avoided.

He looked over at Reuben's barn and the outbuildings surrounding it. The vast corral stretched out nearly as far as he could see. Surely Reuben's youngest son, Benjamin, would receive this land one day. Caleb did not begrudge him this blessing.

He considered yesterday's difficult conversation with Daed, and the one he now planned to have with Nellie. He'd rehearsed it repeatedly.

Wondering why Nellie Mae hadn't returned to the door, he turned to look in and saw her pulling on her coat and scarf.

When at last she stepped out, she looked downright pale. "I can't believe you've come here, Caleb. In broad daylight and all." She was clearly unsettled. "I s'pose we can talk in the bakery shop."

He nodded, recalling the first time he'd gone to Nellie's Simple Sweets last September, bringing her an invitation to ride after the Singing. Their first evening together . . .

They walked in silence, and then she turned toward him. "I was wonderin' how to tell you something . . . and now, well, you're here." She avoided his gaze.

"Jah, and I've got something to say, too."

She glanced back toward the house. "Best wait till we're inside." She picked up her pace, and he wondered if she'd told her father he'd come unannounced.

Once she'd closed the door behind him, they went to sit at a small round table. In the near twilight, she looked as pretty as she had on their first date. "You go first, love," he said.

She touched her neck. "I don't know how to begin." She paused to look hard at him, the first time she'd truly looked at him tonight. "I'm sure you'll be surprised at what I have to say."

"Go on."

"I'm going to join church."

He nodded. "'Tis a gut thing, jah?"

Her face paled again, and she closed her eyes for a moment. "I mean the *new* church, Caleb."

New church? He groaned.

"I gave my heart away today. I can't begin to describe it, really." She looked up at him, tears streaming down her lovely face. "I'm saved, Caleb. I've never felt anything like this."

He shook his head, stunned. "This happened at Preacher Manny's?"

"No."

Jah, gut. Maybe it wasn't too late. Maybe he could still talk her back to good sense.

She pointed toward the barn. "Over there."

He was confused. "Over where?"

Her words formed slowly. "I opened my heart to God's Son in our woodworking shop."

Ach, she's spoiling everything. Everything! "Oh, Nellie, love . . . you know I'm opposed to this salvation talk. I thought you were, too."

"I wish you could know what I know . . . what I'm feelin'."

"Manny's church won't keep you for long," he declared.

"But this isn't about choosin' a church. I'm choosin' a relationship with my Savior, Jesus."

"Ach, Nellie Mae—"

"No, please listen." She grabbed his arm. "It's all in God's Word. We've clearly missed it. Don't you see?"

Perplexed by her strange exuberance, he removed his black hat and ran both hands through his hair. She was making things difficult, if not impossible. "I want to marry you before the wedding season next fall."

She frowned, pursing her lips. "But your father's land?"

"I've given it up—for *you*. There's nothing to keep us from marryin' now."

Her eyes became sad. "Ach, but it's your birthright, after all."

Nodding, he said, "What's done is done. Daed has no say about us any longer."

She seemed to ponder his words, then brightened as she reached across the table for him. "You honestly did that . . . for us?"

He rose and went to her. "I know I can make you happy." He pulled her to her feet. "I promised I'd find a way."

She raised her eyes to his. "Jah, and I do love ya, but . . ."

"But what?" His heart nearly stopped. "This strange gospel can't be what you truly want. Don't let them take you away from me."

She wiped her eyes.

"They've brainwashed you, Nellie."

She looked as beautiful and innocent as the day he'd first smiled at her, back last summer at market.

"You're as stubborn as I was, Caleb. Remember when I was so embarrassed 'bout my parents' interest in Preacher Manny's group? I told you I could never be like that."

"And I believed you."

"But now . . . now I see things more clearly." Her expression was earnest. "Won't you jump the fence with me? Please, won't you come to Preacher Manny's church?"

He shook his head, his heart sinking. "Aw, Nellie, you know I can't do that. And I've got it all worked out—we'll wed in the springtime and then go to Sugarcreek, Ohio, or wherever you want to live. We'll run away together."

Her mouth trembled. "You see only this life, but it's as short as a wisp of breath in the cold air. You see it and then it's gone. Think of Suzy." Her voice sounded sad.

He took Nellie's hand, so small in his. "I know life is short, love—that's why I want to spend it with you."

"What do I have to do to help you see?" Her eyes pierced him. "Suzy died to get my family's attention on heaven."

"Don't say such a thing."

"Truth is, heaven's got a face, and not just Suzy's."

Releasing her hand, he pulled her into his arms. "You scare me, the way you talk."

She clung to him, her cheek wet against his. "You can give up your land for me, but not your heart . . . to the Savior?"

He was weary of her reckoning his future. What had happened to the girl who was willing to do anything for him? "I've given up the land—everything, really—for you, Nellie."

"But you can't just walk away from your land," she protested. "You'll come to resent me for it . . . and for refusing to stay in the Old Ways. Won't you always wonder why I didn't love you enough to join the old church?" She was sobbing now.

Even so, he held her near, hoping his precious girl might change her mind—about Preacher Manny's church . . . and about him.

Dat and Mamma's joint decision to leave behind the Old Ways before the Bann was reinstated tomorrow meant their family would be spared the shunning, something for which Nellie Mae was truly grateful. Come fall, she and Nan would join the New Order church on baptism Sunday. As for Rhoda, it was hard to know what she would ultimately decide; she continued in her Rumschpringe, free from any fear of the Bann.

But the way things were going, Nellie wondered if Rhoda might not leave the Plain community and fully embrace the world. Nellie had such a hankering to see her oldest sister, so she borrowed Dat's horse and buggy. Daily she would pray for both Rhoda and Caleb. To think she'd let her beloved beau walk out of the bakery shop and out of her life. There was no turning back now, not with him so set against the Savior.

Rhoda was already in her nightgown and bathrobe when Nellie arrived at James and Martha's. She seemed happy to see her and took Nellie to her room.

"I've brought you something," Nellie said as she presented her sister with Suzy's diary. "I was wrong to keep this to myself. She was your sister, too." She placed the journal on the bed quilt. "Read it for yourself, if you want. Like a good story, the surprise is at the end, though of course you already know something of that."

Rhoda's face lit up. "Well, I never thought I'd see the likes of this. Denki, sister."

"There's more." She reached into her pocket. "Close your eyes and hold out your hand." Nellie placed the gold bracelet in Rhoda's outstretched palm. "Now open."

Rhoda's eyes sparkled through her glasses. "Ach, what's this lovely thing?"

She explained how the brother of Suzy's boyfriend had bumped into her on the road while trying to locate their family. "You're the one who loves perty things, jah? It makes the most sense for you to have it."

She glanced right then at the dresser mirror adorned with various necklaces, and they laughed in unison. "This is so dear of you, Nellie Mae. Truly it is." Turning the bracelet over in her hand, Rhoda again murmured her delight. Then she put it on, fastening it into place before eyeing it close up. "Looks to be some etching on it."

"Jah. Ever so special, really."

Rhoda invited her to visit anytime, and Nellie sensed she was discontented there. "Tell Nan I miss her, won't ya?" Rhoda said, her eyes sad.

"And all of us miss *you*, 'specially Nan." She looked around the room and then shook her head. "I'd be lyin' if I didn't say I hope you'll consider comin' home . . . real soon."

"Well, I can't let you think that." Rhoda rose and they walked together past the sunroom and toward the back door, where they stood and looked out at the night sky.

Rhoda sniffled as Nellie reached to hug her. "*Da Herr sei mit du*—the Lord be with you, Rhoda."

On the ride home, Nellie fought back tears as her thoughts returned to Caleb and their many nighttime drives together. Oh, but she wished she could somehow influence him away from the grip of the ordinance. But that was his choice to make—or not make. If he jumped the fence eventually, he'd have a dear price to pay. Even though he'd said he had given up everything for her, she knew Caleb could never walk away from his family. David Yoder's hooks were in him but good—just as Caleb supposed Preacher Manny's were in her.

The stars on this clear night twinkled and beckoned against the darkness. Nellie Mae remembered all the times she and Suzy had laughed together under the canopy of twilight, imagining whom they'd marry and what their children might look like. The long jaunts through nearby woods . . .

She hadn't gone to the woods Suzy had so loved since the winter snows, but she would return. Often she had found a reassuring solace there.

The horse drew the carriage along, and the stone mill came into view. Her eyes lingered on the wrought-iron bench near the still-frozen stream, the place where she and Caleb had sat enjoying love's finest hours.

Please, God, help me not regret letting him go. . . .

EPILOGUE

With the dawning of February eleventh, nearly one hundred and fifty people withdrew from the Honey Brook Old Order church, forming two new distinct local congregations. Word has it, according to Dat, that almost a hundred Lancaster County families have left for the New Order, which is beginning to spread to other states, too. I can't help but wonder about the courting couples sure to be caught betwixt and between, as Caleb and I sadly were.

Such a splintering of families and relationships. It's hard to understand how the grace of God can both mend hearts and break them. Belonging to Jesus is often a thorny road.

Mamma is heartsick because Rhoda's taken a second job as a waitress at the Honey Brook Restaurant. Seems my sister needs more money than the Kraybills are able to pay, although Rhoda's still there three days a week. By the looks of her, wearing fancy clothes more often than not, I'd guess she's got herself an English beau, though she's mum on that.

Nan and I have become ever so close, sharing nearly everything, as she used to with Rhoda . . . and I with Suzy. Nan knows Caleb wanted me to run off with him. She knows my answer, as well. There *are* times when I miss him nearly more than I can bear, until I remember his adamant stand against saving grace, and the Scripture warning against being unequally yoked comes to mind. Such a splintering apart it would be had I agreed— our marriage torn in two directions, our children ferhoodled between their mamma's faith and their Dat's Old Ways.

Thankfully Rosanna had the wisdom to see that little Eli and Rosie did not experience a similarly traumatic separation. Tears spring to her eyes when I visit nearly every week, though. Rosanna's quilt sales are thriving once again, and I daresay she has no time for raising babies. She and Elias will get through this murky, painful tunnel, but for now it is one step at a time.

Here lately Preacher Manny's church is jam-packed every Sunday. It's so nice having Rosanna there. She's confided that Elias hasn't talked further

460

about tractors recently, not since his conversion. Wish that were true of my brothers, but Thomas and Jeremiah are planning to get one to share, of all things. When word reached his ears, Dat groaned and said, "Where's all this goin' to end?"

I'd say it's better to soak up Scripture and share a tractor with your twin than to plow behind a mule team and be in bondage to the Ordnung.

There's much to be thankful for, even though my greatest regret, when I consider it now, is my failure with Caleb. I know I'm forgiven, but I gave away my first-ever kisses to him . . . and he saw my hair down, too. There's no way to ever forget that.

I can only wonder how he's doing since our final encounter at Nellie's Simple Sweets. The grapevine's tendrils haven't reached my ears, so evidently he's still in Honey Brook working for his Dawdi.

Occasionally I've wandered down to Cambridge Road and the woodsy atmosphere of the old mill—Caleb's and my private haven. Right or wrong, I allow myself to relive our courtship days . . . and pray the Lord will call him to the truth.

ACKNOWLEDGMENTS

A long this journey, I've met a number of lovely people—research assistants who tirelessly gave of their knowledge, their memories, and their own unique stories. Several who contributed time and energy, digging for hard answers, are the following: Dale and Barbara Birch, Dave and Janet Buchwalter, Frank Casatelli, Nick Curtachio, Fay Landis, Jake and Ruth Bare, and Priscilla Stoltzfus. I am so grateful.

Sincerest appreciation to my first-class editors—David Horton, Julie Klassen, and Rochelle Glöege—and to all of the Bethany House team.

Ongoing gratitude to my husband, Dave, who helps plot every story and makes my writing days less lonely. And to our daughter Julie, who reads the first draft with enthusiasm.

To the people that time forgot, I offer my earnest thanks.

With joy, I offer up this story to the greatest storyteller of all, our Lord Jesus Christ.

The Longing

To sweet Aunt Dottie,

and

in fond memory of her dear husband,

my uncle

Omar R. Buchwalter.

1918–2007

PROLOGUE

Spring 1967

L ike the steady thaw of snow and ice on field and paddock, undoing winter, my sadness has begun to melt away. Six weeks have come and gone since Caleb and I said our last good-byes, and it's nearly time to plant peas and carrots, once the soil is soft enough to take a footprint and be tilled. Time to press on in other ways, too, as I look ahead to joining the New Order church this fall.

Honestly, a great yearning has entered my heart, lingering there in the deepest part of me . . . warming me as I learn to live under the mercy of amazing grace. There are moments, though, when I think of the love Caleb Yoder and I once had and what is now lost to us. At such times, I simply knead the bread dough harder, trying not to fret. With God's help and my family and friends, I'll move forward.

There's no denying it has been a long winter here in Honey Brook, with far too much heartache all round. *Ach*, but I feel as if I'm holding my breath sometimes, waiting for the change of season to bring new life.

As for heartache, my dearest friend, Rosanna King, seems to be doing all right after relinquishing her twin babies, Eli and Rosie, to their birth parents. She's as kind and cheerful as always, but there is unmistakable pain in her eyes, especially when she works on the little cradle quilts she gives away to local midwives. Truly, she longs for her own baby to care for and love. God has certainly allowed some awful hard things in this life, and even with my newfound faith, Rosanna's loss is beyond my understanding.

Not only does Rosanna's plight puzzle me, but my oldest sister's desire for fancy things does, too. Rhoda's made a beeline to the modern world and has herself an English beau, who treats her to fine restaurants and drives

467

her around the countryside in his sporty car. And sometimes in *her* car, according to the grapevine.

Not even Mrs. Kraybill, Rhoda's part-time employer, will shed any light on the rumors when she stops in at the bakery shop. I admit to worrying that Rhoda will get herself hitched up with this *Englischer* and bring new sorrow to Mamma's heart . . . and *Dat*'s, too.

For now, at least, Rhoda's still staying with our brother James and wife, Martha, new members of the well-established Beachy Amish church, not far away. As such, they're enjoying a good many modern pleasures. To think that Rhoda *and* Martha are learning to drive!

And they aren't the only ones. More than a third of the People who originally left the old church have already followed a similar path. My oldest brothers, twins Thomas and Jeremiah, have both purchased cars, unable to agree on the same make and color so they could share one between them. They managed to scrape up the money for a down payment on a tractor, too, which they'll both use.

No telling where all this buying and whatnot will take folk. Truth be told, such a mighty strong pull the world has on us all.

Frankly, I don't boast when I say I have no interest in the fancy life. Thus far, there's little temptation in that direction. How can I miss what I've never had? I do miss Rhoda, though, and long to win her to the Lord one day.

Nan has become my closest and dearest sister now, and I've shared with her the whole prickly story of my courtship with Caleb. She quietly says, "Soon your pain will lift, Nellie Mae." Since she has suffered her own recent heartbreak, I suppose she should know.

I do still wonder if Caleb ever thinks of me. Does he wish things had turned out differently?

I, for one, won't let his determination to adhere to the Old Ways stop me from praying that his eyes might be opened. Often my prayers are mixed with tears, but I refuse to put my hand to the plow and then turn back. I believe I'm called to this new way of living, and nothing will change my mind.

Preacher Manny said last Sunday, in order to be a true follower of Christ, you must allow God to mold you—to remake you—hard as that may be at times. So I read the Scriptures and contemplate the fork in my road, wondering what sort of young woman I'm becoming since I knelt in the sawdust of Dat's woodworking shop nearly two months ago. I know one thing: I'm free from the bondage of the past . . . and the expectations of Caleb's father. I live to honor God, not my uncle Bishop Joseph and more rules than I can possibly remember. And I don't believe it's wrong to talk to the Lord in prayer, like I would to a close friend.

Hopefully the passage of time and the still, small voice of God's Spirit will soften Caleb's heart, too. I'd like to think I pray that not for my sake, but for his alone.

It's strange, really. Even though I carry a lingering tenderness for Caleb, sometimes I have to look down to see if my feet are touching the ground. I feel so light and free and ever so clean that it wonders me how a person can be filled with both joy and a sense of sadness at the same time.

Uncle Bishop, who still oversees our New Order group, and Preacher Manny Fisher, my father's cousin, have decided it's time to add a deacon and a second preacher to help with our growing house church. So the divine lot will be cast twice in a few weeks. Some have already gone to prayer and fasting . . . to be in one accord. I wish I were already a voting member. Not that I have anyone in mind for either office, but it would be wonderful-good to feel more a part of the new fellowship of believers.

These days the *Bann* is back in force and the months of easily switching churches are over. Those who remained in the old church are settled and a bit self-satisfied, too—or at least Dat has hinted as much. It's sad to think they are so closed-up to the notion of salvation through grace, but Mamma says we might be surprised at what's happening deep in their hearts, just as we were surprised about Suzy.

I do ponder such things when I look at her picture, given to me by Christian Yoder, her Mennonite beau's older brother. I gaze at the forbidden image more often than I should, probably, wondering what my parents might say if they knew. I am thankful, indeed, for Suzy's life, short as it was, and for the words of faith and love penned in her diary. Words that have helped to guide me.

All in all, there is peace in knowing that my future—and my salvation—doesn't depend on me. It never did. I'll continue to pray for Caleb and trust I'm not being selfish in that. Meanwhile, I know I can cling to my new faith and to my precious family, come what may.

CHAPTER 1

The debris of winter lay in a messy mat over the ground as the earth beneath groaned to life. Caked mud and the mire of old leaves, dried-up twigs, and downed branches, all tangled together in the chaos left over from the coldest season in recent memory.

Indoors, where embers in the woodstove warmed the kitchen, Nellie Mae scrubbed the green-and-white checked oilcloth. A smudge of cherry cobbler had stained it red near where the edge of Dat's dessert plate had been. She worked on the blemish while Nan washed Mamma's best dishes in the deep sink. Meanwhile, Mamma made quick work of the few leftovers at the counter, commenting again about the "delicious dessert," as if the simple baked dish was extra special.

They'd had an especially fine feast on this Easter Monday noon, even if it was only the four of them seated around the table. They'd sent a written invitation to Dat's parents over in Bird-in-Hand but, not surprisingly, *Dawdi* and *Mammi* had quickly declined. Things had been that way since her parents, Nan, and Nellie, too, had chosen to embrace the teachings of the New Order church.

Resurrection Day, their father now referred to Easter, with a broad smile. Both he and Mamma seemed keen on celebrating the day in a different way than before, though they and the rest of Preacher Manny's New Order group had observed prayer and fasting on Good Friday, just as in the old church. But Nellie had noticed from the very start of the weekend that a certain radiance permeated the observance. Easter was more meaningful than it had ever been in all of Nellie's eighteen years.

Oh, the wonder of it, she thought, wiping down the entire oilcloth even though they sat just at one end of the table now that Rhoda had moved out.

Missing Rhoda and Suzy—one sister gone to the world and the other to heaven—was becoming more bearable. "Life is all about change," Mamma often reminded her, but it didn't make things any easier . . . especially where Nellie's heart was concerned. Even so, Nellie knew that the sooner she got over missing her former beau, the better.

Nan tossed her a tea towel as Mamma left the kitchen. "*Kumm* dry."

Nellie reached to catch it. "Ach, I ate too much. Didn't you?"

"Will you have room for some supper later on?" Nan glanced her way with a curious look.

"Only a smidgen, maybe. We'll have plenty of leftovers, *jah?*"

Nan shook her head. "I was hopin' you'd go with me to the Honey Brook Restaurant, maybe."

"To see Rhoda?"

"Jah . . . I can't help but think our sister must be homesick for us."

Yet Rhoda hadn't bothered to contact them, not even Mamma, for all this time. A sore point, to be sure, and Nellie could have been miffed about it if she let herself. For the most part, she found herself whispering a prayer for Rhoda nearly as often as she did for Caleb.

Hesitating, Nellie asked, "Have you ever been there?"

"Only once." Nan frowned. "With my old beau . . ."

The last time Nellie Mae had talked with Rhoda, she'd taken Suzy's diary to her. Since Rhoda seemed to love jewelry, she'd also given her Suzy's gold bracelet, engraved with that sister's favorite verse. "Sure would be nice to see Rhoda again," said Nellie.

Nan brightened. "Well, I know she's working tonight, since it's Monday. She's there till closing on Tuesdays and some on weekends, too." Nan seemed quite certain of their sister's schedule. "Mamma doesn't mind. I already asked."

"Well, I wish you'd told me before I took my second helping of mashed potatoes and gravy, then." Nellie smiled. "Sure, I'll go with you."

Nan nodded, her hands deep in the suds. "*Denki,* sister." If Nellie wasn't mistaken, tears glistened in Nan's eyes. "Seems odd that she'd be satisfied with her life," said Nan, "out there in the world. . . ."

"Well, she does have James and Martha . . . and the children," Nellie said. "Plenty of family round her."

"Just ain't the same, though."

Nellie agreed. How *could* it be, as close as Rhoda and Nan had always been? For so many years, this house, their father's home, had sheltered them from every possible storm, except those brewing under their own roof. Everything they loved was here—the grand old farmhouse itself; Dat's barn and the horses he raised and trained; the surrounding acreage of fertile land. And the bakery shop. Nellie's Simple Sweets was a haven of sorts in the hollow, between two treed knolls that rose on either side of Beaver Dam

Road like protective barriers against the outside world. For now, at least. Nellie sometimes sensed how temporary her own stay here was—she longed to marry and have her own family someday. *With a husband like Caleb. But with a passion for life . . . and the Lord.*

She thought again of Rhoda and wondered how she could be truly happy being courted by a worldly man. Someone foreign to the Plain community. Surely she would tire quickly of the enticement and long for home.

"I wonder what Rhoda did for Easter." Nan looked at Nellie Mae. "Do you think she dyed eggs and ate chocolate bunnies, like the English do?"

Nellie had wondered, too. "You'd think she would've missed goin' to Preaching yesterday, jah?"

"Would seem so."

She wasn't sure if Rhoda continued to attend the Beachy meetinghouse with James, Martha, and their children. Martha rarely visited since Rhoda's leaving. Such a painful wedge now.

Nellie wished Rhoda might have come to visit for Easter, or sent a note, at least. But maybe her absence was her way of saying she was quite content as she was.

Nan continued washing the last of the dishes, staring down at the water, daydreaming. Suddenly she looked up at Nellie Mae. "I've been wanting to tell ya something," she said softly, glancing toward the doorway.

"Jah?"

Nan brightened. "I've met someone," she said, but her lower lip trembled.

"Ach, Nan . . . you're sad?"

Nan shook her head. "It's my joy I struggle with, sister. Truly, it is. I'm so happy, but . . ."

"But what?"

Nan paused. "Well, to be honest, I'm afraid to be disappointed again. Will this beau hurt me, too?"

Nellie leaned her head against her sister's. "Oh, Nan, I'm worried for ya, honestly." She sighed. "But you mustn't let the past spoil the present . . . nor should you keep mum because of what's happened 'tween Caleb and me."

Long into the afternoon, while Nellie wrote her circle letters and read from the New Testament, she pondered Nan's news. She couldn't help but wonder who the young man could be, hopeful Nan might confide in her in due time. Surely he, too, was of the New Order church.

Nellie let her mind wander, imagining what it would be like to share the same faith as a beau. *Maybe someday I'll know.*

———

The cry of a siren rang out in the distance. That, accompanied by a sudden gale, caught Caleb's attention and he raised his head. Several cows bawled at the sound, shifting in the stalls of his maternal grandfather's barn. Unexpected noises, especially high-pitched ones, disturbed the livestock. He'd observed this even when he'd lived at home, working for his father.

Those days are long gone, he thought, dismissing the far-off distress signal as he emptied the fresh milk into the pumping tank.

He had another hour or so of milking before he returned to the little *Dawdi Haus,* his home these many long weeks while he worked off his "debt of sin"—or so his father called it.

The second urgent wail assailed him as he stood near the last milking stanchion, tired and hungry, as he often was at this hour. This time, the siren sounded closer, but here in the barn, with no way to look out, he couldn't be certain of the direction.

Eager to stay on task—not wanting to delay his grandmother's supper—he dismissed the siren once again. *Best to keep busy.* The thought was a constant refrain since Nellie Mae Fisher had called off their engagement.

What was she thinking?

Lest he fall into discouragement, he refused the defeating thought. He was free now to court a girl from his own church district—someone who gladly held to the Old Ways and appreciated their strict tradition. No longer would he have to plead with Nellie to stay far away from Preacher Manny's group, nor the more liberal Beachy Amish church.

So Caleb was back to looking for a mate while the very girl he'd proposed to was moving in a new direction—away from him. He was miserable working for his grandfather, cut off from his immediate family by his own hand. Even if he could convince someone to marry him, he would have nothing to offer a bride, now that he'd given up his claim to his father's land.

He moved about the milking parlor, comforted by this twice-daily routine—knowing what to expect. The familiar barn smells and sounds relaxed him, just as his older sister Rebekah had often reassured him with her kind words when they were young. But now he was cut off from her, as well, since she'd moved over to Mill Road with the Ebersols. Downright peculiar. How was it they, being Old Order, could tolerate her attending the New Order meetings—even her planning to join that church come fall—but *Daed* could not? Truly, Rebekah had been as harshly ousted from Daed's house as Caleb had been, but for very different reasons.

Things just didn't make sense—not Rebekah's arrogant declaration of "having salvation," nor Nellie Mae's bold claim of redemption. Yet despite the church split and all that had changed because of it, he was as determined as ever to live out his life in the old tradition. *Where I was meant to be . . . even though my loyalty's gotten me nowhere.*

So the gray days continued, and he found no joy in this new life of hard work and loneliness. Still, Caleb had yet to completely regret the ill-fated night with Nellie Mae in the very Dawdi Haus where he was sent to reside. The night he'd crossed a delicate line with the woman he so loved and had planned to marry, asking her to let down her hair for him. *A loving act meant only for her husband's eyes . . .*

Though that night was long gone, he clearly recalled their sweet affection. He hadn't heeded his own inner warning, nor dear Nellie's, to wait for lip-kissing till their wedding day.

The cows were lowing contentedly now, and he moved among them, talking softly, as was his grandfather's habit. He was accustomed to emulating those with more experience and wisdom, the way of doing things passed down by imitation. That's why Nellie's abandonment of their tradition kept him awake at night. It was so foreign . . . not the way of the People, especially not for a woman. Yet, if he let his mind wander back to their earliest dates, her ability to think for herself had been one of the things that drew him to her—and he missed talking to her. *Ach, I miss everything about her.*

It was during his grandmother's skillet supper of sausage, onion, green pepper, stewed tomatoes, and macaroni, that Caleb discovered the significance of the siren's wail.

His grandfather had just commented on the recent rise in feed prices when a startlingly loud rap came at the back door. His older brother Abe burst into the kitchen, red-faced. "Caleb! Kumm *schnell!*—come quick!"

Immediately he leapt from the table, dashing out to the utility room for his coat and hat . . . leaving Dawdi and Mammi to wonder what sudden calamity had befallen them.

———

A light rain had begun to fall, melting the remaining snow on either side of the road as Nellie Mae and Nan made their way to the Honey Brook Restaurant.

"Do ya think Rhoda will be surprised to see us?" asked Nan, holding the reins.

"Well, she said she missed us when I visited her some weeks ago." Nellie wondered if Rhoda had ever considered the verse inscribed on Suzy's bracelet: *Not by works of righteousness but by His mercy He saved us*.

"I hope she won't think we're spyin' on her."

"Well, I doubt she'd admit that." Nellie forced a smile, hoping they weren't making the trip to town only to be rebuffed, if only for Nan's sake.

"Might be best if we don't seem desperate for her to come home, jah?"

Nellie sighed. This was going to be hard, no getting around it. "If she's aloof, I hope you won't take it to heart, Nan."

"Oh no, I'm beyond bein' hurt over her leaving. Honest, I am."

Nellie heard the slight waver in her sister's voice and knew better.

———

"Oh, Caleb . . . Caleb, you're here." His mother's face was ashen as she greeted him and Abe at the back door. "Your father's been hurt," she said, wringing her hands. "I should've gone along in the ambulance," she added as they moved into the kitchen.

"What happened?" Caleb asked.

His sisters Leah and Emmie hovered near Mamm, looking right peaked themselves, and their oldest brother, Gideon, seemed mighty grim at the head of the table.

"Ach, the chain broke on the plow hitch," Mamm explained, "and while your father was down fixin' it, one of the mules kicked him in the head." She faltered, openly weeping. "Your poor Daed . . . so terribly wounded."

Caleb's heart broke as she attempted to describe the accident, and he made her sit down because she seemed like she might just teeter over.

"Abe was out in the field with your father—saw it all—and ran for help to our Beachy neighbors . . . used their telephone to call an ambulance."

"Was Daed breathing?" Caleb asked, sitting at the table with Mamm and the others. A cluster of panicked souls.

Abe nodded. "I checked his breathing and his pulse . . . awful weak. And he couldn't stop shaking."

"Will he pull through?" asked Caleb.

Abe's face fell. "It . . . it's hard to know."

Gideon leaned forward, his voice all pinched. "The medics didn't say one way or the other. But Daed was struggling, that's for sure."

Leah began to cry, and Emmie, Caleb's youngest sister, put her arms around her. "Daed'll pull through . . . he will," Emmie said bravely, but she, too, shed tears.

"One of us must go to the hospital," Caleb spoke up, looking at his mother.

Abe glanced at Gideon. "I should be the one to go. Caleb can stay here with Mamm and the girls, once you head home."

Gideon got up from the table, saying he ought to get back to his own family. "I'll stop in at Jonah's on the way," he said, referring to their other brother. "Maybe he's returned from his errand by now. Sure would hate for him to hear this from anyone but us." He went to Mamm and leaned down to say good-bye, then left.

Abe prepared to leave, as well. Trembling, their mother rose and followed him to the door, pleading with him. "Bring word back as soon as ya know something . . . anything!"

"I'll see what I can find out." Clearly eaten up with worry, Abe nodded and darted out the door.

Caleb led Mamm into the kitchen once again and pulled up the rocking chair for her. "You mustn't fret. We must keep our wits about us."

Trying to be brave, no doubt, she blinked her sad eyes silently, and then with a great gasp, she buried her face in her hands. "Ach, what'll we do if—"

"Mamm . . . Mamm." Caleb stood near her chair, leaning over her now. "Try to remember how strong Daed's always been. Not much can hurt a man like that."

She nodded slowly, wiping her tears. And he wished he believed his own words.

Sobbing loudly, Emmie reached for Leah's hand and they hurried out of the kitchen, toward the stairs.

"Plenty of men have been kicked by a horse and died on the spot," Caleb reminded his mother. "But you heard Abe, Mamma. Daed's alive . . . let's cling to that."

She bowed her head. "Ach, why didn't I go with him? Oh, Caleb." She could no longer speak as she softly cried.

"Everything happened so fast," he said, his heart pounding. He tried to ignore the stranglehold sensation on his chest and throat that fought his every breath.

CHAPTER 2

The interior of the restaurant was bright, with ruffled white curtains adorning the windows. One end of the enclosed porch area made for a cozy dining spot. *For courting couples.* Nellie Mae caught herself and cast away the niggling thought.

Nan spotted their oldest sister first. "There's Rhoda," she whispered, bobbing her head in that direction.

Wearing a pale aqua dress with cap sleeves and a knee-length white apron tied at the waist, Rhoda scurried to deliver a tray of food to a table of four young men.

Nellie forced a smile, fascinated by whatever Rhoda had done to herself. Noticing Rhoda's new eyeglasses and the arc of her eyebrows, she realized their sister had plucked out a significant number of hairs to alter the shape. She wore makeup, too, and was even so reckless as to display much of her legs—the daring hem of her waitress dress just grazed the tops of her knees. *And she's lost weight.*

Rhoda did still have her light blond hair twisted back at the sides and pinned up in a bun, but her prayer *Kapp* was missing—another startling surprise.

Nan twittered nervously, "Did ya think she'd change so quick?"

"Well, people do when they wander away." Nellie glanced at Rhoda again.

Once they were seated, Nan reached for the menu. But Nellie couldn't keep her eyes off Rhoda. A long-ago memory took her back—she and Rhoda as young girls, tugging hard at a faceless doll made by Rosanna's frail mamma. Rhoda had been determined to hang on to that precious doll, no matter what. *"It's mine! Let go! I had it first!"*

Rhoda's little-girl voice rang in Nellie's ears. "She was a bit stubborn even then," Nellie Mae muttered to herself.

Nan lowered the menu, peering over the top. "You all right?"

Quickly she blinked. "I s'pose so."

"Then why do you look so . . . aghast?"

She bent forward, her voice a whisper. "When Rhoda comes over to take our order, you'll see why."

Nan nodded, squinting her eyes in apparent agreement. "Oh, I can tell from here. She's deep into the world, ain't so?"

So Nan had noticed.

As uncomfortable as Nellie felt, she and Nan were here now. And Rhoda had just spotted them across the room, where she waved and smiled before taking another order.

Several more people entered the restaurant—a young couple, then a family of four, who sat down at a table a few yards from Nellie and Nan. A light-haired young man, evidently the older of the family's two sons, caught Nellie's attention. His profile was rather familiar. Goodness, but it was the fellow she'd met so unexpectedly out on the road weeks ago—Christian Yoder, one of Suzy's Mennonite friends.

"Now who are you lookin' at?" Nan was eyeing her, her menu closed and on the table.

"That family over there. Well, don't look now, but I honestly think the younger of the two boys—the darker-haired one—might be the *Mennischte* Suzy dated. I'm pretty sure the older one is the same person I met on the road last February."

Nan's eyes brightened. "Ach, really?"

"Don't stare!" she whispered.

Nan seemed all too eager, literally gawking over her shoulder. "So that's Christian Yoder . . . the one who gave you Suzy's bracelet."

"Nan."

"Oh, all right." Reluctantly Nan turned, and just then Rhoda came over, licking her thumb as she flipped the page over on her order tablet. "How are you *ladies* this evening?"

"We're hungry," Nan said right away, reaching to touch Rhoda's waitress dress. "It's so good to see you!"

"Denki—er, thanks." Rhoda blinked her eyes, her cheeks rosy under her face powder. "I never expected to see yous. . . ."

"I had a hankerin' to come," Nan admitted, still fingering Rhoda's dress. "Hope that's all right."

Seeing that Nan was about to cry, Nellie spoke up. "We thought it'd be fun to visit you here at your work."

Rhoda nodded awkwardly, glancing over her shoulder toward the kitchen. Just as quickly, she turned back to them. "How's Mamma? And Dat?"

"Dat's got some driving horses trained and ready to sell," Nan said. "And Mamma is helping Nellie in the bakery shop quite a lot."

"Still goin' to Preacher Manny's church?" Rhoda looked at Nellie.

"Both of us are. And Nan and I plan to take baptismal instruction this summer."

"Oh, really? When did ya decide *this?*"

Another waitress breezed past, briefly saying something to Rhoda. Rhoda told them she'd be right back, and the two waitresses promptly hurried away.

Nellie wished she might have shared with Rhoda all the wonderful-good things happening deep in her heart. Sighing, she decided to order a bowl of vegetable soup and a grilled cheese sandwich, and when Rhoda returned, she and Nan placed their orders.

Moments later, Nan excused herself to the washroom, and Nellie felt terribly conspicuous and almost wished they'd stayed home. Staring at the salt and pepper shakers, she fidgeted, moving them around. She'd never found herself in such an uncomfortable situation, not that she recalled. Well, perhaps the day she had been out walking, minding her own business until suddenly encountering Christian Yoder in his tan car.

Remembering that day, it took her a moment to realize someone was standing next to her table. Looking up, she saw Christian himself smiling at her, with his presumably younger brother at his side.

"Nellie Mae . . . nice to see you again. We thought we'd come over and say hi." He turned. "This is my brother Zach."

Zach offered his hand, looking a bit bashful. "Nice to meet you, Nellie Mae." He studied her as if searching for a resemblance to Suzy.

Feeling embarrassed, she looked for Nan, wondering what was keeping her. "My sister Nan's here with me." She tried to avoid Christian's gaze. "It would be nice if she could meet you, too."

Zach was nodding, and Christian asked if they'd come to celebrate something special.

She wouldn't say they were here for the sole purpose of visiting their wayward sister. No, she wouldn't divulge that prickly tidbit. "Well, it is Easter Monday, after all."

Christian's face lit up. "And my dad's birthday."

Zach glanced back toward their family's table, and Nellie's gaze followed. Their parents appeared curious, and no wonder.

Christian's eyes remained on her. "Good seeing you," he said again, more softly this time.

Christian and Zach's parents were looking her way again, which made her feel too tense to talk. Unsure of herself, Nellie merely nodded.

Just when she thought she ought to offer them a seat, Nan returned. She looked surprised to see Christian and Zach there and cast a quick frown at Nellie, who introduced her. "This is my sister Nan."

"Hi." Christian reached to shake her hand, as did Zach, smiling.

"Nan, these were some of Suzy's friends," Nellie explained. "From last summer . . ."

Nan nodded with affected courtesy and directed another sharp look at Nellie.

"Would you mind if my parents say hello sometime before we leave?" Zach asked.

Nellie could just imagine her sister's questions, once they were alone again. "Why, sure . . . if they'd like to," she replied, her neck stiff now with tension.

When Christian and his brother headed back to their own table, she reached for the dessert menu right quick, hiding behind it.

"Nellie Mae?"

She sighed; there was no avoiding Nan.

"Nellie, look at me."

Slowly she peeked over the top of the menu.

"Those two fellas looked real pleased, talking to you."

Ach, here we go. . . .

"Honestly, what took you so long in the washroom, Nan?"

"You're ignoring my point." Nan leaned closer.

"Which was?"

Nan shook her head. "You're hopeless." She looked across toward Rhoda, who stood near the table of four young men, obviously flirting as she refilled their coffee cups.

Nellie saw it, too—Rhoda smiling and joking, like she was quite at home. Ever so peculiar.

This is her life now.

Nan frowned and absently touched the end of her fork. "Oh, Nellie . . . I wasn't goin' to say anything yet, but Rhoda just told me something awful troubling in the hallway."

Nellie raised her head, noticing Nan's solemn face. "What?"

"I best say it somewhere in private . . . don't want to burst out cryin'."

"Jah, don't do that."

Rhoda was headed their way now, carrying a round tray of food. When she set it down in front of them, both Nan and Nellie smiled at her. "Denki, Rhoda," they said in unison.

There was a brief glint of welcome in Rhoda's eyes. Maybe seeing them again brought back happy memories. Nellie hoped so. She was counting on them to bring Rhoda back to her senses soon. *Memories . . . and plenty of prayer.*

Once they were alone again, Nellie offered a blessing for the food. Then silently they began to eat. But all through the meal, Nan picked at her food, clearly distracted. What had Rhoda said to make Nan so glum?

Several times during the evening, Christian glanced over at them. Usually it was about the time Nellie looked *his* way . . . but only to ponder his brother. Surely if Suzy hadn't died, her friendship with Zach—and Christian—would have been short-lived. The boys seemed so . . . *English.*

Nellie tried to engage Nan in conversation about other things—even the weather—but to no gain. And then, about the time Nan seemed more herself again, the whole Yoder family rose and walked over to their table. Nellie gulped inwardly.

Her mouth was dry as yarn as Mr. and Mrs. Yoder offered their kind condolences. Christian's steady gaze rested on her all the while. Truth be told, she felt quite relieved when the Yoders finally turned and headed for the door.

"Aw, c'mon, Rhoda, tell us when you get off work," the most flirtatious of the four men said. Running his finger around the lip of his water glass, he looked her over but good.

Rhoda should have been put off by their attention. A fleeting thought crossed her mind: *What would Ken think if he saw me laughing and talking with these men?* But she was not the instigator. They'd struck up a casual conversation, asking what was her favorite entrée on the menu . . . making harmless small talk. Still, she hadn't discouraged it, nor was she flustered by the attention.

A friendly waitress, older and wiser, had warned her: *"Remember how men act around waitresses."*

Even so, she'd gone from no male attention to this—why not enjoy herself? It wasn't like she was engaged to Ken yet, although she would turn off the charm to others the minute that happened. *When* it did.

Hurrying back to the kitchen to check on an elderly couple's order, she glanced at Nan, noticing the way her closest sister leaned forward at the table as she talked to Nellie Mae. Was Nan telling Nellie what Rhoda had shared?

She suddenly felt sad, missing Nan, especially. How long had it been since they'd curled up in their room, confiding their hopes for marriage and babies? Fact was, Nan looked downright dismal, and no wonder. *I shouldn't have breathed a word. . . .*

Nellie Mae seemed preoccupied—and much too apprehensive. Had something changed at home in the time since Rhoda had quarreled with Dat and left? What was wrong? For a moment, Rhoda regretted the distance between her and her two remaining sisters.

Not wanting to cry, she headed to the washroom and stared at herself in the mirror. She removed her glasses, washing a few smudges off the lenses and drying them on the skirt of her uniform. Oh, how she loved her new things . . . her growing wardrobe of for-good as well as casual clothes. She'd even considered buying a pair of dress trousers, the nice-looking pants that English women wore for shopping or for a more relaxed outing.

She washed her hands, letting the warm water run. She'd considered painting her nails—wouldn't that look pretty for the days she put on her waitress dress and half apron?

Heading out the door, she thought again of Suzy's diary. She'd read the surprising last half twice already. In fact, for the second time just last night. She'd had to hide the journal quickly this morning, fearful Martha would discover it. She found it strange that Suzy's wild days had led her to something quite different than she'd set out to find. *She got religion,* as Rhoda had heard it described. *Same as Dat, Mamma, and nearly the whole family.*

"But before all of that, Suzy had gotten herself a fella," she muttered.

Slipping her hand into her pocket, Rhoda felt Suzy's bracelet there, thinking she ought to start wearing it. After all, she was as gussied up as any fancy woman who'd never been raised to know better. *Why not?*

Waiting for some word on his father, Caleb was captive to his own imagination. In his drowsy state, he replayed his final visit with Nellie Mae in her bakery shop, unable to put the dreadful day behind him. He wondered how he might have steered the conversation toward a happy outcome. But no, Nellie had been determined to have her way, unlike any young woman he knew. She'd spurned his love for a newfangled faith that could never endure. He scoffed at the very idea of the new church—the New Order, or whatever they called themselves. Yet somehow, they'd gotten to his beloved.

"She's brainwashed." He hurled his angry words into the stillness of his mother's kitchen. There was some consolation in knowing he had tried to talk Nellie Mae out of joining the new church. Given time, he would have done anything to get her to see the foolishness of her choice. If only she'd agreed to run away with him. If only the church split hadn't ripped the People apart . . . hadn't ripped *them* apart, destroying their hopes for a future as man and wife.

How was I to know it would come to this?

Thoughts of his former sweetheart pressed hard on his mind as he got up and went to the sink for some cold water. He'd lived with this frustration each day since their absurd farewell.

Caleb had no recourse now but to dismiss Nellie completely. Yet, hard as he tried, it was impossible to think of his darling being courted by another man. He clenched his jaw as grief and rage filled him.

It was close to midnight when Abe startled him, shaking him awake. Caleb had fallen asleep near the woodstove, in Daed's old kitchen rocking chair. Rousing himself, he sat up. "How's Daed doin'?" he asked.

"It's bad news, Caleb. Awful bad. He might not even survive the night."

"Ach, this can't be."

"Listen, we can't give up just yet," Abe chided. "There's still breath in him."

"Shouldn't you have stayed?" Caleb asked softly, concerned his father might die alone.

"Believe me, I wanted to, but I thought it best to return right quick for Mamm. Take her back with me . . . just in case. The driver's waitin' outside."

Caleb agreed that Mamm should be at their father's side at this dire time. "You'd best be getting Mamm up, then, jah?"

Solemnly, Abe nodded. "If she's even asleep. No doubt she's up there stewin'." He removed his black hat, brown eyes shadowed in the dim light. "Perhaps that's the hardest thing of all. Not knowing what the mornin' will bring."

Caleb had many questions, but he sat as still as the great stones in his father's field. Shouldn't he go to the hospital, too? Try to make peace with his hardhearted father?

Abe placed a hand on his shoulder. "Go on back to Dawdi's now, Caleb. Get some more rest—you'll need it for what's ahead, no doubt."

Caleb shuddered. *He doesn't think Daed will pull through. . . .*

"Remind Mamm how determined our father's always been," he told Abe. "Don't dash her hopes."

Abe gave a nod and trudged toward the stairs, saying no more.

Slowly Caleb rose and headed into the utility room for his coat and hat, aware of the effort of pushing one foot in front of the other. His tired mind raced with uncertainty—concern that his father's death would leave so much undone between them. And his heart went out to Mamm for all the years she'd stood by the most stubborn man Caleb had ever known.

On the cold ride back to his grandparents' place, he considered the possible changes ahead . . . the harsh reality of his family's predicament. At this dark hour, his father's very life hung by a thread.

CHAPTER 3

Reuben Fisher was surprised when his oldest brother, Bishop Joseph, arrived from the next farm over early the following morning. Reuben was grooming the new foals when Joseph came plodding into the barn, a look of apprehension on his face. "There's been a terrible accident."

Anxious about his aging parents, Reuben braced himself for bad news, the hairs on the back of his neck prickling.

"One of David Yoder's mules kicked him yesterday afternoon—like to have killed him, but it seems he's got himself a hard noggin."

"Will David live?"

Joseph pushed up his spectacles, his eyes serious. "Too soon to say. I expect to hear more from Abe today."

Reuben listened as his brother gave a few more details about the accident. Then Joseph sighed. "Well, I best be goin'. I've got to get word to a few more folks yet this morning." He offered a wave as he departed.

Rushing to the house, Reuben relayed the news to Betsy, who looked as stunned as he felt.

"Oh, Reuben, more sorrow?" She spoke in a whisper as she reached to embrace him, her Bible pressing against his back.

He held her near, aware of her trembling. "You needn't fret, love." He stroked her long, beautiful hair, still down from the night. "Leave all the worry to me. I'll see what can be done to help the Yoders."

She looked up at him ever so sweetly, eyes filling with tears. "I'll do my part, too."

"You're a wonderful-*gut* woman, you are." He leaned down and kissed her. "Take care of yourself today, hear?"

Before leaving, he snatched up his own Bible, wanting it with him in the buggy. There was a quiet confidence in knowing he had God's Word within his reach.

Then he headed out to the barn to get his driving horse, planning to make a quick trip to Preacher Manny's to solicit help from a few of the New

Order men. He would also go to each of his sons to request their assistance with David's farming duties—milking, hauling manure, sowing alfalfa seed in the former wheat field. Such work was never ending, especially during the warm months. He also assumed David and his sons were in the process of sterilizing their tobacco beds with steam, tobacco being one of David's major cash crops. Reuben didn't see how his conscience would allow him to help with that particular job, but he knew plenty of progressive farmers who wouldn't mind pitching in. Even some of the older men were mighty strong in their hands, due to years of working with "the 'baccy."

Last of all, he would stop by to see Elias King. Perhaps Elias would ride with him to visit David at the hospital—a trip Reuben felt compelled to make, no matter the bleak reception that might await him.

Betsy slipped on her bathrobe and hurried downstairs to tell Nan and Nellie Mae of the tragic accident, her voice shaking as she did. To think such a terrible thing could happen—and without warning. She could scarcely bear to think of poor Elizabeth Yoder, who must be heartsick, beside herself with worry. *Ach, what the whole family must be going through.* . . .

"I'll bake a nice, hot dish or two," Nellie said, blinking her eyes.

Nan slowly nodded and leaned on the kitchen table. "And I'll start breakfast . . . then bake some more cookies."

Betsy, too, was eager to help Nellie finish baking the day's offerings for Nellie's Simple Sweets. It was impossible for Nellie alone to keep up anymore, what with the crowd of customers. In fact, she'd thought recently the cozy bakery shop had outgrown its name—Nellie, Nan, and Betsy's Simple Sweets seemed a better fit these days, though the selection was no longer so simple.

Quickly Nan and Nellie Mae decided how they might manage their regular baking with the added meals for the Yoders, and soon the numbing shock of David's accident gave way to purposeful action.

Will the Yoders accept our gift of food . . . and Reuben's offer to help?

Betsy knew it would take a miracle for the Yoders to abandon their so-called shunning of New Order and Beachy folk, even in the midst of their great need.

A thoughtful glance at Nellie's ashen face revealed how deeply the news had affected her now-youngest daughter. Betsy sensed not only Nellie Mae's deep sympathy but her understandably great caution where the Yoder family was concerned. As if it was hard even to speak their names.

It's hard to change horses in midstream, she thought. After all, David Yoder was to have been Nellie's father-in-law.

"I'll cook the food, but I'd rather not take it over there," Nellie admitted softly.

Betsy breathed a prayer of gratitude for Nellie's merciful heart, doing this hard thing. *To show the love of the Lord Jesus . . .*

All the while Nellie chopped potatoes and made small snibbles of a large yellow onion, her thoughts were on Caleb. *How horrid he must feel.*

Oh, his poor, dear mother and siblings . . . and his father, whose life hung in the balance. As she greased the pans for the beef-and-potato casserole and buttered-noodle dish, she wondered what she might be doing differently today in response to this tragedy if she and Caleb were still courting. Wouldn't she rush to his side to offer comfort?

Sliding the baking dishes into the oven at last, she wished there might be something more she could do. But no, she was doing exactly what she ought to—making an anonymous meal.

Her throat was tight with dread. David was a man of conviction and of action, too. Even though he was as sincere as the next man, she believed he was sincerely wrong in the way he'd treated Caleb—and in his firm stance against the new church.

Yet Nellie did not hold even the slightest grudge, though she couldn't help but wonder if Caleb still did, after everything he'd endured at the hand of his unyielding father.

In any case, Caleb surely needed the support of his friends . . . and his extended family. "But it's not my place," she caught herself saying aloud.

She glanced back at Nan to see if her sister had noticed the slip, but Nan appeared lost in her own thoughts. Her usually joyful countenance sagged; doubtless that had more to do with the private chat with Rhoda last night at the restaurant. So far, she hadn't yet divulged what had prompted her concern, but Nellie assumed it had something to do with Rhoda's plans to live a fancy life. What else could it be?

Soon Nan headed out to help feed the livestock, in Dat's absence. Most likely, he was on his way home to wait for the hired driver. Numerous other farmers would surely drop by the Yoders' to offer farming assistance, as word spread. And Uncle Bishop would open up the benevolence fund to help with medical bills, as usual.

Nellie crimped the edges of the crust on one of her many pies as the sun shone hard against the gleaming windows. Dawn was bringing daylight earlier each morning, another vital sign of spring. And with the change of season, there would be much more to do outdoors—tending their own vegetable and charity gardens, weeding flower beds, keeping the lawns well trimmed and neat, and whitewashing fences. She was ready to work outside again, feeling like a cooped-up hen in a chicken house. Eager to keep busy, too. During slow times in the shop, she had even begun writing down favorite recipes. Anything to keep her hands and mind occupied—and her thoughts away from her lingering loneliness for Caleb.

I wish I could be the one to soothe his pain, she thought now, picking up her pace. Deep in her heart, she knew she was grasping for excuses to offer kindness to Caleb. But she must act as though she had never been courted—or kissed—by handsome Caleb Yoder, no matter how desperate or hopeless his father's condition.

———

With Reuben's help, Elias King made swift work of feeding and watering his goats. The younger man seemed pleased to be invited along to visit David Yoder. He slipped briefly into the house to let Rosanna know where they were headed before stepping up into Reuben's carriage. They would wait at the Fishers' for a hired driver to take them to the hospital in town.

Elias was rather solemn in Reuben's buggy. "Such a shame 'bout David. I hope he hangs on." He shook his head. "Denki for askin' me to join ya."

Reuben nodded. "Visiting him is the least we can do."

"Any real hope of us seein' him?"

"Even if not, our goodwill gesture will mean something to Elizabeth, no doubt."

"If she hears 'bout it," Elias said with a knowing look.

"You'd think his children would let their mother know we offered to help with farm work." He informed Elias that he'd gone to see his cousin Manny in hopes of gathering a group of folk to assist the Yoders. "A good way to demonstrate God's love to a stubborn soul," he added.

Elias agreed. "Hard to put ourselves in their shoes just now." Not saying more, he lowered his head, as if in prayer for the unwavering man, now so severely injured.

Reuben joined him silently. *O Lord, bless David with divine mercy and your great compassion. Preserve him so that he might come to know you. And may we be an encouragement to that end.*

Truly, there was little chance of two New Order church members being permitted to visit with David, regardless of how seriously wounded he was reported to be. If the man could think for himself . . . and speak, too, there was no way either Reuben or Elias would step foot in his room, such was the ill will David displayed toward them. Even so, Reuben was glad to make the effort, still faithful to his former friend. He wouldn't think of giving up on David Yoder, no matter.

The steady melting on the road had caused a muddy mess out front and all the way down the road. Betsy recalled Reuben saying how caked up the horseshoes on their driving horses had become. She and Reuben were both fond of the horses, especially those used for pulling buggies. Betsy had known some families who thought of their driving horses as dear pets, even going so far as to give them special nicknames like Josie-girl or Ol' Gertie. She smiled, glad for such reliable transportation this day, the carriage laden with Nellie Mae's delicious meal and several pies, too, along with sweet breads and other pastries. Nellie had been ever so eager to include a broad assortment in the hamper of food.

As if she's making up for something . . .

Betsy could speculate, of course, but she wouldn't go so far as to presume to know what had transpired between her daughter and Caleb Yoder. It wasn't her place to pry. But since Nellie was staying close to home on weekends, most likely she wasn't seeing anyone, including Caleb. To think the young man had been cast out of his own house by his father and sent to live in his grandfather's Dawdi Haus, of all strange things.

Children are such a worry. She thought back to all the fretting she'd done over Suzy. One day she hoped to read her youngest daughter's diary, though she'd not asked Nellie Mae about doing so—nor would she just yet. Nellie had enough on her mind now, without wondering why her mamma was still interested in reading Suzy's private thoughts.

As she rode, Betsy settled back against the front seat, noticing the rise of trees on either side of the narrow road. She envisioned the fiery dahlias she and Nan would plant when the weather was warm and the grass green and soft beneath their bare feet. Such bold flowers looked especially pretty bordered by goldenrod and Queen Anne's lace.

Suzy had loved flowers, wild ones in particular. She remembered her often talking of "their woods," chattering about the many varieties of flowers that bloomed there in all but the deepest parts. The chaos of the forest, the intertwined branches and underbrush that threatened to confuse the casual visitor—all of it delighted Suzy, most of all in early spring. There was something about today, with its fresh, raw smell, that kept Betsy's mind on Suzy, who had once planted wild flowers in the forest with Nellie Mae.

Chuckling softly at the memory, she knew something had lifted in her in the past months. She was free of the heaviest grief. It wasn't that she didn't yearn for Suzy any longer. Oh, she certainly did. But she also envied her girl in a sense, too. Her youngest was sitting at Jesus' feet, soaking up answers to her oodles of questions as readily as she'd spent hours reading Scripture after her conversion.

"What would it take for all of us to hunger for truth?" she whispered.

Closing her eyes, she prayed for a way to reach Elizabeth Yoder. *Let your loving grace shine on her, dear Lord.*

———

Alone with Nan in the bakery shop while Mamma rode to the Yoders', Nellie wondered how long before her sister might open up and share with her. She glanced up from her little recipe notebook, but Nan was concentrating on embroidering a new pillowcase. Nellie returned her attention to the cake recipe she was adding to her growing collection. She had started by writing down the recipes customers requested most often and already had filled up half a notebook.

The bell jingled on the door, jarring the quiet of the shop. She looked up from the counter as three customers stepped inside, obviously excited. "Hullo," Nellie greeted them, recognizing Mrs. Kraybill and two of her neighbors, all nicely dressed.

"How're you today, Nellie Mae?" asked Mrs. Kraybill, sporting a long turquoise coat.

"Just fine. A perty day, jah? How can I help you?"

Nan glanced at Mrs. Kraybill, smiling even though she must surely resent her for taking away Rhoda.

The women purchased one pie each, and Mrs. Kraybill lingered, asking for the recipe for gingersnaps. Opening her notebook, Nellie found the correct page and offered her an index card and pen to jot down the recipe for herself.

Meanwhile, the other ladies discussed the pleasant weather and the social occasions coming up. Some reference was made to the local high school's events associated with May graduation, and Christian Yoder flickered across Nellie's mind.

Not long after, Rosanna King dropped by, asking for five dozen cookies. "Three different kinds, if possible."

Seeing her friend sitting alone in the carriage as it pulled up, and now in the bakery shop, made Nellie want to go and wrap her arms around her. She didn't dare ask how Rosanna and Elias were doing without their twin babies, because that would only prompt the raw emotions to surface. Rosanna was obviously struggling to keep her tears in check.

"I'm having a big quiltin' bee soon. Would you like to come?" Rosanna asked, a small smile appearing. "A Sister's Day—a week from this Saturday."

"Sounds like fun," Nellie was quick to say, and Nan nodded her agreement. "Maybe Mamma would tend the store."

Nellie thought of Rhoda, wondering how to persuade her to come, too. *Unless she has to work at the restaurant.*

Rosanna brightened. "If you want, you could invite your cousin Treva from Bird-in-Hand and her sisters."

Nellie liked the idea; she had been hoping Treva might come visit for some time now. "Jah, I'll see if they can get away."

Nan spoke up. "They could spend the night, maybe."

"A good idea." Nellie smiled. "Maybe Rhoda would join us, too, if she knows about it."

Rosanna agreed, as did Nan, though neither said more. It made Nellie wonder if they both assumed Rhoda was lost to the People. She hoped not. Surely Rhoda's strange behavior would be short-lived.

Some time after Rosanna left with her dozens of cookies, Nellie noticed Nan staring down at the counter, leaning forward on her hands and brooding. "What's wrong?" She went to her side.

Nan's eyes glistened as she looked up. "Oh, I best be tellin' ya, or I'll burst."

Nellie Mae held her breath.

"Rhoda's decided to quit goin' to the Beachy church," Nan said, her lower lip quivering. "She says it's precious time she could be makin' money to pay off her car . . . and other things she's itchin' to do on Sundays."

"Workin' on the Lord's Day?"

"That's what she wants to do."

Nellie had no idea what to think. How could her sister even consider such a thing? She hated the thought of anyone putting money over the

Lord God—and Rhoda in particular, anxious to hurry up and buy all the luxuries she appeared to be craving. If you were bent on doing things your way, there was only one cure, according to Mamma—to simply go and experience what you thought you were missing. That was precisely what Rhoda seemed intent on doing. Of course, still being in *Rumschpringe*, the running-around years before baptism, she could do pretty much what she wanted. *Hopefully, she'll get all that out of her system soon.*

"Rhoda's movin' further away from us all the time, seems like." Nan wiped away her tears before continuing. "Ach, there's more."

Nellie wasn't sure she wanted to hear.

"She's getting rid of her hair bun . . . wants a short hairdo. A shag, she calls it."

Groaning, Nellie reached for Nan's hand. "What can we do?"

"Believe me, I tried to change her mind. But she wants to go fancy. You know how Rhoda is when her mind's made up."

"Do ya suppose . . . did she mention a beau?" Nellie asked. "Maybe he's muddled her thinking."

"She did hint that Mrs. Kraybill's nephew is sweet on her."

"Ach, she's not thinkin' straight if she's letting an Englischer court her."

"Her heart's deciding what her head oughta. And, just so you know, she didn't say not to tell ya, so I'm not breakin' a confidence."

Nellie was actually glad Nan had shared this news, hard as it was. "We'll keep prayin'." She reached into the display case and began blindly rearranging the pies and cakes, distracted by the thought of Rhoda forever leaving the Plain life, seeking out the world.

"What if she dislikes her short bob?" Nan blurted. "What then?"

"Well, once her hair's off, she won't be able to paste it back, now, will she?"

Nan tried to hold in her snicker, and soon they were both laughing. Nan reached to hug her. "Maybe something will keep her from choppin' off her pretty locks, jah?"

Nellie Mae couldn't imagine what.

CHAPTER 4

⌒

B etsy took care unloading the food hamper, gingerly carrying each item to the Yoders' back stoop. When everything Nellie Mae had cooked and baked was set in place on the cold steps, she rapped on the back door.

Fourteen-year-old Emmie came to the storm door, a slight frown on her pretty face.

"I'm so sorry 'bout your father's accident," Betsy began, realizing from the girl's slack jaw that she was either hesitant or worried.

"My parents ain't here. . . . Mamm's with Daed at the hospital." Emmie's voice faltered as she looked longingly at the row of hot dishes and pastries. "Ach, Betsy, it's awful nice of you, but I ain't allowed to . . ."

It was obvious the poor girl had been given strict orders not to accept benevolence from the hand of the New Order folk. "I'll be goin', then." Betsy forced a smile, wanting to make things easy for Emmie, whose mouth was watering, no doubt.

"Here, let me help you." Emmie opened the door and stepped out.

"No, no, that's all right. Really." She didn't want to get Emmie in trouble.

But fair-haired Emmie, more like her mother than her father, offered her a hand with the food anyway, while Betsy silently beseeched the Lord to intervene on behalf of this hurting family. She prayed especially that they might come to an understanding of God's abundant grace, perhaps through Rebekah.

She wasn't so audacious as to dictate her wishes to the Almighty, but she had been kneeling and praying so frequently that Reuben said she'd be wearing out the tops of her shoes even before the soles.

May David and Elizabeth and their family—each one—find this great joy, too, she prayed, lifting the reins as she directed the horse forward, back to the road.

─────

Not wanting a soul to know what she was up to, Rhoda carefully placed three new magazine clippings about distant lands—Africa, India, and

Brazil—in her newly purchased accordion file. She longed to travel some-day, to fly far away in an airplane. She hadn't told Ken or anyone else of this dream as of yet. For now, though, she would settle for faster land trans-portation. And if all went well, this coming Friday she'd have her driver's license and go out for her first solo spin in her lovely car.

She slid the file beneath her bed, close to the wall—the same place where she kept her youngest sister's eye-opening diary. The account of Suzy's running-around time was ever so revealing. To think her life had taken a sharp turn not long before she drowned.

My life's turning, too. Quickly she brushed aside thoughts of Suzy's "sav-ing grace," much preferring to think of Ken now. It was uncanny how Mrs. Kraybill seemed to have known that Rhoda and Ken would be so well suited as a couple.

Stepping back, she checked to see if either the file or Suzy's journal was evident from where she stood near the door. The bed quilt wasn't quite long enough on the side to camouflage her hiding place. She'd sus-pected one of Martha's four children—possibly two-year-old Matty—of having scooted under her bed, since someone had bent the cover of the diary. Matty was certainly one to get into everything, unlike his sister, Emma, nearly six. But of all the children, Emma was the one to watch, since she seemed the most interested in *Aendi* Suzy—"gone to Jesus," as she sometimes said.

Rhoda closed the door securely behind her as she left her room, wanting to talk with Martha. Surely James and Martha were instructing their little ones to respect other people's property.

If only I had a closet with a high shelf. . . . Rhoda made her way through the main-level sunroom and out to the kitchen. She found Martha setting down a plate of warm cookies in front of the children, already at the table. Matty wriggled in his wooden high chair.

She smiled at Jimmy and Emma, who looked up from the table, bright-eyed at the prospect of the treat. "Can I talk to you right quick, Martha?" she whispered. "I'd like to buy a doorknob . . . for my room."

"Oh. Something wrong with the old one? James can repair it if—"

"No . . . it's just fine."

Martha looked confused. "I don't understand."

Rhoda stammered, "Well, I need one . . . with a lock."

"Whatever for?" Martha glanced at the children.

"I'd give you the spare key, of course." How was she to explain her need for more privacy? She'd craved a place all her own even back when she lived at her father's house, tired of sharing a room with Nan.

"Would ya mind?" she persisted.

"James never locks anything. No reason to."

Sighing, Rhoda could see this approach wasn't working.

"Seems to me we need to discuss some things. James, for one, is concerned about you playing hooky from church the past few weeks, not going to Preaching with the rest of the family. And you've been out awful late, too." Martha's eyes gave her away: Both James *and* Martha were peeved but good.

It wasn't like Martha to speak up about such things, but she continued. "You've been spendin' a lot of time with that English fellow."

"He's the sweetest fella, honest he is," Rhoda defended.

Martha shook her head. "Best be takin' it up with your brother."

"All right, then. I'll talk to James later on." Rhoda turned to go, anxious to be done with this conversation. No matter what Martha thought she knew, her sister-in-law hadn't the slightest idea what was going on in Rhoda's personal life.

"When will ya be home tonight?"

"I'm scheduled to close up at the restaurant . . . so it's hard to know." She didn't dare admit she was going out with Ken afterward and that she might not make it back till midnight or later. One of the best things about dating an Englischer was she could see Ken as often as she wished—no waiting for Singings and youth gatherings on the weekends. And since Rhoda didn't have to be at the Kraybills' for work till around noon tomorrow, she could sleep in.

"I hope you know what you're doin'," Martha said.

"Not to worry." Rhoda went and kissed chubby Matty, squeezing his soft cheeks. *I can't wait to have my own little boy.* She could just imagine how cute Ken's and her children would be someday.

Pushing away any feelings of rejection, Betsy Fisher pressed on, not allowing the slightest bit of discouragement to rankle her. She stopped off at James and Martha's, hoping to see Rhoda before she headed off to work at the restaurant.

Wiping Matty's face, Martha told her that Rhoda had just left. She picked Matty up out of his high chair, the tray catching on his pant leg.

"Here, let me take him." Betsy reached for her youngest grandson as he giggled, all smiles, while Martha continued to wash his face, cleaning cookie crumbs off his earlobes.

"Such a messy eater you are, jah?" Betsy kissed his cheek and set him down on the floor to toddle away.

"James isn't too happy with Rhoda lately," Martha said, keeping her voice low. "She's out all hours . . . on weekdays, yet. And she's quit goin' to church, too." She shook her head. "Not sure what's come over her."

"Wasn't Rhoda happy goin' to the Beachy meetinghouse?" Betsy asked. She glanced around, noticing the small radio on the kitchen counter. "If it's the worldly life she's after . . ."

Martha rinsed out her washrag in the sink. "There's more to it, I'm thinkin'."

Nodding, Betsy assumed Rhoda was under the influence of an Englischer, but she wouldn't go as far as to mention that.

Busying herself in the kitchen, Martha said no more and Betsy remembered the many food items out in the buggy.

"Would ya like to have the day off from cooking? I've got a whole hamper of food out in the carriage. I'd hate to see it go to waste."

Martha gladly accepted, undoubtedly putting two and two together, since Betsy had already said she'd stopped off at the Yoders'. "Who'd be crazy 'nough to turn up their nose at Nellie Mae's cooking? She'll make a mighty gut wife someday."

Keeping mum on that, Betsy did not so much as move her head.

"You need help bringing it in?" Martha offered.

Betsy waved her hand. "I can manage." She was glad to leave the extra food with Martha, what with four little ones to feed and Rhoda's living here, not paying room and board, most likely. Besides, bringing the food back home for Nellie to see would only be a reminder of the Yoders' turning up their noses at her heartfelt gift.

When she returned with the last of it, she asked, "Where's Emma keepin' herself?"

Martha called to her daughter, "Mammi Betsy's here to see ya."

Putting the pie on the counter, Betsy heard the patter of feet. She knew that sound anywhere, and here came little Emma, bright as day, running into her arms. "I want to see your latest sewing project," she said after they hugged. And Emma scampered off to show her.

"She'll start school next fall." Martha wiped the table clean. "It'll be mighty quiet round here . . . 'least during the day."

Betsy noticed a sad glint in her eye. "Little girls are hardest to let go." "I'm finding that out."

No matter how old they are, thought Betsy.

She recalled the long strip of saplings Reuben had planted as a wind-break on the northeast side of the house when their first sons, Jeremiah and Thomas, were born. She had held her newborn babes, one in each arm, as she watched Reuben and his brother, then Preacher Joseph, from the upstairs window. How fragile, if not temporary, those wispy trees had looked without their leaves.

And she wondered, *How deep into the world will my Rhoda put down her roots?*

———

What struck Reuben most was the starkness of the hospital. The long, sterile hallways. The lack of decoration was almost a comfort, really—like home somehow. *Yet still mighty foreign.*

The nurses looked awfully young where they sat at a long desklike table with papers around them and stacks of patients' files. There were several telephones and a vase of flowers, too. One of the nurses did a double take as he and Elias walked past.

Then, seeing the words *Intensive Care,* he and Elias located the room where Elizabeth Yoder and her two older sisters kept watch over David, hovering near the bed.

Reuben paused at the door, catching Elizabeth's eye. She seemed to crumple at the sight of him.

"Elias King is here with me," he said, sensing Elias behind him.

David's head was all wound up in white cloths, and his puffy eyes were closed. He lay flat in bed on the near side of a pale blue curtain room divider. Elizabeth straightened, nodding for Reuben to come closer.

"He's under heavy medication for pain . . . and other things. Now that he's survived the night, they say blood flow to the spine is the biggest worry," she explained, looking smaller than he remembered. "David prob'ly won't even know you're here."

Reuben stood motionless at the foot of the bed, aware of the length of David's body taking up the whole of it. Various tubes ran in and out of him, and the effect made the shrewd farmer look even more helpless. All the men in David's family were strong dairy farmers—his grandfather, father, brothers, and every one of his uncles. In the years Reuben had known them, he'd never once heard a Yoder complain about being tied down to the twice-daily milking or any of the other demanding work required.

"He's had lots of tests—X rays and whatnot—to find out more about his brain injury," Elizabeth said. "He isn't able to move his legs at all. The doctor says the longer his legs are paralyzed, the less likely he'll be able to walk again."

Reuben absorbed the news—such a tremendous blow to this proud man. "It's still early yet," he said, wanting to offer hope.

She bowed her head silently.

"Is there anything we can do for you, Elizabeth?" he asked.

The two older women looked at him suddenly, as if he'd misspoken.

"What I mean is . . ." He paused as David's eyes fluttered and then blinked open.

All heads turned, and Elizabeth bent low to speak softly, "You have visitors, dear."

David frowned, his gaze falling first on Reuben and then on Elias before returning quickly to Reuben. "Did ya say . . . you want to . . . help out?" David's voice was raspy, and he struggled to breathe.

"That I did."

David lifted his hand to his forehead and held it there, eyes squinting shut momentarily. Then he said painstakingly, "Have someone get word . . . to Caleb."

Reuben nodded, not sure what David meant.

"Tell him to return home," David added.

Elizabeth looked pained suddenly but never took her eyes off her husband.

With that, David lowered his hand, placing it on his chest, and his eyes closed once again.

Reuben wished he might lead out in prayer right here in the quiet of the dim room. He was fairly certain Elias was already praying silently yet fervently, even as Elizabeth reached for David's hand.

———

Chris Yoder leaned both elbows on his father's desk in the landscaping office late that afternoon. He twirled his pencil over the ledger—the week's garden sales. But he couldn't focus. How could he dismiss his attraction to Nellie Mae Fisher? There was no denying it; he liked her more than he should. She was, after all, Amish. *Like Suzy.*

True, Nellie Mae was different from Zach's girl in that she appeared more conservative than her younger sister, who'd seemed eager to push beyond the boundaries of her Old Order traditions.

Nellie must be dating someone . . . or even engaged, sweet as she is. She was also pretty, though not in the obvious, dolled-up way of most of the girls in his high school.

Thumbing through his father's receipts, he considered the upcoming graduation events at both school and church. The banquet sponsored by their church youth group to honor the high school grads was the most interesting.

He leaned back in the chair to stretch his legs and thought of several girls he could ask—even the pastor's daughter might agree to go with him. Or a seemingly nice girl like Joy Landis from school. Letting his imagination soar, Chris wondered what it would be like to take Nellie Mae as his banquet date.

Of course he would never know, since she would never give an "Englisher" a second look. That was the word Suzy, as well as his Amish cousins, had used to refer to him and his family, but only at first. In time, Suzy in particular seemed to forget that he and Zach weren't actually as Plain as *she* was.

Knowing better than to mention his crush to Zach or anyone else, Chris shrugged the ridiculous idea aside and returned to his work.

Puzzled yet obedient, Caleb packed his things. He loaded his buggy, organizing things on the floor before hurrying over to the main house to let his grandparents know he was returning home at his father's request. This, according to Reuben Fisher, who had stopped by for the few minutes it took to relay the message. Seeing Nellie's father made him wish he might talk to her, too. But a clean break was far better after courting. And since it appeared Nellie hadn't changed her mind, he wouldn't try to win her back. Time might bring some relief to the pain of rejection.

For now he stood in his grandmother's kitchen, where Dawdi was reading *The Budget*, a Plain publication, at the table.

"Well, I'm all packed up," Caleb announced.

Mammi wiped her eyes, nodding her gray head, and Dawdi rose from his chair to clap a hand on his shoulder. "You're doin' the right thing by your father, son."

He agreed but was still conflicted about his father's decision after being cast out so harshly some weeks back.

"Don't worry 'bout us. The neighbor boys'll come help with milkin' and shoveling out manure from the barn, just as before." Dawdi paused, his bearded chin quivering. "Your Mamm needs ya now, and when your Daed returns home, he'll be needin' you, too."

Caleb put on a smile for his grandparents' sake. There was much to forgive and be forgiven for, and he would give it his all. Meanwhile, he must work hard, caring for his father's livestock, overseeing the milking, and plowing the land that had once been intended for his inheritance.

Having refused his birthright to prove his love to Nellie Mae and to be free of Daed's say-so, the land would now bypass him and go to another brother. Or possibly to one of his courting-age sisters' beaus, provided they married and remained in the old church. And what baptized soul would be foolish enough to leave the church now, with the shunning reinstated?

"Be thankful for this chance to serve your ailin' father, Caleb." His grandmother's voice sounded feeble.

A bitter pill to swallow.

"Don't keep your Mamm waitin'." Dawdi rose and walked with him to the door.

His grandfather had come to regret telling on him to Daed. Caleb had seen it in Dawdi's eyes during the time here—the pain of having to report his grandson's indiscretions, however slight, with Nellie Mae.

"Denki, Dawdi . . . Mammi." He appreciated their hospitality, and especially his grandmother's good cooking. "Thanks so much."

"Anytime, Caleb." Dawdi shook his hand. "If ya ever need anything . . . just give a holler."

He nodded, grateful for the offer. Unsure what was ahead of him, he pushed the door open and headed outside to his waiting horse.

No need for a courting buggy now, he thought as he climbed in. *I'll have my hands full taking care of my father.*

CHAPTER 5

R hoda whispered good-night to Ken outside James and Martha's kitchen door, feeling giddy. He reached for her, kissing her squarely on the lips. "I'll see you soon." He gave her another quick squeeze.

She waved and watched him head toward the car, her heart beating fast as she opened the back door quietly. Recalling their exciting first date following the introductory dinner at the Kraybills', Rhoda relived how awkward, even embarrassed she'd felt. The oddity of spending time with an attentive man, let alone an outsider not a single person in her life would approve of—aside from his aunt and uncle, of course—unnerved her when she contemplated it. She was still bemused as to why her employer was so keen on getting them together. Or at least it had seemed that way at the time.

Ken had made reservations for that first date at a fine restaurant in Reading, a thirty-minute drive northwest of Honey Brook. The food was delicious and everything as perfect as she'd ever imagined, but it had just seemed so peculiar to be out in public with a beau. Far different than the Amish custom of dating under the covering of night, alone in a courting buggy with only a horse as a chaperone. But she'd quickly learned to delight in the difference, rejecting the memory of the Amish bumpkins who'd passed her by, and by the third or fourth date, she began to acclimate, accepting Ken's fancy way of doing things.

Of course he knew Rhoda had been raised Plain, but she answered his questions about her background only in the vaguest of terms. She avoided talking about her family and the disappointment and discord that would certainly arise if she and Ken were to marry. She did wonder in which church they would raise their children, but the subject had never been broached. They could work that out later. Keeping things simple—even streamlined—was the surest way to matrimony.

She left her muddy shoes inside the door and proceeded to tiptoe toward her room, one of two former spare rooms just off the sunroom. Holding her breath, she wanted to avoid disturbing the household. Her brother had opened his home to her nearly without question at the outset. He and Martha had been ever so kind, yet here she was defying James yet again.

Moving lightly down the hall, she darted to her room. With a great sigh, Rhoda closed the door and leaned back against it, her heart still pounding.

Good. She'd been as quiet as a field mole. She reminded herself to breathe as she removed her lightweight shawl. Such a wonderful time she'd had again with Ken, who was smart and made her laugh, besides being the most handsome fellow ever. To think he owned his own real estate company, too. She had the Kraybills to thank for meeting him in the first place, but she had herself to thank for attracting and keeping his attention all these weeks.

She hung her wrap on the back of the door, then removed her stockings. The feel of the hardwood floor beneath her bare feet brought to mind Ken's carpeted house. He'd invited her to his lovely historic home on two separate occasions, both times cooking a delicious meal for them in the luxurious third-floor "suite," where he lived. *Imagine Dat or my brothers fiddling about in the kitchen!*

On the first visit, Rhoda had inwardly fretted about not feeling comfortable enough to relax in the tantalizing privacy of the place—like she was doing something wrong and feeling guilty about it. But the second time, this very night, it was slightly less nerve-racking, and she sensed she was beginning to let go of her earlier notions and enjoy Ken's fancy world.

And everything about it was wonderful-good—his choice of music, exotic foods, well-made clothes, and the subtle aroma of his cologne. Even the musky scent of Ken's occasional cigar appealed to her.

Suddenly a single knock came at her bedroom door, and she jumped, startled. "Rhoda . . . are you still up?" It was James.

"Uh . . . jah."

"You decent?"

She looked down at her bare toes and grinned. *All but my feet,* she thought. "Jah, I am."

"Open the door, then."

She did, and there stood her older brother in his pajamas and long blue bathrobe, his hair all *schtrubbich.* "Ach, it's late," she said quickly, hoping to ward off a confrontation.

"Late it is." He leaned on the doorframe. "Why is it you can't seem to abide by my house rules, Rhoda?"

She should've known he'd ask.

"You knew from the start I expected church attendance when you asked to stay here. That and your comin' in before midnight . . . on weekdays, yet." He stared at her, waiting for an answer.

"I'm in Rumschpringe."

"That's the old-time ordinance." He inhaled slowly. "The Beachys are more strict with their young people, and honestly, I think it's mighty gut."

"You're askin' to know where I go and who I'm with?" Such a strange, new way.

"I never said that, but dating's best left to the weekends . . . there's sleep to be had and work to be done during the week, ya know."

She knew, all right; the late nights were catching up with her. "It's not up to me how late I get in. Not really." She was thinking of Ken, who wouldn't be any too pleased at an imposed curfew. He didn't care much for her tying up her Sundays at Preaching service for hours, either. "And I've changed my mind about goin' to church."

"Oh? Returning to Preacher Manny's?"

She paused, feeling almost embarrassed. "I'm goin' nowhere. For now." Once she and Ken were married and didn't have to see each other so late at night, she might start attending again. *Maybe.*

He frowned. "So this is how you got yourself kicked out at home, jah?"

Rhoda felt her face flush. "I'm twenty-two," she said. "Shouldn't I be able to live as I see fit?"

"Why, sure, as long as you find someplace else to do it. And I'll give you a couple weeks to look." He shook his head and turned to leave, muttering about not standing for rebellion under his roof.

Rhoda felt chagrined, even sad. But moments later, as she contemplated the new adventure before her, she secretly felt glad to soon be free of James's expectations.

A small apartment is all I need, she thought, both excited and terrified.

———

Nellie made her way out to the road for the mail Wednesday afternoon, carrying a letter for Cousin Treva to invite her and her sisters to Rosanna King's upcoming Sister's Day. She'd also taken the opportunity to ask about her grandparents, Dawdi Noah and Mammi Hannah. Nellie had been tempted to write, *Do they seem to miss us?* But it was best not to open that all up again since her parents' last face-to-face attempt to convince them to move back home to Honey Brook. So long ago that January visit seemed—one Nellie had missed out on altogether, having stayed too long after the common meal to dote on baby Sadie, her brother Ephram's infant daughter. The babe was already ten weeks old now.

Perhaps she should write to Mammi Hannah herself. She could begin by asking for a few of her best-loved recipes. There had been no need back when she saw her dear grandmother every week and could simply ask if she used butter crackers or biscuits in her cracker pudding, or pecans or walnuts in her morning glory muffins. But now that Mammi was clear over in Bird-in-Hand . . . Nellie sighed at the thought.

She was sure her mother especially missed seeing Dawdi and Mammi Fisher once a week, as was their typical pattern prior to the church split. They'd always sat together following Preaching, during the common meal of cold cuts, bread, and pies. She recalled sometimes slipping over to the table where Mammi Hannah and Mamma chatted with aunts and older cousins. Often Mammi Hannah talked of the "olden days," when boards were put in bundling beds and girls never so much as raised their eyes to a fellow at Singings. Mammi Hannah told stories at quilting bees and canning frolics, too. Once, when she was in Rumschpringe, she sneaked off with a pony cart into town to visit an antique shop, where she'd bought an old, glittering brooch. She'd secretly worn it to bed on her cotton nightgown, taking it off when the sunlight peeked under the window shades, only to hide it beneath her mattress.

Nellie longed to hear Mammi's stories once again. She missed her sweet, crooked smile and her soft laugh. But most of all, she felt less alone about having missed the mark with Caleb—her past sin all washed clean now— when she thought of Mammi Hannah's girlhood pranks.

The Good Book said her heart was white as the driven snow, and deep inside, where no one could steal it away, Nellie had the promise of salvation. The knowledge brought her such joy she wanted to tell everyone.

Opening the mailbox, she discovered letters. Already! So she'd missed getting Treva's letter out. *It'll go tomorrow, then.*

She looked through the mail and was happy to see a letter from Cousin Treva herself. "Well, look at this." Thrilled, she hurried up the drive, toward the bakery shop.

"Anything interesting?" asked Nan when she entered.

"Treva wrote." She handed the letters to her sister.

"Anything for Mamma?"

"Didn't bother to look." Nellie pushed Treva's letter into her pocket, relishing the thought of reading it later.

"I'm afraid Mamma's not feelin' so well. I sent her to the house to lie down."

"Oh? Something she ate?"

Nan shrugged. "Hard to say."

"Maybe it's because of Emmie Yoder's response to the food Mamma took over there. Sure would be upsetting to be turned away. . . ." Only someone as stubborn as the Yoders would turn down Nellie's cooking. But Nellie dismissed the thought.

"Jah, rejected by folk who used to be our friends," Nan added. "The Yoders haven't heeded Uncle Bishop's plea not to shun the New Order folk who left during the grace period." Nan came to sit down at one of the small round tables with Nellie.

Nellie knew this all too well. "How's Rebekah doin', since she moved out?"

"Well, I know it's awful hard living away from her family." Nan glanced out the window, a faraway look in her eye. "And now this sad thing with her father. She must not know what to think. Or do."

"Won't she want to move home to help?" Nellie asked.

"Dat says David Yoder summoned Caleb to return home yesterday."

She blushed suddenly. "He did?" This was the first she'd heard it.

Nan smiled kindly, reaching for her hand. "Honestly, Nellie Mae, you act like a girl in love."

Embarrassed, she looked away. *Guess I still am. . . .*

"Truth is, I believe I'm fallin' in love myself. Little by little." Nan began to share about her new beau—a fellow she'd met at Preacher Manny's church—and Nellie was glad to listen. "He's such a hard worker and bright as can be. Treats his driving horse so wonderful-nice—"

"And you, too, Nan?"

Nan nodded, her face rosy. "Ach, you just don't know."

"Well, I can imagine." Nellie was more than happy for her sister. "I hope he keeps on bein' kind and loving."

"He is that." Nan was nodding emphatically. "I have a feeling he's the one."

"So you'll be tying the knot come weddin' season?"

Nan's eyes were bright with excitement. "Thank the dear Lord, is all I can say." She put her hand on her heart. "I would never have believed a new love could nearly erase the sadness of the old."

"Does this wonderful-gut fella have a name?"

Nan looked at her shyly all of a sudden. "I'd best be waitin' to say."

"Keepin' secrets from your own sister?" She laughed; she'd expected as much.

"Jah, 'specially." Nan gave her a mischievous smile and squeezed her hand. "I do love you, Nellie Mae. I'll tell you in time, I promise."

"Well, as long as you've promised . . ."

With that, Nan turned right into Nellie's arms and gave her a joyful hug. Even so, Nellie couldn't help but worry. *Will this one be Nan's husband someday?*

An hour later, after the bakery shop was closed and supper was laid out on the table—while they waited for Dat to come in from the barn—Nellie read Treva's letter silently.

Dear Cousin Nellie,

I have so much to tell you.

First of all, we've built a new, smaller Dawdi Haus onto ours, and my great-grandparents are moving in. I couldn't help but think of your grandparents this week, with all the hustle and bustle of getting my elderly relatives settled there. We do see Noah and Hannah every other Sunday at Preaching, and Mamma invites your grandmother to quilting frolics, too.

But I have something else even more important to share. Mamma's told me of three expectant women—two in our Old Order church district, one New Order—who've heard the sad story of your dear friend, Rosanna King, and been moved to act. Each of them is offering to give her baby to your childless friend. Can you believe it? It does seem odd for me to be the one passing this news along, but Mamma assures me it's all right to mention. In fact, she'd like for you to tell Rosanna yourself, close as you two are.

None of the women knows yet about the others, so I would think Rosanna could talk to each of them individually and then decide without anyone else ever needing to know. Mamma and I will keep this news quiet here.

Oh, I do hope it is right for me to tell you this, Nellie. See what your mamma says, though. There's always safety in wise counsel.

Nellie groaned. If Treva had a mind to talk with Rosanna herself about this, Nellie would want to protect Rosanna, not sure her friend was ready to attempt to adopt another baby. She sighed, considering the amazing news. To think *three* mothers-to-be felt enough compassion for heartbroken Rosanna to bear a child for her and Elias!

Same as her cousin Kate Beiler . . .

Nan came over and stood nearby. "You feelin' all right?"

She hated the thought of Rosanna's going through what she had with her cousin again—first being promised a baby, then having the twins taken away. "Did I make a sound?"

"Jah, like you might be sick."

Nellie smiled. "Well, I didn't mean to." She folded up the letter. No sense bringing Nan into this yet. "Is Mamma goin' to eat supper with us?"

Nan turned. "I'll check on her."

Nellie resumed her reading, finishing her cousin's remarkable letter. But the rest of the news—the division of a nearby church district due to growth, and farmers already seeding the oat crop—couldn't compare to the notion of the Bird-in-Hand women wanting to give Rosanna a baby. And two of them were members of the old church. What on earth?

Do I dare tell Rosanna?

Long after dishes were done and Dat had read the Scriptures and led them in prayer, Nellie waited for a private moment with Mamma in the kitchen. At last Dat obliged by making himself scarce, going upstairs to retire for the night. Nan had already gone up.

"I'd like to ask you somethin'," Nellie said before her mother could follow the others.

Mamma motioned for her to sit at the table.

After relating the contents of the letter, Nellie asked, "What should I do? I mean, think of it: This puts poor Rosanna in an awful place . . . you know, if something should happen and things fall through."

"And things just might." Mamma's face was serious. "Sometimes the answer to our prayers isn't always clear. Sometimes it's 'no,' or 'just trust.' "

Nellie smiled. Naturally her mother would think this. And the more Nellie learned from Manny's sermons and her own Bible reading, the more she, too, would approach things similarly. "I'm most concerned for Rosanna's frail state right now. She still cries, missing Eli and Rosie."

"Well, it's prob'ly too soon, then."

"So I best keep mum on it?"

Mamma sighed, rubbing her neck as she thought it over. "You'd just hate to see her get thrown more sorrow on top of what she's already suffered. Maybe just wait a bit . . . see if these women are truly serious."

Nellie Mae fiddled with her cousin's letter, considering Rosanna's fragile heart. "If Treva and any of her sisters accept my invitation, they'll be here next Saturday for Sister's Day."

"My goodness. I can't remember the last time we saw her. Can you?"

Nellie shook her head. "We exchange letters so often it doesn't seem that long ago, but I think it must be at least several years."

Mamma stretched and yawned. "Too long, I 'spect."

"Well, I best be headin' for bed . . . there's a little gathering at Rosanna's tomorrow, too. We'll quilt some of her cradle quilts to give away."

"She sure keeps herself busy, ain't?"

"Maybe too busy, really."

"Oh, but bein' so is a real blessing when you're grievin'," Mamma said with a small smile. "It's a real gut thing, truly 'tis."

Nellie looked at her mother and knew she was speaking of herself.

CHAPTER 6

Nellie was surprised to see Rebekah Yoder at Rosanna's work frolic the next morning, given her father's frail condition. Nevertheless she and six other young women had come for a few hours, all of them sitting around Rosanna's kitchen table and working on separate cradle quilts of pale yellows, greens, and blues.

Rosanna's sister-in-law Essie was not in attendance, nor were any of her other relatives from the old church. Nellie felt a twinge of sadness for Rosanna, who had once spoken of this very possibility—close relatives avoiding her and Elias because they'd embraced the New Order.

A hard price to pay . . .

Nellie had been visiting Rosanna each week since the return of her twin babies to their biological parents, John and Kate Beiler. And although Rosanna appeared strong, Nellie knew from the things her dear friend had shared that Rosanna still struggled terribly with the loss of little Eli and Rosie.

Such a brave and thoughtful thing for Rosanna to do, making baby quilts, Nellie thought, sitting across from Rosanna, whose eyes were fixed on her quilt. Her slender fingers worked the fabric, the needle rapidly moving up and down. Rosanna donated the small quilts to Amish and Mennonite midwives, who presented them at the birth of a new baby. Though the quilts were meant to be anonymous, the grapevine suspected Rosanna, and if anyone asked, she did not shy away from acknowledging the truth.

Nellie pondered again Cousin Treva's letter. *So surprising.* Still, she couldn't imagine opening up that precarious door only to have it slam shut again, as she and Mamma had discussed last night. Rosanna's cousin Kate had broken her heart, and Nellie did not want to be a party to a repeat of any such thing.

Nevertheless, there was the niggling thought in the back of her mind that perhaps she was making a mistake in not telling Rosanna the astonishing news. If she did keep it quiet and her dear friend got wind of it later—perhaps from Treva herself—would Rosanna be hurt to discover that Nellie had known?

Shifting in her chair, she forced her thoughts to Rebekah, who sat next to Rosanna at the table. Seeing her made Nellie wonder if Rebekah was permitted to help her dear mother, who must need her now more than ever. *What about Caleb? Surely he, too, is suffering under this new burden.*

Nellie felt downright tense, with a hint of a headache. She tilted her head back and forth before returning her attention to stitching up the rest of the baby quilt.

As time passed, the talk around the table became surprisingly cheerful. It was as if they were making a conscious effort to avoid the painful topic of David Yoder's accident.

Looking about the table, Nellie realized that each one present called herself a saved believer. The awareness brought her joy, and she took pleasure in the feel of the needle between her fingers and the pretty colors in the fabric, all remnants from other quilting projects. Some as old as four years, back when Rosanna was a young bride of only seventeen.

The chatter slowed some, and when all that could be heard was the pulling of thread through fabric and the snipping of scissors, Rosanna spoke up, inviting all of them to her planned Sister's Day. "Bring along your sister or a close friend and *her* sister, of course. We'll have us a *wunnerbaar-gut* time with a light lunch at noon and plenty of pies." Smiling, she looked right at Nellie, who nodded and let her know she'd be happy to bake a half dozen or so different kinds.

Rosanna's smile broadened. "We all know how delicious our Nellie's pies are, ain't so?"

· This brought a round of smiles and bobbing heads, and Nellie felt a bit embarrassed, though her heart warmed anew for Rosanna. Such a precious friend deserved the happiness of many children. *Just as Mamma had—nine in all.*

Nellie wondered if anyone had ever offered a healing prayer for Rosanna—the kind Preacher Manny spoke of in his very practical sermons. Nellie wouldn't be so bold to ask Rosanna unless the subject came up naturally . . . and only if they were alone, just the two of them. Yet in her heart, she felt impressed to add Rosanna's healing to her growing prayer list. The Lord God could strengthen her friend and enable her to carry a baby to term. Prayer was the best gift Nellie could offer.

Chris Yoder headed outside to the school parking lot to his car, especially enjoying his off-campus privileges during lunchtime. Today he was hungry for a big juicy hamburger and some hot French fries with salt and pepper. While he ate, he planned to scan the paper for his current events class this afternoon, since he hadn't had time to catch up last evening. *Physics,* he groaned inwardly, wondering why some teachers had to pile it on.

On the way out for some fast food, he passed the Honey Brook Restaurant and the idea taunted him again—was he bold enough to ask Nellie Mae Fisher to his graduation banquet? Why this nagging thought, despite his every attempt to brush it away?

The whole situation was strange. *First Zach falls for an Amish girl . . . and then I meet her sister.* How wise was it to even consider getting to know Nellie better? He could imagine what his father would say, but not Zach. He didn't need his younger brother to remind him that his interest was laughable. Actually, Zach might even be troubled by any reminder of the girl he'd lost. It didn't help that Nellie Mae was Suzy's sister.

Settling in with his lunch, he scanned the front-page headlines. Escalating soldier casualties in the Vietnam War and the upcoming Eastern Division finals between Philly's 76ers and the Boston Celtics got top billing.

Chris flipped over to the local-news section and stopped to read an article about an Amish farmer who'd survived a kick to the head by his mule. Longtime dairyman David D. Yoder of west Honey Brook had been left tragically paralyzed by the freak accident.

"David Yoder?" he said aloud. *Dad's cousin!* He scanned the column again. It had been some years since his family's last trip to the Amish farm, but he hadn't forgotten their many Saturday afternoon visits. Staring out the window, he remembered flying through the barn on the rope swing with Caleb and his older brother Jonah. He had forked hay into the stable area for the new calves, too, and helped with milking chores, much to the amazement of the boys—and their parents. Cows were very sensitive to strangers, but they'd taken to Chris like he was one of Caleb's brothers.

He'd been nine or ten the last time, a Saturday before the Yoders were to host Preaching service. He remembered the excitement as the Amish bench wagon pulled up to the house. The men had removed all the walls on the main floor of the Yoders' house before hauling in long wooden benches to set up a temporary place of worship. The wagon contained piles of Amish hymnals, too, and dozens of extra dishes for the big meal afterward.

Chris and his own brothers quickly became as caught up in the fun of the preparations as his many cousins. The Yoders had provided popcorn and cold apple cider for everyone who helped, and he and Caleb—the cousin closest to him in age—had enjoyed more than their fair share. While Chris's older brothers pitched in to help, he and Zach had played hide-and-seek with Caleb under the benches as they were stacked in the yard.

Chris wondered how much had changed since the days of his own Grandpa Yoder, who'd left the Amish to marry an English girl. Because Grandpa hadn't joined the Amish church, he had not been shunned, and Chris's father's family could visit their Plain relatives whenever they pleased.

Suddenly curious to drive out to the Yoder farmhouse, Chris also felt compelled to offer his help during this trying time. *And I wouldn't mind seeing Caleb again, either.*

He wondered if his father's cousins had a strong faith to draw on.

Yeah, I think it's time I got in touch with my Amish roots. Chris grinned, and Nellie Mae popped into his thoughts yet again.

———

The day had been plentiful with sunshine and clear skies since her brother James dropped Rhoda off at the Kraybills'. She had admired the big clapboard house, the detached garage, and the stretch of land behind the Kraybills' property, but mostly, she was eager to see her Buick again. *My ticket to freedom.* She had driven it with Mrs. Kraybill instructing her at least a dozen times now, and with her brother James—before he'd laid down the law to her.

She'd come a long way since January's snows, when she'd accidentally backed into the Kraybills' front yard, running over the children's snowman. Yet she wanted to be fully prepared for both the driving test and the written one.

Ken was urging her to take the test soon, so she could drive independently to meet him places and drop by his house for supper, too. Her heart pitter-pattered whenever she thought of Ken . . . and his beautiful house. Although they hadn't been dating long enough to be quite that serious yet, she wondered when he might pop the question, as the English often referred to a proposal of marriage.

Hurrying now to finish dusting the downstairs rooms, Rhoda dismissed her romantic notions and set about doing a thorough cleaning. In a while, she hoped to take a few minutes to look over the apartment ads. Smiling to herself, she recalled it hadn't been so long ago she was poring over the ads in search of a car. *That turned out just fine,* she thought, congratulating herself as she carefully moved the many knickknacks, one by one, on the old desk in the living room.

I'm getting my dearest wishes . . . and tomorrow I'll have my driver's license. If all goes well.

Numerous times since having first met Ken here, in this very house, she'd stopped and pinched herself to see if this was all a mere dream. Working for the Kraybills was indeed providential. She still embraced that mind-set, though she wondered if Ken might be right. He viewed things differently— that life was more about what you made of it in the long run. That's what counted, he said.

It's all up to me, she reminded herself.

With that in mind, she eyed the newspaper, ready at last for a coffee break. Feeling good about striking out on her own, she opened to the ads and noticed several apartments available immediately. One not so far away caught her attention, though she wondered if she could afford it.

Mrs. Kraybill wandered into the kitchen. "What are you looking to buy now?"

"Well, I'm being shown the door, so to speak." She explained that James was much too strict for her liking. "Ken's not terribly pleased about his rules, either."

Upon hearing her nephew's name, Mrs. Kraybill tilted her head, eyebrows raised. "Oh, the two of you are becoming serious?"

Rhoda wasn't used to discussing private matters. "I think it's safe to say we like each other."

"And your brother's opposed to your seeing someone outside the Plain community?"

"That's putting it mildly." She'd heard Ken say this before and liked the ring of it. "So now I'm hunting for an apartment." Mrs. Kraybill leaned down to look where Rhoda was pointing. "What do you think of this one?"

Mrs. Kraybill read the ad. "Well, if it's as nice as the description, you could be very happy there." She straightened, eyeing her curiously. "I'm sure Mr. Kraybill wouldn't mind if you'd like to rent the spare room from us, Rhoda. Until you get on your feet."

Does she mean till I'm married?

"Oh, nice of you to offer," she replied. "I'll let you know soon."

She wasn't too keen on the idea, but she didn't want to be impolite, either. Truth be told, she wondered if it was such a good idea to live under her employers' roof, no matter how kind.

Thankfully, Mrs. Kraybill didn't press further. Perusing several more ads, Rhoda realized she was actually excited about looking for a place to call her own—never mind that James was forcing her out. Perhaps Ken would be willing to take her to see the apartments listed in the paper after their supper date tonight.

And if not, maybe I'll discover how serious he is, she thought, wondering if this turn of events might even spur him to ask her to marry him.

CHAPTER 7

H is favorite radio station blaring, Chris took in the sights as he continued on Beaver Dam Road past the narrow bridge, near the spot where he had first met Nellie Fisher. He noticed, for the first time, a small sign posted along the road—*Nellie's Simple Sweets*. Could it be her shop?

Not giving in to the temptation to slow down, he headed toward the stone mill. He knew better than to let his mind wander back to the two times he'd talked with her. Suzy's sister was off limits to him. Anyone knew that.

But what was he supposed to do? Wash her from his mind—those appealing brown eyes, her sweet innocence?

The afternoon was bright as he passed the old stone mill. His mother had often pointed out the historic building, with its millpond and the wide creek that ran parallel to the road. Though not far from his own neighborhood, this stretch of countryside felt strangely removed from the familiarity of town. Few trees obstructed the sun's rays, which splashed gold onto the road. Everywhere he looked, nature seemed to be springing back to life.

Squinting, he reached up for his sunglasses, sliding them off the visor. The deeper into the country he drove—a place of grazing land and the silhouettes of silos and barns—the more clearly he pictured David Yoder's farm. A long swing dangled out front, hanging high from the tallest maple.

He'd once snuck off to a water hole with Zach and Caleb, leaving their clothes strewn along the trail—all but their undershorts. They'd climbed high into a sycamore tree to leap off the thick middle branch into the cold, clear water below.

What adventures we had!

So many memories of their country visits were racing back that Chris had to purposely slow down, his excitement fueling his speed.

———

Reuben was put off by the Yoders' refusal of his most recent offer to help—"*We'll stick to our family's aid,*" the oldest son, Gideon, had told him—and he relinquished his frustration to prayer. He was not alone in his predicament; a good many other New Order farmers had been turned away, as well. Prior to the church split, the People had always united when a tragedy struck, regardless if the victim was family or not—in or out of the old church—with the exception of the Bann.

But now? The Yoders seemed to be making a point of the division, and just when they needed the most assistance.

Overwhelmed with concern, Reuben knelt beside the love seat in the upstairs bedroom. "O Lord, make my heart soft toward the Yoders . . . come what may." He prayed for salvation to come to David's household, for physical healing, and for divine help for the whole family. Claiming the promises of God, he stayed on his knees.

After a time, he rose and felt the familiar urge to extend himself yet again to David. *I'll do your bidding, Lord.*

He hurried outdoors, going to the horse barn to trot his two best driving horses around the training track. Two farmers from Chester County would be arriving soon, interested in dickering. Reuben needed to sell more than two horses this spring if he was to keep his head above water, but as he now endeavored to do in all aspects of his life, he would trust God for the outcome.

––––––

Before starting the afternoon milking, Caleb headed to the house for some ice tea. He'd seen his sister Leah making some earlier as he'd brushed past her, adding oodles of sugar, just the way he liked it. He entered the kitchen; with both Mamm and Daed away, the house felt too quiet. He wondered how Daed was holding up, lying in a hospital bed, unable to shift or even feel his legs.

My brothers have all been to see Daed. . . .

Truth was, he couldn't bear the thought of seeing his father waste away, being cared for by English folk he merely tolerated. Yet they were undoubtedly making him comfortable with pain medication . . . and keeping him alive. He didn't know all the ins and outs of his father's condition. Mamm said little enough when she returned home, and none of his older brothers was given to talk. Of the three, Abe was most often around, overseeing things as best he could, though like Gideon and Jonah, he had his own farm to keep going, and a growing family.

Caleb was aware of a small shadow gathering inside him, taking up residence in the middle of his chest, threatening his very breath at times. He must not give in to it, must not let those big black crows nest there.

Not wanting to get bogged down with thoughts of his harsh father, he drank the sweet tea straight down and then headed back to the barn. It was already close to four o'clock, and Daed had the whole herd of dairy cattle on a strict milking schedule, with one milking at four in the morning, and the second at four in the afternoon. *"Like clockwork,"* Daed had once stated. And his father usually had to state things only once.

Caleb's right arm had taken a beating today, during a difficult birthing early this morning. In an attempt to limber it up, he waved it around and around, like a pitcher preparing to throw a ball. He smiled momentarily. He hoped to slip away to play some softball come summer, if he found any spare time while Mamm and his sisters were busy shelling, snapping, and pickling the produce from their vegetable garden—an acre or more, which he needed to till up before long. Attending Singings and other youth gatherings was already out, no matter that he was courting age. Despite her past smiles, Susannah Lapp had snubbed him after Preaching service recently. No doubt she'd heard he had given up his father's land and had nothing left to offer a bride now. "Not that I care," he muttered, rubbing his bruised arm. The poor calf had been turned wrong and taken hours of labor to birth. He was thankful his arm had withstood the near bone-crushing contractions long enough to move the valuable calf deep within its mother. He'd nearly lost the beautiful creature.

Hurrying across the wide backyard, he almost welcomed the thought of the strenuous days of work stretching before him. He still had several tons of hay to unload, hay that had been hauled in from neighboring barns, since the drought had wreaked havoc with dozens of local hayfields last summer. He recalled Nellie's talking at length about it, too. Goodness, but he remembered in vivid detail every conversation he'd ever had with Nellie Mae. Was that how it was at the end of things . . . you remembered too clearly the beginning?

Just as he reached the barn, Caleb heard a car creep up the lane. An unfamiliar tan sedan slowed and then stopped near the back walkway.

A fellow about his age jumped out, hair like shocks of wheat. "Hello, Caleb!" he called, waving.

Caleb recognized him immediately as his second cousin. "Hullo, Christian!"

Grinning, Christian approached him, his gaze taking in the entire area. "Looks just like I remember."

"All but the barn . . . that needs a good paintin', I daresay." He put out his hand. "Good to see ya."

"Same here. Last time was . . . where?"

"In town at the hardware store, seems to me. A jingle, as you called it, was playin' on the radio behind the counter." Caleb stepped back to appraise his cousin, all spiffy in dark jeans and a brown suede jacket. "What brings you here?"

Christian pursed his lips, displaying the first hesitancy since he'd arrived. "I'm real sorry about your father's accident, Caleb. I read about it in the paper."

Caleb's back stiffened, uncomfortable with sympathy. "We don't get the English newspaper. Never have."

Christian looked over at the house. "I wasn't sure I'd find your place. It's been a while. . . ."

Suddenly impatient, Caleb was eager to start milking. "Well . . . I'd show you around," he said, thumbing toward the barn, "but we're kinda shorthanded these days, what with Daed in the hospital. So I'd better—"

"Could you use some help?"

"What?" He stuffed his hands in his pockets. "Actually . . . no."

"Seriously. I've got some free time, and I *have* milked before."

Caleb did recall his father's showing Christian how years ago. *How old was I then?*

"I'm sure I still remember." Christian grinned again. "Besides, it would give us a chance to get reacquainted."

Reacquainted? Caleb was befuddled again. Normally, Caleb would have sent him on his way, just as he had the new church folks who'd frequently come by since Daed's accident. Men who were thought to be too keen on converting them, like the whole lot at Manny's church had done to Nellie Mae and her family. Like them, Chris seemed entirely too friendly, yet what could it hurt? He *was* family, though English, and milking was a big chore for one man.

He found himself shrugging. "S'pose if you really want to. You remember how to approach the cows?"

Christian nodded with evident confidence. "I never forget!" Christian walked along with him to the barn.

"Well, let's see how the cows respond to you, okay? They're quite wary of strangers, ya know."

It turned out Christian really did remember, and after only a few tips he was working his way between the rows of the heaviest milkers.

More than an hour had passed by the time Caleb took his cousin over to the milk house for a short break.

"You weren't kidding." Caleb showed him the bulk milk tank. "You didn't forget much at all. Actually, kind of a miracle, seems to me."

Christian slapped his pants free of straw. "Hey, I forgot how much I like it here."

"Smells nasty." Caleb chuckled. "At least that's what city folk say."

Christian shook his head. "I must be crazy. I've always liked the smell of manure in the springtime."

They laughed and then Christian turned to Caleb. "So when do you milk again?"

"Four o'clock tomorrow mornin'. You comin' to help *then?*"

Christian chuckled. "No, but seriously, I could come after school several times a week."

Caleb stared at his long-lost cousin, mulling over his unexpected offer. The fellow was as likable as the day was long. There was something disarming about him . . . something refreshing, too. *What could it hurt?*

He glanced at Christian's shoes. "Next time, tennis shoes might not be so good."

Christian lifted his right foot; dried manure was stuck to the bottom. "Yeah, I see what you mean."

"You'll need work boots."

"Is that a yes?" Christian asked, breaking into a broad grin.

Caleb slapped him on the back. "We'll make a farmer out of you yet, Christian."

"Fine with me . . . and please call me Chris."

Caleb hoped he'd done the right thing by John Yoder's boy . . . hoped, too, that Daed wouldn't get wind of Chris's helping anytime soon.

———

Rhoda wanted to skip for joy, but she demurely walked down the steps of the Department of Motor Vehicles. She'd worn her floral cotton skirt and tan sweater set, with a long single braid hanging down her back and her hair parted on the side, instead of the traditional middle part. Above all, she did not want to be thought of as Plain. Not today!

A colleague-friend of Ken's had followed her and Ken here to the town of Reading, the closest location for her driving test. Ken and his friend had already returned to the real estate office in Strasburg. Secretly, Rhoda was glad, eager to enjoy her first solo drive now that she'd passed both her written and driving tests with what the official had said were "flying colors."

Flying colors. What a peculiar idea!

Hurrying to her car, she opened the door and slipped into the driver's seat. "I did it!" she said, leaning back and laughing.

Feeling confident now that the tests were a thing of the past, she pulled out of the parking lot, relieved not to have had to parallel park, as she'd done earlier. Her only slight weakness, the testing official had said, explaining that many new drivers improved that skill over time.

Heading south on Business Route 222, she was anxious to get back to rural Honey Brook before going to work at the restaurant. She'd brought along her change of clothing, still marveling that she'd landed the waitress job while wearing her Amish garb. *Must've been providential,* she thought, catching herself. Did she believe that anymore? She wanted to go fancy in every way, but try as she might, it was hard, if not impossible, to dismiss that part of her upbringing.

Rhoda came to a stop sign. She actually welcomed the sight, but not because she enjoyed slowing down or stopping. Rather, she enjoyed shifting gears, having gotten the rhythm of the clutch and accelerator down as smooth as vanilla custard.

After another twenty minutes, the landscape began to open up, but she did not allow herself the luxury of looking out the side windows. She was focused on the road ahead . . . and on her future, as she saw it unfolding in her mind.

"First, I pay off this car . . . then I save up for my travels. *Our* travels," she corrected herself, thinking of Ken. He was, after all, the perfect choice for a husband.

At the intersection of Route 10 and Beaver Dam Road, she slowed, looking both ways before accelerating again. She noticed several farmers out doing early plowing with teams of mules, and she thought of Dat and her brothers. Ephram would wait awhile longer to start plowing, because he liked the soil to be softer, but Thomas and Jeremiah—James, too—could plow anytime now with their new tractor. She felt a brief pang of sadness. She missed seeing her parents and her sisters, too, but her new, fully modern lifestyle was far more exciting than theirs could ever be.

As she neared her father's farmhouse on the left, Rhoda noticed a family of ducklings close to the road. She slowed the car, waiting for them to toddle across to the other side. "Be careful, little ones," she warned in the voice she used with her nieces and nephews. "Be ever so careful. . . ."

When the familiar horse barn and house came into view—her father's house—she purposely did not look. She was determined to keep her gaze straight ahead. No good reason to look back; even the Bible said as much.

———

During a short lull at dinner between the salad and the main entrée, which required a few more minutes in Ken's oven, Rhoda folded her hands tightly in her lap beneath the white linen tablecloth. She looked at Ken, all spruced up, as he sometimes described himself—and her—when they dressed up. What should she say about her dilemma, if anything?

His eyes searched hers. "Are you all right, Rhoda?" He slid his hand across the table, palm up, but she continued to press her hands together.

"I'm moving out of my brother's house."

Ken's eyes widened and he frowned. "After such a short time?"

His response put her even more on edge.

"I just need to leave, that's all."

He sighed, withdrawing his hand. "Well, if you need a place, one of my renters gave me notice yesterday. I'll have a vacancy downstairs, on the second floor. It's a spacious place with its own bath but won't be cleaned and ready for another three weeks."

Second floor?

"Nice of you to offer . . . but I haven't decided what I'll do just yet." She considered what her mamma might say about living in the same house as her beau, although a floor apart. *Avoid the appearance of evil.*

No, her mother wouldn't understand. Neither might the Kraybills, especially as Mrs. Kraybill had been so kind to offer their spare room. Now Rhoda was flummoxed, unsure what to do.

James would ask why I don't just abide by the rules, she thought, shrugging that aside.

"I think you'd be very comfortable in that room," Ken said from across the small table. "But seriously, no pressure."

After dinner, Ken insisted on making ice cream sundaes. "Do you want the works?" he asked. "Chocolate syrup, nuts, whipped cream . . . and the cherry on top?"

"Sounds good. Denki . . . er, thanks."

When he brought her bowl around and placed it on the table in front of her, he leaned down and kissed her. "Congratulations, Rhoda. You're a licensed driver now."

She blushed, happy about passing her test, and nearly as happy with his sweet kiss. Truth was, the written test had gone quite smoothly, after studying the booklet so many times with both Ken and his aunt.

She smiled too broadly and Ken caught her eye and grinned. "You know the Pennsylvania rules of the road better than most high school students taking driver's training, I do believe."

He was humoring her and she loved it. She relished the attention Ken gave her. She loved him with no real gauge of such emotion from the past, never having had someone so interested in her before.

And now they were spending time once again in his wonderful house. She assumed he must love her, too, because his kisses seemed to say as much, although he hadn't declared it with his words. But then, Mamma often said, "Actions speak louder than words." Maybe that applied when it came to falling in love, too.

For no apparent reason, Ken winked at her. Then he reached for her hand, and this time she accepted. "You seem tired."

"I've been thinking. What would you say if I had my hair cut?"

He scrutinized her with a mischievous expression. "I would never presume to tell a lady what to do with her hair."

She didn't want to say she'd already arranged the appointment for tomorrow morning, before she had to be at work around noon. "All right, then. But it'll be short."

"A drastic change?" He paused. "I've never even seen it down."

You probably shouldn't.

"How long is your hair, Rhoda?" His eyes had softened to the point she felt he might be sorry if she followed through with the haircut.

"Past my waist."

"Really?" His eyes lit up.

"But not for much longer."

He smiled thoughtfully. "No matter what you have done to it, you'll always be pretty to me."

Ach, pretty . . .

She felt like dancing, even though she'd never danced a step in her life.

CHAPTER 8

Saturday morning held an air of expectation as Rhoda drove herself to the beauty shop. Even the sky seemed a deeper blue, and the song of robins had awakened her—a right good sign.

Today was her special day, and she knew precisely how she wanted her hair to look, like that of a movie star she'd seen in a magazine left behind at the restaurant. She'd discovered it while closing up one night recently. She had been struck by how long and graceful the actress's neck looked with such a short bob, complete with wispy bangs.

Unlike the actress—Suzanne somebody—Rhoda was not a brunette. Nor was she at all interested in dying her blond tresses a dark brown.

She only hoped she would not regret this bold move today—her hair was the final link to her formerly Plain appearance. Knowing Ken was in agreement with her decision encouraged her.

An hour later, Rhoda stared at herself in the beauty shop mirror, touching her hair repeatedly, surprised at how short and bouncy it was. Not only was the weight of it gone—and the weight of what her bun had signified—but she felt an overwhelming sense of defiance. She gave the beautician a nice tip and stepped outside to her car, parked at the curb.

She relished the breeze blowing through her short 'do and realized her life had already changed completely. Cutting her hair was only one more step toward her hope of becoming a fully fancy woman, a life that had begun with her purchase of this wonderful car.

Slipping into the driver's seat, she somehow felt even freer than the day she'd left Dat and Mamma's house. Moving her head from side to side, she adjusted her rearview mirror to admire herself once again.

She pushed her glasses up and slid the key into the ignition, never tiring of the sound of the engine starting up. *Ach, what power.* She signaled and looked over her shoulder to check for oncoming traffic, then pulled into the street, rejecting thoughts of tedious horse-and-buggy travel. *All of that's behind me now*. She was headed directly to Ken's house, eager to see him—and for him to see her new look, as well.

At the first traffic light, she noticed a scruffy fellow wearing tiny "granny glasses," standing on the curb, holding out his thumb, his hair long and stringy. She knew from listening to Ken talk that this young man was a hippie—"a flower child." The name struck her as peculiar, yet another English term that made no sense to her. Feeling sorry for the man, she considered picking him up, but something hazy and odd about his eyes made her think better of it.

The light turned and she focused on the road ahead, enjoying the drive. She glanced now and then at the speedometer, as both Ken and James had instructed her. Thinking of her brother again, she felt a sudden mix of emotions. James had asked her to leave his house. So many sacrifices she'd made for her new life, though surrendering two feet of burdensome hair was not one of them.

The sight of Ken's big house inspired her as she parallel parked on the street. The stonemasonry work made her think of the houses on Beaver Dam Road, near her father's own sprawling farmhouse.

Glancing up, she saw Ken standing in the doorway, waiting. She ran her hands through the back of her hair, checking the mirror quickly, liking what she saw, and then got out of the car. She called to him as she hurried up the flagstone steps. "Well, I did it . . . what do you think?"

"It's nice . . . really cute." He cocked his head humorously. "You look like someone in the movies."

"Oh?" she said coyly. "Who's that?"

"She starred in a horror flick—an Alfred Hitchcock movie." He snapped his fingers. "Not the lead actress, but a pretty brunette. . . ." He looked at her, studying her again as she angled her head demurely from side to side. "Ah yes—Suzanne Pleshette. She was in *The Birds*." He leaned over and kissed her cheek. "You're simply dazzling, darlin'."

She had no reason not to believe him, and let out a little laugh, nearly frightened at this latest victory. "Thanks ever so much," she said when he repeated how pretty she looked. "Well, I'd better head off to work."

"It's definitely you, Rhoda." Ken was nodding as he waved, all smiles. "I'll drop by in a while, if you'd like."

She smiled her response.

"See you later," he called.

Everything she'd longed for was coming true.

Rosanna King had awakened extra early to redd up the house the morning before Sister's Day, scrubbing the floors in the kitchen, sitting room, and front room. More than a dozen women were coming, including Nellie Mae and her sister Nan and their Bird-in-Hand cousins Treva and Laura.

She needed this time to sweep the dust bunnies out of the corners, dust the furniture, and wipe down the windowsills. If she'd felt up to it, she might have washed all the downstairs windows—inside and out—but she must conserve her energy.

Before it was time to make the noontime dinner for Elias, Rosanna felt drawn to go to the nursery upstairs, where Eli and Rosie had slept. *All those many weeks they were ours*.

She stood there, taking in the cozy room with its single dresser and blanket chest filled to the brim with receiving blankets and baby afghans she'd made. The lump in her throat turned to sudden tears, and she sat in the middle of the floor in a heap. The matching oak cradles made for their twins soon blurred as she wept uncontrollably.

Hugging herself, she rocked forward and back, thinking of her babies in Kate's and John's arms now. She remembered the last time she'd seen precious Eli, nestled in Kate's embrace across the room from her, where she'd held little Rosie for the final time. It had been the day the bishop had called the two couples to his house—the day Rosanna had relinquished both babies back to their original parents.

She could not erase the images from her mind. Hard as she tried, she kept seeing her sweet babies . . . Eli, Rosie . . . even all the nameless ones she'd lost since her first failed pregnancy.

And silently she promised herself not to let on to Elias what she now knew to be true: Another wee babe lived within her. But for how long? The knowledge brought her no joy. "Is this my lot in life, Lord?" she prayed, knowing she must somehow prepare herself emotionally and physically for the likelihood of yet another miscarriage.

She cried out to God for grace to bear the impending loss, loving her baby for the few short weeks it was safe in the haven so near her heart. Her very soul felt bound up in this life, just as it had been with each of the others, and she felt she might simply break apart. Oh, the desperate way she loved her forming child, though she was never, ever to see him or her, or to hear her little one's cry for nourishment and love.

"How many more times, dear Lord?" Rosanna sobbed. "How many?"

Over the lunch hour, while the pies for Sister's Day were baking, Nellie asked Nan to help her make up the bed in the spare room. Nan, who had been darning several of Dat's socks, hurried upstairs with her. "I ironed the bedsheets and pillowcases yesterday, so they'll be extra nice," Nellie said.

Nan's face shone. "Treva must be looking forward to comin' to our neck of the woods, jah?"

"She's curious 'bout the bakery shop, too, I think."

"Is that why she's comin'?" asked Nan.

Nellie suspected the reason had more to do with hoping to find a baby for Rosanna than with the shop. "Well, we've been writing letters all these years, so it's certainly time she visited."

"Seems odd, really." Nan scrunched up her face. "To think we have cousins we know mostly through circle letters and whatnot."

"Well, when there're more than a hundred of them—and they don't all live round here—it's hard to keep up."

"Even so. Family's family."

She looked at Nan, who was making square corners on the bottom sheet, and suddenly thought of Nan's best friend. "Do you think Rebekah Yoder will come tomorrow . . . with a friend or a cousin?"

"I'm sure she won't bring her sisters Leah or Emmie."

"I hadn't thought either of them would go." She wondered how poor Elizabeth was getting along, traveling back and forth between the house and the hospital, as she was rumored to do daily. Her husband's survival was no longer in question, but his paralysis remained. "Any news on David Yoder?"

"Only what Rebekah told me yesterday—that her father's comin' home today or tomorrow."

She couldn't imagine what a sad reunion that would be for the whole family, and especially for Caleb. She assumed he was working the dairy farm, since he was back at home. He would be seeding the tobacco beds real soon, as well. His father, like quite a few others, depended on that cash crop, which required the help of nearly the whole family and a "dark-to-dark" work schedule. Anymore, though, Preacher Manny was speaking out against growing tobacco, and plenty of farmers were agreeing with him that it was just "feedin' the devil's crowd."

Plumping the pillow on her side of the guest bed, she waited for Nan to do the same. Then together they pulled up the old quilt—the bold Bars pattern, in shades of deep blue, red, and palest pink—and tucked it beneath the pillows. She stepped back to appraise their work.

"Too bad Mamma didn't let Rhoda move into this empty room," Nellie said softly. "Maybe she would've stayed put."

"Ach, you can't know that." Nan leaned on the footboard.

"Rhoda's her own person, and she's makin' that mighty clear."

Nan hung her head. "Maybe we should talk less 'bout it and pray more."

"Jah," Nellie agreed. "Well, s'pose it's time to check on the pies."

Nan went ahead, and Nellie stayed to open the window to let the room air out a bit. She looked to the west, drinking in the view of the meadow, hoping it would please her cousins, too. It wouldn't be long now till Treva and Laura arrived.

Nellie sighed. She half wished she'd told Rosanna that her wait for a baby could well be over.

No, I can't do that to her, she decided. But what could she tell Treva was the reason she'd held back such astonishing news?

Caleb felt strangely like two different people, standing in the barn looking through the milk house window as the van pulled into the drive—bringing his father home. There was the Caleb who'd been tending to the brand-new calf, coaxing it to nurse from its mother, wanting to hurry to the house to help Mamm—and the others—get his father settled. His wounded father was home after eleven long days in the hospital, although he would have to return regularly for rehabilitation.

The other Caleb kept himself in check, lest he rush outside and look like a bumbling fool in front of Daed and the family. *That* Caleb knew the right thing to do but was nearly frozen with fear and frustration . . . even guilt. *If I'd been home, would the accident have even happened?* he'd asked himself a dozen times. Yet it was his father's doing that he'd been absent that evening, living over at Dawdi and Mammi's place.

Cast out for loving Nellie Mae.

He watched his sisters hold the door open for the wheelchair to pass through, and surprisingly, it cleared. Mamm's face was as solemn as he'd ever seen it. He knew from observing her jerky movements that she was as frightened as he was. This wasn't the usually confident and poised mother who could weather any storm.

If only he could describe how wretched he felt, knowing his father was

severely injured . . . and frail as could be. If only he could utter his deepest
fears to someone, whether they understood or not—just saying them might
bring some sense of relief. But he was reticent to breathe a word, especially
to his brothers, and Mamm had worries enough of her own. Rebekah, now,
she was a different story—the smart one, long gone as she was and staying
away, just as he sometimes wished he had. Yet now he was back, running
the farm for Daed, under Abe's oversight. That brother most likely stood to
inherit everything someday, since he was renting his farm and their older
brothers already owned theirs.

How foolish I've been. Yet Caleb felt powerless to change the circumstances. At night he dreamed maddening dreams where he was ensnared
in a pit, unable to move or get out.

He would have much preferred to dream of Nellie Mae, despite knowing she was forever lost to him. At least then a hope of some beauty and
goodness could be evident in his recurring nightmares. She, of all people,
might understand how he felt today.

Caleb heard the sound of Chris's car rolling up the drive later that afternoon, right on schedule. It was nearly time for the second milking of
the day, and Caleb had yet to make it to the house to welcome his father
home. *Just as well,* he decided. "Hullo again," he greeted his jovial cousin
as he pushed open the barn door.

Chris grinned. "Time to extract milk from the milk makers."

"You're far too excited about this." Caleb laughed and led him to the
milking parlor.

"It's great to be back." Chris took a deep breath and held it, catching
Caleb's eye. They broke into guffaws.

"We've got nose plugs on hand for English folk."

"Seriously?"

"No," Caleb admitted, instigating more laughter.

They shoved open the back barn door, and the cows began to move toward their assigned stalls. Quickly, Caleb started latching them into their
individual stanchions.

"It's restful here," Chris said, moving between the rows of cows to wash
down udders in preparation for attaching the milkers.

"Well, the roosters are raucous at times, cows complain, dogs bark—"

Chris chuckled. "So you'd compare them to blaring horns, squealing
brakes, and the endless hum of the city?" He patted the bulging side of a cow.

"You've got me there," Caleb replied.

"Coming here is about as peaceful as it gets, other than early morning, when I have my devotions."

Caleb nearly groaned. So Chris was one of *those* Christians. He should have suspected this of his Mennonite cousin; he'd heard this about Preacher Manny's group, too. *The troublemakers . . .* He still despised what they'd done to his Nellie—feeding her such nonsense.

"What about you, Caleb?" asked Chris, disappearing beneath the cow. "Where do you find peace?"

He felt his chest tense up. Instead of answering, he shrugged and then steered the topic to the mild weather. He brought up the growing season and tobacco seeding just around the corner, anything to avoid Chris's question. "Still catchin' up, really. Hadn't been home for nearly two months." He glanced at the row of heavy milkers on the other side of the barn, aware that Chris was looking his way.

"Two months is a long time," his cousin said.

"Just workin' for my grandparents, is all." He opened his mouth to say more but thought better of it.

"You weren't needed here?"

Caleb rubbed his lower back and stretched. "We don't see eye to eye, Daed and I."

Chris paused. "When I was little, your father used to play volleyball like his life depended on it."

Caleb guffawed. "That's how he does everything."

Chris squatted to reach under the cow again. "Sure hope his health improves."

"No one seems to know what'll happen." Caleb hesitated to mention what he feared. "Doctors say he could be paralyzed for the rest of his life. But with his rehabilitation sessions . . . maybe those'll help get him back on his feet."

Chris nodded and turned his talk to the past, asking Caleb what he thought of having such fancy cousins. Fact was, Caleb had never given it much thought, having little interest in the outside world. Yet despite their obvious differences, including Chris's keen interest in "God's Word," Caleb was surprised by how comfortable he felt with him. He appreciated his tenacity and hard work, too. Chris had come twice already since his first visit last week, when he had stayed a good two hours, keeping close tabs on the feed for the cows and helping to put on the milkers. Chris was strong from working for his father at their family-run nursery and landscaping business, something he did several hours during the week and all day Saturday. Even so, he'd made it clear he was available to help Caleb with some afternoon weekday milkings, provided he was able to keep up with his homework.

Chris had a real special way with the herd. Yet as surprisingly well as this little arrangement was working out, Caleb couldn't help but wonder what would happen once his father got wind that an outsider was lending a hand.

Most likely my days with Chris are numbered.

CHAPTER 9

Cleaning up for supper, Caleb heard his mother calling. He quickly dried his hands and hurried through the sitting room to the bedroom just off the front room, where Abe and Gideon were helping lift Daed from his wheelchair to the small bed on the far wall.

The wound on the right side of his father's head was still bandaged, and the rest of his face seemed somewhat swollen. Fading bruises marked his temples.

"Steady the wheelchair, won't ya, Caleb?" asked Mamm softly.

He squatted down and set the brake. *They should have done that sooner*, he thought, wondering why Mamm had called for him. Soon enough he knew, and it was just as he might have guessed. Daed's gaze fell on him momentarily before his father looked away, never acknowledging Caleb at all. Then, turning toward Gideon and Abe, Daed spoke quietly . . . slowly thanking Caleb's brothers for all they'd done.

Caleb experienced a jumble of emotions, but he straightened and pushed out his chest, daring his father to ignore him once again.

When Daed finally did acknowledge him, he offered a brief nod. Nothing more.

Is this how it's going to be?

A few minutes later, when Mamm was setting the table, she offered a quick apology. "Your father's out of sorts, ya must know, son."

Jah, well, he's always been that, thought Caleb.

"*Willkumm*, Treva . . . and Laura," said Mamma as Nellie Mae opened the back door to greet their cousins. "We've been expectin' you."

"Hullo, nice to see ya," Treva said with a big smile, removing her black outer bonnet. Her face was flushed with excitement.

Mamma ushered them inside, and Nellie took their long shawls and hung them up on the wooden wall pegs. "How was your trip over?" asked Nellie, taking the shared suitcase from Treva and setting it in the kitchen.

"Well, we did get stuck in some traffic, but overall the car ride went by quick," replied Treva, glancing at her younger sister. "Laura, here, was a bit nervous, though."

"First time?" Mamma asked.

Laura nodded somewhat bashfully.

"Oh, go on, you were so nervous . . . holdin' on like we were doomed." Treva shook her head in pretended disgust and then smiled.

Mamma glanced at Nellie and suggested she take them upstairs to see their room for the night.

Nellie Mae nodded, motioning for her cousins to follow. Treva chattered away all the while, and Nellie understood better why it was she was such a frequent letter writer—Treva loved to express herself, no getting around that. Maybe she'd ask Treva to rattle off some of her favorite recipes, too.

Smiling politely, Nellie couldn't wait for the wonderful-good supper Mamma had planned. And for Rosanna King's big quilting bee tomorrow.

———

Saturday breakfast was plentiful, with blueberry pancakes, scrambled eggs, bacon, and German sausage—a typical early morning meal and not just putting on the dog for company. Dat made a comment about how "extra light" Nellie's pancakes were, and everyone agreed.

Once at Rosanna's, it was clear how well she had planned for the special frolic. She had already spent numerous hours doing the piecework and appliqué, stitching the many rings down till they were as pretty as a picture. The middle, a thin layer of cotton batting, was already in place, and the plain tan backing had also been skillfully fitted.

Twelve chairs were positioned around the large quilting frame, and everything necessary for the quilting was on hand, including the cardboard templates for the intricate figural motifs designed and passed down through the generations. There were even two tin templates, heirlooms from Rosanna's quilter grandmothers.

"You've done a beautiful job with all the piecework," Nellie said, pointing to the array of pastel colors. "When on earth did you find time for all this?"

"Oh, there's plenty of time, believe me." Rosanna laughed, but she looked a bit peaked. "I enjoy the work."

"You feelin' all right?" Nellie whispered.

"I'm fine."

Nellie noticed the gray shadows under Rosanna's eyes. *She needs more distractions . . . like today's frolic.*

"Well, I'd be happy to help serve the pies at noon. Or do anything else to help you today."

"Denki, Nellie Mae . . . I appreciate it." Then Rosanna hugged her unexpectedly, a short little embrace.

"You sure you're—"

"Nonsense." Rosanna waved her away and headed into the kitchen.

She's not herself. Nellie turned to see Treva and Laura standing and talking with Nan and Rebekah Yoder. "Would ya like to all sit together?"

Laura looked at Treva as if awaiting her lead. "We'll sit wherever you say," Treva spoke up quickly. She smoothed the auburn hair that peeked from beneath her Kapp and touched the rings in the quilt. "Downright perty, jah?"

Laura nodded and followed, and Rebekah stayed put, still talking in low tones to Nan.

After a time, they settled down to work. Treva had brought along her own thin needle, brass thimble, and a cloth measuring tape in a small packet, as had several others.

The prattle rose and fell with the rhythms of a lively sermon. And Treva filled the occasional lulls with her own chatter—just like her letters, she was newsy and interesting.

Later, during the noon meal, while Nellie Mae cut each pie into eight helpings and dished up ice cream, Treva singled out Rosanna. "Did Nellie say anything to you about . . . well, something a bit personal?" Although Treva had lowered her voice to a whisper, the question was loud enough for Nellie and anyone else present to hear.

Nellie Mae cringed. *No, don't bring that up!*

Treva continued. "Did she tell you 'bout my neighbor, next farm over, and two women in our church district . . . what they're hopin' to do?"

Rosanna shook her head. "No."

Nellie cast a warning glance at Treva, who asked Rosanna and Nellie to go with her into the empty sitting room.

Rosanna agreed, frowning at Nellie. "What's she talking 'bout?"

When all was clear, Treva leaned in close to them both. "All three women have offered to give you a baby, Rosanna." Treva nodded, as if to punctuate her declaration. "None knows 'bout the other, but they each want you to visit. You could go and meet them—decide which woman should be the one."

Rosanna's eyes dimmed suddenly. She stared at Nellie as if in disbelief. Nellie reached for her friend's hand. "Ach, Treva," she said, glaring at her cousin. "Come, Rosanna, we best be talkin' this over . . . alone."

Quickly they headed for the front room, leaving Treva behind. "Are you sayin' you knew of this . . . and said nothin'?" Rosanna whispered, her tone tense.

"Oh, Rosanna . . . I just learned of it last week. I was frightened, honestly. I didn't want to open the door to more sadness for you and Elias." She shook her head. "Please, believe me."

Glancing over her shoulder, Rosanna trembled. "Is your cousin ever so sure?"

"'Bout the women's intentions?" Nellie nodded. "Seems so."

Rosanna leaned into her and wept.

Before the final quilting stitch was made midafternoon, Rosanna had decided to indeed travel to Bird-in-Hand to meet the women. Nellie worried that Rosanna might suffer further heartache just from the visits, let alone agreeing to receive one of the babies once he or she was born.

Treva leaned forward to ask, "Would you want to come along with Rosanna?"

Nellie offered a smile. "If that's what she wants."

Rosanna's tears sprang up again, and she nodded silently, her lips pursed tightly together.

Bless her heart . . . does she even know what she's getting into?

Knowing Rosanna as she did, Nellie was somewhat surprised her friend hadn't said she'd wait to discuss the idea first with Elias. And surely she would, as close a couple as they were. *Far closer than any husband and wife I know . . . 'cept Dat and Mamma.*

Rebekah Yoder and Nan offered to help Rosanna take the quilt off the frame after the guests began to leave. Then, come Monday, they would drop by to finish off the edges by adding a colorful, contrasting one-inch border.

Nellie offered to sign and date the wedding quilt in a chain stitch, one of her favorite kinds of stitching. "Do you have a bride-to-be in mind?" she whispered.

"Let's leave it as is—just today's date for now." Rosanna's face looked nearly gray.

"Oh, Rosanna, you've overdone it." Nellie touched her elbow. "Here. Sit and relax, why don't ya?"

"*Nee*—no. I best be keepin' busy."

Nellie wondered why she wouldn't let the rest of them remove the quilt and dismantle the frame. "Just for a minute?" she pleaded.

Rosanna shook her head, going straight for the quilt and frame, almost as if she were miffed. This hurt Nellie no end, but she tried not to let on and volunteered to help her and the others with the quilt while Laura headed to the kitchen for another piece of pie.

Turning off the road that Monday afternoon might have been crazy, but it was too late now. Chris was already headed into the drive leading to the country bakery shop. Not normally given to impulsive decisions, he knew only one thing as he stepped out of his car: Strange as it seemed, he wanted to talk to Nellie Fisher again. Besides, he hadn't tasted shoofly pie in a long time, and he was pretty sure his parents and Zach would enjoy something homemade *and* Amish. Who wouldn't? And anyway, he had plenty of time before he had to be at David Yoder's for milking. This new connection to the Plain community was a great idea—something he'd overlooked for too long—getting reacquainted with relatives, learning about his own heritage. *Getting a peek into Nellie Mae's world, too.*

Pushing open the door, he was startled to see five Amishwomen standing behind a counter, three of them smiling a glowing welcome. Two he recognized as Nellie Mae and her sister Nan, whom he'd met at the Honey Brook Restaurant. The other two young women looked like they might be related somehow, but he knew Suzy had talked of having only three older sisters. The last woman was much older and quite plump, with wisps of gray hair mixed among the blond visible beneath her prayer cap.

"Hullo," she said, her blue eyes reminding him of Suzy's. "May I help you?"

Nellie and her sister glanced at each other shyly, as if to say, *What's he doing here?*

When he asked to purchase a shoofly pie, the older woman—Mrs. Fisher, he guessed—pulled out a deep-dish pie. "Wet bottom's the best, I have to say." She offered another big smile. "And we also have two fruit pies today. Do ya like Dutch apple?"

Eyeing the shoofly pie in her hands, he hesitated—Dutch apple was one of his father's favorites, and both smelled fantastic. Suddenly he was unsure which to buy.

"Both are just delicious." She tilted her head.

Nellie Mae surprised him by speaking up. "You could take two pies and decide which one you'd like to buy another time, maybe."

He looked at her, taking in her fresh beauty—her clear-as-silk complexion and kind and sensitive eyes. "Sure, why not?" He smiled at her specifically, and she smiled back, her eyes brightening as she did.

He felt his face redden. *She's on to me*, he thought. Then, reaching for his wallet, he said, "I'll take both pies, please."

Nellie's friendly manner made his heart beat faster. While he waited for them to box the pies, he looked around at the shop, which wasn't as stark as he might have guessed. The tables and chairs scattered around were a nice touch, and the uncurtained windows let the light pour in.

Feeling all sets of eyes on him, he turned and paid for the pies. "Good-bye," he said. "And thanks!" He headed out the door, aware of the jingling bell as he left.

Chris didn't dare glance back toward the shop as he approached his car. *Guy time straight ahead—afternoon milking.* He laughed at himself, thinking of all those Amishwomen in one place, gawking at him. "Man, do I need to get a grip."

Nellie Mae hardly knew what to say, embarrassed as she felt. The bakery shop was much too quiet now that Chris Yoder was gone, even though Treva and Laura now sat at one of the round tables, flipping through Nellie's recipe notebook and chattering a blue streak about the bakery business.

Mamma was looking out the window at Chris, who was putting the pies in his car on the passenger's side before getting in on the other.

Ach, that was awkward, thought Nellie Mae.

It crossed her mind that he might have come here hoping to talk with her again. But why would that be? He was clearly an outsider—and quite a befuddled one at that. *Uncomfortable with so many of us helping him, that's for sure.*

She smothered her urge to giggle and watched him back the car up slowly. He took the driveway at a snail's pace, glancing over at the house a couple times.

What the world? She felt a bit nervous as he slowed even more out front, where the long porch stretched across the house and met the sidewalk. Then Chris made his way to the road, finally turning east.

Betsy sighed and sat down to rest a bit. Nellie and Nan had gone to the house with Treva and Laura to help them prepare to leave for home, and here came Fannie—Jeremiah's wife—with her youngest, Jeremiah Junior, looking to purchase a big batch of cookies for a sewing bee she was having tomorrow. "A whole group of us Beachy churchwomen are getting together," she made it known to Betsy. "I heard Rosanna King had herself a doin' over there last Saturday."

Nodding, Betsy checked to see how many dozen cookies were left. "Jah, Nellie and Nan went with Treva and Laura." Picking up a box, she asked, "Would ya like a mixed variety?"

"Whatever Nellie has left will be wonderful-gut," Fannie replied, hoisting her son on her hip.

"How've you been, Fannie?" asked Betsy as she gathered up the many cookies, glad her daughter-in-law was cleaning them out so there'd be no day-olds to sell tomorrow.

"Just fine . . . and you?"

"Oh, as busy as ever."

Fannie pulled out a wad of dollar bills from her pocket. "Here, take what you need." She kissed the toddler's head.

"It's so gut to see you. And you, too," Betsy playfully wrinkled her nose at her grandchild. Then she counted out only a few dollars and carried the cookies around to the front of the counter.

"Nice seein' you, too, Mamm." Fannie leaned up and gave her a kiss on the cheek. "Sure miss you and Reuben at church . . . since we pulled up stakes from Preacher Manny's."

"Come over anytime. Yous are always welcome." She reached out a finger to tiny Jeremiah, who grasped it. "Here, let me walk you out."

Fannie accepted. "How are you and Daed takin' the news about the Yoders? I just feel so terrible 'bout what happened. Poor, poor Elizabeth. I know ya used to be fairly close."

Betsy sighed. " 'Tis a shame all around, that's for sure."

"I heard they've got themselves a new fellow workin' with Caleb. And he sure ain't Amish, neither."

"Are you certain?"

"Well, Jeremiah was over there last week, offering help. Jonah turned him down flat—that one's got a bit of his father's edge to him. But when Jeremiah went out to the barn to talk to Caleb awhile, there was a blond-haired young man, dressed all fancy—well, not in fine getup, I don't mean that—but he surely wasn't Amish. Even so, he was washin' down the herd for milking while Jeremiah was there, chewin' the fat with Caleb."

"Blond, you say?"

"Jah. Jeremiah said his name was Christian, and he could've passed for Caleb's twin."

Betsy pondered this as she set the cookies in the buggy. She took her grandson from Fannie, holding him while she got settled. "Ya know, this very fella might've dropped by here earlier. Just a few minutes ago, in fact."

Fannie looked surprised. "Well, now, that's mighty odd. Wonder what he wants, comin' here."

Who's to know, she thought. "I'll ask Reuben and see what he thinks."

An Englischer helpin' the Yoders? A more peculiar piece of news Betsy couldn't imagine.

CHAPTER 10

Since long before dawn, Reuben had been praying for unity among the brethren, whether Old Order, New Order, or Beachy.

His prayers had deepened for David Yoder, a mere shell of a man. It pained Reuben to recall David lying there so helplessly in the hospital, Elizabeth nearby. Wanting to trust the blessed Lord for all his concerns, he headed outside to sit with the Good Book in his makeshift office, a small area at one end of the barn.

After reading for a good half hour, he reviewed his notes on the particularly fine Morgan that he hoped to sell today. *That's three now this spring,* he thought, mighty thankful.

When the sun slipped over the horizon, he went out and hitched up his best mare to the buggy. Then he went back upstairs to tell groggy Betsy that he planned to go and have breakfast with Ephram, wanting to keep in touch with him. *My only son still in the old church. . . .*

Several magnolias were already thick with buds and loaded down with robins in Ephram and Maryann's side yard as Reuben reined the horse into the lane. He was coming for breakfast unannounced, which he knew was fine with his son and daughter-in-law. The young ones, too, would make over him, and oh, how he enjoyed that. He planned to build some more martin birdhouses in a few weeks, inviting a different grandson to help with each one. But that could wait—he had other things on his mind this morning.

When Maryann glanced up from the stove and saw him, she smiled and came to open the door. "Ach, come in, Dat. Awful nice seein' ya!"

Soon toddlers Katie and Becky were tugging and pawing at his pant leg. "Up, Dawdi . . . up!"

Ephram rose from the table. "*Guder Mariye,* Dat! You're just in time for breakfast."

"Smells wonderful-gut," Reuben said, carrying little Katie to her place at the table. Becky ran over to Maryann, fussing till her mother reached down and kissed her curly head and set her in her high chair.

"*Kumm esse,*" Ephram said, waiting for Reuben to pull out a chair and sit at the opposite end. *Down here at the foot of the table, reserved for us old folk,* thought Reuben with a chuckle.

The silent prayer was short, and soon Maryann was passing a platter of scrambled eggs made with cheese, and then a plate of home-cured ham, some French toast, sticky buns, and blueberry jam. There was black coffee and cream right from the cow, as well as fresh-squeezed orange juice.

"Goodness, were you expectin' company?" Reuben asked.

"Well, Dat, you're hardly that!"

"Mamma cooks like this every mornin'," said one of the school-aged boys.

"That's right." Ephram looked at Maryann.

Her pretty face turned several shades of red. "Awful good of you to come," she said softly.

The children ate without making a sound, except for smacking lips and an occasional burp. Maryann had trained them well—to be seen but not heard. He wondered how long before they might come to realize the differences that so painfully existed between the old church and the New Order.

When offered it, he took a second helping of Maryann's cheesy eggs, ever so delicious, and another cup of coffee, this time with a dot of cream, which made the children snigger. Ephram did the same, clear up at the head of the table, as if imitating, although he was not one to go along with others for the sake of pleasing them. Reuben had been reminded of that stubborn trait during the contentious days of the church split, when Ephram had remained fixed in his resolve to stick with the old church. *I've got my work cut out for me in the coming years, getting him to see the light.* Still, Reuben believed in the power of prayer. The mightiest force of all.

After breakfast, they moseyed out to the woodshed, and Ephram mentioned being tired of the drab, brown colors that lingered on, reminders of the hard winter. He picked up an ax and handed one to Reuben. "I tilled the wife's vegetable garden yesterday . . . she's already got lettuce, peas, carrots, and her parsley planted." Ephram made small talk as he set up a log. Then, bringing the ax down with a mighty blow, he split it in half.

"Soon we'll be tilling the fields for potatoes and corn." Reuben made quick work of his own log.

"Thomas and Jeremiah will be using their tractor, no doubt," Ephram muttered. "So many new freedoms, anymore." He paused for a moment. "And lots of folk have used them as license to branch out to other things."

"When freedom comes, one must use good judgment," Reuben said.

Ephram pushed his straw hat down hard and slammed his ax into the tree stump nearby. "That church split you and Preacher Manny got started, well, it's opened up a whole bunch of doors that should've stayed shut, Dat."

"Are ya sayin' give them an inch and they'll take a mile?" Reuben quit chopping, too, wiping his brow with the back of his arm. "Listen, son, I didn't come here to squabble." He picked up his ax again.

"Well, then, tell me: Where's God's will in all this disjointed mess?" Ephram asked. "If I can be so bold, I believe the Good Lord gave me a sensible head on my shoulders."

"Won't deny that."

They locked eyes. "That's why I've stayed put in the church of my baptism."

Reuben reached for another log. "I understand why you'd want to stay."

"And why's that, Dat?"

"For one thing, it's all you know. It's familiar."

Clearly put out, Ephram quickly changed the subject. "Did ya hear David Yoder's boy has himself some fancy help?"

Reuben shook his head. "Doesn't sound like him a'tall."

"I saw the young fella myself the other day, forkin' out the muck with Gideon and Caleb."

"Who is it?"

"No one said." Ephram shrugged. "But he ain't Amish, and that's all I need to know."

"Sure wish I could help David during this time." He scratched his head. "He's not keen on having New Order farmers over there, doing chores."

"I guess if David doesn't want your help, you'd best walk away."

Reuben wondered if Ephram was suggesting the same was true for him. Things had gotten rather tense all of a sudden. He set his ax aside. "Well, I have horses to tend to, so I s'pose I should be sayin' so long."

"All right, then." Ephram waved.

Reuben lifted off his hat for a moment to fan his head. He walked to his horse and buggy, mentally putting Ephram in God's hands. *Best place for him, Lord . . . for all of us, really.*

———

Rhoda helped Martha clear the breakfast dishes until she caught sight of little Matty's messy face. "Oh, look at you, sweetie." She got a clean, wet washcloth and wiped his cheeks and mouth as he grinned up at her. Then she set to work on the table, wiping it off and catching the crumbs in her hand. Tossing the crumbs into the dishwater, she leaned close to Martha. "Just wanted you to know, uh . . . I'll be movin' out real soon."

Martha looked surprised. "So you've found a place?"

"Well, nothing's for sure yet, but I have two possibilities."

"And is one of them to return to your father's house?" Martha's eyes probed, piercing her.

I won't go back, Rhoda promised herself anew, glancing at Emma and Matty playing together, and suppressing her sadness.

"Makes good sense, doesn't it?"

"Honestly, I just can't." Sighing, she wished things could have been different and that she'd been given the freedom she longed for while living there. But that was all water under the bridge, even though she missed Nan and Nellie Mae terribly. "S'pose I should get to work."

"Have a gut day, Rhoda."

She blew kisses to the children and thanked Martha for breakfast; then she hurried to get her coat. The phone rang and Martha answered.

"Rhoda, don't leave quite yet. It's for you." Covering the receiver with her hand, Martha whispered, "It's a man."

Ken? Oh, she hoped so, but she felt awkward accepting his call in front of her sister-in-law. Thankfully, the children were nicely occupied in the next room, and Martha was polite and excused herself after handing her the phone.

"Hullo?"

"How's my girl this morning?"

My girl . . .

She peeked around the corner to see whether Martha was out of earshot. "Well, hi, Ken. You just caught me."

"I wanted to talk to you before you left the house."

Maybe he was calling to ask for another date. How she loved the convenience of the telephone and the feel of it in her hand! Not to mention having Ken's voice so close to her ear.

"I was thinking about dinner tomorrow night. How about prime rib?" he asked.

She leaned against the wall, enjoying the sound of his voice as he talked about wine and all the delicious food they would enjoy. She herself had only had one small sip of a very sweet wine in her whole life, but if Ken felt it topped off a meal, she didn't mind trying some.

"You know, Rhoda, you never said why you're leaving your brother's place," he surprised her by saying.

"Oh, you know how older siblings can be."

He chuckled. "Well, would it help if I got you in earlier at night?"

He's a sharp one.

Secretly she'd hoped her leaving James and Martha's might move things along more quickly toward her ultimate goal. So far, though, Ken had not even hinted at marriage—this in spite of Rhoda's attempts to make herself into the sort of modern woman she assumed he'd want in a wife.

Really, she could scarcely believe how well she was pulling off the transformation. She'd steadily lost close to a pound every four days by eating only fruit and juice at breakfast, and a big salad at noon—thanks to the chef at the restaurant on the days she worked there, and Mrs. Kraybill and Martha. While she still craved lots of fattening foods, she was ecstatic about her evolving shape.

But when it came to thinking about weight and her overall appearance, Rhoda remembered back to her delight at Ken's having chosen to date her even when she was beyond pleasingly plump. And that made her smile.

CHAPTER 11

Having deliberated long enough, Rosanna was ready to make plans to travel to Bird-in-Hand, hoping to meet the women behind Treva's astonishing revelation. She'd shared with Elias what she wanted to do, and although he brightened a bit at the prospect of another child, he was also tentative. *"I don't want to see you endure more heartbreak, love,"* he'd said.

She walked down the road and noticed the meadow grass trying its best to green up, and the bursting buds on trees. Spotting the small communal telephone box hidden by a large oak tree, she hurried to it and placed her call to a driver to set up a trip for tomorrow, thinking she might first stop in at Treva's and then go with her to meet the women. The feel of the telephone receiver in her hand always made her nervous, and today was no different.

While she waited for an answer on the other end, she thought how nice it would be for Nellie Mae to go along tomorrow. Sighing, she recalled how hurt Nellie had seemed by the way things had unfolded on Sister's Day. Rosanna felt bad about that. Part of it was due to her own struggle, knowing she would soon lose the baby growing within her. Yet that was no excuse for treating Nellie so.

If only I'd told her the truth . . .

But there was no need to tell a soul, really. No need for anyone else to experience the too-familiar pain.

After calling for a driver, she strolled back toward the house. She resisted the urge to cradle her stomach, to somehow comfort the fragile life growing inside. She cherished every day it continued. At least now Rosanna trusted she'd know this child in heaven if not here on earth.

She thanked God for bringing the light of Scripture to her heart and to Elias's. Its truths had led them out of past bondage and into the liberty of such things as feeling free enough to talk to her Savior in prayer.

Because of this, more than any other springtime, Rosanna observed the aromas of April's freshening landscape and the clusters of songbirds, each with a unique call. And the way the sky appeared increasingly blue as each week passed . . . the way the sun came to rest in the mulberry trees at sunset. The neighbors would soon turn their heifers out into the grassy meadow, and woodcutters would scout out the woods for dry timber.

Spring's never been more stunning.

She hoped she was doing the right thing by going to meet Treva's acquaintances. She'd asked for a divine warning, for something to stand in her way if she was not to go. So, moving ahead cautiously, Rosanna felt her way through this painful maze, her bittersweet memories of Eli and Rosie still lingering.

———

Betsy laid out her dress pattern with some help from Nan while Nellie looked after the bakery shop. She planned to cut out a new dress and sew most of it today, since her for-good dresses had seen better days.

Reuben came in the back door just then, looking for another big mug of coffee. She stopped everything and poured some for him as Nan finished pinning her pattern to the blue fabric. Then, with a quick smile, Nan headed out the door to the shop.

"Well, such gut timing," she admitted to her husband.

He reached for the coffee, nice and black, the way he liked it. "You have a kiss for me, Betsy . . . is that it?" He leaned forward and puckered up.

"Oh, you silly." She bent down and kissed him soundly. "I wondered if you'd heard 'bout Caleb Yoder having an outside fella helping with milking of an afternoon."

" ' Tis mighty curious, I daresay. Just heard it from Ephram."

"So it *is* true." She moved back to the table and picked up her scissors, leaning over to cut out the dress. "I think the same young man might've stopped in here . . . bought himself some pies."

Reuben glanced out the window. "Here?"

"Jah, Nellie sold him two of her pies yesterday afternoon."

"Well, now . . . wonder what David thinks of all this." He shook his head and made his way toward the back door again.

Betsy picked up her pace, determined to cut out the dress before it was time to lay out the noon meal.

———

With Abe's help, Caleb lifted his father from his wheelchair onto the downstairs bed, where he preferred to rest, following the noon meal. Like clockwork his father slept each day for more than an hour, something he had never done, at least prior to his accident.

Abe stepped out of the bedroom, leaving Caleb alone with Daed, whose face was still marred with fading bruises. Caleb was careful to move his father's legs just the way he'd requested, even though Daed could not feel anything from his waist down. But he could speak his mind without wavering—his tongue wasn't paralyzed.

Daed leaned his head up, bracing himself with his long arms. He scowled down at his rumpled trousers. "Ach, straighten them, Caleb," he barked.

Nodding, Caleb lifted first one foot, then the other, pulling the pant legs down. He remained calm as he untied and removed the heavy shoes to place them at the bottom of the double bed, stumped as to why Daed didn't simply wear his bedroom slippers. After all, he never left the house and stayed mostly in the kitchen near Mamm, where he read *The Budget* or watched her bake and cook and clean all day.

Then, before Daed could remind him to get the quilt that was folded over the blanket rack near the bureau, Caleb reached for it and spread it over his father's legs with great care, almost forgetting there was not a speck of feeling there.

"Don't leave me alone for too long." Daed closed his eyes. "Like the other day."

Caleb stared at the floor, grinding his teeth. Was it ever possible to meet Daed's expectations?

"Are you listenin' or still mooning over that Fisher girl?" Daed's words gnashed at him. "Don't leave me here to rot," he repeated.

His brothers and Leah and Emmie were in and out of the room all the time. Why was Daed picking on him? But no, he wouldn't let his father's sharp remarks discourage him.

Caleb felt strongly that his older sister Rebekah could be of some good help indoors when Gideon, Jonah, and Abe were too busy with farm work—especially on days when Leah was away working at the neighbors'. Even if Daed wouldn't allow Rebekah to live here, wouldn't it make sense for her to help sometimes with everything all topsy-turvy?

"Well, what're you waitin' for?" Daed said, one puffy eye open. "Start sowing all them tobacco seeds. Won't be long and you'll need to transplant, ya know. You, your brothers, and all their families. As many as you can get to help."

Caleb nodded, but resentment hung like armor around his shoulders. "Anything else you need for now?"

Daed waved his hand, still big and strong from all the years of raising tobacco.

"I'll check on you in a couple of hours, then."

A guttural grunt was the response.

Now's not the time to bring up Rebekah. . . .

He was glad he'd kept his cousin Chris's visits quiet, too, wondering why neither Mamma nor any of his brothers had said a word to Daed. If anyone had, surely his father would have mentioned his disapproval by now.

As he left the room, he pulled the door partly shut, leaving it open a crack, as Daed insisted. He felt mighty sorry for Mamma, who was at his father's beck and call even more so than before. Caleb had even helped with the heavy part of spring housecleaning, washing down walls and windows with his mother and sisters, since it was their turn to hold Preaching service—all of this while Daed looked on, seemingly disgusted that his son would stoop to women's work. But Caleb didn't mind; he had to fill up his hours somehow to avoid thinking too much about Nellie Mae.

At times, he could kick himself for not leaving town when he'd had a chance. With *her* . . . if she'd agreed. But he'd made the mistake of staying on and waiting for Nellie to come to her senses, hoping she'd realize she was mixed up in the wrong church. To no avail. And the longer she stuck it out in that new church of hers, the more unreasonable she was sure to become.

Nellie was so delighted to see Rosanna turn into the lane, she ran out of the shop and waved. "Hullo, Rosanna!"

Her friend was slow to climb out of the buggy, and a fleeting thought crossed Nellie's mind that she might still be under the weather. "I'm not here for pastries this time," Rosanna told her.

"No need to buy a thing."

Reaching for her hand, Rosanna asked, "Would you consider goin' with me to Bird-in-Hand tomorrow?"

This did Nellie's heart good. "I'll see if Mamma or Nan can manage the shop without me. Maybe both."

"Goodness, you must have lots of customers."

"You have no idea." Nellie hugged her. "Oh, I'm glad you're not mad at me."

"Well, why would I be?"

They grinned in unison, and Nellie led her inside to sit at the table nearest the window. "Care for some warm tea . . . or coffee, maybe?"

Rosanna shook her head right quick. "None for me."

This was a surprise. Since when had Rosanna given up her favorite hot drinks? Nellie joined her at the table, wondering what she could offer her instead. "How 'bout some juice, then?"

"Apple juice, jah—sounds good."

Nellie nodded. "I know we have some. Just wait here."

Quickly she made her way to the house, returning back to the shop with a small pitcher of the juice. But she was alarmed to see Rosanna brushing away tears. "Dear Rosanna, whatever's wrong?"

"I'm ever so frightened . . . just like you were when you read Treva's letter."

Nellie patted her hand. "Of course you are."

"What'll I say to them . . . I mean, think of it: How do I pick the mother of my baby?" Rosanna's face was streaked with tears, and her Kapp was off-kilter.

"God will give you wisdom." Nellie took her friend's hands. "Just ask." She bowed her head and began to pray softly. "Dear Lord in heaven, you see into our hearts—both Rosanna's and mine. You know how unsure Rosanna is just now. So I ask for help tomorrow, as Preacher Manny says we ought to pray. And may your will be done. Amen."

When they opened their eyes, Nellie saw her mother walking from the house toward the bakery shop. "Mamma knows of Treva's letter—I shared it with her. Is that all right?"

Rosanna nodded, sighing. "Denki for the prayer, Nellie Mae. I like the way you're comfortable talkin' to the Lord like He's sittin' right here with us."

"Well, He is . . . ain't so?"

Rosanna smiled now. " 'Where two or three are gathered,' jah?"

Mamma came in the door, and Rosanna motioned for her to sit with them, asking if she'd mind watching the shop tomorrow so Nellie could travel to Bird-in-Hand.

"Are you ever so sure 'bout going, Rosanna?" asked Mamma, her face pinched with concern.

Rosanna looked at Nellie, smiling again. "Nellie Mae prayed 'bout it . . . and, jah, I'm mighty sure."

"Well, then, who am I to say differently?" Mamma reached over and gently squeezed both of Rosanna's hands.

Nellie bit her lip, fighting back her own tears.

CHAPTER 12

Sheryl Kreider hadn't exactly caught his eye, but the junior *was* pretty, a girl Chris had known in the church for nearly all his life. The graduation event was six weeks away, and he figured he should ask *someone*, since the entire youth group turned out for these things, seniors or not—like one big, encouraging family. It did worry him that Sheryl might think he was interested in going out with her more than once. In reality, there was no one he cared for like that. No one in his world, at least.

Thinking back to his spur-of-the-moment stop at Nellie Mae's bakery shop, Chris felt ridiculous. He knew he wasn't crazy enough to ask her out, interesting though she was. Zach had been quizzing him about where he disappeared to several afternoons a week, but Chris refused to own up, saying only that he was helping a friend in need. All the same, it was getting harder to dodge Zach's questions without raising even more. No sense throwing him back into missing Suzy all over again, with talk of their Amish cousins.

He spied Sheryl at her locker between fifth and sixth period as she was spinning through her combination, her brown shoulder-length hair pulled back in a loose bun beneath the formal Mennonite head covering. He did a double take; her profile reminded him of Nellie Mae's.

Enough of that, he told himself, heading down the hall to ask Sheryl to the banquet.

Rosanna hoped each of Treva's acquaintances would like her and see her as a good choice to raise a baby. *Lord willing,* she thought while walking across the side yard with Nellie Mae as Treva tied up the horse.

Soon the three of them were entering the large brick farmhouse to meet the first woman, a faithful member of the Old Order Amish church. The young mother of four preschoolers was named Emma Sue Lapp, and the way she said her first two names pushed them together into one.

Rosanna listened as she chattered about her lively children, enjoying the woman's delicious chocolate chip cookies. As they visited, Rosanna held

Emma Sue's youngest boy—a towheaded one-year-old—thinking all the while how terrible it would be to take away his baby brother or sister. Visions of Cousin Kate's other children making over Eli and Rosie hit her ever so hard, and she shivered and looked away from the tot still in her arms. Seemingly untroubled, the little boy leaned into her, close to where her own wee one grew.

Rosanna tried to keep her focus on Emma Sue. The cheerful woman was making it overly clear that her husband was in favor of giving Rosanna this next baby, "as long as it's a girl."

Feeling out of sorts and terribly presumptuous, Rosanna was relieved they couldn't stay long. Right now, when she considered again why she'd come today, she felt nearly heartsick.

"We'll have us a light meal at the next house," Treva said, glancing at Rosanna, who sat sandwiched between her and Nellie Mae in the front seat of the buggy.

Thank goodness neither asked what she thought of Emma Sue. It was all Rosanna could do to sit still and not suggest that they turn back.

Even so, she'd come this far. Why not go ahead and meet the others?

By noon, Rosanna was all in. She wanted to be more grateful, or at least show it. But she felt sad as they pulled into the lane where Rosie Miller lived.

Rosie met them at the door. The thoughtful yet rather outspoken woman had already been blessed with eight children, four boys and four girls. With another baby on the way—the little one she was willing to give to Rosanna and Elias—her home would certainly be full. Treva pointed out how interesting it was that her name fit so well with Rosanna's, evidently forgetting that Rosie was also the name of the baby girl whom Rosanna had dearly loved.

But Rosanna wouldn't allow herself to make an emotional connection between the adult Rosie and the baby she missed so much that she sometimes awakened in the night, her face wet with tears.

Yet something didn't set well with Rosanna about this Rosie. Perhaps it was her too-aggressive way. She worried Rosie's baby might have a similar temperament, when what she desired was a tender-hearted child. Something she knew Elias would cherish in a little one, as well.

The third mother-to-be, Lena Stoltzfus, was a quilting friend of Nellie's grandmother Hannah Fisher, who also lived nearby. Rosanna wished there might be time to stop in and visit with Nellie's Dawdi and Mammi. Lena's connection to Nellie Mae's family immediately caught Rosanna's interest, and she hung on to the woman's every word.

Lena's face glowed as she spoke of "the Lord's guiding hand," and Rosanna wondered if she was trying to say that God had impressed on her to have a baby for Rosanna, just as Cousin Kate had claimed. With the memory of that still too fresh, Rosanna became increasingly tense. Lena was not as young as either Rosie or Emma Sue, and she wanted to know that this baby—her seventh—would be "raised up in the knowledge of the Lord." At that, Treva let out a little gasp, and Rosanna nodded quickly in agreement.

On the buggy ride back to Treva's parents' house, where Rosanna and Nellie Mae were to meet their driver, Rosanna thanked Treva. "I appreciate you so much."

"Glad to be of help." Treva smiled. "If anything gut should come of it."

When they arrived at the house, they waited inside for the driver, sitting at the kitchen table while Treva's mother poured a glass of lemonade for them.

"If I might be so bold, do you have a preference out of the three?" Treva asked.

Rosanna didn't want to appear ungrateful. "I need time to ponder the day," she managed to say. *And more time to grieve over Eli and Rosie . . . and my own sweet babe right here*, she thought, letting her hands rest on her lap. "All this has come up so fast, ya know."

"Well, sure it has," replied Treva, looking somewhat disappointed. No doubt she'd hoped to be involved in making things better for Nellie's friend.

Nellie Mae spoke up. "It's such a big decision after all you've been through."

Rosanna reached for her lemonade. "Nearly too much just now." She suddenly felt like she was slipping away, like she wasn't actually here in the flesh. *Or maybe I only wish it.*

"No one's sayin' you have to decide today," Treva said, glancing now at Nellie Mae.

"Given Rosanna's recent heartache, why don't we let all this settle for now?" Nellie Mae suggested.

Treva seemed to understand, slowly nodding her head. Then Treva and her mother began to discuss quilting bees, asking Nellie Mae when she'd be attending the next one in Honey Brook.

Not feeling very sociable, Rosanna merely listened and was glad when she heard the driver pull into the lane.

———

"You've gone *ferhoodled*, Ken!" Rhoda let the word slip; then, eyes wide, she clapped her hand over her mouth. Leaning back in her chair, she smiled apologetically across the table. "Ach, I didn't mean it."

Ken leaned forward, blue eyes soft in the candlelight. "What did you say?"

She laughed a little and wiped her mouth with the napkin, attempting to compose herself. Dare she say he was both crazy and mixed-up? After all, he'd just poked fun at her wonderful secret—her dream to travel one day—adding he had no intention of ever hopping a plane himself. "What's so wrong about wanting to fly in an airplane?" she asked.

"Don't get me wrong." He paused, regarding her with a bemused smile. "You just don't seem, well . . . like a jet-setter to me."

"That's precisely why I want to, though. Don't you see?"

"But why not be yourself instead?"

"Well, I am. This is who I *want* to be." *Though a far cry from who I was raised to be.* "You know, my bishop uncle would call me hell-bent for wanting to fly."

He squinted across the table. "Seems rather disapproving."

"Some might think so." More and more she believed that much of what the bishop said—and some of the preachers, too—was hard to take. Not so much what Preacher Manny had shared from *his* heart, though—those sermons, for some reason, had struck a chord in her. But she didn't want to talk about church, since Ken wasn't interested. And, too, she didn't want to spoil their time together—this special dinner, complete with candles. Just what was her boyfriend up to?

"So, are you going to tell me what ferhoodled is?" He winked, and her heart felt like it might melt.

"What's it sound like?"

"All mixed-up?"

"Sure. That's it, then," she teased.

He rose and went to her, taking her hands and pulling her to her feet. "I'm mixed-up, all right. You do that to me, I'll admit."

She smiled, enjoying the attention she'd come to expect.

He glanced at her hair again. "You look so different, Rhoda," he whispered, reaching up to touch it.

"You like it, then?"

"It's pretty . . . so smooth—like silk."

They laughed together. Then he cupped her face in his hands. "You're perfect, Rhoda . . . just the way you are."

Reluctantly she pulled away, unsure how to respond. Should she say he was the most handsome fellow she'd ever known?

He surprised her by speaking first. "If you'd like to see the room for rent, I'll show you now."

"Oh . . . all right." But her heart sank a little. Did he want her to rent from him instead of thinking ahead to marriage?

"The tenant's gone for the evening. We'll just take a look, if you'd like."

"You sure it's all right?"

"He knows I need to find another renter."

Ken slipped his arm around her waist, and they walked down the hallway to the long, gleaming staircase to the second floor.

Mammi Hannah had seemed so delighted to see them, she'd talked Nellie Mae and Rosanna into staying for supper, much longer than they'd intended. Thanks to the community phone booth, Rosanna had managed to reach nearby neighbor Linda Fisher, Jonathan's wife, who was glad to tell Elias she'd be home after supper.

Rosanna relaxed a bit as she enjoyed the tasty beef stroganoff and buttered peas, warm dinner rolls with strawberry-rhubarb jam, and applesauce cake. Mammi Hannah gladly shared her recipes with Nellie while they lingered at the table over coffee and second helpings. Meanwhile, their driver had other folk to pick up, so it worked out for him to return later.

"Sure was surprising to hear of David Yoder's accident," Dawdi Noah said, stirring sugar into his coffee. "But a body never can tell what's ahead."

Nellie Mae nodded.

"Such a sad thing 'tis." Mammi shook her head.

"Well, David's a fighter, no question on that," Dawdi said, his beard twitching. "He might just surprise everyone and walk again . . . who's to say?"

Nellie knew that what distressed her grandparents most wasn't David Yoder's paralysis—it was the choice her parents had made to join the new church. This was the reason they were living clear over in Bird-in-Hand instead of next door in her parents' Dawdi Haus, as planned. She hoped something she might say, or do, would make them think twice about the religious stir in several areas of Lancaster County, and in other states, too. Some called it a "move of God." Others shook their heads in utter confusion, like Dawdi and Mammi. She hoped they'd soon know the amazing things she and her family—and many others—were learning from scripture and from the pertinent sermons preached each Lord's Day.

"Lots of prayers are goin' up for David Yoder," Nellie said softly. "Healing for his body, for one thing . . . and his spiritual healing, too."

This brought an immediate hush to the table.

Nellie felt a sudden boldness. "If the truth were known, David Yoder just might be pondering, deep down, all the talk of a personal relationship with the Lord. Lots of folk seem hungry for it."

"Now, now, Nellie Mae." Dawdi's eyes pierced hers.

"I'm serious," she continued. "Why squelch the questions . . . the longing?"

"How's your sister Rhoda doin'?" asked Mammi. The effect of her grandmother's stroke was still evident in her slightly slurred speech.

Nellie knew she was being shushed in a kind sort of way, but Rhoda was not the most pleasant subject. "I don't know much about her these days." Both Dawdi and Mammi nodded.

Surely they've heard she's living with James and Martha. . . .

"We saw Mrs. Kraybill the other day over at the General Store. She mentioned something about her nephew and Rhoda. Sounds like your sister has an English beau." Dawdi set down his spoon and folded his knobby hands over his coffee cup. "First Suzy, now Rhoda?"

Feeling awkward, Nellie looked at Rosanna and sighed. None of this was a secret. "Rhoda's finding her wings, I daresay. But Suzy . . . well, honestly, she found hers in the Lord Jesus." She began to recite some of Suzy's favorite Scripture verses, sharing the things Suzy had prayed about . . . all of it. When she was finished, Mammi's eyes were moist, but Dawdi seemed unaffected.

"No one's ever mentioned this side of things 'bout your sister," Mammi said. "I just don't know what to think."

Rosanna nodded. "Suzy was in love with the Lord, that's for sure."

Dawdi frowned, his brow knitted tightly under his thinning bangs. "Talkin' like that about the Almighty? Ach, that's *unsinnich*—senseless!" He shook his head.

"I used to feel the same way, Dawdi," Nellie dared to say. "But now I see that the truth is set before us . . . in God's Word. It's impossible to turn away." *At least for some* . . . Her heart broke to see her grandparents struggle so with the whys and wherefores.

Rosanna reached for Nellie's hand. "Elias and I, too, believe we have been saved by the grace of the Lord." Tears glistened in her friend's eyes. "You can be, too."

Dawdi frowned, and Mammi mumbled under her breath.

Verses Nellie had memorized sprang to mind, but now was not the time to speak them. The resistance was ever so strong here, where the old church still reigned.

CHAPTER 13

This is one of the largest bedrooms in the house." Ken pointed to the high ceiling as Rhoda stood beside him in the doorway, peering in, conscious of Ken's arm around her. "The windows face the southeast, so if you have indoor plants, they'll do nicely along that wall." He motioned to the windows, draped in a tweedy gold fabric. The views of Strasburg were nearly as lovely as those from Ken's upstairs suite.

Rhoda attempted to place herself in the room in her mind, wondering how it might be to wake up here each morning, knowing Ken was living on the floor above her. Would she hear his footsteps early and late, be aware of his comings and goings? The modern space was so different from the farmhouse where she presently resided with James's family. She thought of her darling niece and nephews. *I'd miss them so much if I moved here.*

Ken looked at her. "So, what do you think?"

"It's nice and roomy." She couldn't help admiring the present tenant's arrangement of furniture.

"Don't forget there's a private bath—with a tub and a shower."

The television in the corner caught her curiosity. How exciting it would be to own one. *Someday,* she thought, looking now at the pretty pole lamp and other pieces of furniture. Would she develop a style of her own? Since she didn't have many things, she'd have to invest in a bed and a chest of drawers, as well as a small sofa or love seat to entertain guests. *Will Ken visit me here?*

Sighing, she stepped back. She'd had her heart set on living upstairs with Ken as his bride, sharing the larger space of rooms. She mustn't let on how disappointed she felt, or she would seem presumptuous.

"When the room's vacant, you're welcome to see it again. Maybe by then you'll have a better handle on what you'd like to do." He closed the door, locking it with his master key.

If they married, would they ever have the entire house for themselves, for their growing family?

It was then she realized he'd never talked of having children. Was he as fond of them as she? There hadn't been any playful times with the Kraybill children—Ken's own young cousins—that first night she'd met him for dinner there. No talk of them from his perspective, either.

He reached for her hand when they came to the landing at the top of the long flight of stairs. "I'll pour us some after-dinner wine to go with the surprise dessert," he said. "Would you like that?"

Wine . . . during dinner and after?

Well, who was she to interfere? This was Ken's way, and she welcomed even the most foreign aspects.

"Do you accept tenants with young children?" she asked as he pulled out a chair for her at his table. The dining room seemed too dark, and she smiled when he pressed the dimmer switch and raised the light a bit before lighting the candles once again.

"There." Stepping back, he smiled. "Much better." He went to the kitchen, where he pulled out two dessert plates and two small glasses. "What was the question?"

"Are children welcome here?"

He grimaced. "Dogs and kids are liabilities for investment properties."

"What do you mean—a liability?" she asked.

"To rephrase it, they're a pain in the proverbial neck," he stated flatly, carrying the two dessert plates with a generous slice of pie on each. "Most kids are more bother than they're worth." He placed the cherry pie and single scoop of ice cream in front of her. Then, picking up his fork, he looked across the table without batting an eye.

She felt nearly ill. She thought of his own relatives' children. They were entertaining and smart and responsible. In short, lots of fun. "Are you fond of your young Kraybill cousins?"

"What's this? Twenty questions?" He stared at her across the candles.

Realizing she was on the verge of spoiling a perfectly good evening with a wonderful man who seemed to dote on her, even love her, maybe, Rhoda picked up her fork and made herself take a bite of Ken's cherry pie. Even though she had absolutely no appetite now.

Dat says children are a blessing from God.

He rose to pour the dessert wine, and she nodded her thanks as he handed her a glass with a small amount. Holding her breath, she slowly sipped it, as she'd seen him do. She felt terribly tense, like she was falling with no way to stop herself.

Betsy felt chilly and wanted the afghan she sometimes draped over her lap while Reuben read the Bible to her. Quickly she made her way upstairs to the blanket chest at the foot of the bed. Opening the lid, she stepped back, surprised at the sight of the small sachet pillow—the "headache pillow" Suzy had made for her—lying on the top of the quilts and crocheted afghans.

How'd this get here?

She recalled having gone to sleep with it one recent night, only for it to have fallen to the floor by morning. Of course, that's where Reuben must have found it, and he'd slipped it back into the chest.

She stared at Suzy's delicate handiwork. Did Reuben have special mementos or memories of their Suzy? He scarcely ever spoke of her. Was the pain of loss still too raw . . . too tender? Or had his grief found solace in the knowledge their youngest now resided at the feet of the dear Savior?

Finding Suzy's favorite spring quilt several layers down, she tucked the sachet pillow into one of its folds and left it safely stowed in the blanket chest. Then, locating the small afghan, she closed the lid and headed downstairs, looking forward to the scripture reading . . . and time spent alone with Reuben later tonight.

The boys seemed exceptionally fidgety during Wednesday evening class, and following the Bible study—geared to junior boys—Chris asked only three questions to test their attention level. After more bantering, he asked for prayer for his father's cousin, mentioning that a mule had kicked David Yoder in the head. In typical boyish fashion, several bucked their own heads.

To his surprise, Billy Zercher, usually the loner, hung around after the others left. "I've never heard of a mule kicking someone." His eyes blinked rapidly. "How'd it happen?"

"He was fixing the chain on the plow."

Billy was fiddling with his fingers. "Is he Amish?"

The kid was pretty perceptive. "Yeah. Why did you ask?"

"Well, they use mules out in the fields, don't they?"

He smiled. "That's right. Have you seen them?"

"Sometimes, from a distance."

He watched Billy head for the door. The boy stood there, as if waiting for Chris to say more. That's when an idea hit. "Say, Billy, how would you like to visit a working Amish dairy farm sometime?"

The boy's eyes lit up. "For real?"

"Ask your mom."

"Oh, she'll let me go . . . if you're taking me." His eyes registered near-glee. Chris was heartened.

Suddenly turning shy again, the boy waved and left.

Chris gathered up the Bibles and stacked them in the cupboard, hoping Caleb might agree. He'd been amazed by how much he looked forward to spending time with his cousin, and he hoped to make more connections with Caleb, to influence him toward the Lord. Befriending him was simply the beginning.

If only it were just as easy to get better acquainted with Nellie Mae. Maybe he'd actually get over his crush if he knew her better. *Only one way to find out.* Was it possible to win her confidence enough to ask her for ice cream sometime, or to go for a walk? How weird would it seem for her? For him?

Was it time to tell Zach what he was thinking? He was reluctant to do anything that might plunge his brother back into the pits of depression.

On the way toward the church lobby, he spotted Sheryl with a girl friend. Thinking it was time he became more friendly with his future date, he smiled, waiting until she finished her conversation. Sheryl's eyes lit up as she made her way to him, and he struggled with guilt for having set things in motion.

"Hi, Sheryl."

She smiled prettily, her eyebrows arched slightly with apparent delight. "How are you?" She spoke so softly he had to lean close to hear her.

"The school year's winding down," he said, even though small talk was the last thing he wanted.

She nodded. "Another month till the banquet."

"Six weeks, yes."

Smiling, she glanced at another friend who waved to her as they passed. "What color dress are you planning to wear?"

"Pale blue," she said.

He made a mental note. "All right . . . sounds nice." He smiled, wondering how other guys did it, making conversation with a girl they knew but didn't *really* know. For all the years they'd grown up together in this church, he'd never bothered to become better acquainted with Sheryl . . . till now. Why, Zach probably knew her better than he did. His younger brother had always been more outgoing, more comfortable with girls.

Maybe that's why Zach and Suzy clicked. Both were more extroverted than he, which wasn't saying much. *Outgoing like Nellie Mae,* he mused with a genuine smile. Instantly Sheryl brightened, probably believing that his joyful expression was meant for her.

All during the drive home, Chris felt lousy. He could kick himself for putting Sheryl in such a pitiful spot. He sure had a lot to make up for. *Her corsage better be extra special*, he decided.

But wait—if he went all out on flowers, wouldn't that send a too-encouraging message? He groaned aloud as he drove toward home.

CHAPTER 14

Rosanna took her time laying out a half dozen large quilts at market day on Thursday. Thanks to Elias, she'd arrived early enough to claim the display table closest to the sweets, a popular stopping place for shoppers. This way she also wasn't very far from several other women from Preacher Manny's church who were selling pickled green tomatoes, beets, and peppers.

She spotted some women from the Beachy church already setting up, as well. "Hullo!" She waved quickly and smiled, thinking how thankful she was Elias had changed his mind about tractors and cars—and about joining the more liberal Beachy Amish. Such a push and pull that would have caused in their home, just as for any couple divided over beliefs. For now, she felt sure Elias was quite satisfied to attend the New Order church, where the ordination of a second preacher was to take place this Sunday, following the sermon and songs of worship.

She had been praying in earnest for God's will in the selection of this preacher. As with the old church, the man chosen by drawing lots need not be a learned man, nor one trained in speaking. The greatest difference in the New Order church was that all candidates nominated by the membership had to be willing to study scripture and spend time preparing sermons. Memorizing God's Word was also emphasized, which was encouraging to Rosanna, who felt like a thirsty sponge during Preacher Manny's sermons.

She anchored the display table with the quilts' color schemes, placing the bold-colored ones at each end—a red and royal blue Bars pattern and her Sunshine and Shadows quilt all done in plums, blues, and golds. The softer, more muted colors and designs were for the center of the table. She'd learned this from her aunt, an expert quilter and her mother's oldest sister.

Usually Rosanna sold out of everything by around noon. She wished that might be the case again this week. Elias had an errand to run over near White Horse, and she was hoping the timing of his return might coincide with her being ready to head home.

Feeling sluggish again, Rosanna sat behind the table, satisfied the quilts were marked and situated nicely. In her frequent daydreams, she often thought of the many lovely baby things she could make, should the Lord allow her to birth a son or daughter. She would gladly use her quilt money for plenty of yarn and fabric.

Following yesterday's visit to Bird-in-Hand, she found it nearly impossible to stop thinking about Emma Sue, Rosie, and Lena—such considerate women. But was she ready to take another woman's child as her own?

A bright-eyed young lady stopped by the table, and Rosanna dismissed her earlier musings. She hoped the general weakness she felt now might dissipate so she would not have to reassure Elias again that she was going to be all right. Each morning lately, he lovingly inquired. Yet she wanted to protect him, so she still kept this pregnancy to herself.

"Oh, isn't this a striking quilt," the customer said. "Is it the Log Cabin pattern?"

"Jah, 'tis." She pointed to the large square quilt.

"Is it definitely Amish-made?" the woman asked.

Rosanna nodded. "I laid it out myself."

"Your work is exquisite." The woman fingered the edge of the quilt. "Do you ever do custom work?"

"I'd be happy to make something for ya." She reached for her tablet and a pen, accustomed to sewing quilts to suit a buyer's fancy. She delighted in the process of choosing patterns and colors and laying out the unique designs, as well as the quilting itself. Every aspect was wonderful-good, including bringing the finished quilts to market. "Which pattern would you like?" she asked.

"Can you make an Album Patch for me?"

"What color scheme?"

The woman thought about it for a moment. "As long as there is some green in it—as a background, perhaps—and yellows and pinks, too, any mix would be fine."

"Sounds perty," Rosanna said, envisioning the many pieces within each of the twenty-five squares—as expensive to make as the lovely Dahlia pattern, with its individual gathered petals.

"I once saw one at an antique quilt sale and it went for nearly seven hundred dollars," said the customer.

"Well, mine won't cost you near that." Rosanna explained that the fine wool batiste and wool cashmere of the old days were no longer available. "Now we use polyesters and scraps of old dress fabric, pieces from men's for-good shirts, and other odds and ends. I even purchase quilt squares just for my work. Does that sound all right?"

The woman's smile spread across her face. "Oh, this is so exciting." She took out her wallet and made the down payment in cash, saying she'd pay the rest with a personal check.

Rosanna agreed to the method of payment. She had been told she was too trusting, but that's how her mother was and her grandmothers, too. And they'd never run into a snag with Englischers, that she knew of. "I'll give you my address, and you can come pick it up either at my house or here—at market—three weeks from today. I'll do a nice job for you."

The woman wrote her own name, address, and phone number on another index card Rosanna handed to her. "Thank you so much. You just don't know how you've made my day."

Rosanna glanced at the card. "I hope you'll be pleased, Dottie," she said, a twinge of pain in her middle. She smiled through the impulse to flinch as she handed the woman her own address. "Have a nice day."

After that customer, there were several more sales, including two sisters—Julie and Wendy—who wanted custom-made quilts, as well as crib quilts. Rosanna offered to make a baby quilt in the Ocean Wave pattern at no charge. The sisters were quite surprised at this, but Rosanna insisted and they told their friend Bonnie to purchase the most expensive quilt there, "to make up for it."

By eleven o'clock, when Rosanna reached under the table for her lunch sack, she felt so hungry and dizzy, she was glad to be seated. She'd thought of going to see a doctor, but she knew such a visit would be sure to worry Elias.

As she slowly ate, she happened to notice her cousin Kate with her niece Lizzy, standing at the far end of the row. They were each holding one of the twins as they talked to the young Amishwoman best known for her jams and jellies, Rebecca from nearby Hickory Hollow.

Try as she might, she could not keep from staring at Kate and Lizzy . . . and the babies. Goodness, were they growing! She stopped to think how old they'd be now. *Born November seventh and today's April tenth . . . so they're already five months old, bless their dear hearts.*

She began to cry, unable to stop the flow of tears.

"Ach, Rosanna—you all right?" the woman at the next table asked, coming to lean over her.

She could not speak, shaking her head and patting her chest, trying to compose herself.

Indicating the half-eaten sandwich in her hand, the woman asked if there was something spicy in it. "Do ya want a drink, maybe?"

Rosanna nodded, relieved when the woman marched off to get a cup and some water. By then, Kate and Lizzy had evidently moved around to the other side, because Rosanna could no longer see them. *Just as well.* She had to pull herself together, or she might begin to really sob. *And oh, would I ever, if I caught sight of the twins' sweet faces.*

Then she was getting up, compelled by an irresistible drawing. *I must see Eli and Rosie . . . must touch their little hands. Ach, I can't help myself.*

The woman carrying the water intercepted her journey, taking her arm and leading her back to her table and the single quilt remaining—the softly muted Nine Patch in the center. "There, now, this'll make ya feel better."

"Denki," she eked out as she sat down, grateful to be off her feet once again.

"You look altogether peaked." The woman eyed her. "You got someone comin' for ya later?"

Quickly she nodded. "My husband will fetch me." She was so thankful for the water as she took several small sips. Hoping to set her mind on other things, she considered the money she'd made this day and the delightful new customers—pretty Dottie and the two sisters, Julie and Wendy, and their friend Bonnie. She pondered each face, each comment . . . all this to keep her focus away from the fact that her darlings were here at market, in this very building.

If Elias hadn't arrived a few minutes later, Rosanna didn't know what she might have done. Created a scene, perhaps? She wanted to think she would have kept her emotions in check. But oh, the powerful tug on her heart toward Eli and Rosie.

For now, though, Elias was folding up the single quilt and looking at her curiously, asking if she was any better than she'd been earlier this morning. He supported her elbow as they made their way over to the small window to pay the percentage owed the establishment.

Then, as they walked to the exit, she told him she'd seen Eli and Rosie, and he slipped his arm around her and said not a word. All the while, she hoped against hope they would *not* run into Kate and Lizzy and the babies, she was so wrung out with emotion. *Help me make it home in one piece.*

Elias held her hand nearly all the way. The gentle sway of their old covered carriage lulled her into repose, and she leaned her head on her husband's strong shoulder.

When they arrived home, she went to lie down and rest, and Elias tenderly tucked her into bed, looking mighty concerned as he sat on the bed next to her, stroking her arm.

In spite of feeling quite comfortable now, Rosanna could not erase the
memory of the babies snuggled happily in Kate's and Lizzy's arms. And she
knew, without a doubt, she could not consider "adopting" another woman's
wee one just now. *Maybe not ever.*

———

Chris Yoder couldn't wait to drive the back road leading to his Amish cousins' spread of land. He liked the openness and the farm activity on both sides as
Amish and English alike were busy moving sludge around in their barnyards,
creating shallow ditches for runoff to accommodate the spring thaw. Chris
recalled seeing David Yoder and his older sons do the same thing, years ago.

Recently Caleb had said their driving horses had begun to shed—another
sign of spring. Chris found himself looking for such things more closely since
coming out to help. While Caleb and Abe were usually around working
somewhere, occasionally Gideon or Jonah would come for a few hours at a
time, too. Thankfully, the other brothers took his helping in stride, though
only Caleb really seemed comfortable talking with him.

When Chris pulled into the drive, he was surprised to see the bench
wagon parked there. He couldn't imagine David and Elizabeth hosting
church this Sunday, not the way David had to be assisted. But then, he had
no idea how this community operated. They seemingly continued to do
the things they'd always done, even though the head of the family was so
seriously injured. Really, the whole situation boggled his mind, this family
subsisting without the help of an in-home nurse or therapist. When he'd
talked with Caleb about his father's desperate condition, Caleb had merely
said it was their way. *"Life goes on, no matter."*

Shifting into Park, Chris turned off the ignition. When he looked up, he was
shocked to see Caleb's father being lifted out of the bench wagon on a makeshift stretcher lined with a narrow mattress and hoisted by the four brothers.

He hopped out of the car and caught up with them, walking slowly behind
as the entourage lumbered toward the back door. Not wanting to interfere,
he waited on the back stoop, puzzled by what he'd witnessed. When Leah
opened the door and asked if he'd like to come inside, he told her he would
wait there for Caleb.

"My brother might be a while yet."

Until today, he had not been invited inside the house since he was a
child. "I'll wait, thanks," he said. He'd gotten the impression from Caleb
that it might be best if he didn't stir up the waters.

Soon two older men with long brown beards emerged from the house, talking slowly in Pennsylvania Dutch. The men nodded their heads when they caught his eye but kept walking. He stood there awkwardly, overhearing snatches of someone talking rather loudly inside. Actually grumbling—then a holler—and he assumed Caleb's father was having difficulty getting situated in his wheelchair again.

Quickly Chris moved out of earshot. Not knowing where to go to avoid catching private exchanges, he headed to the barn and watched the determined parade of cows as they moved into the milking parlor, amazed again at how each animal independently moved to its own stanchion.

While he waited, he wondered if maybe David Yoder had just returned from a doctor appointment. *Had to be.* And he instantly knew how he could help lessen such an ordeal for his father's cousin, the poor man.

He heard voices and turned to see Abe and Caleb coming into the barn. Swiftly the brothers began to secure the stanchion bars into the locked position while the cows fed on hay. Chris could have helped do that in their absence, but Caleb had said last week that the cows were still getting used to him, and Chris did not want to spook them.

He didn't have to ask about his suspicions. Once Abe got to milking, Caleb mentioned how hard it was for his father to go to his weekly rehabilitation sessions in the bench wagon.

Right then Chris offered his dad's van, the vehicle they used to make deliveries for the nursery, for the trips.

Caleb turned, stunned. "You'd do that?"

"Sure, why not? I can easily drive your father back and forth, as long as it's after school hours. I know Dad won't mind. I've already talked to both my parents about what I'm up to here."

"Well, his next appointment's set for Tuesday morning," Caleb said. "I'll see if it can be moved to the afternoon. I'm sure Daed'll be willing to go with you—beats his other option all to pieces. He complained today he'd never go back if he had to lie on that stiff board again."

"Do you think you could make a ramp for his wheelchair?" Chris suggested.

"Good thinkin'. We'll look into it." Caleb nodded. " 'Tween you and me, it pains me to see my father suffer so. Denki, Chris."

Caleb's eyes held a mix of pain and gratitude. *I hope I'm helping to ease the stress around here—not adding more,* Chris thought, wondering what else he could do without infringing on his cousin's life.

CHAPTER 15

All afternoon, Mamma kept talking about scurrying off to see Martha, hoping to also run into Rhoda, but she was still there working in the bakery shop near closing time. Nellie, presently waiting on customers, was eager to talk privately with Nan, if Mamma *did* actually leave. Either that, or Nellie would have to wait till evening. She and Nan had enjoyed several nighttime discussions about scripture while curled up on Nan's bed. Together they'd nearly memorized the first five chapters of the gospel of John.

Moving toward the door, Mamma said a quick good-bye and hurried toward Dat and the waiting horse and carriage.

"Honestly, I thought Mamma might up and change her mind and stay home today," Nan said, looking out the window.

"Ach, funny. I was thinkin' the same thing."

"So, you've got yourself a secret to share, is that it?" Nan's eyes twinkled.

"Well, I've been thinking 'bout all the times you've asked me to go along to the New Order barn Singings."

Nan leaned near, a droll expression on her face. "Are ya sayin' you might be ready?"

"Nee."

"Then what?"

"It's just that I'm anxious to see your beau . . . if only from afar."

Nan laughed. "Oh, you're the sneaky one, ain't so?"

Nellie tried not to grin. "How much longer must I wait, sister?"

"He is mighty good-lookin', I'll say that much."

"But lots of fellas are."

"He's not as bold as some, though, so I doubt he'd ever meet me at the barn door . . . just so *you* can catch a glimpse of him."

"All right, then, you'll have to tell me who."

Nan crossed her arms in jest. "I don't have to tell you any such thing."

"Ain't that the truth."

Brightening again, Nan teased, "But if you guess his name, I will."

Nan had her but good. "It'll take far too long to name off all the youth in the new group. And I doubt you'll give me another hint, knowin' you."

"Not a one!" With that, Nan again burst out laughing.

"Well, if you're getting married come fall, I s'pose he'll be a baptismal candidate, jah?"

"Now you're gettin' warmer."

Nellie Mae considered all the young men who were the right age to join church. Mostly their second and third cousins came to mind. "You're not in love with a Fisher relative, are ya?"

Nan's eyes bugged out, and she tried to compose herself.

This was fun. "Dat's cousins have quite a few courting-age sons. . . ."

"Never mind. I won't tell you even if you do guess."

"Aw, Nan."

"Best not say, for now."

"Oh, and I was that close, too."

Nan had that twinkle again. "You only think so."

"Ach, you're the feisty one, ain't? Guess I'm just going to have to go to Singing with you, then."

"Wonderful-gut! That's what I was hopin' you'd say."

Nellie Mae shook her head. *What am I getting myself into?*

"Life's full of twists and turns," Caleb told Chris as they entered the milk house. "I never expected my father to end up in a wheelchair. I figured he'd still be out cutting tobacco when his time came."

"Must be hard, seein' him that way."

"One thing's for certain," Caleb said. "It makes you think twice."

"What does?"

Caleb shrugged, knowing that a discussion about sickness and death was like opening a barn door to Chris's undoubtedly strange ideas. At the moment, though, he didn't care. "We deal with so-called tragedy differently than Englischers, you might know."

"But you're human. You still suffer."

"Usually in silence," Caleb said quietly. "Sometimes I wonder . . ." He paused, shaking his head, unwilling to voice his frustrations. He stared out the window, wondering how they'd gotten to this.

Chris cleared his throat. "I don't blame you. You might think you know how you'll react to something as terrible as your father's accident, but until it happens, you can't really know at all."

Turning away from the window, he was surprised at Chris's response. He'd become accustomed to seemingly prideful statements from some of the New Order folk—*the saved folk*. But Chris seemed different. Why?

As if in response to Caleb's questioning stare, Chris bowed his head for a moment, running his hands through his thick blond hair. "I'll tell you . . . Suzy Fisher's drowning was the worst thing that's ever happened to our family. The hardest thing on Zach and me."

"Did you know her very well?"

Chris paused, as if wanting to be careful how he put this. "For the short time my brother dated her, I'd say I knew her fairly well, yes."

Caleb searched Chris's face. "You were there when she died, weren't you?"

Nodding, Chris stepped away from the bulk milk tank, and Caleb cautiously opened the lid to check on the stirring mechanism. "I'll just say that it shook our faith—my brother's more than mine," said Chris. "Why would God allow such a wonderful young girl to drown? We'd heard debates on suffering, but . . ." He hesitated. "Until it hits home, all the talk in the world is simply that . . . talk."

"So what happened? I mean, how did you keep on, you know . . . believing like ya do?" asked Caleb.

Chris shrugged. "We decided to take God at face value, so to speak. It's hard sometimes, but in the Bible it's clear—what's waiting for us . . . after this life, is impossible to understand or fathom. But most important for us . . ."

Caleb waited.

"We knew we'd see Suzy again."

Caleb swallowed hard. He wouldn't let on how he felt—downright helpless. Even alone. "My father says we can't know for certain where we're goin'. But we can hope for heaven, come Judgment Day."

"Well, I disagree."

Chris seems so sure. "Why's that?"

"Because God's Word tells us differently."

"Since Daed's accident, I admit to thinkin' things that might shock the bishop." Caleb forced a nervous laugh.

"Well, I'm not your bishop, Caleb."

He turned slowly, taking a long look at his modern cousin. "Maybe that's a good thing." Caleb smiled.

They continued to work together like close brothers. And, later, when it came time for Chris to leave, he mentioned a boy in his church class who might benefit by spending a few hours at the farm.

Caleb agreed to ask his father about having Billy Zercher visit sometime with Chris. But what Caleb really wished for was to invite Chris to stay on for supper. *Anything to keep him here longer.*

Caleb sat whittling in the corner of the tobacco shed after supper. A gray barn cat sauntered through the open doorway and nuzzled her head against his leg. Dusk closed in around them, and Caleb found some tranquility in the stillness of nightfall. Peace was something he longed for, especially now.

He'd left the house for a reprieve from watching Daed in his wheelchair at every meal. His father was so determined to cut his own meat or reach for his glass, but needing help from Mamm to steady him. He seemed to be losing more muscle tone and mobility even in his arms and upper body as the days passed. But he remained at the head of the table—where a crack in the wood reminded all of them of his fierce temper. Now the paralysis had pushed Daed's ire to a frightening rage over his weakness as he still strove to control his household with a strong hand. His willingness to allow Caleb to help out was purely practical, Caleb knew, and nothing more.

"My father's not getting better," Caleb told the cat. She turned her head sideways, looking at him with yellow-green eyes. And he sighed. "I must be desperate if I'm talkin' to you."

He leaned back against the shed wall gingerly, muscles sore after a long day of unloading stored hay for the neighbors. Lately, he seemed to meet himself coming and going—getting up before dawn and staying up too late, contemplating his lot in life.

It hadn't been more than a few weeks ago that his father and brothers had been pressing the cured and stripped tobacco leaves into a bale box, packaging it for auction. Daed had always sold his "Pennsylvania 41" to a broker from the Lancaster Leaf Company. The dark-colored, gummy leaf made for good cigar filler, according to his grandfathers, and some fine chewing tobacco, too. He'd tried the latter, but only on the sly, as a rite of passage when he turned sixteen.

The worst thing about raising tobacco was all the labor. When Caleb's older brothers were busy with harvests of their own, a whole group of farmers had to drop everything to help Daed cut the "leaf." It was backbreaking labor to hand-cut the stalks one at a time, leaving the cut leaves on the ground for the sun to soften, before stabbing them onto the long laths and stacking them on the cart for hauling to the curing shed. It was a great deal of work for the return, he knew, having heard his father complain through the years.

Caleb yawned, staring up at the empty rafters. He did not miss hauling the forty-pound laths required to hang the tobacco leaves on the long rails here in the shed. Nor did he miss the insufferable temperatures beneath the tin roof. Late summer's heat was a true test of a man's endurance, he knew firsthand. He never had trouble falling asleep during that season.

But these days sleep was slow in coming, if it came at all. He'd struggled with maddening insomnia since his father's return from the hospital. The minute Caleb closed his eyes, no matter how exhausted he was from the day's work, his brain kicked into high gear. Even now his brain whirled with Chris's kind offer to drive Daed to rehabilitation.

Sighing, Caleb forced air through pursed lips. He ought to be well rested before he approached his father on this. He wouldn't speculate how that conversation might go.

Truth was, everything had changed since his father's head got in the way of that ornery mule. There were days when Caleb felt he might suffocate. Had the Lord God reckoned to punish him?

Ironically, Caleb actually missed working alongside Daed—filling silo, helping birth calves. And soon there would be plowing and planting. His father would not be present in the fields all day, muttering his ongoing grievances and whatnot. But Abe would be. And Gideon and Jonah and some older cousins, each taking shifts. Everyone but Daed.

Probably not for the rest of his life.

Caleb whittled harder, taking out his frustrations on the piece of wood as twilight fell. He considered the hour difference between the People and the modern folk who moved their clocks up a full hour each April, lengthening the end of the day, instead of the beginning, when work was best accomplished. The fancy practice was called "fast time" amongst the Amish because it pushed everything forward. *"Not at all the way God intended,"* Daed had always said.

Fast time meant more daylight hours for not only work but for play and courting, too, even though most fellows waited till twilight to go out riding with their girls.

He wondered if Nellie Mae was looking ahead to the weekend and the Sunday Singing. No doubt she was pairing up with a new fellow by now. There were plenty of New Order boys to make for a nice choice of a mate, if a "saved" husband was what she was after.

His knife cut deep. Looking down at the misshapen wood, Caleb gave up trying to whittle it into a small horse. Flicking the strips of wood off his lap, he realized anew that he would never have the chance to talk with Nellie Mae again if she met up with one of those "redeemed" fellows. And come Sunday, the new church would have another minister and deacon, too. Apparently Preacher Manny's group was thriving, not dissolving as he'd hoped.

He reached down to rub the mouse-catcher's neck. "My girl's gonna end up marryin' some preacher-man . . . you just watch and see." The cat leaned into his hand, purring hard. "Well, she *was* my girl. Now she's free as a bird. . . ."

It still hurt, though he doubted a single soul knew just how badly.

CHAPTER 16

A gentle rain fell as Nellie Mae sat with Rosanna at the kitchen table on this gloomy Friday afternoon. At Mamma's urging, she'd left the bakery shop to visit her dearest friend, who still looked so pale, Nellie was sure she'd caught a springtime bug.

Nellie stirred the freshly made peppermint ice tea. "Sure is soggy out there," she said.

"Elias said the fields were startin' to dry out, so this shower's nice." Rosanna glanced out the window.

Nellie watched it rain, enjoying the peaceful sound. "It's makin' down pretty good."

Getting up for a plate of oatmeal raisin cookies, Rosanna said, "Before I forget, I want to show you an old quilt pattern I found." She set the cookies down and left the room. Soon she returned with a tattered magazine. "Lookee here." Rosanna pointed to a picture of a turn-of-the-century cradle quilt. "Perty, ain't so?"

"What's the pattern?" Nellie had never seen this one, but she wasn't up on the older patterns. Mammi Hannah would know, though—she was a walking dictionary of quilt patterns—sometimes comically referring to herself as having "quilt pox," she loved quilting so much.

"It's called Grandmother's Dream and was made from twill-weave wool."

"And a Lancaster County pattern, yet." Nellie looked at the picture more closely. "Will you try to copy it?"

"If all goes well, I'll make three of them—as thank-yous."

It dawned on her what her friend was up to. "Oh, that's so thoughtful of you, Rosanna."

"Well, I don't know 'bout that . . . but I *do* want to make something nice for Emma Sue, Rosie, and Lena. They were so kind to me."

Nellie Mae waited, hoping Rosanna might say which woman she was considering for her baby.

The steady patter of rain on the roof was the only sound as Rosanna reached for a cookie. She glanced at Nellie as if she had something on her mind but couldn't quite say it.

At last, Rosanna sighed and moved the quilt picture to the side. She kept her hand on it, breathing slowly. "If I told you something, Nellie Mae, would ya promise to keep mum?"

Nodding, Nellie ran her pointer finger and thumb across her lips.

"This is ever so hard," she whispered, locking eyes with Nellie.

"You can trust me with your decision," Nellie said. "Honestly."

"No, no . . . ain't that."

Nellie searched her friend's eyes, seeing the pain there. "Are you all right, Rosanna?"

"I'm with child again." Rosanna leaned into her hands, covering her face. "Not even Elias knows."

Nellie's heart broke for her.

"It'll disappoint him so . . . when I lose this baby, too." Rosanna wiped her eyes. "Best not to get his hopes up again, ya know?"

"Oh, Rosanna . . ."

"Pray that I'll have the grace to bear this yet again." She wept uncontrollably. "Or for healing, if it be God's will."

Nellie fought down the lump in her own throat. "I'll pray . . . you can count on that."

"I mean now. Would ya?" asked Rosanna. "The Lord healed the woman with the issue of blood . . . what sort of disease was that?"

Nellie had also read the New Testament story. "All I know is she believed that if she could touch the hem of the Lord's robe, she'd be made well."

"Oh, I wish He could walk among us today."

"Well, He does," Nellie Mae said.

Rosanna brushed away her tears. "You sense His presence?"

"These days, jah . . . since He lives in my heart."

Rosanna nodded silently, unable to speak.

"We can show His love to each other—and to others—as we walk through the hardest valleys."

Rosanna searched for a hankie in her dress sleeve.

"Like the one you're walkin' in now." Nellie leaned closer. "Have you thought of askin' the elders to lay hands on you, like the Scriptures say to us?"

"But we're here now. And the Lord promises to be with us when we come in His name, jah?"

Nellie studied her. "You must believe that God will heal you if we pray together."

"It's mighty hard, I'll admit that." Taking a deep breath, Rosanna seemed to brighten a bit.

Nellie Mae didn't feel skilled enough to offer a powerful prayer, like the ministerial brethren might. She merely took a breath and did her best. "O Lord, my friend Rosanna here wants a baby with all of her heart—just however you might see fit for that to happen. And she wants to be strong enough to carry her baby till it's time for the birth." Nellie paused, hoping she was choosing the right words.

Only the Lord knows my heart . . . and Rosanna's.

Nellie continued, filled with a deep love for her friend. "But more than any of this, Rosanna longs for your will to be done. She wants it more than everything else. Amen."

———

Betsy wished to be in a prayerful attitude all during this gray and rainy day of working in the shop. She had been mindful of communion for a full month now, Sunday being one of its twice-yearly celebrations, with the ordination service following. In preparation for taking communion with the membership, she had committed to memory a good portion of First Corinthians, the eleventh chapter. But it was the twenty-eighth verse that convicted her most.

But let a man examine himself, and so let him eat of that bread, and drink of that cup.

She had no known sin in her heart, yet she wasn't perfect. Only the Lord was that. And there was this awful rift between Rhoda and the family. How she longed to somehow heal the breach. *Ach, the folly of worldliness . . .* Rhoda's selfish living still hurt terribly. Yet she chose to forgive her willful, wandering daughter.

Several times she had even made the trip to see Rhoda at James and Martha's, only to find her already gone.

What can I possibly do to smooth things over?

Nan held the door for her as they entered the bakery shop with the still-warm pies and cookies. Quickly she and Nan arranged the fruit pies and two coconut cream pies in the display case. The cookies were set out on platters with plastic wrap over the top to keep them nice and moist.

"I do hope Rosanna's all right," Nan said softly.

Betsy counted out a baker's dozen for each variety of cookie. "I 'spect Nellie Mae's visit will do her some good."

"Rosanna's a strong believer. I daresay she's been praying 'bout the women over yonder."

"Nellie must've told you, then?"

Nan smiled. "Anymore there isn't much Nellie doesn't share with me." *Both girls have lost close sisters . . . they've come to depend on each other.* "God's so good to give me Nellie Mae," Nan added.

Betsy couldn't have agreed more, and she reached for Nan, wrapping her arms around her girl. "Oh, I'm so glad you're all right, Nan. You know, I was awful worried after your beau broke things off."

"Well, no need to, Mamma. I'm fine now." Nan continued talking about the church and youth gatherings, how she couldn't wait to read Scripture with Nellie at night. "We go upstairs after Dat reads to all of us and memorize verses."

Oh, the joy! "I daresay the younger you are when committing Scripture to memory, the better you'll remember it . . . for a lifetime."

"I can see that. Ev'ry poem I ever learned when I was a little girl, I can still recite."

"Ach, see?"

"What poems do you remember from childhood, Mamma?"

Betsy raised her finger to her cheek. "Here's a sobering one I was taught from the *McGuffey Reader*: 'Tobacco is a filthy weed. It was the Devil sowed the seed. It leaves a stench wher'er it goes. It makes a chimney of the nose.' "

Nan was nodding her head. "Ain't that the truth!"

"And it rhymes, too."

They had a good laugh, and when she looked up, Betsy spied a tan car pulling into the driveway. Lo and behold if the selfsame blond fellow who'd come Monday didn't climb out, running through the rain, straight for the shop door.

Well, lookee here. . . .

———

Nellie wanted to stretch her legs, since Rosanna was resting. She pulled her raincoat up over her head and ran out to see Elias's new baby goats. She found one of the mothers, a beautiful brown-and-white doe, nuzzling her little one playfully. Nellie was taken by the gentle way the nanny goat had with this baby, who soon began to nurse. The kid still had its horns, so it was less than ten days old, which was when Elias would dehorn it.

An earthy scent hung heavily in the air, and she thought of David Yoder's herd of dairy cows, wondering how Caleb was managing since his father's accident. She caught herself. *He's at the edge of my every thought.*

She heard the creak of a carriage and the sound of approaching horse hooves and saw Elias pulling up to the barn. He jumped out of the buggy and quickly unhitched the horse in the midst of the rain. *He's lost some weight.* Rosanna had said he'd skipped meals recently for the purpose of fasting and prayer. Nellie had assured her that once *Gmee*—the big church gathering this Sunday—was over, he would eat again and gain the weight back. She'd seen Dat and her brothers do much the same when they went to their prayer closets, doubtless pleading in part for God to withhold the divine lot from them, so solemn a responsibility it brought. Yet praying for God's will, too.

After a time, Nellie returned to the house. She was relieved to see Rosanna had awakened and her color was some better. When Elias came inside, he headed upstairs, saying he'd come down after supper.

"God's called him to prayer for the future of our church," Rosanna explained, tucking a loose hair under her Kapp.

Nellie Mae had never heard of the Lord calling someone to pray for something specific. Always before, the bishop had been the one to admonish the membership to do so.

"Honestly, Nellie, I've never seen Elias so bent on something. And he's decided against seeding tobacco this year, too."

"Seems Preacher Manny's message is catchin' on, then."

"Jah, for sure, even though the crop's always been a good mortgage lifter, as the tobacco farmers like to say." Rosanna set a pot on the stove and then washed her hands.

"Some folk still cling to bringin' in the 'baccy, you know."

"Sure they do. It'll take some time before things change much round here, no doubt." She reached for her wooden cutting board and gathered up the vegetables intended for the evening meal. "All that talk aside, Elias and I've found a real home in the new church. We've had some good fellowship with two older couples who are like spiritual parents to us."

Since Elias's and Rosanna's families had remained in the old church, their being looked after by older believers was a blessing.

"Well, I can hardly wait for September," Nellie said right out.

"To join church?"

Nellie smiled, ever so anxious for her baptism. Until that day, she was exempt from the ordination process, so she and Nan and other non-baptized youth would keep the young children occupied outdoors while their parents chose a worthy man to nominate. If a man received three or more votes, his name went into the lot. Of those men, one would eventually draw the old hymnbook containing the scripture signifying he was God's man. *Just as in the old church on Gmee Sunday,* she thought, glad Uncle Bishop had decided to ordain a second preacher.

"Must be our church is growin'," she said.

"Oh, is it ever." Rosanna steadied the celery with her left hand, cutting firmly through the stalks with her right. "That's why this ordination comes at such a good time. And I'm not the only one who thinks so."

"Mamma says there's not to be any talk 'tween members 'bout who should be nominated," Nellie said.

Rosanna nodded. "We're to make it a matter of prayer."

"Nonmembers can pray 'bout all this, too?"

"Whether you're a member yet or not, you want God's will."

Nellie finished chopping carrots and reached for the onions. "How long before we'll have our own bishop, do you think?" She'd wondered this for months, ever since Uncle Bishop Joseph had lifted the Bann from the People, temporarily allowing those who wanted to join the New Order to leave with mercy.

"Elias thinks it'll take a few years to make us a bishop."

"It must keep Uncle Bishop busy, overseein' two church districts."

Rosanna nodded. "I daresay the ministerial brethren carry a love-burden we can't begin to understand."

"Dat's said much the same," Nellie acknowledged.

"Your father's a wise man—Elias often looks to him for counsel, as well as Preacher Manny. Manny's concerned we not 'go soft,' taking anything for granted concerning our salvation . . . lest our deeds deceive us." Rosanna stopped her chopping to look at Nellie. "I wasn't sure I should say anything, but your Aendi Anna came to see how I was doin' . . . you know, after Elias and I met with her bishop husband and John and Kate about . . . the babies. It was just so nice of her . . . considering everything."

Nellie was glad to hear this. "My aunt always loved you, Rosanna."

"She was so dear, comin' to check up on me. If Anna were younger, she could be like a mother to me . . . 'cept for one thing."

"Disagreeing that you can say you're saved?" Nellie asked softly.

"No matter what anyone thinks, the split is still dividing the People," Rosanna said.

For some it's more heartbreaking than for others, thought Nellie.

Together they dumped all the prepared vegetables into a big pot, and Rosanna added ample salt and pepper before setting on the lid and lighting the gas stove.

"You know, Anna did tell me, without a blink of an eye, that she and the bishop read the Bible out loud every day," Rosanna said.

Nellie thrilled to hear this.

"Something they've been doin' for a while . . . but she made a point of saying, mind you, that they wouldn't think of studying or discussing the verses." Rosanna wore a mischievous smile.

"Nor memorizing, either?" Nellie could hardly keep herself in check.

"I truly believe the Lord's at work in their hearts," Rosanna said softly.

Reassured that supper was well underway, Nellie gave her friend a quick kiss on the cheek. "Good-bye—and take good care." How she hoped and prayed Rosanna would not lose this baby. "I'll look forward to seein' your pretty Grandmother's Dream quilts next time, Lord willing."

"Be careful out on the wet roads," her friend called. "And come again soon!"

With a wave, Nellie hurried across the soggy yard to retrieve her horse from the stable.

CHAPTER 17

H is mom's eyebrows rose and remained aloft when Chris carried the boxed coconut cream pie into the kitchen and, with a flourish, set it on the counter.

"Are we celebrating something . . . again?" She smiled, opening the lid and breathing in the luscious aroma.

"Do we need a reason to eat a delicious pie?"

"Must be you're sweet on a cook somewhere," Zach teased, sauntering over to peer at the treat. Then, his eyes darting comically, he sneaked a swipe at the creamy white peaks with his finger.

"Hey . . . watch it." Chris swatted him away.

Zach was nosing around, eyeing the plain white box. "Where *are* you getting these? Three pies in one week?"

Chris simply smiled. "Just eat it already."

Mom reached for the knife rack. "We'll have our dessert before dinner," she said with a smile.

Zach grinned and bent close to the pie.

"Oh, you . . . you're goin' to inhale it next." Mom pushed him back playfully.

Chris loved having his mom around. She'd never considered any job but that of homemaker. *Like Nellie Mae Fisher surely will be.*

Startled, he attempted to push away the thought while Mom cut thick wedges of Nellie Mae's mouthwatering handiwork. He'd sure missed seeing her at the shop today.

After Chris enjoyed every morsel, Zach followed him to their shared room and plopped down on his bed with a demanding look on his face. Chris knew he'd better come clean with his brother. After all, he'd already told their parents about his visits to their Amish cousins.

"Listen, the pies came from a country bakery," he said.

With an obnoxious smile, Zach raised his eyebrows. "And . . . ?"

"And . . . what?"

"You're not so big on pies," Zach shot back. "C'mon!"

Chris sighed. "There *is* someone. . . ."

Zach laughed. "I knew it!" Then he frowned. "Wait a minute. I thought you were flipped out over Sheryl Kreider. Weren't you at her locker the other day?"

"Well, I *did* ask her to the banquet."

"So, are you two-timing someone else?" Zach's eyes twinkled.

Chris sprawled out on his bed, across from Zach's. "Listen, man, can you be serious for once?"

"Oh, this is *good*." Zach leaned up on his elbow. "So . . . who's the other girl?"

Chris paused a moment. "Look, I don't want to get something all stirred up again."

"What are you talking about?"

"Suzy Fisher."

Zach shook his head, frowning. "Wh . . . I don't get you."

"The girl I like is Amish."

"Translation, please?"

Chris decided to just say it. "The other girl is . . . Suzy Fisher's sister."

Zach tilted his head, looking baffled. "No way."

"Nellie Mae. But I'm not sure what to do about her. I mean, you know how it is." He looked at his brother, who was nodding thoughtfully, evidently still taking all this in.

"Yeah," Zach said, "I know."

Rhoda slipped out of bed, having already slept for several hours. She'd come in plenty early last night, thanks to Ken's insistence. Now she crept to the kitchen for a glass of milk, careful not to awaken the children.

Sitting in the light of the moon, the sky having cleared since her date with Ken, she stared out the window. She felt awfully sad. Ken might think of it as having a pity party—she'd heard him say much the same regarding one of the real estate agents at his company, who complained when her sales fell short of making her Realtor of the Month.

But Rhoda's malaise was about herself and Ken. How had she managed to miss his disinterest in having children?

He was, after all, father material. Wasn't he? Perhaps he just didn't see it in himself. Maybe if he spent more time around his cousins, it would help him to discover his paternal instincts.

Moonlight fell on soon-to-be-planted cornfields, and Rhoda stared out at its beauty. She felt sure she could move Ken to her point of view, at least in time. That's when she decided maybe it *was* a good idea to rent the room from him.

James would want a decision soon—he wanted her things moved out by next Tuesday. There was no changing *his* mind on anything, unless . . . Maybe she could buy herself some time.

What if I went to church with them this Sunday?

———

Rosanna busied herself with the newly commissioned quilt projects acquired at market. But since tomorrow was communion and ordination Sunday, she was mindful to divide her time amongst cutting colorful squares for the quilt Dottie had ordered, reading the Good Book, and praying for guidance.

The nagging pain in her lower back had faded somewhat today. And her cheeks seemed a bit rosier when she'd looked in the mirror. Overall, she felt stronger than she had for some time.

The mail arrived and she hurried outside, though she was not yet expecting a circle letter back from either her aunts in Smoketown or her cousins down in Conestoga. When she spied a letter postmarked Bird-in-Hand, she was curious.

Eagerly she tore open the envelope, surprised to see it was from Lena Stoltzfus, the kindhearted New Order woman Treva had introduced to her. The expectant mother and quilting friend of Nellie's grandmother had written it just yesterday.

She began to read.

Friday, April 11, 1967
Dear Rosanna,

   Greetings in the name of our Lord!

   I enjoyed meeting you so much, knowing we share a like faith. Oh, but I would've liked to sit down with you alone when you visited here—to share my peculiar story.

   Not long ago, while I was praying, I felt strongly that I was to give my seventh baby to the Lord, like Samuel of old. Of course my husband and I have dedicated all of our children to God, but this baby—I truly believe it's a boy—is meant to be raised in the house of the Lord.

At the time, I had no idea what that meant, but when it came to my ears that a young woman in Honey Brook had repeatedly miscarried, then lost her two adopted babies because of her newfound faith, I wondered if God meant for me to give him to you, Rosanna. To be raised in the fear and admonition of the Lord.

The more I prayed, mind you, the more I felt this child would be a great blessing to you and your husband. I believe that as strongly today as I did that day more than two months ago.

Bless you, dear Rosanna. I hope to hear from you soon, whatever you decide.

Your sister in Christ,
Lena Stoltzfus

P.S. The baby is due in mid-September.

Rosanna attempted to read the last couple of paragraphs again, but her eyes filled with tears. *More than two months ago.* So Lena had been in deep prayer around the time Eli and Rosie went back to Cousin Kate. . . .

She felt reassured that this woman had not acted impulsively. Because of that and this amazing letter, Rosanna knelt to pray for her, unsure how to respond to Lena's generous offer. Her heart beat a little faster, thinking what it would be like to someday hold Lena's son in her arms. *If it is your will, Lord.*

———

Following his father's afternoon nap, Caleb took extra care getting him settled in the kitchen, with assistance from Abe, who left quickly. His brother obviously struggled with Daed's helpless state. They all did, but Abe seemed to show it more than Mamm or the girls. Caleb, however, always stayed by to do his father's bidding, especially if Mamm was out running an errand or attending a quilting bee, as she was today.

Surprisingly, Daed's only request was for a full glass of cold water within arm's reach. He would sit while he waited for Mamm's return. She had somewhat apologetically reminded Daed before leaving early this morning that this was the big month for quiltings. Caleb had even wondered if Mamm was suffering from cabin fever, although she'd been outdoors plenty to plant many of the garden vegetables with his sisters. She'd announced just last night that the radishes were up already . . . some lettuce was peeking out of the soil, too—"*a bit early.*" Mamm's eyes had shone at the telling.

She's making her own happiness. . . .

"Abe and I are buildin' a ramp for your wheelchair, Daed," Caleb said.

"What's that for?" Daed growled.

"You'll need it to get to your rehab sessions."

His father's eyes brightened briefly, like a light flickering on, then off.

"Your English cousin's son offered to drive you in a van, so you'll get there right quick . . . more comfortably, too." He held his breath, waiting as if for the next shoe to drop.

"Who do ya mean?"

"Christian Yoder."

Daed smiled faintly. "My cousin John's boy? Well, what do ya know."

Before Daed could change his tune, Caleb mentioned that Chris had been coming several times a week to help with milking and other chores. "He's workin' mighty hard. And just so good round the herd, too."

Daed nodded and closed his eyes in repose—either that or he was recalling former days.

Should he forge ahead and risk asking to have Chris's young friend, Billy, come for a visit? Slowly he went to sit on the corner of the table bench, facing his father. "Chris would like to bring a grade-school youngster out to see the farm sometime, Daed. Just for a few hours. What do ya think?"

"This here Chris is a good boy, ain't?"

Caleb was quick to nod. "A big help, jah."

"Well, I can't say I'm happy 'bout using outside help." He drew a slow, deep breath, eyes cast downward. "I just don't know. . . ."

Caleb's heart sank. "Chris Yoder *is* blood kin," he reminded him.

Another long groan. "That he is. I s'pose it's all right on both counts. After all, John Yoder and I go back a long ways, though I haven't seen him in years."

Stunned by how well his father had responded, Caleb allowed himself to breathe more easily.

"When can I lay eyes on this long-lost cousin's boy?"

"Chris'll take you to rehab next Tuesday afternoon. Gideon will help Abe cover the milking so I can ride along."

"Well, better hurry and get that ramp ready, then."

With that, Caleb headed for the back door, relieved. On the way out to the barn for the saw, he thought of going back and asking if Rebekah might also be permitted to help out during daylight hours.

Then, thinking better of it, he decided he best leave well enough alone.

CHAPTER 18

Nellie Mae couldn't wait to close up the shop today. She'd sent Mamma down to the house to relax while Nan made supper—fried chicken, noodles and gravy, and green beans with ham and onions. Pulling the shop door closed, she walked toward the house, drinking in the raw, damp smell of overturned soil. Farmers would be out plowing and planting soon, and that made her think of Caleb.

Inside the summer porch, she wiped her bare feet on the rag rug at the door and put a smile on her face. Then she rushed past Nan in the kitchen and made her way upstairs to her room. All day she'd had it in her mind to get Caleb's old letters out of hiding and reread them. *To help me move forward without him*, she thought. *Nothing more.*

Yet now that she had a few moments to herself, she feared she might open up an even deeper hurt, seeing his loving words . . . the strong slant of his handwriting.

Sitting on her bed, she reached for her Bible instead and began to read Psalm 89. *I will sing of the mercies of the Lord for ever: with my mouth will I make known thy faithfulness to all generations.*

"O Lord," she prayed, "I broke up with Caleb . . . for you. And once again, I give him—and our love—back to you." *Again and again*, she thought, realizing it was still nearly a daily occurrence.

Heartened, she read half of the chapter, the phrases soothing her. Then, resisting the urge to ponder the past, she went to look for her mother. Seeing her parents' door ajar, she called softly, "You busy, Mamma?"

"Come in." Her mother held a piece of paper, the Bible in her lap.

"Didn't mean to interrupt—"

"I'm preparing for communion council tomorrow."

"Same way as the old church?"

Her mother nodded. "Some things are similar, jah. There's a time of soul-searching beforehand." She held up the page. "Come, look at what you'll be asked to think 'bout as a member next fall . . . before the foot washing and communion service."

She sat next to Mamma on the love seat, near the window. "I know the bishop always asked if the People were of one mind before communion Sundays."

"Unity's necessary for this most holy ordinance." Mamma showed her the five written questions, and the verse printed in Preacher Manny's own hand at the top: *For as often as ye eat this bread, and drink this cup, ye do show the Lord's death till he come.*

They discussed the bread and the "wine," which for them was grape juice, and read aloud the first question to be given prayerful consideration. " 'Are you willing to be at peace with God, wholly trusting in Jesus Christ and living a life without spot or blemish, by the power of the Holy Spirit?' "

Mamma smiled sweetly. " 'Tis my heart's cry." Tears sprang to her eyes. "Oh, Nellie Mae . . . it's the second question that hurts me so. And I've been considering it all month, seems."

Nellie soon understood as she read aloud, " 'Are you aware of any unresolved relationship, where someone is carrying something against you?' "

"Rhoda is hurt, surely she is," said Mamma, sighing. "What can I do to make it right?"

Nellie patted her hand. "It was never your fault Rhoda left."

"Still, I must try to talk to her . . . I simply must."

They shared further—Mamma was convinced she could not partake of holy communion if she did not speak with Rhoda today. "To offer forgiveness, if nothing else."

"Well, I'll take you to see her, if that's what you want."

"Oh, would you, Nellie Mae?"

She gave her mother a hug. "I'll tell Nan we'll be havin' supper away from home this evening."

"Let Dat know, too."

Nellie hurried out to the horse barn, praying Rhoda might have an open heart toward their mamma. Swiftly she hitched the horse and buggy, thinking about someday partaking in communion—the emblems of the Savior's body and blood. She was touched deeply, tears falling down her cheeks.

"O dear Lord, if only Caleb could understand. If he could just realize what you did for each of us," she whispered as she stroked the mare's long neck.

———

As she waited for the cook to complete her order for table number four, Rhoda spotted her mother and sister coming in the restaurant door. Stricken by the solemn expression on Mamma's face, Rhoda wanted to hide in the kitchen. Instead, she determined to be brave and simply "face the music," as Mrs. Kraybill sometimes said.

Nellie caught her eye, waving shyly as the hostess showed them to an inviting booth. *Now what'll I do?*

She had no choice but to be polite, and she wanted to be kind. But really, *another* visit from her family—and this time Mamma, too? Was eating out just so appealing now that she was a waitress?

Putting on a smile, she breezed over to their table. "How are you, Mamma . . . Nellie Mae?"

Her mother looked up, her beautiful face alight. "Oh, Rhoda, dear . . . are you our waitress?"

"What would you like to order?" She flipped her order pad over to a blank page.

Nellie said nothing, and Mamma kept looking at her, as if she hadn't heard Rhoda at all.

"We have several specials tonight," Rhoda said, rattling them off. The sight of Mamma brought her final evening at home right back in one sweeping rush: The horrid way she'd talked to her father, her haughty attitude, and her impatience to leave the house. Doubtless Mamma recalled all of it.

"Would you mind terribly if I talked to you before we order our supper?" Mamma asked.

The weight of the world landed on her. Her mother was going to confront her about coming home, she just knew it. "I can't . . . well, I'm at work."

"For pity's sake, Rhoda, we came all this way," Nellie piped up. "Won't ya hear Mamma out?"

"Only a few minutes?" Her mother's eyes were bright with tears.

Reluctantly Rhoda slid in next to Nellie Mae. "What is it, Mamma? Is someone ill . . . or worse?"

Her mother lowered her eyes, and her shoulders rose slowly as she inhaled. "No one's ill physically, no. But I am heartsick, daughter. I've come to ask your forgiveness . . . to make things right 'tween you and me."

Surprised, Rhoda said, "You don't understand." She sighed and continued. "This isn't easy to say, Mamma, but my leaving has little to do with you . . . or the family. It's nothing you've done at all."

"But why, then?" asked Mamma. "It's not natural for a single woman to live away from her father's house. Just ain't."

She'd expected her mother to feel that way. It was all she knew. "I'm fine. No need to worry."

Mamma reached across the table. "Will you forgive me . . . all of us?"

"For bein' Plain? That's something we—you—were born to. None of us had any say in the matter." She moved quickly out of the booth, perplexed. "It's not something I can forgive you for, Mamma."

Her mother bowed her head.

"It's all right, Mamma." Nellie cast a disappointed glance at Rhoda. "You did what you came for . . . now we best be orderin' our supper."

After a moment's hesitation, Mamma chose a meatloaf dinner from the menu, and Nellie Mae asked for the fried chicken.

Later, after they'd finished and she'd switched on her professional demeanor once again, Rhoda offered them a look at the desserts, but both her mother and sister said they were "plenty full."

Rhoda felt nearly sick as they paid their bill, unsure if she should accompany them out to the horse and buggy or remain inside at her post. But with the intense uncertainty came a familiar wave of frustration, and all she could do was watch them move toward the door.

What sort of woman refuses her own mother? Rhoda hurried into the hallway and to the washroom to check on her makeup, fearful her sudden tears had smudged her fancy face.

April sunsets were colorful, replete with reds and gold. And Nellie was particularly glad for the long light in the evening as she and her mother left the restaurant and headed toward home, the horse's *clip-clopp*ing helping to rid her of tension. "You're not sorry we went, are you, Mamma?" she asked.

"It was good to see Rhoda, even if she's not herself."

"You did all you could," Nellie said, holding the reins nice and steady.

"I hardly recognized her, really."

Nellie sighed. "Well, she has lost a little weight. And her hair's cut short . . . and styled right fancy."

"It's more the way she holds herself . . . her way of talkin'."

Nellie agreed. "More fancy than Plain." Rhoda had seemed resistant to their request, too, not wanting to sit down and talk. Was their company so unwelcome?

"The world's rubbed off on her." Mamma sniffled a little.

Nellie dared not glance at her mother or she, too, would cry. "Let's try 'n' think happy thoughts. Tomorrow we'll have us a deacon and another preacher."

Mamma perked up. "The church is thriving, that's for sure."

They rode along serenely for several miles, taking in the beauty of the fields and the ever-changing sky. But out near Route 10, a ways from town, where the road opened up with less traffic, two cars—joyriding, more than likely—passed by a mite too close, one after another, like they were racing.

Nellie steadied the reins and held her breath as the horse veered, causing the carriage to careen dangerously over the center line. "Oh, Lord, help us," she cried out as Mamma gripped her arm.

She struggled to control the horse, using the reins and calling to the mare, "Get over, girl!"

But the horse reared up and then began to gallop. "Come on, girl," Nellie said more softly, her heart in her throat. She'd heard of too many carriages being tipped over in the midst of a dangerous situation. *I can't let that happen!*

Attempting to slow the horse by repeated pulls on the reins, she finally managed to get the mare over to the side of the road. Her arms were limp with fright, and all she could say was "Thank the dear Lord. . . ."

She looked at her mother's face, white with near dread. "Ach, Nellie, you managed so well." Mamma folded her hands in her lap. "I doubt I could have done the same."

Nellie Mae felt some relief following the close call, yet she was still shaken all the same. She wondered when her heartbeat might ever return to normal.

She clicked the horse forward again and asked Mamma, "Do you ever pray for protection when you start out on the road?"

"Well, I do now . . . since I started reading the Bible ev'ry day."

"Not before?"

"We weren't taught to pray for the covering of protection when I was growin' up. There's plenty of scripture about calling on the name of the Lord for salvation, for guidance, for His loving care—changin' the tide of evil or preventing harm," Mamma explained. "So many passages, really. We just didn't know what was there before."

"Passages like some Suzy wrote in her diary?"

Mamma fell silent.

"Ach, I should've kept quiet."

Eyes serious, Mamma shook her head. "Actually, I'm glad you brought that up, Nellie, because I've been meanin' to ask if I could read Suzy's diary. To ease the grief that lingers in me."

"Well, it's only the last part of the diary that's of any comfort, truth be told. Even so, Rhoda has it now."

Brightening, Mamma said, "Better yet. Jah, such good news."

"I'm sure Rhoda's read it through by now, although she hasn't said so."

"No matter. I can wait."

Nellie recalled Rhoda's rather distant remarks earlier and wondered why Suzy's words had not seemed to soften her heart. Was her sister so steeped in the world of the English that she was deaf to the still, small voice of God?

Her time with Elias following supper was one of Rosanna's favorite hours of the day. Tonight they sat at the table discussing the communion-council questions, pausing when they came to the third one: *Are you willing to live in love, forgiveness, and peace with your brothers and sisters in Christ and with all people, as far as it is in your ability to do so?*

Rosanna felt a tug in her spirit. "I have absolutely no peace 'bout something."

"What is it, love?" Elias's eyes searched hers.

She sighed, trying not to cry. "To tell you the truth, I don't know what to do 'bout taking a baby from yet another woman. I just feel so numb." She found Lena's letter in her pocket and handed it to Elias. "This came today, complicating matters even more."

She waited as he read, watching his expression change from surprise to brief consideration, and back to astonishment. "I say we commit this to the Lord."

Trembling, she reached for his hand. "There's something else, Elias. Something I should've told you sooner."

"You're shaking, love. What is it?"

"I'm with child again," she whispered, scarcely able to form the words.

His eyes grew wide. "Ach, Rosanna . . ."

"I've known for a while, but I couldn't think of takin' communion without telling you."

He leaned toward her, kissing her cheek and then taking her hand in both of his. "Now, why would you keep such a wonderful thing to yourself?"

She pressed her lips together as she struggled not to cry. "I wanted to bear the pain alone, to spare you when . . . if . . ."

He rose quickly and crouched beside her chair. "You must promise me never again to suffer so, my darling. You're carrying our baby, created by God . . . by our love for each other."

Nodding, she yielded to his arms, resting her face against his. *Trust* . . . *trust*, she told herself. *Do not fear.*

"We'll pray every day for the baby's safety," he whispered.

She felt his chest heave as Elias drew her near—as though he, too, was terribly frightened.

CHAPTER 19

C aleb's bantam rooster began to crow, awakened not by the brightness of the moon moving out from behind a cloud, but by the noisy arrival of a carriage. Caleb had been up for nearly a half hour reading a few verses from the old family Bible, merely to start out the Lord's Day. *No other reason,* he told himself, although here lately he was intrigued by his cousin Chris's exuberant talk of the Good Book.

Caleb went to the window and saw a young woman emerge from the carriage, her head bowed. Was it . . . could it be his long-lost sister? He leaned closer to the window and realized it was indeed Rebekah. "What do you know!"

She had not darkened the door since leaving nearly three months ago. Quickly he headed down the stairs, to the back door, chagrined at not having kept in touch as he'd promised that miserable Sunday night in late January. Things had gone awry shortly thereafter, spiraling out of his control. There had been no time for his headstrong sister, with so many problems of his own.

"Well, look at you." He opened the door.

She smiled. "You're up early."

"I might be the only one awake in the house." He stood near the cookstove, thinking he ought to fire it up to take off the chill. For Daed, especially. "What brings you here?"

"It's communion Sunday—at Preacher Manny's, that is. And even though I'm not a member just yet, I want to have a clean slate, so to speak." She eyed him hesitantly. "Caleb . . . I want to make peace here. If at all possible." Her light blond hair was still parted down the middle and combed back smoothly on top, the twisted strands on the sides pinned beneath her white netting Kapp. He'd thought his sister might have begun to look different by now, spending time with the defectors. "Are ya starin' at me?" she asked softly.

"You look exactly like you did before you left."

"Well, what did ya expect? Ain't like we're fancy folk. We dress Plain and still use horse and buggy." She smiled. "It's the spiritual teachings that are the big difference . . . and I daresay, Caleb, if you gave it a try, you'd find it wonderful-good, too."

He shrugged, put off.

"How's Daed since . . . the accident?" she asked.

"Go and see for yourself," he dared her.

She flung off her shawl. "Be serious, Caleb. It won't be that easy to make amends."

"With Daed?"

"Well, not with *you*." She poked his arm, mischief in her eyes.

"Ach, I miss seein' ya," he admitted. "You oughta come to see Mamm some. You have no idea how hard things are for her—Daed's unable to move without help and all."

"I'm here for that, as well. But do you think I'll be welcomed back?"

He shook his head sadly. "Truth is, I doubt it . . . not if you're bent on stayin' with the heretics."

Her eyes dimmed. "Why do you call us that? You can't condemn what you don't know firsthand, now, can you?"

It occurred to him that she was in touch with Nellie Mae every week at church, or so he assumed. He found himself straining to hold back, even inching away from her, not wanting to ask what he was dying to know.

"What is it?" Her eyes searched his. "You all right, Caleb?"

He forced a chuckle, waving away her question. "I'll see if Daed and Mamm are up yet."

———

Rhoda awakened to the sound of wood thrushes bickering loudly in the pasture. A sudden breeze rang the dinner bell hanging on the back porch from a rope high in the eaves. Stretching in the warmth of her bed, she remembered it was Sunday and thought again of attending church with James and Martha. She could help with the babies in the nursery, which might soothe her a bit. Oh, how she wished she could wipe Ken's offhand remarks from her memory!

Getting up, she washed and dressed in Plain attire for the day. It was impossible to push her short hair into a bun, so she merely parted it down the middle and secured it on the sides with bobby pins. Then, putting on her Kapp, which she had not worn in quite some time, she hurried downstairs to start breakfast for Martha before the rest of the family awakened. For herself, though, she would lay out only fruit—grapefruit, apple slices, and half a banana. She wouldn't take any sugar in her coffee, either, nor allow herself a single bite of Martha's scrumptious cinnamon rolls, baked yesterday evening.

A boring breakfast is my lot. . . .

Even Emma seemed to notice her Amish garb as the little girl came running into the kitchen to give her a good-morning hug. Eyeing her but good, Emma grinned shyly, her eyes drifting to the undoubtedly disheveled appearance of Rhoda's too-short hair. She quickly guided Emma to the drawer for her apron, tying it around her waist before her niece gave her yet another hug, as if to say, *I'm glad you look more like yourself today, Aendi Rhoda.*

Sitting at the table to await the rest of the family, Rhoda listened to Emma's chatter about going to "God's house" and wished Ken could allow his own heartstrings to be tugged by such an adorable child.

When James and Martha came to the table with the rest of the children, James's eyes lit up momentarily at seeing Rhoda dressed so conservatively, ready for church. And Martha's smile never once ceased all during breakfast.

The same noisy birds were still quarreling even after the morning meal, their song occasionally rising amidst the ruckus—*ee-oh-lay, ee-oh-lay*—as Rhoda walked to her car. Although she still hoped to stay on with James and Martha, she would not stoop to groveling, in spite of her church attendance today.

Her words were not the only thing she had to convince James. Though headstrong, he was quite responsive to Martha—unlike her brother Ephram, who paid little mind to what his wife ever thought.

So I'll play my cards right—for now, Rhoda decided as she drove to the Beachy meetinghouse, quite pleased with herself and her growing collection of wordly phrases.

She hoped her willingness to don a cape dress and apron—and to attend her brother's church—this beautiful Lord's Day morning might just soften his heart.

———

Rosanna couldn't help noticing the size of Preacher Manny's black sheepdog as she and Elias pulled into his yard Sunday morning. Sitting guard presently on the front porch steps, as if observing all the gray-topped buggies,

the dog was a fixture. Nothing moved him, including the comings and goings of the teen boys who were busy leading driving horses to the stable to
water them for the long day ahead.

Eventually she took her seat in the kitchen for council with other women
church members. They turned in handwritten sheets of paper giving their
individual answers to the communion questions, and clusters of the membership were asked to answer as Preacher Manny read the list of questions.

She was glad she'd shared openly with Elias last evening. As unworthy
as she felt apart from God's mercy and grace, today Rosanna believed she
was ready, indeed, to take communion.

It was during the time of congregational singing that she sensed a near-
tangible sweetness in the room; tears of repentance shone on the faces of
some. And following communion, during their traditional foot washing,
she delighted in the miracle of unity displayed among the membership.
She knelt to tenderly wash Betsy Fisher's callused feet, considering the
many families separated during the span of time since they'd made their
choice to follow the way of salvation. *So many of us heeding the prompting
of the Holy Spirit . . .*

When it was time to dry Betsy's feet, Rosanna prayed silently that Ephram
and Maryann Fisher, and Rhoda, too, might come to find the Savior in a
personal way. With a warm smile, Betsy stooped to slip on her stockings
and shoes again, and they traded places as Betsy, in turn, knelt to wash
Rosanna's feet. Betsy wept as she did so, her head bowed for the duration of
the foot washing. When at last she had finished, she looked up and nodded
to Rosanna, her eyes gentle and kind.

Nellie Mae was happy to baby-sit a group of hushed small children. She
used her white handkerchief to do clever tricks to entertain them—one
minute making imaginary mice, then the next twin babies who slept side
by side in a hankie cradle. The little girls' eyes were bright with glee, although they knew better than to make more than a quiet sound out here
in the barn.

When at last communion was over, she took the children back to the
house to reunite them with their parents. Happy to help further, Nellie
offered to work in the kitchen to get the common meal laid on the table.
Preacher Manny's wife was glad for the extra assistance and asked her to
retrieve a variety of cheeses from the summer kitchen.

Going for the cheese, which needed some preparation yet, Nellie Mae happened to glance out the back window. There, near the barn, she spied Preacher Manny's nephew standing not so far away from Nan. The attractive young fellow was actually grinning and flirting in an understated way.

Well, now, is this Nan's beau? Curiously she watched as he stepped closer to Nan and slipped her a note.

Nan quickly pushed it into her dress pocket and walked away, head high, as if merely strolling to the outhouse. Out of respect for her sister's privacy, Nellie wiped the smile of delight off her face before continuing to the kitchen, still savoring her discovery.

Nan'll wonder how I know, Nellie thought as she sliced the cheese thinly on the cutting board. *I'll have such fun teasing her!*

"What're you lookin' so happy about?" Rosanna came over and hugged her arm.

"Oh, nothin' much."

Rosanna's eyes were puffy but bright. "Romance in the air? The possibility for a beau, maybe? New Order marrieds look awfully handsome with their neat beards."

Nellie blushed and laughed. "No, there's no beau. Not for me."

"Aw, Nellie Mae . . ." Rosanna leaned close. "There *is* a Singin' tonight."

She knew that all too well, thanks to Nan.

"Elias's handsome cousin Jacob will be attendin'."

"It just ain't fair for me to go, honestly," Nellie managed to say.

"Why's that?"

She sighed. With so many womenfolk milling around, it was impossible to explain. " 'Tis just best for now. That's all."

Rosanna smiled. "You'll know when you're ready. . . ."

Appreciating Rosanna's insight, Nellie nodded. "All in God's hands."

Ken should see me now, Rhoda thought as she snuggled a baby close. The morning service had lasted longer than was usual, yet she didn't mind. Feeding and changing the infants in the nursery was a joy, even though it had been some weeks since she'd attended the Beachy church. And she truly enjoyed being back. *Even more than I thought . . .*

The baby boy in her arms was fussy now. Rhoda began to walk, whispering in Amish to the wee one, realizing it had been months since she'd spoken her first language to anyone but family. She hadn't been able to erase from her mind Mamma and Nellie Mae's visit to the restaurant yesterday. Not for a minute.

Sighing, she sat down to rock the child, hoping that a change in his position might help to calm him. "I've hurt my mamma terribly." She muttered her woes.

One of the other women asked if she was all right. Rhoda nodded and suddenly realized she was crying. Stroking his little head, she faced the wall, attempting to compose herself.

Not only have I disappointed my family, I've disappointed myself. . . .

———

Reuben was the last man to make his way into Preacher Manny's temporary house of worship this Lord's Day. His delay was intentional, as he had been outside pacing behind the barn. Several others had been there with him, all of them doubtless begging God to pass them by. So heavy was the burden of ministering to the People . . . the lot brought with it a lifelong pledge, one that came with no financial compensation for being on call at all hours. That, however, was not so much Reuben's worry as was his concern over wayward Rhoda . . . and even Ephram and Maryann, who still embraced the old tradition. He wondered if he shouldn't have asked not to be considered for either the office of deacon or preacher. Yet likely all his worry was for naught. Truly, the very idea of presuming that anyone would nominate him felt prideful.

He sat down on the backless bench next to his son Benjamin to wait his turn to nominate a man to fill the office of deacon. Once that man was divinely appointed, they would all line up and repeat the same process for the ordination of a preacher—whispering the name of an honorable man to Preacher Manny.

Reuben had always kept his mind trained on matters at hand, but today he noticed several of the men, including Elias King, fidgeting three rows ahead. *We're all restless till this is over. . . .*

He was somewhat reticent to nominate for preacher the man he felt was the most deserving of all the married men. Naming a choice for deacon was another thing—while it was sobering to have the lot fall on you, that particular position did not carry the immense responsibility of preacher. *A near-crushing blow to most.* Some men lost sleep for decades after the lot struck them.

Bishop Joseph rose and stood before them, reading from First Timothy, chapter three. " 'Likewise must the deacons be grave, not double-tongued, not given to much wine, not greedy of filthy lucre; holding the mystery of the faith in a pure conscience. And let these also first be proved; then let them use the office of a deacon, being found blameless.' "

The bishop went on to admonish the wives of the prospective deacons: " 'Be grave, not slanderers, sober, faithful in all things.' "

Bowing his head, Reuben pondered the verses of instruction, praying for God's will to be made known in this place.

Women members formed a line on one side of Preacher Manny's farmhouse, while the men did the same on the opposite side. Betsy watched as their neighbor, the newly elected deacon, Abraham Zook, stepped forward. "Whisper only one name for preacher at the door," he reminded them. For womenfolk it was one kitchen door; for men, it was the other. Neither the bishop nor Preacher Manny could have a vote, but Manny would be standing there in the kitchen to hear the name, which he would pass on to Bishop Joseph once he closed the door. The bishop, for his part, would write each candidate's name on a piece of paper. Any name that was whispered three or more times would be included in the lot.

Betsy's heart pounded as she approached the kitchen door, which was slightly ajar. She dared not look ahead but kept her gaze on the floor. Her mind was on Reuben, hoping he would not be in the preacher's lot. He had enough on him already, what with his sons scattered to the four winds, or so it seemed. *And with our wandering Rhoda. A big worry,* she thought.

She put her hand on her heart and stepped forward. Softly she spoke the name of the man she believed most praiseworthy and then she meekly moved away, returning to the house by way of the front door.

Inside, she joined the others in the large front room who'd already offered their *Stimmen*—votes. No one, except the bishop, would ever know how many votes each man had received.

When Bishop Joseph, solemn as night, came at last into the room and offered a prayer of blessing upon what they were about to do, Betsy squeezed her eyes shut. Afterward, the man of God chose five exceptionally worn *Ausbund* hymnals and placed a single piece of paper inside only one of them. Each hymnal was then secured with a matching rubber band, and the books were arranged on the table.

Bishop Joseph asked, "Does either Preacher Manny or Deacon Zook want to reshuffle the hymnals?"

Silently Preacher Manny stepped forward and made a stack of the books before laying them out on the table to reorder them. He moved aside, allowing the new deacon to do the same. When the ministers appeared satisfied the books had been sufficiently shuffled, the bishop announced the names of the five men in the lot. Elias King was the first named, and Rosanna gasped, a reaction repeated by the next three wives as their husbands' names were called.

Not my Reuben, Betsy hoped, her hands moist.

Bishop Joseph stopped to wipe his eyes. Then, looking at the congregation, he said gravely, "And last . . . Reuben Fisher."

Betsy reached to clasp her daughter-in-law Ida's hand next to her. *Ach, dear man.*

She swallowed hard, fully conscious of the seriousness of the hour . . . and the weight of duty about to befall their soon-to-be chosen servant. The men whose names had been called could no longer refuse the lot, because they'd already promised at their baptism to serve as ordained ministers, should the divine lot strike them.

Betsy was aware of her own heartbeat as the bishop reverently spoke the familiar words, "Are those in the lot here, seated before me, in harmony with the ordinances of the church and the articles of faith?"

Each man answered, "Jah," and then knelt to beseech the Lord to use the biblical process to show which one was to be the minister.

Betsy bowed her head and recalled the day Reuben's cousin Manny had been struck by the lot. His wife and many of his immediate family had wept, their grief something that no one among the People would dare to slight.

When the prayer was finished, Reuben bowed his head as the oldest of the five men went to the table to select one of the hymnals. After a time, he heard that man shuffle back to the bench and sit down.

The next two men each took turns choosing one of the hymnals, but the lot was still not cast.

Only two of us remaining. . . .

Holding his breath, Reuben walked forward to the table. He thought of the added responsibilities ahead should he be chosen by the Lord, and an enormous weight seemed to press on him as he picked up a book.

When the bishop removed the rubber band, Reuben reverently searched the pages for the slip of paper bearing the telltale Bible verse. The lot was not there.

His breath returned and he made his way back to his seat. Then, realizing the outcome before Elias ever rose to take the remaining hymnal, Reuben heard the sound of weeping as it swept through the room—the ritual mourning. His heart went out to Elias and Rosanna—both so young to receive this divine call, and already so brokenhearted. . . .

Elias's shoulders heaved as he returned the book to the bishop and stood for the bishop's charge. "In the name of the Lord our God and this church, the ministry of preacher has been given to you, Elias King. You shall preach God's Word to the people, and encourage and instruct them to the best of your ability." The bishop went on to list other expected duties before concluding, "May the almighty God strengthen you in this work, with the help of the Holy Spirit. Amen and amen." Bishop Joseph then shook Elias's hand and greeted him with a holy kiss.

Immediately following, the members were instructed to pray and "to encourage Elias and his good wife, Rosanna," and the half-day gathering swiftly came to an end.

Reuben searched the congregation for Betsy and noticed how relieved she looked. He couldn't help wondering how they both might be feeling now had the lot struck Reuben instead of Elias, who was expected to give himself—his time, energy, and insight—for the good of the flock. *All the days of his life.*

———

Elias and Rosanna spoke not a word as they rode. Silence reigned except for the clatter of the buggy wheels on the pavement, punctuated by the steady *clip-clop-clip*ping of their horse.

Fully aware of her husband's humble heart, Rosanna wiped tears away. *Dear Lord, give Elias the patience of Job, the wisdom of Solomon, the faith of Abraham.* . . .

When Elias reached for her hand and offered a meek smile, she made an unspoken pledge to help her husband however she could, for as long as she lived.

A sudden and sharp pain shot through her stomach. She started but suppressed the urge to cry out.

"What is it, love?" Elias turned.

"Ach . . . the baby." She cradled her middle, trying not to cry—refusing to allow fear to overtake her.

Elias drew her near. "O Lord, protect our child. And if it be your will, strengthen . . . and heal my wife. I call upon your name, Lord Jesus Christ," he prayed.

Rosanna was comforted by her husband's confidence, yet her own doubts threatened to assail her. *Don't let me lose the baby today, Lord*, she pleaded, thinking of Elias's ordination. *Please, not today.* . . .

CHAPTER 20

O n the way to the Sunday night Singing, Nellie noticed tire tracks in James and Martha's cornfield. "Sure seems odd that James uses his tractor for fieldwork instead of just in the barn like some farmers," she told Nan from the front seat of the family buggy. "Guess he wants to do more than fill silo."

Nan nodded, holding the reins. "It's hard gettin' used to all the modern equipment round Honey Brook."

Nellie noticed the stubble from last year's cornfield covering the ground, keeping the green from springing up. *Less need for horses anymore, it seems.*

Her thoughts turned to the Singing. She half wished she'd stayed home and planned the flower beds with Mamma instead.

I'm thinking like a Maidel, for sure.

Crows were *caw-caw*ing in the underbrush, and redwing blackbirds cackled out near the pond behind the new deacon's place. How quickly word would spread of Abraham Zook's and Elias King's ordinations. She wished she might have been sitting next to Rosanna when the lot fell on Elias. She would have cried right along with her.

When the youth had finished with the evening's songs, more than half the fellows sought out girls, moving swiftly across the barn floor. Nellie caught sight again of Ezekiel Mast, Preacher Manny's dark-headed nephew. He strolled confidently to Nan and discreetly touched her hand, his engaging smile and the way his whole face brightened when he spoke to her revealing his intentions. Nan seemed to make no attempt to hide her own brilliant smile, either.

Now that the organized part of the event had concluded, Nellie assumed she would be returning home in Dat's carriage, leaving Nan to ride with Ezekiel in his open buggy. Waiting to let her sister know she was about to leave, Nellie stood there until Nan glanced her way. She motioned toward the barn door and Nan nodded. Satisfied, Nellie turned to depart.

She reached to slide the rustic barn door open, and Jacob King slipped in next to her. Elias's tall and good-looking cousin offered an enthusiastic smile, his big brown eyes intent on her. The heat rushed to her face when she realized how close he was. Rosanna had undoubtedly put a bug in his ear, and for that Nellie was even more mortified—although it wasn't the first time someone had tried to matchmake. *He is awfully cute,* she thought as he heaved open the barn door with one easy shove.

"Goin' out for some air?" He fell into step with her.

"Thought of heading home."

He glanced up at the sky. "But the night's mighty young yet, jah?"

She'd heard that before. All the fellows said it with a new girl when they were at a loss for words. He was definitely going to ask her to go with him in his courting buggy.

Should I? How would Caleb feel?

Jacob glanced down at her, still smiling encouragingly. She felt so uncomfortable walking this way with a new fellow—like she was betraying her former beau.

Suddenly she said, "Jacob, please wait just a minute." She ran back to the barn, motioning for Nan to come quick.

Nan hurried over to her. "I thought you'd left."

"Well, I did, but . . ." She hesitated. "There's someone waitin' outside for me. Ach, Nan . . . this is just so awful."

"You'll be fine. The first date after a breakup is the hardest." So Nan had guessed Nellie might have an opportunity to go riding. "I'll tell ya what, if our buggy's still sittin' out there when I'm ready to leave, I'll drive it home and walk to meet . . . well, my beau, somewhere later."

"No need to be secretive 'bout Ezekiel Mast, ya know."

A smile spread across Nan's face. "Well, don't be goin' and telling anyone."

"Like who?"

"Like anyone," Nan said, eyes twinkling. "And I'll keep mum 'bout Jacob King, too, jah?"

"So you saw him." Nellie sighed. "Now, listen: I haven't decided what I'll do tonight. Honestly, I shouldn't be here at all."

Nan frowned and then leaned closer. "Why not go with Jacob just once? See if he makes you forget Caleb."

Nellie squeezed Nan's hand, wondering if Jacob had given up on her by now. But when she stepped outside again, he was still in the vicinity, talking to his horse, petting the animal's long neck—waiting for her.

Nearly afraid to move from her comfortable position in bed, Rosanna lay as motionless as a log, her breaths coming in shallow sighs. She let her body sink into the mattress, embracing its consolation. Aside from her many miscarriages, she had never endured such gripping pain, pain that caused her to clench her jaw to keep from crying out, curling her toes beneath her pretty, handmade quilts. But she must not allow herself to relive those terrible, wrenching times. *Try to think on the Lord*, she told herself. *The Lord and Elias.*

Her dear husband had been so kind to her, it nearly made her cry. She remembered how he'd sat on the bed, holding her hand tenderly as he prayed, entrusting her and their baby to God's will.

Eventually she fell into a deep sleep, dreaming of holding the twins once again, and waking to find Elias near, his arm draped over her protectively.

Rosanna awakened hours later and realized her pain was somewhat lessened. Yet she couldn't trust that it was over, even though she longed for this frightening afternoon to pass.

Elias brought up some tea for her to drink and helped her to sit up slowly, murmuring loving words . . . taking such good care. Truly, she loved him all the more. "There, now, you're goin' to be all right." His lips brushed her forehead. "The pain's subsiding, jah?"

"How'd you know?" she asked.

He reached for her hand. "Your eyes are free of it, love."

"Perhaps a false alarm." Tears sprang to her eyes. "Ach, Elias, I've never heard you pray so earnestly."

He nodded, looking down at their entwined fingers. "I believe the Lord heard the cry of our hearts, Rosanna."

She sipped the tea, letting the warmth fill her slowly as she relaxed in the presence of her husband . . . the newly ordained preacher.

It was already dark when Chris headed for home following the Sunday evening meeting with the Mennonite Youth Fellowship. They'd discussed plans for their annual Lord's Acre fund-raiser coming up this summer, deciding which vegetables to grow for sale.

Zach and a few of the kids from MYF had decided to go out for sodas, including Sheryl, who'd glanced Chris's way as if wondering why he, too, wasn't going. He'd smiled at her as he left, but now, thinking about it, he must have seemed aloof. With all the hours he was putting in at the landscaping office and David Yoder's farm, he was finding it tough to stay focused on his studies and eventual academic future at Eastern Mennonite School in Harrisonburg, Virginia. He was especially interested in their cross-cultural study programs. He was glad they'd added seminary courses less than two years ago, since he hoped to enroll in those once he had his four-year degree.

Chris had been driving only a short time when he noticed in the distance an Amish buggy parked off the road, not many blocks from the ice cream parlor in Honey Brook. He tapped on the brake. He hadn't seen many Amish courting couples milling about yet; the evenings were still too cold. Most of the time they kept to themselves anyway, staying on the back roads, far from prying eyes. He was curious about their secretive dating customs, which Caleb had alluded to in passing. How strange that no one was supposed to know whom you were seeing until the preacher "published" your wedding date and time just a few weeks before the actual wedding.

Slowing down even more, Chris could see a young Amish couple on the shoulder of the road, surveying their broken-down carriage. Without thinking twice, he signaled and slowed to a stop, parking a safe distance behind. The last thing he wanted to do was startle them.

Hopping out, he walked up to the young man, who looked about his own age. "Anything I can do to help?" asked Chris.

"Well, it ain't somethin' that can be fixed tonight. Denki anyways." The boy tipped his straw hat, seemingly frustrated. "I'm goin' to unhitch the horse and lead him home over yonder." He pointed toward the farmhouse in the middle of a vast meadow to the south.

Chris assumed that meant the girl was going to walk with him, but a chilling wind was picking up now. "You sure I can't give you two a lift?"

The young man glanced at his date, whose face was veiled by the shadow of her black bonnet. "Nellie Mae, would ya want to catch a ride home with this Englischer?"

Nellie Mae? Chris was struck cold.

"Nellie Mae Fisher?"

"Jah, how'd ya know?" asked the boy, scrutinizing him.

She held her hands stiffly in front of her. But now that she had turned, he could see that she was definitely the very girl he'd been unable to stop thinking of since they'd met on the road in early February. "Hello, Nellie Mae," he said, suddenly unaware of her date.

She nodded. "Hi, Christian."

The Amish fellow eyed him suspiciously and then looked back at her. "You two know each other?"

"We've met before," Nellie Mae said, still looking at Chris.

"Well, I s'pose it's all right, if you know him," said the boy.

She seemed hesitant, glancing back at her date. "Jah, then," she said. "I'll go on home."

"You'll get there more quickly," the boy urged her.

"All right." She gave a halfhearted wave to her young man before turning to follow Chris, who was still trying to decide if this was just dumb luck or what.

He went to the passenger side and opened the car door, waiting for her to gather in her long skirt before closing it securely. *Whatever you do, be cool,* he warned himself, not wanting to seem too keyed up.

"Your friend . . . he'll get home okay?" he asked Nellie as he started the car.

"He lives close enough, really. Just over there a ways." She pointed. "Not sure how we broke down. This happens lots on dates." She laughed softly. "You just never know with a horse. . . ."

"You'll have to help me find your house in the dark."

"Oh, ain't so hard. To tell ya the truth, I'm glad to be headin' home earlier rather than so late."

He glanced at her as she made small talk. "Your boyfriend seems like a nice guy."

She looked back at him shyly. "Well, Jacob's not my beau. Just a fella who . . ." Her voice trailed off. Then she continued. "He's nice enough—I don't mean that."

Nodding, he felt a surprising sense of relief. He continued to listen, figuring it was smart to let her do the talking.

"How'd you like the pies?" she asked out of the blue.

"Well, they disappeared real fast."

She let out a little laugh. "Ach, there are more where those came from."

He was pleased by her exceptionally friendly manner. But she was clutching the door handle, keeping her eyes ahead on the road.

"You're not afraid to ride in a car, are you?"

"I rarely ride up front, is all. When I go with paid drivers, it's usually in a van. And we often travel in large groups if we have to go anywhere that's not so safe for the team."

"The team?"

She laughed softly, a melody to his ears. "What we call the horse and carriage."

"Of course." Now *he* was laughing, and much too comfortable with her for his own good.

"Would you mind terribly . . . well, will you tell me more 'bout my sister Suzy and your brother Zach?" she startled him by asking.

His thoughts flew back to the times he'd been with them. "Zach thought she was it, you know . . . and Suzy seemed to think the same about him."

"Do ya think they would've ended up hitched, if she hadn't drowned?"

"I know that Zach was praying about a life mate right before he met Suzy." *Like I did not long ago.* He could see her out of the corner of his eye, sitting there demurely.

She turned to look at him. "Zach's faith led Suzy to Jesus." She sighed, releasing the door handle now and folding her hands. "Suzy wrote 'bout it in her diary, which I decided to read. I broke my promise to her on that, but I know she would forgive me. The scriptures she wrote and things she heard at a nearby campground—all of it—put a longin' in my heart for more. Ach, well, I'll be frank with you, Christian—I wanted to know what Suzy had found."

Stunned that she was so open to talking about the Lord, he listened intently. Nearly all the Amish he'd ever encountered, Caleb and his family included, spoke little of having a personal faith. And they definitely shied away from discussing scripture.

"I'm a follower of Christ," Nellie Mae said boldly. "So are my parents and Nan, the other sister you met." She mentioned several married brothers and their wives who were also saved. "But they're much less conservative—for the time bein', anyway."

He realized now why he was drawn to her, apart from her appealing and natural beauty. Nellie's love for the Lord shone on her face, and he must have known it subconsciously from the first day.

"When did *you* become a Christian?" she asked. "Besides the day you were named 'Christian,' that is."

He smiled at her little pun. "I was young when God called me. I didn't wait—I opened my heart and gave Him my whole life right then. Like my dad and mom did when they were also children."

"Your parents seem very nice, too." .

Was she trying to say that *he* was nice?

"I'm glad my parents and Zach met you and Nan at the restaurant that night."

"Did your father like celebrating his birthday out in public like that?" Her voice was softer now.

He had no idea what she meant. "Do you and your family usually observe birthdays at home?"

"Oh, always. But we keep it very simple, with a special dessert only occasionally—no cake with candles, like fancy folk." She paused, perhaps catching herself. Then she went on, as if not fully realizing that a "fancy" person was at the wheel, driving her home. "There's usually homemade ice cream, and the children receive small gifts like at Christmas. And we sing 'Happy Birthday,' too. When we were little, Suzy once gave me a pretty little plate to put on our dresser on my birthday." She sounded slightly sad all of a sudden.

He waited, hoping she might continue, but she fell silent for the whole rest of the drive.

Later, after Chris let her out at the end of her driveway at her insistence, he replayed the whole evening in his head. He couldn't have planned it better. Glancing at the passenger seat where Nellie had sat, he shook his head.

What is it about her? Why is she so unforgettable?

CHAPTER 21

———

Chris wanted to arrive punctually at the Yoder farm Tuesday afternoon. He spotted Sheryl Kreider at the traffic light in town and, feeling bad about not talking with her Sunday evening, he waved, perhaps a bit too enthusiastically.

She smiled and returned the gesture. *Good.* At least she wasn't ticked off. He didn't want to be without a date for the banquet.

One thought led to another, like dominoes cascading down, and Nellie Mae came to mind as the light turned green. He still was amazed at the strange turn of events, meeting up with Nellie Mae and her "fella." If any aspect of the night had been altered at all—from Zach's decision not to ride home with him to Chris's choosing not to go out to eat after MYF—the chance of his driving her home would have been a big fat zero.

All the same, he'd be better off not daydreaming too frequently about a girl who was off limits to him. Reaching for the radio knob, he found his favorite station, 94.5 WDAC, "the voice of Christian radio." He hoped to play some of that soul-stirring music for David Yoder and Caleb while they rode together to Lancaster for rehabilitation.

Help me always to be a light for you, Lord. . . .

Nearing the outskirts of Bird-in-Hand on the drive back from David Yoder's rehab session, Chris heard David snoring. He and Caleb had made sure he was securely strapped into the locked wheelchair, positioned toward the back of the van.

Caleb glanced over his shoulder from his spot in the front next to Chris. "These sessions take a lot out of Daed."

"And I'm sure they will for a while." At first Chris had sat in the waiting area and studied while Caleb and his dad were in the rehabilitation room, but then Caleb had returned to wait with him. They'd talked for a short time, until the magazines lying on the lamp tables seemed to catch Caleb's attention. So Chris had returned to his history textbook.

Now that they were able to talk more confidentially, out of the public eye, he wanted to ask Caleb about his father's prognosis. "Is there some hope your dad's condition will improve over time?"

"No updates lately. Daed might make some minor progress here and there, but . . ." Caleb shook his head. He looked out the window and then back down, as if unable to express something. At last he spoke in measured tones. "Like I said before, it's kinda impossible to prepare for something like this."

Chris nodded, wishing he could make a difference in his cousin's outlook. "Your father seems determined, though. That's positive."

"Jah, well, determination's always been one of Daed's strengths."

Caleb went on to speak of the many doctors involved in his father's care and "the helpful way the People give to families in crisis—like ours now." He talked up a blue streak as they headed toward Honey Brook.

When they were within a mile or so of the farmhouse, Chris asked, "Do you have extra help lined up for milking on the days we go to rehab?"

"Gideon and Jonah help when they can, and my sister Rebekah is comin' now, too, three days a week. Even Leah and Emmie are pitchin' in some with the farm work." Caleb chuckled. "Abe's got us all workin' hard, that's for sure."

"Your dad must be proud of how well his children are all handling things."

Caleb shrugged. "It's hard to say with Daed." He removed his straw hat, running his hands through his hair. "You know, I enjoy havin' you out for milkin', Chris." He paused. "Not sure how to say this, but . . ."

Chris glanced at him, wondering what Caleb might have on his mind.

"Truth be told, these days, my life's not about much 'cept work and sleep . . . and then more work. Same thing, day in and day out." Caleb fingered his hat on his knees. "Once my brothers leave for home before suppertime, that's the end of my day, pretty much . . . as far as someone to talk to."

"No time for friends . . . or a girl?"

Huffing, Caleb shook his head. "That's it in a nutshell . . . and there's no girl. Not anymore, there isn't."

Unsure what to say, Chris kept his eyes on the road, his ears open.

"She's in love with someone else—well, *something* else." Caleb lowered his voice, and Chris saw him look over his shoulder nervously. "But my father didn't approve anyways, so that's that."

"Sorry, man."

"Jah, so am I."

They were nearing the turnoff to the Yoder farm. "Listen, Caleb . . .
anytime I can help so that you can get away from the house for a while,
just let me know."

"No need for that," Caleb stated. "I have to admit I'm not quite ready
yet to return to the Singings."

"Singings?"

"Two Sunday nights a month the young folks get together, sing for a bit,
then pair up and go ridin' round the countryside in the dark." Caleb pushed
his hat back onto his head. "When you find the girl you like best, you ask
her to marry. Then, come fall, you get hitched durin' wedding season, 'tween
November and December."

"You can marry only two months out of the year?" This came as a surprise.

"After baptism . . . jah." He said it so solemnly, Chris wondered if he was
hinting at his own aborted plan to wed.

They turned into the driveway, and Chris heard Caleb's father rousing
behind them.

"Oh, by the way, my Daed agreed to let you bring Billy out to see the
farm," Caleb said quickly.

"That's great, thanks. I'll check when he can come with me." Chris was
grateful, but Caleb's gloomy expression made him wonder if more might
have been revealed about the former girlfriend Caleb seemed to still care
about, if only there had been more miles to today's trip.

It boggled his mind to think he might be the one and only friend in this
trying season of his Amish cousin's life.

———

Tired from hours spent breaking a strong mare but convinced the Lord
wanted him to make another attempt to visit David Yoder, Reuben made
his way toward the man's dairy farm in his old, rickety market wagon, since
Nellie Mae needed the family buggy to visit Rosanna King. The afternoon
had turned out nice, with the sun as bright as that of a summer's day . . .
the sky clearing as far as his eye could see to the west.

He'd awakened early and tilled manure from the barn into their two
gardens first thing, including the charity garden planted for the purpose
of growing produce for their new minister, Elias King. Betsy had already
planted Swiss chard, lettuce, onions, and horseradish. She and the girls
would tend it, as well as an abundance of planted celery, *"just in case,"* Betsy
had said with a smile. A creamed-celery casserole was standard fare at a

wedding feast, and they would need plenty for all their guests. He assumed Betsy had Nan in mind; that daughter seemed to be out with a beau nearly every weekend now.

Reuben neared the Yoders' place, hoping not to be turned away this time. *The poor man needs to know we care!*

When he reined the horse to the left to make the turn into the driveway, he spied a large gray van parked there, blocking the way. Lo and behold, if David Yoder wasn't being brought down out of the van on a wooden ramp built for his wheelchair. "Well, I'll be." From the looks of things, he had himself some outside help, all right. Reuben took a good look at the tall, blond fellow, clearly English. Was this the young man Ephram and Betsy had mentioned? He certainly did resemble Caleb quite a lot.

Not wasting any time getting down from the wagon, Reuben tied up the horse, his curiosity getting the best of him. The process of getting David safely out of the van was painstakingly slow, and he walked over to see if he could be of help to Caleb and his fancy sidekick.

"Hullo, Reuben," Caleb greeted him.

Reuben nodded. "How are yous doing?"

Just then David himself spoke up, tilting in his wheelchair. "I'm all tuckered out, Reuben."

"My father's just returned from his rehabilitation," Caleb explained politely. His eyes held the full story. The session had apparently been grueling.

"I'll come another day, then," Reuben said, but before he turned to leave, Caleb quickly introduced him to "Christian Yoder, my second cousin."

"Good to meet you, Christian." He shook the English fellow's hand.

"And, Chris, this is Reuben Fisher. . . ." Caleb's voice drifted off. Reuben wondered if he'd been about to add *Nellie Mae's father*.

Christian studied him. "Fisher, you said?"

"That's right."

"You wouldn't, by any chance, know of a bakery shop called Nellie's Simple Sweets?" Christian asked, eyes fixed on him.

"Why, that's my daughter's little place—well, she does most of the bakin', anyways."

Christian's face beamed, but he quickly became more subdued.

"Nice meetin' ya," Reuben said as Caleb pushed the wheelchair around the side of the house.

"Very nice to meet you!" Christian called over his shoulder.

Such enthusiasm.

"What the world?" Reuben muttered on the way back to his horse and wagon.

"You must've stopped in at Nellie's shop," Caleb said once they'd gotten Daed back inside and resting in his room. He handed his cousin a glass of lemonade.

"I've been a couple times, yeah. I bought some pies to surprise my family," Chris said, taking a seat out near the woodpile. "The best I've ever tasted."

Caleb wished to goodness Chris hadn't brought up Nellie's wonderful-good baking. Nobody's compared, that he knew of. Not even his own mother's tasty desserts held a candle to Nellie's. "Ever have her peach pie?" he asked, making small talk.

Chris shook his head. "Not in season right now."

"Jah . . . long out of season." Caleb knew he shouldn't have said it like that, as if he were trying to reveal more than he really cared to.

Chris rose, still holding the lemonade glass—empty now. "Well, I'd better let you get back to your family," he said. "I need to return my dad's van."

"I sure appreciate it—and I know Daed does, 'specially."

"Not a problem," replied Chris. "Maybe sometime your dad and mine can get together again."

"I think Daed might like that." Caleb walked with him toward the large van.

"I wonder if Nellie's bakery shop is still open—do you know?" Chris looked at his wristwatch.

Caleb used to know the minute Nellie closed her shop, but that was another time. Things might have changed. "Can't say I do."

"Well, maybe I'll stop by and see."

Caleb couldn't help but notice the unfamiliar glint in Chris's eye, and he wondered just how well his cousin knew Nellie Mae Fisher.

———

"Ach, why don't you stay for supper?" Rosanna pleaded.

Nellie Mae didn't want to overextend her welcome. "You sure I'm not imposing?"

Rosanna smiled sweetly. "Maybe we can get in another hour or so of quilting afterward. All right?"

She'd come to help Rosanna stitch up the three baby quilts meant for the expectant women in Bird-in-Hand. "I'll stay if you want," she said. "But only if you let me cook supper."

"No, no . . . I'm not an invalid," laughed Rosanna. "I can help."

So they agreed to make supper together, and Rosanna chattered about how much better she was feeling. "I wish you could've heard Elias pray after I had such pain on the ride home Sunday afternoon."

Nellie smiled. "I put your name and the baby's at the top of my prayer list."

Rosanna sliced four hard-boiled eggs to make deviled eggs, grinning. "Seems to me, with all of us prayin', just maybe this time I'll keep my baby."

"The Lord knows how you long for a son for Elias."

She removed the golden yellow yolks and began to mash them with some homemade salad dressing. "I honestly don't have my hopes up much at all, Nellie," she said softly.

"It's normal to be cautious."

"S'pose so . . . which is why Elias and I've decided to accept Lena Stoltzfus's baby." Rosanna looked up at her. "Well, that's not the only reason."

"What do you mean?"

"The main reason was the content of her letter. Elias pointed out to me that it was rather prophetic." She mashed some mustard into the mixture and then added salt.

Nellie waited to hear more, stunned at her friend's change of heart.

"Lena seemed to know—maybe the Lord showed her as she was writing—that the divine lot would fall on Elias last Sunday."

Nellie Mae stopped peeling potatoes to look at her. "You don't mean it!"

"She wrote about wanting her babe to be raised in 'the House of the Lord.' "

"Well, how on earth did she know?"

Rosanna shook her head, shrugging slightly. "Would ya like to read the letter?"

"No, that's all right." A little shiver ran down her back. Truth be known, Nellie was stunned. Why was Elias hoping to raise Lena's baby while praying so hard for Rosanna's and his own child, asking God to help her carry it to term?

CHAPTER 22

It was prayer-meeting night at the Beachy church in Honey Brook. But Rhoda sat in Ken's comfortable living room in Strasburg, her feet up on the plush ottoman as she sipped a thick vanilla milkshake she'd made for herself, against her better judgment.

"You prefer that shake to, say, some dessert wine?" Ken teased, winking at her. He placed his wine glass on the coffee table and slid over next to her on the sofa.

She pouted. "I've all but busted my calorie count for today, so I might as well stick with what I've got here." She'd already indulged in a juicy steak, grilled out on the balcony by none other than "the chef," as Ken playfully referred to himself.

"Aw, honey, you'll get back on the wagon again."

She didn't ask what that meant. Truth was, she was miserable, and when she was this blue, she ate. Not healthy fare, but fatty foods like this thick milkshake made with loads of ice cream, extra sugar, and topped with oodles of real whipped cream. Not to mention the two cherries.

He slipped his arm around her. "Why the sad face?"

Dare she tell him? He was altogether thoughtful and wonderful tonight. *Even so . . .* Taking a deep breath, she knew this was not the time to talk about her desire for a family.

"I'll be all right," she whispered, her face close to his. *When we're married and planning our first baby . . .*

He kissed the back of her hand. "Are you worried about moving away from your brother's? Because the room I showed you will be vacant by Friday. Just say the word and it's yours."

She wanted far more than to be Ken's tenant.

"We'd see each other every day." He smiled.

Sitting up straighter, she pulled away gently. "Ken . . . please, can we talk this over?"

"What's to talk about? You need a place to live. How hard is this?"

She nodded but inside she felt tense. *What would my family think?*

"I'm falling in love with you, Rhoda. We'll have more time together . . . to get to know each other."

I'm already in love with you. She faced him, letting him kiss her gently. "I don't want to do anything that would look . . . well, questionable," she said.

"How can it be wrong to rent a room from your soon-to-be fiancé?"

Her heart beat faster. Was he nearly ready to propose? She couldn't help but smile up at him.

He'll change his mind about a family once we're married, she thought, wrapped up in his arms.

———

His cousin seemed restless when Chris arrived after school Friday with Billy Zercher in tow. Billy had been rather quiet on the first part of the drive, as he usually was in the junior boys' class, but as soon as the Amish farms came into view and the road opened up, Billy became more talkative. Then if he didn't hit it off surprisingly well with Caleb, who seemed to brighten as he took Billy on a tour of the place. In no time, Billy was calling him Cousin Caleb.

Rebekah caught up with Chris in the barn once Caleb took Billy over to the milk house to show him where the milk was cooled and stored. "I hoped I'd have a chance to talk with you again." She wiped her hands on her long, black work apron, her hands still dirty from her work in the vegetable garden. "I wanna say how glad I am for Caleb that he has you to talk to."

Chris smiled. "I enjoy talking to him, too."

She seemed to study him. "You know, back when we were little kids, I always thought you and Caleb could pass for brothers. And I still think that sometimes when I see you two workin' together." She tilted her head, her eyes thoughtful. "You've prob'ly heard about our church split. It's been hard on all of us, but on Caleb more than most." She paused, looking down. "I guess I shouldn't be sayin' anything, 'tis such a private subject, but Caleb and his girl got caught in the middle of that. It really hurt to see him end up, well, single again . . . even though I understand why they broke up."

He didn't know how to respond, or even if he should. Fact was, he'd only heard bits and pieces from Caleb, who was guarded about church talk . . . and his former girlfriend.

"She is the most hardworking, pleasant girl I think I know," Rebekah was saying. "I was lookin' forward to having her as my sister-in-law."

Just then Caleb returned with Billy, who was holding a glass of fresh cow's milk. "Look what Cousin Caleb gave me," Billy said, eyes shining.

Chris couldn't keep from grinning at this usually forlorn boy. "Did you get to see how the lines carry the milk to the big tank?" he asked Billy, who nodded his head, still smiling bigger than Chris had ever seen him.

He's definitely out of his shell!

Chris suddenly wondered if Billy might like one of Nellie's delicious cookies to go with his milk—he hoped she would be at her shop this time. Chris could feel his own smile widen at the thought.

———

As April gave way to May, the lengthening days became ever busier. With the help of James and Benjamin, Dat prepared the cornfield for planting, and Nellie and Nan took turns helping Mamma with early morning weeding in the family vegetable garden and the charity garden pledged to Preacher Elias. Keeping up with the necessary baking was a challenge without the help of either Suzy or Rhoda, but somehow the three Fisher women managed. Life was a flurry of action since spring had sprung, yet with warmer days finally enticing them outdoors, Nellie made time for after-supper walks with Nan. The plentiful wild flowers reminded them of Suzy.

Nellie wondered how Rhoda was getting along over in Strasburg. Martha had said she'd moved last month into a big house owned by her beau, a real estate agent. *"I hope this worldly man doesn't break her heart,"* Martha had whispered to Mamma. Nellie also was concerned. She knew all too well how difficult breaking up could be.

As for Nan, her face literally shone whenever Nellie Mae looked her way. Even right this minute, all smudged with dirt from the garden, Nan was glowing.

"We could be in for a hot day." Nellie stopped to catch her breath and observe the blazing gold of the sunrise beyond the potato field.

Nan paused, too, staring down at the long rows of celery before them. "Why do ya think Mamma insisted on planting so much celery?"

"Isn't it obvious?" Nellie smiled.

"She must guess I'm serious about a beau."

"Well, aren't you?"

Nan blushed. "Oh, Nellie . . . Ezekiel's just the best ever. I love him so."

"You wear your happiness on your face," Nellie said. "I daresay you've been through the mill and back."

"Well, and so have you." Nan started to hoe again. "But I think there's someone who's more than just a little interested in you these days."

Nellie was afraid of this—worried, really. Christian Yoder had become a regular customer of the bakery shop, a fact not lost on Nan or Mamma.

"You'd think Chris Yoder's mother doesn't know how to bake at all." Nan looked at her askance.

She had to respond. Truth was, she'd felt Chris's interested gaze more than once. She'd also contemplated the time he'd driven her home, when Jacob King's buggy broke down. "As nice as he seems, he's surely got himself a girlfriend," Nellie said casually.

"Jah, I would say so." Nan was grinning to beat the band. "If only in his imagination."

"Oh, now, I hope you don't mean what I'm thinkin'."

"Well, what *do* you think, Nellie Mae?"

She didn't honestly know, and the more she tried to dismiss his weekly visits, the more peculiar they seemed. To compound things, Dat had mentioned some time ago that he'd met up with Chris over at the Yoders'. Word had it he was working in the barn and milking with Caleb, for goodness' sake.

"You ignoring me?" Nan asked.

She laughed nervously. "I think Chris is just a friendly fella. And he knows good bakin' when he sees it . . . well, *tastes* it."

That brought more laughter from Nan, and they finished weeding the celery and then headed for the lettuce rows, knowing Mamma was keeping an eye on the baking pies. Nellie was thankful the awkward conversation was over.

———

Nellie sat on her bed that evening, all wrapped up in her bathrobe and wishing she'd taken Rosanna up on reading Lena Stoltzfus's letter. She simply could not understand why Elias and Rosanna were willing to take another such risk, accepting Lena's baby as their own. *If Rosanna were thinking clearly, she wouldn't. Not after the nightmare with her own cousin.*

But Nellie had no choice but to trust her friends' judgment, and since Elias had evidently said the letter was discerning, she shouldn't question that. Especially now that Elias had been ordained by God for the new congregation. Still, she would keep praying for protection over Rosanna's fragile heart.

She opened her Bible to find the picture of Suzy she'd slipped between the pages of John, in chapter three—the chapter that had been the turning point for Dat and Mamma last fall. Looking now at Suzy's face, she sighed, wishing she knew what her sister had known about Christian and Zachary Yoder.

What a strange thing, Chris's visit to the bakery shop each week. Every Thursday afternoon now he came happily to purchase a pie or two—"for my family," he would say, looking right at Nellie Mae with his endearing grin. She couldn't help but wonder when Mamma might make something of it like Nan had today.

Surely Suzy would have felt uneasy at first about going with a boy outside the Amish community. Yet according to her diary, she had been drawn to the Yoders. Quite strongly, in fact. Perhaps because she was fed up with worldly Jay Hess. Nellie remembered having read the final section enough times to know that Chris and Zach were honorable and good. *As fine as any young men I've ever known*, Suzy had written.

Did being honorable and good mean Chris would seek her out, just as Zach had pursued Suzy? Why should Chris look outside his own church for a girlfriend? Perhaps he was only curious about the Amish family that might have been Zach's in-laws had Suzy lived.

She pondered this as she reached beneath her pillow for the snipped-off Kapp strings—the ones from the last head covering Suzy'd ever worn. Holding them as she gazed fondly at the face of her blue-eyed sister, so full of God's love in this picture, she breathed a prayer for wisdom.

———

The clink of china and silverware and the muted talk of couples and their youth group leaders and sponsors blended into the background as Chris held a chair for his date. Their being seated at the head table had come as a surprise to him, although he should have expected it, since his scholarship was going to be announced.

"How's this for front and center?" he joked with Sheryl, who, in a floor-length soft blue dress, looked prettier than he'd ever seen her. Nearly all the other young women were dressed just as conservatively for their church's version of a senior prom, though there would be no dancing here.

"Did you think we'd be sitting here?" she asked softly.

He offered a quick yet heartfelt apology when he saw how ill at ease she was. To distract her, he pointed out the attractive program beneath her napkin and fork, and together they looked at the order of events. There would be a delicious dinner and dessert, then a guest speaker, a cappella singing by the attendees, and special remarks by key youth advisors. All in all, it made for a big night.

They bowed their heads for the blessing when the minister took the podium. Throughout the meal and awards, Chris felt like he had to carry the conversation, what little there was of it between him and his date. He'd known painfully shy girls before, but he'd never spent an entire evening with someone as quiet as Sheryl. Somewhat frustrated, he imagined for a moment what the event might have been like had Nellie been sitting to his right. It was nearly impossible to picture her at this white linen–covered table. Not a single young woman present wore the traditional garb of the Amish.

For everything that was good, even sweet, about Sheryl, he looked forward to next Thursday, when he planned to stop in at the bakery shop again and surprise his mom with yet another tasty dessert. Of course, she was on to him, even though he'd played down his interest in the "young Amish cook."

When his name was called from the podium to announce his academic scholarship to Eastern Mennonite School, Chris forced himself to focus on the present. Sheryl was smiling at him, clapping with all the others.

Gratefully he rose and made his way to their senior pastor, who, smiling, gripped his hand and said, "Well done, Chris . . . the Lord bless you."

He thanked him and returned to his seat, excited about his college plans.

The rest of the evening was a blur of conversations with friends from the youth group. He did his best to include Sheryl, who stood at his side throughout.

When he arrived home later, Chris was exhausted. Such an important evening should have been joyful, yet it had turned into an endurance contest. By comparison to his graduation banquet, the mere twenty minutes he'd spent taking Nellie Mae Fisher home seemed more thrilling—and all because of the company.

I've got to get Nellie into my life, he thought, taking the stairs two at a time.

CHAPTER 23

R euben strode through his cornfield on the last day of May, the day before another Lord's Day. Having two preachers and a deacon for the New Order church had boosted the morale of the congregation. Not that it needed boosting, as the house church was packed each Sunday. All of the witnessing they were doing was certainly seeing a gathering in of souls. Even so, the Old Ways still held an iron grip on many of the People, including David Yoder, who was either too weary to visit with him or eating "in private," according to Elizabeth, whenever Reuben stopped by. He had felt like he was making some slight progress toward a connection with David the day the man had spoken directly to him after returning from rehab—but no longer. Reuben felt like a weekly intruder, but he also believed the Lord wanted him to persist, regardless of any frosty reception.

Not one to shy away from a challenge, Reuben took a minute to pray again for David. After all, it took determination to do anything worthwhile, including breeding and breaking horses to sell to other farmers. That attitude had made him a reliable source for driving horses all around Lancaster County and to the east. Farmers came from as far away as Maryland and New Jersey to talk turkey with him about his horses, many of which were bred from lame racehorses he had restored to health and trained for buggy driving.

Jah, persistence is the key to anything worth doing. But the last time he'd gone to see David, even young Rebekah had turned him away, adding quietly how sorry she was that her father did not wish to see him.

"I'll keep offering my friendship," he'd told her.

"Now, I'm not tellin' you to quit comin', mind you," she'd said, a glint in her eye. "Just relaying what my father said." Rebekah had even followed him out to the buggy, waiting till he was inside before adding, "God will bless you, Reuben Fisher. You have been a faithful friend to my father, which hasn't been true of some of his own kin."

Reuben hadn't known what to make of that, but he assumed it had much to do with the demanding and likely ticklish task of caring for David.

The accident had undeniably taken its toll on the whole family. But with this continuous barrier to his attempts to visit David, there was little he could do, except pray. And hope.

He leaned down and pulled up a tall weed, carrying it along with him through the furrowed rows of corn on either side of his feet. As he walked, he prayed over that vast field and the potato field up yonder, asking for a bountiful harvest, after last year's drought. "We sure could use a good crop, Lord. But good or bad, may your will be done."

The sky was devoid of color now, as white as the eggs laid by the purple martins in the two new birdhouses he and Benny, his six-year-old grandson, had built together last winter. Reuben had sent the birdhouses home with James's boy, who had nearly burst his shirt buttons with pride.

Now if Reuben could just find some time, he would ask if his father might not enjoy building a few with him. *For old time's sake.* He rarely saw his parents anymore, but he made a point of writing every week, though he never received a letter back. *They're still miffed, no doubt. . . .*

Thus was the way of things, he was discovering. You stake your claim with Christ and risk the loss of family and friends. He breathed in the familiar earthy tang of dirt and manure at the far perimeter of the field, near the edge of the forest, and tossed the weed from his callused fingers into the wood.

Narrow is the way.

But Reuben was not to be defeated, even though he was somewhat discouraged—a good, long reading of God's Word should cure that. *Surely David is discouraged, too, day in and day out in that wheelchair,* he thought, wishing he might share the encouragement of scripture with the man.

"Help me have patience, Lord," he prayed. "Soften David's heart."

———

Rhoda made a flourish of counting her tip money, raising her right hand high as she placed each bill on the pile. She was ever so glad she'd worked all of Saturday at the restaurant. Glad, too, her boss had noticed how conscientious and helpful she was, often offering to do things that other waitresses weren't as willing to do, like sweeping the floor before closing time. Her customers appreciated her diligence, as well, and her attention to detail was paying off in better tips.

Now if she could only get her checkbook to balance. She glanced up, looking around at the room she'd managed to furnish with a bit of help from Mrs. Kraybill, who'd given her a small sofa and several lamps she'd had stored in the attic.

Even James and Martha had come through with an old bedstead, although it hadn't come with a mattress. She'd had to purchase one outright, borrowing a small sum from Ken, which she hated to do. He was more than happy to help, but that fact didn't make her any less discouraged. Truth was, she was in debt to the hilt. "I need a rich husband," she said to herself with a little laugh.

Opening her notebook, she checked off each bill she was able to pay right now, too aware that the beginning of June was just around the corner. *I'm slowly going under*, she thought, adding up her obligations, including her rent to Ken. The hand-to-mouth existence was getting the better of her, and she wondered if she might manage to add more hours at the restaurant. Or better yet, get another housekeeping job.

She sighed. Adding more hours to her workweek meant less time to spend with Ken. He'd already begun to complain. "If I'm to persuade him to marry me, I need to be available to court," she murmured.

To think I gave up a free room at James and Martha's. Goodness, I did the same at my father's house, too.

She pictured Nan and Nellie Mae out tending to the garden, working the soil and running the shop. Dat's corn would be ankle-high by now, and there would be nights when her sisters fell into bed nearly too tired to put on their nightgowns. She had also known such fatigue. She was even tired now, but her weariness stemmed partly from a sense of great concern—even fear. Yet all was well, wasn't it? She had her car, she'd gotten a man, and she had two good, albeit part-time jobs. But there seemed to be scant happiness to accompany all of that, and not a single dime had been saved toward her dreams of travel.

She found herself lying awake at night, thinking about Nan—had she gotten over the loss of her beau? Was Mamma still in deep mourning for a sister Rhoda rarely thought of anymore?

Sighing, she closed her notebook, going to the drawer where she kept Suzy's journal. Opening it to the page she'd marked, she read: *"Be not faithless, but believing."* She'd turned to the line more times than she cared to admit.

Suzy had been fascinated with doubting Thomas, as some referred to the disciple who couldn't believe until he pressed his hand into the Lord's wounded side. Evidently Suzy had been curious about the verse, too—enough so that she'd copied and underlined it.

Rhoda did wonder how Suzy had managed to go from dating a very worldly fellow to a nice Mennonite boy. She pondered her sister's steps and missteps. The way she saw it, Suzy's final months were a series of choices that made little sense.

At least she wasn't broke like me.

Rhoda slipped her stash of money into an envelope for depositing on Monday, conscious of the sudden lump in her throat.

Nellie Mae meant not a speck of harm when she decided to open her heart to Nan and show her Suzy's picture.

Nan blinked her eyes. "Ach, where'd you get this?" she gasped, leaning close to look.

Nellie plunged ahead, telling Nan that, at Zach's insistence, Chris Yoder had given her the photo back in February, along with Suzy's bracelet.

"He wanted you to have Suzy's picture?" Nan regarded her like she'd done something sinful.

"He thought we might want it to remember her by," she explained.

Nan refused to touch the picture, but she continued to look at it longingly, like it might disappear. "She seems so happy, doesn't she?"

Nellie Mae couldn't disagree. "I think she was." She went on to say what Chris had told her about his younger brother and Suzy's close relationship. "They loved each other dearly."

Nan bit her lip, frowning. "I'm glad you showed me, but I almost wish I hadn't seen it."

"I never wanted to upset you. That's why I've kept it secret till now."

Nan scratched her head. "I honestly don't know what to think."

They both knew photographs were prohibited for the Old Order, but nothing had been said about whether or not they were allowed in the New Order church. "I'd rather not bring it up to anyone else," Nellie said, still holding the picture. "I'd hate to part with it. I have to confess it's become precious to me."

Nan nodded, glancing at it again. "Maybe that's why pictures weren't allowed . . . before."

"I'm not sayin' that I couldn't do without it."

"Even so, do you wish you'd never seen it?" Nan leaned back on the bed, her head resting against the footboard, arms folded across her chest.

"It's not an idol to me, if that's what you mean." She clasped the picture to her heart. "I'm sorry, Nan. I don't mean to be short with you."

Nan's eyes were sober. "Maybe there's more to it, sister." She sat up quickly. "Hear me out before you jump to conclusions, all right?"

Nellie pushed a pillow behind her. "I'm listening."

"Is that picture more dear to you because of Suzy . . . or because of who gave it to you?" Nan asked.

She should've seen that coming. "Well, if you're accusing me of liking an Englischer just because he gave me Suzy's picture—"

"I didn't say that."

She huffed. "In so many words, you did. You can't deny it."

Nan rose and stood at the window; then she slowly turned to face her. "Are you sayin' you don't care for this fancy fella?"

Nellie was hurt. "How could you think that?"

"I think it, sister, because I see it on your face."

Nellie was stunned. Did Nan see or know something she herself did not realize? *Am I falling for Chris Yoder, of all things?*

The Lord's Day was a tiring one for Nellie Mae. And today Rebekah Yoder had returned home with the Fishers after the common meal, as she sometimes liked to do. Nellie was happy for Nan, who'd missed seeing her friend regularly now that Rebekah was helping her family during the day when she wasn't working for the Ebersols.

Glad for some time to herself, Nellie curled up on her bed to answer circle letters as Nan and Rebekah's happy chatter filtered down the hall.

She was most eager to write to Treva, and as soon as she finished her other letters, she started one to her Bird-in-Hand cousin.

Sunday, June 1, 1967
Dear Treva,

It seems like a long time already since you visited here for Sister's Day. I'm so glad we've had letters to stay in touch. Are you keeping busy? I surely am, what with the bakery shop and tending to the vegetables this year—our gardens are larger than ever. Hopefully, the Lord will see fit to bring them and our crops to a plentiful harvest.

Elias King has settled into his new role and is preaching some mighty fine sermons. I wish you could hear them! Speaking of the Kings, you might already know this, but Rosanna has told me to share with you that she and Elias have accepted Lena's offer of a baby. He's due in the middle of September, the Lord willing. (They and Lena speak of him as a boy.) Rosanna and Elias have already named him Jonathan, which means "God's gift." It seems fitting, since it was my father's cousin Jonathan Fisher who first shared the Good News over here in Honey Brook.

As for me, I am praying that Lena's baby will be a strong and healthy child, whether a boy or a girl.

She stopped writing, careful not to share too much. Except for the midwife, Ruth Glick, Rosanna had told only Elias and Nellie that she was with child. Ruth had urged Rosanna to see a medical doctor, and Rosanna had agreed, not surprised when the doctor called for bed rest if further pains persisted. Her friend had confided to Nellie her daily fear that she might lose this baby after carrying him or her for four months—indeed, the longest time yet.

Nellie wondered if Elias viewed Lena's baby as a cushion of sorts, so he and Rosanna would not be too devastated if they lost their own. Yet surely Rosanna would tell Lena at some point that she was also in the family way. And what then? Would Lena follow through with her offer?

Finishing her letter, Nellie placed it in her top drawer to mail later. She touched the small blue plate on her dresser, looking fondly at it. *Is Suzy's picture—and everything I love of my sister's—an idol?* She pulled the ever-present Kapp strings from her pocket. "Are these, too?"

She roamed about the room, going to the window to look out on the emerald fields as far as she could see, out to the lush rolling hills along the bright horizon. Had she fooled herself in believing she was past her grief?

Feeling restless, she went to ask Dat if she might take the family buggy out for a ride. As she hitched the horse to the carriage, she pondered what Nan had said about the expression on her face when she spoke of Chris Yoder.

She glanced at the bakery shop and recalled his last visit—if one could call it that. He had been all business as he chose a pie and then paid for it. But he had also looked her way more than necessary and lingered momentarily, as if there was something else on his mind.

She couldn't deny how much she'd enjoyed their conversation in his car back in April. Sometimes she even wondered if he hoped to have another such chance.

The afternoon was perfect for a ride out toward the old mill to the east, and even though she should have known better than to drive down that particular road, she felt compelled to seek out the millpond and the treed area, in all of its green and resplendent beauty.

She hadn't expected to see people walking along the millrace or near the old stone mill, but there was one couple holding hands, veiled a bit by the dense underbrush and leafy trees. Surprised that the sight of them didn't upset her as it might have months ago, Nellie urged the horse along. Always before she'd felt so sad at what she and Caleb had lost . . . how separated they were by their beliefs.

Am I resigned at last to not having him in my life?

It did seem that things remained unsettled between her family and the Yoders. Her kind, caring father had been trying for over two months to visit with David—she'd heard Dat and Mamma discussing it enough times in the kitchen to know Dat had yet to meet with any success. Caleb's father was hard to understand and seemingly unmovable. Was he so stubborn as to continue in his hardhearted ways even when dependent upon others for his daily needs?

Deep in thought and allowing the horse to lead her, Nellie was startled to see Caleb's house coming into view. In a sudden panic, she slowed, searching for a quick turn to the left or to the right, but there were no crossroads. It was not a good idea to try to make a turn on this narrow road, although she recalled Caleb's having done so one night last fall, both to her amazement and to Caleb's obvious relief when he completed the dangerous maneuver.

"Ach, not good," she muttered, wishing for her winter bonnet to hide her face as she approached the lane leading to the Yoders' house.

Elizabeth or one of the girls had planted bright red and white geraniums in the front flower garden, along with pink coralbells and white Shasta daisies, too. The lawn was well manicured and edged along the walkways, showing no sign of neglect. She glanced toward the house and felt a twinge of sadness for David Yoder's terribly altered life. She wished to tell the whole family just how sorry she was.

Yet I'm cut off from them. . . .

She thought not only of Caleb and his family but also of Rhoda and her strides into the world . . . and Ephram, holding fast to the Old Ways, much like the Yoders.

If only all the People could know the truth that ruled her own life: *The Lord's dying breath has given me life.*

She burst into tears, so great was the tenderness she felt toward those who still clung to tradition. With all of her heart, Nellie wished she could sit down and share with each one what the Lord meant to her. *Especially Caleb and his poor hurting family.*

CHAPTER 24

⸻

The days dragged on in one sense yet seemed to fly by in another. Caleb and his brothers weren't needed nearly as often to move their father to the wheelchair, since Daed mostly stayed in bed. Even with continual treatment, their father's and the doctors' efforts seemed futile. And the realization that Daed's health was declining struck Caleb mighty hard as he and Chris prepared for milking on this mid-June afternoon.

He and Chris had become good friends but, although there was much he wanted to tell his cousin, Caleb held back, lest he be misunderstood, especially where Nellie Mae was concerned. No matter how fond he was of Chris, his regrets over Nellie Mae were no one's business. And anyway, his cousin smiled much too broadly for his liking whenever Nellie's Simple Sweets was mentioned.

"My dad wants to visit your father," Chris told him before leaving for home, after milking was done. "We could drop by this Sunday after church, if that's okay."

Caleb shook his head. "Well, I'd hate for you to make a trip out here for nothin'. You know how it is . . . Daed's not so keen on visitors."

"Well, we're not talking about Reuben Fisher here. Wouldn't your dad be more willing to see his own cousin?"

"Jah, prob'ly. Though it's been a long time."

"Wonder why they drifted apart."

Caleb shrugged. He didn't know but could guess—likely something to do with the ongoing debate over the *hope of* versus the *assurance of* salvation. But Daed wouldn't mind so much what his fancy cousin believed. John wasn't trying to change his colors like Reuben and Manny's other followers had attempted to do.

Since Daed's accident, Caleb had personally had to turn away numerous folk from the New Order church, none of them having been received even once. Daed had made his stand and wasn't budging. Of course, with John Yoder being kin and all, who was to know? "Well, if you just drop by, maybe he would be more agreeable."

Chris opened his car door and climbed in. "Then that's what we'll do." He waved as the engine roared to life.

"See ya Sunday!" Caleb called, watching the car make the turnaround before heading down the lane toward the road. All the while, Chris's arm stuck out of the window, held high in a sweeping gesture similar to Caleb's own way of waving good-bye.

Sure hope Daed doesn't turn them away.

Heading for the house, Caleb sat on the back stoop, staring down at Mamm's handiwork there in the small garden near the walkway. Years ago, they'd pressed some of their old shoes into the soil, making little plant holders for petunias and marigolds. The shoes were holding up just fine, withstanding the wintry elements each year.

The sight of his outgrown boyhood shoes brought back memories of better days. *Before Daed's accident.*

At times, when anger threatened to overtake him, he wished they'd sold away the offending mule. But Daed had been the one to insist they keep the animal. Far be it from Caleb to say otherwise.

Not aware of the hour, he looked up and saw Rebekah coming up the driveway on foot, carrying a cake holder. "Hullo, *Bruder!*" she called. "It's almost suppertime, ain't so?"

"You brought me some dessert?" He chuckled and rose to meet her, always glad to see his most cheerful sister. "What kind of cake?" He leaned down as they walked, comically trying to nose his way in for a peek.

"Now, you just wait and see." She hurried toward the back door and then paused, a worried look on her face. "Tell me . . . how's Daed doin' today?"

He winced, dreading to say. "Not so good, I'm afraid."

"The cake might perk him up."

"It'll take more than that."

She grimaced. "I wonder if he'll listen while I read my favorite Bible verses."

"Well, *I* can read to him." He caught himself, not wanting to reveal that he'd been curious to read for himself the chapter in John so many of the New Order folk had talked about at the outset of the split. Truth be told, Chris's fondness for scripture had him thinking a bit.

She eyed him. "What'd you say?"

"The Good Book—anyone can read it to Daed. That's all."

She grinned at him, reaching for the door. "Well, what's keepin' *you,* then?"

Her words haunted him all during supper. But each time he glanced toward the head of the table, it was all he could do to keep smiling, for his mother's sake. And for his sisters', too, surprised that Rebekah was permitted to partake of the meal with them.

Yet there was no getting around it: Daed was failing—weakening physically and emotionally—before their eyes.

———

Rhoda was delighted at the tenderness of the pork chops she'd made for Ken. There were mashed potatoes, gravy, and buttered carrots and peas. She'd baked dinner rolls, plump and flaky. More often than not, they ate supper by candlelight in his third-floor suite, where they enjoyed the view from the large windows and each other's company.

Ken mentioned reading in the paper about a midair crash of two airplanes reported over the radio. Rhoda wondered, *Is he trying to discourage my dream of traveling by plane?*

"Many people were killed." He picked up his knife to cut his meat.

"That's dreadful," Rhoda agreed, "but it doesn't scare me away from wanting to fly. Maybe if I had children, I would think differently, but—"

He looked up at her sharply. "Old Order Amish girls don't fly . . . it's against their upbringing."

"But I'm finished with that life," she said.

"Are you?" He narrowed his eyes. "Finished with the God-thing, the apron strings, the brats, the whole nine yards?"

She felt her lips part but was shocked into silence. She was only leaving the Old Order. She'd never said she had given up God or her dreams of a family.

He searched her face. "Well? Are we through with all the hints about kids?"

She felt as frustrated as she'd ever been in her life. Getting up, she walked to the sliding-glass doors, staring out at the grill and the plush patio furniture. Everywhere she looked, things were colorful, pretty, neatly arranged. Ken had plenty of money, certainly. Why didn't he want plenty of children? At least a few? She struggled not to cry.

She felt his gaze on her and glanced back at him.

"You look like you're going to be ill," he said.

"When I think of the life my family would have me live, I do feel sick. But when I think about the kind of life you seem to want . . . with no little ones, I feel just as ill. If not more so."

Hadn't Ken been the one to say life was what you made it? Well, she was determined to make a life with him. She straightened her shoulders and took a deep breath. "I want to have a family someday." She turned to face him. "A big family."

He frowned. "It's a dead issue, Rhoda. There is no room for debate on kids, I can assure you."

Now she was crushed. "What's so terrible about babies?" Her neck was hot. Why did he feel so strongly about this?

He sat tall and still at the table. "I thought you wanted to leave all that outdated tradition behind you. Be a modern woman."

"I never said that. Sure, I wanted to make a new life for myself . . . and then I met you, Ken. It seemed like our friendship was meant to be. Providential, as my people say."

He scrutinized her; then he shook his head in disgust. "Come on, Rhoda. There is no such thing as 'providential.' God is just a comfortable myth. We've talked about this before. Your family really brainwashed you, didn't they?" He crumpled his napkin and tossed it down.

"No." Tears filled her eyes. She knew he wasn't fond of their long Preaching services, but how could he not believe in God himself? No matter how hard she had tried to embrace Ken's views, she simply could not dismiss the reality of the Creator.

"What did you think? That you could change my mind?" She cringed at the cutting tone of his voice. "Change *me?*"

She wouldn't confess she'd thought that very thing. She wouldn't tell him she'd been sure, once they were married, she could convince him what a wonderful father he'd be. Or that she'd imagined the two of them and their children attending church together. How stupid she felt now. How deceptive. "I'm sorry, Ken. It was wrong of me to let things go so far between us."

"No," he said quickly. "I was wrong . . . to think this could ever work out." He sighed loudly. "I just don't seem to understand women—ever!"

She groaned audibly, and Ken glared at her. But she had no more to say, so she walked to the door. "I'll let myself out."

He didn't follow to see her leave, or ask if they could talk further. He just let her walk away, and all the while she wanted to kick herself for believing in a pipe dream, another one of Ken's English expressions. Well, now it was hers, too.

What a ridiculous thing to move to Strasburg, only in hopes of getting married. She hurried to her room and closed the door. *Now what?* She went to sit on her bed. *Am I stuck here, with this lease to Ken?*

She buried her face in her hands.

"I'll put all the jam away." Nellie Mae stacked several glass jars and stored them in the utility room cupboard while Mamma went and sat next to Dat. It was nearly time for Bible reading, and already her father was thumbing through the Good Book, looking for the spot where he'd left off last evening.

"Mamma, you've been pushin' yourself too hard lately." Nan glanced over her shoulder as she washed dishes.

"Well, picking strawberries is always the biggest chore," Mamma said.

"I can't believe how much jam we've put up," Nan said.

"Don't forget the pies," Dat joked, smacking his lips.

Nellie wondered if Chris had ever tasted strawberry-rhubarb pie. *Just delicious.* She reprimanded herself for thinking of him so familiar-like; then she grinned.

"Maybe you should take one of my pies over to the Yoders' tomorrow, Dat," she said, knowing her father still hadn't gotten a foot in the door. "Maybe a strawberry pie will do the trick."

"Something's got to give." Mamma touched Dat's arm gently.

Nan placed Mamma's big kettle on the rack to be dried. "Rebekah says her mother cries a lot," Nan told them.

"Aw, Nan . . . did she now?" Mamma said, a frown marring her face.

"Well, word has it David's goin' downhill," Dat added.

This news deepened Nellie Mae's sorrow for the family. "What'll happen if . . . ?" She couldn't bring herself to finish.

"I say we pray right now." Dat motioned to them.

Nan dried her hands quickly, and the four of them joined hands while Dat, who could scarcely speak for his tears, asked the Lord to extend David's life—so he might find Jesus before it was too late.

Silently Nellie Mae prayed the same for Caleb, hoping her former beau would not follow in his father's stubborn footsteps.

Reuben excused himself to go upstairs after Bible reading. Betsy said she'd stay down in the kitchen with the girls, which was just as well, as he found he could beseech the Lord better when praying alone.

He pulled out his prayer list, beginning with his own father, who was up in years. How he missed talking to . . . learning from, gleaning lost wisdom from the man. Then he prayed for each of his sons, their wives, and their children—those born and yet to be born.

Last of all, he whispered Rhoda's name. "Bring my daughter to her senses soon, O Lord."

So many needs. He wiped his eyes and continued to kneel like a trusting child at his side of the bed.

After a time, when his burden had lifted some, he went to the dresser and found his writing tablet. Tearing out a sheet, he began to write to his father.

Friday, June 20
Dear Daed,

Hello from Honey Brook. Here I sit, writing to you and missing you. I think of you and Mamm so often, hoping you're both well.

The thought popped into my head that we might build a martin birdhouse together, you and I. Benny and I did just that not so long ago. We had a wonderful-good time, and I couldn't help but recall how you and I did the same thing when I was but a boy.

I'll be glad to bring all the necessary materials—get me a hired driver to haul everything over to your place. Betsy could bring a hamper of food and visit with Mamm, if it suits her. What do you think of that?

I'll wait to hear from you. And if you don't reply, I'll simply write again next week.

May the Lord be with you over there in Bird-in-Hand.

> *Your son,*
> *Reuben Fisher*

Folding the letter, he was not ready to give up on either his father or his old friend David. Nor would he turn his back on daughter Rhoda, although it seemed she'd done so to them.

Expelling his breath, Reuben rose and slipped the letter beneath the gas lantern on the dresser. Thankfully, the dear Lord had not given up on him.

Or any of us.

———

Caleb had been waiting for his English cousins to arrive, trying not to be too anxious as he glanced out the front-room window every few minutes.

He tried to picture his father's first cousin John. It had been years since he and his wife and their five boys had come to visit. There was no apparent reason for them not to have further fellowship . . . none that he knew of, other than their obvious differences. He'd never once heard his father speak ill of his Mennonite relatives. If anything, Daed held them in high regard; otherwise Chris would not be allowed to work here alongside Caleb and his brothers.

He looked across the expanse of the front room toward the door that led to Daed's small room. The door was slightly open, and Caleb could hear his father muttering to himself, something he'd begun to do more recently, definitely disturbed by his circumstances. *Who can blame him?*

Caleb often tried to put himself in his father's shoes, but it just wasn't possible. He was quick on his feet, strong, and energetic, and youth was on his side.

Seeing Chris's car pull into the driveway, he went to his father's bedroom door, peering in through the crack. *Good, he's awake.* Caleb hurried out the back way to greet Chris and his father, hoping Daed might agree to see them. If he refused, he hoped at least that he would not shout as he had the other day when Preacher Manny had dropped by after Nellie's father, Reuben Fisher. The man had to have some grit in him to keep coming back for more rejection.

Chris and his dad were getting out of the car as Caleb went to meet them. He was immediately taken by their Sunday attire, the dark suits and ties they'd probably donned to attend church. In fact, they were so fancy looking, he worried it might be off-putting to Daed. *Either that or he'll view it as a compliment.*

"Hi again, Caleb." Chris offered the same friendly smile he always did when he arrived. "You remember my dad, don't you?" He motioned toward his father, a tall, slender blond man who stretched out a hand to firmly shake Caleb's.

"Good to see you again," Caleb said, leading the way toward the house. "My father's awake . . . but I should warn you—"

"No worries. I've already told Dad," Chris interjected.

Caleb felt some relief. "Mamm's upstairs resting. So are my sisters." He opened the back door. "It's just the three of us downstairs . . . and Daed."

Chris offered a sympathetic nod, hanging back to let his father go first as they headed through the kitchen. A plate of sandwiches was laid out on the table in anticipation of their arrival.

"Would ya like anything to eat or drink first?" Caleb asked, mindful of his role as host.

"Thanks for the offer, but we'll wait till after we've spoken to your father, if you don't mind," John said graciously. Chris's father seemed calm and poised, and Caleb thought unexpectedly of Nellie Mae, who had always been so hesitant, even frightened around Daed.

Moving toward the small bedroom, he paused, glanced back at Chris, and then pushed the door fully open. His father was staring at the ceiling, eyes glazed from boredom and pain. "Daed . . . your cousins are here," he said.

Daed lay propped up on the bed with an abundance of pillows, thanks to Mamm, who'd gotten him situated before heading upstairs. Caleb expected his father's booming voice of disapproval to erupt at any moment. Instead, Daed eyed his cousins before smiling faintly. "Have yous come for my funeral?"

John lost no time moving toward the bed. He leaned down to shake hands. "We came directly from church," he said. "That's why we're wearing monkey suits."

"Well, pull up a chair." Daed motioned with his hand.

Caleb was shocked. No tantrum today? By the looks of things, it seemed Daed might even enjoy this visit. He was listening peacefully as John began to reminisce about the old days and their childhood visits to Uncle Enos's. "Remember that old fishing hole, out behind the rickety barn? We cut our way to ice-fish one winter."

Daed blinked his eyes in response. "Gut days, jah. Mighty gut."

The two older men did most of the talking, and Caleb could sense that Chris was pleased at the way things were going.

Daed's voice suddenly grew stronger. "It's awful kind of you, John, to loan that fancy van of yours . . . for my trips to rehabilitation."

"Glad to do it. Just give Chris a holler."

Daed breathed in long and slow, looking now at Chris. "And your boy's been a big help here. I owe ya both."

"Nothing doing." John moved his chair closer.

"Well, I'm glad you came today, so I could say Denki in person." He drew another long breath before continuing. "You see, I won't be needin' your vehicle any longer, John. Won't be goin' in for treatments anymore, neither."

Caleb perked up his ears. *What?*

"But they're essential, right, David?" John frowned, folding his hands. "They'll strengthen you over time."

Daed shook his head weakly. "Well, there ain't much time left for me, so I won't be pushin' myself out the door any longer. They can carry me out when I'm dead and gone, that's what."

Caleb was embarrassed. Even if Daed believed he wouldn't live much longer, it wasn't right to say so in front of company.

"Surely you don't want to throw in the towel, do you?" John asked, gesturing to Chris. His cousin took the hint, glanced at Caleb, and rose, stepping out of the room.

Caleb followed quickly behind, not knowing what Chris's father intended to say to Daed. But obviously it was personal.

He caught up with Chris out in the kitchen, and he reached for two apples in the bowl on the table, handing one to his cousin. "Here, help yourself to a sandwich, too," he said before heading toward the back door.

Chris complied and followed. "Your father's dejected," he said soberly. "He's made a bad turn since his last rehab session, hasn't he?"

"Haven't seen him like this before today, to tell you the truth." Caleb directed Chris toward the tobacco shed, where they could sit on some old stools in back. "Maybe it's time I slipped Reuben Fisher in to visit my father . . . if they're to see each other again before—"

"So Reuben and your dad were friends at one time?" Chris looked surprised.

"They go back a long ways."

"And now? Evidently Reuben's very anxious to see your dad." Chris took a bite of his sandwich.

Chris could always be counted on for a line of questions, always wanting to get to the bottom of things. "Well, there's a lot of history there. Daed's upset because Reuben's Fisher cousins—Jonathan and Preacher Manny—got an upheaval started when they decided the Good Book was not only to be studied but memorized and discussed, too. Every which way."

Chris's eyes grew wide. "Are you sayin' you're not supposed to do any or all of the above?"

"Scripture isn't s'posed to be fussed over, no."

"Not even talked about?" Chris's face registered disbelief.

"The ministers do that at Preaching service, every other week. Mostly they expound on the Sermon on the Mount." *Why should I have to defend the church fathers?* "For the rest of us, scripture is only meant to be read."

Chris seemed appalled. "But it's inspired by God—every word. Isn't that what you believe, Caleb?"

Uncomfortable now, Caleb welcomed the sound of a large flock of birds flying low overhead, and he craned his neck to look. All the while, he wondered why John's father had left the Amish decades ago. As curious as he was, he wasn't going to ask. Another day, maybe.

Chris had never been so pointed before. Even so, Caleb did not feel antagonistic, not as he might've had someone like Reuben or others from the new group come tooting the dangerous horn of salvation through grace. No, the way Chris talked typically wasn't threatening. And now he suddenly felt as he had when his own "saved" sister, Rebekah, had mentioned reading the Bible to Daed earlier. "There are times when I'm befuddled," he confessed, " 'bout what to believe."

Chris nodded, shifting his weight on the stool. "I hear you. But there *is* something to hang on to—something that doesn't change. *Someone* who can be counted on, no matter what's going on in your life."

This sounded too much like the way Nellie Mae had talked. Caleb could still picture her standing so prettily behind the display counter in her bakery shop, her face glowing—why?—his arms gentle around her despite his fierce desire to protect her from being swept up in the fanciful talk.

And here he was again—his own cousin about to spout off more of the same.

Yet Chris was respectful. He didn't just forge ahead with what he was surely impatient to say. He waited for Caleb to nod or say something, to give consent. But Caleb was determined to be true to the old church, aware of the pull on him. Above all, he must be loyal to the only church he knew, or cared to know. For this reason, he budged not even an inch.

But long after Chris and his father drove away, Caleb could not escape his cousin's words: *"Someone who can be counted on . . ."*

CHAPTER 25

A few hours before suppertime, Daed asked Caleb to call Mamm so he could talk with her alone. Caleb nodded and left the bedroom his father had claimed as his own since the accident. *He needs a doctor*, he thought, wishing Daed hadn't decided to abandon his treatments.

Ever since Daed's cousins had left earlier today, Caleb had wondered what Daed and John had discussed. He didn't understand how Daed could simply give up and not want to get stronger.

I won't think about this now!

He knew the cows would be lined up at the gate, waiting for their feed— and for milking. Today being the Lord's Day, it would take him at least twice as long, since his three brothers usually stayed put at home Sunday afternoons.

Rebekah hadn't arrived yet, either, so he'd have to get Leah and Emmie to help, unless the neighbors wandered over to pitch in, as they sometimes did on weekends.

Caleb set off to the pasture to open the gate for the cows, glancing toward the cornfield, still watching for any extra help. He wondered if Daed and Gideon had already discussed what would happen if his father were to die. Would Abe continue to run things? Would Jonah? Which of his siblings would care for Mamm in her old age? Perhaps Daed was talking to Mamm about that even now, holed up as they were in the small main-floor bedroom.

To keep from fretting, he pondered the bishop's sermon—the longer of the two sermons this morning. Not a single time today had he dozed off. The bishop was changing his way of preaching, repeating scriptures that seemed foreign to Caleb. Had anyone else noticed? There was no getting Mamm's or Leah's opinion, since they'd taken their turn staying at home with Daed. And anyway, for the most part, he didn't discuss church-related matters with his mother and sisters. Only Rebekah had ever shown any interest in such things, but he couldn't talk to her now, not since she'd gone to live with the Ebersols. *Since she'd gone off the deep end . . .*

Caleb was washing down the fifth cow in the first row when here came Leah, Emmie, and Mamm. He looked away when he saw how puffy and red Mamm's eyes were. "I don't want to be gone long from Daed," she said quickly, which created even more apprehension in him.

What's happening? Is it possible my father's dying?

After milking, and before a light supper of sandwiches, red beet eggs, and celery sticks with peanut butter, Rebekah sat down with Caleb at the far end of the table. As was her way, she smiled freely.

Placing a plateful of cookies in front of him, she said, "I baked your favorites yesterday."

He reached for a chocolate chip cookie, eyeing the peanut butter ones, as well, but she slid the plate back quickly. "You'll spoil your supper, Caleb Yoder."

"Where have I heard *that* before?" He glanced at Mamm, worry slapping him in the pit of his stomach each time he noted her serious demeanor. She was even more solemn than earlier. *Why?* He wanted to fool himself into thinking it was merely her usual response to the Lord's Day; she'd always been a stickler for observing Sundays reverently. But something told him her glum spirits had more to do with Daed's deteriorating condition. That and whatever they'd discussed alone.

Mamm sat with them for the silent prayer, which Caleb offered as the only male present at the table. Then she rose and dished up food for Daed. "I'll be helping your father with his meal tonight" was all she said before leaving the kitchen.

Once the door to Daed's room was latched shut, Rebekah leaned forward. Her smile faded. "I don't mean to frighten yous, but Mamma's told me Daed believes his days are numbered."

Leah gasped, covering her mouth with her hand, and Emmie shook her head, mouthing, *No.*

"He's settin' his house in order," Rebekah continued, looking toward Caleb now.

"What's that mean?" Caleb managed to ask.

"Well, I know you may not understand this, but if I may be so bold . . ." She paused, her eyes on Leah and Emmie. Then she faced Caleb again. "The way I see it, God's beginnin' to answer the prayers that have gone up for our family . . . and for Daed, 'specially."

Unable to grasp her point, Caleb stared at her. "Meaning what?"

"Evidently Daed's makin' peace with God . . . in his own way." Rebekah reached for her sandwich.

"But he did that at his baptism," Leah said, "back when he joined church as a youth."

Rebekah glanced at Caleb. "Well, if you go walkin' with me in a bit, I'll tell you more 'bout what I mean. And the reason for the break in the old church, too, in case you don't know."

"Had something to do with a big debate," Caleb said. He hadn't meant to sound so dismissive.

Rebekah's face lit up—the same glow he'd seen on Nellie Mae's face the day they'd said their good-byes. "Jah, the split was about saving grace," she said. "And makin' a public confession of it."

"I'll take a walk with ya, Rebekah," said Leah, her voice surprisingly bold.

Caleb wasn't interested in Rebekah's views of the church split. He already knew far too much about all of that.

———

Rosanna saw the tobacco farmer first as the man turned into their lane. *Coming for counsel with Elias, no doubt.* She touched Elias's hand as they lingered at the table, having a piece of strawberry pie.

"Mind if I go out and talk to him?" Her husband rose quickly.

"Supper's through," she said softly, and Elias got up from the table and headed for the back door. No question, he was taking his ordination seriously, even to the detriment of his own work, just as Preacher Manny and others of the ministerial brethren did. Elias not only embraced his divine calling, but his was truly a caring heart for the congregation.

The Lord knew what He was doing when He chose him. . . .

Rosanna carried the dishes to the sink, surprised again at how much stronger she felt lately. *Will I keep this wee one, Lord?* It was the question she dared not ponder too much, for she was so much in love with this baby, conceived in the midst of her great sadness over the loss of the Beiler babies. Little Eli and Rosie were growing like weeds now—she'd seen them again from afar, all bunched up with John and Kate and their other children in their carriage, on the way to Preaching service this very morning. She hadn't winced at the sight of them sitting on Kate's and her oldest daughter's laps but waved as they came up closer on the road. Elias had done the same, and after the two buggies passed, neither he nor she had mentioned the twins or John and Kate. In fact, they'd said nary a word, which seemed odd to

Rosanna now, thinking back on it. Yet what a blessing to realize her darling also held no animosity.

Washing the last dish, she reached for a tea towel. She glanced out the window, observing her husband. Perhaps he was discussing tractors and what they could and could not be used for in the fields, the subject of much talk these days. Now that fieldwork was going on all over Honey Brook, this fellow probably assumed he could make some time by using his tractor for transportation on the road, as she'd heard of others doing. Such was not permitted by the new ordinance, and several families had left the New Order church over this issue, joining up with the Beachys, who allowed more liberal use of tractors.

For herself, she much preferred to think about all the pretty yarn she planned to purchase this week with the money from her quilts. She wanted to begin crocheting baby afghans for Lena's baby, whom Lena intended for the Amish midwife to bring directly to the Kings', following his birth. Lena had started referring to herself as the "baby carrier," declaring Rosanna the mother appointed by God. Because of her own secret pregnancy, Rosanna felt rather sheepish reading Lena's touching letters, even though she cherished each one and saved them in a pretty wooden box Elias had built for her as a recent birthday gift.

Another glimpse outside showed Elias was still engaged in conversation, his arms folded—likely he would be busy for a while longer. Perhaps Rosanna should take this time now to reply to Lena.

With a prayer in her heart, she sat down to pen her most private thoughts, words that might completely change Lena's mind.

Sunday, June 22
Dear Lena,

I can't tell you how often I've been in prayer here. I truly believe with you that your baby is to become Elias's and my own. And we will care for him as lovingly as we would a flesh-and-blood son.

There is more for you to know and to understand, though—something ever so dear to me. You see, I, too, am with child. It is my hope and prayer that I will carry the baby in my womb to term, something that has never happened before. Yet, if things continue as they are—and oh, how we pray they will—I'll begin to show soon, and there will be talk wending your direction that I am in the family way.

I have only a small hope that this little one, who lies so close to my heart, will be born alive. Our baby's sisters and brothers all reside in heaven now, with our Lord, whose will we desire in all things. Elias says he likes to think the angels are caring for them till we can get there to do that ourselves.

In the meantime, I am being ever so careful, seeing a doctor and taking bed rest, too, praying that this time these things will make a difference. Will you keep me in your daily prayers, just as I pray for you, dear sister in the Lord?

Thinking about Lena's possible reaction, she dared not write for much longer. It might have been wiser to wait to tell this news to Lena in person, but the doctor had put the nix on any travel right now for more than twenty minutes at a time. And she needed someone to go along with her for even those short trips, which meant she'd be asking Linda Fisher to go with her to the yard-goods store this week.

Hoping Lena would not be disheartened by word of the pregnancy, Rosanna finished her letter and signed off, deciding to put her feet up while she awaited Elias's return inside. In her heart of hearts, she hoped this revelation would not change Lena's mind. But why should she worry about that, when it was the Lord who'd prompted Lena to offer her child in the first place?

I must remember the scripture to not be anxious.

Caleb paced near the window and waited in the kitchen for his mother to emerge from Daed's room, hoping she might tell him more about Daed's conversation with his cousin John. Could Daed be softening? Knowing his father, Caleb didn't see how that was possible.

Even impending death wouldn't deter Daed from his life course. The Old Ways were stamped on his heart. *"You're either in the church or out. There's no betwixt and between,"* his father had always said.

In a few minutes, Mamm came into the kitchen, her face tearstained. She motioned for Caleb. "Your father's askin' for ya."

He steeled his heart and made his way to the small room, where he stood in the door before entering. Daed looked to be sleeping.

Silently Caleb sat on the cane chair across from the bed, watching his father's chest rise and fall. He sat there, hands folded, and understood for the first time something of the misery Nellie Mae and her family had endured when they lost Suzy.

Chris had said a person couldn't prepare for something like a death in the family. No matter how you thought you might react, you never truly knew till the time came.

Has it come already? He leaned forward, checking to see if his father was indeed breathing. *Slowly, jah . . . mighty slow.*

But lest he become fearful, sitting in a room with death nipping at his father's heels, he let his thoughts fly away to his cousin Chris. Truly, he was the happiest person Caleb had ever known, and he found himself comparing him to Rebekah.

So what was it they had that he lacked? They both claimed to be saved, he knew that. They also talked of a freedom they experienced. Nearly everything they did or said was somehow linked to God's Son, their "Lord and Savior."

From where he sat, he could see Rebekah and Leah through the window, returning from their walk. He wondered what things Rebekah was filling Leah's head with now. Since her return visits, Rebekah had gone out of her way to attempt to influence each of her sisters for the new church.

Caleb smiled, allowing a speck of momentary pride. *She'll have a hard time cornering me.*

Closing his eyes, he shut out the image of his helpless father. The last thing he wanted to hear today was a deathbed appeal.

After some time had passed, his father whispered, "Caleb."

Jerking to attention, he sat up. "I'm here, Daed."

"My cousin came to set me straight. . . ." His father's voice faltered, then began again, stronger now. "He showed me what a stubborn soul I've been."

Caleb didn't know how to respond. Never before had his father admitted his wrongdoing, his too-stern ways. Such odd behavior—was it a result of being confined to this room and a wheelchair?

"Today I'm puttin' my house in order, before it's too late. And I want to start with you, son." Daed smiled sadly. "You've endured unnecessarily harsh treatment over the years. You did nothin' to deserve such severity. And I'm sorry."

He's apologizing? Caleb was stunned. The words sounded out of place on his father's lips. And yet, the old temptation to be resentful, even bitter, reared its ugly head.

"You must surely think I've gone ferhoodled." Daed drew a slow breath, his eyelids fluttering. "But it was hellfire that put the fear of God in me. I want you to hear it from me. Otherwise if it's secondhand, you might doubt it."

"No need to, Daed. You get some rest now, ya hear?"

"Caleb . . ."

"You're not yourself," he insisted. "You've suffered terribly."

"No, son, listen to me."

He clenched his jaw. All of Nellie Mae's arguments for her faith came rushing back. The strange and ridiculous way she'd behaved, throwing away their love, breaking their engagement for Manny's church. Caleb chafed against the "alien gospel," as he'd heard it called by his Daed and others. And now had his own father succumbed to it?

Daed continued. "I know it goes against the grain . . . to say I've been granted salvation." He reached for a glass of water and his hand shook as he sipped through the straw. "John finally got me to see the truth. Ach, what a persistent soul . . . for so many years."

How can this be?

"John said if I asked the Lord, He would make me a new creation, givin' me His gift of grace and makin' me fit for heaven. I know God's forgiven me . . . and I'm hoping I might ask the same of you."

Caleb shook his head, still uncomprehending. "Daed, I . . ."

"You don't have to say anything now, Caleb. But I would like ya to do somethin'." His father inhaled slowly. "I must speak to Reuben Fisher. Go fetch him and bring him here to me . . . straightaway."

Such a strange request on top of even stranger words—nothing like Caleb had prepared himself to hear. "Jah, I'll go."

With that, he left the room.

———

Shocked to see young Caleb looking mighty grim at the back stoop, Reuben immediately believed David had passed away. Mighty thankful to learn he was mistaken, he reached for his straw hat, agreeing to ride to the Yoders' in Caleb's courting buggy, oddly enough.

All Caleb had said was his father had asked to see him—nothing more. But as they rode, Caleb described his Daed's declining health, as well as the man's firm belief his end lurked just around the corner. Caleb was forthright, saying he had no idea what his father wanted with Reuben.

At first Nellie thought she must be dreaming where she sat at the window, reflecting on the day's sermon.

When she heard a horse and carriage come rushing into the drive, she turned and looked out, amazed. She gasped at the sight of Caleb Yoder sitting tall in his courting buggy. *Well, what on earth?*

She remembered the last time he'd come unannounced. But knowing how fragile his father's health was, she worried.

Moments later she heard Dat's voice downstairs. Then, of all things, if Caleb didn't whisk Dat away, driving lickety-split back down the drive, toward the main road.

She had no reason not to assume that David had passed away, but if that were true, why was Caleb taking Dat back with him? At this, Nellie was beyond befuddled, and she dropped to her knees in prayer.

———

When Reuben arrived at the Yoder farm with Caleb, Elizabeth greeted him somberly and led him to a downstairs room, where David lay on the bed, flat on his back, eyes shut. "He's resting," Elizabeth reassured Reuben and then left.

Reuben considered the situation. Here he was finally at David's bedside, after months of repeated rebuffs. *Why has he called for me?*

David's wrinkled eyelids fluttered open and he fixed his gaze on Reuben. "Denki . . . thank you for comin'."

"Glad to, David." He nodded.

"I daresay I don't have long for this world," David said in low tones. "I've been given a warning this day . . . by an English cousin of mine." He drew a labored breath. "I'm in danger of eternity without God unless I repent." He closed his eyes, and a tear squeezed out and slid down his ruddy face. "I'm guilty of callin' you a fool, Reuben Fisher. . . . I've looked down on you for chasin' after this new faith, thinkin' you and the others were bent on destroying the People with prideful ways. Turns out . . . I was the one in the wrong."

Reuben was dumbfounded.

David reached out his hand. "I plead for your forgiveness."

Reuben gripped David's hand, the lump in his throat crowding out his very breath.

"You're entitled to your way of thinkin', Reuben—if it's assurance of salvation you want, then so be it." David's face was ashen; he was spent.

"I forgave you months ago, David. Truly, I did."

David blinked his eyes open, then shut, then open again. "I was the fool."

"We're brothers."

"That we are . . . I've laid down my will for God's," David said softly.

"At long last." A tear trickled down his cheek. "I wanted you to hear this directly from me."

Overjoyed, Reuben clung to David's hand.

David went on. "I'll die in peace, whenever the Lord wills it."

"Maybe He'll raise you up . . . make you whole."

"No need for that now. Dying has brought me life, Reuben. Tell all the People, won't ya?"

If Reuben had not heard this with his own ears, he might not have believed it. "I'll tell the brethren first."

"And ask your cousin Manny to stop by. I need to be speakin' to him, too." David went on, his voice a throaty murmur. He was saying he wanted to ask both the bishop and Preacher Manny to preach at his funeral. Reuben took mental notes, not questioning whatsoever as David uttered his last wishes. This was a man who had always known what he wanted, and he was going to have it. Reuben would see to that.

Betsy stroked her husband's hair as they rested together later that night. "What you're tellin' me is nothing short of a miracle," she said.

"I've been thanking God for His mercy," her dear husband said.

She kissed his face. "Wouldn't it be somethin' if David lives for longer than he expects?"

Reuben smiled. "I hope that, too."

"Meanwhile, what'll Elizabeth do? Surely she knows from David's lips what he's told you."

"Oh, she knows."

"Will she follow in her husband's footsteps?"

"Who's to say?" Reuben looked up at her. "The Lord is at work."

And Caleb . . . what of him?

She realized how such a fork in the road for the Yoder family—which would certainly include the Bann—might change things for Nellie Mae, as well. Betsy assumed Nellie had started attending Sunday Singings again with the New Order youth. It was also rather apparent from his frequent visits to the shop that Caleb's cousin Chris Yoder was sweet on their dear girl, though probably that would prove a passing fancy.

It wasn't as if Nellie was sitting around waiting for her first beau to catch up to her spiritually. All the same, Betsy couldn't begin to know what was in her daughter's heart.

CHAPTER 26

———

Nellie Mae was alone in the bakery shop when Christian Yoder inched his car right up to the front and parked. She couldn't have planned the timing any better if she'd had a thing to say about it. Actually, she was surprised at her happiness to see him . . . and he was right on schedule, too. After all, this was Thursday afternoon; she *should* be expecting him.

Watching him get out of his car, she suddenly questioned if his afternoon visit was the reason for Nan's and Mamma's disappearance earlier. *Well, surely not,* she thought, a bit bemused.

He strode up with confidence, as though on a mission. And for the first time, he lacked the look of adolescence evident in most fellows his age. His hair was neatly combed, as always. *As fair-haired as Caleb,* she thought.

For a moment, she wondered what it might be like for the three of them to be friends. Naturally, that was no longer possible, in spite of the amazing news Dat had shared of David Yoder's embracing salvation. Even so, she thought of Caleb and experienced a fleeting envy at Chris's weekly contact with him.

The door opened, and Chris smiled his way inside. "Hi again, Nellie Mae."

"Hullo, Chris."

He took in the small shop with a glance and was not subtle about noticing she was there by herself. "What pies do you have today?" he asked.

"Well, if it's pies you're interested in . . ." She caught herself for being so bold. "I do have several kinds of cookies, too."

His eyes searched hers. So much so that she felt nearly ill at ease; yet she did not look away as she might have with a stranger. "Nellie, I've been thinking." He paused, as if weighing his words. "And please be honest with me . . . if I'm overstepping . . ." His voice trailed off. He seemed unnerved.

What's he going to say?

His smile reappeared. "What I mean is, how would you like to go for ice cream sometime . . . with me?"

He was obviously ferhoodled, so she wanted to make this easy for him.

"When were you thinkin'?" she asked, realizing too late that she should've said something less forward.

His smile spread clear across his handsome face. "So, you *do* like ice cream. . . ."

She tried without success to keep her own smile in check. "Ach, who doesn't?"

"When would you be free to go?"

"Well, only after dark . . . of an evening. That's *our* way, though. Is that what you had in mind?" She felt terribly odd taking the lead this way, but she had no choice—not if they weren't going to be found out. *And, oh, we will be.* Surely they would, the way Nan had talked about Chris while weeding the garden with her that day in May.

Nearly staring a hole through her, he pressed his hands on the counter. "I'd like to get to know you better. But I also want to respect your . . . customs."

She nodded. "After dark, then."

"Is tonight too soon?" His gaze softened, as if with hope.

"Tonight's just fine." She told him that she would meet him up the road. "I'll come on foot," she said. He agreed . . . and left without choosing a pie or cookies or any sweets at all. She refused the giggle that threatened to burst out as she watched him hop into his car again.

Mamma mustn't find out what I'm up to, Nellie thought, deciding she'd only go with Chris Yoder just this once.

———

Adding a few extra hours of waitressing each week would be precisely what Rhoda needed to help get out of her financial bind. After a little over a week of not seeing Ken Kraybill—not even encountering him in the hallways of his own house—Rhoda had realized their dating relationship was most likely finished. *Time to move on,* she decided as she returned a smile to the two fellows at one of her restaurant tables.

One of them seemed quite nice, and she imagined what it might be like to have dinner with him. She found it surprising that she didn't miss Ken as much as she thought she might. Of course there were moments when she missed talking with him, especially last Friday night, after getting off work. Still, she was convinced there was a fine, good-looking man for her somewhere out there. Someone who wanted to marry and start a family.

I wouldn't mind if he likes to watch television, too, she thought. She'd acquired a taste for *The Lucy Show* while baby-sitting the Kraybill children once the little ones were tucked into bed.

When she'd asked about working more than her regular hours, Mrs. Kraybill had agreed to put her at the top of her list for baby-sitters—*"but only if it doesn't interfere with your social life,"* Mrs. Kraybill had said. Her employer seemed aware that Ken was no longer in the picture, which was interesting to Rhoda. She wouldn't have pegged him as the type to talk to his aunt about matters of the heart.

Rhoda considered whether she might somehow scrape together enough money to buy a small TV set, so she'd have something entertaining to do on the evenings she wasn't working late. That is, if she didn't land a new beau soon.

"Would you like to order dessert?" she asked the men at her table.

"What's your favorite?" asked the blond man.

"Maybe we'll order something for you, if you'd like to join us." The taller man patted the seat.

She blushed. "Do I look like I'm off work?" Then she laughed.

They nodded enthusiastically. "C'mon, don't you want some pie or ice cream?" asked the first fellow. "You know you do."

As appealing as a break sounded, she wasn't going to while away her time and get herself fired.

Trying to be more professional, she asked, "What would the two of you like?"

The more handsome of the two leaned forward, eyes twinkling. "A banana split sounds good," he said. "And bring an extra spoon, just in case." He winked at her and then pulled out a card from his shirt pocket. "Call me anytime."

She accepted the card, noticing his name—Ted Shupp—and that he owned a welding shop on the outskirts of Honey Brook. Come to think of it, she'd seen it. "We don't have banana splits on the menu," she told him.

Ted pretended to pout. "Aw, can't you go and whip up something, Rhoda?"

She was surprised he knew her name and then realized it was pinned on her dress. She laughed at herself, but the flirty Ted must've thought she was laughing at him, because he waved her over closer. "Tell you what: I'll take you out for a banana split later, okeydokey?"

She gave him a careful look, trying to decide if this attractive fellow could be trusted. She didn't want a repeat of her dreadful night with Glenn Miller last winter. "I'll meet you at the ice cream parlor at nine o'clock," she said, thinking it wiser to drive herself tonight.

Nellie Mae thought of any number of reasons she might have given Chris Yoder to refuse his ice cream date. Yet here she was, scurrying up the road, hoping neither Nan nor Mamma suspected where she was going. And how could they not suspect something? After all, she'd waited till dusk to slip away without saying good-bye—a telltale sign she was meeting someone.

I can hear Nan now, when she corners me. She smiled, knowing however prying her sister might be, no amount of teasing would keep Nellie from meeting Chris tonight. *Caleb's cousin, no less.* The thought had clouded her thinking during supper. Was she only willing to spend time with Chris because he was related to her former beau?

She recalled how comfortable she'd felt around Chris the evening he drove her home—she'd nearly forgotten she was with an outsider. Maybe it was because she, too, was on the periphery, by Old Order standards.

She noticed the field grasses in the warm twilight. When had they grown to nearly waist-high? She hadn't gone to the woods at all since last fall, although she'd promised herself she would. Was she so hesitant to see the uncoiled ferns of deep summer . . . the rainbow of wild flowers? The sweetly scented air would be filled with the sounds of crickets at this time of day. All happy reminders of Suzy.

She sighed, realizing her nightly dreams of Suzy had ceased. And worse, she hadn't noticed, till now.

Suzy's description of the last weeks of her life was still clear in Nellie's mind, though—weeks that Chris's brother Zach had helped to make some of her very best.

Jah, there are plenty of reasons to have ice cream with Christian Yoder tonight, Nellie told herself.

The ride to Honey Brook was as pleasant as the last time she'd ridden with Chris. He'd greeted Nellie with an infectious smile, as he always did at the shop. Then, once she was settled inside, he hurried around the front of the car and jumped in behind the wheel, fast as a wink. Maybe to set her at ease, he asked if she minded listening to his favorite radio station, which turned out to be one that played fast hymns. At least, he said they were church songs, but the fancy-sounding melodies could've fooled her, despite lyrics that seemed drawn from the Bible.

The music got them talking for a while about the kinds of songs he sang as a member of his church. "You've already joined?" she asked.

"When I was sixteen. Our church allows baptism when someone professes faith, but most parents, like mine, want their children to be older before they become voting members."

"Sixteen's not too young, really. I know lots of girls, 'specially, who take the baptismal vow as soon as they're allowed to court."

He seemed to understand. "Our church requirements are different from yours, I'm sure."

She found it interesting he knew something of Amish practices. Perhaps it was due to his father's family tree.

The more Chris talked, the more she realized he was very settled in his church and seemed to have a deep sense of purpose.

Why *had* he asked her out?

When they arrived at the ice cream shop, she wondered if they would go inside to eat or if he would prefer to stay in the car. After all, she was wearing a Plain dress, unlike Rhoda, who she'd heard flounced all around town in her worldly getup.

No, I must not think more highly of myself.

When Chris came around to open her door, she smiled, pleased. *He's not embarrassed at all.*

It was a chore to rein in her smile as they headed to the sidewalk leading to the little shop. This being a weeknight, she hadn't expected the place to be so busy. But then, school was out for the summer. She'd nearly forgotten to ask Chris about his graduation last month and made a mental note to mention it later.

"What's your favorite flavor?" he asked, his eyes intent on her as they waited in line.

"Mint chocolate chip." She could almost taste the rich, creamy ice cream made on the premises—as delicious as the homemade kind she and Nan took turns cranking in their old ice cream maker on hot nights. "What's yours?"

"Coffee," he was quick to say. "I don't drink it, but I love the taste of coffee in ice cream."

She inched forward in the line with him. "It's funny, but coffee brewing smells just wonderful-good, yet the actual drink tastes bitter to me."

He nodded in agreement.

"I use coffee in my Chocolate Christmas Cookies, though. And they are delicious, if I do say so myself." She felt her cheeks grow warm. It wasn't like her to boast.

He smiled down at her. "I don't doubt it. How many recipes do you have?"

She shrugged. "I don't know. Oodles. I've even started writing out some of them."

His eyes lit up. "That's great. Are you making a cookbook? Recipes from Nellie's Simple Sweets?"

She shook her head, pleased but embarrassed by his enthusiasm. "Ach no. Just jotting them down for the customers who ask." She quickly changed the subject. "Suzy wasn't much of a baker, but she loved to make all kinds of ice cream. Nearly as soon as the bumblebees flew, she'd want to make it—around the time we started goin' barefoot in the spring."

"Suzy was keen on bare feet," he said.

"Oh jah, and she was always pushing the time for when we'd shed our shoes. Suzy loved the feel of barnyard mud squishing 'tween her toes." She caught herself. "Sorry . . . I don't mean to chatter on so."

"Isn't talking the best way to get acquainted?"

Her face reddened again. Goodness, but she liked him.

They were having such a laughing-good time already, and Rhoda scarcely even knew Ted Shupp. He walked over to her car after she'd pulled up and waved to him, opening her door. "Nice wheels," he said admiringly.

"Thanks," she said, blushing a little as she stepped out.

"This place is sure hopping tonight," he commented.

She noticed several Amish courting buggies toward the back of the lot and wondered who was out on a weeknight.

"Ever ride in one of those contraptions?" Ted asked.

She already liked Ted, but she wasn't ready to go into the whole story of her family background. "I sure have." She laughed. "I have friends who are Amish."

"Hey, me too." He grinned, and she was struck again by how comfortable she felt around him, which must surely be a good sign. "Who do you know that's Plain?"

She pulled a name out of her head, that of one of their former preachers. "Oh, the Zooks."

He chortled. "Aren't there a hundred and one Zooks around here?"

She nodded slowly, stepping back on the slippery path of pretense. "More Zooks than you can count, prob'ly," she said, walking beside him as they headed into the pink, red, and white ice cream shop.

I best watch myself. . . .

Jazzy, upbeat music wafted through the ice cream shop. Nellie felt like bobbing her head, as Chris was doing.

He caught himself and smiled apologetically. "I have to admit to liking cheerful music." He began to describe the appealing gospel-style music he'd heard at the Tel Hai Campground tabernacle.

"Suzy went there," she said suddenly. "Last summer."

"She loved that little place." He glanced upward, as though thinking back. "Suzy walked to the altar there, in fact."

Nodding, Nellie admitted she'd read Suzy's account of that happy day.

"How would you like to go with me sometime?" he asked, blue eyes shining. "I'm sure you'd enjoy it."

She'd wanted to attend the open-air services ever since learning of her sister's fondness for the rustic setting, but she'd never dreamed she would have the opportunity. Not with Chris, the very person who'd first invited Suzy, of all people!

Then she remembered she'd promised herself only one date with him. It made no sense to encourage Chris. Green though she was around English fellows, she was not so naïve that she couldn't see how fond he was becoming of her.

"A revival meeting's beginning in a few weeks—we could get in on the start of it, Nellie Mae." The way he said her name, part pleading, part admiration, startled her.

She wanted to ask Chris if he felt strange being seen with her, but maybe she was jumping ahead too quickly, becoming too personal.

"Would you like to go?" He was pressing for an answer between spoonfuls of ice cream. "We could come here afterward."

"But we hardly know each other."

He stared at his dish. "Well, I don't know about you, but it seems to me we've been friends for . . . well, quite a while."

She couldn't deny that, or the fact she felt drawn to him, as well. "Even so, I'm Amish. Surely this must be a problem."

She found herself holding her breath.

What'll he say to that?

"My grandparents were Amish, so it's not like I'm a fancy, worldly man, or whatever it is your People might think of me." His eyes were solemn but tender. "Just a few decades ago, my father's father was Amish. My father and David Yoder are first cousins."

Wanting to ask, yet cautious, she said, "How's David doin' since his accident?"

He bowed his head; then slowly he raised his eyes to meet hers. "My dad and I went to see David last Sunday afternoon. He's struggling . . . he's giving up."

"Ach no." Her heart sank.

Chris nodded sadly. "Caleb's worried—all the family are. You can see it in their eyes, the way they move around the house, taking care of him. Elizabeth rarely smiles," he added.

"Hopefully Rebekah can bring some joy to them," she said. "I've heard she's helpin'. She's my sister Nan's closest friend."

"I've seen her sometimes—she comes by during the day."

"It's just so sad." She didn't want to dwell on this topic, although she cared deeply for the Yoders. She wondered, too, why thus far Chris had made no mention of David's recent conversion.

Chris began to share about his church youth group and the Wednesday night Bible studies. Nellie lost herself in his words. How she enjoyed spending time with a date who loved the Lord.

She wanted to ask him about the passage in Romans she and Nan had discovered recently—one all about grace, which was still becoming a reality to her. And she would have brought it up, but at that moment she heard a familiar voice. Glancing at the door, she was surprised to see her sister Rhoda coming in with an Englischer, both of them laughing.

Is this her serious beau?

Then, just as quickly, she was more concerned about the possibility of Rhoda's seeing her with Chris Yoder. She turned to face Chris again, her back to her worldly sister.

They were sharing an enormous banana split, the two of them dipping with long fountain spoons into the mounds of ice cream topped with whipped cream. Rhoda thought it dear of Ted to sit beside her in the booth. He had a great sense of humor and, now that he wasn't hanging around the other guy, was much less a flirt—not that she minded the occasional wink or playful comment. So many nice qualities about him—he was polite and complimentary—and he was even better looking than Ken Kraybill.

Funny I should think of Ken.

She again marveled at Ted, sure she had found the perfect way to forget the pain her former beau had caused her. "Do you like kids?" she asked, spooning up her next bite.

"You bet I do. The more, the better." He leaned close, like he might kiss her cheek. "How many babies do you want, honey?" He was so near to her, she could smell his cologne.

"As many as the Good Lord sees fit, I'm guessing."

He laughed. "The way I see it, the Lord doesn't have much to do with all of that."

She smiled back at him, puzzled, thinking that sometimes there was a secret code to the Englischers' way of talking. Even so, something told her he might be just a little fresh, sitting this close. Yet she didn't budge. She'd been lonely since she and Ken split up, and having Mr. Ted Shupp be so attentive was just as nice as it could be.

The couple at the table behind them got up and left, and she leaned back in the pink booth, Ted's arm around her shoulders now. That's when she spotted her sister Nellie Mae with a fancy fellow. "Well, I'll be snookered," she said, excusing herself.

Boldly, she approached them, eyeing Nellie suspiciously from behind. She leaned over and smiled. "Why, goodness' sake! Nellie Mae . . . what're you doing here?"

Her sister instantly turned pale. "Oh, hullo, Rhoda . . . how're you?"

Then, as if remembering her manners, Nellie sputtered out an introduction. "This here is . . . Christian Yoder, a friend of mine."

"Hi there." Rhoda offered her hand. "I'm Nellie's sister, Rhoda Fisher."

Chris nodded, smiling politely. "Weren't you our waitress for my father's birthday dinner?"

"Oh, so *that's* where I first saw you. Christian Yoder, you said?" The name seemed familiar to her . . . but then, there were an awful lot of Yoders in these parts.

"Mostly it's Chris." He glanced now at Nellie Mae, who seemed to be shrinking on her side of the table.

"Are you eating alone?" Nellie asked her.

Rhoda realized what she'd done—setting herself up to be questioned later by Ted. She sure didn't want that. Talk about spoiling things for herself, and mighty fast! "It's my first date with someone, so I'd better get going." She inched back, dying to return to Ted but still very curious about what Nellie might be up to. "Just wanted to say hi. Great ice cream here, ain't?"

"Nice to see ya, Rhoda," said Nellie. "I'll tell Nan I saw you—it'll make her ever so happy." Nellie Mae looked forlorn as she mentioned Nan, and it made Rhoda feel lousy for abandoning her dearest sister. *I wonder how*

Nan is, really, she thought, pasting on a big smile for Ted as she scooted in next to him once again.

First date? Nellie didn't quite understand, unless perhaps Rhoda meant this was a new beau. She wasn't about to turn and gawk, but she would have liked to meet her sister's friend, just as she'd introduced Chris to Rhoda.

She and Chris fell back into conversation, discussing everything from Chris's college scholarship to his youth group fund-raisers. As nice as he was, suddenly she felt terribly uneasy. Her parents would be upset, and Nan, too, if they heard she was out with an Englischer. How long before news of Nellie's "fancy beau" would find its way to the Amish grapevine?

Across the way, she noticed Rhoda and her friend moving through the maze of tables, heading for the door. Nellie expected her sister to look over and wave, but Rhoda was preoccupied with her new boyfriend, laughing loudly as she held his hand.

"I'd love to go to the tabernacle with you, but I better not," she told Chris after he'd brought up the revival meetings again.

His face drooped. "Well, it's hard to describe, but I think you'd really like it. Lots of youth attend."

Nodding, she knew intuitively that if Suzy had loved it, so would she. But she refused to break her mother's or her father's heart. There had been far too much sadness amongst the People for one year, and her seeing Chris was sure to raise eyebrows and bring unnecessary anxiety. "I should be getting home now," she said, torn between the lovely idea of seeing him again and knowing their relationship had the potential to lead to yet another parting.

He rose quickly and gently escorted her to his car, not pressing the matter further.

Chris had witnessed the marked change in the tide. Somewhere in the space of time between Rhoda's coming to their table and when she and her boyfriend exited the ice cream shop, something had changed drastically in Nellie Mae. Hard as he tried, he could not determine what had happened to alter her openness toward him.

He knew of a longer route back to Beaver Dam Road and chose that way, wanting to get things back on better footing before the night was over. But how? If he brought up Rhoda's lack of Plainness, how would that serve to get Nellie talking again?

"I really wish you'd think about going to the tabernacle with me," he ventured.

She gave a small sigh. "It's kind of you." Then she surprised him by saying she didn't want to bring sorrow to her parents. She spoke more softly now—gone was the confident, talkative girl he'd brought to town. Was it her encounter with Rhoda, who apparently was no longer Amish, that upset her?

They drove without speaking for a time. Then, when he thought he might not get her to talk again, she looked over at him. "Besides your family history, how is it you know so much about . . . the Amish church?" she asked.

He was glad to explain. "David Yoder and my dad always liked to sit around after dinner at their house when I was a kid. They loved debating the rules of the Amish ordinances and my father's belief in the grace of the Lord. My dad often said he knew what his Amish cousin believed nearly as well as David did himself."

"Ach, really?"

"When David started to talk about dying last Sunday, my dad shooed Caleb and me out of the room and laid out the Gospel to him one more time."

She shifted herself to face him, as if eager to hear more.

"Dad told his cousin that following the rules of a church or a bishop wouldn't get him past the pearly gates. 'You need Jesus,' Dad told him flat-out."

"What did David say to that?"

Chris hesitated, not wanting to sound critical. "I don't know how well you're acquainted with my dad's cousin, but—"

"Quite frankly, most folk know he's stubborn."

"That's putting it mildly. Even with death starin' him in the face, at first he was as closed-minded as he's always been." Chris thought how ironic it was that a mule's kick to such a hardheaded man hadn't softened him up much. "But God can crack the hardest heart, and David cried out to Him . . . and repented."

"Too bad it takes a calamity to get a person's attention." Nellie's voice quivered. "Suzy's death brought my family to their knees, I know that for sure. I'm so thankful God was able to use this accident to get David's notice . . . and his heart."

Hearing her express herself so sweetly made Chris want to reach for her hand. *I have to be out of my mind.* By tomorrow, he guessed, he'd be glad if he kept his hands firmly on the steering wheel, where they belonged.

CHAPTER 27

N an was waiting for her in the hallway when Nellie Mae tiptoed up the stairs. "Did you go out with you-know-who?" She was smiling, clad in her long cotton nightgown.

"Well, it won't happen again, so you don't need to fret."

"So, you *were* with Chris Yoder!"

Nellie hurried to her room. "Is this the same sister who made me wait for weeks to know the name of my future brother-in-law?" She nearly closed the door on Nan's nose and then opened it right quick to pull her inside. "I'll just say this much—Chris told me more about the day David Yoder opened up to Christ. We mustn't quit praying for him or the rest of the family."

Nan agreed, waiting for more information—Nellie could see it in her too-eager eyes.

"Other than running into Rhoda, who looked to be in good spirits, there's nothin' else to tell." She yawned and stretched her arms. "Now I'm tired . . . and so are you."

"Jah, s'pose it is bedtime." Before Nan left for her room, she grinned and said, "If you need advice 'bout, well, just anything, I'm willin'."

"Good night, sister," Nellie said, reaching up to undo her hair.

The weekend passed quickly for Rhoda, who couldn't believe how nice it was to have a new beau with a flair for romance. He stopped by the restaurant with flowers for no reason, and the day after waited till she was off work to take her to dinner.

Since meeting Ted a week ago now, she'd already stopped in at the welding shop twice to talk to him and simply "hang around," as he put it, with a twinkle in his eyes. Today, though, when she arrived, hoping to surprise him before heading to work at the restaurant, she noticed a couple of pretty girls already doing just that, and Rhoda wondered if they were there to see Ted or one of the other guys. Watching from her car, she felt a pang of jealousy when she saw Ted go over and put his arms around both of them. *Like he does with me!* One of the girls leaned against him flirtatiously.

Deciding not to stay, she drove away, as offended as she'd felt the day Curly Sam Zook had dropped her like a hot fried potato.

Best not be counting my chickens before they're hatched!

Seized by an overwhelming desire for a milkshake and salty French fries, Rhoda drove straight to the nearest fast-food place.

Just this once.

The dream began as the dearest Rosanna had ever dreamed. A covering of radiant leaves showered around her as she strolled merrily through the golden wood. She savored the earthy scents of autumn and cradled her swollen stomach, where her darling babe grew.

A gentle gust swept across her face, making her apron billow out around her ankles. She felt the sun . . . ah, the sweet, warm sunshine. The day of her baby's birth was drawing closer. *Elias will be ever so happy.*

At first she didn't see her—the wee baby curled up in the blood-red leaves. Then she stopped to look and cried out, "Oh, surely not!" *No . . . not my precious little one. My baby, on the ground, lifeless . . .*

She awakened with a start and, sitting up, realized she must've made a sound.

"Rosanna?" came Elias's sleepy voice. "You all right?"

"I had a horrid dream."

"Ach, you're crying, love." He sat up with her, drawing her near, and she buried her face in his warm embrace.

"Shh . . . it was a nightmare . . . jah?"

She dared not say just how awful the dream had been . . . how frighteningly real. No need to burden Elias, whose own pillowcase was sometimes wet with tears in the morning, so heavy was the burden he faithfully carried for the People. And now here she was waking him.

Is it a forewarning?

Lena's thoughtful letter had arrived earlier that Friday, the looked-for reply to Rosanna's. Lena had seemed overjoyed to hear of Rosanna's pregnancy, calling it "wonderful-good news" and thanking the Lord for this "gift," praying Rosanna would have the health to deliver a full-term baby. Yet Rosanna's own baby news had not changed a single thing in Lena's thinking.

In the distance, the crack of fireworks from the town's Fourth-of-July celebration punctuated the present silence.

"I'm here, love." Elias pulled her gently down with him, cradling her in his strong arms. "Just rest."

She nodded, trembling at the vision of the beautiful baby girl . . . dead on the forest floor.

O Lord, please let it not be so. . . .

———

Caleb stayed at home with Mamm on the Lord's Day to help with Daed while Leah and Emmie attended Preaching. Though both the bishop and even Preacher Manny had dropped by, nothing more had been said about his father's wishes for the funeral. And Caleb remained chagrined at Daed's sudden change of heart, as well as Mamm's reluctance to discuss the events of the Sunday two weeks ago.

He'll come to his senses, Caleb told himself. *He's off-kilter.*

To Caleb's surprise, today Daed seemed able to hold his head more erect and wanted to come to the table for the noon meal. And strength did seem to be returning somewhat to his upper body as they all sat at the supper table presently. Caleb also noticed how much longer his father bowed his head for the silent blessing . . . and when he asked for various dishes to be passed, his words were unexpectedly soft and kind.

Was Daed experiencing a miraculous turnaround, just as Chris Yoder had prayed? And where would all this talk of miracles lead them, anyway?

When Daed asked to be wheeled back to his room, Caleb rose quickly. Alone together in the bedroom once again, he sat waiting for Abe to drop by and help move Daed back into bed.

Motioning for Caleb to close the door, Daed said, "I have something to say to you, son."

Caleb braced himself, not ready for another confession. His father looked so feeble in his wheelchair.

"I've said before that I've been a hard man." Daed raised his eyes to Caleb's. "I was bullheaded to force you away from your girl. Wasn't my place."

All the anger Caleb had felt—all the pain and loss—came flooding back. He didn't want to talk about Nellie Mae now, least of all with a man he scarcely knew anymore.

"I rejected your choice of a mate, somethin' mighty sacred." Daed stared down at his rough hands. "You should've been allowed to marry the girl you chose. The one you loved."

Caleb gritted his teeth, unable to make heads or tails of this. After thwarting his longed-for plans at every turn, did Daed hope to gain his forgiveness so easily? This wasn't the time to inform Daed of Nellie's choice. That *she*, not Daed, had cut things off in the end. Caleb breathed deeply, studying his father—still shocked at the words coming out of his mouth. Was the new belief Nellie embraced—that tore their love apart—truly now Daed's own?

Daed continued. "I've talked with your brothers—each one. And you can rest assured there'll be no hard feelings from them." He made no attempt to restrain his tears, which ran down both sides of his wrinkled face. "Son, my land is yours for the taking."

Caleb felt the air leave him. Had he heard correctly? "Ach, I wasn't expecting this."

"I know, Caleb . . . I know. But there's a big difference now. There are no strings attached. You're free to farm it for as long as you live."

Caleb was speechless. He'd never seen such benevolence in his father. Truly, something deep had altered in him.

With much effort, Daed offered his hand. "I failed you, son," he said. "Can you ever forgive me?"

Without giving it a second thought, he clasped his father's hand. "Dat . . . this is all so sudden. . . ."

Slowly, Daed nodded his head, his beard bumping his chest. "But I believe you'll see . . . in due time . . . what I'm talking 'bout." With those puzzling words, his trembling hand suddenly dropped, too weak to grasp any longer. "You'll see."

The land he'd always wanted, even coveted, was to be his—if Daed was in his right mind, that is. Caleb would be foolish to refuse the very thing he'd longed for, yet he felt mighty distrustful as he sat staring at this father who'd changed nearly before his eyes.

"I love you, Caleb . . . whether you forgive me or not."

Once again, Caleb was bewildered, unable to recall ever having heard his father declare such a thing.

———

For sure and for certain, Nellie enjoyed Rebekah Yoder's Sunday afternoon visits almost as much as Nan. Today she'd stayed for supper, and since it would be daylight for a few more hours, Nellie suggested the three of them go walking in the woods. "The red columbine should still be blooming," she told Nan, knowing her sister would remember the brilliantly scarlet blossoms that had always been Suzy's favorite.

It was a hot and muggy July day, the first Sunday of the month, and blue sky was divided by a buildup of clouds to the west. All three girls had worn their winter bonnets to shield their faces from the sun.

"How's your father doin' today?" Nan asked Rebekah as they hiked through the paddock, toward the meadow.

"Well, it was a bit surprising when I stopped in to see him earlier. He seemed some better, actually." Rebekah glanced at Nellie Mae. " 'Tis such a blessing to be welcomed by him again. Ya know, he's offered to let me move back home, if I want to. Caleb says I should take him up on it before he changes his mind." She chuckled.

Delighted as she was to hear this news, Nellie tensed up at the mention of Caleb.

"I was out walkin' with my sister Leah just two Sundays ago, talking about Daed's makin' peace with God and explainin' the reasons for the church split," Rebekah continued. "Ach, such a thorny thing. Most of the youth have little idea what went on, or what even caused it."

"I daresay 'twas a mighty confusing time for all of us," Nan said.

"My father's saying he wants as many of the People present at his funeral as will come—everyone from the New Order and the Beachys, too," Rebekah said.

"I wonder why." Nan stopped to pick a black-eyed Susan and spun it between her fingers.

"Has the bishop been to see him?" Nellie asked, curious what David Yoder was cooking up.

"Jah, the bishop and Preacher Manny, both. The two of them met with my father." Rebekah shook her head, removing her bonnet and fanning her face. "To think Daed is willing to talk to a New Order preacher, of all things. Only the Lord could make that happen."

Nellie wondered if David had softened at all toward Caleb. She still felt dreadful when she thought of him giving up his treasured inheritance, grasping anew what Caleb sacrificed to prove his love for her. The whole thing made her stomach tie up in knots.

Quite by surprise, Chris Yoder came to mind. She liked the fact that he shared her faith—ever so appealing—in contrast to Caleb's disapproval of her new beliefs. She found much to admire about Chris, although they should limit their conversation to his weekly visits to the bakery shop from now on.

Even so, Nellie couldn't help but think how exciting it would be to go with him to the very tabernacle where Suzy had first encountered the Lord.

———

Caleb carried a glass of water into Daed's room, placing it on the lamp table near the bed. As usual, he'd brought a straw to make drinking easier, since his father wanted to hold his own glass—in some ways, his father was as bent on being independent as ever.

Going to the window, Caleb noticed a long V-shaped line of birds fly over the house, and he watched them travel east till they were black specks in the distance. The evening sun remained high in the sky at nearly seven o'clock, and Caleb reached up to pull down the green shade.

"Come . . . sit with me, son." His father's eyes were open again.

Caleb reached back to raise the shade slightly, surprised at the request. "Thought you might want to retire for the night." He set a chair next to the bed.

"Not yet, no. There are still things I must say." His Daed was quiet for a moment, and Caleb wondered what on earth his father had in mind. He had been avoiding him some, hoping not to be cornered with another request for forgiveness. *It's too late to put everything right.*

Weak as his father appeared, his gaze held steady, and Caleb had an uncomfortable sense that he suspected the fight within. "Don't follow in my obstinate ways. Give your life over to the One who died for you . . . and for me. Nothin' else you do is worth a lick otherwise."

"Daed . . . I just don't understand what's happened . . . this way of thinkin'. You were so opposed to talk of grace and salvation before."

His father's breathing seemed shallow now, and his eyes were closed once more. "Don't wait to believe, Caleb," he whispered, folding his hands over his chest. "Preacher Manny was right . . . all along. Honest, he was."

Unable to sit any longer, Caleb rose and went to the window again. Did his father expect him to abandon the Old Ways as quickly as he seemingly had?

"None of this adds up," Caleb muttered.

He didn't know how long he remained there, but some minutes had passed and he sensed something amiss—even absent—in the room. Daed's arduous breathing had subsided. And when he turned to look, he saw the pallor of death settle over his father's face. Gone was the fight for each lungful of air; his eyes were closed with the sleep of the ages.

How easily he passed. . . .

Caleb felt like an intruder suddenly—shouldn't Mamm have been the one present to hear Daed's last words? Moving to the bedside, he looked more closely and saw a slight smile on Daed's lips. A good death, as some might say.

Standing there, he felt a sense of peace, followed by his own regret. He had withheld forgiveness from his father . . . and now Daed was dead.

He stared down at the folded callused hands and laid his own there lightly.

"Don't wait to believe, Caleb. . . . *Preacher Manny was right."*

Caleb shuddered at the memory of his father's final request and went to tell his mother.

———

By the time they returned from the woods, carrying handfuls of red columbine to give Mamma, Nellie was spent. After the long church service this morning and with Rebekah's visit, she'd missed sitting down to write her circle letters and her weekly letter to Cousin Treva. She felt tired for some unexplained reason. Unless, was she somehow allowing herself to be burdened by Caleb's concern for his father? Connected in grief?

She'd enjoyed the walk to the woods, where Rebekah had revealed her hope to marry in November, during wedding season, as Nan smiled knowingly at Nellie Mae.

With a happy sigh, Nellie looked forward to spending the evening hours with Mamma. Nan and Rebekah would soon be heading together to the Sunday Singing.

It was some time later, after Nellie had taken down her hair and was brushing it before bedtime, that someone came riding into the drive, bringing word that David Yoder had died not but a few hours ago.

CHAPTER 28

The morning of his father's funeral, Caleb found his mother weeping over the kitchen sink. Her hair was still flowing past her waist, and it appeared that she'd come downstairs for some juice. Still wearing her nightclothes and bathrobe, she must have thought she would be alone.

Not wanting to startle her, he went to stand near, unsure how to comfort her. "I'm mighty sorry 'bout Daed's passing," Caleb managed to say.

She looked at him with pleading eyes. "Did he make his peace with ya, Caleb?"

He nodded slowly.

A sad sort of smile crept across her lined face. "It was the most peculiar thing." She drew a long breath. "I believe your father must've had heavenly visions—did he tell you?"

"First I've heard it."

She glanced nervously toward the doorway. "He asked me several times the day he died, while I sat with him, if he was 'in glory yet.' I didn't know what to make of it. And then, closer to his time of passing, he seemed ever so joyful."

He wondered if she'd noticed Daed's small smile when she came in right after his passing. Or had he only imagined it?

She put a hand to her trembling lips, her eyes filling with tears. "He changed so, toward the end. Honestly, I hardly knew . . ." She couldn't go on.

"Maybe the medicine was the culprit," Caleb was quick to say. Certain drugs could alter one's thinking. Had that been the case for Daed?

"Your father asked forgiveness for bein' *Hochnut*—all puffed up. He regretted treatin' folks as he did. Ya know what a stickler he was for the ordinance."

This jolted Caleb. So his father had apologized to Mamm for the very thing he'd accused the new church believers of? He'd told Caleb many times that the New Order and Beachy people seemed to think they were better, because they "knew the Lord." That had irked him no end.

Footsteps on the stairs brought their conversation to a close when Leah and Emmie came into the kitchen to prepare the pancake batter. The milking was already done, thanks to Jonah and several sympathetic neighbors. Caleb had been glad for the help, not wanting to awaken his sorrowful sisters on a day that would undoubtedly stretch on for all of them. And as distraught as she already was, he didn't see how Mamm would make it through the three-hour funeral and the burial service.

Just three short days ago, Daed was alive and sitting at the head of their table. He'd had a momentary reprieve from some of his physical weakness . . . enough to carry him through to his passing. The body required energy to die, or so Caleb had once heard.

Where was his father's spirit now that his body was soon to be committed to the ground of the nearby cemetery? Was he indeed in heaven?

Caleb made his way upstairs to clean up, pondering Daed's abnormal behavior. Was it possible he'd found a personal connection with the Lord, like Cousin Chris claimed to have? *Like all the supposedly saved folk . . .*

―――――

Word had spread rapidly, and Caleb's father's wish was granted. The Yoder farmhouse was packed to standing room only with those faithful to the old church, as well as many who'd gone to the New Order and the local Beachy Amish church. Because he sat close to the front with his Dawdi, brothers, and nephews, Caleb was not able to see how many English neighbors were present, nor if Chris and his family were in attendance.

He put mental blinders on, narrowly focusing on the casket before him. Here, in the front room of his father's own house, where so many Preaching services had been held all through the years.

Bishop Joseph gave the first and shorter sermon, as Daed had evidently requested. But soon it was clear that the service was a departure from the norm, as one long scripture after another was read, and not from the old German Bible, either. Hearing such sacred words in English jarred Caleb— and others, he was mighty sure.

Why had Daed asked for this? And why had the bishop agreed?

After a full hour, Preacher Manny rose. The second, longer sermon was to begin.

Immediately it was clear that this portion of the service would also depart from tradition, the very thing Daed had defended for so long. "Coming to Christ means you are no longer in denial," Preacher Manny commenced.

Denial of what? Caleb froze in his seat.

"David Yoder lived a life pleasing to himself. He requested that I speak to you all today to the best of my ability about the kind of faith that became his before the end." Preacher Manny held a piece of paper in his hand, his dark hair shiny and clean for the occasion. "David told me to my face that he never knew why he balked so hard at the reality of saving grace, till it struck him between the eyes. He said God had to use a mule to get his attention."

A low stir rippled through the room.

"Truth is, David laid down his will for God's. And although he didn't live long enough to personally share his newfound faith with each of you, his belief in the saving power of Jesus will resonate from his grave."

Caleb wanted to look and see how his mother was holding up, over there with Rebekah, Leah, and Emmie, and all her daughters-in-law, too—cushioned by the womenfolk.

Preacher Manny continued speaking to the congregation in conversational tones, another departure from their usual way. "If David Yoder were alive today—and strong enough to speak here—he'd want you to know that life is too short to bicker over church ordinances, or to think more highly of ourselves than we ought. Doing so is an abomination in the sight of God."

Caleb's neck ached with tension, and he wondered how soon Preacher Manny would get back on track, if he would at all.

Preacher Manny looked out at the congregation, his eyes moving slowly over them before returning to his notes. "With tears of joy, David made a profession of faith two weeks ago. He believed, in the final days of his life, that God's grace was a gift from the Father's hand—not something to be spurned, but to be received as the loving blessing it was intended to be. These are the words I read to him when I last saw him, words he openly laid claim to: 'Not by works of righteousness which we have done, but according to his mercy he saved us, by the washing of regeneration, and renewing of the Holy Ghost.' " Preacher Manny wiped his eyes with his handkerchief, composed himself, and went on. "So, beloved family and friends of our brother David Yoder, it is only through God's mercy we are made new, a precious gift indeed."

Caleb wanted to escape, but he had no place to go. He was compelled by his upbringing and his mother's would-be shame to remain . . . to endure this unimaginable sermon. *What will the brethren think?*

It was talk like this that would get his family shunned . . . and yet, the bishop himself was allowing it. Why should a son question the wishes of his dying father?

Thinking now of his English cousin, Caleb knew Chris would be in full agreement with a sermon like this. And Nellie Mae might well be whispering amen, too.

He stared at the long handcrafted coffin, narrow at both ends. Daed was nestled in there, wearing his for-good clothes. Mamm and her sisters—and other womenfolk—had bathed and dressed him in all black, but for his best long-sleeved white shirt.

He remembered his father's outstretched hand . . . the humble way he'd asked for forgiveness. And the bequest of land—what Caleb had once so coldly rejected had been unexpectedly offered anew with no conditions attached. Was this the very sort of mercy Manny spoke of?

Sitting straighter now, he returned his attention to the preacher, who opened the German Bible to John chapter eight, verse thirty-six. Then, following that short reading, he moved to the English Bible and read the same words. " 'If the Son'—meaning our Lord and Savior—'therefore shall make you free'—this is the salvation our hearts yearn for, beloved—'ye shall be free indeed.' " Preacher Manny's eyes brimmed with tears, and he took out a white handkerchief to wipe his eyes. "Our brother David is no longer trapped in a broken body. He is present with the Savior . . . the very One whose words he denied for most of his lifetime." He breathed deeply, clearly moved. "And our brother is free in ev'ry way now. He worships the living God even as we gather here to mourn his passing."

Caleb recalled his father's good death. Was Mamm right about what she assumed? Had his father experienced glimpses of heaven before dying? *"If the Son shall make you free, ye shall be free indeed. . . ."*

The verse echoed in his mind . . . the selfsame words he'd read on his own several times now. According to this verse, in some inexplicable way, Daed had found a spiritual freedom in the last days of his life.

This was the first funeral Nellie Mae had ever attended that seemed more like a Preaching service—certainly the messages being delivered were quite unfamiliar to a third of those in attendance. She felt strongly that David Yoder's death might either unify or further divide the People.

She looked toward the back of the room, where Chris and Zach sat with their family. A few other Englischers were there, as well, including a couple regular customers of the bakery shop.

But today it was Caleb she found herself drawn to, utterly sad for him. A tear trickled down her cheek, and she glanced his way again and saw he was looking at her, his countenance pained. She wondered if he'd had any previous warning about what would be said today by either Uncle Bishop or Preacher Manny. Had David Yoder shared any of this directly with Caleb? If not, how was such a service setting with the family—Caleb in particular, who'd adhered to his father's tenacious beliefs even when it meant the death of their relationship.

All in God's hands now.

Aware of the apprehension in the room, she closed her eyes, pleading for divine mercy to settle over the congregation. Nellie added a silent prayer of thanks for the miracle of salvation in David Yoder's heart, grateful to Chris and his father for their part in this wonderful turn.

CHAPTER 29

Nellie Mae was determined to be a good sister, even if it meant appearing to be meddlesome. She had to know if Rhoda was aware of David Yoder's death and felt the need to go and visit by herself. After all, Rhoda was surely as lost as David had been, and she was still her dear sister, no matter how far into the world Rhoda wandered.

With this in mind, she left Mamma in charge of the shop and went on foot to the Kraybills' house midmorning, hoping to see elusive Rhoda there.

She spotted a black-and-white car parked off to the side of the driveway and guessed it was Rhoda's. Seeing this reminder of her sister's fancy life, she wondered what David Yoder might share with all of them about that, after four days in Glory.

"Hullo!" she called to Rhoda, who was carrying trash out the back door.

"How're you, Nellie Mae?" Her sister shielded her eyes from the sun. "What brings you here?"

"I hoped you might have a minute to talk."

Rhoda frowned. "Well, Mrs. Kraybill's expecting me to finish cleaning."

Nellie followed her to the kitchen door. "I won't keep you long. I just wanted to know if you'd heard that David Yoder passed away last Sunday."

Rhoda shook her head. "Ach, I hadn't." She opened the door, and for a moment, Nellie wondered if their conversation was to be cut short. Then Rhoda kindly held the screen door, motioning for Nellie to go inside first. "Maybe we could sit at the table for a bit." Going to a tall refrigerator, Rhoda opened it and brought out a pitcher of orange juice, already made.

"I'll make it snappy," Nellie said. She couldn't help noticing the modern kitchen, with its shiny dishwasher and double oven—ever so bright and cheerful, too. "Ya know, David Yoder turned to Jesus before he died . . . made his peace with God." She paused, wondering if she'd make matters worse if she said what was on her mind. "I sure hope you're happy with your . . . um, fancy life."

"Why, sure I am." Rhoda sipped some juice. "How'd David die?"

"He was kicked in the head by one of his mules some time ago."

"Oh . . . that's just terrible." She shook her head. "So many dangers on a farm."

"So many dangers in the world, too," Nellie said softly.

Rhoda gave her a sharp look. "Are you here to ask me to come home?" she said. "Mamma has, you know—a couple times. I wondered if she'd sent ya, maybe."

Still hesitant to speak her mind fully, Nellie Mae turned the juice glass around, staring at it. "It'd sure put a big smile on Mamma's face, I know. Nan's and Dat's, too. But since you haven't joined church, that's all up to you."

"Honestly, I couldn't go back even if I wanted to." Rhoda explained she'd signed a year's lease with her landlord.

Dat had taught them well—there was no sense in talking about breaking a legal promise—or any promise, for that matter. "So, after a year's up, would ya consider it?"

Rhoda shrugged and glanced away, toward the vast green meadow visible through the window. "'Tween you and me, I hope to find me a nice husband by then." But she looked ever so glum now. "Though I haven't had much luck with that yet, either."

"I could say the same." Nellie offered a small smile as she rose from the table. "Denki for the juice. Sorry to keep you from work."

"Tell Nan I think of her a lot." Rhoda touched her arm. "Tell Mamma, too."

"Well, you're not a stranger—you could tell them yourself."

There was a faraway look in Rhoda's pretty green eyes, and Nellie wanted to throw her arms around her. *If only she wasn't so stubborn . . . bent on her own way.*

Together the two sisters walked out the back door and down toward the narrow road. Nellie buttoned up her lip, finding it mighty curious that Rhoda had clearly forgotten about the cleaning she was being paid to do.

In spite of having declined yet another date from Chris, Nellie hoped he might stop in at the bakery shop that Thursday afternoon. Just as before, Mamma and Nan made themselves conspicuously scarce near the time he usually appeared.

Chris strode up rather comically, offering his familiar grin. "How's the prettiest baker in Honey Brook?" he asked, his eyes serious.

Blushing, she looked away.

Chris pointed to the notebook on the counter. "Are these your recipes?"

"Jah. I was just adding to them." She was relieved his intense gaze was no longer focused on her. "S'pose I should just put together a little book as you said, since so many customers have asked."

"If you want to, I could help you print and bind it. I know someone who could help us."

Us? He wanted to include himself in the imaginary project? There was no question that he was thoughtful . . . even sweet. And she felt more certain than ever that he liked her—he wouldn't keep coming by every week if he didn't.

"Denki, Chris . . . that's nice of you."

He smiled, pausing before continuing. "Have you thought any more about going to the tabernacle meeting?" Before she could respond, he added, "I'd like to take you—considering I was the one who first invited Suzy there last spring." He explained how he'd given Suzy the flyer, inviting her to the meetings. "But maybe your sister wrote about that, too."

Nellie nodded. *Should I give in?*

The whole time he stood there, Chris never once looked at either the pies or the delicious cookies. And when he didn't ask again, she hoped she hadn't miffed him. Sure, she wanted to go. Despite all the reasons she'd talked herself out of another date before, she was secretly glad he'd come by to ask again.

"Thanks for invitin' me," she said softly, unable to avoid his clear gaze.

"Then, you'll go?" His eyes twinkled with irrepressible delight.

Nellie couldn't keep from smiling her joyful reply.

CHAPTER 30

The days following his father's funeral were heavy with heat, humidity, and strenuous work—threshing small grains took up the hours from dawn to dusk, as well as hoeing the tobacco patches. Caleb's extended family pitched in and helped with both as Amish and English farmers up and down the road continued cultivating their potato fields and cornfields.

Stifling hot evenings were spent outdoors with picnic blankets spread on well-trimmed lawns. Amidst the creak of rocking chairs and hushed chatter of teenagers, Caleb's nephews and nieces chased lightning bugs, putting them in canning jars. An occasional harmonica tune wafted over the dense midsummer air as the family sat on the porch, trying to escape the heat and longing for sundown. Nights were nearly as muggy as the daylight hours, bringing little relief. Those sleeping in upstairs bedrooms were sometimes forced to shed their nightclothes, hoping for the slightest breeze.

Caleb found the absence of his father surprisingly difficult. Daed's last words still stirred in his memory. More than once, while sitting in his room next to the open window late at night, he had reached for a pen and paper to start a letter to Nellie Mae. He wanted to share his keen understanding of her loss of Suzy more than a year ago. He longed to tell her that his love for her remained, that he missed her more than his words dared communicate.

Each time, though, he realized again how futile it was to attempt to link across the short distance to her. And with that knowing came the wadded-up paper and the aggravation of realizing the gulf between them was much too wide now. Besides, according to the grapevine, Nellie had already moved on—attending Singings with the New Order church youth. He'd even heard she'd been seen out with an Englischer. Was she taking the same path as Suzy? After all, she was every bit as pretty. *And truly delightful in every way . . .*

But it was past time to forget her. And there was no time at present to think of courting anyone new, not till after the laborious tobacco harvest was past . . . if even then.

———

Nellie Mae walked beside Chris up the narrow aisle to take seats on the rustic benches at the little tabernacle at the Tel Hai Campground. The wooden platform was low and smaller than she'd envisioned from Suzy's account, but it was the fervor in the singing that captured her attention as many young couples and other folk crowded into the open-air meeting. She was happy to be outside on such a warm Saturday evening, although thunder rumbled in the distance.

The sermon text was the nineteenth chapter of Job: " 'Oh that my words were now written! Oh that they were printed in a book! That they were graven with an iron pen and lead in the rock for ever! For I know that my redeemer liveth, and that he shall stand at the latter day upon the earth: And though after my skin worms destroy this body, yet in my flesh shall I see God. . . .' "

As the evangelist explained the verses, she realized his conversational style was similar to Preacher Manny's. Nellie was grateful to be in a church where the preaching was vital for daily living. Thinking of the verse just read, she thanked the Lord once more for bringing David Yoder to the knowledge of salvation . . . just in time, too.

Sitting next to Chris, she imagined what Suzy might have felt, coming here the first time . . . the evening she'd felt so uneasy. Thankfully, she had returned a second time and answered the Savior's call at the altar up front.

After the final prayer, people began to rise and Nellie noticed quite a few Amish couples, the girls in their long cape dresses and aprons. There were Mennonites, too, some of the girls wearing the formal head covering, others without the Kapp, their hair pulled back in a loose bun.

Later, on the drive to the ice cream shop in Honey Brook, Chris asked if going to the tabernacle had made her sad . . . because of missing Suzy. He mentioned that he'd seen her cry several times.

"I wasn't thinkin' so much of my sister as I was David Yoder's family. Elizabeth, 'specially . . . and poor Caleb."

"Well, he seemed all right today when I saw him during milking. Grieving, yes, but not openly."

She sniffled at the mention of her former beau. "It's just that . . . well, Caleb's been through a lot this year." She didn't know how much Chris and Caleb talked. Did he even know Caleb had been sent away by his father?

"He's shared a few things."

She wondered if Chris knew about her and Caleb's breakup. "We were once engaged," she admitted. "But then our church broke apart."

Chris's smile vanished. "So you're the girl. . . ." His voice sounded pinched, even pained.

She felt uncomfortable—she wouldn't be rude and go on about how they'd met or how long they'd courted. Chris was her date tonight.

"What happened . . . after the church split, I mean?" he asked.

"Well, Caleb wanted me to keep to the Old Ways."

"So you came to the Lord after the church folk scattered?"

"Jah, and strange to say it, but the Lord came between Caleb and me. That's all I'd best say."

Chris became uncommonly quiet as they drove the moonlit back roads. She realized she'd upset him somehow.

Some time later, he said, "I'm sorry for Caleb—losing his father . . . and his girl." Chris looked over at her, his gaze lingering.

"I'm glad he has you for a friend, Chris." She went on to say that she prayed daily for Caleb to know the Lord.

"So do I," he admitted.

When they arrived at the ice cream shop, she hoped they might talk about other things. She didn't want the evening to end on a sad note, especially after having enjoyed the service so much—and Chris's company.

"What flavor will it be tonight?" he asked as they approached the counter.

She eyed the many choices on the board behind the counter. "Strawberry sounds good. Denki."

"Branching out a little, I see." He placed her order and then paused. "I'll have what you had last time—it looked so good."

They found a table in the back, more private than before, and she was quite relieved when he made not a single further mention of Caleb.

Later, when Chris drove her home, Nellie noticed he took the long way, as he'd done before. She enjoyed the starry sky and the moonlight on the fertile fields while soft music played on his radio. It was impossible to justify accepting another date from him, but goodness, he looked her way nearly as often as Caleb had when they rode out on nights like this in his open buggy.

"I'd like to see you again, Nellie Mae," he said as he parked along the wide shoulder, near her house.

"You mean next Thursday at the shop?" She couldn't keep her smile in check.

"Yes, that too." He got out and came around to open her door. "I'll walk you down the road a ways, okay?"

"Nice of you, Chris . . . but it's a plenty bright night."

"Well, is it all right if I want to?"

She wouldn't think too far ahead. She'd simply relish this moment. How she'd enjoyed this special night filled with memories of Suzy and her faith . . . and ice cream with Chris. Somewhere, in the back of her mind, was the constant thought of her former beau, but she pushed it away. Feelings for Chris Yoder had grown in her heart in such a short time.

What does it mean? Am I finally over Caleb?

———

Rosanna King sat alone at the kitchen table, looking out at the glow of the moon on waist-high corn that ran in long, even rows beyond the side yard. To keep the insects from flapping and fluttering against the window, she'd decided against lighting the gas lamp. Besides, it was ever so late to be up.

She had painful cramping again tonight, although she couldn't tell if it was due to the baby or indigestion. The midwife had suggested saltine crackers at such times, so here she sat nibbling on one—snacking and praying.

Visions of a funeral and burial threatened her peace. If she were to have a stillbirth now, she would have to endure both, being so much farther along. But on the brighter side, if all went well, in just ten more weeks, their baby would be safe in her arms.

Will you allow me this miracle, Lord?

Lena had written another very encouraging letter, including a prayer she'd composed just for Rosanna. So touched was she by it, Rosanna had tucked it into the pages of her Bible to reread whenever she felt the panic lurking.

Here lately she did not suffer from panic as much as she did fatigue. So far she had spent nearly half the day in bed and was becoming quickly weary of it. Even so, she was willing to do more than that for her precious babe.

If Elias wasn't so busy with tilling potato fields, she might mention the need for a short trip to the doctor again. But making even that drive frightened her. Perhaps she'd ask Linda Fisher to use her telephone to call the midwife tomorrow when Linda stopped by with lunch. Or, better yet, stay to pray with her yet again. Truly, the Beachy woman who'd first introduced Rosanna to the idea of salvation full and free was as dear as any believer she knew.

Meanwhile, she ate crackers, letting the salty blandness soothe her stomach and hoping . . . praying these alarming spasms might cease.

CHAPTER 31

O n his way to Elias King's, Reuben passed three vegetable stands and a child's deserted bicycle with its small wicker basket dangling from the handlebars. Today he would till Elias's twenty acres of corn with a team of eight mules. He knew by the warmth of the dawn that this next-to-last day of July would be a scorcher. *Should be done by sunset.*

He'd awakened earlier than usual to finish up some of his own chores before heading to Elias's. Knowing he'd have little time to rest today, he leaned back in the buggy seat as he rode, taking in the fields, verdant and thriving, in all directions. It sure looked to be a good year for potatoes and corn . . . even tobacco for the old church farmers who were still growing it. Thus far, God was answering prayer for a bountiful harvest.

When he came within shouting distance, he was glad to see lights in the Kings' kitchen windows, which meant Rosanna might be up and feeling better.

Soon, though, he discovered it was Elias who was making himself some oatmeal and toast. "Rosanna's plumb tuckered out," Elias told him. "Doctor wants her in bed till the baby comes."

"Must be awful hard on her, seein' how the summer's been so hot."

Elias nodded, finishing up his breakfast. "Still, we're not nearly as bad off as we were last year round this time."

Remembering the severity of the drought, Reuben finished the coffee Elias had poured for him. "Looks like this year could be different, Lord willin'."

"Let's be mighty thankful for that." Elias wiped his mouth on his sleeve. "Best be getting to work, jah?"

Reuben carried his coffee mug to the sink before he followed him outdoors. On the way up the earthen ramp to the second story of the bank barn, Elias asked if he would remember Rosanna in prayer. "Truth be told, her health—and the baby's—are in the back of my mind all the time."

Reuben promised to pray. "The Lord sees the desire of your heart—yours and Rosanna's."

"I'll try to keep that in mind." Elias nodded. "Denki."

"Anytime, preacher."

———

They were driving home from the nursery on a day Chris had worked in the landscaping office.

Zach yawned loudly, leaning back on the headrest. "I helped Dad put together a knock-out landscaping plan today. He seemed pleased," he said. "Looks like I've got my focus back."

"Great to hear it. Would you mind if I asked you something about you and Suzy?" asked Chris.

"Fire away."

"Did you guys ever talk about your future—how to make it work if you were to marry someday?"

Zach's head popped back up. "Where'd that come from?"

"The culture clash, you know. Wondered how that would fly."

"Easy. Suzy was finished with Amish life."

"You knew this?"

"Sure." Zach stretched his right arm out the open window, yawning again. "She was all geared up to leave. Just didn't know how to switch from wearing Plain clothes to more modern ones without causing an uproar at home." Zach frowned, facing him. "Why are you asking?"

Chris didn't want to say.

"Hey, fine, go ahead and clam up." Zach folded his arms across his chest.

Chris was surprised Zach was so sure about Suzy's plan for going modern. He couldn't imagine Nellie Mae as anything but Amish. Oh, he'd tried, but he was sure that wasn't happening—not in his head, and not in reality. She was so Plain, in fact, it was a waste of time to think of her otherwise.

So, if I'm to keep seeing her, I might need to grow a beard. . . . He grinned at the image of himself decked out like an Amishman, but he had no interest in joining the horse-and-buggy crowd.

If only he'd thought all this through before he'd fallen so hard . . . but then he might have missed his chance to get to know her at all.

Frustrated as Chris was, he wouldn't deny his feelings. He needed to figure things out—the sooner, the better.

———

Betsy was surprised and elated to see her mother-in-law at a pickling bee over at Martha's the first week in August. Several women had gathered to put up dills and bread-and-butter pickles, with Martha and the two younger women making and stirring the hot brine, while Betsy and Hannah prepared the cucumbers. Little Emma and her younger brothers got underfoot in their efforts to help, creating lots of chuckles all around.

It had been such a long time since she'd seen Hannah. She sat right next to her and they chattered nearly all morning. Glad for a bit of a break from the bakery shop, she asked Hannah what had brought her here today—it was rare that she or Noah ventured this direction anymore.

"Oh, I've been missin' Honey Brook, is all. Seemed like a good time to take Martha up on her invitation." A small, sad smile played across her wrinkled face. "And Noah and I wanted to offer our sympathy to Elizabeth after we heard of David Yoder's passing."

Betsy didn't want to get her hopes up, but she was glad to see her mother-in-law accepting an invitation from family to visit again—from a Beachy home, no less. She wished they'd move back. *Where they belong.* After all, the Dawdi Haus was still vacant. And even if Reuben's parents wouldn't consider living with them, there was always Ephram and Maryann, who'd remained firmly planted in the old church.

She contemplated again David Yoder's conversion and had a strong belief that Elizabeth might soon follow in his footsteps. Elizabeth had asked her meaningful questions following the burial service, and Betsy had shared with her some of the verses that had touched her so deeply in the third chapter of the gospel of John.

God's Word will accomplish the good pleasure of the Lord, she thought, recalling another favorite passage she'd discovered recently in Isaiah. She trusted it would be true for dear Elizabeth and the rest of her family.

———

Food, and lots of it, brought her such comfort here lately, despite the fact that she'd already gained a good five pounds—pounds Rhoda had dropped with great effort and satisfaction in the previous months. But with bills pouring in, including the latest, for the small television she'd impulsively purchased, she'd immediately turned to food, especially the grease-laden fast food she craved. In any case, eating kept her from crying . . . over the loss of Ken and Ted and all the uncaring Amish boys who'd ever looked her way, only to reject her.

She sobbed about being stuck in Strasburg, with the long drive to work at both the restaurant and the Kraybills', and she cried because she had no one to talk to, missing her cozy sisterly chats with dearest Nan. When she was wholly honest with herself, she even admitted missing Dat's long, drawn-out nightly Bible reading.

Leaving the restaurant after work on this blazing afternoon, Rhoda was tempted to make a left-hand turn and head out east, toward Beaver Dam Road. *For old time's sake.*

But did she really want to return there?

The thought of having to let her hair grow back—that miserable middle part and tight bun—made her squirm. And the unstylish dresses and the long black aprons she'd worn whether cooking or not. What was the apron for, anyway? She wore one at the restaurant and at the Kraybills', but there was a reason for it when she was working. Even then, she could scarcely wait to untie it and toss it into the hamper the minute she was finished for the day.

Thinking of Mrs. Kraybill, she had a hankering to stop in and talk to her. After all, the woman had encouraged her flight to the world in every imaginable way. Without her influence, who knew where Rhoda might be today. Most likely not living in a second-floor room, hearing her former beau clomp around overhead while he played his music too loud—up there living his happy, single, and childless life, content to be without her.

All this time I thought he cared. . . .

Sighing, Rhoda fought back tears and drove straight to the house where she'd once hidden this beautiful car she drove. Where all of her fancy ideas had gotten their start.

———

His mouth parched from a long day in the sun, Caleb went to the well and pumped several cupfuls of water, gulping them down. Hungry for supper, he headed to the house to rinse the rest of the grime off his hands.

Leah and Emmie were setting the table, carrying food over from the cookstove. "Where's Mamm?" he asked, going to the sink.

Emmie glanced his way, a worried expression on her face. "She's in Daed's old room."

Concerned, he dried his hands and tossed the towel onto the counter. He found her kneeling at Daed's bedside, weeping.

Placing a hand on her shoulder, he stood there silently. He'd never seen her cry like this before, and it convicted him for his own lack of sorrow. He was sorry about his father's death—it wasn't that—and he missed Daed's presence in the house. But he hadn't wept. Not at the burial, where he'd helped shovel heavy clumps of dirt into the gaping hole for Daed's coffin, nor at the surprisingly unorthodox funeral service.

He waited while Mamm dried her eyes and rose to sit on the edge of the bed. Patting the spot next to her, she gave him a smile.

"You all right, Mamma?"

She sighed. "I'm glad you're here. There's something your father told me. . . . I can't get it out of my mind."

Had his own mother also endured sleepless nights with Daed's words turning continually in her head?

"Your Daed kept sayin', 'Preacher Manny was right,' until I didn't know what to think." Profound grief was evident in her eyes, and deep lines marked her face. "But it was his tears, Caleb—he couldn't stop lamenting. He urged me to attend the new church . . . said I would find what he'd been missin' till the last few weeks of his life."

Caleb understood her confusion. He, too, still struggled to grasp that his father—the man who had forbidden him to marry Nellie Mae—had embraced the very faith that had once made Nellie and her family unsuitable in his eyes. How could it be? How could a hard, stubborn man like his father change so drastically?

"I'm honestly thinkin' of going this Sunday," Mamm said.

Startled by this, he wished he might persuade her differently. "What'll the bishop say?"

"Well, I've talked to his wife, Anna, already. Seems the bishop has taken to heart much of what Preacher Manny shared at the funeral."

This made not a smidgen of sense. How could it?

"Anna and the bishop have been reading together every night," she whispered.

He held his breath. "Reading what?"

"The Good Book, of course." She referred to it in reverent tones, just the way Nellie Mae had . . . the way Chris did.

"Well, I read it, too, but I'm not thinkin' of switching churches. Are you, Mamm . . . truly?"

She covered her mouth, trembling.

"Ach, don't tell me . . ."

"I just know if your father hadn't been injured—if he was robust and healthy and alive today—he wouldn't have talked that way. God used his paralysis—and his impending death—to lead him to accept new life . . . eternal life."

He looked at her. "You believe this for truth?"

Nodding, her eyes glistened again. "Never more than now."

Sitting here in the room where his father's life had ebbed away, Caleb wished he'd at least made some attempt to confess his deception during the latter days of courting Nellie Mae. And the shifty way he'd handled things, willing to do anything to get his father's land. But he'd let the moments tick away, not heeding the inner nudging.

And I let Daed die without knowing that I freely forgave him.

"Daed confessed his shortcomings toward me. I should've done the same," he said quietly. "I just never thought he would slip away so fast."

She listened, reaching for his hand. "I'm ever so sorry."

"Should've made things right when I had the chance."

She leaned her head on his shoulder. "That's exactly what your father told me, Caleb. 'Make things right with the Lord while time's on your side. . . .' "

In the solemn stillness, Caleb was keenly aware of his own lack of time. Did he dare wait for the light of truth Nellie Mae had told him about, there in her shop? Did he know without a doubt—*who could possibly know?*—he would survive a mule kick to the head? Or any other freak farm accident, for that matter, and not be plunged into eternity without God?

"If the Son therefore shall make you free, ye shall be free indeed."

Was it possible? Could he, too, have the assurance of eternal life, just as Daed had so urgently declared?

"I oughta think good and hard 'bout this," he whispered.

CHAPTER 32

Nellie Mae suggested Mamma sit out on the front porch with her, wanting to just relax and look out over the neatly trimmed front lawn. Down on the road, market wagons traveled back and forth, and there were several young children on scooters.

Dragonflies settled on the pond across the way as dusk played hide-and-seek with the sun. And dark, rich soil peeked out between the rows of corn to the north. Far to the horizon, the ridge of hills turned slowly gray, then black, as the sun made its slide to earth.

"I've been wantin' to show you something, Mamma." Slipping her hand into her pocket, she pulled out the secret picture. "It's Suzy," she whispered.

Mamma gasped. "Oh, goodness!" Her mother held it away from her eyes, squinting a bit. "Well, doesn't she look happy?"

"Her beau took this picture before she drowned," said Nellie quietly.

Mamma sniffled. "Did ya ever see such a sweetness in her eyes?"

Nellie clasped her mother's hand and they were still for a long moment, sharing the secret that had troubled Nellie so.

"Oh, I can't tell you how nice it is seein' her face again," Mamma said.

"What must I do with this—now that you know I have it?" Nellie asked. "Does the New Order prohibit such things? I'll be starting baptism instruction next week, ya know."

"Well, if it was just me, I'd say if you don't sit and stare at it, or let it come 'tween you and the Lord"—Mamma smiled now—"you might keep it in your Bible, maybe. A good reminder of what Suzy's dyin' brought us." Mamma reached into Nellie's dress pocket and pulled out Suzy's Kapp strings. "As if you need another souvenir, jah?"

Together they smiled knowingly, and their laughter rose and scattered on the wings of twilight.

Chris was heading for the car after finishing up the milking with Caleb. "Hey, don't leave just yet," Caleb called to him. "I'd like to show ya something in my room."

"Sure, but I have some college paper work to do with my dad, so I'll need to get going."

"It'll only take a minute."

Upstairs, on his dresser, Caleb showed him the deed to Daed's land. "Man, is this some relic or what!" Chris said, noticing the yellowing around the edges.

"Passed down through the generations." Caleb's smile extended from ear to ear. "My father wanted me to have it—Abe just brought it by."

Chris looked out the window and whistled. "Wow—what do you plan to do with all the land?"

"Well, grow cash crops, for certain, and have plenty of grazing land for the dairy cows. Maybe raise horses, like Reuben Fisher."

Like Reuben . . .

Chris caught the curious glint in his cousin's eyes. *He's still thinking of Nellie Mae.*

"What about tobacco?" He was curious, knowing that the crop had been the family's staple for generations.

"Well, tobacco harvest is comin' up fast . . . but after this year, I'm not sure." Caleb motioned for him to take a seat near the open window. "Mamm's urging me to raise other crops . . . hoping I'll make the right choice on that." He went to sit on the edge of his bed. "To be blunt, plenty's goin' to change round here . . . and right quick, too."

Chris wondered what he meant.

"I've made a hard decision," Caleb said. "My father seemed to change overnight . . . he became downright *niedrich*—humble—before he died. I have to say it got my attention."

Chris leaned forward, listening.

"My father not only willingly gave me his land, Chris . . . he gave me something else. Something better." Caleb got up and went to the dresser, picking up the deed again. "Our great-grandfather—yours and mine—owned this property. Did you know that?"

Fascinated, Chris looked at the old deed again.

Caleb pointed to the former owner. "Right there, see? Christian C. Yoder. Guess what the middle initial stands for."

Chris laughed. "No way."

"Kinda spooky, jah?"

Caleb handed it to Chris. "Yep, your name's on there, too—must've been your namesake." He spoke of all the blood kin who'd lived out their lives here in this house, on this land. "All of them following the Old Ways to the best of their ability, then dyin' and never knowing what my father experienced in the last days of his life. Never knowin' the assurance of their salvation.

"Before Daed died, he pleaded with me to make the faith he found my own." Caleb's face shone. "I'm glad to say I finally took him up on it. I'll see my Daed again someday. And I know now it's not a prideful thing to say I'm born again—since the Lord himself paid the price for me."

Chris gave him a firm handshake. "Now, that's the best news, cousin. Hey, we're brothers now."

Caleb smiled. "Sounds good to me!"

Thursday afternoon, on the way over to Caleb's, Chris stopped in at Nellie's Simple Sweets. He'd considered what he wanted to do and hoped Nellie Mae might agree to see him again. After all, revival meetings were still in full swing at Tel Hai.

Besides, he was anxious to see how she might react to his invitation. He recalled her lingering tenderness toward Caleb, even though Chris was certain she was happy to be in his company now.

At first, she seemed surprised to see him, since he usually came later in the afternoon. She was walking over from the house, carrying several medium-sized boxes—filled with fruit pies, he assumed.

He rushed to help. "Here, let me take those."

"Are ya back for more desserts?" Her quick smile gave her away. She *was* glad to see him.

"I was hoping you'd go again to the revival meeting this Saturday night."

She paused, like she might be thinking it through. Then she said, "All right. Sounds nice."

Filled with a growing sense of excitement, he carried the pies to the bakery shop. He tempered his grin when he saw Nellie's mother behind the counter in the bakery shop today.

He greeted her, and Mrs. Fisher held his gaze, smiling. "Can I interest you in two pies today, Mr. Yoder?" she teased.

Deciding to try something new, he bought a peach cobbler. Then, waving good-bye to both Nellie Mae and her mother, he headed back to his car. He noticed Nellie standing in the window. He waved again and was tempted to memorize the outline of her, carrying it in his mind all the way to Caleb's.

After milking was done, when they were washing up in the milk house together, Chris mentioned the surprise he had out in the car. Caleb perked up his ears, and Chris went to get the peach cobbler, still warm from the sun.

Coming into the kitchen, he placed it on the table, and Caleb's eyes widened. "I see you've been to Nellie's bakery shop."

Chris could hardly contain his pleasure. "This is just one small thank-you for letting me hang around with you here, in the country." He dished up ample portions and served the dessert first to Caleb, then to himself. "I also thought you might like a tasty reminder of someone's baking skills."

"Well, believe me, this here's somethin' you don't soon forget."

They exchanged banter about their favorite foods—pies and pastries included—and Chris's plans to head to college soon.

Then Caleb said, "You know, I used to be able to talk with Nellie 'bout most anything. She has no idea what's happened to me."

"That you're saved, you mean?"

Caleb nodded. "Honestly, it's still hard to think of it just that way."

Chris listened.

"Even so, I know I've already lost her." Caleb reached for another scoop of cobbler. "And rightly so."

Seeing the look of longing in Caleb's eyes, Chris inhaled deeply. "Listen, Cousin—"

Caleb's laugh was hearty. "Hey, it's *brother*, remember?"

"Brother it is." Chris stared at his Plain cousin, who so closely resembled himself in so many ways. "You know, Caleb, you've shared some personal things with me about you and Nellie Mae. . . ."

Caleb's head jerked up, his fork poised in midair. "Jah?"

"Well, I've been thinking . . . and I realize it's time I leveled with you. . . ."

Rhoda parked her car up the road and walked along the shoulder, down to the house. The horse pasture on this side of her father's house was shaded with cottonwoods, all lined up in a straight row. She'd leaned against the trunks of those very trees, counting slowly to one hundred, while her sisters ran and hid, back when they were all little girls.

Breathing in the sweetness of honeysuckle, she dared to let her eyes roam over the rambling paddock and the neatly trimmed front yard. It looked to her like the picket fence had been newly whitewashed, and she was struck by a pang of sadness, not having been around to help with a chore she'd always enjoyed.

She tried not to look at the house directly as she made her way up the drive, as self-conscious as she'd ever been in her pretty blue skirt and blue and yellow floral-print blouse, her short hair free and floating against her cheeks.

What'll Dat say when he sees me all fancy like this? She could only imagine the jolt to his heart.

Hoping she would not cause more pain for her parents, she hurried through the grass and crept into the barn. The acrid sting of manure mixed with the sweat of the horses overwhelmed her—she'd forgotten the smells of her father's beloved trade.

She moved past the stable toward the little woodworking shop, where she spied Dat bent over his wooden desk in the corner, poring over his logs of birthing schedules and training programs.

Pausing at the threshold, she leaned against it. *This is it . . . the end of all my so-called fun.*

She pushed up her glasses. "Dat . . . it's Rhoda," she said softly.

He turned, his startled expression turning into a full smile. "Well, well. Gut to see ya, daughter."

"You too." She felt the lump in her throat. "You have a minute?"

He rose and pulled out a chair. "For you, Rhoda, I'd say far more than a minute."

She found courage in his reaction to her being here. "I'll get right to the point." Struggling not to cry, she looked down. Oh, she needed his acceptance, his love. And she needed the openness of fields and pastureland once again—even the woods appealed to her now that she'd been gone so long. Being cooped up in a one-room apartment wasn't at all what her heart craved. "I was terribly wrong, Dat. . . ."

"Rhoda, whatever you've done—"

"Truth is, I'm just plain miserable." She looked at him, this man who worked harder than anyone she knew. He'd never asked for anything special or unreasonable—only that his children yielded to his covering as their loving father. "The worst of it was breaking your heart," she said. "Yours and Mamma's. For that, I'm most sorry."

He tugged on his beard, his eyes piercing hers. "Would you like to come home, daughter?"

She wanted to laugh. No, cry. "Where would I park my car?" She knew it sounded ridiculous, even prideful to think she could live here again, yet have much of her own way.

A slow smile reached across his tan face. "Well, last I looked we've got a nice big woodshed."

She could tell by his sincere, steady gaze that he wasn't kidding. "You'd let me come home and still be . . . well, a bit fancy?"

He leaned forward, resting his elbows on his legs. For a moment he stared at the floor filled with sawdust and chips of wood. "Just how fancy do ya mean?"

She'd thought it all through. "Well, I'd like to attend the Beachy church—if they'll have me back—and dress more Plain than I am now, of course." She stared down at her favorite skirt and pretty white sandals. *Willing to give an inch so you can have a mile, Dat must be thinking.*

"I'll keep working hard for the Kraybills'. If you want me to quit the restaurant, I'll do that. And, once I get back on my feet, I'll start paying you room and board."

He waved his hand and shook his head. "Ach, just help your mother and sisters all you can. How's that?" He got up with a grunt and walked with her all the way down the lane and out to see her new car. And before she opened the door, he asked, "Heard you've got yourself some sort of lease where you're stayin'?"

"Mrs. Kraybill's agreed to handle that with my landlord." She'd covered all her bases, at least for now. Her brother James liked the idea of having her television, and any other fancy cast-offs she wanted to sell him at a discount. That way she wouldn't have a pile of questionable items sitting out in a yard sale, making Dat and Mamma a laughingstock.

"I must confess that I've prayed for unity amongst the People till the cows come home." He closed the car door for her and leaned on the open window. "But charity always begins at home, ya know." She saw tears in his eyes, and her heart lifted.

"Denki, Dat . . . ever so much. You've made my day!" She couldn't believe she'd just said one of Ken's favorite expressions.

Waving, she pulled onto the road, waiting until she was out near Route 10 before she gave in to her joyful tears.

Nellie, Nan, and Mamma stood next to the bakery shop window, all bunched together, their noses nearly touching the pane as they watched

Dat walk down toward the road with Rhoda. "What could they be talking 'bout?" Nan asked.

Nellie realized she had been holding her breath. "Ach, do ya think Rhoda might be thinkin' of coming home?" she nearly gasped.

Nan did a little jig next to her, sniffling and then pressing her lips together. "I won't cry . . . I just won't!"

Mamma, more serene, slipped a plump arm around each of them. "Don't ever doubt it, dear ones . . . you're seein' firsthand how God answers prayer."

Oh, please let it be so! thought Nellie, squeezing Nan's hand.

CHAPTER 33

R osanna eagerly awaited the sound of Elias's footsteps on the stairs, especially during the noon hour, when he so kindly carried up a large tray of food for the two of them. The families from their church had been faithful in keeping them supplied with hot meals for both lunch and supper.

Such a blessing . . .

Elias had repositioned the bed from its original spot, so she could look out the window when she tired of reading or needlework. At times, she could even watch Elias out in the field, as the second cutting of alfalfa was in full swing.

She tired so easily anymore that sometimes it was all she could do to stay awake when Nellie Mae dropped by to read aloud from the Bible. Yesterday, Rhoda—who'd just returned home—had come to visit for a few hours, sitting upstairs with her and crocheting baby things right along with Rosanna. Such good company she was, and what stories she told on herself—ever so amusing. Sobering too.

Today, when Elias brought up a delicious meal of hamburger puffs topped with cream sauce, green beans, and a side of cabbage slaw, he sat and talked with Rosanna about the possibility of inviting Rhoda to stay with them, for pay, when Lena's baby was born. That way, she'd have someone to help with Jonathan—as they'd named him already, hoping he would in fact turn out to be a boy—while she waited for her own little one to arrive.

If all continues to go well . . .

"Will you want Lena to come for a while, too, maybe?" Elias asked, shoveling a bite into his mouth.

She cringed, thinking of her cousin Kate's coming too often last year. "As a wet nurse, ya mean?"

He nodded, his mouth still full.

"Maybe . . . I'll ask her if she'd feel comfortable staying for the first few days." But then she thought of all the children Lena had to care for at home.

Surely there's a wet nurse close by.

Once her own baby was born, Rosanna wondered if she might not have plenty of breast milk for two wee ones. But if not, she would resort to infant formula, just as she had with Eli and Rosie.

"Looks like the Lord's goin' to give us the desire of our hearts," Elias said, reaching for his glass. "With Lena's baby not much older than ours, Lord willin', it'll be nearly like having twins all over again."

She blew a kiss to him. "And I s'pose you'll be quite satisfied if we end up with two little girls, jah?"

Elias leaned over to give her a kiss. "You do have a way of makin' a man chuckle, love." He reached down and stroked her hair, still loose from the night. "I best be headin' back out. But I'll be in for supper later."

"Take plenty of cold water along in your thermos," she called to him, watching her darling go.

Rosanna planned to spend even more time praying for her preacher-husband, what with the church youth already having begun their study of the Confession of Faith and the New Order *Ordnung* in preparation for baptism. Elias was working alongside Preacher Manny to learn all he could, and right quick, too, as he instructed the young applicants about being in right relationship with the Lord and one another.

Nellie Mae's joining church, she thought with a smile, ever so happy about that. *Now, if you'll just see fit to send her a kind and good husband, dear Lord. . . .*

Her father's horses rhythmically moved their heads from side to side, lowering their noses into the tallest grazing grass in the high meadow. Dat had once told Nellie they did this to watch the insects spread out below them as they moved forward. She wasn't sure if he'd said that in jest, but she liked the idea all the same.

Nellie watched from her bedroom window as the horses nuzzled one another and then meandered forward, finding their way along, letting first one mare lead . . . then another.

She felt something like them as they drifted toward the barn for watering. First Caleb had led her, so to speak, and then Chris. Both young men were special to her, but neither was right. She knew this now; she'd spent long hours pondering her upcoming date tonight with Chris.

Having taken care to brush her hair fifty extra strokes, she pinned it back just so. Sure, she was enamored with Chris. Well, she had been until she'd really thought about the possibility of courtship. Which of them would budge, if they were to become serious? Was it even practical to think of Chris settling into the Plain community his grandfather had chosen to leave? *How's it possible for us to manage as a couple?*

But even if he did decide to leave his modern life and join her here, she believed she still cared too much for Caleb. She wasn't ready to be wooed by a new love—might never be. So, when the time was right, sometime this evening, she would tell Chris the truth . . . that she liked him, and quite a lot, but she loved Caleb. And maybe she always would.

Thus far God had given her the grace to bear her sadness. Yet she wouldn't stay marrying age for too many more years. Even so, she must trust the Lord, who does all things well, as Mamma so often reminded her and Nan. *And now Rhoda, too.* Such a delight it was to see her sister settle quickly—and happily—into James's former room down the hall, the very spot she'd asked for and been refused. But something had changed in Mamma . . . in Dat, too. They were more tolerant, and Nellie had noticed the number of necklaces hanging on the edge of the old dresser mirror was fewer than before. Rhoda had placed Suzy's bracelet front and center, however, saying it was a big part of why she'd come home. Rhoda had also begun sewing new cape dresses and aprons, and Nellie secretly wondered if she might someday up and sell her car, too.

Just that morning Rhoda had returned Suzy's diary, and Nellie Mae had passed it right off to Mamma.

"Where're you headed?" Nan poked her head into Nellie's room.

"Over to the little tabernacle at Tel Hai—ever go there?"

Nan nodded. "Ezekiel's talkin' of going sometime."

"This is my last time to go . . . with a fella."

Snickering, Nan covered her mouth. "Ach, you're always talking 'bout the last you'll do such and so."

"Well, I mean it this time."

A frown crossed her brow; then she reached for Nellie's hand. "I hope what I have to say won't upset you." Nan sighed. "Ezekiel and I've set our wedding date for the first Thursday in November . . . the sixth."

"What's to be sad about?"

A smile broke on Nan's face. "I'm hopin' you'll consider being one of my bridesmaids. You and Rhoda."

"Oh, Nan, I'd love to!" She gave her sister a quick hug. "You and Ezekiel will be such a cute married couple, ya know?"

They stood smiling at each other, arms still entwined. "Only one thing could be better 'bout that day for me, Nellie . . . that's if you had a best beau there for you to fellowship with during the wedding feast."

The feast would last long into the evening and be followed by a special barn Singing with the wedding party and all the youth in attendance—a right good and happy time, for sure.

She nudged Nan to the window. "Look out there. Watch the horses . . . see how they trust the one in the lead?"

Ever so still, they watched. At last Nellie said, "They're not in any hurry to get where they're goin'. And neither am I."

"Dat always says essential things can be learned from nature, if we pay attention. Journeying with the seasons the Lord set into motion."

Jah, journeying with the Lord . . .

After a time, Nellie moved toward the door. " 'Tis nearly dusk, so I best be goin'."

"Is it Chris, then, tonight?" Nan whispered.

Nellie Mae gave her a nod. "Pray for me . . . it won't be easy." She thought how much harder it would be to say good-bye to someone if they were further along in their courtship. Like she and Caleb had been . . .

There was such a stitch of sadness in her soul at the painful memory of their last conversation together. Her beloved's rejecting the dear Savior . . .

Nan walked her to the end of the hall. *"Da Herr sei mit du*—God be with you, sister."

"Oh, He is, Nan." She patted her heart. "Rest assured . . . He surely is."

———

The night was especially still and heavy with nature's perfume—a scent as sweet and pure as that of wild honey.

Nellie made her way down the drive, turning right at the road. She'd slipped through the redd-up kitchen to fleeting glances from both Dat and Mamma, though as was their way, they asked no questions. But from now on, she wouldn't be sneaking out anywhere. Her dates with Chris Yoder would soon be a thing of the past.

She guessed he might try to dissuade her—try to talk her into giving their friendship more time. He did seem interested in knowing her better, even though if they were to continue their friendship, it would have to be by letter. Soon he would be leaving for Virginia to attend college.

But she wanted to share with him the truth—what lay in her heart. *Oh, but I don't want to hurt him.*

She recalled the freshness heralded by the fragrant morning as she worked out in the blackberry patch early today, alone and talking to God. A red-tailed hawk had flown overhead and hung in the high current, its call sounding almost like the *mew* of a new kitten. And she'd wept, her tears falling to the soft soil. Even so, she knew this difficult deed she was about to do was the right thing.

At the bend in the road, Nellie looked for Chris's car along the wide shoulder—their appointed meeting spot. She noticed an open buggy parked there—at first glance, it looked like Chris sitting atop, holding the reins. She looked away, knowing she had to be mistaken. What would he be doing with a courting buggy? Unless . . . had he borrowed one for a joke? But no, she couldn't imagine that.

Certain she must be imagining things, she kept her head down, embarrassed, eyes still on the road. The crickets had begun their evening song, and Nellie listened, aware of the beauty to be found in the fragile twilight.

Love is ever so fragile, too. . . .

How could you open your heart fully to someone new when it already belonged to another? That very realization had overtaken her in the blackberry patch this morning.

She heard someone call, "Nellie Mae?"

Looking up, she let out a little gasp, startled to see Caleb sitting in the buggy, smiling down at her.

"Word has it a pretty girl would be walkin' this way at dusk." He leapt down from his perch. "I'd say that's right about now."

She couldn't help herself—she laughed. Chris and Caleb in cahoots. For how long?

But she didn't have to know. The surprise was purely delicious, like mixing favorite ingredients together and getting a blue-ribbon pie.

"I hear there's a wonderful-good meetin' over at the Tel Hai tabernacle . . . want to go with me, Nellie Mae?" he asked.

She saw the sincerity in his beautiful hazel eyes. Now she was crying . . . tears of greatest joy. Caleb was here . . . *here* where Chris had agreed to meet her, of all amazing things. "That's why I came," she said, overcome with delight.

He helped her into the left side of his shiny black buggy and then sat down next to her. "There's so much I want to tell you. . . ."

With that, he picked up the reins and clicked his tongue.

The laughter she'd first suppressed at this most unexpected reunion slipped out softly, mingling with Caleb's own. A welcome breeze swept across their faces as nightfall gathered in around them.

"You once said you believed in miracles," he said.

"Now more than ever." Oh, she could hardly wait to sing joyful praises that night, blending her voice with those of the other worshipers, and her darling's!

Only one thing mattered now: She was with Caleb as the horse pulled them forward, toward the little tabernacle beneath the stars.

EPILOGUE

February 1968

Just imagine my excitement when both Preachers Manny and Elias agreed to help my darling catch up with the other twelve baptismal candidates as we prepared to join the New Order Amish church. Once his father led the way, the truth of the Lord became real to Caleb, and it was impossible for him to deny it for long. Or so he's told me, all smiles. As a result, Caleb and I made our kneeling vows to God on the fourteenth of September last year, becoming church members together. After he was greeted by the ministerial brethren, his face shone with purest joy as he looked my way. Up until that wonderful-good day, there had not been a more sacred moment for either of us.

As the Lord planned it, Rosanna's adopted son, Jonathan, came into the world that very evening—and with little to-do, according to Lena Stoltzfus, who kept her word without hesitation. Bright-eyed and weighing nearly nine pounds, fair-haired Jonathan seemed to bond immediately with Rosanna on the second day of his life, when Lena herself presented him. And just as was her desire, Rosanna was soon able to nurse him, once she gave birth to her tiny blue-eyed daughter, who came a bit early. A true miracle, according to the midwife. Praise be!

So Jonathan and Lena Grace are only one day shy of three weeks apart. "Two precious gifts," Rosanna says as she holds one in each arm, cooing and carrying on. Ach, how it does my heart good to see it.

My oldest sister is the busiest mother's helper ever, according to Rosanna. She hopes to keep Rhoda around for a while longer—at least till Caleb's and my own little one is born in late September, marking the month two years ago that salvation came to my father's house.

Sweet Nan and her husband are in the family way, too, which isn't surprising, as my sister and I put our heads together and planned a double wedding. And, oh, it was the finest Indian summer day there has ever been, like a divine sign, truly. Even Mamma thought so. I stood up for Nan as her bridesmaid while she made her vows to Ezekiel Mast just moments before I made my own to dearest Caleb. It was only fitting, being that Nan's older than me.

As for Dat's ongoing hope for unity, Uncle Bishop has surprised the People—some more than others—by softening his stand on studying and discussing Scripture, departing from the typical way of the Old Order. Truth is, the words spoken at David Yoder's funeral shook up quite a few folk, including Ephram and Maryann. Dat says the Lord knew what it would take—that the rather pointed and sobering sermons were necessary to nudge the most reluctant of all my married brothers in His direction. It's safe to say that freedom in the Lord—with less emphasis on man-made regulations—is becoming rather contagious round here. More prayer meetings and Bible studies are cropping up all the time, and in the most unexpected places. There's no denying it: God is at work in all of our hearts.

I can't think of anything that would please Suzy more. Honestly, I think of her most often now when Caleb reads Chris's letters from college. I'll never forget how Chris and Zach played such an important part in leading my sister to faith. And I still find it curious that the Lord used my interest in Chris—and his in me—as a wonderful reminder of Caleb while we were apart.

Just recently Chris wrote describing his ministerial studies, and I recalled that he'd once shared wanting to do something big for God. To think that his and Zach's befriending Suzy started such a stir amongst the People, like a dewdrop falling into a vast sea, rippling out to touch so many thirsty souls.

At the close of Chris's letter, he mentioned having heard that a Miss Rhoda Fisher was signed up for college days weekend in April—two months from now. Evidently Rhoda is confident about passing her GED test—the class is the sole place she goes in her car anymore, preferring to take Dat's horse and buggy the rest of the time. Of course, if Rhoda does attend the Eastern Mennonite School, I won't have her wonderful-good help with Caleb's and my first baby. But Mamma will surely make up for that, if need be.

Meanwhile, I sew and crochet for our little one to come while reciting aloud my recipes to Elizabeth, my dear mother-in-law, who kindly helps me write them down. We're hoping to finish my *Nellie's Simple Sweets Cookbook* before it's time to plant my vegetable garden. Dat and Mamma closed the bakery shop after Caleb and I moved into his parents' big farmhouse, ending one more happy chapter in my life. Now I'd much rather cook and bake for my husband. Every so often, Caleb sneaks up behind me in the kitchen to reach around my ever-widening middle and whisper loving words, his nose tickling my neck. He likes to talk to our baby, too, which makes me smile. Oh, the Lord is so good to bring us together as man and wife. To think we'll soon be a family of three!

Caleb's mother moved right away to the Dawdi Haus after our wedding, an unspoken way of showing her hope for grandbabies—Lord willing, one right after another. It'll be especially fun for Rosanna and me to raise our wee ones together, so close in age they'll be.

As for Caleb's sister Rebekah, she managed to keep her beau a secret longer than most brides-to-be, publishing the wedding date after church just one week before Nan's and my wedding day. She and her husband, one of Susannah Lapp's cousins, live within walking distance of Caleb and me. So my husband enjoys seeing his sister, and I'm becoming a close sister-in-law to Nan's dearest friend.

Last week, between quilting frolics, Cousin Treva wrote that she noticed two new purple martin birdhouses standing tall in Dawdi and Mammi Fisher's side yard. Dat has the most interesting way of turning his father's heart back toward Honey Brook. Mammi Hannah has also sent a nice batch of recipes in answer to my request, and she has been writing to Mamma quite a lot since seeing her at Martha's for the pickling bee last summer, recently hinting at moving back "home." Although now with all the religious stir amongst my married brothers—wanting more of Scripture, as well as fancier things—who's to say my grandparents might not just end up at the Dawdi Haus next door to my parents, after all.

Early in the morning, when I do my bread baking, I ponder my love for Caleb . . . and his growing love for the Lord.

For folks who say miracles don't exist, I've imprinted in my mind the happy day when my father walked Rhoda clear out to the road, to her pretty car. And I offer prayers of thanksgiving for Rosanna's tiny, full-term daughter, as well as the blessing of Lena Grace's brother, Jonathan—both miracles, indeed. What a joy that our young preacher and his wife have themselves a cuddly pair to raise and love—a farmhand in the making for Elias, and a cute little dishwasher and quilter someday for Rosanna.

But above all, I marvel at the change saving grace has brought to the lives of the People—'specially David Yoder, whose transformation might have been the greatest of all. Word has it, if the Lord can save such an obstinate, hardhearted soul—soften him before his family's very eyes—then why should any of us ever doubt God's power?

Yesterday evening following supper, while thick snowflakes fell, Caleb discovered a note his father had written and stuck inside the old family Bible. *God no longer sees me as a sinner. Because of His Son's blood sacrifice, He looks at me . . . and sees Jesus there instead.*

Caleb and I had to wipe away tears, and we clasped hands and looked at each other, amazed at this precious legacy of faith for our family. We decided then and there it must be framed. We'll hang it on the kitchen wall so all who sit at our table can see the reason for our enduring happiness. Even before we realized it, our deepest longing has always been for the Savior, our dear Lord Jesus—for sure and for certain.

AUTHOR'S NOTE

THE COURTSHIP OF NELLIE FISHER is a work of fiction inspired by the intriguing events of 1966, when the Lancaster County New Order Amish church was birthed.

Among the many helpful individuals I've conferred with, I am especially thankful to Ike and Fay Landis and to my husband, Dave, who assisted with unearthing fascinating research, as well as by taking his red pen to my manuscript. I am also grateful to my wonderful editors, David Horton, Julie Klassen, Rochelle Glöege, and Janna Nysewander, along with meticulous reviewers Ann Parrish and Barbara Birch.

I owe the greatest debt of gratitude to my Savior and Lord, the Light to my path, and Joy to my journey.

> O the deep, deep love of Jesus,
> vast, unmeasured, boundless, free!
> —SAMUEL TREVOR FRANCIS, 1875

B EVERLY LEWIS, born in the heart of Pennsylvania Dutch country, fondly recalls her growing-up years. A keen interest in her mother's Plain family heritage has inspired Beverly to set many of her popular stories in Amish country, beginning with her inaugural novel, *The Shunning.*

A former schoolteacher and accomplished pianist, Beverly has written over eighty books for adults and children. Her novels regularly appear on *The New York Times* and *USA Today* bestseller lists, and *The Brethren* won a 2007 Christy Award.

Beverly and her husband, David, make their home in Colorado, where they enjoy hiking, biking, reading, writing, making music, and spending time with their three grandchildren.